"Humans aren't allowe... sniffed. "You'll have to wait at the servants entrance with the others."

"I'm on state business," he told her firmly. "Zelia will want to see me at once. If you won't let me in, go find her. Tell her Arvin is here to see her with an urgent message about . . ." He paused. How to word it . . . ? "About diseased rats in the sewers."

The slave tried to stare him down, but her resolve at last wavered. She turned away and snapped her fingers. "Boy!" she shouted. A boy about eight or nine years old, carrying a glass decanter of pink-tinged water, emerged in response to the doorkeeper's call. "This man claims to have been summoned here by one of our patrons," the doorkeeper told the boy, placing emphasis on the word "summoned," perhaps to remind Arvin that, while he might be a free man, he was ultimately at the beck and call of the yuan-ti. "Find the yuan-ti Zelia and deliver this message to her." She relayed Arvin's message. "Return with her reply."

The boy ran off down the main tunnel. Arvin waited, stepping to the side and dropping his gaze as two yuan-ti entered and were greeted with low bows by the doorkeeper. The boy came running back, this time without the decanter.

"Mistress Zelia says to bring the man to her," the boy panted.

ENTER
THE
HOUSE OF SERPENTS

FORGOTTEN REALMS®

More Books by
The New York Times Best-selling Author

LISA SMEDMAN

THE LADY PENITENT

Book I
Sacrifice of the Widow

Book II
Storm of the Dead

Book III
Ascendancy of the Last

R.A. SALVATORE'S
WAR OF THE SPIDER QUEEN

Book IV
Extinction

SEMBIA

Heirs of Prophecy

LISA SMEDMAN

HOUSE OF SERPENTS

VENOM'S TASTE **VIPER'S KISS** **VANITY'S BROOD**

House of Serpents Omnibus

Published by Wizards of the Coast LLC.

FORGOTTEN REALMS, WIZARDS OF THE COAST, and their respective logos are trademarks of Wizards of the Coast LLC in the U.S.A. and other countries.

Printed in the U.S.A.

Cover art by Raymond Swanland
Map by Rob Lazzaretti

Venom's Taste originally published March 2004
Viper's Kiss originally published March 2005
Vanity's Brood originally published March 2006

First Printing: October 2009

9 8 7 6 5 4 3 2 1

ISBN: 978-0-7869-5364-6
620-25128000-001-EN

U.S., CANADA,
ASIA, PACIFIC, & LATIN AMERICA
Wizards of the Coast LLC
P.O. Box 707
Renton, WA 98057-0707
+1-800-324-6496

EUROPEAN HEADQUARTERS
Hasbro UK Ltd
Caswell Way
Newport, Gwent NP9 0YH
GREAT BRITAIN
Save this address for your records.

Visit our web site at www.wizards.com

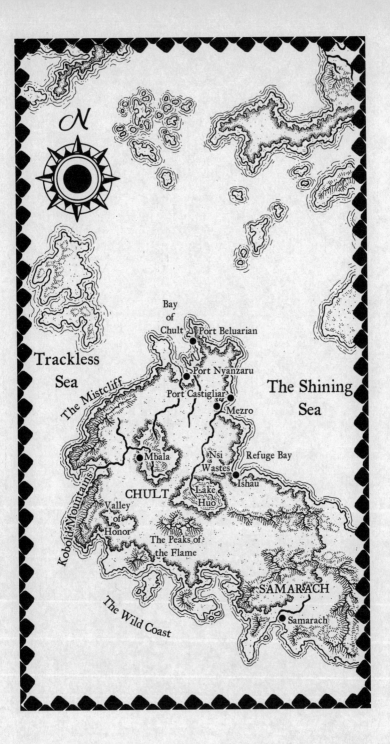

BOOK I

VENOM'S TASTE

PROLOGUE

S O THIS IS TO BE MY COFFIN, ARVIN THOUGHT.

Had he been capable of it, he would have groaned in despair. He was sprawled on his back inside a leaky rowboat, too weak to lift himself out of the cold, filthy water in which he lay. Even blinking was beyond him. With eyes too dry for tears, he stared at the bricks that drifted past a short distance above him—the arched ceiling of the sewage tunnel. Water sloshed against him as the boat nudged against a wall with a dull thud. Then the lazy current scuffed the boat away from the wall again and dragged it relentlessly onward.

It was not so much the knowledge that he was dying that filled Arvin with impotent grief—even though twenty-six was far too young for any life to end—it was the thought that his soul would begin its journey to the gods fouled with this intolerable stink. The sewage tunnel was slimed not just with centuries of human waste, but also with the pungent excretions of the serpent folk. The stench of the water eddying back and forth across Arvin's hands, plucking wetly at his hair and wicking up through his clothes, was unbearable, it brought back childhood memories of being unable to get clean, of tauntings and humiliation. Even Bane, god of crushing despair, could not have dreamed up a more perfect torment for Arvin's final moments.

He felt no pain, unlike those whose screams he could still hear echoing distantly from farther up the tunnel. There was just a dull heaviness that dragged him further toward unconsciousness with each passing moment, gradually slowing his thoughts to a trickle. Body and mind seemed to have become detached from each other, the one lying limp and unresponsive in the boat while the other spun in slow spirals, like water going down a drain. Pain would have been welcome; it might have blotted out the thoughts that were turning slow circles inside his mind.

Why? he asked himself, thinking back to the events of only a short time ago, of his meeting with Naulg in the tavern. Why was I . . . so careless? That woman. . . .

The thought drifted away as consciousness fled.

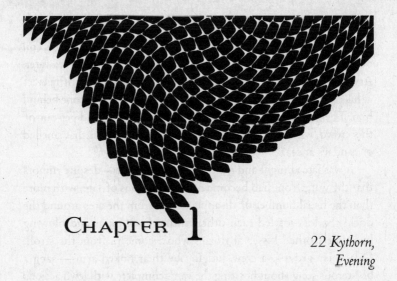

CHAPTER 1

ARVIN REACHED INTO HIS MUG AND FISHED A SMALL, SPECKLED EGG out of his ale. He set it on the wooden table in front of him and, with a quick flick of his forefinger, sent it rolling. The egg wobbled to the edge, teetered, and fell, joining the sticky mess that littered the sawdust on the tavern floor.

He sighed as he raised the mug to his lips. Eggs. Why did the barkeep bother? Some humans had a taste for them—or rather, a taste for pretending to be something they were not—but Arvin despised the gagging, slippery feel of raw egg sliding down his throat. Next thing you knew, the Mortal Coil would be offering half-and-hares— ale mixed with rabbit blood.

The ale was surprisingly drinkable this evening; the barkeep had either forgotten to water it, or he'd washed the mugs. Arvin sipped it slowly, hoping he wouldn't have to wait all night. The pipe smoke drifting in blue swirls against the low ceiling was already thick enough to make his eyes water. The twine in his breast pocket didn't like the smoke much, either. Arvin could feel it twitching within its tightly stitched leather pouch. But at least the air was cool, a welcome relief from the muggy heat of a summer evening.

The Mortal Coil occupied the cavernous, circular basement of one of the warehouses that lined the Hlondeth waterfront. The tavern had been named for its ceiling, carved to resemble an enormous coil of rope. At high tide the room's southern wall sweated seawater. Arvin, seated on a bench that curved along that wall, sat stiffly erect at his table, loath to let his shirt brush against the damp stone behind him. The sooner Naulg arrived, the sooner Arvin could get out of this crowd, with their tarred hair and unwashed clothes that smelled of tendays at sea.

It was late at night and the tavern was crowded—despite rumors that the waterfront had become more dangerous of late, with more than the usual number of disappearances from the area around the docks. Sailors jostled each other, tilting back mugs and blowing loud, ale-frothed kisses at doxies who'd come in from the stroll. One noisy group—a crew, judging by their linked arms—sang a boisterous song about hoisting the yard, complete with lewd actions that made the double meaning of the chorus clear. On the other side of the room, another crew had shoved the tables aside and were lined up for a game of toss-knife. A dagger suddenly spun through the air between the two lines of men, zigzagging back and forth across the gap as each man caught and tossed it as rapidly as he could. Halfway down the line, one man suddenly howled and yanked his hand back against his chest, letting the dagger fall behind him. Blood dribbled from his clenched fingers as the others pounded him on the back, laughing at his misfortune at having to buy their next round of drinks. The wounded sailor, staggering under the thumps of mock congratulation, slowly opened his hand and stared, blinking and suddenly sober, at a fingertip that dangled from a thin thread of flesh.

Arvin winced. A dull ache flared in his finger as he involuntarily clenched his left hand. He opened his fingers and rubbed the smallest one, massaging it through the soft black leather of his glove. Years had passed since the Guild had cut off the last segment of that finger as retribution for intruding on their turf, yet the stub still smarted, especially if the weather was about to change. The wad of felt stuffed into the fingertip of Arvin's glove provided some padding for the lumpy scar tissue but not enough.

Waiting, sipping his ale, he smiled grimly at the irony. Back when Arvin was a teenager, living on the few coins he was able to filch from unguarded pockets and purses, the Guild had come close to depriving him of what was to become his livelihood. Thank the gods they'd found the rope he'd made and recognized his talent before they cut off the rest of his fingertips. Now, years later, they valued his skills highly—so highly they wouldn't let him go. They'd arranged for him to rent a warehouse at a ridiculously low price and saw to it that he was able to acquire whatever exotic and expensive materials he needed in return for the right to be his only "customers"—and the right to a steep discount.

Speaking of customers, where was Naulg?

Arvin glanced around the room but saw no sign of the rogue. His eyes darted to the entrance as someone in yellow—a color Naulg often wore—came down the ramp, but it turned out to be a woman in a yellow dress. A yuan-ti, human in overall appearance, with long red hair, but with skin covered in a sheen of green scales that thinned to a freckle of green on her face and hands. She moved with a grace that contrasted with the rolling gait of the sailors and the pouting slouch of the doxies. Despite the fact that she was female and wearing a dress that hugged the sensual curve of her hips like a second skin, the sailors kept their hands to themselves. Several scrambled out of her way, automatically dropping their glance to the ground and touching their foreheads in a subservient gesture that their ships' yuan-ti masters had ingrained in them, one painful lash at a time.

Arvin watched the woman out of the corner of his eye as she settled at a table two down from his, her back to the wall. When she flicked a finger impatiently for ale, the barkeep hurried to her side, setting a mug in front of her. He took her coin quickly, jerking his hand back as she reached for the mug, then bowed and backed away. The woman lifted the mug to her lips, tipping it until the egg inside the ale slid into her mouth, then swallowed it, shell and all, with one quick gulp. A forked tongue flickered as she licked her lips appreciatively.

As she glanced in Arvin's direction, he noticed her eyes. They were sea green flecked with yellow. As they met Arvin's they emitted a flash of silver, momentarily reflecting the lantern light like those of a cat. Aware that she was staring at him, Arvin hastily averted his eyes. Yuan-ti often slummed at the Coil, but when they did, they came in groups and looked down haughtily on the "lesser races" who frequented the place. What was this woman doing in the tavern on her own, quietly sipping an ale? She, like Arvin, seemed to be waiting for someone.

If she'd been human—and wearing even a scrap of green—Arvin might have worried that he was the object of her search. The druids of the Emerald Enclave usually stuck to the wilderness but were known to occasionally enter a city to sniff out wizardry—and Arvin's craft required him to work with wizards on a regular basis. He did so only at arm's length, through a middler, but the druids would hardly believe that if they discovered the ensorcelled twine in his shirt pocket.

This woman, however, seemed to have no interest in Arvin. After her brief scrutiny of him, she no longer glanced in his direction. She was obviously looking for someone else.

A second glimpse of yellow attracted Arvin's attention to the tavern entrance—Naulg. Small and dark haired, Naulg had eyebrows that formed an unbroken line over his squared-off nose. He had a big grin on his face—and one arm firmly around the waist of a doxy who snuggled tightly against his side. With his free hand, he reached up and rubbed first the inside corner of his right eye, then the outside corner—the sign that he was looking for somebody. It was an unnecessary formality, since he and Arvin had known each other for years, but Arvin played along. Placing an elbow on the table, he rested his chin on his fist and raised his little finger so that it touched his lips. *I'm your man.*

Naulg shoved his way through the crowd, dragging the doxy with him. He found an empty chair at a nearby table, dragged it over, and sat in it, pulling the woman down into his lap. As they settled themselves, Naulg waved for two ales, one for himself and one for Arvin. He insisted Arvin join him in a drink. The doxy looked impatiently around as if she'd rather complete her business with Naulg and move on to the next tumble.

Despite the perpetual frown his heavy eyebrows gave him, Naulg was a likable fellow, with his easy grin, boldly colored shirt that drew the eye, and generous nature. He and Arvin had met when both were boys at the orphanage, during Arvin's first year there. Naulg had shared his meal with Arvin after a larger boy had "accidentally" knocked Arvin's trencher out of his hand. He'd been the only one to show friendship toward Arvin without wanting something else in return. They'd developed a close bond immediately and cemented it by twining their little fingers together like snakes.

Naulg had run away from the orphanage a year later—and had never been caught. His escape had been an inspiration to Arvin through the years that followed, and Arvin had always wondered to where Naulg had fled. After Arvin's own escape, he'd at last learned the answer. It was ironic that both men had wound up under the thumb of another, even more repressive organization—though Naulg didn't seem to see the Guild that way. To him it was a game, an adventure. To Arvin, the Guild was a rope around his wrist—one that kept him as bound to Hlondeth as a slave was to his master.

The doxy's shrill laughter jerked Arvin sharply back to the present. Staring at her, he decided that she would make a better rogue than Naulg. She was pretty, with fluttering eyelashes and long dark hair that coiled in soft waves around a milk white face, but there was something about the hard glint in her eye that told Arvin she could hold her own. He disliked her immediately—perhaps because of the faint odor that clung to her—a ripe smell that reminded Arvin of spoiled meat. Of course, the smell might have been coming from Naulg, who was scratching absently at the back of his neck, revealing a large sweat stain in the armpit of his shirt.

"It's finished, then?" Naulg asked, ignoring the distraction of the doxy nuzzling his ear.

Arvin reached into the breast pocket of his shirt and pulled out a leather pouch that had been sewn shut with small, tight stitches. Keeping it hidden under his palm, he slid it across the table, leaving it beside Naulg's mug.

Naulg prodded the pouch with a finger and watched it bulge as the coil of twine inside it twitched. "Are there words that need to be spoken?"

Arvin shook his head. "Just cut the stitches and slip the pouch into a pocket. It'll do the job."

The doxy whispered something in Naulg's ear. Naulg laughed and shook his head.

"Be patient, woman. We'll be alone soon enough." Then, to Arvin, "Good. The middler already has your coin. You can collect it any time. I'm sure the goods will perform as promised."

"When will you be . . . using it?"

"Tonight,"—his grin broadened and he winked at the doxy—"much later tonight."

He picked up his ale and raised his mug to salute Arvin; his wide, sweeping gestures suggested he'd already had one too many.

Arvin nodded. He could guess what the twine would be used for—assassin vine almost always went for the throat—but maybe Naulg had something else in mind. Maybe he just meant to use it to bind someone's wrists.

Arvin twitched his mouth into a grin and covered his discomfort with a hearty joke. "Just be sure you don't let pleasure get in the way of business."

Naulg laughed. " 'Idle hands make merry,' " he quipped.

Arvin smiled. "You mean 'mischief,' " he said, correcting the motto that had been drummed into them at the orphanage. Then he *tsked*. "Brother Pauvey would weep for you."

"Yes, he would," Naulg said, suddenly serious. "He would indeed." He paused then added, "Can we talk later?"

Arvin nodded. "I'd like that."

Naulg shifted the doxy from his lap and rose to his feet, slipping the pouch into a trouser pocket. The doxy staggered slightly, as if she'd had too much to drink, but Arvin noted the quick, sharp glance she gave the pocket where Naulg had stored the pouch. If she was a rogue, as Arvin suspected, one quick stroke of her hand would see it gone, especially if Naulg was . . . distracted.

Arvin had labored for two full tendays to make the twine—and he'd spent good coin on the spell that kept the tendrils of assassin vine fresh after their harvesting. Braiding them had been like working with writhing snakes; if he'd let one go even for a moment, it would have coiled around his throat. If the twine disappeared, would Naulg demand a replacement?

As Naulg headed for the door, doxy in tow, Arvin decided to protect his investment. At least, that was what he told himself he was doing. He waited until the pair were halfway up the ramp then rose to his feet.

❧

Hlondeth by night was a city of whispers. Its cobblestoned streets had been worn smooth by the endless slither of the serpent folk. High above, the ramps that spiraled up the outside of build-ings to join viaducts that arched across the street were alive with the slide of scales on stone. Soft hisses of conversation whispered out of round doorways and windows. From the harbor, a few hundred paces away, came the crash and sigh of waves breaking against the seawall, rhythmic as breathing.

The streets alternately widened and narrowed as they curved between the city's circular, dome-roofed buildings, continuously branching into the Y-shaped intersections that were unique to Hlondeth. Cloaks rustled against walls as people squeezed against buildings in the narrower portions of the street, making room for Naulg and his doxy to pass.

The buildings on either side of the street they were walking along glowed with a faint green light—a residual glow left by the magics used to quarry the emerald-colored stone from which Hlondeth had been built. Its light, not quite bright enough to see by, gave a sickly, greenish pallor to the doxy's skin, making her look even less appealing than she had in the Coil.

Arvin had been keeping a careful distance behind Naulg and his doxy. He lost sight of them momentarily as the street took yet another sinuous twist then spotted them a few paces later as they entered one of the small, circular courtyards that dotted the city. At its center was a lightpost, wrought in iron in the shape of a rearing cobra. The cobra's mouth held an egg-shaped globe, which should have been glowing brightly, flooding the courtyard with light, but this one had dimmed, leaving the courtyard in near darkness. Arvin saw at once why the globe had remained untended. The residence whose walls formed the courtyard had windows that were boarded over and dark lines of soot smudged the walls above each window. Its main entrance was in shadow, but even so, he could still make out the yellow hand that had been painted on the door. Clerics had cleansed the building with magical fire more than fifty years ago, but like so many other buildings in Hlondeth that had been subjected to a similar fate, the residence remained vacant. The fear of plague was just too strong.

Arvin watched as the doxy steered Naulg toward the darkened doorway. Naulg either didn't notice the faded symbol on the door—or was too engrossed in the woman to care. Judging by the way he was fumbling at the woman's skirts, it looked as though they were going to complete their transaction then and there. Arvin waited just outside the courtyard, watching and wishing he were somewhere else. If he'd been wrong, it would just be a short while—Naulg's bragging notwithstanding—before the doxy would be on her way again.

Arvin stiffened, realizing he could no longer hear the rustling noises. Something was wrong; Naulg was no longer moving. Then Naulg's body fell out of the doorway to land with a thud on the cobbles. He lay, stiff as a statue—paralyzed. Nothing moved except his eyes, which rolled wildly in their sockets.

Arvin would have to be careful; the doxy obviously had magic at her disposal. He touched the clay bead he wore on a thong around his neck. The unglazed bead, about the size of a hen's egg and carved with circles representing a pupil and iris, was a cheap copy of the good luck charms known as cat's eyes. It was the last gift his mother had ever given him. "Nine lives," he whispered to himself, echoing the words she'd spoken that day.

As the doxy bent down over Naulg, Arvin reached under his jacket with his left hand and drew the dagger that was sheathed horizontally across the small of his back. He turned it in his gloved hand, ready for throwing, then whispered the command that activated the glove's magic. The dagger disappeared.

Arvin walked boldly into the courtyard, hands apparently empty at his sides. Out of the corner of his eye, he searched the shadows on either side, alert for any accomplice the woman might have.

"Get away from him," he ordered. "Leave now, and I'll forget I ever saw this."

He expected the doxy to startle, but instead she looked up boldly. Arvin saw with a shock that her face had changed. Instead of being smooth, her skin was pocked with dozens of overlapping scars. So, too, were the hands that gripped Naulg's trousers. Arvin jerked to an abrupt halt, heart hammering in his chest as he recognized the scars for what they were—the hallmarks of disease.

In the moment that he stood, rooted to the ground with surprise, the doxy sprang into action. One of her hands rose and she began to chant. Arvin reacted a heartbeat later, speaking the glove's command word as he raised his hand. But even as the dagger point became solid between his fingers, the doxy completed her spell. Blindness fell over Arvin like a heavy curtain, leaving him blinking.

He threw the dagger—only to hear it thud into the door behind her. At a word, the magic weapon unstuck itself and flew back to his hand; even blinded, Arvin had only to grasp the air in front of him to catch it by the hilt. Now the doxy was whispering a second spell—and approaching him. Afraid of catching her contagion, Arvin jumped sideways, sweeping the air in front of him with the dagger to keep her at bay. The tip of his dagger caught and sliced through something—her clothing?—but then his foot caught on a loose cobblestone and he tripped. He landed hard, cracking his cheek against the cobblestones.

He started to rise, all the while slashing blindly with the dagger, but then a hand shoved against his back. He sprawled forward into a tight space that must have been the doorway, and an instant later felt something hard smack into his face. Dazed, he realized it had been the door opening.

He tried to get up again, but a foot slammed into his back, forcing him back to the ground. Strong hands wrenched at his arm then banged his hand against the ground in an attempt to loosen his grip on the dagger. Frightened now, realizing he might lose the magic weapon, Arvin spoke the command that made it vanish into his glove. With luck, the doxy and her accomplice would simply take the coin in his pocket and run, leaving Arvin to recover from her spell.

But it seemed Tymora did not favor him this night. Instead of patting him down, the doxy's accomplice wrenched Arvin's hands behind his back and lashed his wrists tightly together. Then Arvin felt the hands shift to his ankles. He kicked violently but to no avail; whoever the doxy's accomplice was, he was strong. He trussed Arvin up neatly, like a swine ready for slaughter. He said something in a low voice to the doxy, and they both chuckled. Arvin thought he caught a name: Missim.

"Take what you like and leave," Arvin yelled—in a voice that was tight with fear. "I'll keep my mouth shut. Neither the militia nor the Guild will—"

The jerk of being hoisted into the air cut off the rest of Arvin's plea. As he landed across the accomplice's shoulders, he swallowed nervously, suddenly aware that words wouldn't save him. This was no ordinary bait and jump.

What in the Nine Hells had he blundered into?

Arvin tensed as the accomplice shrugged him off his shoulders and let him fall. Tensing was the wrong thing to do; Arvin hit the ground hard, cracking his head against stone. When the sparkles cleared from his blinded eyes, he tried to lever himself into a sitting position, but the ground was too slippery. He succeeded only in fouling his face and clothes with muck before falling back down again.

Judging by the smell, he was in the sewers. The stench was overwhelming; it filled his nostrils and throat, making him gag. The feel of sewer muck on his clothes and skin was worse than being covered in crawling spiders and renewed his determination to escape. He thrashed even more frantically, half expecting a blow from his captors at any moment, and eventually managed to sit up—albeit awkwardly, with his wrists tied firmly behind his back and his ankles lashed together.

If he could only see, he might conjure his dagger back into his hand and start to cut himself free, but blind as he was, he had no way of knowing where his captors were. One of them might have been standing right behind him, ready to pluck the dagger out of his hand.

Then he heard chanting. Men's and women's voices together, perhaps a half-dozen of them. He tilted his head, listening. It sounded like they were close—no more than a pace or two away—and all together in the same spot. He turned so his hands were away from them and considered calling his dagger back into his glove. Should he risk it?

Suddenly his sight returned. Arvin saw that he was sitting inside a circle of yellow lantern light on an island of stone at the center of a large, water-filled chamber. The island itself was perhaps a dozen paces wide and no more than a handspan above the surface of the water that filled the chamber; in the shadowy distance he could just make out brick walls and a half-dozen arched tunnels leading away from this place.

Five figures—three men and two women, all dressed in grayish green robes with frayed hems and sleeves—were kneeling in a circle around a small wooden statue a couple of paces away. One was the doxy who had rolled Naulg. All had skin that was heavily pocked with thumbprint-sized scars. One of the men had a face so disfigured with disease that his eyes were mere squints; another—a hulking giant of a man—had hair that grew only in patches between the scars.

Turning his head, Arvin saw Naulg—no longer stiff with paralysis, but bound hand and foot as Arvin was. They were not the only captives. Three other unfortunates lay on the stone nearby: an older sailor with tarred hair pulled back in a tight bun; a boy of about twelve who was crying with soft, hiccupping sobs; and a woman Arvin remembered seeing inside the Coil earlier that evening, soliciting the sailors. She was struggling fiercely against her bonds, her hands white as the cord bit deep into her wrists, but the sailor appeared to have given up. He lay with eyes closed, whispering a prayer to Silvanus.

Arvin caught Naulg's eye then jerked his head backward to draw Naulg's attention to his hands. *Which way is out?* he signed in finger-speech.

Naulg glanced from one tunnel to the other and then shrugged. *Can't swim. Drown.*

Arvin ground his teeth. They lived in a port city, and Naulg couldn't swim? He glanced around, seeking other options. Just beyond the spot where their captors chanted, a rowboat was tied up. It seemed to be riding low in the water; its gunwales could barely be seen above the lip of the stone island.

Boat, Arvin signed back.

Naulg glanced at it out of the corner of his eye and shook his head. *Too far,* his fingers replied.

Arvin winked. *Wait. I signal. You. . . .* He stared purposefully at the lantern and twitched one foot. Their captors had set the lantern down halfway between themselves and their captives, close enough that Naulg could kick it if he wriggled just a little closer.

Arvin wiggled his fingers to draw Naulg's attention to his gloved left hand. "*Shivis,*" he whispered, calling the dagger into it. Turning the weapon, he carefully positioned its edge against the cord that bound his wrists.

Naulg grinned and shifted—slowly, and without making any sound—just a little closer to the lantern. The female captive, having followed their hand signals avidly—though presumably without understanding them—edged closer to Arvin. She turned her bound hands toward him and gave him a pleading look.

Arvin ignored her and continued his work with the dagger. His hands were numb from being bound, his fingers fumbling as he sawed at the cord. The dagger slipped, slicing into his wrist, and he nearly dropped it.

The chanting stopped. The pockmarked people rose to their feet and turned toward the captives, each holding a small metal flask with ridged sides that was shaped like the rattle of a snake. Arvin jerked the blade frantically up and down against the cord that held his wrists, heedless of the jolts of pain as its point jabbed into his forearm. He felt the cord start to part. But then the larger man with patchy hair kicked Arvin in the chest, knocking him onto his back. Arvin gasped as the blade sliced a hot line across the small of his back and lost his grip on it. He wrenched with all of his might against the cord, but though it gave slightly, it refused to break.

Arvin squirmed, trying to find the dagger again, but now the larger man was kneeling on his chest. Thick fingers pried at Arvin's lips, forcing his mouth open. Arvin tried to bite him—then immediately thought better of it, not wanting to sink his teeth into the man's pockmarked flesh, which exuded the same tainted-meat smell the doxy's had. Realizing this, the larger man laughed. He shoved Arvin's head to the side, forcing his cheek against the stone, and held him there while he popped the cork out of the flask with a thumb. Then he jammed the flask into Arvin's mouth. A vile-tasting liquid rushed out of it, making Arvin gag. He tried to wrench his head away and spit, but the larger man forced his jaw shut. The bitter liquid slid down Arvin's throat like a snake finding its hole.

"Embrace him," the pockmarked man chanted. "Enfold him, endure him."

The man's four companions were also chanting. Above the drone of their voices, Arvin heard the female captive shouting violent curses and the boy screaming. The larger man released Arvin suddenly and clambered to his feet then reached down for Arvin's ankles. Instead of wasting time kicking, Arvin fumbled for the dagger that still lay under his back and at last managed to close his fingers around it. He tried to saw at his bonds as the large man dragged him across the island toward the statue, but the dagger was nearly ripped out of his hand as it grated against the stone. Just before it left his fingers he spat out the command word that made it vanish. He'd try again in a moment, but first, a distraction.

"Naulg," he shouted, "now!"

Then a wave of agony gripped him. It felt as though a hand were reaching into his guts, twisting them. Arvin's skin suddenly went ice cold and violent trembles raced through his limbs. His jaw clenched and his neck spasmed, jerking his chin down against his chest.

The larger man dropped Arvin's ankles and grabbed his hair, forcing his face closer to the statue. Arvin was trembling so violently he could barely see the thing. It looked like the statue of a woman, but the wood was so rotted and worm eaten it was impossible to make out more detail than that. Still holding Arvin's hair, the larger man coughed into his free hand and smeared his phlegmy palm against first Arvin's forehead, then that of the statue. "Mother of Death, take him, torment him, teach him."

All of the other captives were screaming now as they too were dragged toward the statue; Arvin could hear Naulg's voice among them. Then he heard a loud clatter. Flashes of light spun across the ceiling as the lantern rolled. It hit the water with a loud sizzle, and the chamber was plunged into darkness. Immediately, Arvin called the dagger back to his gloved hand. This time, despite the violent shaking of his hands—or perhaps aided by it—he was able to saw through the cord. His hands sprung apart. One arm clutching the ferocious ache in his belly, he spun around and plunged the dagger into the pockmarked man behind him. He wrenched himself away, leaving the man gasping, and slit the cord that bound his ankles. Then he began crawling toward the sound of Naulg's screams.

Someone was in his way—Arvin's outstretched hand encountered the soggy hem of a frayed robe and a pair of legs. He thrust his knife into one of them and heard a grunt of pain. Then the person whirled. A woman's voice began chanting; Arvin recognized it as that of the woman who had posed as a doxy. She was casting a spell. Arvin, already doubled over with pain, felt its magic strike his mind like a gong. Over the ringing in his ears came a single, shouted command: "Retreat!"

Compelled by its power, he scrambled backward across the slippery stone. He was barely able to crawl, so fiercely was he trembling; the pain caused by whatever they'd forced him to drink was almost overwhelming now. Suddenly there was nothing under his hand—he'd been driven all the way back to the lip of the island. He tumbled off the edge, twisting as he fell. Instead of splashing into water, he landed sprawled inside something that rocked back and forth as he landed in it—the rowboat. Cold, stinking water slopped inside, soaking his shirt and pants as he lay on his back. Arvin heard a wet tearing noise as the line that moored the boat to the island parted as easily as rotted cloth. Then the boat, nudged by the current, began to float away.

Naulg and the other captives were still screaming. Arvin, however, only dully felt the agony that had gripped his body a few moments before. It had been replaced with an overwhelming weakness. He tried to sit up, but found he could not; his body no longer responded, not even so much as a finger twitch. Dully, he tried to make sense of what was happening, but his thoughts were as frayed as the pockmarked peoples' robes.

Dying, he thought. I'm dying. I thought I could escape, but all I was did was crawl into my coffin.

23 Kythorn, Darkmorning

Arvin's eyes sprang open as a sharp hissing noise filled his ears. Where was he? Had he been dreaming? No. He was wet, and shivering, and surrounded by the overpowering stench of sewage. He could feel its slime on his skin; inside his wet, clinging clothing; in his hair. And he could feel something more—something heavy lying on his chest. A moment later it shifted, revealing the source of the hissing noise he'd heard a moment ago. It was a snake twice the length of his arm and as thick as his wrist.

Two unblinking eyes stared into his.

Startled, Arvin sat up—only to crack his head against a low ceiling. He fell back into whatever he was sitting in, and it rocked to one side, nearly spilling him out. He saw that he was lying in a decrepit-looking rowboat, its gunwales almost touching the brickwork overhead. Worried it would sink, he kept as still as he could. The snake, meanwhile, turned and slithered across Arvin's body, down toward his feet.

Arvin turned his head to the right and looked through the space between the boat and the ceiling. He saw that the side of the boat was butted up against vertical iron bars that were rusted with age. Beyond these he could see the harbor, crowded with ships. From somewhere outside and above, he heard the voices and footsteps of sailors walking along the seawall that lined the waterfront. Turning his head to the left, he saw a darkened, water-filled tunnel. From some distant point inside it, he heard what sounded like falling water.

After a moment's confusion, Arvin realized where he was—and remembered what had happened. Despite having been fed what he could only assume was poison by those crazed, pockmarked people, he'd survived. The pain and trembling—and the lethargy that had followed—were gone. Some time while he lay uncon-scious, his body must have conquered the toxin. He was alive and healthy—and covered in a stench that made his skin crawl. Somehow the rowboat he'd fallen into had made it, without swamping, down the series of spillways that carried Hlondeth's sewage to the sea.

"Nine lives," he whispered, touching the bead at his throat.

Was Naulg still alive? How much time had passed? The gods only knew how long Arvin had lain unconscious in this boat. The only thing he knew was that it was still night. He listened, straining his ears to catch the sound of distant screams, but heard only the low gurgle of water and the *plop-splash* of what was probably a rat dropping into the sewage.

The snake, meanwhile, slithered across his ankles and up over the edge of the boat and began to coil up one of the bars. Was it just an animal, or a yuan-ti in serpent form? And what was it doing in the boat with him? Arvin touched its scaly body with his fingertips. "Who are you?" he asked. "What—"

The snake paused and turned to look at Arvin. Light from the harbor glittered off its green scales. A slender blue tongue flickered in and out of its mouth as it tasted the air. Its eyes remained locked on Arvin's for several long seconds, as if taking his measure. Then it drew back and slithered up the bar toward the seawall above. In another moment it was gone.

Quickly, Arvin took stock. The ensorcelled glove was still on his left hand, and—he spoke the glove's command word twice and the dagger appeared in his hand then disappeared again—he hadn't lost his dagger. Nor had his captors taken the braided leather bracelet that encircled his right wrist. All three of his magical devices were still with him.

He'd need them if he was going to rescue Naulg.

The chamber with the island of stone would be farther up the sewer line. If Arvin remained flat on his back and pushed with his hands against the ceiling, he could send the rowboat back up the tunnel. Carefully, not wanting to swamp the boat, Arvin placed his hands flat on the ceiling above.

Then he paused. Would he really be able to find his way back? The sewers were said to be as much of a maze as the streets above them, with more twists and turns than a nest of coiled snakes. By the time he found Naulg—assuming he did—Naulg could very well be dead.

Then there was the prospect of facing the pockmarked people again. Plague had always terrified Arvin; he didn't want to expose himself to it in what was likely to be a lost cause. And really, Arvin didn't owe Naulg anything. When Naulg had escaped from the orphanage, he hadn't come back for Arvin. He hadn't even sent word. Instead, he'd forgotten Arvin—until fate threw them together a second time. If it had been Naulg who had escaped, Arvin wouldn't have counted on the rogue to rescue him; he'd have expected to be on his own.

Just as he had been in the orphanage.

Except for that brief time when Naulg had befriended him.

But those screams. . . . Could Arvin really turn his back on Naulg and not expect to hear them echoing in his memory for the rest of his life?

Arvin had to rescue Naulg. That was who he was. Foolish and loyal, just like his mother.

He just hoped he didn't wind up dead, as she had, because of it.

He started to guide the rowboat back up the tunnel, but after moving it only a short distance, he noticed something. The gap between the gunwales and the brickwork above was getting smaller. The tide was rising, backing up the water in the sewage tunnel. It would be only a matter of moments now before the gunwales were touching the ceiling. Then the boat would fill with water and sink.

That was it, then. The tide had decided for him. In a few moments this tunnel would be flooded and there would be no way for Arvin to make it back to the chamber where Naulg was—not until low tide, by which time it would probably be too late, anyway.

Arvin wasn't going to be able to find that chamber again. . . .

Unless, of course, the pockmarked people returned to the Coil for more victims. And there was a slim chance that they might, since at least two of the victims—Naulg and the woman who had implored Arvin to cut her bonds—had been plucked from there. With luck, they'd assume Arvin was dead. If he could spot one of them at the Coil, he might be able to follow him back to the chamber.

The ceiling grated against the gunwales, shutting out the harbor lights like a coffin lid closing. The water in the tunnel was nearly at ceiling height now and streaming into the boat. Time to get out of here.

Arvin rocked to his right, deliberately swamping the boat, and grabbed for one of the bars as he was spilled into cold, stinking water. The bars were spaced far enough apart that he might just squeeze through them, especially with sewage lubricating his skin. Clinging to the bar to keep his head above the rapidly rising water, he jammed his shoulder through the gap between two bars. By turning his head and exhaling, he was just able to squeeze through.

He climbed the brickwork of the seawall, levered himself up over the edge, and stood up, looking around to get his bearings. Then he set out, dripping stink in puddles around his feet, in the direction of the Mortal Coil.

CHAPTER 2

23 Kythorn,
Darkmorning

As Arvin walked along the seawall toward the Mortal Coil, suspiciously eyeing everyone who passed under the streetlights, four sailors staggered toward him. He stepped to one side, intending to allow the group to pass, but as they drew nearer, one of them took a long, bleary look at Arvin then loudly guffawed. His two companions all turned to see what the joke was; an instant later they sniffed and pinched their noses. They began shouting drunken oaths at Arvin, telling him to haul his stink downwind.

Arvin felt his cheeks grow hot and red. Suddenly he was a boy again, enduring the taunts of the other children in the orphanage as they made fun of the punishment he'd been subjected to—the touch of a wand that had made his skin stink worse than a ghoul's. The punishment was a favorite one of the priests and had been inspired by the martyrdom of one of Ilmater's innumerable, interminably suffering saints. Arvin had tried to scrub the magical stink off, scraping his skin raw with a pumice stone and standing under the tap until he was shivering and wrinkled, but still it had persisted, filling his nose with a sharp reek, even lingering on his tongue until he wanted to gag. Even shaving his hair off hadn't helped—the other kids had only incorporated his shaved head into their taunts, pointing at the stubble and calling him "rotten egg."

A dribble of filthy water trickled down Arvin's temple. He flicked his wet hair back and felt the dribble transfer to the back of his neck. At least, this time, the smell would wash off.

And he was no longer a cringing child.

Grabbing the largest sailor by the shirtfront with his bare hand, Arvin summoned his dagger into his glove and jammed the blade up the man's nostril. As the point pierced flesh, a trickle of red dribbled out of the nostril onto the man's upper lip. "Shall I cut your nose off, then?" Arvin said through gritted teeth. "Would that alleviate the smell? Or would you and your friends prefer to take your insults somewhere else?"

The man's eyes widened. He started to shake his head then thought better of it. "Easy mate," he gasped. "We'll ship off."

Arvin stepped back, removing his dagger. The sailors staggered away, the bloody-nosed one muttering curses under his breath.

Arvin stood for a moment in silence, watching other late-night revelers stagger along the seawall, wondering if any might be hiding pockmarks under a cloak of magic. The taunts of the sailors had made him realize one thing, at least. The only way he was going to locate any of the pockmarked people was by using his nose to pick out their sour, sick odor. Enfolded in sewer stink, he didn't have a hope of doing that.

Sighing, he strode away to find a bathhouse.

A short time later, Arvin felt human again. The bathhouse—a circular stone chamber where patrons basked lazily in hot, swirling steam while slaves soaped and scrubbed them—had been worth the delay. Arvin—scrubbed pink and smelling of good, clean soap—dressed in a fresh change of clothes and felt ready to face any challenge.

Even a descent back into the sewers to find Naulg.

He returned to his only starting point: the Mortal Coil. It was still some time before dawn, and business at the Coil was slow, most of the sailors having staggered back to their ships to sleep off their revels. No more than a dozen patrons sat at tables. One of them Arvin recognized immediately: the yuan-ti woman with red hair who had been drinking there last night.

The woman, who had changed into a dress made from a

shimmering green fabric a few shades lighter than her scales, looked up as Arvin entered the tavern. He didn't think she'd recognize him from yesterday evening—he'd gotten his hair cut short at the bathhouse. Even had his hair still been shoulder length, odds were she wouldn't remember seeing him. Arvin's average build and pleasant, "anyman" face gave him a natural talent for disappearing into a crowd. It was a godsend in his line of work—though with it came the annoyance of people frequently mistaking him for someone else.

The woman was still staring at him. Arvin crossed the first two fingers of his right hand while holding it discreetly at his side. *Guild?*

The woman made no response. Instead, she turned away.

A thought occurred to Arvin. Last night, the woman had seemed to be searching the crowd for someone. Had she, too, lost a friend to a pockmarked abductor? Was that why she'd returned to the Coil? If so, she might be willing to join in the search for Naulg. At the very least, she might have noticed something that Arvin had missed.

Arvin crossed to her table and bowed deeply, waiting for her to bid him rise. When she did, he gave her his most winning smile and indicated the empty chair opposite her. "May I join you?" A familiar prickling sensation tickled the base of his scalp—a feeling that always boded well in this sort of situation. She would invite him to sit down. He was certain of it.

The yuan-ti tilted her head as if listening to something—another good sign—but didn't speak. For a moment, Arvin was worried she'd dismiss him out of hand—yuan-ti were prone to doing that, with humans. But then she nodded and gestured for him to sit. A faint smile twitched her lips, as if she'd just found something amusing. Then it disappeared.

Arvin sat. "You were here last night," he began.

She waited, not blinking. Arvin had grown up in Hlondeth and was used to the stares of the yuan-ti. If she was trying to unnerve him, she was failing.

"Do you remember the man I was sitting with—the one in the yellow shirt?"

She nodded.

"The woman who was sitting on his lap, the doxy, have you seen her since then?"

"The pockmarked woman?" Her voice was soft and sibilant; like all yuan-ti, she hissed softly as she spoke.

Arvin raised his eyebrows. "You saw her sores?"

"I saw through the spell she'd cast to disguise herself," the yuan-ti answered. "From the moment she entered the tavern, I recognized her for what she was."

Arvin was appalled. "You knew she was diseased? Why didn't you warn us—or call the militia?"

The woman shrugged, a slow, rolling motion of her shoulders. "There was nothing to fear. Plague had touched her then moved on, leaving only scars behind."

"But her touch—"

"Was harmless," the yuan-ti interrupted. "Her sores had scarred over. Had they been open and weeping, it would have been another matter entirely."

"What about her spittle?" Arvin asked.

The yuan-ti stared at him. "You kissed her?"

"My friend did. Or rather. . . ." He thought back to the phelgm that had been smeared on his brow. "The doxy kissed him on his forehead. Would that pass the plague to him?" He waited, breath held, for her reply. Had he fought off the poison he'd been forced to drink, only to be condemned to death by disease?

The yuan-ti gave a faint hiss that might have been laughter. "No. Tell your friend not to worry. The plague that left the pockmarks was long gone from her body. From *all* parts of her body."

She said it with such certainty, Arvin believed her. Relief washed through him. Knowing that he'd been touched by people who themselves had been touched by plague had filled him with dread. He wasn't old enough to have witnessed the last plague that swept through the Vilhon Reach; the "dragonscale plague" had been eradicated thirty years before he was born. Like most people, though, he feared to even speak of it. The disease, thought to be magical in origin, had caused the skin of those it touched to flake off in huge chunks, like scales, leaving bloody, weeping holes.

Shuddering, he ordered an ale from the serving girl who approached their table; then he turned back to the yuan-ti. "You seem to know quite a lot about disease."

"In recent months I've made a study of it."

Arvin's eyes narrowed. "Is that so?" A suspicion was starting to form in his mind—that it was the "doxy" this woman had been looking for last night, or one of her pockmarked companions.

"Did you follow us after we left the tavern?" Arvin asked bluntly. He waited tensely for her answer; perhaps she could describe the place where the pockmarked people had entered the sewer system. If he knew that, he might be able to find the chamber where—

"There was no need. I had a . . . hunch that I'd see you again this morning and hear your story." Her eyes bored into his. "Tell me what happened last night after you and your friend left the Mortal Coil."

Arvin stared at her, appalled by her indifference. She'd sat and watched as Naulg was led away by a dangerous, diseased woman—and done nothing. At the very least she might have warned Arvin not to follow them. Instead she'd let events unfold, content to question the survivors afterward.

"Some 'study of disease,'" Arvin muttered under his breath. Then, meeting the yuan-ti's unblinking eyes, he asked, "Who are you?"

"Zelia."

Arvin supposed that must be her name.

"Who do you work for?"

Zelia gave a hiss of laughter. "Myself."

Arvin stared at her, frowning. When it was clear she wasn't going to add anything more, he made a quick decision. He had little to lose by telling her his story—and everything to gain. Perhaps she might pick out some clue in his tale that would help him find Naulg. She seemed to know more—much more—than she was letting on, but then, yuan-ti tended to give that impression.

Omitting any mention of his transaction with Naulg, Arvin reiterated the events that had taken place a short time ago: his fight with the doxy and her accomplice, finding himself in the sewage chamber, being force-fed the poison, the terrible anguish it had produced, and escaping in the rowboat. He watched Zelia closely as he told his tale, but her expression didn't change. She listened most attentively as he described the chamber where the force-feeding had taken place, stopping him more than once to ask for more detail, including full descriptions of the people who had abducted him. She made him describe each person's appearance and exactly what had been said.

Arvin concluded with a description of the statue. "The wood was rotted, but it was definitely a statue of a woman. The hands were raised, as if reaching—"

"Talona."

"Is that a name?" Arvin asked. He'd never heard it before.

"Lady of Poison, Mistress of Disease, Mother of Death," Zelia intoned.

Arvin shuddered. "Yes. That's what they called her."

"Goddess of sickness and disease," Zelia continued, "a lesser-known goddess, not commonly worshiped in the Vilhon Reach. Her followers only recently surfaced in Hlondeth."

"Last night was a sacrifice, then," Arvin said.

"Yes. It is how they appease their goddess. They appeal to Talona to take another life, so she will continue to spare their own."

"That's why they fed us the poison."

"Yes," Zelia said. "Sometimes they use poison and sometimes plague. Usually, a mix of both."

Arvin felt his face grow pale. "Plague," he said in a hoarse voice. Had there been plague mixed with the poison they'd forced him to drink? He gripped the edge of the table and stared at his hands, wondering if his skin would suddenly erupt into terrible, weeping blisters.

Just at that moment, his ale arrived. The serving girl set it on the table then stood, waiting. Arvin stared at the mug. He suddenly didn't feel thirsty anymore. Realizing that the serving girl was still waiting, he fumbled a coin out of his pocket and tossed it onto her tray. He'd probably just paid her too much, judging by the speed with which she palmed it, but he didn't care. His thoughts were still filled with images of plague: his lungs filling with fluid, his body burning with coal-hot fever, his hair falling out of his scalp, his skin flaking away in chunks. . . .

"Will Talona claim me still?" he croaked.

Zelia smiled. "You feel healthy, don't you?" She waved a hand disparagingly. "If there was plague mixed in with the poison, it's been held at bay by the strength of your own constitution. You slipped out of the goddess's grasp. Talona has lost her hold on you."

Arvin nodded, trying to reassure himself. He did feel healthy— and strong. Refreshed and alert, despite having had no sleep last night. If he had been exposed to plague, he was showing no signs of it—yet.

A question occurred to him. "Why are you so interested in this cult?" he asked.

"They're killing people."

"They're killing humans," Arvin pointed out. "Why should a yuan-ti care about that?"

All he got in reply was a cold, unblinking stare. For a moment, he worried he'd gone too far. Did he honestly care why Zelia was "making a study" of disease, or on whose behalf? Really, it was none of his business. He quickly got back to the matter at hand—trying to learn something that would help him find Naulg.

"Does this cult have a name?" he asked.

Zelia gave a slight, supple nod. "They call themselves the Pox."

"Can you tell me anything else about them? How I can find them again, for example?"

Zelia smiled. "What would you do if you found them?"

"Rescue my friend."

Zelia frowned. "Rushing in will only alert the Pox to the fact that someone is watching them," she told him. "And it would serve no purpose. Your friend is already dead."

When Arvin began to protest, she held up a hand. "As would you be, if you hadn't proved stronger than the rest. But there is a way for you to avenge your friend's death. Would you like to hear what it is?"

Arvin's eyes narrowed. He could tell when he was being manipulated. How did this woman know for certain that Naulg was dead? Like Arvin, he might have fought off the draught of plague. He might still be alive—and a captive. Arvin nodded.

"I want to know more about the Pox—things that only a human can uncover," she continued. "I'd be willing to pay for that information, providing the human was smart and knew how not to tip his hand."

Arvin feigned only a passing interest by crossing his arms and leaning back in his chair. "How much?"

Zelia took a sip of her ale—not quite quickly enough to hide her smile. Her teeth were human—square and flat, rather than the slender, curved fangs some yuan-ti had. "Enough."

It was Arvin's turn to stare. "Why do you need a human?" he asked at last.

"The cultists won't accept any other race into their ranks."

Arvin wrinkled his nose in disgust as he realized what she was asking him to do. "You want me to join their cult? To worship that foul abomination of a goddess? Never!"

Zelia's expression tightened. Too late, Arvin realized what he'd just said. "Abomination" was the word that humans elsewhere in the Vilhon Reach used to describe the yuan-ti who had the most snake-like characteristics. It was an insult that no human of Hlondeth ever dared use. It commonly provoked a sharp, swift—and fatal—bite in return, or a slow constriction.

Arvin swallowed nervously and half-closed his gloved hand, ready to call the dagger to it, but Zelia let the insult pass.

"To *pretend* to join their cult," she said.

Arvin shook his head. "The answer is still no."

"Is it because of your faith you refuse?" she asked.

For one unsettling moment Arvin wondered if she was refer-ring to Ilmater, if she knew about his time in the orphanage and the endless attempts by the clerics to instill in the children under their care a sense of "eternal thankfulness for the mercy of our lord the Crying God." Then he realized that Zelia was simply asking a general question. "I don't worship any particular deity," he told her. "I toss the occasional coin in Tymora's cup for good fortune, but that's all."

"Then why do you refuse?"

Arvin sighed. "I'm a simple merchant. I import ropes and nets. For this job, you need an actor—or a rogue."

Zelia's eyes narrowed. "It's you I want. You survived the disease the Pox infected you with. In their eyes, that makes you blessed."

"I see." He decided to see how badly she wanted these cultists. "I lost one thousand gold pieces last night. Would you be willing to pay that much for me to spy on them?"

Zelia gave a dismissive wave of her hand, as if the figure he'd just named were pocket change. "Certainly."

"Five thousand?"

"Yes."

"Ten?"

Zelia gave him a tight smile. "If you produce the desired results, yes—and if you follow orders."

With difficulty, Arvin kept his expression neutral. As he collected his thoughts, he sipped his ale and considered her offer. Ten thousand gold pieces was a lot of coin—enough to get him out of Hlondeth and free him from the Guild's clutches forever. But he wondered for whom Zelia was working. Someone with deep pockets, obviously—perhaps someone with access to the royal coffers. Unless she was lying about the coin, and didn't intend to pay anything, which was more likely when you came right down to it. A classic bait and jump—offer the victim anything he asks for then give him more than he bargained for.

"Well?" Zelia asked. "Will you do it?"

Arvin shuddered, remembering the terrible pockmarks on the cultists' skin. Was that how his mother had looked as she lay dying? He decided he couldn't bear the foul touch of their fingers again, even if they carried no taint. Even for ten thousand gold pieces.

"No," he answered. "Not for all the coin in the Extaminos treasury. Find someone else." He set his ale down and started to rise from the table.

Surprisingly, Zelia didn't protest. Instead, she took a long swallow of the ale in front of her, gulping down the egg inside it. When she was finished, she licked her lips with a tongue that was longer than the average human's, with a slight fork at the end of it . . .

A blue tongue.

Arvin felt his eyes widen. He sank back into his seat. "You were the snake in the rowboat."

"Yes."

"You neutralized the poison?"

Zelia nodded.

"Why?"

"I wanted you alive."

"Knowing—thanks to your 'hunch'—that I'd return to the Coil, and I'd tell you my story," Arvin said.

"Yes."

Anger rose inside Arvin, flushing his face. "You used me."

Zelia stared at him. "I saved your life."

"The answer's still no. I won't join the cult."

"Yes you will," Zelia said slowly. "Seven days from now, you will."

She said it with such certainty that it gave Arvin pause. "What do you mean?" he asked slowly.

"After I neutralized the poison, I planted a 'seed' in your mind," Zelia said. "A seed that takes seven days to germinate. At the end of those seven days, your mind will no longer be your own. Your body will be mine—to do with as I will." She leaned across the table and lightly stroked his temple with her fingertips then sat back, smiling.

Arvin stared at her, horrified. She was bluffing, he told himself. But it didn't *feel* like a bluff. Her smile was too confident, too self-satisfied—that of a gambler who knows he holds the winning hand. And now that she'd drawn his attention to it, Arvin could feel a faint throbbing in his temple, like the beginning of a headache. Was it the "seed" spell she had cast on him, putting down roots?

"What if I agree to join the cult?" he asked. "If I do that, will you negate the spell?"

Zelia hissed softly. "You've changed your mind?" Her lips parted to add something more, but just then, from somewhere behind Arvin, there came a shout of dismay and the sound of chairs being scuffed hurriedly back—and the clink of chain mail.

Turning on his chair—slowly, so as not to attract attention to himself—Arvin saw a dozen men in armor descending the ramp: Hlondeth's human militia. Each wore a helmet that was flared to resemble the hood of a cobra, with a slit-eyed visor that hid the face from the nose up. The bronze rings of their chain mail shimmered like scales as they marched into the tavern. They were armed with strangely shaped crossbows. Arvin observed how these worked a moment later, when a boy in his teens leaped from his chair and tried to run to a door that led to the tavern's stockroom. At a gesture from their sergeant—a large man with a jutting chin and the emblem of two twined serpents embossed on the breastplate he wore—one of the militia pulled the trigger of his crossbow. A pair of lead weights linked by a fine wire exploded from the weapon, whirling around one another as they flew through the air. The wire caught the youth around his ankles, sending him crashing into a table.

The silence that followed was broken only by the sound of a mug rolling across the table and falling with a soft thud into the sawdust below. Then, as the man who had shot the crossbow strode across the room to apprehend the runaway, the sergeant spoke.

"By order of Lady Extaminos, I am commanded to find crew for a galley," he announced. "Those who have previously served in the militia are exempt. Roll up your sleeves and account for yourselves."

A handful of men in the tavern dutifully began to roll up their sleeves, exposing the chevrons magically branded into their left forearms by battle clerics—chevrons that recorded the four years of service required of every human male in Hlondeth. Arvin, meanwhile, glanced around the tavern, his heart pounding. A galley? Their crews had even less expectation of coming home again than the men who were sent to the Cloven Mountains to fight goblins. Arvin wasn't so foolish as to get up and run; he'd get no farther than the bare-armed youth who was being hustled toward the exit. The one avenue of escape—the wide, sloping ramp that led up to the seawall above—was blocked by militia, who were only letting men with chevrons leave the tavern.

More worrisome still was the man who stood beside the sergeant. He wore neither helmet nor armor, and carried no weapon other than the dagger sheathed at his hip. He had strange eyes with a curious fold to the eyelid—Arvin's mother had described the peoples of the East as having eyes like that. Judging by his gray hair and the deep creases at either side of his mouth, he was too old to be a regular militiaman. He stood with one hand thrust into a pocket—closed around a concealed magical device, perhaps—as he scrutinized the faces of the men in the tavern, one by one.

This was no press gang. The militiamen were searching for someone.

Arvin swallowed nervously and felt the bead he wore shift against his throat. "Nine lives," he whispered. Reaching down, he began to unfasten his shirt cuff. As he pretended to fumble with the laces, he turned to Zelia.

"I won't be able to spy for you if I'm aboard a galley," he whispered. "If you have any pull with the militia, use it now."

Zelia's lips twitched into a slit of a smile. "You accept my offer?"

Arvin nodded vigorously as a member of the militia approached their table.

"Too late." With a supple, flowing motion, she rose from her chair. Cocking her head in Arvin's direction, she spoke to the man approaching their table. "Here's one for you." Then she strode away.

As the man's visored eyes locked on him, Arvin felt the hair at the back of his neck rise. His hand froze on his shirt cuff. Even if the press gang was a sham, the fact remained that he'd never served his time with the militia. In order to keep up the pretense of the press gang, they'd have to arrest him. They'd toss him in jail, where, in seven days' time, Zelia's spell would take effect.

Arvin couldn't allow that to happen. The only way he could find out whatever Zelia wanted to know about the Pox, and save himself, was to remain a free man.

The militiaman raised his crossbow. "Roll up your sleeve."

Arvin forced his lips into a smile. "There's been a mistake," he began, rising to his feet. "I served my four years, and they branded me, but a year ago I contracted an illness that"—his mind raced as he tried to think up a story the man would actually believe—"that left me terribly pockmarked." He dropped his voice to a confiding whisper. "I think it was plague."

Arvin widened his eyes in mock alarm, but it didn't have the expected result. The militiaman stood firm and unflinching. He'd obviously heard similar excuses before.

Arvin pressed on hurriedly. "Only recently did I earn enough coin for a tithe. The cleric who healed me did a wonderful job—he actually restored my skin to an unblemished condition. But in the process, he erased my chevrons. See?"

Rolling up his sleeve, Arvin showed the man his bare arm. As the militiaman looked at it, Arvin felt the base of his scalp begin to prickle. Quickly, he caught the militiaman's eye and gave him a friendly grin. "Listen, friend, it's true that I haven't served," Arvin said. "But you could let me go this time—right? Since this isn't really a press gang and I'm not the man you're looking for."

Slowly, the militiaman's expression changed, until his smile mirrored Arvin's own. "Don't worry," he whispered back. "I won't tell them about you."

"Thanks," Arvin said, rolling down his sleeve. "I knew I could count on you, friend." He turned then and began walking toward the ramp, as if the militiaman had granted him leave to go. Zelia was just exiting; the militiamen blocking the ramp parted to let her pass, leaving a gap in their ranks. Arvin lengthened his stride, but then the gray-haired man turned his full attention in Arvin's direction. Arvin saw the man's strangely shaped eyes narrow slightly as he glanced down at Arvin's gloved hand then up at his face again. His expression hardened.

He's recognized me as Guild, Arvin thought, fighting down panic. Or he's mistaken me for whoever the militia are looking for. Either way, I'm in trouble. If only I could distract him for just an instant. . . .

The prickling sensation he'd felt at the base of his scalp a moment ago, when he'd charmed the militiaman, returned—this time deep in Arvin's throat. Within heartbeats it became so strong that Arvin began to hum involuntarily. A low droning filled the air—a sound like that of a bow being drawn against the low bass string of a musical instrument. The militiamen and their sergeant all glanced around as if trying to find its source, but its effect on the gray-haired fellow was even more dramatic. He suddenly lost interest in Arvin and stared at the far wall, a far-off look in his eyes, as if he were completely engrossed in it.

Now! Arvin thought. Seizing his chance, he bolted. He sprinted through the gap in the ranks, and, as one militiaman lunged out to grab him, made the most of the man's mistake by grabbing the fellow's hand and using the man's own momentum to tumble him into the fellow behind him. He heard the *snap whiz* of a crossbow being fired—and a sharp exhalation just behind him, followed by curses, as the wire-linked weights wrapped around the man he'd just tumbled. Zelia, farther up the ramp, turned to see what the commotion was. As Arvin sprinted past her, he saw her eyes widen. Then Arvin was around a bend in the ramp and running up it as fast as his pumping legs would carry him.

He emerged onto a seawall limned red by the rising sun—the start of another hot, muggy day. He ducked left into a narrow street, and as soon as he was a few paces down it, leaped headlong at a wall. Fingers splayed, he activated the magic of the leather cord knotted around his wrist. His fingers and boot toes found cracks in the stonework that ordinarily would have offered no purchase, allowing him to scramble up the building like a cat climbing a tree.

Below and to his left, two militiamen emerged onto the seawall.

Arvin froze, not wanting to betray his position with movement. One of the men stopped, crossbow at the ready, to stare down the narrow street Arvin had entered, but Arvin was already level with the building's third story—well above where anyone would reasonably expect him to be. The militiaman looked away.

"Nine lives," Arvin panted, grinning.

Then the gray-haired man stepped into sight beside the militiaman. He held an unusual object in his hand—three finger-sized crystals, bound together with silver wire and pulsing with a faint purple glow. Arvin had never seen anything like it before. The militiamen heeded the call of one of their fellows, ran farther up the seawall, and ran off, but the gray-haired man stood, still staring at the crystals. Then, slowly, he looked up.

Right into Arvin's eyes.

"There he is!" he shouted, pointing.

Arvin cursed and resumed his climb up the wall. The top of the building was just above him—one quick scramble and he was on the roof, a spot where the crossbows wouldn't be able to take him down. He ran lightly along the slate tiles, in a direction they wouldn't expect—back toward the seawall. From below, he could hear the gray-haired man shouting directions.

With a sinking heart, Arvin realized the man had guessed the direction in which he was headed. Arvin abruptly changed direction—and heard the man below shout that the quarry was going *this* way, not *that* way. Cursing, Arvin changed direction again, sending a tile skittering down the rooftop, but that telltale sign was the least of his worries.

The gray-haired man below had magic that could track Arvin, whichever direction he ran. Arvin's only hope was to somehow get out of its range.

CHAPTER 3

ARVIN RAN TOWARD THE REAR OF THE WAREHOUSE, HIS FEET slipping on the tiles. The rooftop was domed, forcing him to run with one leg slightly cocked and his other against the metal gutter that ringed the roof, his arms extended for balance. He made for the rear of the warehouse, toward the point where the curve of the building across the street forced the street to narrow. A split-second glance told him he was in luck; the ramp that spiraled up the outside of that building was one story lower than the warehouse rooftop.

He sprinted the final few steps and hurled himself into the air. He landed on his feet on the ramp of the building opposite, but momentum carried him forward, sending him crashing into the wall. Hot sparks of pain exploded in his nose as his face slammed into the smooth, hard stone. As he staggered down the ramp, nose dripping blood, he startled two men in tattered trousers and sweat-stained shirts who were hauling a two-wheeled handcart up the ramp. Each man had several days' growth of stubble—not quite enough to hide the **S** that had been branded into his left cheek.

Shouts came from the street below. A quick glance over the edge of the ramp told Arvin the militia had rounded both sides of the warehouse and were almost in a position to shoot up at him. Arvin had to get off the ramp—and quickly.

He ran headlong at the two slaves, shouting, "Out of my way!" Shoving his way between them, he leaped onto the handcart. He'd intended only to scramble over it and continue running down the ramp, but the force of his landing jerked the poles out of the slaves' hands. Suddenly the cart was rolling down the slope, poles scraping the stone behind it. Arvin teetered on top of its load, sacks of grain from the Golden Plains. His eyes widened as it careened toward the edge, but before he could jump, one wheel thumped against the low, outside lip of the ramp. The jolt staggered Arvin, nearly spilling him from the cart.

Guided by the scrape of its outside wheel against this barrier, the cart changed direction slightly, its path curving as it followed the ramp. The cart picked up speed, its outside wheel grinding like a millstone against the rock, and Arvin smelled friction-scorched wood. Barely able to keep his balance, arms flailing, he rode the cart down the ramp like a man standing on a galloping horse.

Wire-linked weights shot past over his head as one of the militiamen below loosed a crossbow in his direction. Then he was around the curve of the building, and the bottom of the ramp came into sight.

At its base were two more slaves, just turning a second handcart onto the ramp. Near them stood an overseer who Arvin assumed was human until he opened his mouth to hiss in surprise, baring curved fangs. The two slaves, eyes wide at the sight of the runaway cart, dived to one side, abandoning their own cart. Arvin could see it was time to do the same. He crouched and leaped off the back of his cart. As he landed, skinning the palms of his hands and tearing one trouser knee, he heard the sound of splintering wood followed by the soft hiss of spilling grain.

Arvin leaped to his feet and sprinted past the slaves, who were cringing under a venomous spray of curses from their overseer. Another pair of wire-linked weights crashed against the wall next to Arvin, spurring him onward. He could hear shouted orders and running feet behind him as he pelted through an intersection, choosing a route that led away from the harbor. He turned up one side street, then another. At the next intersection, he changed course yet again, this time heading back toward the harbor. A few more twists and turns and he'd lose them. But somehow, the militia didn't seem to be falling behind. Then he heard the shouts of the gray-haired man, telling the militia which way Arvin had gone. Cursing—he still wasn't out of range of the fellow's magic, it seemed—Arvin ran on.

Up ahead was a wider intersection from which came the smells of overripe fruit and goat dung. In it, street merchants were setting up their wares. Women shook out dusty blankets and laid them on the cobblestones, claiming their selling space for the day. Heavily laden goats stood with heads lowered, picking at the scraps of rind and peel left behind from the previous day, while older children unloaded produce from bulging sacks on the goats' backs, setting it out in neat piles on the blankets their mothers had spread.

All of this Arvin took in at a glance as he pounded toward the Y-shaped intersection. He also noted the buildings that framed the intersection: a sprawling pottery factory with smoking chimneys jutting out of its roof, a slaughterhouse with freshly skinned rabbits hanging from its eaves, a tinsmith's factory from which came the din of hammers pounding on metal, and a narrow two-story tower housing a business Arvin recognized—a spice shop.

Its owner was Guild—a man who, like Arvin, sold products other than those on display. Viro had olive skin and dark, thinning hair with traces of yellow powder in it. He was just unlocking the curved wooden shutters that fronted the spice shop when he heard Arvin running toward him and glanced back over his shoulder.

Arvin's fingers flicked quick signs in the Guild's silent language. *Need to hide. Distract?*

Pretend back door, Viro signed back. *Stay inside. Loft.*

Arvin panted his thanks and ran into the shop.

The interior was only dimly lit; Viro had yet to open its shutters to let in the dawn's light. The smell of freshly extinguished candles drifted through the dusty air, together with the sweet scent of cinnamon and the sharp tang of ground coriander. The spices were held in enormous, open-mouthed clay pots that had scoop handles sticking out the tops; Arvin deliberately snagged one of these as he ran by, sending it clattering to the floor amidst a scatter of black pepper. He hoped the pepper wasn't too exotic or expensive; he'd have to pay Viro for it later.

He ran to the back door and flung it open. Then he doubled back and clambered up a rope ladder that led to a wooden platform—the loft where sacks of unground spices were stored.

Outside the shop, he could hear Viro shouting protests at the militia. "No! There's valuable merchandise in there. You can't run through there! Stop!"

The militia, urged on by a babble of voices as street merchants pointed out which doorway Arvin had run into, ignored Viro. A heartbeat after Arvin had pulled the last rung of the ladder up into the loft and flung himself down, out of sight, they burst into the shop.

"The back door!" one shouted. "He must have gone that way."

Peering down through a knothole, thankful that blood was no longer dribbling from his injured nose, Arvin watched as two militiamen ran out the back door. The third man—their sergeant—held back, eyeing the thigh-high jars of spice as if trying to decide whether they were big enough to hold a man. Spotting the scoop that had fallen, he drew his sword and thrust it into the pepper inside the jar, stirring up the black powder. Suddenly he began blinking rapidly, and gave an enormous sneeze. He yanked his sword out and kicked the jar instead, knocking it over. Pepper cascaded onto the floor.

Arvin silently groaned; the cost of his freedom had just gone up significantly. But at the same time he smiled at the man's discomfort; the sergeant was sneezing violently. Arvin knew just how that felt. One of the times he'd run away from the orphanage he'd hidden inside a bakery and accidentally wound up pulling an entire sack of flour down from a shelf he'd tried to climb. The rupture of the sack over his head had set off a sneezing attack. As a result, the bakers had discovered Arvin, but the spilled flour had been a blessing in disguise. It had coated him from hair to heel, hiding the ink on his wrists that identified him as belonging to the orphanage. Unfortunately, he'd been recognized for what he was when he stepped outside into the rain and the flour washed off.

Below Arvin, the sergeant turned as someone walked in through the front door. Arvin's heart sank as he saw it was the gray-haired man. Behind him came Viro, wringing his hands.

"That's pepper!" Viro wailed, staring at the toppled jar. "Ten silver pieces an ounce!" The protest sounded genuine—and probably was.

Viro glared at the back door of his shop, as if trying to spot Arvin. "When you catch that rogue, drag him back here. He's got to pay for what he's spilled."

The sergeant ignored him. "Where did he go, Tanju?"

The gray-haired man—Tanju, his name must be, though the word sounded foreign—closed his eyes and raised the wire-bound crystals to his ear as if listening to them. A faint sound, like that of chimes tinkling together in the wind, filled the air. Arvin wondered just who in the Nine Hells he'd been mistaken for. Whoever it was, the men below certainly wanted to find him. Arvin glanced frantically around the loft, looking for an escape route. Morning sunlight slanted in through the shutters of a small window a few paces away. Rising to his hands and knees, he began a slow, silent crawl across the spice sacks toward it.

In the room below, the purple glow of the crystals intensified. Then, just as Arvin reached the window and began turning its latch—praying all the while it wouldn't squeak—the purple glow dimmed.

Arvin heard Tanju's voice drop to a low whisper. Viro immediately began a loud protest. "Where are you going? He's not up—"

Viro's protest ended in a sharp grunt. Arvin winced, realizing the fellow had probably just been punched in the gut. An instant later, the creak of boards and the slight clink of chain mail completed the warning Viro had begun. The sergeant was climbing toward Arvin's hiding place. Someone else—probably Tanju—was striding toward the back door, presumably to call back the other militiamen.

The time for stealth was long gone. Leaping to his feet, Arvin booted the shutter open and dived headlong through the window. He landed in a controlled tumble on the flat, soot-encrusted rooftop of the pottery factory and sprang once more to his feet, this time smudged with black. He glanced behind him—just in time to see the sergeant lean out the window with a crossbow—and threw himself behind a chimney a heartbeat before a crossbow bolt shattered the roof tiles where he had been standing. The sergeant wasn't carrying one of the immobilizing crossbows. He was shooting to kill.

Arvin touched the bead that hung around his neck for reassurance and glanced across the rooftop, estimating how far he'd have to run. The militia had obviously given up on merely capturing him. They meant to kill him instead. "Nine lives," he whispered, dropping his hand, but it was more of a question, this time. Had his luck finally run out? He heard the creak of sinews tightening and the winding of a crank. The sergeant was reloading his crossbow.

Breaking from cover, Arvin sprinted across the roof. There were chimneys every few paces, emitting thin, hot smoke laden with glowing sparks that settled on his hair and skin. Ignoring these pinpricks of pain, he zigzagged from one chimney to another, all the while making for the center of the building, which was open to the sky. The open area was a circular courtyard filled with stacks of newly made pots and firewood for the kilns. No one was in it at the moment.

This courtyard looked like a dead end—but Arvin knew it must have doors leading out of it. He could always double back through the factory and escape onto the street again.

As he ran toward the lip of the roof, Arvin scanned the courtyard below, looking for a place to jump down. There: that pile of straw looked soft enough.

Just as he started to jump, something *whooshed* past his head and the sharp edge of a fletch scraped his ear. The crossbow bolt sailed on across the courtyard, but its close passage unnerved Arvin and threw him off his stride. He tripped over a lip of decorative tile that undulated around the inner edge of the rooftop and fell headlong into the courtyard.

He crashed down onto the lid of an enormous clay pot. It stood inside the courtyard—most of it underneath the overhang of the roof, but with just enough of it protruding that Arvin had landed on it. The wooden lid Arvin had fallen onto was as wide as a feast table. He'd landed facedown on top of it with his head, one arm, and one leg dangling over the edge of the pot. He'd heard something crack when he landed and felt pain flare in his collarbone, but it wasn't sharp enough for the bone to be broken. Dazed, he rolled onto his back and found himself looking up at the underside of the rooftop. Above, someone was making his way cautiously across the roof, coming in his direction—the sergeant.

Arvin rolled over a second time—farther into the shadow of the overhang—then rose to his elbows and knees, his back brushing the rooftop above him. He glanced quickly around the courtyard. A few paces away from the pot on which he was perched were double doors leading into the factory. These doors were just starting to open—but whether it would be a factory worker or a militiaman who came through them would be a coin toss. Arvin spoke his glove's command word and his dagger appeared in his left hand. He dropped flat onto his stomach, hoping they wouldn't spot him.

Suddenly, the lid tilted underneath him. Arvin grabbed for the rim of the pot but missed. Flailing, he tumbled down into its darkened interior and landed in something wet, soft, and squishy. The lid struck the underside of the overhanging roof with a dull thud, teetered an instant, and then fell back into place. It had closed—but not completely. A thin crescent of morning light shone down into the otherwise dark interior of the pot.

Arvin lay in what felt like soft, wet earth. The smell of wet clay surrounded him. The squelch of it between the fingers of his bare hand and inside his trouser legs as he sat up reminded him of the sewers, and he shuddered. For the second time that morning, he was covered in muck. But at least the clay didn't stink. Instead it had a pleasant, earthy smell.

The running footsteps reached the edge of the overhanging roof then stopped.

"Do you see him?" the sergeant shouted down.

"No," another man's voice shouted back—the person who came through the door had been a militiaman, after all. "But he's got to be hiding here somewhere. Tanju will sniff him out. We'll soon have that rebel in our grasp."

"Just remember the bounty that goes to whoever takes him down," the sergeant called back. "And keep your eyes sharp."

"For ten thousand in gold, you bet I will."

Ten thousand gold pieces? Arvin whistled under his breath. That was some bounty. As he slowly sank into the clay in which he sat, he wondered again who they'd mistaken him for. He didn't dare stand up; the sucking noise of his legs pulling out of the clay would betray his location. And he was starting to wonder if he would ever be able to climb out of the pot. Its walls were concave and thickly coated with clay. It had partially dried to a crumbly consistency, but underneath this skin was a damp, slippery layer. And the pot was enormous; even standing, Arvin wouldn't be able to reach its rim. A jump would allow him to catch hold of it—assuming his feet and legs didn't become so deeply mired in clay that jumping became impossible.

His dagger had landed point down in the clay beside him. Slowly, wary of squelching the clay, he drew it out. Armed again, he felt better, but only slightly. With his ungloved hand, he reached up to touch his bead—and found it rough to the touch.

Superstitious dread washed through him as he realized what must have happened. When he'd struck the edge of the pot, the bead had cracked. Holding it at the end of its thong, he stared down at it. He couldn't see much in this dim light, but the front of the cat's eye appeared to have a deep, jagged line running across it. The damage could be temporarily mended—all Arvin had to do was fill the crack with some of the clay he was sitting in—but the timing of it frightened him. His mother had said the bead was a good luck charm—that as long as Arvin kept it close, it would provide him with the nine lives of a cat.

Had he just used up his last one?

He could hear the murmur of voices—both men's and women's. They had to be those of the potters, emerging into the courtyard to find out what was happening. One voice rose above the rest—Tanju, calling up to the sergeant, asking him exactly where he'd last seen the man they'd been pursuing.

"He jumped down from here," came the answer from above. "And I can guess where he's hiding. You there—fetch a ladder so we can look inside the pot."

Arvin gritted his teeth. In another moment the lid would open and the militia would lean over the edge to feather him with crossbow bolts. Readying his dagger for throwing, Arvin vowed to take at least one of them with him. He waited, heart racing, almost forgetting to breathe.

He heard running footsteps—and a breathless voice, announcing that a ladder could not be found. Arvin opened his mouth to whisper a prayer to Tymora for favoring him—then halted as he noticed the light filtering down into the pot through the crack where the lid was askew. The light had a distinctive purple glow.

"Is he inside?" the sergeant asked from close above.

The purple glow came nearer; as it did Arvin heard a low humming noise. It must have been Tanju, humming to himself as he worked his magic. Above it, Arvin heard the clink of mail; the militiamen must be standing just outside the pot, waiting for Tanju's pronouncement.

The humming stopped. "No," Tanju called back. "All I see is darkness. The pot is empty. He must have escaped from the courtyard."

The purple glow dimmed.

Arvin felt his eyes widen as the sergeant shouted down at his men, ordering them to search the factory. Despite his magic, Tanju hadn't been able to find Arvin, this time. Something had saved him—but what?

Arvin stared at the clay caked onto the walls of the pot and the inside of its wooden lid. The clay had a peculiar undertone to its smell, one that he was at last able to place. It was heavy and metallic—lead.

Suddenly, Arvin understood. He'd heard that lead would block certain magics; the spells Tanju was casting must have been among these.

Breathing a sigh of relief, Arvin touched the bead at his throat. His mother's blessing still held; he hadn't used up his last life, after all . . . yet.

Whispering the two words that had become his personal prayer, Arvin started to rise to his feet but then thought better of it. Though the militiamen had jogged away, for all Arvin knew, the sergeant might still be waiting on the rooftop above, watching to see if the man he'd been pursuing would emerge from some other, hitherto unspotted hiding place. No, Arvin would wait until he was certain everyone was gone.

Which would give him plenty of time to think about a few things. He thought about Naulg—who probably *was* dead already, since a yuan-ti hadn't conveniently taken an interest in him and neutralized the poison in his body. And he thought about Zelia and whether she'd been lying about the spell that would allow her to take over Arvin's body in seven days' time. There was a slim chance she'd been bluffing—but Arvin wasn't willing to bet his life on it. No, the only safe course was to find out everything he could about the Pox, report his findings to Zelia, and pray that she'd show him mercy. Or rather, since Zelia didn't seem like someone inclined toward mercy, to pray that she'd recognize Arvin's worth and spare him, just as the Guild had.

In the meantime, there was this little matter of being hunted by the militia—and their tracker. That was going to complicate things.

Arvin settled back into the wet clay with a sigh, waiting for the silence that would be his signal to scramble out of the pot.

Chapter 4

*23 Kythorn,
Fullday*

ARVIN STOOD IN HIS WORKSHOP IN FRONT OF A HALF-COMPLETED net that was suspended from a row of hooks in a rafter. Beside him on the floor was a ball of twine spun from yellow-brown dog hair. He worked with a length of it, knotting the silky stuff into row after row of loops. One end of the twine was threaded through a double-eyed wooden needle, which Arvin passed through, around, and over a loop, forming a knot. With a quick jerk, he tightened the knot then went on to the next.

He worked swiftly, unhampered by his abbreviated little finger. Knotting nets and braiding ropes was a craft he'd honed over twenty years, at first under duress in the orphanage then later because it was what he did best—and because it was what the Guild wanted him to do. His hands were much larger than they'd been when he started, but his fingers were no less nimble than when he had been a child. They seemed to remember the repetitive motions of net knotting of their own accord, allowing his mind to wander.

His thoughts kept looping back to the events of last night. To Naulg—dead, he was certain—and his own fortunate escapes. Tymora had smiled upon him not once, but twice. Eluding the militia had been equally as miraculous as his escape from the Pox.

He'd waited in the clay storage pot for some time, until he was certain the militia were gone and none of the factory workers were about. Then he'd scrambled out of the pot, quickly washed off most of the clay with water from a barrel in the courtyard, and crept back to his warehouse. He'd changed for the second time that morning into fresh, dry clothes then prowled the city, peering down stormwater grates, looking for some clue that would lead him to the Pox. He'd hoped to lift one of the grates and slip into the sewers, but every time he found a likely looking one, a militia patrol happened by, and he was forced to skulk away.

His search was further frustrated by the fact that he didn't dare go anywhere near the sewage tunnels that emptied into the harbor—or anywhere else in the vicinity of the Coil—not for some time, at least. Zelia might be there, or worse yet, the militia sergeant and Tanju. The former looked like a man with a long memory and a short temper, and the latter was a frighteningly efficient tracker. Arvin didn't want to repeat the morning's chase and narrow escape.

Realizing that he wasn't going to find the Pox on his own, he'd turned, reluctantly, to the Guild. He'd made the rounds of his usual contacts, dropping a silver piece here, a gold piece there, putting out the word that he was looking for information on newcomers to the city—newcomers who were heavily scarred with pockmarks. Then he'd retired to the workshop he'd built between the false ceiling and rooftop of the warehouse the Guild had rented for him. Exhausted, he'd fallen into a deep sleep. When he woke up, it was long past highsun; the air felt heavy and hot. Deciding that he might as well continue with his work, he'd soon lost himself in the soothing, repetitive steps of netmaking.

The net he was working on suddenly vanished. Arvin waited patiently, keeping his fingers in exactly the positions they had been when the twine blinked into the Ethereal Plane. A few heartbeats later, the twine reappeared and he continued at his task.

In its raw form, the blink dog hair was unstable, shifting unpredictably back and forth between the Ethereal and Prime Material Planes, but when the net was complete, a wizard would attune it to a command word. This done, the net would then blink only when its command word was uttered. Then Arvin would deliver it and collect his coin.

Arvin had no idea who had commissioned the net. The order

had been passed along by a middler who already had the coin in hand and who would take delivery of the net when it was done. Arvin would never know if the product would be used for good or ill—for restraining a dangerous monster or for ensnaring a kidnap victim—nor did he want to know.

When Arvin had first begun working for the Guild, nearly twelve long years ago, he'd quickly realized that the magical twines and ropes and nets he had a hand in creating were used in crimes ranging from theft to kidnapping to outright murder. Not wanting blood on his hands—even at one remove—he'd begun to include deliberate flaws in his work.

Those flaws had been discovered, and an ultimatum delivered. Arvin could continue to produce product for the Guild—*quality* product—or he could go under the knife again. It wouldn't be a fingertip he'd be losing this time, but an eye. Perhaps both eyes, if the flaw caused a "serious difficulty" like the last one had.

Arvin had nodded and gone back to his work. He kept smiling as he passed the finished goods to his customers—even when he knew they were destined to be used to kill. In the meantime, he'd begun padding his orders for material, setting some aside for himself. A slightly longer section of trollgut here, a larger pouch of sylph hair there. The extra material was used to create additional magical items that he'd cached in hiding places all over the city. One day, when he had enough of these collected, he'd gather them all up and leave Hlondeth for good. In the meantime, he continued to serve the Guild.

At least this time, with the net he was weaving, he wouldn't have to meet the customer face to face. It was better not to get to know people, to keep them at a distance, even old friends like Naulg. Trying to help Naulg had only gotten him into trouble. Arvin should have heeded the painful lessons he'd learned in the orphanage.

He'd been only six when he'd been sent there as a "temporary measure"—a temporary measure that had lasted eight long years. Before leaving on the expedition that had turned out to be her last, Arvin's mother had arranged for Arvin to stay with her brother, a man Arvin had met only twice before. This uncle, a wealthy lumber merchant, had cared for Arvin for two months after his sister's death. Then he'd set out on a business trip across the Reach to Chondath. He'd placed Arvin with the orphanage "just for a tenday or two," but when he returned from this trip, he hadn't come back to collect Arvin.

At first Arvin had assumed that he'd done something wrong, that he'd angered his uncle in some way. But after running away from the orphanage, he had learned the truth. His uncle wasn't angry, just indifferent. Arvin had arrived at his uncle's home with fingers blistered from net knotting and tears of relief in his eyes—only to have his uncle pinch his ear and sternly march him back to the place again, refusing to listen to Arvin's pleas.

That was the first time Arvin had been subjected to the ghoul-stench spell. It wasn't the last. After Naulg's escape, Arvin had attempted one escape after another. Some failed due to the orphanage's reward system, which encouraged the children to spy on each other. Later, when Arvin learned to avoid making friends, even with the newly arrived children, his escapes had failed due to poor planning or bad luck. Prayers to Tymora had averted some of the latter, and an increasing maturity helped with the former. Over time, Arvin learned to wait and prepare, and his escape plans grew more cunning and complex. So, too, did his skill at knotting, weaving, and braiding, until he was almost never punished for being too slow, or for mistying a knot.

Arvin continued working on the net, letting his painful memories drift away in the repetitive thread-loop-loop-tie of netmaking. After a time, his emotions quieted.

Then he saw something out of the corner of his eye—a movement where there should have been none. He whirled around, left hand reflexively coming up to a throwing position until he realized his glove was lying on a nearby table. His eyes scanned the low-ceilinged workshop. Had the length of trollgut on the workbench across the room suddenly flexed? No, both ends of the gut were securely held in place by ensorcelled nails.

Through a round, slatted vent that was the workshop's only ventilation he heard a cooing and the flutter of wings. Striding over to the vent, he peered out and saw a pigeon on the ledge below. That must have been the motion his eye had caught—the bird flying past the slats. Three stories below was the street; none of the people walking along it were so much as looking up. Above—Arvin craned his neck to look up through the slats—was only the bare eave of the rooftop, curving out of sight to either side of the hidden room that housed his workshop. Satisfied there was no cause for alarm, he wiped sweat from his forehead with a sleeve and returned to his work. He picked up his netmaker's needle and rethreaded it with a fresh piece of dog-hair twine then began to loop and tie, loop and tie.

"So you escaped."

Arvin whirled a second time. "Zelia!" he exclaimed.

The yuan-ti was standing against the far wall, her scale-freckled face partially hidden by a coil of rope that hung from one of the rafters. She stepped out from behind it and stared at Arvin with unblinking eyes, her blue tongue flickering in and out of her mouth.

Arvin darted a glance at the spot on the floor where the hidden trapdoor was; it hadn't been opened, nor should it have been. Arvin was the only one who knew about the three hinged boards in the net loft ceiling, adjacent to a "roof" support post, that opened into his workshop.

"How did you find me?" he asked.

Zelia smiled, revealing perfect human teeth. "Your blood was on the ramp. Fortunately for you, I collected it before anyone else did."

"And you used it in a spell to find me," Arvin guessed. But how had she gotten into his workshop? More to the point, had she brought the militia with her? Were they waiting in the streets below?

Zelia's eyes flashed silver as they reflected the light from the lantern that hung from a nearby rafter. She gave a breathy hiss of laughter that somehow overlapped her words. "I've decided against having the militia arrest you," she said.

Arvin startled. Had she read his thoughts? No, it was an easy thing to have guessed.

"I'm going to take you up on your offer," she continued. "Find out what I want to know—without alerting the Pox—and I'll remove the mind seed."

"What do you want to know?"

"What the Pox are up to—over and above the obvious, which is poisoning people. What is their goal? Who is behind them? Who is really pulling the strings?"

"You don't think they're acting on their own?"

Zelia shook her head. "They never could have established them-selves in Hlondeth without help."

"Where do I begin?" Arvin asked. "How do I find them?"

"When I locate the chamber you described, I'll contact you," Zelia said. "In the meantime, there are resources you have that others don't. Put them to work."

"Use my . . . connections you mean?" Arvin asked.

"No," Zelia said, her eyes blazing. "Say nothing to the Guild."

"Then what—"

"You have a talent that others don't."

Arvin shrugged then gestured at the nets and ropes and delicately braided twines that hung from the rafters and from pegs, leaving not one blank spot on the wall. "If it's an enchanted rope you want, I can—"

Zelia moved closer, her body swaying sinuously as she made her way around the hanging clutter. "You're a psion."

Arvin felt the blood drain from his face. "No." He shook his head. "No, I'm not."

Zelia's eyes bored into his. For once, the unblinking stare of a yuan-ti was getting to him.

"Yes you are. In the tavern, when we first met, you tried to charm me. And later, you used psionics to distract the militia."

A cold feeling settled in the pit of Arvin's stomach. He opened his mouth but found himself unable to deny Zelia's blunt observation. For years, he'd told himself that his ability to simply crack a smile and have people suddenly warm up to him was due solely to his good looks and natural charisma, but deep down, he'd known the truth. What had happened this morning—when Tanju had been distracted in the tavern—had confirmed it.

Arvin's mother had been right about him all along. He had the talent.

"The Mortal Coil," he began in a faltering voice. "That droning noise. . . ."

"Yes."

Arvin closed his eyes, thinking back to the day he'd finally succeeded in running away from the orphanage. He'd been in his teens by then—hair had begun to grow under his arms and at his groin, and the first wisps of a beard had begun on his chin. His mother had always warned him that "something strange" might start to happen when he reached puberty. Arvin, surrounded by the rough company of children "rescued" from the gutters by the clerics of Ilmater, had developed his own crude ideas of what she'd been referring to—until that fateful day, just after his fourteenth birthday, when he'd found out what she'd really meant.

It had happened at the end of the month, on the day the clerics renewed the children's marks. The children had been summoned from their beds, and Arvin contrived to place himself last in line—an easy thing to do, since those at the end of the line had to wait longest to return to their beds. As the cleric who was applying red ink to the children's wrists worked his way down the line, staining the symbol of Ilmater onto the wrists of each child with quick strokes of his brush, Arvin stood with fingers crossed, wishing and wishing and wishing that somehow, this time, he might be overlooked.

One by one, the children were painted and dismissed, until only Arvin remained. Then, just as the cleric turned toward Arvin, brush dripping, something strange happened. It started with a tickling sensation at the back of Arvin's throat. Then a low droning filled the air—the same droning that had filled the tavern this morning.

Suddenly, the cleric had glanced away. He stared at the far wall, frowning, as if trying to remember something.

Arvin seized his chance. He stuffed his hands into his pockets, deep enough to hide his wrists, and turned away. Then he began to walk out of the room, as if dismissed. From behind him came not the shout he'd expected, but the sound of a brush being tapped against a jar. The cleric was cleaning his brush and preparing to leave.

Later that night, when he was certain the other children in his room were asleep, Arvin had climbed down from a third-floor window using the finger-thin rope he'd secretly braided over the previous months. After four days of hiding in a basement, what remained of the previous month's mark had faded enough for him to venture out onto the streets. He was free, and he remained that way for several tendays . . . until the Guild caught him thieving on their turf.

Thank the gods he'd still been carrying his escape rope at the time. The rope appeared ordinary, but woven into it were threads that Arvin had plucked from a magical robe owned by one of the orphanage's clerics. The resulting rope had chameleonlike properties and magically blended with its surroundings—allowing it to dangle against a wall, undetected, until the moment it was needed. One of the rogues who had captured Arvin had tripped over it—and cursed the "bloody near invisible" rope. The other rogue had paused, dagger poised to chop off another of Arvin's fingertips, then slowly lowered his dagger.

"Where did you get that rope, boy?" he'd asked.

Arvin's answer—"I made it"—had saved him.

In the years since his escape from the orphanage, Arvin had deliberately avoided thinking about what had happened to the cleric that night. He'd hadn't been willing to face the truth. He hadn't wanted to wind up like his mother, frightened by her own dreams—and dead, despite her talent for catching glimpses of the future.

Arvin opened his eyes and acknowledged Zelia. He could no longer deny the obvious—even to himself. "I do have the talent," he admitted.

Zelia smiled. "I could tell that by your secondary displays—by the ringing in my ears when you tried to charm me, and later, by the droning noise. Beginners often give themselves away."

"That's the thing," Arvin hastily added. "I'm not even a beginner. I haven't had any training at all."

"I'm not surprised," Zelia said. "Psions are extremely rare, especially in this corner of the world. Their talent often goes unrecognized. Even when a high-level power is manifested, it is usually attributed to some other magical effect."

"High-level power?" Arvin echoed. He shook his head. "All I can do is make people like me. I have no control over it. Sometimes it works . . . and sometimes it doesn't. And once, no, twice ever in my life, I was able to distract—"

"You could learn more. If I taught you—which I would, if you prove that you're worth the time and effort."

That startled him. Zelia was a psion? Arvin had always assumed his mother had been the only one in Hlondeth—maybe in all of the Vilhon Reach. But here, it seemed, was another.

That surprise aside, did he *want* to be trained? He had dim memories of his mother talking about the lamasery, far to the east in Kara Tur, that she had been sent to in the year her woman's blood began. The discipline and physical regimen she'd been subjected to there had sounded every bit as strenuous as that imposed by the orphanage, but strangely, she'd spoken fondly of the place. At the lamasery, she learned the discipline of clairsentience—an art she'd used in later life during her work as a guide in the wild lands at the edges of the Vilhon Reach. She'd been in great demand in the years before Arvin was born.

Yet her talent had come with a price. Some of Arvin's earliest memories were of being startled awake by a sharp scream and trying to comfort his mother as she sat bolt upright in the bed they shared, eyes wide and staring. She'd muttered frightening things about war and fire and children drowning. After a moment or two she'd always come back to herself. She would pat Arvin's hair and hug him close, reassuring him that it was "just a bad dream." But he'd known the truth. His mother could see into the future. And it scared her. So much so that she'd stopped using her psionics around the time that Arvin was born and had spoken only infrequently about them. Yet despite this, her nightmares had continued.

"I don't know if I want to learn," he told Zelia.

"You're afraid."

"Yes."

"Why?"

"I don't want to see my own death," Arvin answered.

Zelia's lips twitched. "What makes you think you will?"

"My mother did—though a lot of good it did her. She thought the vision would help her to avoid dying. She was—"

"Clairsentient?" Zelia interrupted.

Arvin paused. That wasn't what he'd been about to say. He had been about to tell Zelia that his mother had been wrong in her belief that even the most dire consequences could be avoided, if one were forewarned. He'd been about to tell Zelia about that final night with his mother—about seeing her toss and turn in her bed and being able to make out only one of the words in her uneasy mutters: plague. The next morning, when he'd nervously asked her about it, she'd tousled his hair and told him the nightmare wasn't something to be feared—that it would help keep her safe. She'd given him his cat's-eye bead and left on the expedition she'd only reluctantly agreed to guide. Later Arvin had learned what this expedition had entailed—guiding a group of adventurers who wanted to find a cure for the plague that still lay dormant in the ruins of Mussum. They hadn't entered the ancient city, but its contagion had found them nonetheless.

Just as her dream had foretold.

"The talents of mother and child do not always manifest in the same way," Zelia said, breaking into his silent musings as she moved closer to him. "You may turn out to be a savant or a shaper or even a telepath. Their talents lie in glimpsing and shaping the present, not the future. Would that be so frightening?"

Arvin had never heard of savants, shapers, or telepaths before, but understood the gist of what she was saying. Not all psionic talents came with the terrible visions that had plagued his mother. "I suppose that wouldn't be so bad," he conceded.

"I can also see to it that you receive your chevrons. You'll never have to run from the militia again."

"Those chevrons are impossible to fake," Arvin answered. "You must have powerful connections."

Zelia smiled, but her eyes remained cold and unblinking.

"Why the sudden change?" Arvin asked. "Why promise me so much—when before you were content to threaten me?"

Zelia moved closer. "I find that it's most effective to use both the stick"—she brushed his cheek with her fingertips—"and the carrot. At the same time."

Arvin's skin tingled where she'd just touched it. Zelia was an attractive woman, for a yuan-ti. A very attractive woman. Not only that, she was powerful—and well connected. But if his guess was right about her serving House Extaminos, he had little reason to trust her. The expression "deceitful as a snake" hadn't come from nowhere. Humans in the service of the ruling family had to watch their backs constantly, never knowing when a fang might strike. And because they were working for the royal family—whose members could do no wrong—their poisonings were always "accidental."

No, working for Zelia was going to be just as demanding—and nerve-wracking—as working for the Guild. Arvin wanted to escape Hlondeth, not mire himself even deeper in it.

"You're not going to remove the mind seed, are you?" he asked.

Zelia shook her head. "Not until I get what I want."

"Where can I find you if I learn anything?" Arvin asked.

"Ask for me at the Solarium," she said. Then, bending gracefully, she inserted a finger into a knothole in the floor and pulled the hidden trapdoor open. She straightened, stepped through the hole, and fell out of sight. Arvin rushed to the trapdoor in alarm, and saw that she had assumed her serpent form. She was hissing loudly—and falling as slowly as a feather. Her sinuous green body lightly touched the floor, and she slithered away between the dusty coils of rope and spools of twine stacked in the warehouse below.

Arvin started to close the trapdoor then had second thoughts. Until he heard back from the Guild, he had nothing to go on, no way of locating the Pox. Sand was slipping through the hourglass. In less than seven days, Zelia's spell would activate.

No, he corrected himself, not a spell, a power—a psionic power. But psionic powers were like spells, weren't they? They could be negated.

But how? Arvin ground his teeth. Despite the fact that his mother had possessed the talent, psionics was something about which he knew very little. Maybe, by following Zelia and observing her, he could learn more.

Arvin scooped up his glove from the workbench and yanked it onto his hand. Then he clambered through the trapdoor and slid down a rope. He ran across the warehouse floor, toward the door that was slowly swinging shut.

CHAPTER 5

*23 Kythorn,
Fullday*

ARVIN PULLED OPEN THE FRONT DOOR OF THE WAREHOUSE AND stepped out into the humid summer heat. He glanced anxiously back and forth but saw no sign of Zelia, in either yuan-ti or serpent form. The street was filled with people, most of them human. One of the Learned, his ability to read and write proudly displayed by the two red dots on his forehead, swept past in a silken cloak, nose in the air. A stonemason, hammer and chisel hanging at the belt of his leather trousers, shouted at a brace of four slaves yoked to a rumbling cart bearing a snake-headed statue carved from cream-colored alabaster—one of the many statues that had been carved for the restoration of the oldest part of the city. Women returning from the public fountain in the plaza just down the street to Arvin's right swayed across the cobblestones, pots of water balanced on their heads, while children lugged smaller vessels along beside them.

Across the street, young Kolim, the seven-year-old son of the woman who owned the bakery up the road, was pressing his palm against the stonework of the building opposite. When he removed it, the stone's magical glow, triggered by the momentary darkness, was revealed. Spotting Arvin, Kolim hurried across the street, pulling from his pocket a loop of string with a bead on it.

"Hey, Arvin!" he called, threading it over his fingers as he ran. "I can do that string puzzle you showed me. Hey, Arvin, watch!"

"Later, Kolim," Arvin told the boy, gently patting him on the head. "I'm a little busy just now."

The section of city the yuan-ti preferred to live in lay to the left, uphill from the harbor. Arvin closed the door behind him and strode in that direction. He spotted a woman with green scales coming toward him and, for a heartbeat or two, thought it was Zelia returning to the warehouse, but it turned out to be another yuan-ti, this one with darker hair and a snakelike tail emerging through a slit in the back of her skirt. Wrapped around her neck like a piece of living jewelry was a tiny bronze-and-black-banded serpent with leathery wings, one of the flying snakes imported from the jungle lands far to the south. As if sensing Arvin staring at it, the winged snake flapped its wings and hissed as its mistress walked by.

Zelia was nowhere in sight—she'd probably maintained her serpent form and slithered away. Either that or she'd gone in the opposite direction. Sighing, Arvin slowed his pace.

He was just turning to go back to the warehouse when he heard a man standing in a nearby doorway give a low, phlegmy cough. Arvin glanced in the fellow's direction, expecting to see someone aged, but the man who had just cleared his throat was even younger than he. And not a human, either, but a yuan-ti—albeit one with a fair amount of human blood in him. The fellow had olive skin, black hair, and a heavy growth of beard that nearly hid his mouth. Arvin could see the small patches of silver-gray scales dotting his forehead, arms, and hands. He wore black trousers and a white silk shirt with lace around the cuffs and neckline. Arvin walked past him, automatically lowering his eyes in the yuan-ti's presence—and suddenly caught a whiff of something he recognized: a sour, sick odor.

The smell that lingered on the skin of members of the Pox.

Arvin had worked among rogues long enough to instantly stifle his startle. He continued walking past the "yuan-ti," deliberately not looking at him. Arvin's escape of the night before had not gone unnoticed. The Pox were looking for him. And they'd found him.

"Lady Luck, favor me just one more time," Arvin whispered under his breath. "I'll fill your cup to the brim, I promise." He continued to walk steadily down the street toward the front door of his warehouse, shoulders crawling as he imagined the cultist behind him, about to reach out and touch his shoulder with filthy, plague-ridden hands. . . .

As Arvin approached the door, he suddenly realized something. The cultist wasn't behind him. Risking a glance back, he saw that the man was still lounging in the doorway down the street. He wasn't even looking at Arvin. Instead his attention seemed to be focused on the women who were drawing water from the public fountain.

Arvin paused, considering. Was the cultist's presence outside the warehouse mere coincidence?

He decided not to take any chances.

Arvin stepped inside the warehouse and scooped up a coil of rope. Then, with the rope looped over his left forearm, he walked up the street toward the cultist. The man paid no attention to Arvin's approach. Either the cultist's presence here truly was coincidence—or he was as good at hiding his emotions as any rogue. He glanced at Arvin only at the last moment, as Arvin stepped into the doorway with him.

"Hello, Shev," Arvin said in a hearty voice, greeting the fellow with what was a common name among the yuan-ti of Hlondeth. "So good to see you! The thousandweight of rope you ordered has just come in with the shipment from *shivis*."

As Arvin spoke the glove's command word, the dagger appeared in his hand. He jabbed the point of the weapon into the man's side and let the rope looped over his forearm slide down to hide it. "Let's go to the warehouse," Arvin continued in his falsely hearty voice. "I'll show it to you."

The cultist startled then flinched in realization that Arvin meant business. He allowed himself to be marched down the street, toward the warehouse door. Not until he'd stepped inside did he suddenly spring away. Arvin, however, had been expecting something similar. He had, accordingly, steered the cultist slightly to the left as he marched him through the door. As the man jumped, he barked out a command word. A coil of what appeared to be ordinary hemp rope lashed out toward the cultist, spiraling around him like a constricting snake. Confined in its coils, the cultist toppled like a felled tree and landed in a patch of sunlight that slanted in from one of the barred windows above. He immediately opened his mouth to cry out for help; in response Arvin threw his dagger at the man. The blade sliced open the cultist's ear and thudded into the wooden flooring behind him; at a whispered command, it flew back to Arvin's hand again.

"Be silent," Arvin growled as he closed the door behind him. "And I might let you live."

The cultist did a credible job of imitating a yuan-ti. "Release me," he spat arrogantly, glaring as he blinked away the blood that was trickling into his right eye. "And I might let *you* live."

Arvin chuckled. "I know what you are," he told the man. "You might as well drop your disguise. I can see—and smell—Talona's foul touch all over you."

The cultist hissed in anger, still trying to convince Arvin that he was really a yuan-ti then gave up. The magical disguise in which he'd cloaked himself dissipated, revealing a young man whose mouth was so disfigured by scars that his lips would not close. A faded gray-green robe with frayed cuffs and a torn neck covered all but his hands and feet, which were covered in pockmarks. Arvin made a mental note not to touch the magical rope that entangled the fellow; perhaps even to burn it, despite the expense that had gone into its manufacture. He bent over a burlap sack and carefully wiped the cultist's blood from his dagger.

The cultist strained against the rope for a moment but only succeeded in causing it to constrict further. He glared up at Arvin. "What do you want?" he said in a slurred voice.

"I'll ask the questions," Arvin countered. "For starters, why were you watching me?"

"Watching you?" The cultist seemed genuinely puzzled. He tried to purse his disfigured lips together, but they formed an uneven, ragged line. Staring down at the fellow, Arvin suddenly felt sorry for him. This man had been handsome, once, but those lips would never again know the soft caress of a woman's kiss.

Surprisingly, the cultist laughed. "You pity me?" he slurred. "Don't. I *sought* the embrace of the goddess."

Arvin felt a chill run through him. "You did that to yourself deliberately?" he asked. He'd given little thought to the motivations of the Pox. He'd assumed they were driven to worship Talona after illness claimed them in the hope that she would free them from their afflictions. He'd never dreamed that anyone would afflict himself with plague on purpose. Yet that was what this fellow seemed to be saying.

He thought of the liquid they'd forced him to drink. "The liquid in the metal flasks," he said, thinking out loud as he stared at the terrible pockmarks on the cultist's skin. "Is this what it's supposed to do to people? Make their skin . . . like that?" He resisted the urge to touch his own skin to make sure it was still smooth.

The cultist started to speak then gave another of his phlegmy coughs. He glanced around as if about to spit. Without intending to, Arvin backed up a pace.

The cultist gave him a penetrating look. "You've seen something, haven't you? Something you shouldn't have." He paused for a moment, and his expression turned smug. "It doesn't matter. Cry all the warnings you like—it won't help you. Talona will soon purge this city, sweeping it clean for the faithful. We will rise from the ashes to claim it."

Arvin shivered, suddenly realizing what the Pox must be up to. Last night's ritual hadn't been an isolated sacrifice. Thinking back to the rash of disappearances that had taken place in recent tendays around the waterfront, Arvin realized that he and Naulg weren't the first to be subjected to the Pox's vile ministrations. Nor would they be the last. The Pox meant to spread plague throughout the entire city.

But if that was their goal, why hadn't their victims been turned out into the streets, where they would spread their contagion to others? Perhaps, Arvin thought, because they had all died. But if they had, why weren't the cultists dumping their bodies in the streets instead?

Maybe the cultists were saving them up, intending to scatter them throughout the city like seeds when they had enough of them.

As Arvin stood, these dark thoughts tumbling through his mind, he became dimly aware of noises from the street outside—the chatter of voices, the *rumble-squeak* of carts, the voices of women returning from the fountain.

The public fountain, one of dozens from which Hlondeth's citizens drew their daily drinking water.

The one the cultist had been watching when Arvin spotted him.

Arvin suddenly realized the answer. If the Pox wanted to spread contagion, what better way to do it than by tainting the city's water supply? All they had to do was carry to each fountain a little of whatever was in the flasks and tip it into the fountain under the pretense of filling their vessels. But would this work—or would the volume of water in the fountain dilute the plague, rendering it ineffective? How much did a person have to ingest for it to kill?

Perhaps that was what the Pox were trying to find out.

As Arvin stared down at the cultist, his expression hardened. If the Pox had their way, forty-five thousand people would die— perhaps more, if plague spread beyond Hlondeth into the rest of the Vilhon Reach. The gods had just placed what might be the key to preventing these people's deaths in Arvin's hands. All he had to do was find out where the Pox were and report that to Zelia. She would take care of the rest.

"Where are the other cultists?" he asked. "Where do you meet?"

The man gave a phlegmy laugh. "In the Ninth Hell."

Arvin hefted his dagger, wondering if pain would prompt the truth. Probably not. Anyone who deliberately disfigured himself like this had little consideration for his own flesh.

The cultist's disfigured mouth twisted into a lopsided grimace. "Go ahead," he countered. "Cut me again with your fancy dagger. Perhaps a little of the blood will spray on you, this time, and you'll know Talona's embrace. Throw!"

As the cultist mocked him, Arvin's mind exploded with rage. He whipped up his dagger and nearly threw it, only stopping himself at the last moment. His temper suddenly cooled, and he realized what the cultist had just attempted. He'd cast a spell on Arvin, compelling him to throw his dagger. Only by force of will had Arvin been able to avoid fulfilling the cultist's wish to be silenced.

Slowly he lowered the dagger. That had been a narrow escape, but it reminded him of something. Perhaps there was another way, other than threats, to get the man to talk—by charming him.

Arvin had felt the first sputters of this power—which, until his conversation with Zelia a short time ago, he hadn't admitted was psionic—back when he was a boy. Back when his mother was still alive. She'd discovered him cutting one of her maps into parchment animals and had raised her hand to strike him. Frightened, he'd summoned up a false smile and pleaded in the most winsome voice a five-year-old could summon—and had felt the strange sensation prickle across the base of his scalp for the first time. His mother's expression had suddenly softened, and she'd lowered her hand. Then she'd blinked and shaken her head. She'd tousled Arvin's hair and told him he'd very nearly charmed himself out of a punishment—that he showed "great promise." Then she'd taken his favorite wooden soldier and tossed it into the fireplace, to teach him how bad it felt when another person damaged something that was yours.

He hadn't been able to manifest that power again until he reached puberty. He'd charmed people in the years since then, but his talent was unreliable. Sometimes it worked . . . sometimes it didn't. But that time with his mother, it had arisen spontaneously.

Why?

Suddenly, Arvin realized the answer. Strong emotion. Like a rising tide, it had forced his psionic talent to bubble to the surface.

Standing over his captive, Arvin tried to summon up an emotion equally as strong as the one he'd felt that day. Then, he'd been motivated by fear; this time, he let frustration carry him almost to the edge. He embraced the emotion and combined its rawness with the urge to get the man to talk to him. Why couldn't he get the cultist to speak? The fellow was his *friend*. He should *trust* Arvin. The prickling began at the base of his scalp, encouraging him.

Arvin squatted on the floor next to the man. Deliberately he let his frown smooth and his voice soften. "Listen, friend," he told the cultist. "You can trust me. I drank from the flask and survived. Like you, I am blessed by the goddess. But I don't know how to find the others. I need to find them, to talk to them, to understand. I yearn to feel Talona's. . . ." He nearly lost his concentration as he spoke the goddess's name then found his calm center again. "I need to feel Talona's embrace again. Help me. Tell me where I can find the others. Please?"

When Arvin began his plea, the cultist's eyes had been filled with scorn and derision. As his expression softened, a thrill of excitement rushed through Arvin. Untrained he might be, but he was doing it! He was using psionics to mold this man to his will!

The excitement was his undoing; it broke his concentration. The cultist jerked his head aside and broke away from Arvin's gaze then began blinking rapidly. He heaved himself into a sitting position, fingers straining between the coils of rope as he reached for Arvin, who jumped back just in time. Then the cultist's eyes rolled back in his head.

"Talona take me!" he cried. "Enfold me in your sweet embrace. Consume my flesh, my breath, my very soul!"

Though Arvin was certain the cultist was not crying, three amber tears suddenly trickled down the man's pockmarked cheek. With each wheezing exhalation, the cultist's lungs pumped out a terrible smell, worse than that of a charnel house stacked with decaying corpses. Arvin staggered back, afraid to breathe but unable to run. He stared in terrified fascination as the sores on the cultist's body suddenly burst open and began to weep. Violent trembling shook the cultist and his robe was suddenly drenched in sweat. Even from two paces away, Arvin could feel the heat radiating off the man's body. With horrid certainty, he realized what the cultist had just done—called down a magical contagion upon himself. Had Arvin been crouched just a little closer, and had the man succeeded in touching him, it would have been Arvin lying on the floor, dying.

The cultist's body was swelling like a corpse left in the sun. In another moment his stomach would expand past the breaking point; already Arvin could hear the creak of flesh preparing to rupture . . .

And he was just standing there, staring.

Arvin flung open the warehouse door. As he slammed it behind him, he heard a sound like wet cloth tearing and the splatter of something against the inside of the door. He breathed a sigh of relief at yet another narrow escape, and touched the bead at his throat.

"Nine lives," he whispered.

He stood for a moment with his back against the door, staring at the people in the street. If the cultist's boasting was true, their days were numbered. Did Arvin really care if they died of plague? He had hundreds of acquaintances in this city but no friends, now that Naulg was gone. He had no family, either, aside from the uncle who had consigned him to the orphanage.

The sensible thing to do was report what he'd just found out to Zelia and see if she would remove the "seed" from his mind. Whether she did or didn't, he'd clear out of the city as quickly as possible, since staying only meant dying.

If Zelia had been bluffing, Arvin would be safe—assuming that the plague the Pox were about to unleash stayed confined within

Hlondeth's walls. Even if it didn't, clerics would stop the spread of the disease eventually—they always had, each time plague swept the Vilhon Reach. Maybe they'd lose Hlondeth before they were able to halt the plague entirely, but that wasn't Arvin's problem.

Then he spotted Kolim, sitting on the curb across the street. The boy had his string looped back and forth between his outstretched fingers in the complicated pattern Arvin had taught him. He was trying—without much success and with a frown of intense concentration on his face—to free the bead "fly" from its "web."

Arvin sighed. He couldn't just walk away and let Kolim die.

Nor could he walk away from something that might produce orphans for generations to come. He thought of his mother, of the trip that had taken her to the area around Mussum. That city had been abandoned nine hundred years ago, but the plague that had been its ruin lingered in the lands around it still.

If Mussum's plague had been prevented, Arvin's mother might never have died. Had there been one man, all those centuries ago, who had held the key to the city's survival in his hand—only to throw it away?

Arvin realized he really didn't have a choice. If he left without doing as much as he could, and plague claimed Hlondeth, the ghosts of its people—and everyone who ventured near it and died in the years that followed this—would haunt him until the end of his days.

Including the ghost of little Kolim.

Sighing, he trudged up the street to find Zelia.

CHAPTER 6

23 Kythorn,
Fullday

ARVIN STRODE ACROSS ONE OF THE STONE VIADUCTS THAT ARCHED over Hlondeth's streets, glad he didn't have to shoulder his way through the throng of people below. The narrow, open-sided viaduct didn't bother him the way it did some humans. He was agile enough to feel sure-footed, even when forced to squeeze to the very edge to let a yuan-ti pass.

Ahead lay the Solarium, an enormous circular building of green stone topped with a dome of thousands of triangular panes of glass in a metal frame that was reputedly strengthened by magic. The sun struck the west side of the dome, causing it to flare a brilliant orange.

The viaduct led to a round opening in the side of the Solarium. The human slave sitting on a stool just inside it rose to her feet as Arvin approached. She had curly, graying hair and wore, in her left ear, a gold earring in the shape of a serpent consuming its own tail. It helped distract the eye, a little, from the faded **S** brand on her cheek. She held up a plump, uncalloused hand to stop Arvin as he stepped inside the cool shade of the doorway.

"Where do you think you're going?" she demanded.

Arvin peered past her, down the curved corridor that led to the heart of the building. Side tunnels with rounded ceilings branched off from it, leading to rooms where the yuan-ti shed their clothing. The air was drier than the sticky summer heat outdoors and was spiced with the pungent odor of snake. He was surprised to find no one but this woman watching the entrance; he'd expected at least one militiaman to keep out the rabble.

"A yuan-ti asked me to meet her here," Arvin told the slave. "Her name is Zelia."

The slave sniffed. "Humans aren't allowed to use this entry. You'll have to wait at the servant's entrance with the others."

Behind her, within the Solarium, a yuan-ti that was all snake save for a humanlike head slithered out of a side tunnel. It turned to stare at the humans with slit eyes, tongue flickering as it drank in their scent, then slid away down the corridor in the opposite direction, scales hissing softly against the stone.

Arvin stared down at the slave. She might be twice his age, but he was a head taller. "I'm on state business," he told her firmly. "Zelia will want to see me at once. If you won't let me in, then go and find her. Tell her I'm here."

The slave returned his glare with one of her own. "The Solarium is a place of repose," she told him. "You can't expect me to burst in and wake our patrons from their slumber, looking for some woman who may or may not exist."

Arvin fought down his impatience. Slave this woman might be, but she'd been at her job long enough to consider herself mistress of all who entered the doorway, be they slave or free folk.

"Zelia has red hair and green scales," Arvin continued. "That should narrow down your search. Tell her Arvin is here to see her with an urgent message about. . . ." He paused. How to word it . . . ? "About diseased rats in the sewers." He folded his arms across his chest and stood firm, making it clear he wasn't going anywhere until his message was delivered.

The slave tried to stare him down, but her resolve at last wavered. She turned away and snapped her fingers. "Boy!" she shouted.

From a side tunnel came the patter of footsteps. A boy about eight or nine years old, carrying a glass decanter containing pink-tinged water, emerged in response to the doorkeeper's call. He was barefoot and dressed only in faded gray trousers that had been hacked off at the thigh; his knees and the tops of his feet were rough, as if he'd scraped them repeatedly. His hair was damp with sweat, and the **S** brand on his cheek was still fresh and red.

"This man claims to have been summoned here by one of our patrons," the doorkeeper told the boy, placing emphasis on the word "summoned," perhaps to remind Arvin that, while he might be a free man, he was ultimately at the beck and call of the yuan-ti. "Find the yuan-ti Zelia and deliver this message to her." She relayed Arvin's message. "Return with her reply."

The boy ran off down the main tunnel. Arvin waited, stepping to the side and dropping his gaze as two yuan-ti entered the Solarium and were greeted with low bows by the doorkeeper—who all the while kept one eye on Arvin, as if expecting him to dart into the Solarium at any moment. The boy came running back, this time without the decanter.

"Mistress Zelia says to bring the man to her," the boy panted.

The doorkeeper was busy directing the yuan-ti who had just entered to one of the side rooms, but Arvin saw her eyebrows rise at the news that Zelia would see him. As the yuan-ti departed down a side corridor, she glared at the boy. "Take him to her, then," she snapped, "and be quick about it." She aimed a cuff at the back of the boy's head, but the boy ducked it easily.

"This way," he told Arvin.

Arvin followed him down the corridor. The farther along it they went, the hotter and drier—and muskier—the air became. Arvin couldn't imagine having to spend his whole life working in this snake stink. It was already making his temples pound. "Here," he said, fishing a silver piece out of a pocket and holding it out to the boy. "Keep this somewhere safe, where the others won't find it. Maybe you'll have enough to buy your freedom, one day."

The boy eyed the coin in Arvin's hand suspiciously.

"Nothing is expected of you," Arvin reassured him. "It's just a gift."

The boy plucked the coin from Arvin's hand and tucked it into his own pocket then grinned. As they reached a point where sunlight flooded into the corridor from the large room beyond, he dropped to his knees, tugging on Arvin's shirt as he did so. "We're not allowed to stand," he whispered.

Arvin wasn't sure if this rule applied to free men, but he complied.

Dropping into a kneel, he followed the boy into the main room of the Solarium, trouser knees scuffing against the floor.

The sunning room of the Solarium was even larger than he'd imagined. The enormous circular chamber, capped by its high dome of glass, was bathed in hot, bright sunlight. Perhaps a hundred or more yuan-ti lounged on a series of low stone platforms on the floor, while snakes of every color and size—either more yuan-ti or their pets—hung from the delicate framework of wooden arches that connected one platform to the next. Some of the yuan-ti could pass for human at a distance while others had obvious serpent tails, heads, or torsos. They lay naked in the bright sunlight, men and women together, in some cases coiled in what Arvin would have assumed were sexual unions were it not for the slow, sleepy languor that pervaded the place. Human slaves—most of them young children—moved between the platforms on their knees, offering the yuan-ti sips of blood-tinged water or thumb-sized locusts, impaled on skewers and still twitching.

The boy led Arvin toward a platform near the center of the room where Zelia lounged with three other yuan-ti who looked almost human. The boy then backed away. Zelia lay on her side, coiled in a position no human could have emulated, her torso bent sharply backward so that her head was pillowed on one calf. She had a lean, muscled body that was soft and round in just the right places. Arvin noted that her scales gave way to a soft fuzz of red hair at her groin and that her breasts were smooth and pink, quite human in appearance. He found himself imagining what it would feel like to have Zelia's body coiled around his—to feel the contrasting textures of rough, scaly skin and smooth breasts—then realized that Zelia had lifted her head to glance sleepily at him. Arvin, still on his knees, his head level with the ledge on which Zelia lay, dropped his gaze. He concentrated on the floor and waited for her to bid him to speak. The air seemed even hotter and drier than it had been a moment ago; Arvin found himself wetting his lips, just as the yuan-ti around him were doing.

Zelia chuckled, as if at some private joke. "You've been hunting sewer rats?" she asked, eyes still half-hooded with sleep. Her tongue tasted the air. "Yet you smell sweet."

"One of the rats came out of the sewers," Arvin said. "I caught him."

Zelia sat up swiftly, her eyes glittering. "Where is he?" The three yuan-ti behind her stirred in their repose, disturbed by her sudden motion. One of them—a man who might have been handsome, save for the hollow fangs that curved down over his lower lip—rolled over and laid an arm across Zelia's thigh. She slid her leg out from under it.

"The rat is dead," Arvin answered.

Zelia gave an angry hiss.

"But not by my hand," he swiftly added. "His . . . mistress claimed him. But before he died, I managed to learn what he and the others plan to—"

"Not here," Zelia cut him off with a fierce whisper. She glanced pointedly at the three other yuan-ti who shared the platform with her. "Follow me and keep silent."

She slid off the platform in a flowing motion and moved toward the exit—walking at an apparently unhurried pace and nodding her goodbyes to those she passed, but hissing softly under her breath as she went. Arvin followed on his knees, which were already sore despite the trousers that padded them. He wondered how the slave children could stand it, scuffing about on bare knees all day long. He supposed they got used to it, just as he'd gotten used to cramped and blistered fingers when he was a child.

When they reached the corridor, Zelia quickened her pace. Arvin leaped to his feet and trotted after her then waited while she pulled on sandals and a dress scaled with tiny, overlapping ovals of silver. After she had dressed, she led him down a ramp and out onto the street.

They walked uphill for some time past enormous mansions. Human servants and slaves hurried through the streets, intent upon their masters' business, but parted quickly to make way for Zelia when they saw her coming. The yuan-ti who lived in this part of Hlondeth strolled leisurely along the viaducts that arched above, enjoying the view out over the city walls and the harbor.

As he jostled his way through the crowd that quickly closed in Zelia's wake, Arvin wondered why she had chosen the street-level, more crowded route. Perhaps because she wanted to avoid having to stop and chat with other yuan-ti, or perhaps because she didn't want any of those above getting a close look at the human who was accompanying her.

Zelia at last turned off the street and ascended a narrow ramp that spiraled up the side of a tower that was several stories tall. Arvin followed her. The roof of the tower turned out to be flat. It was surrounded by a wrought-iron railing covered in flowering vines. Bees droned lazily among tiny blue flowers. Arvin wondered if the tower was Zelia's home—if so, she certainly came from a wealthy family. She paused at the top of the ramp to unlock a gate with a key taken from a belt purse at her hip. The gate squeaked open under her touch.

Arvin followed her through the gate into what turned out to be a rooftop garden. On the rooftop were several enormous clay pots, planted with shrubs that had been carefully clipped into shapes reminiscent of coiled serpents. The bushes had obviously been grafted together from several different plants; the colors of the flowers changed abruptly at several points along the length of each coil, mimicking the banded pattern of a snake.

At the center of the rooftop was a fountain. Its gentle splashes filled the air with a cool mist. Arvin wet his dry lips, wishing he could take a sip of the water. Perhaps that would help the headache that was still throbbing in his temples. This was probably one fountain the Pox wouldn't be able to get to, but still. . . .

Zelia closed the gate behind them. "We'll have privacy here," she said.

Arvin nodded uneasily as the gate's lock clicked shut. Despite the vines that screened the railing, he'd noted the intricate pattern of its metalwork. The wrought iron formed an inscription, which, judging by the one character Arvin could make out, was written in Draconic. Arvin couldn't read Draconic but had once painstakingly memorized a handful of its characters so that he could include them in his knotwork. It was a language well suited for sorcery. He hoped—and this hope was reinforced by Zelia's assurance of privacy—that whatever magic the rail worked was designed to keep people out, rather than in.

Zelia turned to him and spoke without preamble. "Tell me what happened."

Arvin did, describing how he'd spotted the cultist in the street, and then he told her everything that had followed from there. He expected Zelia to raise her eyebrows when he told her his conclusions about what the Pox were up to—tainting Hlondeth's water supply—but she merely nodded. If anything, she seemed slightly disappointed by what he'd just told her.

"The cultist said Talona would purge the city 'soon,' " Arvin noted. "I don't think he'd have gloated that way if they planned to taint the water supply months from now. It sounded as though they were going to put their plan into action within a tenday, at most. I hope that will give you time to—"

Zelia held up a hand, interrupting him. "Your conclusions are . . . interesting," she said. "I suppose time will prove whether they're correct."

Arvin frowned, not understanding Zelia's apparent lack of concern. "Humans aren't the only ones who drink from the public fountains," he told her. "Not all yuan-ti live in mansions with private wells. Some are sure to quench their thirst at the fountains, and though they may be immune to poison, they can still die of plague—and spread it to others. Unless. . . ." He paused, as a thought suddenly occurred to him. Did Zelia know something that he didn't? Did yuan-ti have a natural immunity to plague, as well as poison?

Even if they did, a city with ninety-five percent of its population ill or dying wouldn't serve their interests.

When Arvin reminded her of this fact, Zelia gave him a cold smile. "I am well aware of the role humans play in Hlondeth," she told him. "And I agree. The cultists must be stopped."

Arvin nodded, relieved. It was out of his hands. He could step back and let Zelia—and the powerful people who backed her—deal with the crisis from here on in.

"I suppose it will be a simple matter of stationing militia at every public drinking fountain and arresting the cultists as they appear," he said, thinking out loud. "Or are you going to try to capture them before they make their move?"

"Capturing them will only solve part of the problem," Zelia said. "The cultists are just one playing piece in a much larger game. I still need to find out who is behind them."

Arvin frowned. "If you stop them, will it matter?"

"Someone wants to upset the balance of power," Zelia said. "My job is to discover who. Find that out—and you'll earn your freedom. And all that I promised you earlier."

Arvin nodded. He'd expected her to say that. Why remove the mind seed when it was such an effective tool? "I have an idea that might help me to infiltrate the Pox—once we find them," he told her. "The cultist who died today in my warehouse used magic to alter his appearance, but I got a good look at his face after he dropped the spell. If I described him to you, perhaps you could use your psionics to alter my appearance. I could pass myself off as him and—"

"You would never be able to carry it off," Zelia said. "One false gesture or word, and the Pox would use their magic to see you as you truly are. You will have to present yourself as you are—or rather, as how they want to see you: someone who survived their draught of plague and now wants to join their cult."

Arvin grimaced. He'd been afraid she'd say that. "Won't they also have magic that will allow them to see through my lies?" he asked, thinking back to the spells the clerics at the orphanage had used.

"If you choose your words carefully, you won't have to lie," Zelia told him. "A cleverly worded half-truth—plus a little charm—will carry you a long way."

Arvin nodded. That much, at least, was true. "Have you been able to locate the chamber I told you about?"

"I think so," Zelia told him. "Or at least, I've located a chamber in the sewers that matches the description you gave."

Arvin wet his lips nervously. Finally he would be able to find out whether Naulg was alive—or dead. "Did you see my friend there, or . . . his body?"

"The chamber was empty. But the cultists may return to it at middark, the time they seem to prefer for their sacrifices."

Arvin nodded. "Where is it?"

Zelia ignored his question. "Until then, you will wait here with me. As middark approaches, I will begin observing the chamber. As soon as I see any activity, you can set out."

Arvin chafed, wishing he could just get this over with—but he could see that Zelia wasn't going to tell him where the chamber was until she was good and ready. In the meantime, he needed to prepare. He hadn't exactly gone to the Solarium ready for an excursion into the sewers. If he was going to confront the Pox, he'd need to equip himself.

"There're some items I'll need," he told Zelia. "If I promise to meet you back here at Sunset, can I go and get them?"

Zelia stared at him for several long moments, hissing softly to herself. Silver flashed in her eyes as they caught the sun. "Go," she told him, unlocking the gate. "Purchase your potions, but don't be late."

Arvin was halfway down the ramp before what she'd just said sank in.

He hadn't told her he intended to buy potions . . .

Not out loud, anyway.

23 Kythorn, Sunset

Arvin sat cross-legged in the rooftop garden, watching Zelia exercise. She was naked, with her hair bound in a loose knot at the back of her neck, but she didn't seem to mind him watching her; yuan-ti didn't have the same concept of modesty that humans did. He'd never seen anything quite like the convolutions she was putting her body through—a series of poses that bent her torso, arms, and legs into positions he was certain no human could ever achieve. She held each pose for several moments, muscles quivering from the strain and sweat beading at her temples, then suddenly her body flowed into the next position in one smooth and supple motion. One moment her ankles were wrapped around her neck tighter than a knot as she balanced on her palms, seemingly sitting in midair, the next she was in a handstand, her body straight as an arrow. Down she swept to hover at the horizontal a palm's width above the ground, balancing her rigid body on her hands, then up went her head and feet to meet in an arch over her back.

Arvin expected her to be exhausted when she finished, but instead she seemed invigorated. Her eyes sparkled and her cheeks were flushed a healthy pink, enhanced by the light of the setting sun.

"Those exercises," Arvin said. "They remind me of an acrobat I saw once—though he was nowhere near as graceful."

"They're called *asanas*," Zelia answered.

"Do you do them every day?"

"At sunset, without fail," Zelia said, slipping on her dress. "They focus the mind."

"My mother meditated each morning at sunrise," Arvin said. "These—*asanas*—are for the same purpose, aren't they? To aid your psionic powers?"

"They restore my ability to manifest my powers," Zelia answered, "much like a cleric praying or a wizard reading his spellbooks."

"I see," Arvin said. During her routine, Zelia had gone through a *lot* of different poses. She must have had quite a number of psionic powers at her disposal. If he wanted to learn how to master his psionics—to do more than merely charm and distract people—Zelia would be an invaluable instructor. "You said you'd teach me to use my talent," he reminded her. "Do you think you could teach me one of those *asanas?*"

Zelia untied the thong that had held back her hair and shook out her long red tresses. "It takes years of practice to learn to do them properly," she answered. "You need to master not only the movements of the *asana* itself, but also the mental focus that goes with each pose. You might be able to crudely mimic one of the simpler *asanas*, but—"

"Will you teach me a simple one, then?" Arvin asked. He rubbed his temples. It hadn't been his imagination, earlier; his head was throbbing. He really could feel the mind seed putting in roots. "At the very least, it'll give me something to . . . distract me."

Zelia stared back at him, and for a moment Arvin wondered if she was going to dismiss his request as ridiculous and impossible. Then her lips twitched into a smile. "Why not?" she said at last. "It might prove amusing. An interesting test of your potential. I'll teach you the *bhujanga asana*. Take off your clothes."

Arvin blushed. "It that absolutely necessary?"

Zelia's eyes narrowed. "Do you want to learn—or are you wasting my time?"

"I want to learn," Arvin hurriedly assured her. "But my bracelet and amulet stay on."

Zelia raised an eyebrow. "Everyone draws the line somewhere," she said. "But your glove must come off."

Arvin fumbled at the buttons of his shirt then peeled it over his head. He unfastened the belt that held his sheathed dagger and set the weapon to the side then sat and pulled off his boots and his glove. Finally he unfastened the laces of his trousers, let them fall in a heap at his feet, and stepped out of them. He stood with hands cupped in front of himself, hiding his nakedness. Zelia seemed oblivious to it, however. Her eyes never strayed from his.

"Lie down," she instructed, "on your stomach."

Arvin did, gratefully. The stone of the rooftop was warm against his bare skin.

"Place your hands, palms down, under your shoulders," Zelia continued.

Arvin did. Zelia walked behind him and nudged one of his ankles, adjusting his legs. Arvin's ankle tingled where her bare foot had touched it. "Feet together, and point your toes," Zelia said. "Now arch your back—slowly—and tilt your head back until you are looking straight up at the sky."

Arvin did as he was instructed, arching until his stomach and throat were taut. He stared up at the rapidly darkening sky, wondering how long he'd have to maintain this position.

"Continue to hold the pose," Zelia said.

Arvin did. Above him, the first glimmers of starlight became visible as sunset slid into evening. Slowly the sky darkened, changing from purple to a velvety black. Arvin held the pose, expecting further instruction, but Zelia merely strode around him, adjusting his pose with a nudge here, a pressing down of her palm there. Each time she touched him he felt a flush go through his body, making it difficult to concentrate on the pose. His mind wandered to the stories he'd heard about the delights and terrors of sleeping with yuan-ti women. About their sensual, twining embraces, their reputed ability to coax a man on past his limits—and their rumored tendency to, in the heat of passion, inflict a fatal bite. Legend had it that, in the convulsions of death, the man experienced a release unlike anything he'd ever—

"Concentrate on the pose," Zelia hissed. "Keep your mind in the present."

Obediently, Arvin tore his mind away from fantasy.

Zelia stood, arms folded, staring down at him in silence.

As the evening continued to lengthen, Arvin began to wonder if Zelia was toying with him. Was she ever going to tell him what to do next, or just leave him frozen in this pose until he collapsed? The muscles in Arvin's lower back were starting to bunch with strain, and his stiffly extended arms had begun to tremble. The human body wasn't built to hold a pose like this for so long. But at least it took his mind off the throbbing in his head that had been pestering him most of the day. Compared to this new pain, the headache was inconsequential.

"Hold the *asana*," Zelia droned. "Feel the energy in your lower back—in your *muladhara*. That's where the energy lies, coiled tight like a serpent."

Arvin concentrated on his lower back but could feel only the tension in his muscles, which were starting to burn. It wasn't working. Already it must be halfway between sunset and middark—surely this had gone on long enough. He let his arms bend, just a little, to ease the strain.

"Maintain the pose!" Zelia snapped, her voice like a whip.

Arvin straightened his arms at once. He could do this, he told himself. It was just like climbing a wall—a very high wall. You climbed so far, until your muscles were burning and you thought you couldn't support yourself a moment longer; then you looked down and realized how far you'd fall if you let go. And you kept going.

He refused to give up. He could do this. He had to. He was physically stronger than Zelia and determined to succeed. He wasn't about to fail at something she'd made look so easy.

More time passed. His arms began to tremble. His muscles had gone beyond burning, to the point where they felt like water.

"Move through the pain—send your mind to a place beyond it," Zelia instructed. "Send it deep, to the base of your spine. Search there for your *muladhara*. Find it."

Gritting his teeth, Arvin did as he was told. Rallying his flagging will, he blotted out the agony of his muscles and turned his mind inward. He sent his awareness sliding down his spine, to a place in the small of his back and concentrated on it, refusing to acknowledge anything else. He pushed himself through the pain . . . and suddenly was beyond it.

There. Was that it? He felt, in the small of his back, a hot, tight sensation that reminded him of the prickling he felt in his scalp when he manifested his charm. It was coiled around the base of his spine, a focused energy waiting to be unleashed.

"You've found your *muladhara*?" Zelia asked. "Good. Now let the energy uncoil."

Arvin continued to stare up at the sky, which blurred as his vision became unfocused. Then suddenly, the knot of energy that was coiled at the base of his spine sprang open. A wave of energy surged through his body like a flash of wildfire. It was a feeling that came close to sexual release—except that the energy stayed within his body, tingling deep within every pore and hair.

Arvin laughed out loud, delighted. "I've done it!"

Zelia let out a slow, surprised hiss as Arvin sat up. "With a single *asana*," she said softly. "Incredible."

"Teach me more," Arvin said, flush with the energy that was coursing through his body.

"Very well," Zelia said, sounding edgy. It was as if Arvin's success had irritated her somehow. "Let's see if you can learn one of the simpler powers—the Far Hand. Hold the position and send the energy you've summoned to a point on your forehead, between your eyes."

Arvin did as instructed, mentally guiding the energy up his spine. It seemed to find a resting point all on its own, coiling just inside his forehead, between his eyes.

Zelia stepped in front of him, holding something: his magical glove. Seeing it in her hand, he nearly lost his concentration.

"Maintain your focus!" Zelia snapped. "Keep the energy tightly coiled, until it's time to use it."

Realizing that she had chosen a valuable possession deliberately, to test him, Arvin gritted his teeth and found his focus again.

"Good. Now reach out with the energy; direct its energy with your gaze. Take the glove from my hand."

Arvin tried but could not. "I . . . don't think I can," he gasped.

Zelia's lips curved into a tight smile.

Prodded by anger—she didn't *want* him to succeed—Arvin tried harder and felt the energy in his forehead loosen . . . just a little.

Zelia backed away from him, retreating until she was up against the vine-covered rail that surrounded the rooftop. She continued to hold the glove in front of her. "Give up?" she smirked.

Arvin shook his head and continued to concentrate. Once again, the energy loosened—but not enough. The glove in Zelia's hands twitched then lay still.

Zelia's eyes widened. "Try again," she said, serious once more.

"Send the energy out all at once . . . now!" As she spoke, she tossed the glove over the edge of the rooftop.

"No," Arvin gasped.

The energy that had been spiraling between his eyes suddenly rushed out through them. He saw a bright streak of silver flash out toward the glove. His vision filled with sparkling light. When it cleared, the line of light was gone. The glove, however, was hovering above the rail. Tentatively, with slow jerks, he drew the invisible energy back toward him, reeling it back into his mind. The glove was tugged along with it and moved through the air toward him with short, choppy movements then fell onto the ground in front of him.

"You can relax now."

Arvin sagged onto the ground and let the tension flow from his muscles. Sitting up, he tilted his head to stretch his neck. "I did it," he said. "I learned a new power."

"Yes." Zelia stared at him with a thoughtful expression, as if his success had surprised her. "That's enough for one night," she said curtly. "It's almost middark. I must see if the cultists have returned to the chamber."

Arvin nodded, suddenly exhausted. Trembling slightly, he pulled his clothes back on. He'd expected the invigorating rush of energy to continue, but all he wanted to do was sleep. He hoped the headache would let him. When he'd finished dressing, he sat again, his back against one of the potted plants. He found himself fighting to keep his eyes open. Even his curiosity about what Zelia was doing—sinking into a cross-legged position with the soles of her feet uppermost, just as his mother had done when she meditated—couldn't keep him awake.

As Zelia stared off into the night sky, hissing as she summoned up the psionic power that would let her peer into the sewer chamber, he fell asleep . . .

And into the strangest dream.

CHAPTER 7

23 Kythorn,
Middark

Arvin lay on his side, knees drawn up to his chest and arms coiled around his legs. He was midway between sleep and wakefulness—aware that he lay on a rooftop, his breaths slow and even as they hissed in and out of his mouth, yet with his mind entangled in the strands of a dream. It was a strange sensation, almost as if he were awake and observing the dream from a distance—a dream that was as vivid as waking.

In the dream he was a child—a serpent child. He was slithering down a corridor as fast as he could, contractions rippling through his body as he pushed with his scales against the smooth green stone of the floor. Behind him loomed a human child of about five years of age—two years younger than Arvin—with braided hair and a slave brand on her cheek. She was laughing as she chased Arvin into a carpeted dining hall, her eyes glittering with excitement. Arvin, hissing with delight at having eluded the lumbering human, heaved the front half of his torso upright and began to slither up onto a table. Too late. The slave girl bent down and yanked the carpet, sending Arvin tumbling. Then she leaped forward and slapped his tail with her palm.

"Tag the tail!" she shrilled. "Tag the tail and you're it!"

Arvin felt rage course through him. No. It wasn't fair—the slave had cheated. She hadn't given him enough of a start. His body drew back into a coil; then he lashed out. His fangs sank into the girl's arm, and he tasted the sweet, hot tang of blood.

The slave girl gave a strangled gasp and staggered backward, staring at the twin beads of blood on her forearm, then collapsed onto the floor. "I thought . . ." she gasped, her tongue already thickening in her mouth. "We . . . friends. . . ." Then her eyes glazed.

Arvin's tongue flickered in and out of his mouth. The slave girl lay still on the floor, no longer breathing. Dead.

Regret trickled through him. Perhaps he shouldn't have been so hasty. Who was he going to play with, now?

Arvin shifted, turning over in his sleep. The night air was growing cooler, less muggy. He squirmed over to a section of rooftop that retained a little of the day's warmth; his body drank it in. A part of him realized that he had moved like a snake, undulating hips and shoulders in order to shift himself. . . .

The dream shifted. Now Arvin was kneeling on a low stone platform in the middle of a room richer than any he had ever seen. It had a high, domed ceiling held up by gilded columns, windows draped with silk curtains that fluttered in the evening breeze, and walls painted with *Origin* frescoes—a series of images showing the World Serpent looking down upon the snakes, lizards, and other reptilian races issuing from Her cloaca.

Arvin was weary with the exhaustion that follows an intense rage. His hands were raw from having pounded his fists repeatedly against his sleeping platform, and his skin was moist and itching from the acidic sweat that had oozed out between his scales. He'd hissed until his jaw ached, thrown his dinner against the door— splatters of egg and shell clung to its polished wood—and still his mother hadn't relented. He was *not* going to be given another slave with whom to play. Not until he learned to coil his temper. Until he learned to master his emotions. Until he stopped acting so *human*.

That had punctured his pride. Humans were stupid, blundering creatures. Look how the yuan-ti manipulated and dominated them, just as humans and the other lesser races dominated animals. It was the natural order of things. It—

The door opened. Arvin looked up at the strangest human he'd ever seen. The man was short, dark skinned, and bald—and so wrinkled his face looked as though it had shrunk beneath its skin. Yet he was lean and well muscled. His only article of clothing was a loincloth, nearly as dark as he was. Around one wrist was coiled a finger-thin turquoise serpent with translucent yellow wings: a flying snake from the jungles of Chult. Arvin stared at it, transfixed, as it raised its head and hissed. He'd *wanted* one of those for *so long.* . . .

The bald man moved his hand up and down, causing the flying snake to flutter its wings. All the while, he stared at Arvin, not speaking.

In a distant part of the family manse, Arvin heard a wind chime tinkling. Yet the breeze that had been ruffling his curtains had stopped. The clouds must have cleared; sunlight was shining in through the window now.

"Desire," the bald man said in a deep voice that was at odds with his thin frame. "I can feel it radiating from you, like heat from a sun-warmed rock. Your emotions run deep and swift—very unusual, in a yuan-ti."

Arvin stared at the impudent human, wondering when he was going to hand over the flying snake—perhaps he should just take it from the man, instead. The pet was obviously an apology from his mother for her overreaction about the slave girl.

The bald man raised his free hand and flicked a fingertip against the snake's nose. The tiny serpent recoiled, hissing. He flicked its nose again, and this time the snake bared its fangs. Arvin stared, appalled, as the man gave the snake's nose another flick, sending it lashing back and forth. He flicked his finger at it again, and again, and again, until Arvin was certain the snake would sink its fangs into the offending human at any moment. Yet, though the snake hissed its fury, mouth wide and venom dripping from its fangs, it did not strike.

The bald man gave a toss of his hand, sending the snake fluttering into the air. Arvin raced across the room, hoping to catch it, but the snake was too quick. It flew out the window. Arvin turned to glare at the human, teeth bared.

The bald man held up an admonishing finger. "Control," he said.

Now Arvin understood. The bald man was yet another tutor, come to drill him in moderation and self-restraint. A *human* tutor, this time, to further humiliate him. "The flying snake held its temper," Arvin hissed back at the man. "So what?"

The bald man chuckled. "You misunderstood my demonstration," he said. "I held the snake's temper. With mind magic. But before I could do that, I had to learn to control my own." He stared for several long moments at Arvin without speaking then asked, "Is this something you would like to learn?"

"Yes," Arvin hissed, speaking aloud in his sleep. "I want to learn."

Suddenly the dream became more chaotic. He was no longer a yuan-ti child, but himself—Arvin—an adult human. Yet strangely, his skin was covered in serpent scales. They were as brown as the bald man's skin had been, and crisscrossed with bands of reddish brown. No, that wasn't a scale pattern on his arms but a series of red thongs, looped around his body and slowly tightening. Zelia, dressed in a gray robe and skullcap, like the ones the priests at the orphanage had worn, was holding one end of the cord and slowly pulling it toward herself, coiling the cord around one wrist as she hauled it in. She stood on the ball of one foot, her other leg twisted up against her chest, the ankle tucked behind her neck. "Control," she said, the word somehow coming out as a hiss. Her jaws opened wide. Hot, stinging venom dripped onto Arvin's temple as she leaned over him, mouth opened, fangs bared—

Arvin's eyes sprang open. Suddenly he was wide awake. Someone was leaning over him, touching his shoulder. A dark silhouette in the moonlight with long, loose hair.

Throwing himself to the side, he called his dagger into his glove. In an instant he was on his feet—and then he recognized Zelia. "By the gods," he gasped, holding his weapon between them. "What did you just do to me?" He rubbed his temple and winced. The headache was still with him.

Zelia remained kneeling, hands on her knees. "What do you mean?"

Arvin blinked, trying to clear his head of the disturbing images. "That dream. I was. . . ."

"Someone else?" Zelia asked, rising slowly to her feet.

Arvin nodded. "A yuan-ti. A child. A . . . girl." The latter was something he'd only just realized—that he'd been female in both of the dreams.

"Sometimes when a psion sleeps, a power manifests spontane-ously," Zelia told him. "You obviously manifested a telepathic power that allowed you to peer into another person's mind and listen in on her thoughts. That it was a yuan-ti is hardly surprising in a city with more than two thousand of us. Your mind tried to make sense of what the power showed you and turned it into a dream."

Arvin stood, considering. Was that what he'd just been doing? Looking in on another person's thoughts and knotting them into his dreams? It hadn't *felt* like a dream. Not until the last, chaotic part that had woken him in a cold sweat. That last segment was easy to explain—it was a jumble of his old memories and fears, combined with fragments of what had happened earlier today, including the headache that just wouldn't go away. But the first part had felt like . . . a memory.

Arvin stared at Zelia. "It wasn't just any yuan-ti," he said slowly. "It was someone trained in 'mind magic.' That girl was you—wasn't it?"

Zelia smiled. "I must have been thinking about my childhood." Her smile abruptly vanished. "The Pox have returned to the sewer chamber."

"They have?" Arvin asked, all thoughts of the dream driven instantly from his mind. He looked up at the sky and saw that it was past middark. "Was my friend with them?"

"I saw two men. Neither was your friend. It looked as though they were waiting for something—or for someone."

She gave him directions to the sewer entrance he would use. It was just a short distance away, inside a slaughterhouse—one that had recently been shut down by the militia after its owners were caught butchering cattle that had succumbed to the rotting hoof disease and passing it off as quality meat.

"How appropriate," Arvin muttered. He slid his dagger into the sheath at the small of his back and picked up his backpack. He pulled out one of the potions he'd purchased earlier, a clear liquid with a sweet scent that lingered in the air even though the tiny bottle that held it was stoppered. The rogue who had sold it to him had assured Arvin it would purge any disease from his body, even ailments that were the result of clerical magic.

Arvin transferred the bottle to his gloved hand and whispered the word that made it disappear into an extradimensional space where it could neither be seen nor smelled. The last thing he needed was for one of the Pox to spot the bottle and recognize what it held.

He put on the backpack and nodded at Zelia. "Tymora be with me, I'll have some answers for you soon," he said. Then he realized something. "How will I get a message to you?" he asked. "Do I meet you back here?"

"No," Zelia replied. She opened her belt pouch and pulled from it a stone that glittered in the moonlight. It was dark blue, flecked with gold, about the size and shape of a thumbnail, and flat on one side. Arvin nodded, recognizing it by its distinctive color: lapis lazuli, with inclusions of pyrite. He extended his right hand, palm up, for the chip of stone.

Then he stiffened in surprise. He was no gem cutter. How in the Nine Hells had he known what type of stone it was?

Zelia tipped it into his palm. Arvin used a finger to flip it over. Its rounded surface was cool and smooth, but the flat surface was warm.

"When you have something to report, this will allow you to manifest a sending," Zelia said.

Arvin gave her a puzzled look. "What's a sending?"

"A psionic power—one the stone will allow you to manifest, even though you haven't learned it yet," she continued. "You can send a brief message to me—no more than two dozen words, and only once per day—and I can reply to you, in turn. The distance separating us is not a factor; your message will reach me, no matter where I might be."

"And no matter where I might be?" Arvin asked.

Zelia nodded.

"I see," he said. "It's a contingency plan. In case something happens to . . . prevent me from returning."

Zelia's answer was blunt. "Yes. In order to use the stone, you must place it over your third eye."

"My what?"

"You used it earlier tonight, when you manifested your teleki-netic power. Place the flat surface of the stone here"—she touched a finger to a spot between her eyes, just above her nose—"and it will adhere."

Arvin stared at the lapis lazuli, wondering if there was more to it than Zelia was telling him. "Can I put it on later?" he asked. "If the Pox see it—"

"They won't know what it is. Only another psion would recognize it. But put it on and take it off as you wish. You need only think the command word—*atmiya*—and it will adhere or release. Just don't lose it."

"Why? Is it expensive?"

Zelia's lips twitched in what might have been a smile. "Yes."

Arvin stared at the stone. If he did run into trouble—if he wound up a captive, bound hand and foot and without his dagger to cut himself free—having the stone already in place on his forehead would allow him to call for help.

The question was would Zelia answer?

"All right," he said. "I'll use it—but I won't put it on until I need to contact you." He slipped the stone into his shirt pocket, tucking it safely inside a false seam.

24 Kythorn, Darkmorning

Arvin eased himself through a window and drew the shutter closed behind him. He stood a moment, letting his eyes adjust to the gloom and his nose adjust to the smell. The slaughterhouse stank of old blood, animal excrement, and spoiled meat. The stench was so over-whelming he nearly turned to leave, but he steeled himself by thinking of what would happen in less than seven days and pressed on.

He made his way toward the center of the building, avoiding the stained hooks that hung from the ceiling. As he stepped over one of the troughs used to catch the slaughtered animals' blood, his foot bumped against something in the darkness. Flies rose into the air with a soft buzzing noise. Looking down, he saw it was a cow's head, its tongue purple and protruding and both eyes missing. The putrid smell rising from it made his eyes water.

The troughs all led to the same place—a grate in the floor near the center of the building. The spaces between its rusted bars were nearly clotted shut with chunks of decaying flesh, but the crust of blood that had sealed the edges of the grate was broken. Someone had lifted the grate since the slaughterhouse had been shut down.

He removed a hooked tool from his belt and used it to lift one side of the grate. Grabbing the edge of it with his gloved hand, he moved it aside—carefully, so it wouldn't clank against the stone floor—then stared down into the shaft that led to the sewers. He could smell and hear water gurgling somewhere below, but the shaft was as black as a snake's heart.

Wetting his lips, he shrugged off his backpack and set it on the ground beside him then rummaged inside it for the second potion he'd purchased. It was in a vial made from glass of such a deep purple it appeared almost black. Arvin pried out the wax that sealed it and sniffed the vial's contents. It took him a moment to place the scent: night-blooming flowers, underlaid with a hint of something earthy—a root of some sort.

He tipped the potion into his mouth and swallowed. It tasted honey sweet, with an aftertaste of loam. A heartbeat later, the room seemed to lighten. Murky shadows became distinct objects. A vertical line of darkness was revealed as a chain hanging from the ceiling, and a dark mound in one corner resolved itself into a fly-speckled tangle of cow's legs, minus the hooves. As the darkvision potion took its full effect, the room seemed to become as bright as day—except that everything was devoid of color. The hooks in the ceiling were a dull gray, crusted with blood that was a flat black. Looking down at his own hands, Arvin saw that his skin appeared gray—a lighter gray than his shirt.

This, he mused, must be how dwarves see the world most of the time. Only when they ventured out of their underground strong-holds into sunlight would they see color. No wonder they were such a dour race.

But this was no time for idle thought. The potion would only last so long.

The shaft the grate had covered was square, barely wider than his shoulders. It descended some distance to a horizontal tunnel through which foul-looking water flowed. There was a gap between the murky surface of the water and the ceiling of the tunnel—quite a bit of a gap, almost as much space as Arvin was tall. The tunnel must be one of the main sewage lines.

A hook in the slaughterhouse ceiling, just over the shaft, told the story of how the cultists had descended to the tunnel below. The curved bottom of the hook was free of blood; the cultists had obviously tied a rope to it.

Arvin decided to do the same. His bracelet would have allowed him to climb down, but he didn't relish the thought of clinging to a wall so grimed with dried gore. He pulled from his backpack a trollgut rope he'd retrieved from its hiding place earlier that night, when he'd gone to buy the potions. It was rubbery and slightly warm to the touch. He tied the unknotted end to the hook and slipped the rest of its coiled length over his shoulder. Gripping the rope just under the hook with one hand, he transferred his weight to it. With his other hand, he lifted the grate and stood it at an angle on the floor, next to the opening. Then he spoke the rope's command word.

The magical rope lengthened, sending Arvin into a descent down the shaft. He let the grate close above him; its edge pinched the rope as it closed. He descended for a few heartbeats more; then, as soon as the soles of his boots touched the water, he spoke the rope's command word a second time, halting its magical growth.

He hung there a moment, looking around as he twisted on the rope. He immediately spotted what he'd expected to see—a convenient ledge that ran along one wall of the tunnel. He clambered onto it then used his dagger to cut the rope back to its original length. The freshly grown section of rope immediately began to rot; in a short time, it would fall off the hook, away from the spot where the grate pinched it, and all traces of Arvin's entrance would be gone. The original section of rope was still intact and could be used again another day. Arvin carefully stored it in his backpack and set off down the ledge, bending over slightly to avoid banging his head against the rounded ceiling.

After a short distance, the tunnel curved. As Arvin crept around the bend, he spotted the chamber to which he and Naulg had been taken. He'd expected to see the two cultists Zelia had just spotted, but the island of stone at the center of the chamber was bare, devoid even of the hideous wooden statue. Where had the two cultists gone? There was no sign or sound of anyone inside any of the other five tunnels that radiated away from the circular chamber, and this tunnel was the only one with a ledge to walk along. Had he arrived just a little too late? Had the cultists left through the tunnel Arvin stood in, passing beneath the grate even as he crept into the slaughterhouse?

He crouched and examined the ledge, but it held no clues. The sewage that mired its surface held no footprints but his.

Deciding he would wade out to the island, Arvin fished out of his pocket a spool of thread with a lead weight tied to one end. He walked to the mouth of the tunnel and lowered the weight into the water until it hit bottom then grasped the thread just above the point where it entered the water. Lifting it, he measured the depth of the water. It was well over his head.

That gave him pause for thought. How had the cultists who had captured them reached the island of stone that lay in the middle of the chamber, especially hauling captives along with them? They hadn't swum—their robes had been dry, as had the clothes of Arvin and the other captives. And they hadn't rowed there in the boat in which Arvin had escaped. It had been neither big enough, nor sound enough. It had obviously been tied up in the chamber, quietly rotting, for years. The hems of their robes had been wet, however, as if they'd dragged in water. Had the cultists *walked* across the water to the island, using magic? If so, the two cultists Zelia had spotted might have strolled away down any of the tunnels, whether they had ledges or not. But which?

As if in answer, a low groan echoed out of the tunnel immediately to the right of the one in which Arvin stood. He tensed, recognizing the sound of a man in pain. Naulg?

He had to find out.

The wall between the tunnels was brickwork, its crumbling mortar offering numerous finger- and toeholds. Activating the magic of his leather bracelet, he began climbing along the wall, glancing over his shoulder frequently. All he needed now was for the cultists to show up. He could hardly claim to have come to join the Pox if he were found skulking around.

Reaching the mouth of the other tunnel, he slipped around the bend and continued into it, still climbing horizontally along the wall. A short distance ahead was a small, square door, up near the ceiling of the tunnel. As Arvin neared it, he saw that the door was open slightly; it gave access to a low-ceilinged corridor. The door was made of wood but was faced with bricks; when closed, it would blend with the wall of the sewage tunnel and be nearly impossible to spot.

Like the sewage tunnels, the secret corridor beyond the door curved; Arvin could see only a few paces inside it. The floor just inside the corridor was smeared with sludge; someone with sewage on his clothes had entered it recently. Arvin paused, clinging to the wall next to the door. Was this corridor where the groan had originated?

He climbed into it, making as little noise as he could. Once on his hands and knees, he drew his dagger. Weapon in hand, he crept up to the bend—and hissed in alarm as he came face to face with a body.

The man lay on his side, unmoving, eyes closed. He was older, with tarred hair pulled back in a tight bun and a face that was vaguely familiar. Only as Arvin reached out to touch the man's stubbled cheek—which was still warm—did he remember where he'd seen the fellow before. He'd been one of the five captives the Pox had taken last night. Like Arvin, he'd been forced to drink from one of the flasks.

Arvin jerked his fingers away from the corpse. Had the old sailor died of plague? Arvin's heart raced at the thought of sharing this narrow tunnel with a diseased corpse. He was breathing the same air the man had just groaned from his lungs—breathing in disease and death and. . . .

Control, he told himself sternly. Where is your control?

The self-admonishment steadied him, that and Zelia's reassurances that he was immune to the plague in the flasks, his body having already fought it off once. Or had it? His headache had dulled, a little, but it still nagged at him. Perhaps it wasn't the mind seed after all but the start of a fever. And he did feel a little light-headed—though that might have been due to the sewer stench.

Forcing himself to touch his amulet with the fingers that had just touched the dead man's cheek, he uttered the words that had always given him courage in the past: "nine lives."

Then he noticed something—a smear of blood on the floor of the tunnel, just beyond the corpse. Curious, Arvin shifted position so he could see the sailor's back and spotted the fletched end of a crossbow bolt protruding from a spot just below the right shoulder. Had the old man tried to escape and the cultists shot him in the back?

Oddly enough, the thought fueled Arvin's hopes. If the old sailor had remained alive for this long—and had felt well enough to attempt escape—perhaps Naulg was still alive, too.

Arvin had just started to crawl past the body when he heard a groan issue from the man's lips. He froze, halfway over the sailor, as the man's eyes flickered open.

"It hurts," the sailor whispered.

Arvin's eyes flickered to the crossbow bolt. "You've been shot," he told the old man. "I don't think. . . ." He didn't have the heart to say the rest—that he doubted the fellow would live much longer.

The old man stared at the wall, not seeing Arvin. "My stomach. It hurts," he whispered again in a voice as faint as death. "Gods curse them . . . for doing this to me. I just want . . . the pain . . . to end."

"It will, old man. It will." Arvin wanted to pat the shoulder of the sailor, to console him, but was afraid to.

The old man was whispering again—fainter, this time, than before. "Silvanus forgive me for. . . ."

Arvin could have leaned closer and heard the rest, but he was fearful of getting too close to the man's plague-tainted breath. Instead he drew back, holding his own breath.

A moment later, he realized the old man had also stopped breathing.

From somewhere up ahead, Arvin heard the metallic hiss of a sword being drawn from its sheath. Worried that Naulg might be the next to die, he crawled past the corpse and on up the corridor as quickly as he could.

CHAPTER 8

24 Kythorn,
Darkmorning

As Arvin hurried down the corridor on his hands and knees, the stench increased. It wasn't just the odor of the sewers that was clogging his nostrils, but something far worse—the reek of putrefying flesh, vomit, and sweat. Bile rose in his throat. He fought it down. He hurried on, blinking away a drop of sweat that had trickled into one eye. It wasn't just the exertion of crawling rapidly through a low-ceilinged corridor that had caused him to break out in a sweat. The air was definitely getting warmer, more humid. Up ahead, he could see the glow of lantern light. It turned the brick walls of the corridor from gray to dusky red.

There had been silence for some time after the sound of the sword being drawn, but now he could hear retching noises. Then a woman's voice, tense and low. "Something's coming, Urus. Hurry! Get up!"

Just a few paces ahead, the corridor gave access to a large chamber. Arvin saw a man, down on his hands and knees, vomiting. A woman was bent over him, tugging on the back of his shirt with one hand. Both wore high boots slicked with sewage to the knee. Judging by the crossbow that lay on the ground next to the man's knee, they were the ones who had shot the sailor.

He hadn't been their only victim.

A bull's-eye lantern lay on the ground beside the kneeling man, its light painting a bright circle on a cultist in faded gray robes who was slumped in a heap against one wall, his chest bloody. Judging by the slit in his robe, he'd been killed by a sword slash. A large basket lay on the floor beside the cultist. Freshly butchered chunks of meat had spilled out of it. One of them was recognizable as a human foot.

The man on his hands and knees was middle-aged and broad shouldered with dark, curly hair and a full beard. The woman was younger—in her early twenties—and slender, with a narrow face framed with waist-length hair that hung straight as a plumb line. She wore a man's trousers tucked into her boots and held a bloody sword. She tugged frantically on the man's shirt with her other hand, trying to drag him back to the corridor in which Arvin had halted, but without success. Her eyes were locked on the chamber's only other entrance: an archway that led into a darkened corridor tall enough for a human to walk upright. From it came a slurping sound, as if something large and wet were being dragged across the floor.

Arvin peered through the archway. His darkvision revealed what looked like a grayish mound, moving slowly toward the chamber. It hunched and sagged as it moved, sections of it bulging out like bubbles trying to burst through thick oil then sinking flat in a fold of flesh as the rest of the mass surged over them. As the thing drew closer to the lantern light, colors were revealed. Gray resolved into greenish yellow, the color of diseased flesh. Red pustules dotted the body of the thing, as did molelike tufts sprouting wiry black hair. The creature had no eyes, no mouth. Here and there, a bone jabbed momentarily out of the flesh like a thrusting sword, causing a dribble of pus-tinged blood, then was drawn back into the mass with a wet sucking sound as the mound surged forward.

"Torm shield us," the woman croaked as the thing bulged out of the archway. "What is *that?*"

The man glanced up as the fleshy mound squeezed its bulk through the archway and tumbled into the room with a sound like a bag of wet entrails hitting the floor. The mound hesitated, pulsing first in the direction of the two living humans, then toward the cultist's corpse. The kneeling man tried to climb to his feet but was only able to rise partway before clutching at his stomach and doubling over again. His back heaved as he gave in to nausea, retching over and over again. One hand gestured weakly, urging the woman to leave him.

The young woman, gagging in the overpowering stench that filled the chamber, at last let go of his shirt. But instead of turning and running, as Arvin expected, she stepped between her companion and the mound, readying her sword.

"You fool," Arvin whispered to himself. "Get out of there!" He'd already started backing down the corridor through which he'd crawled, though he could not tear his eyes away from the horrific creature that was only a pace or two away from the woman. The stench of the thing was terrific; Arvin's eyes watered as he fought to keep himself from vomiting. Control, he told himself fiercely. You can control—

No he couldn't. His stomach was twisted by a wave of nausea that felt like a dagger stabbing into his gut. He vomited onto the floor, splattering his hands and knees.

The woman was shouting something. Suddenly, Arvin felt the humid air around him grow slightly cooler. As he fought down the next wave of nausea and managed to look up, he saw her leap forward, thrusting with her sword. The blade plunged into part of the mound that had been bulging toward her. An ice white burst of magical energy erupted from the sword, instantly freezing the flesh around it. The creature's skin cracked like a frozen puddle that had been stomped on. Then the woman yanked her sword free, sending a scattering of frozen blood tinkling onto the floor.

The mound hesitated, sucking its wounded flesh back into itself. Then it exploded into motion. It surged forward, driving the woman back. Her companion had just enough time to glance up at the thing that was towering over him like a pulsating wall—and the mound collapsed on top of him, suffocating his scream.

"Urus!" the woman screamed in a strangled voice. "No!" She leaped forward, thrusting her sword into the side of the mound a second time. A blast of magical cold radiated through the creature's flesh, causing a section of it to expand and crack apart as it froze. But despite this new wound—and a third, and a fourth—the fleshy mound refused to retreat. It remained firmly on top of the spot where her companion had been crouched, its bulk filling the far half of the chamber. From beneath it came a muffled tearing noise, punctuated by the sharp crackle of breaking bone.

The sound drove the woman into a frenzy. She flung herself at the mound, thrusting with her sword. The weapon plunged to the hilt into the pulsating wall of flesh—and the pustule it had entered exploded, spraying her with pus. The mound pulsed forward in the same instant, engulfing her hand just as the magical cold erupted from the sword. She gasped as the flesh that surrounded her hand froze.

Arvin, meanwhile, fought his own battle against the nausea that was cramping his stomach. Move through the pain, he told himself, staring at the vomit-splattered brick between his hands. A part of his mind noted that the floor was gray again; the lantern must have been engulfed by the mound. Forcing the stray thought away, he concentrated on blotting out the cramps in his stomach. The mind is master of the body, he told himself, repeating the phrase his tutor had drilled into him. It is in control. Gritting his teeth, he tried to force his mind past the nausea . . .

And found himself vomiting—this time, on his glove.

Staring at it, he remembered the potion that was hidden inside its extradimensional space. The potion was designed to remove disease—would it also cure nausea? It was worth a try.

Summoning the vial to his hand, Arvin ripped the cork out with his teeth. He drank the potion in one swallow, welcoming its honey-sweet taste . . .

And suddenly, the nausea was gone.

Hissing in relief, he looked up. The lantern had indeed gone out; he viewed the chamber with darkvision alone. The woman had lost her sword and stood flexing frostbitten fingers, trying to make them work again. The mound had engulfed the cultist's corpse and was consuming it, giving her a brief reprieve. But even as Arvin watched, it began to slide toward her with a slow, certain malevolence. The woman retreated, backing toward the corridor Arvin occupied, her undamaged hand extended behind her as if she were feeling her way. Arvin wondered why she didn't just turn and run then realized that, unlike him, she couldn't see. She didn't have a chance.

Unless he helped her. Which would mean abandoning what might be his one chance to slip around the mound and into the corridor at the far end of the chamber—a corridor that might lead him to Naulg.

Or to a dead end, with a flesh-eating monster at his back.

"This way!" Arvin shouted to the woman, crawling forward as quickly as he could. He sprang out of the corridor and grabbed her, forcing her down into a crouch, then shoved her into the low corridor. "Move!" he barked. "Get out of here."

She did.

Out of the corner of his eye, Arvin saw the mound looming above him. He leaped out of the way an instant before it toppled onto the spot where he'd just stood—then cursed, realizing the mound had forced him into a corner, away from the exit. His only hope was to somehow drive the thing back, to force it to draw away from the mouth of the corridor that led back to the sewers. He slashed with his dagger at the bulge and felt the blade slice through soft, quivering flesh. But the mound was undeterred by the wound. It reared up until it touched the ceiling, towering above Arvin. As it did, the wound Arvin had just inflicted upon it gaped open. Staring into the depths of the creature, Arvin saw a gore-streaked ball of bone with two dark pits where the eyes had been—a partially digested head—and a rounded shaft of metal, wrapped with leather.

The grip of a sword hilt.

And not just any weapon, but the one that inflicted magical cold. He started to reach for it then realized it was buried deep inside diseased flesh and yanked his hand back.

Instead he sent his consciousness deep into himself and found his third eye—and the energy that lay coiled there—and flung that energy outward. A bright line of sparkling silver light burst from his eyes and coiled itself around the sword hilt then yanked it free. Grabbing the hilt with his gloved hand, he stabbed the blade into the bulge that blocked the corridor mouth.

Thankfully, the weapon's magic was still working: a burst of cold erupted from the blade, instantly freezing the protuberance. Arvin twisted the sword, using it like a lever, and the frozen bulge of flesh snapped off, revealing the exit. Unfortunately, the sword broke, as well. Dropping it, Arvin dived into the tunnel headfirst. Just in time—as he did, he heard the heavy slap of flesh hitting the wall behind him. A bulge of flesh forced its way into the corridor and brushed against one of his feet. Soft, squishy flesh engulfed his boot, nearly reaching his ankle before he could yank his foot free.

Spurred on by fear, Arvin crawled away as quickly as he could. Behind him, he heard bones cracking as the mound tried to force its bulk into the narrow corridor. As he retreated, the sounds of the creature slapping itself against the walls fell farther and farther behind—it couldn't fit into so small a corridor, Tymora be praised.

Up ahead, around a curve of the tunnel, Arvin could hear a scuffing noise and the rasp of a scabbard dragging on brick. He caught sight of the woman he'd just saved as she was crawling past the body of the old sailor. Leaving it behind, she rounded the bend in the corridor. In another moment she would reach its end.

"Wait!" Arvin shouted as he eased his way past the corpse, loath to touch it. "You're going to fall into—"

A splash told him his warning was too late. Reaching the end of the corridor himself, he looked down into the tunnel and saw the woman thrashing about in the sewage, her long hair plastered to her body. "I'm up here," he called out, reaching down to her. "Take hold of my hand." She startled at the sound of his voice, but accepted his hand readily enough when he grabbed hers and used it to lever herself up into a standing position. The sewage turned out to be no more than knee deep.

She let go of his hand and clawed away the wet hair that was plastered to her face then spat several times, a disgusted expression on her face. Then she fumbled at the pouch on her belt, lifting its flap and tipping sewer water out of it. From out of the pouch, she pulled a small metal flask, its sides ridged like the rattles of a snake—the same kind of flask the Pox had used to force-feed Arvin plague-tainted water. She ran her fingers across the top of it, checking the cork that sealed it.

"Where did you get that?" Arvin asked.

His tone must have been sharper than he'd intended. The woman squinted up in his general direction, a wary look in her eyes. She took a step back, her free hand brushing her scabbard—she stiffened as she found it empty. "Who are you?" she asked, suspicion thickening her voice.

Arvin summoned up a smile, even though she couldn't see it. He needed to keep her talking. She might have seen other cultists—or even Naulg. A warm prickling began at the base of his scalp. "I'm a friend," he told her. "I followed you and Urus. I thought you could use some help."

Arvin saw her head tilt as if she were listening to something—a good sign. An instant later, her expression softened. "Thank the gods you came after us," she gasped. "I *told* Gonthril that sending just two of us was a bad idea, but he wouldn't listen." She tucked the flask back into her pouch and tied it shut.

"I'm glad I found you in time," Arvin said. Seeing her wet clothes clinging to her almost hipless body and noting that the belt that held her scabbard was much too large for her, he revised his estimate of her age to late teens. She was awfully young to be adventuring down in the sewers. Even with a chaperone.

"I'm glad you found us, too," she said. Then she shuddered. "Poor Urus. That *thing. . . .*"

"I've never seen anything like it," Arvin said. "Have you?"

"No. Whatever it was, I think the cleric was on his way to feed it," the woman said, a grimace on her face. "If I hadn't had my father's sword. . . ." She shuddered again then stared blindly up in Arvin's general direction. "Have we met?" she asked. "Or are you in a different arm of the Secession?"

Arvin made a mental note of the word—it sounded like the name of an organization, but it was one he'd never heard of before. "We haven't met," he answered honestly. "My name's Arvin."

"I'm Kayla." She glanced around, squinting as she tried to penetrate the absolute darkness. "I can't see anything—can you?"

"Yes."

"Good. Then you can help me find my way out of these gods-cursed sewers. I need to get back to Gonthril and make my report. He'll be glad to hear we were right about the clerics being down here."

"Good work," Arvin said, playing along. Gonthril was, presumably, the leader of whatever group this woman belonged to, and he seemed to be interested in the Pox—interested enough to send people into the sewers to search for them. Why was anyone's guess.

"Gonthril asked me to keep an eye out for someone while I was down here," Arvin told Kayla. "A dark-haired man whose eyebrows join above his nose. Have you seen him?"

"Who is he?"

"Someone who might be able to help us," Arvin said, keeping his answer deliberately vague.

Kayla shook her head. "I haven't seen him."

"How long have you been down here?"

"Since sunset. We tried to enter the sewers earlier, but the militia were everywhere."

Arvin nodded. She'd been in the sewers quite some time, then. "Did you see any other clerics besides the one with the basket?"

"No."

"How did you know where to find him?"

"We didn't," Kayla said. "It was just Tymora's luck. We were snooping around in the sewers—we'd seen one of Talona's clerics come down here earlier. When we spotted the opening that led to the hidden corridor, we decided to follow it."

"I see," Arvin said, disappointed. Though Kayla had been forth-coming, she hadn't told him anything about the cultists that he didn't already know. Perhaps others in her organization would know more.

One thing was bothering Arvin. "That second fellow—the old sailor—why did Urus shoot him?"

The mention of her companion's name started the woman's lip trembling. "He attacked us."

Arvin frowned. "Are you sure the old man wasn't just trying to escape—to get by you?"

Kayla shook her head. "He was *with* the cleric. When Urus and I surprised them in the chamber, the cleric shouted at the old man to attack us and started casting a spell. I was able to stop him before his prayer was complete, but the old man managed to bite my arm before Urus could shoot him. He ran off while Urus was reloading . . . and that *thing* showed up."

Arvin frowned. "The old man *bit* you?" he said.

"You don't believe me?" Kayla shoved up her sleeve. "Look."

Arvin stared at the crescent-shaped bite mark on her wrist.

"His bite was venomous," Kayla continued. "He must have been yuan-ti—one that could pass for human in lantern light. If it weren't for this, I'd be dead." She touched something that hung from a silver chain around her neck—a pendant made from a black gem. That it was ensorcelled to ward off poison, Arvin had no doubt. But had the old man's bite truly been poisonous?

He gave the bite on her wrist a closer scrutiny. The wound lacked the distinctive puncture marks that hollow, venom-filled fangs would leave. "The old man was diseased, you mean," he corrected.

Kayla shook her head. "It wasn't disease—the effects were too quick. As soon as his teeth broke the skin, my entire arm felt as though it were on fire."

Arvin nodded, losing interest. The real question was whether the old sailor had joined Talona's cult or been magically compelled by the cleric to attack. Whichever it was, he must have been one of the two men Zelia had spied earlier on the stone island. She'd assumed that both were cultists even though only one was wearing robes. The old man obviously hadn't been acting like a prisoner—and he certainly hadn't been bound.

"We should get moving," Kayla said.

Arvin nodded. "Is there an exit nearby?"

Kayla found the wall of the tunnel by touch and ran her palm up it to locate the edge of the corridor in which Arvin crouched. Then she pointed up the sewage tunnel, away from the chamber with the stone island. "That way. There's a shaft that gives access to the street, about four hundred paces up the tunnel. It's at the base of the next spillway."

Arvin glanced down at the water, the surface of which was dotted with half-dissolved lumps that drifted gently with the current. The sewage was deeper than his ankle-high boots; he grimaced at the thought of climbing down into it. "I'm going to climb along the wall," he told her. "You can hold onto my shirt and follow me. All right?"

Kayla nodded.

They set out, Arvin making his way slowly along the wall, Kayla holding on to his shirt. Several times she slipped and nearly pulled Arvin into the sewage with her, but his bracelet allowed him to stick tight to the wall.

As he led her up the sewage tunnel, he considered his options. He could wait near the stone island to see if any other cult-ists showed up, could slog around in the sewers in the hope of stumbling into some of them—or he could leave with Kayla. The charm he'd placed on her would be effective for some time, and she could probably be talked into taking him along with her when she reported to her leader. This Gonthril fellow must know more than Kayla did. If Arvin could charm *him* into sharing what he knew, perhaps two knots could be tied with a single twist. Arvin might learn the answers to Zelia's questions *and* might gain some insight into where Naulg was . . .

Without having to face the cultists.

CHAPTER 9

ARVIN LIFTED THE GRATE A FINGER'S WIDTH AND PEERED UP AND down the darkened street. They were inside the yuan-ti section of the city; mansion walls towered on either side. A slave was sweeping dust from an elaborate, column-fronted entryway to the right. A second slave with a handcart was picking up garbage from the street.

Arvin tipped the grate sideways and passed it down to Kayla, who had braced herself inside the narrow shaft with her back against one wall, her feet against the other. Arvin was just above her, in the same position, his backpack turned so that it hung against his chest. When both slaves had their backs to the opening, he clambered out of the shaft, took the grate from Kayla, and helped her up after him. A moment later the grate was back in place, and they were strolling in the opposite direction from the slaves, just two people out for a walk in the darkness that preceded dawn.

As they passed a light standard, Kayla glanced at Arvin. Seeing her eyes widen, he worried that she might have realized that he wasn't a member of her group after all.

"Amazing," she said. "You could be Gonthril's brother." She paused then added, "Are you?"

"No," Arvin said, not wanting to get caught up in a lie that would quickly unravel on him. "The resemblance is coincidental. I'm always getting mistaken for—" He paused, suddenly realizing something. *That* was who the militia had thought Arvin was that morning: Gonthril. A "rebel," the sergeant had called him. . . .

A rebel with a ten thousand gold piece bounty on his head. And Kayla was about to lead Arvin straight to the man. The next little while could prove interesting—and possibly lucrative.

He nudged Kayla into a walk again. "Let's keep moving. If anyone sees you like that. . . ."

Kayla nodded. "There's a fountain up ahead. I can wash up a little."

They quickened their pace, taking a side street to the fountain. Arvin stood watch as Kayla rinsed the worst of the sewage off herself by ducking into the spray, and they set off again. Arvin expected a lengthy, downhill walk, but Kayla instead led him uphill, deeper into the yuan-ti section of town. Several times they saw militia out on patrol and had to turn up a side street to avoid them. Once, while doing this, they blundered into a group of slaves. Arvin stuck his chin in the air haughtily and hissed at them, giving the impression that he was a yuan-ti. They touched their foreheads and turned aside, discretely ignoring the squelching sound Kayla's wet boots made and the odor that lingered in her wake.

"Not bad," Kayla commented. "You've even got the sway in your walk."

Did he? After she'd called his attention to it, Arvin realized she was right. He'd been swaying his shoulders and hips back and forth as he walked, without intending to. The realization that this must be the mind seed at work sent a chill through him. He rubbed his temple, feeling the ache that lurked just under the skin.

Kayla led him ever upward, into one of the oldest parts of the city, navigating by its most conspicuous landmark—the enormous, fountain-topped dome of the Cathedral of Emerald Scales. Eventually they passed under one end of an ancient, monumental arch that stretched from this street to the next—an arch that was undergoing restoration. Kayla stopped near the pillar that supported this end of the arch. It was surrounded by wooden scaffolding that in turn was sheeted with cloth. She glanced around then lifted a flap of the cloth and tilted her head, indicating that Arvin should slip behind it. He did, and saw that the pillar's decorative scalework was being rechiseled. The cloth must have been hung to prevent dust and stone chips from littering the street below.

Arvin ran a hand over the rough, half-finished carving. The arch was a snake in the process of shedding its skin. Then Kayla ducked behind the cloth with him. She winked at him, one hand on a bar of the scaffolding. They were obviously about to climb it. "Ironic, isn't it?" she whispered. "That scaly bitch is looking all over for the man who's treading on her tail, and he's hiding under her belly all the while. It's one of Gonthril's favorite tricks—hiding in the places she'd least suspect."

Arvin grinned back at her, pretending that he knew what Kayla was talking about. As he followed her up the scaffolding, however, he started to get an inkling. The higher they climbed, the more he could see of the surrounding area through gaps in the cloth draping. He found himself looking down on one of the private gardens of the Extaminos family, now closed for renovations. Its age-pitted walls dated back more than eight centuries, to the time of Lord Shevron, the man who had beaten back the kobold hordes that had besieged the city in 527. This act had ensured House Extaminos's standing for centuries to come. Indeed, for the past three centuries, all of Hlondeth's rulers had been members of House Extaminos, right up to Lady Dediana, the city's current ruler . . .

Who, like most of her predecessors, was yuan-ti.

Arvin understood who the "rebels" were. He'd heard rumors of a group of men and women who wanted to restore the city to human rule. They wanted to turn back the centuries to a time before Lord Shevron had made his pact with the scaly folk. They might as well try to turn the sun back on its course in the sky or cause lava to flow *into* Mount Ugruth. But they'd certainly stirred up the militia with their efforts.

Kayla reached the top of the scaffolding and clambered into one of the gaping serpent mouths that fronted the arch. She turned to help Arvin inside. When he climbed in after her, he was surprised to see that the arch was hollow—to help reduce the weight of so much stone, he supposed. He crawled along behind her through its corridor-like interior, hissing with pain each time he banged a knee against the uneven floor. More than once, his backpack caught on the rough stone ceiling and had to be yanked free. His darkvision was gone; the potion had worn off during the walk here. The only light came from the gaping serpent mouth behind them and a similar opening up ahead. He followed Kayla—who seemed quite familiar with the route—as she led the way through along the darkened passage.

When they reached the second serpent mouth, Kayla stopped. Arvin peered past her and saw they were directly over the private garden, which was illuminated only by moonlight. Its walls, like the monumental arch, were surrounded by scaffolding—part of the massive restoration project that had been undertaken by Dmetrio Extaminos, eldest prince of the royal family, in recent months. Rumor had it Dmetrio had already spent more than a million gold pieces on the project, which seemed destined to tear apart and remortar every building in the old section of the city, stone by stone.

Kayla leaned out of the mouth of the stone serpent head and whistled a tune. A moment later, an answering whistle came from below. The end of a rope rose into view outside the serpent's mouth. Recognizing it, Arvin cracked a wry smile. He'd woven it from sylph hair, a little more than two years ago.

At least one of his customers, it seemed, hadn't been Guild. Or if they were Guild, they were also working the other side of the coin.

Kayla motioned for Arvin to grab the rope. Instead, he took a cautious glance down. Only one person stood in the garden below—the man who held the other end of the rope. The fellow looked harmless enough, with a balding head and ale belly, but appearances could be deceiving. For all Arvin knew, the staff the man had propped against a bush next to him could be a magical weapon of some sort. Getting past him would be the first challenge on the way to meeting Gonthril. Arvin would need a backup, if he were unable to charm the fellow.

"Sorry," Arvin told Kayla with an apologetic smile. "Heights make me nervous." As he spoke, he slipped a hand behind his back and grasped the hilt of his dagger. At a whisper, the dagger disappeared into his glove.

"Go on," Kayla urged. "It isn't far."

Arvin winced, still pretending to be nervous, then grasped the rope. He swung out onto it and clambered down. Kayla followed.

As soon as they were both on the ground, the balding man ordered the rope down. As it looped itself neatly over his outstretched arm, he frowned at Arvin and picked up his staff. "Who's this, Kayla? And where's Urus?"

Kayla's lip began to tremble again. "Dead," she said in a quavering voice. "I'd be dead, too, Chorl, if Arvin hadn't come along when he did."

"I've come to speak to Gonthril," Arvin said. The familiar prickle at the base of his scalp began, and he smiled. "I'm not with the Secession, but I have similar interests—and some information I'm sure Gonthril will want to hear." Seeing a skeptical narrowing of the balding man's eyes, he quickly added, "Information about Talona's clerics—and what they're up to. Kayla managed to get her hands on a flask that one of them was carrying."

The man's eyebrows rose. "Did she?" He glanced at Kayla, who nodded eagerly. "Well done. Well, come on, then."

Arvin let out a soft hiss of relief. His charm had worked. Or had it? As he followed Kayla through the garden, he noticed that Chorl fell into step behind him. The balding man was keeping a close watch on Arvin—closer than Arvin liked.

The garden was laid out in a formal pattern. A path, bordered by flowering shrubs, spiraled in from the main gate to the center of the garden. Bordering this path were slabs of volcanic stone, their many niches providing shelter for the tiny serpents that called the garden home. At the center of the garden was a gazebo, its glass-paned roof reminiscent of the Solarium. The gazebo's wrought-iron supports, like the light standards in the street, took the form of rearing serpents, except that the globes in their mouths hadn't glowed in centuries. Its floor was a mosaic, made from age-dulled tiles. It was covered with what Arvin at first took to be sticks. As he drew closer, though, he saw that they were tiny, finger-thin snakes, curled around one another in sleep. The snakes obscured part of the mosaic, but Arvin could still make out the crest of House Extaminos: a mason's chisel and a ship, separated by a wavy red line.

Chorl stepped forward and used the end of his staff to flick away the tiny snakes. He was needlessly rough with them, injuring several with his harsh jabs, and Arvin found his anger rising. He balled his fists at his sides, forcing himself to hold his emotions in check as the tiny snakes were flung aside.

Chorl stepped up onto the spot the snakes had just been evicted from and pulled from his pocket a hollow metal tube. Squatting, he rapped it once against the tiled floor. The rod emitted a bright *ting*, and the air above the floor rippled. Then a portion of the floor—the section of the mosaic depicting the ship—sank down out of sight. Arvin peered into the hole and saw a ramp leading down into darkness.

Kayla stepped to the edge of the hole. "I always enjoy this part," she told Arvin. She sat on the lip of the hole then pushed off, disappearing into it. The sound of her wet clothes sliding on stone faded quickly.

Chorl nudged Arvin forward with the end of his staff. "Down you go," he ordered. Arvin hissed at the man and angrily knocked the staff aside. Who did this fellow think he was, to order him about?

Chorl was swifter than Arvin had thought. He whipped the staff around, smacking it into Arvin's head. A burst of magical energy flared from the tip of the staff, exploding through Arvin's mind like a thunderclap and leaving him reeling. Eyes rolled up in his head, unable to see, Arvin felt the staff smack against his legs, knocking them out from under him. He tumbled forward, landing in a heap on the tiled floor.

Arvin's backpack was yanked from his shoulders. He felt the end of the staff force its way under his chest, levering him over onto his back. He tried to speak the command that would make the dagger appear in his glove, but his lips wouldn't form the word. The staff thrust inside the collar of Arvin's shirt and shoved, sending him sliding toward the hole. He found himself at an angle, head and shoulders lower than his hips and legs.

Chorl leaned over him. "You may have charmed Kayla, you scaly bastard, but it didn't work on me." Another shove and Arvin was sliding headlong down a ramp.

Up above, he heard Chorl's shout—"Snake in the hole!"—and the sound of stone sliding on stone as the trapdoor slid shut.

He hurtled along headfirst through darkness, unable to stop his slide down what turned out to be a spiraling tunnel with walls and floor of smooth stone. At the bottom was a small, brick-walled room, illuminated by a lantern that hung from the ceiling; Arvin skidded to a halt on its floor. The room's only exit, other than the tunnel he'd just slid out of, was blocked by a wrought-iron gate that had just clanged shut. Still lying on his back, Arvin craned his neck to peer through it and saw Kayla being hurried away down a corridor by two men. She glanced back at Arvin, her face twisted with confusion, as they hustled her around a corner.

Arvin sat up, gingerly feeling the back of his head. A lump was rising there. It burned with the fierce, hot tingle of residual magical energy.

"Stand up," a man's voice commanded.

Turning, Arvin saw a man standing behind the wrought-iron gate. He was Arvin's height and build, had short brown hair, and was no more than a handful of years older than Arvin. His resemblance to Arvin, now that Arvin's hair was also cut short, was uncanny—so much so that Arvin could understand why Kayla had taken them for brothers. The only difference was that this fellow's eyes were a pale blue, instead of brown, and shone with such intensity that Arvin felt as if the man were peering into his very soul.

"Gonthril?" Arvin guessed.

The man nodded. The sleeves of his white shirt were rolled up, revealing bare forearms. He, too, had avoided service with the militia. He patted the lock on the gate with his left hand. Rings glittered on every finger of it. No wonder Tanju had mistaken Arvin for Gonthril in the Mortal Coil, he must have assumed the glove was hiding those rings.

"The gate is locked," Gonthril told Arvin. "You can't escape."

Arvin held out his hands. "I have no intention of escaping," he told Gonthril. "I'm a friend. I came here to ask you about—"

"Don't try to twist my mind with your words," Gonthril barked. "I'm protected against your magic. And just in case you're thinking of slithering out of there. . . ." Letting the threat dangle, he drew a dagger from a sheath at his hip and turned it so it caught the lantern light. The blade glistened as if wet, and was covered with a pattern of wavy lines.

If Gonthril expected a reaction, Arvin must have disappointed him. He stared at the dagger, perplexed. "Am I supposed to know what that is?"

"Go ahead and assume serpent form," Gonthril said in a low voice. "You'll find out, soon enough, what the blade does."

"Serpent form?" Arvin repeated. Then he realized what was going on. Chorl—and now Gonthril—had mistaken him for a yuan-ti.

And they hated yuan-ti.

"You've made a mistake," Arvin told the rebel leader, wetting his lips nervously. "I'm as human as you are."

"Prove it."

Gonthril, standing just a few short paces away, must be able to see that Arvin had round pupils, but obviously believed that Arvin's clothes hid patches of snake skin or a tail. Realizing what he had to do, Arvin slowly began shedding his clothing. He started with the belt that held his empty sheath, letting it fall to the ground, then kicked off his boots. Shedding his shirt and trousers and at last tugging off his glove, he stood naked. Arms raised, he turned in a slow circle, letting Gonthril inspect him. He finished by briefly sticking out his tongue, to show that it was not forked.

"Satisfied?" he asked.

"I see you've had a run-in with the Guild," Gonthril observed.

"Fortunately, only one," Arvin said, picking up his glove and pulling it back on. Gonthril seemed to be finished with his inspection, so Arvin continued to dress.

When Arvin was done, Gonthril pulled something from his pocket and tossed it into the room—a ring. It tinkled as it hit the floor near Arvin's feet.

"Put it on," Gonthril instructed.

Arvin stared at it. The ring was a wide band of silver set with deep blue stones. He recognized them as sapphires—something he shouldn't have been able to do, since he didn't know one gemstone from another. "What does the ring do?" he asked.

"Put it on."

Arvin wet his lips. He could guess that the ring was magical and was reluctant to touch it, even though Gonthril had just done so. Still, what choice did he have? He needed to convince Gonthril that he was a friend—or at least that he was neutral—if he ever wanted to get any information out of him. He bent down to pick up the ring. No sooner did his fingertips brush its cool metal than it blinked into place on his forefinger. Startled, he tried to yank it off, but the ring wouldn't budge.

Gonthril smiled. "Now then," he said. "What were you doing in the sewers?"

Arvin found his mouth answering for him. "Looking for Naulg."

"Who is Naulg?"

Arvin was unable to stop the words that came out in short, jerky gulps. "A friend. We met years ago. When we were both boys. At the orphanage."

"What was *he* doing in the sewers?"

"He was captured. By the Pox. The clerics with the flasks. They made him drink from one. As a sacrifice to their god. They made me drink from one, too."

"Did they?" Gonthril's eyes glittered.

"Yes," Arvin gulped, forced by the ring to answer the question, even though it had obviously been rhetorical.

"What happened after you swallowed the contents of the flask?"

In short, jerky sentences, Arvin told Gonthril about the agonizing pain the liquid had produced, being dragged before the statue of Talona, fighting his way free, falling into the rowboat and escaping, losing consciousness—and coming to again, only to realize he'd left Naulg behind. He started to talk about going back to the Mortal Coil, but Gonthril cut him off with a curt, "That's enough." He stared at Arvin for several moments before speaking again.

"Are you human?" he asked at last.

"Yes."

The first two fingers of Gonthril's right hand crossed in a silent question: *Guild?*

"Yes." The ring jerked a further admission out of him: "But I don't want to be."

That made Gonthril smile. He nodded at Arvin's gloved hand. "Given the way they treat their people, I don't blame you." Then came another question: "Who are you working for now?"

Arvin could feel his lips and tongue starting to produce a *z* sound, but somehow the answer—Zelia—got stuck in his throat. "Myself," he told Gonthril. "I work for myself."

"Are you a member of House Extaminos?"

"No."

"How do you feel about the yuan-ti?"

Arvin didn't need the ring to answer that one honestly. "I don't like them much, either."

That made Gonthril smile a second time. "Why did you come here?"

"I wanted to talk to you. To learn more about the cultists. I thought you might be able to tell me something. Something that would help me save my friend. Like where I can find the cultists."

Gonthril shrugged. "On that point, your guess is as good as mine." He reached into his pocket and pulled out a small metal flask—either the one Kayla had recovered from the cultist, or one exactly like it. "Do you know what's inside this?" he asked.

Arvin shuddered. "Yes. Poison. Mixed with plague."

"You drank it, and it didn't kill you?"

Arvin found himself paraphrasing what Zelia had told him. "I have a strong constitution. The plague was driven out of my body. Talona was unable to claim me."

Gonthril stared at Arvin, a speculative look on his face. "Interesting," he said. "You called her clerics by a name—the Pox. Tell me what you know about them."

Arvin summed up what little information he had, concluding with, "They're a cult. Of Talona. They want to kill everyone in the city."

"How?"

"By tainting the public fountains. With what's in those flasks."

"When?"

"I don't know. Soon, I think."

"What do you know about House Extaminos?" Gonthril asked.

Arvin frowned, confused by the sudden turn the conversation had taken. His mouth, however, answered of its own accord. "They rule Hlondeth. They've lived here for centuries. Most of them are yuan-ti. Lady Dediana—"

"I didn't ask for a history lesson," Gonthril said, holding up a hand to stem the flow of words. "I meant to ask if you knew what their role is in all of this."

"What do you mean?" Arvin asked.

"A member of the royal family was observed meeting with Talona's clerics. They turned over several captives to him. Human captives. Including one of our members. Do you know anything about that?"

"No," Arvin answered honestly. He mulled this new information over in his mind. Zelia had been certain that the Pox weren't acting on their own, that someone was backing them. Could it really be House Extaminos? Why would the ruling house want to spread plague in its own city? Unless there was a coup in the works.

"Which member of the royal family?" Arvin asked.

Gonthril's eyes narrowed. "Why would you want to know that?"

"I suspect a yuan-ti might be behind the Pox. I want to know who it is."

"Why?"

"Because I need. . . ." Arvin's voice trailed off as a fierce throbbing gripped his temples. Compelled by the ring, he'd started to answer honestly—to tell Gonthril that he needed to report this information to Zelia—but another answer was also trying to force itself out through his lips at the same time. That he needed to know if *Sibyl* was involved. Who that was, he had no idea—the name had just popped into his head. He knew where it had come from—the mind seed. Already, just a day and a half into the transformation, it was starting to take over his mind in subtle ways, to force his thoughts along channels that were foreign to him. And dangerous. The instant the Secession found out about his link with Zelia, Arvin would be a dead man.

With an effort that caused sweat to break out on his forehead, he forced himself to give an answer that would satisfy both himself and the mind seed. "I want to learn which yuan-ti are involved because it will help me stop the Pox," he told Gonthril. "Are you sure it was a member of House Extaminos?"

"We're sure. We observed him passing a dozen flasks—identical to this one—to one of Talona's clerics, in exchange for the captives. But given what you've just told me, I'm confused. Delivering plague to clerics who can call down disease with a simple prayer makes no sense. It would be like carrying fire to Mount Ugruth." He stared at Arvin, one eyebrow raised. "Would you like to know what's *really* inside the flask?"

"Yes," Arvin said, his answer uncompelled by the ring. "I would."

"So would I." Gonthril lowered the flask. "Two final questions. If I let you out of that room—let you move freely among us—will you attack us?"

"No."

"Will you betray us to the militia?"

Arvin smiled. "The ten thousand gold piece bounty is tempting," he answered honestly. "But no, I won't give you away. Not while you have information that can help me find my friend."

That made Gonthril smile. He gestured, and the ring was suddenly loose on Arvin's finger. "Take the ring off, and come with me."

24 Kythorn, Sunrise

Arvin sat on a low bench inside a room a short distance down the corridor from the one Gonthril had used to question him. He was flanked by two members of the Secession—Chorl, with his magical staff, and a younger man named Mortin, who had a day's growth of beard on his chin. Gonthril stood nearby, arms folded across his chest as he watched a wizard lay out his equipment. Gonthril didn't seem to regard Arvin as a threat—he had his back to Arvin—but Mortin had drawn his sword and Chorl held his staff ready. Neither of them took their eyes off Arvin.

Arvin stared at the wizard. He'd never met one face to face, but this fellow looked just as he would have imagined. He was an older man with wispy gray hair, thick eyebrows waxed into points, and a narrow face that was clean shaven save for a goatlike tuft of white on his chin. The hand that stroked it had fingernails that were trimmed short, save for the little finger; that nail was nearly half as long as the finger itself. His shirt was large and hung loose over his trousers, giving it the appearance of a robe, and was fastened at the throat by an intricately wrought silver pin. The worn leather slippers on his feet had turned-up toes.

The table on which he was setting up his equipment took up most of the room. On it, the wizard had already set out a small pouch of soft leather, a bottle of wine, a feather, a mortar and pestle, and a pair of silver scissors. He opened the lid of a well-padded box and pulled from it a chalice with a bowl the size of a man's fist. He set it carefully at the center of the table then lifted the lantern down from its metal hook on the ceiling and set it next to the chalice. He closed the lantern's rear and side shutters, leaving a single beam. It shone on the chalice, illuminating the clear glass.

The wizard held out a hand. "The flask," he said.

Gonthril handed it over. Holding it in one hand, the wizard began to chant in a language Arvin didn't recognize—a lilting tongue in which soft-spoken words seemed to spill over one another with the fluidity of a tumbling brook. As he spoke, he held his free hand over the flask and made a pinching motion with fingers and thumb. Arvin heard a soft pop as the cork jerked out of the flask and rose into the air. Directing it with his fingers, the wizard sent it drifting away from him. Mortin drew back slightly as the cork moved toward him then relaxed again as it settled onto the table. Gonthril, meanwhile, watched closely as the wizard poured the contents of the flask into the chalice.

Arvin recognized the bitter odor of the liquid. He grimaced, remembering how it had been forced down his throat. As it trickled into the chalice, it was as clear as water, but as it filled the vessel, it changed color, becoming an inky black.

"Ah," the wizard said as he peered down at it. "Poison." He squatted, peering through the chalice toward the lantern, then nodded. "And a strong one, too. The light is almost entirely blocked."

"What about plague?" Arvin asked nervously. "Is there any plague in—"

"Shhh!" The wizard held up a hand, silencing him. His eyes, however, never left the chalice. The color of the liquid inside it was changing, turning from black to a murky red. In a few moments, it was as bright as freshly spilled blood. The wizard peered through the side of the chalice, his eyebrows raised.

Gonthril leaned forward. "Well, Hazzan?"

The wizard straightened. "The liquid contains no plague," he answered. He stared thoughtfully down at the chalice. "This is a potion . . . one that contains poison. The poison must be a component."

Arvin hissed in relief. No plague. That was good news—one less thing to worry about. Meanwhile, his head continued its dull throbbing. He resisted the urge to rub his forehead.

"Can you identify the potion?" Gonthril asked the wizard.

"We shall see," Hazzan answered. He picked up the pouch, untied it, and tipped its contents into his palm. A handful of pearls spilled out. He chose one and placed it inside the ceramic vessel then put the rest back into the pouch. With smooth strokes of the pestle, he ground the pearl he'd chosen into a fine powder. Into this he poured wine. He stirred the mixture with the feather, using its shaft like a stick. Then he laid the feather down and picked up the mortar. He raised it to his lips and drank.

When he lowered it, his pupils were so large they seemed to have swallowed the irises whole. Staring at a spot somewhere over Arvin's head, Hazzan located the chalice by feel. He gripped it with one hand and dipped the tip of his overly long fingernail into the liquid. Then he began to chant in the same melodious, lilting language he'd used before. When the chant was finished, he stood for several moments, his lips pursed in thought.

Abruptly, his pupils returned to normal. He raised his fingernail from the liquid and snipped the end of it off with the scissors, letting the clipping fall into the potion.

Gonthril leaned forward, an anxious expression on his face. Mortin mirrored his leader's pose, barely breathing as he waited for Hazzan to speak. Chorl, meanwhile, kept his eyes on Arvin.

"It's a transformative potion," the wizard said at last. "With a hint of compulsive enchantment about it. But predominantly transformative."

"A potion of polymorphing?" Gonthril asked.

Hazzan shook his head. "Nothing so general. Its properties are highly focused. The potion is designed to transform the imbiber into a specific creature, though I can't identify which. But I can tell you this. Whoever drank this potion would be dead long before the transformation occurred. One of its components is a highly toxic venom." He looked up from the chalice to stare at Gonthril. "Yuan-ti venom."

Gonthril pointed at Arvin. "This man drank an identical potion—and lived."

Hazzan turned to Arvin. "Are you a cleric?"

"No," Arvin answered. "I'm not."

"Did a cleric lay healing hands on you?"

Arvin wet his lips. He was glad he wasn't wearing Gonthril's truth ring anymore—though perhaps he could have avoided giving the game away, since Zelia was a psion, rather than a cleric. "No."

"Are you wearing any device that would neutralize poison?"

Arvin thought of Kayla—of the periapt she wore around her neck. He touched the cat's-eye bead that hung at his throat for reassurance.

Hazzan noticed the gesture immediately. "The bead is magical?"

Arvin shrugged.

Hazzan cast a quick spell and pointed a finger at the bead. Then he shook his head. "It's ordinary clay. A worthless trinket." He lowered his hand. "It is possible that the potion you were forced to drink was different from the rest. Perhaps it lacked the venom."

"The flask was identical to this one," Arvin said. "The potion smelled like this one, too. And it certainly *felt* like I'd been poisoned. The pain was excruciating. It felt as though I'd swallowed broken glass."

"Yet your body fought off the venom," Hazzan mused. "Interesting." He turned to Gonthril. "He could be yuan-ti. They're naturally resistant to their own venom."

"I knew it," Chorl growled. He shifted his staff.

Arvin hissed in alarm.

"Chorl, wait," Gonthril said. He placed a hand on Chorl's staff. "It's possible, sometimes, for humans to survive yuan-ti venom. And to all appearances, this man is human—despite his strange mannerisms."

Chorl glared at Arvin. "So what? He's still a danger to us. He knows where we—"

"He's an innocent caught up in all of this," Gonthril countered. "The ring confirmed his story."

Chorl's eyes narrowed. "Why does he hiss like that, then, and lick his lips? He even moves like a yuan-ti."

Arvin glared at the man. Chorl's constant hectoring was starting to annoy him. "I *am* human," he spat back. "As human as you."

Chorl's lip curled. "I doubt it."

Hazzan suddenly snapped his fingers. "The potion," he exclaimed. "So that's what it does—it transforms humans into yuan-ti."

Arvin felt his eyes widen. "No," he whispered. He started to wet his lips nervously then realized what he was doing and gulped back his tongue. Then a thought occurred to him. Maybe Zelia *had* been bluffing. Maybe there was no mind seed. She might have guessed what the potion did, realized it would work this transformation on Arvin, and tried to claim credit for it. If it was the potion that was causing the hissing and the lip licking, what would be next? Would Arvin's spittle suddenly turn poisonous, like that of the old sailor he'd found dying in the tunnel?

Realizing he was starting to panic, he forced himself to calm down. Would it really be so bad to turn into a yuan-ti? They were the rulers and nobles of Hlondeth; Arvin would certainly move up the social ladder if he became one. And in addition to their venom—handy, in a close-quarters fight—yuan-ti could assume serpent form at will. And they had magical abilities. They could enshroud themselves in darkness, use their unblinking stares to terrify others into fleeing, and compel others to do their bidding—a more powerful version of the simple charm that Arvin liked to use. They could entrance both animals and plants, causing the former to lose themselves in a swaying trance and the latter to tangle themselves about creatures or objects. And, as Zelia had demonstrated, they could neutralize poison with a simple laying-on of hands.

That thought led him to a realization. If the potion was intended to turn humans into yuan-ti, it would be useless if everyone who drank it died from the venom it contained. Which they didn't. The old sailor had survived. Had Naulg?

Maybe.

And if Naulg was still alive and slowly transforming into a yuan-ti, would he wind up embracing Talona's faith, as the old sailor had? Or . . . had the sailor really become a convert? Thinking back to the old man's final words, Arvin concluded that was not the case. The sailor had invoked Silvanus's name as he lay dying—hardly something someone who had embraced Talona would do. No, the old man had probably been magically compelled by the cultist—for some time, probably, since the cultist no longer felt the need to keep him bound hand and foot.

A thought suddenly occurred to Arvin—one that sent a shiver through him. He caught the wizard's eye. "You called the potion something else, a 'compulsive enchantment,' " he said. "What does that mean?"

"A compulsive enchantment allows a wizard to dominate his victim," Hazzan answered.

Gonthril was quickest to catch on. "That bastard," he gritted. "He doesn't just want to turn us into serpent folk. He wants to turn us into his slaves."

Chorl's grip on his staff tightened. "This man might already be in Osran's power," he said, gesturing at Arvin. "All the more reason to—"

Gonthril silenced him with an angry glare. As Chorl flushed suddenly, Arvin realized what had just happened. In his anger, Chorl had let slip something he shouldn't have—the name of the yuan-ti who had been seen meeting with the Pox.

Osran Extaminos, youngest brother of Lady Dediana.

Arvin pretended not to have noticed the slip. "Can you dispel the potion's magic?" he asked Hazzan. He curled the fingers of his gloved hand, readying it for his dagger, as he waited for the wizard's reply. If the answer was no, he'd have to fight his way out.

Hazzan stroked his beard. "Possibly."

Gonthril took a deep breath. "For the sake of Hlondeth's true people, Talona grant it be so," he whispered. Then, to the wizard, he said, "Try."

Hazzan rolled up his sleeves then extended his right hand toward Arvin, pointing. Staring intently into Arvin's eyes, he began casting a spell. The incantation took only a moment; the final word was a shout. As it erupted from his wizard's lips Hazzan flicked his forefinger and Arvin felt a wave of magical energy punch into his chest. It coursed through his body like an electric shock, making his fingers and toes tingle and the hair rise on the back of his neck. Then it was gone.

Gonthril peered at Arvin. "Did it work?"

"Let's find out." Hazzan picked up the chalice and tipped the potion out of it, pouring it into the mortar. Then he pulled a scrap of cloth out of a pocket and wiped the inside of the chalice clean. He then held out a hand. "Give me your hand," he told Arvin, picking up the scissors.

Arvin drew back, unpleasant memories of the Guild filling his thoughts. "What are you going to do?"

"He needs a sample of your blood," Gonthril told Arvin. "To see if the potion is still in it."

"All right." Arvin answered reluctantly, placing his hand in Hazzan's. "As long as it doesn't cost me another fingertip."

Gonthril chuckled.

"A small incision should do," Hazzan reassured him. "I just need a few drops of blood, enough to cover the bottom of the chalice."

He winced as Hazzan sliced into his finger with the blade of the scissors—deliberate cuts always hurt more, it seemed, than those inflicted in a fight—but kept his hand steady over the chalice. A few drops of blood leaked into it, splattering against the clear glass.

"That's enough," Hazzan said.

Arvin pressed against the cut in his finger, staunching the blood. He sat back down and stared at the bowl of the chalice. Strangely, though the blood had been red as it had dripped into the bowl, now it looked clear as water—so clear that for a moment he thought the blood had disappeared. He leaned forward, peering down into the mouth of the chalice again, and saw that it was indeed drizzled with bright red blood. Surprised, he started to let out an involuntary hiss—and saw Chorl's frown deepen.

Hazzan—once again peering through the side of the chalice at the lantern—nodded. "The spell worked," he told Gonthril. "The potion has been neutralized."

Chorl stared at Arvin. "Why's he still hissing, then?"

Gonthril stared at Arvin thoughtfully. "I don't know."

Arvin did. It was the mind seed. Zelia hadn't been bluffing, after all.

"I still say we should get rid of him," Chorl urged.

The rebel leader shook his head. "Arvin will stay with us, for the time being. There may be ways in which he can aid our cause. But keep a close eye on him, Chorl, and let me know if he does anything suspicious. If he takes any hostile action against us, or attempts to escape, I leave his punishment to your discretion."

Arvin matched glares with Chorl, and for a moment actually considered summoning his dagger into his hand and plunging it into the man's heart. But this done, the odds of Arvin being the next one to die would be very high indeed. Mortin held his sword at the ready, the wizard could blast him with magic, and the gods only knew what the rings on Gonthril's fingers were capable of doing.

No, there were other, better ways to deal with the situation. Arvin relaxed his grimace into a smile and tried to summon up the familiar prickle of psionic energy. None came. And for good reason, he suddenly realized. He was exhausted, on the verge of collapsing on his feet. Only rarely had he been able to charm anyone under these conditions.

No matter. He could always do it later, when the odds of escape were better.

"Don't worry," he assured Gonthril. "I'll behave."

"Do I have your word you won't try to escape?" Gonthril asked.

Arvin smiled to himself; he wasn't bound by the ring any longer. "You have my word," he said solemnly.

CHAPTER 10

24 Kythorn,
Sunset

I N HIS DREAM, ARVIN MOVED THROUGH A CROWD OF LAUGHING people who stood in a vineyard outside the city, their faces painted a ruddy orange by a bonfire that sent sparks spinning up into the night. Some stood and watched, tipping back bottles of wine, while others danced, arms linked as they moved in giddy circles around the bonfire. Several held small rectangles of wood, painted red and inscribed with a single word: "Chondath." These they threw into the fire, together with spoiled fruits and limp, moldy vegetables. The air was filled with smoke, sparks, and the hissing noise of food being blackened by flame.

The humans called it the Rotting Dance. It was a celebration of the defeat of Chondath in the Rotting War of 902, of the rise of the city-states of the Vilhon Reach. Hlondeth had gained its independence nearly three centuries before necromantic magic laid waste to the empire's armies on the Fields of Nun, and its people had suffered the aftermath of that battle—a plague that spread through the Vilhon Reach, afflicting those it touched with a disease that caused even the smallest of cuts to turn gangrenous. But its citizens celebrated the Rotting Dance just the same. Humans needed very little excuse for frivolity. Emotion was just one of their many weaknesses.

Arvin weaved his way through the humans, his tongue flickering in and out of his mouth as he tasted the excitement that laced the night air. Whenever he saw a man that caught his eye—one who was strong and well muscled, with lean hips and a glint in his eye that showed he was of a better stock than the average human—he worked his magic on him. "Come," he whispered, staring intently into the man's eyes. "Mate with me."

One of the men Arvin selected already had a mate picked out for the evening—a human a few years older than Arvin, and prettier, by human standards. No matter. When she protested, Arvin merely stared at her. She began to tremble then, with a small shriek, dropped the man's arm, surrendering him to Arvin, and fled into the night.

A part of Arvin's mind, observing the dream from a distance, recoiled at the thought of propositioning men. But to his dreaming mind, the act felt as natural as his own skin. He swayed through the crowd, the five men he had chosen trailing in his wake, each of them yearning to stroke his scales, to touch his newly budding breasts, and to press themselves against his curved hips. Flicking his tongue, tasting their desire, he felt a surge of power. He might be just fourteen years old and in his first flush of sexuality, but he was in control. He owned these men, as surely as a master owns slaves.

He led the men to a secluded spot in a nearby field and, as they converged on him, unfastened the pin at his throat and let his dress fall around his ankles, shedding it like an old skin. As the men stepped forward eagerly, pressing themselves against him and tearing at their clothes, he drew a curtain of darkness around them. Then he pulled the men to the ground, where they formed a mating ball with Arvin at its center. A hard body pressed against his and was wrenched away, only to be replaced by another—and another—as the men wrestled with each other in an attempt to mate with Arvin. The smell of their sweat and of crushed grapes and torn earth filled Arvin's nostrils as he slithered through the tangle of bodies, coiling around first one man, then another, taking each of them in turn. Acidic sweat erupted on his own body, soaking his hair and lubricating his scales—and burning the thin, sensitive skin of the humans who twined and fought and thrust against him. As ecstasy surged through Arvin again . . . and again . . . and again . . . he gave vent to his passion, screaming and throwing his head back then lashing forward to sink his fangs into throats and thighs and chests. One by one the men coiled around him abruptly gasped, stiffened, and fell limp as poison usurped passion.

When it was done, Arvin lay on his back on warm, sweat-soaked soil, his forked tongue savoring the taste of blood on his lips. He smiled, satisfied that there would be no one to tell his guilty secret—that he felt an unnatural attraction toward an inferior race. A heavy body lay across him; he shoved it to the side. Then he assumed snake form and slithered off into the night, leaving the tangled remains of his lovemaking cooling on the ground behind him.

Arvin's eyes sprang open as he was wakened by the urgency in his loins. He found himself lying on a straw pallet in a dimly lit room. A pace or two away, Mortin sat with his back against the wall, eyes closed, his sword on the floor beside him. For a moment, as Arvin stared at the handsome young man, dream and waking seemed to blend. Had he really just mated with Mortin and killed him? No . . . Mortin was still breathing; he'd merely fallen asleep. He was a member of the Secession, not a reveler, and he was guarding Arvin—though he was doing a poor job of it.

Arvin sat up, rubbing his temples. The headache that had been plaguing him was back again, despite his sleep. Doing his best to ignore it—and the unsettling dream—he forced his mind to the here and now. He was human, he told himself—and male—not a lustful yuan-ti female, as he'd been in the dream.

A yuan-ti female with the power to work magic with a mere thought.

Zelia.

Arvin cursed softly. Had the mind seed caused him to listen in on her thoughts again in his sleep? It seemed strange that, once again, he had picked up her memories, rather than her thoughts about more pressing matters, but maybe that was the way yuan-ti minds worked. Maybe all that lazy basking in the sun prompted them to dwell on the past, rather than the current moment.

Speaking of which, what time of day was it? Arvin's visit to the wizard had been around sunrise. Afterward, Gonthril had given him a meal and some wine to wash it down. He'd even returned Arvin's backpack—after a thorough inspection of its contents by Hazzan, who seemed fascinated by Arvin's trollgut rope. Then Arvin had curled up to sleep, alone in the room except for Mortin, who had remained behind to keep a watch on him.

It must have been well into fullday. The need Arvin felt to relieve himself told him that he'd slept a long, long time. As he yawned, a suspicion started to dawn in his mind, fueled by the grogginess he felt. He'd been drugged. Maybe that was why only Mortin had been left to watch him—Gonthril had expected Arvin to sleep much longer than he did. If it weren't for the wild dream that had jolted him into wakefulness, Arvin might have slumbered for some time still.

As he sat on his pallet, thinking, he noticed he was swaying back and forth. Not only that, but he was wetting his lips again. His tongue felt shorter and thicker than it should have been . . . no, than it had been during the dream, he corrected himself. The stray thought alarmed him. The mind seed was still firmly rooted, despite the fact that Hazzan had cast a dispelling on him. Was there no way to get the gods-cursed thing out of his head?

He hissed as anger frothed inside him. Anger at the Pox for what they'd done to Naulg and their other victims. Anger at Osran Extaminos for inviting the cultists into the city. And, most especially, anger at Zelia for what she'd done to him.

If he was ever going to free himself of the mind seed, he needed to get going.

Arvin stood and put on his backpack. Thankfully, Mortin was still asleep. Moving silently past him, Arvin crept to the door. Not only was it unlocked, but the hinges of the door didn't creak when he slowly pulled it open. And—Tymora be praised—the hallway beyond it was empty.

Arvin closed the door behind him and let his eyes adjust to the hallway's gloom. Slipping out of the room had been too easy. Perhaps the Secession were toying with Arvin. Chorl might be just around the bend, happy to have an excuse to kill him.

Wandering the corridors unescorted seemed like an excellent excuse to Arvin.

He summoned his dagger into his gloved hand and crept down the hallway.

The first room he came to was a smaller version of the one he'd just left; through its open door Arvin could see sleeping pallets on the floor. Those in Arvin's field of view were empty, but the sound of a man's voice came from inside. It sounded as though he was singing a low, dirgelike hymn.

A lantern in this room was burning brightly, flooding the corridor with light. The doorway reached from floor to ceiling. There was no way for Arvin to sneak past it and not be seen by whoever was inside the room. Unless he had his back to him, of course.

Crouching, he held his dagger just above the floor and moved the blade slowly into the doorway. By tilting it, he could see a reflection of the inside of the room—a narrow, blurry reflection, but one that told him that Tymora's luck was still with him. The man's back was indeed to the door. He was bent over someone in a pallet; a moment later Arvin heard a woman's faint groan. Curious, he risked a peek.

It was Kayla on the pallet. Her face was flushed, her hair damp and tangled. She lay on her back, turning her head back and forth, groaning softly.

The sight sent a chill through Arvin's blood. Had Kayla succumbed to the disease that had pockmarked the cultists—or some other, even more terrible illness? The fleshy mound she'd fought had been one enormous, pus-filled bag of disease, and she'd been splattered with its fluids—perhaps that was what had laid her low.

Whatever the cause, at least a cleric was tending to her—the man who had his back to Arvin. If the fellow was wearing clerical vestments, however, they were of a faith that Arvin didn't recognize. They included a black shirt and long gray kilt that was belted with a red sash. Black leather gloves lay on the floor beside him. The cleric's dark brown hair was plaited in a single braid that hung against his back. One of his hands held Kayla's; the other was raised above his head. His sleeves were rolled up, revealing a patchwork of blotchy scars, faded to a dull white, on his forearms. They looked like old burn marks.

"Lord of the Three Thunders," he chanted, lowering his hand to touch Kayla on the forehead. "Free this woman from fever's grip. Heal her so she may live to carry out your divine justice."

The healing spell was almost finished. Any moment the cleric might turn around and see Arvin peering into the room. Arvin slipped past the doorway and continued down the corridor.

The rest of the doors he passed were closed. It was only a short distance to the spiraling tunnel that led back to the surface. Arvin wasn't sure how he was going to get the trapdoor in the gazebo floor open, but he'd deal with that problem when it presented itself.

As he drew near the room where the wizard had analyzed the potion, he heard voices coming from behind its closed door. One was unmistakable: Gonthril's. He was giving instructions on how the Secession would sneak into a building. Arvin paused to listen, excitement making his heart race. There was a good chance the Secession were planning a raid on wherever the Pox were holed up—Arvin might at last be able to learn where the cultists were hiding. But try as he might, Arvin couldn't puzzle out which building they were talking about. The only clear detail was that they were going to strike during the very heart of the evening—at middark.

No matter. Arvin could always wait in the garden above then follow them. Assuming he got that far.

He tiptoed past the door to the wrought-iron gate, which was closed. The room beyond it was in near darkness; the lantern that hung from the ceiling had its wick trimmed low. Arvin gently pulled on the gate. It was indeed locked, as he'd expected. He vanished his dagger into his glove then unfastened his belt. Digging a fingernail into a slot in the tongue of the buckle, he pulled out a hook that clicked into place. Inserting his pick into the hole in the lock plate, he twisted until he felt one pin click back . . . then a second . . . then a third. . . .

He grinned as the bolt sprang open. He tried to open the gate. . . .

He couldn't move.

Not a muscle. His eyes continued to blink and his chest rose and fell—albeit only in short, shallow breaths—and his heart thudded in his chest. But the rest of his body was as still as a statue. Realizing he must have fallen victim to a spell, he strained against it until sweat blossomed on his temples and trickled down his cheeks, but still he couldn't move.

Stupid. He'd been stupid to think they'd simply let him walk away. He should have paid attention to the warning voice that had told him it was all too easy.

Meanwhile, the voices continued from behind the door. It sounded as though Gonthril was wrapping up the meeting. At any moment, the door would open—and Chorl would have all the excuse he needed to kill Arvin.

Arvin could hear Chorl's voice coming from behind the door. "I'm in favor," Chorl growled. "It will send a message to that scaly bitch—that she's not safe anywhere."

Another voice—one Arvin didn't recognize—raised an objection. "I still think we should ambush him in the street."

"He'll be on his guard there," Gonthril answered. "Especially after what happened to the overseer."

"That was just thieves, trying to steal whatever it was the work crews found in the old tower," someone else protested.

"Those thieves killed a yuan-ti—one who served the royal family," Gonthril said. He sighed; Arvin pictured him shaking his head. "The only place he'll let down his guard now is within the walls of his own home."

"It's suicide," the other man grumbled. "We'll never get inside."

"Yes we will," Gonthril said in a confident voice. "One sip of this and we'll be able to slip right past the guard. They won't suspect a thing. They'll think we're his little pets, out for a middark soar. We'll even have the right markings."

Suddenly a voice whispered in Arvin's ear. "I think you've heard enough."

Had Arvin been capable of it, he would have jumped at the touch of a hand on his shoulder. Held frozen by magic, all he could do was wonder who in the Nine Hells had crept up so silently behind him.

He heard a whispered chant, felt momentarily dizzy, and was standing in a room—a brightly illuminated room, next to the pallet on which Kayla lay. Her eyes were closed and her chest rose and fell smoothly. The flush of fever was gone from her face.

Arvin, still unable to move, could feel a hand on his shoulder—that of the person who had just teleported him. He could guess who it was. The cleric. The fellow spoke in a normal tone, no longer whispering. "That was poetic justice, don't you think?"

The hand fell away from Arvin's shoulder. Suddenly able to move, Arvin whirled to face the cleric. The green eyes that stared back at him were filled with mirth.

"What do you mean?" Arvin asked.

The cleric tipped his head in the direction of the hallway. As he did, an earring dangling from his left ear flashed in the light; the three silver lightning bolts hanging from it tinkled together. "By unlocking that gate, you locked your own body."

Understanding dawned on Arvin. "There was a glyph on the gate, wasn't there?"

The cleric nodded.

Arvin slid a wary glance toward the door to the room and saw that it was shut. It had no visible lock, but he was willing to bet its handle bore a glyph that was similar to the one on the gate he'd just tried. His imagination came up with unpleasant possibilities—turn the handle and have your head turned completely around. Until your neck snapped.

"What happens now?" he asked the cleric.

"We wait."

"Until . . . ?"

"Until Gonthril and the others have finished their night's work," the cleric calmly replied.

"Where are they going?" Arvin asked.

"To scotch the snake."

Arvin stared at the cleric, suddenly understanding. It wasn't the Pox the Secession were going after, but the yuan-ti who had supplied them with the potions, Osran Extaminos. And it wasn't just any building Gonthril had been talking about infiltrating, but the palace. The man who had been objecting to this scheme had been right. A plan to kill a prince inside the royal palace was indeed suicide. A desperate gamble. Yet it was a risk, apparently, Gonthril was willing to take. He must have been hoping that Osran's murder would cut off the source of the potion and save the city.

And he might just be right about that. Though Arvin couldn't help but wonder if the old adage would prove true. Scotch the snake, and watch another two crawl out of the hole. "Backers," Zelia had said. Plural.

Then there was the question of the cultists and why they had hooked up with a yuan-ti. As Gonthril had pointed out, why carry fire to a volcano? The cultists were perfectly capable of creating disease on their own, as the man who had killed himself in Arvin's warehouse had so aptly demonstrated. Why then, would they feel the need to obtain "plague" from an outside source?

Suddenly, Arvin realized the answer. That name he'd heard one of his attackers use, just before he'd been bundled off to the sewers, wasn't a person's name, after all. It wasn't "Missim" that he'd heard, but "Mussum." The city that fell victim, nine centuries ago, to a plague so virulent that to this day it continued to claim lives.

That was what the cultists believed was in the vials. The most potent plague in all of Faerûn—one that even they, in their most fervent prayers, would be hard-pressed to duplicate. They hoped to unleash it on Hlondeth, reducing it to a city of corpses. Instead they were being tricked into emptying a potion into its water system—one that would turn every human in Hlondeth into a yuan-ti, making it truly a "city of serpents."

A city of slaves.

Realizing the cleric was standing in silence, watching him, Arvin decided to play on the man's sympathies. "A friend of mine is in trouble," he began. "The Pox fed him the potion that turns humans into yuan-ti. He's the reason I was down in the sewers and"—he gestured at the sleeping Kayla—"the reason I was there to save Kayla's life. He's also the reason I was trying to leave, just now. I need to find him, before it's too late."

"A noble endeavor," the cleric said, nodding. "But I can't let you go. Too many other lives are at stake."

"Please," Arvin said, feeling the familiar prickle of psionic energy at the base of his skull. He gave the cleric his most pleading look. "I'm Naulg's only hope."

The cleric's expression softened. "I. . . ." Then he shook his head, like a man suddenly awakening from a dream. A smile quirked the corner of his lips. "A psion," he said. "That's quite rare." He folded his arms across his chest. "I'm sorry, but the answer is still no. And don't try to charm me again."

Arvin fumed. Just who in the Nine Hells did this human think he was?

Arvin hissed then leaped forward with the speed of a striking snake, intending to sink his teeth into the man's throat. The cleric, however, was quicker. He barked out a one-word incantation and whipped one of his scarred hands up in front of his body, palm outward. Arvin crashed face-first into a glowing wall of magical energy that rattled his teeth in their sockets.

Suddenly sobered, he staggered away, rubbing his aching jaw. The anger that had boiled in him a moment ago was gone. Mutely, he glanced at the glove on his left hand, wondering why he hadn't tried to summon his dagger to it.

Of course. The mind seed. He had reacted as Zelia might have done.

The cleric slowly lowered his hand. With a faint crackling, the magical shield around him disappeared. "Now that you've come to your senses, let's pass the time like civilized men," he told Arvin. "Gonthril told me part of your story; I'd like to hear the rest. But here's a warning. If you try to attack me again, you'll spend the rest of the day as a statue."

Arvin didn't bother to ask whether the cleric meant that literally—whether he was threatening to turn Arvin to stone—or whether he was simply promising to reimpose the spell that had held Arvin motionless earlier. Either way, Arvin didn't really want to find out. He spread his hands in a peace gesture.

"Fine," he said. "Let's talk."

CHAPTER 11

ARVIN PACED BACK AND FORTH LIKE AN ANIMAL IN A CAGE. HE'D been trapped in this room for ages with a man he could neither charm nor fight his way past. He wanted to be out *doing* something. Only two days had passed since Zelia planted the mind seed, but already Arvin was starting to lose control. If he didn't do something soon he might make another dangerous—possibly fatal—mistake. And there was a chance, it seemed, that Naulg might still be alive. But all Arvin could do was weave his way back and forth, back and forth, across the floor.

He and the cleric—Nicco, his name was—were alone in the room now. Kayla had awakened some time ago, as refreshed as if she'd never succumbed to fever at all. She'd been summoned from the room by Gonthril, presumably to join the suicidal raid on the royal palace. Arvin supposed that was the last he'd ever see of her.

Arvin had passed the time by telling Nicco his story—omitting any mention of Zelia, since the news that he was gathering information for a yuan-ti was hardly going to endear him to the rebels. Thinking of her—and the mind seed— made him wonder. Hazzan's dispelling hadn't broken its hold over Arvin, but perhaps clerical magic might succeed where wizardry had failed.

"I've been thinking about the potion," Arvin began. "Hazzan's dispelling doesn't seem to have worked. I still seem to be turning into a yuan-ti. In mind, if not in body."

Nicco nodded grimly. "You do seem to be under some sort of magical compulsion—from time to time. Right now, I'd say you were your own man. But when you attacked me earlier. . . ."

"I'm sorry about that," Arvin repeated. "I wasn't . . . in my right mind."

"Apology accepted."

"You recognized me as a psion earlier," Arvin said. "How?"

"You cast a charm spell without using either a holy symbol or hand gestures. Some wizards and sorcerers can cast spells with stilled hands or silenced lips, but the faint ringing sound I heard when you tried to charm me confirmed my guess. You're a psion."

Arvin's hopes rose. "Not many people know what a psion is."

Nicco shrugged. "I'm widely traveled."

"Have you dispelled psionic powers before?"

"Yes . . . why?"

Arvin smiled. Maybe Nicco *could* help him. "I've been wondering if the potion I was forced to drink might have contained a component that was psionic, rather than sorcerous," Arvin said. "If it did, Hazzan might have overlooked it. I was wondering if prayer might succeed where wizardry failed."

"It might," Nicco said slowly. "If it is the Doombringer's will."

"The Doombringer? Is that the name of your god?"

"In my country he is known as Assuran, Lord of the Three Thunders, but here they call him Hoar."

"I . . . think I've heard of him," Arvin said.

"He is the righter of wrongs," Nicco said with a grim smile. "I heard you whisper Tymora's name earlier. Like that goddess, Hoar is a bringer of luck—bad luck, but only to those who have called it down upon themselves by their own actions. He seals their doom—and in the process, saves those who are doomed."

"That's how I feel, right now," Arvin said somberly. "Doomed."

"Talona's clerics did wrong you," Nicco agreed. "The Doombringer will surely be moved to set matters right."

Arvin let out a long, slow hiss of relief. The sooner Zelia's mind seed was out of his head, the better.

Nicco stared at him. "Hoar's blessings come with a price."

Arvin gave the cleric a wry smile. "Nice of you to be up front about it. What is it?" He pictured a healthy tithe, or several tendays of fasting, self-flagellation, and prayer. The clerics who ran the orphanage had been big on flagellation.

"You must do everything you can to bring those who have wronged you to justice. And it must be in as . . . appropriate a manner as you are able. 'Blood for blood'—that is Hoar's creed."

Arvin nodded. It was easy to come up with a suitable punishment for the cultists. Slipping into their water a potion that would polymorph them into sewer rats, for example. But if Nicco's prayer succeeded in purging the mind seed, would Arvin be expected to also enact vengeance upon Zelia? What could Arvin—an untrained psion—possibly do to someone so powerful? For that matter, did he even want to take revenge on her? She'd saved his life by neutralizing the poison that had nearly killed him, after all. And she had offered to train him in psionics and ensure that the militia would never claim him, in return for information on who was backing the Pox—information Arvin now had.

"I'll do what I can," he told Nicco.

That seemed to satisfy the cleric. "Sit," Nicco instructed. "Hold in your mind the thoughts of vengeance you just imagined."

Arvin did as instructed, seating himself on one of the pallets and picturing the cultists turning into rats. Nicco knelt in front of him and rested three fingertips on Arvin's chest. Then he began to pray. "Lord of the Three Thunders, hear my plea. A great wrong has been done to this man. Set it right. Dispel the magic that is transforming him. Drive it from his body by the might of your thundering hand!"

The cleric closed his eyes then, dropping into silent prayer. Arvin heard a crackling sound—and a tiny spark erupted from each of Nicco's fingertips and shot through the fabric of Arvin's shirt. Arvin jerked back as they stung his chest.

Nicco smiled and dropped his hand. "The Doombringer has answered."

Arvin pulled his shirt away from his chest and saw, with relief, that his skin was still intact. He let out a long, slow hiss—then realized what he'd just done. His headache wasn't gone either. "I don't think your prayer worked," he told Nicco. "I feel . . . the same."

Nicco scowled. "Impossible. You felt Hoar's power at work. Whatever remained of the potion will be neutralized, now."

Arvin nodded. The potion indeed might be neutralized, but the mind seed was still in place. Zelia's psionics must be more powerful than either Hazzan's spells or Nicco's prayers.

He eyed the door, wondering when the rebels were going to return. He wanted to be well on his way before Chorl came back. Could Arvin convince Nicco that he posed no threat to the Secession, that he should be allowed to leave? Perhaps . . . if Nicco could be persuaded that he was an ally, a friend. But that would be difficult, without charming Nicco. Instead, Arvin would be forced to rely upon more conventional means. Conversation.

Fortunately, there was always one sure way to get a cleric talking.

"Tell me more about your faith," he told Nicco. "How did you come to worship Hoar?"

Nicco gave Arvin a searching look. Then he shrugged and sat down on a pallet next to the one on which Arvin was sitting. "In Chessenta, slaves are not branded," he began. "The only mark of their servitude is a thread around the wrist."

Arvin had no idea what this had to do with Nicco's religion, but his interest was piqued at once. "A magical thread?" he asked.

Nicco smiled. "No. An ordinary thread."

"But what's to stop the slave from breaking it?"

"Nothing," Nicco said.

Arvin frowned, puzzled.

"Slavery isn't a cruelty, as it is here, but a retribution," Nicco continued. "Here, innocent men and women are forced into servitude against their will and work until the day they die. In Chessenta, the term of slavery is fixed. It is imposed, following a public trial and a finding of guilt, as punishment for breaking the law. The criminal is a slave until his sentence is up then becomes a free man once more. The work slaves are set to can be hard and dangerous, but sometimes, if a slave performs well, his master may negate his sentence by breaking the thread." He paused, and the glower returned. "Of course, that is how it is supposed to work."

"Ah, I understand now," Arvin said. "You worship Hoar because you were once a judge."

"Not a judge," Nicco said, "a criminal."

Arvin tactfully avoided asking what crime Nicco had committed. Years of dealing with the Guild had taught him the value of silence at such moments—and a sympathetic nod, which he gave Nicco now. "You were unjustly accused," he ventured. "That's why you turned to Hoar."

Nicco shook his head, causing the lightning bolts in his earring to tinkle. "I was unfairly *treated*," he corrected. "I worked hard and well at the glassblowing factory, and yet the overseer, instead of breaking my thread, falsely accused me of vandalism. Every time a piece of glassware broke due to some flaw—and there were plenty, since the iron, tin, and cobalt powders he purchased to color the glass were cheap and filled with impurities—I was punished. When I dared challenge him, he further insulted me by chaining me to my furnace, as if I were not a man of my word. So short was my chain that he shaved my head, to prevent my hair from being singed."

Nicco paused to toss his head angrily, setting his long braid to dancing against his back. Arvin, meanwhile, stared at the cleric's arms, understanding now where the patchwork of scars had come from. They were old and faded. This had happened long ago.

"I, too, was a slave . . . of a sort," Arvin said. "When I was a boy, I wound up in what was supposedly an orphanage, but was in reality a workhouse. They worked us from dawn until dusk, weaving nets and braiding ropes. Every night when I went to sleep, my hands ached. It felt as though each of my knuckles were a knot, yanked too tight." He paused and rubbed his joints, remembering. He'd never discussed his years at the orphanage before, but telling Nicco was proving surprisingly easy.

"My term of servitude was supposed to end when I reached 'manhood,' " Arvin continued. "But no age was ever specified. My voice broke and began to deepen, and still I wasn't a man. My chest broadened and hair grew at my groin, but I was still a 'child.' " He held up his fingers, flexing them. "They weren't going to let me go. I was too good at what I did. I knew I had to escape, instead."

Nicco's eyes, which had dulled to a smolder, were blazing again. "I, too, was eventually forced to take that road," he said. "When it was clear that my overseer would never treat me fairly, I began to pray to Assuran—to Hoar. I prayed for justice, for divine retribution. And one day, my prayers were answered."

"What happened?" Arvin asked, curious.

"The overseer tripped. At least, that's what the other slaves saw. I was the only one to see Hoar's hand in it. Or rather, to hear it—to realize what it meant. The overseer fell headfirst into the furnace next to mine—just as thunder rumbled above. Varga, the slave working at that furnace, pulled the overseer out, but by the time he did the man's face was burned away. Despite the intervention of a cleric, he died later that day."

Nicco bowed his head. "It was Hoar's will."

"Did things get better after the overseer's death?" Arvin asked.

The scowl returned. "They became worse. Varga was accused of having pushed the overseer into the furnace. The evidence given was that Varga did not immediately help the man—that he waited until the overseer was burned beyond help. In fact, it was surprise and shock that caused Varga to stand gaping, not malice. I testified to this at his trial. And I told them the truth—that it was I who had killed the overseer."

"What happened then?"

Nicco sighed. "The judge didn't believe me. He misunderstood. He thought I meant that I had pushed the overseer—and noted that my chain was too short for me to have reached the man, even using my glassblowing pipe. I tried to explain that I had killed him with prayer, but the judge wouldn't listen. I had taken no clerical vows—I had never once set foot in the temple. The judge decided that I was lying to spare the life of the accused.

"When I saw that the judge remained unconvinced, I tried to explain to my master what had happened. He believed me—but he said I was too valuable a worker, whereas Varga was 'dispensable.' And *someone* had to be punished for the crime."

Arvin shifted uncomfortably, guessing what was coming next. "The other slave was found guilty?"

"He was—and of the murder of an overseer, a capital offense. Varga was put to death the next day. According to law, our master chose the form of execution. He chose drowning. He might have left it at that, but he was as cruel a man as the overseer. He ordered it done in the factory, in front of all of the other slaves, in a quenching bucket—mine."

Nicco stared at one of the walls, his green eyes ablaze with rekindled fury. "That night I prayed. I begged Hoar to give me the means to avenge Varga's death. I swore I would devote my life to Hoar's service, if only he would give me a sign. The next morning, the Lord of the Three Thunders answered. The padlock on my chain clicked shut as the new overseer closed it—then fell open a moment later, just as thunder rumbled overhead. Then there came a second thunderclap, and a third—the sound of Hoar calling me to his service."

Arvin wet his lips. "And you answered?"

Nicco nodded. "I did the unthinkable. I broke my vow of servitude and ran away. Hoar guided my steps to Archendale, to a temple in the Arch Wood."

Arvin nodded his encouragement. "You didn't run away. You ran *to* something." As he spoke, jealousy stirred. If only *he'd* had something to run to, after escaping the orphanage. How different his life might have been. Instead he'd run straight into the clutches of the Guild—from the fat into the fire.

"That's true," Nicco agreed. "It helps to think of it like that." He paused then continued his tale. "I spent the next two years in prayer. During that time, Hoar provided me with a vision of vengeance. The idea came to me during a thunderstorm, when I was caught in a torrential rain. I created a magical item—a blown-glass decanter that I crafted myself, exquisitely shaped and colored. I returned to Chessenta, disguised by magic, and spread the rumor that I had something rare and wonderful for sale—a decanter of unknown but extremely powerful magical properties. I made sure my former master heard of it. The price he offered was ridiculously low, but after putting up a show of haggling, I accepted it. I delivered the decanter to his home. As I left him in his study—a windowless room—I used a spell to lock the door behind me. When he removed the stopper, expecting a jinni to emerge and grant his every wish, all that came out was water."

Arvin leaned forward, caught up in the story. "What happened then?"

Nicco gave a grim smile. "Once removed, the stopper could not be replaced. The water filled the room. He drowned. Blood for blood—or in this case, a drowning for a drowning. Justice."

Arvin found himself nodding in agreement, which surprised him. He wasn't the sort of man to dwell on the past, to let it fester as

Nicco had. The thought of devoting two years of his life to a scheme of revenge was utterly foreign to him. Despite his treatment at the orphanage, he'd never once had thoughts of exacting revenge upon the clerics who had humiliated him—not serious thoughts, anyway. Instead he'd avoided that part of the city. Best to let sleeping snakes lie. But now he found himself caught up in Nicco's tale, wetting his lips as he savored the taste of revenge secondhand . . .

. . . which scared him. Arvin didn't want to answer the call of such a grim and vengeful god. Part of him, however, enjoyed the cruel, poetic justice Hoar meted out.

The part that was thinking like Zelia. But it gave him an idea.

"Nicco," he asked slowly, pretending to be thinking out loud, "does your god ever forgive?"

The cleric folded his arms across his chest. "Never."

"So . . . if I sit here and do nothing to rescue Naulg—a friend since my days at the orphanage—a friend who was as grievously wronged by the Pox as I was. . . ." He paused and wet his lips nervously. "I can expect Hoar's retribution?"

Nicco was smart enough to see exactly where Arvin was going. "I can't let you leave."

"I won't betray the Secession," Arvin said. "I give you my solemn oath on that—my personal word of honor. You can trust me. I won't break my 'thread.' All I want to do is save my friend." And myself, he added silently.

Seeing a flicker of indecision in Nicco's eyes, Arvin pressed his emotional thrust to the hilt. "Chorl doesn't trust me—he wants me dead. He's just looking for an excuse to punish me for a crime I haven't even committed—and nothing either you or Gonthril will say will persuade him that I'm innocent."

Nicco held up an admonishing finger. "Don't you think Gonthril knows that?" he asked. "Why do you think Mortin was assigned to guard you? Unfortunately, you awakened early. You weren't supposed to 'escape' until middark."

"I get it," Arvin said slowly. "I was to be a distraction, to draw the militia away from . . . wherever it is Gonthril and the others have gone." He thought a moment. "I take it you're abandoning this hiding place?"

Nicco smiled. "We already have. You and I are the last ones here."

"So what happens now?" Arvin asked. "Do we sit and wait for middark?"

Nicco nodded.

"Why not let me go early? I won't betray the Secession—their interests are my interests. Like them, I want the Pox stopped."

Nicco sat in silence for a long moment before answering. "Will you agree to let me place a geas on you that will magically seal your oath?"

Arvin hesitated, uncomfortable with the thought of a compulsion spell being placed on him. A geas was dangerous—if you broke its conditions, it could kill you. Was it worth it, just to be on his way a little sooner? Middark wasn't all that far away. But what if Gonthril changed his mind about Arvin's usefulness in the meantime, or if Chorl returned?

"Do it," he said.

Smiling, Nicco rose to his feet. He placed three fingers on Arvin's mouth and whispered a quick prayer. Arvin felt magic tingle against his lips where Nicco's fingertips touched them.

Nicco stared into Arvin's eyes. "You will not reveal any information about the Secession."

So far, so good. This was what Arvin had expected.

"You will not reveal the names of any members of the Secession," Nicco continued. "Or provide any description of their appearance, or. . . ."

The terms of the geas were surprisingly thorough —too thorough. Arvin winced as he heard the final part of the oath.

" . . . or speak the name Osran Extaminos."

How in the Nine Hells was Arvin going to make his report to Zelia?

24 Kythorn, Evening

The Terrace was busy this time of night. After a hot, humid summer day, Hlondeth's wealthier citizens were at last relaxing and enjoying themselves in the more bearable temperatures that evening brought. Seated at tables under softly glowing lights, they had a view across the city, with its towers and arches shimmering a faint green, down to the harbor below, where ships crowded together so closely their masts looked like a forest. Beyond them was the Churning Bay.

Arvin, flush with energy after having performed the *asana* he'd learned from Zelia, watched the slaves who bustled between the tables, trays balanced on one hand above their heads, serving tea and sweets. At last he spotted the slave he wanted to speak to—a young woman with a slight limp. He slipped into a seat at one of the tables she was serving. When she approached, she showed no sign of recognizing him, even though he'd ordered two of Drin's "special teas" from her just yesterday. She set a small glass on the table in front of him. Inside it was a chunk of honeycomb. Then she asked which of the teas he'd like her to pour.

Arvin glanced over the collection of teapots on her tray and shook his head. "None of those," he said. "I want a special blend." He pretended to wave the tray away, but as he did, his fingers added a word, in silent speech: *magic.*

The slave was good; her expression never changed. "What flavor, sir?"

Arvin dropped his hand to the table, drumming it with his fingers to call her attention to his hand. "Let's see," he mused. *Need*—"Perhaps some mint"—*speak*—"and chamomile"—*Drin*—"and a peel of cinnamon."—*now.*

"That's an expensive blend," the slave countered. "And it will take time to fetch the ingredients."

"I'm prepared to pay," Arvin said, tossing a silver piece onto her tray. "And I'm happy to wait. Give me some black tea to sip in the meantime. And I'll take two of those poppy seed cakes. I'm famished."

The slave set a teapot and two cakes down on his table and limped away. Arvin sat, sipping the honey-sweet tea. Despite his hunger, he found himself doing little more than nibbling at the cakes. Their taste was every bit as good as always, but somehow they seemed flat and lifeless in his mouth. He had to wash each mouthful down with a hefty gulp of tea.

Waiting in the warm night air was making Arvin lethargic. He closed his eyes, listening to the hum of conversation around him and drinking in the scent from the flower baskets that lined the Terrace. It was a welcome change from the sewer stink he'd been floundering around in lately. He dozed.

A chair scuffed. Arvin opened his eyes to find Drin sitting across the table from him. The potion seller looked worried, as always. His narrow face with its deep vertical grooves between his eyebrows gave him a perpetual frown. His wrists were narrow and his fingers long—that and the slight point to his ears suggested that there might be a wood elf hiding in the branches of his family tree. He smiled at Arvin—a quick twitch of his lips—and leaned forward. "You wanted to speak to me?"

Arvin nodded and spoke in a low voice. "Do you have anything that can undo mind-influencing magic?"

"Clerical magic or wizardry?"

"Neither," Arvin answered.

Drin's eyebrows raised. "Then what——"

"Do you know what a psion is?"

Drin gave him a guarded look. "I've heard of them. They cast 'mind magic.'"

"That's right. I want something that will block a psionic power."

Drin thought a moment. "There's no 'tea' that does that. None that I know of," he said. He glanced around then dropped his voice to a whisper. "But I think there might be a ring that blocks such spells."

"Would it work against one that's already been cast?"

"I'm not sure. It's not my area of expertise."

Arvin wet his lips. "Could you obtain a ring like that for me?"

Drin shrugged. "Maybe. But it would take time to find out. The . . . merchant I need to speak to won't be back in Hlondeth for at least a month." He dropped his voice to a whisper. "The druids have been busy."

Arvin drummed his fingers on the table in frustration. Coming to Drin had been a long shot—a gamble that hadn't paid off. But perhaps Drin could tell him something about the potion the Pox were using—something that might help Naulg. Assuming Arvin was able to find him again, that was.

"One other thing," Arvin said. "There's a 'tea' that I'm trying to find out more about. A very rare blend. It comes in an unusual container—a small metal flask that's shaped like the rattle of a snake. Do you know anything about it?"

"I'm sorry, but I can't help you," Drin said. "I've never heard of a tea like that."

The guarded look was back in Drin's eyes; the potion seller was lying. "Listen, Drin," Arvin said, dropping his voice to a whisper. "A friend of mine *drank* some of that tea, and it's had an . . . unpleasant effect on him. I'm trying to help him." Focusing on the potion seller, silently willing him not to leave, Arvin felt the prickle of his psionics coming into play. "All I want is information," he pleaded. "Just some friendly advice—anything you think might help. I'm willing to pay for it." He placed ten gold pieces on the table.

The wary look in Drin's eyes softened. He leaned forward and scooped up the coins. "Let's move to a quieter table," he said. "One where we won't be overheard."

Arvin smiled.

They moved to a table at the back of the Terrace, well away from the other customers. When they settled into their chairs, Drin continued. "I can't tell you much," he said. "I've only seen a flask like that once before, in a 'tea shop' in Skullport, a few months ago. The man behind the counter said it came from the Serpent Hills."

Arvin hissed softly to himself. The Serpent Hills lay far to the northeast, up near the great desert. Once the area had been the seat of a mighty kingdom, but now the yuan-ti who lived in those desolate hills were forced to ally with lesser reptilian races just to survive. The yuan-ti kept vowing to retake what had once been the capital of their kingdom, but the humans who had unwittingly encamped upon the ruins stood in their. . . .

Arvin shivered, suddenly uneasy. Once again, the information had come from nowhere; it had just popped into his mind. He had never traveled beyond Hlondeth, yet he was able to picture the hills, the river that wound its way between them, and the enormous stone arch that spanned it—part of a coil that reached from one bank to the other. . . .

He wrenched his mind back to the present. "How much do you know about the potion the flask contained?" he asked Drin.

"Only what the seller told me. That whoever drank it would be able to perform 'mind magic' that would duplicate a yuan-ti's innate magical abilities." He paused, and the creases in his brow deepened still further. "I sensed that there was something he wasn't telling me, but I was still interested in buying."

"Did you?" Arvin asked.

Drin shook his head. "I was outbid by another buyer, a yuan-ti slaver by the name of Ssarmn. Apparently he's someone big in Skullport—someone you don't refuse. The seller told me I shouldn't be angry at being cut out of the deal, because the potion had an additional, undesirable effect on humans. It turned them into yuan-ti. Permanently. And there was more. Once the potion took effect, anyone who was transformed by it would unquestioningly obey any true yuan-ti who happened to give orders."

Drin sat back in his chair and shrugged. "I thought the seller was trying to pacify me, so he wouldn't lose my business; we've had dealings with each other for years. But maybe he was telling the truth. Is that what happened to your friend? Did he sprout a tail and grow scales?"

"Nothing so obvious as that," Arvin said. "At least, not yet. His saliva turned venomous, but otherwise he appears human."

Drin stared at Arvin then nodded. "Where did he get the potion?"

"He was forced to drink it. By a cleric."

"One of Sseth's?"

Arvin shook his head. "No. The cleric was human."

"Why did he force your friend to drink it, then? Did he think it would make your friend obey him?"

"I'm not sure," Arvin said. He thought back to what Kayla had said about the old sailor—about him instantly obeying the cultist's command to attack. That compulsion could equally have been produced by a clerical spell. If what Drin had just said was true—if the potion in the rattle-shaped flasks compelled its victims to obey yuan-ti, but not humans—Naulg wouldn't necessarily be a mindless servant of the Pox. Arvin just might be able to free him, even with the potion in Naulg's system.

Unless a yuan-ti showed up at an inopportune moment.

Arvin was starting to have a clearer picture of what was going on—and why Osran Extaminos was involved. He was tricking the Pox into transforming the humans of Hlondeth into his willing servants. With an army of thousands at his disposal, Osran could easily snatch the throne away from his sister and would wind up ruling a city filled with complacent citizens.

A city of slaves.

"Did the seller in Skullport say whether there was a countermeasure that could negate the potion?" Arvin asked. "A counterpotion, for example?"

Drin shook his head. "If there is, I don't know of it."

Arvin sat back, disappointed. He wet his lips. "Thanks for the information," he told Drin.

The potion seller rose to his feet. "Glad to give it," he said, giving Arvin a knowing wink. "I hope it helps your 'friend.'"

CHAPTER 12

24 Kythorn,
Evening

ARVIN WALKED THROUGH THE NIGHT WITH HIS HANDS THRUST INTO his trouser pockets, oblivious to the people who passed him on the narrow streets. At long last he had the information Zelia wanted, but he couldn't give it to her, thanks to the geas Nicco had placed on him. Nor was he any closer to finding Naulg. None of his contacts in the Guild had seen the Pox, or heard any word of them—or smelled them.

In a short time—it was fast approaching middark—the rebels would be making their assassination attempt on Osran Extaminos. Arvin toyed briefly with the idea of trying to reach Osran first, to see if he could charm information about the Pox out of the yuan-ti prince. But trying to sneak into the palace on the same night as an assassination attempt would be nothing short of suicidal.

No, there had to be another way to find the Pox, something Arvin hadn't thought of yet. If only Tymora would smile upon Arvin and cause him to cross paths with another of the cultists, he might be able to learn where they were hiding. He wouldn't make the same mistake as last time. This time he'd follow the cultist rather than try to question him. Asking questions had only caused him to lose his warehouse. Someone was sure to have noticed the stench of the corpse by now and called in the clerics to. . . .

Arvin slowed, suddenly realizing something. He'd questioned the cultist, but he hadn't searched him. There hadn't been time. For all Arvin knew, there might have been something on the body that would lead Arvin straight to the cultists. And thanks to Zelia, Arvin had a tool he could use to search the body from a safe distance.

Arvin hurried to his warehouse. It didn't take him long to get there—the streets were emptying of people as middark approached. He passed the public fountain and turned into the intersection his warehouse fronted. He saw that the front door was still shut—and unmarked. He bypassed it, holding his breath as soon as he caught the rotten odor coming from behind the door, and made for one of the barred windows, instead. Leaping up, he grabbed the bars, supporting himself, and peered in. The corpse—or rather, what was left of it—was still tangled in the magical rope. It lay on the floor just inside the door. The cultist's tunic was disheveled, but Arvin could see that it had at least one pocket.

He concentrated, drawing psionic energy up into his "third eye." He sent it out and saw a streak of silver light flash toward the corpse. As soon as it touched the pocket Arvin gave it a mental yank and heard the fabric tear. Three items spilled out: a leather sling, a lumpy-looking pouch that probably contained sling stones—and a key.

Immediately, Arvin coiled his mental energy around the key. He yanked, and the key lifted in the air and sailed toward the window. Springing back from the wall, Arvin landed on the street below, pulling the key out between the bars. It landed with a dull clink on the cobblestones at his feet.

Arvin stared at it, his heart racing. This was no ordinary key, intended to fit the door of an inn or warehouse. It was made from a peculiar reddish metal, was as long as Arvin's index finger, and had teeth that were an odd shape. They were jagged and triangular, instead of square. It probably opened a lock that was equally unusual. Possibly the door to whatever building the Pox had chosen for their hiding place.

Arvin carefully picked it up—with his gloved hand—and spoke the glove's command word, sending the key into extradimensional space. Then he set out for the artisan's section of the city. That was where Lorin, the Guild member he'd purchased his belt buckle from, had his workshop. Lorin was a master locksmith; if anyone knew what lock this key fit into, he would.

24 Kythorn, Middark

Arvin banged at the shutters of Lorin's workshop. After a few moments they opened. Lorin's apprentice—a slender boy in his teens with mouse brown hair as fuzzy as frayed rope—stared out at Arvin, yawning.

"Is Lorin here?" Arvin asked. Silently, his fingers added, *I'm Guild.*

The apprentice shook his head. "He's out on business." He stressed the last word, adding a wink to it, then yawned again.

"When will he be back?" Arvin asked, irritation rising in him.

"I dunno. Maybe tomorrow morning. Maybe the next day."

Arvin hissed in frustration. Tymora wasn't with him tonight, it seemed. Should he wait—or try to find another locksmith? The trouble was, Lorin was the only one he knew for certain was Guild. "Fetch him," he demanded. "At once or I'll—"

Only at the last moment did Arvin realize what was happening. It was the mind seed again, intruding upon his thoughts, stirring up his emotions like a nest of spitting vipers. With an effort, Arvin forced himself to calm down. "Sorry," he apologized, rubbing his temple. "But it's important. Can I leave something here for Lorin?"

"What?" the apprentice asked.

"A key—one I'd like him to identify, if he can. I'll pay well for whatever information he can provide." To back up his words, he passed the apprentice a gold piece.

The apprentice suddenly wasn't sleepy any more. He pocketed the gold piece and held out a hand. "Leave the key with me."

Arvin shook his head. "You mustn't touch it," he cautioned. "It came from the pocket of a dead man—a man who died of plague."

The apprentice's face paled. He drew back from the window, and for a moment Arvin worried that he'd slam the shutter in Arvin's face. But after a moment's fumbling inside the workshop, he reappeared. "Plague," he said with a shudder. "No wonder you're so edgy." He held out a ceramic jar, which he uncorked. "Put the key in this."

"Good idea." Arvin summoned the key into his gloved hand and dropped it inside the jar, which the apprentice hurriedly corked.

"Tell Lorin I need the information as soon as possible," Arvin instructed. "It's urgent. The life of a Guild member is at stake."

The apprentice nodded, his eyes serious. "I'll tell Lorin about it as soon as he gets back," he promised.

"Thanks." Turning away from the window, Arvin set off down the street, seething with barely subdued frustration at the delay. It was unacceptable, intolerable. . . .

He'd walked some distance before he realized that he was hissing—and that worried him. The mind seed's hold was intensifying. Arvin was thinking more and more like a yuan-ti—reacting like one, too. His dreams, crowded with Zelia's memories, were no longer his own. Even in his waking moments it was difficult to hold on to *himself.* He never knew when he was going to lose control, when the mind seed was going to twist his thoughts and emotions in a direction that frightened him. His mind was like a tiny mouse half-swallowed by a snake. Squeal though the mouse might, it was only a matter of time before its head disappeared down the serpent's throat.

Arvin wet his lips nervously then grimaced as he realized what he'd just done. At least he was still noticing the odd mannerisms.

He wandered the streets with no clear destination in mind. What he really needed was someone to talk to—someone in whom to confide. He had dozens of associates among the Guild, but that was all they were—customers and contacts. Naulg was the only one Arvin could call a friend. There weren't any women to whom Arvin could turn. Wary of ever getting too close to anyone, he'd never formed a permanent bond with a member of the opposite sex. He'd rarely slept with the same woman twice, let alone become a lover and confidant to one.

Yet he needed help—that much was clear.

Nothing, it seemed, could dislodge the mind seed. Wizardry had failed, prayers had failed, and there was no known potion that would work against it. Then his footsteps slowed as he realized there was one form of magic he'd not yet tried.

Psionics.

From childhood, he dimly remembered his mother once mentioning that psionic powers could be "negated." Presumably, this was a process akin to a wizard or cleric dispelling a spell. If Arvin could find a psion—one who was willing to help him and who was powerful enough to counter the mind seed—perhaps he could free himself from it. But where was he going to find a psion? In his twenty-six years in Hlondeth, Arvin had only met one, other than his mother. Zelia. Was there really no one else, or had Arvin just not recognized the subtle signs?

The secondary displays, for example. Zelia and Nicco had both recognized Arvin as a psion by the ringing sound they'd heard when Arvin had manifested his charms. Zelia had attributed the secondary display to the fact that Arvin was untrained, implying that more powerful psions didn't produce any such telltale traces. But what if she'd been lying? On several occasions, Arvin had noticed her eyes flashing silver as they "reflected" the light—even when the light was behind her. Was that a secondary display, too?

As Arvin thought about it, he realized there was someone else who had produced something that might have been a secondary display when working his "magic"—Tanju, the militia tracker. When Tanju had tried to view the inside of the enormous pot Arvin had fallen into, Arvin had heard a low humming similar to the drone that Arvin's distract power produced. He'd assumed Tanju had been humming to himself, but the noise might have, in fact, been an involuntary secondary display. And there was the bundle of crystals Tanju had been carrying. . . .

With a start, Arvin realized he knew what they were: a "crystal capacitor," a device for storing psionic energy. The capacitor was charged using a complex series of *asanas*, which directed energy from the *muladhara* up into. . . .

Arvin shook his head. He was doing it again. Linking, thanks to the mind seed, with Zelia's memories and drawing information from them.

He saw that his wanderings had carried him to the vicinity of Zelia's rooftop garden. He could see the tower between the buildings up ahead. How in the Nine Hells had he allowed himself to wander so near to it?

He turned abruptly, intending to stride away in the direction from which he'd just come, and nearly collided with a man who had been walking a few steps behind him. The fellow had his neck craned to look up at the buildings ahead of him and saw Arvin only at the last moment. He gave an irritated hiss—which made Arvin take a second glance at the fellow. All Arvin needed was to run afoul of a yuan-ti. But this fellow appeared wholly human—and he had four chevrons branded into his arm. Yuan-ti were never called for militia service.

Muttering his apologies, Arvin walked on. He'd gotten no more than a few paces before a hand reached out of the shadow of a ramp to grasp his arm.

A hand covered in fine green scales.

"Zelia!" Arvin gulped as she stepped out into the street. "What a coincidence. I was just heading back to the tower to look for you."

Her lips crooked in a smile. "I can see that," she said. "Obviously you have something to report, something important enough to have come in person, rather than using a sending." She stared unblinkingly at him. "What have you learned?"

Arvin thought furiously. What *could* he tell Zelia? "You were wrong about the flasks," he began. "They don't contain plague."

Zelia merely stared at him. "No?"

"They contain a potion."

"What kind?"

"One that transforms humans into yuan-ti. It comes from the Serpent Hills, possibly by way of Skullport. A contact of mine saw a flask similar to the ones the Pox carry, a few months ago in a potion seller's shop. He tried to buy it, but before he could, it was purchased by a slaver."

"What was the slaver's name?" Zelia hissed.

"Ssarmn."

Zelia hissed thoughtfully. Apparently she recognized the name.

"That's all I've been able to learn so far," Arvin concluded.

"Is it?" Zelia asked.

"Yes," Arvin answered evenly. He stared at Zelia. The last thing he needed was for her to question him, to force him to tell her about the Extaminos connection to the Pox. If he did, he'd be a dead man. Deliberately, he forced Osran's name out of his mind—but not quickly enough.

Zelia's eyes suddenly flashed silver. She gave a long, slow hiss. "Osran? I suspected there was a bad egg in the brood."

As she spoke the name aloud, Arvin felt a stabbing pain in his throat. Doubling over, he began to cough. Dark droplets flecked the ground; when he swallowed, he tasted blood. He felt a chill of fear course through him as he realized what was happening. The geas was taking hold, even though he hadn't spoken the name aloud—hadn't even intended for it to be overheard. He swallowed again, his throat raw. Hoar, he pleaded silently. I didn't mean to. Please don't kill me.

Zelia didn't even ask what was wrong with him. She just stood, smiling like a snake that had swallowed a mouse. Arvin, meanwhile, felt the pain in his throat ease—just a little. Then his coughing stopped. Hoar, it seemed, had heard his plea and spared him.

Arvin touched the bead at his throat. "Nine lives," he whispered. He followed it with a silent thank-you to Hoar.

At least it was middark. Tymora willing, the assassination would already have taken place and the Secession would be on their way out of the palace.

"Zelia," Arvin said, finding his voice again as the raw ache in his throat at last subsided. "I've given you what you wanted. Remove the mind seed. Get out of my head."

Zelia's eyes blazed. "You dare make demands?" she hissed. "The seed will remain in place—at the very least, until I've had a chance to put a few questions to Osran."

Unbidden, an image flashed into Arvin's mind. Of just what Zelia meant by "putting a few questions" to Osran. First she'd place a lock on his higher mind, causing a mental paralysis that would render him unable to take any physical actions. Then she'd slither into his mind. She'd poke and prod into the darkest crevices of his thoughts, finding his weaknesses and fears. One by one, she'd bring these into the light of full awareness. She'd nudge his helpless mind this way and that, forcing him to dwell upon that which most demoralized him, filling him to the brim with fear. Then, when she'd forced her victim to retreat into a tight coil of despair, she'd beat the last of his will down with her questions. What did it matter, she'd say, if he revealed his secrets to her? All was lost, hopeless, bleak. He was doomed. *She* was in control, not him.

Arvin dwelled upon the image, gloating. It felt good to be the one in command. To savor the raw, weeping anguish of another that he so thoroughly dominated. He remembered the first time he'd ever used his psionic powers to reduce someone to sniveling helplessness—his former master. The master whose psionic powers Arvin had so easily surpassed. The human had proved as fragile as an egg when Arvin at last tired of toying with him. . . .

Arvin felt sweat trickle down his temples. He shivered, despite the warmth of the night air. He wrenched his mind back to the present, away from Zelia's memory, and glanced around.

Zelia was gone. Having gotten what she wanted from him, she'd slithered away into the night without another word.

Arvin pressed his forehead against the stone wall next to him, savoring its coolness. It helped ease the throbbing of his headache. Through half-closed eyes, he saw the pale green shimmer of residual magical energy the stones contained. The color matched the scales on Zelia's skin—and reminded him that he could no more shed her than the stone could shed its luminescent glow. Nicco had been right. Arvin *was* doomed.

No. He was thinking like one of Zelia's victims. There was still hope if Tanju could be persuaded to help him. But how to make contact with the tracker? Tanju might be quartered at the militia barracks, or he might not. Being an auxiliary, rather than a regular member of the militia, might have its privileges. If Arvin tried to ask one of the militia where Tanju was, he would probably be mistaken for Gonthril again, and the chase would be on.

And Tanju would be summoned to help track him.

And if, in his flight to "escape," Arvin swung through the section of the city that contained the palace, he might just draw enough of the militia away from it to enable Gonthril and the others to make their escape after the assassination attempt. And in the process, make amends to them for having let Osran's name slip.

Grinning, Arvin set off in the direction of the palace.

25 Kythorn, Darkmorning

Arvin clung, panting from his rapid climb, to the underside of a viaduct. In the street below, three members of the militia pounded past, never once thinking to glance up as they ran directly beneath his hiding spot. Escaping them had been too easy, he thought. Despite the hue and cry they'd raised after spotting "Gonthril," they hadn't called out their tracker. Tanju was nowhere in sight.

This was getting ridiculous. Arvin had allowed himself to be seen in at least a dozen different locations, without success, and it was almost dawn. He'd have to find some other way to flush out Tanju.

Climbing back down the pillar that supported the viaduct, Arvin jogged in the opposite direction the three militiamen had just taken. As he made his way up the winding street, he caught glimpses of the tower that rose high above the central courtyard of the royal palace. The tower was capped with an enormous statue of a cobra, its flared hood covered in overlapping scales that were said to be slabs of solid gold. The eyes of the statue—which flashed red in daylight, but which by night looked like dark, brooding pits in the golden head—were rumored to be chunks of ruby as large as a human heart. No rogue had ever climbed the tower to find out if that was true, however. Just getting into the palace compound was problem enough. The walls were protected by magical glyphs far more powerful—and deadly—than the one Arvin had fallen victim to in the Secession's hiding place, and the grounds were patrolled by officers from the human militia. Assuming the rogue actually made it inside the palace, he would have to run a gauntlet of its yuan-ti guard: high-ranking clerics from the Cathedral of Emerald Scales.

Arvin shook his head, wondering how Gonthril and the Secession had ever hoped to get that far. But even if they had failed in their mission, it wouldn't matter. Zelia knew that Osran Extaminos was the backer behind the Pox. When she was finished with Osran, the cultists' supply of transformative potion would be cut off, and Hlondeth's citizens would be saved.

Saved, of course, with the notable exception of Naulg, and the other poor wretches the Pox had already used for their experiments.

Arvin, thanks to the mind seed, was equally doomed—unless he could find Tanju.

If only Arvin had access to Zelia's powers—and not just her emotions and memories—he might be able to search for Tanju using psionics. That would certainly improve his odds of finding the tracker. A simple sending would do. . . .

Slowing to a walk, Arvin hissed an oath. He reached into his pocket and pulled the lapis lazuli from its hiding place. Had he the means to find Tanju in his hands all this time—or rather, in his pocket? When Zelia had told him the lapis lazuli would allow him to manifest a sending, he'd assumed she meant that it would only allow him to contact her. But perhaps that was an incorrect assumption.

He stared at the stone, trying to will the answer from the seed that was buried deep within his mind. It only took a moment before the answer bubbled to the surface: the stone could be used to manifest a sending . . . to anyone.

Smiling, Arvin slipped into the shadow of a ramp then touched the flat of the stone to his forehead. "*Atmiya*," he said, speaking its command word out loud.

The stone grew warm against his skin. His forehead tickled as if tiny stitches were being sewn into his flesh, securing the lapis lazuli in place. He tried picking at the edge of the stone with a fingernail but could find no edge; it was embedded in his forehead. Suddenly worried, he thought the command word. Instantly the tickling sensation was gone. The stone fell from his forehead and he caught it in his hand. He rubbed his forehead, expecting to find a hole, but his skin was smooth, not even dented.

Once his heart had stopped racing, he returned the stone to his forehead and repeated the command word, locking it in place. Then he closed his eyes and concentrated, calling to mind Tanju's face. Gray hair, strangely slanted eyes. . . .

After a few moments, he felt a familiar prickling of psionic energy at the base of his scalp. The image of Tanju he held in his mind seemed to solidify; it was almost as if Arvin were staring at him in the flesh. The tracker lay on his side with eyes closed and head cradled on one arm, his face bathed in the dim glow of either a lantern or a low-burning fire. *Tanju,* Arvin thought. As he gave mental voice to his words, the lapis lazuli began to vibrate softly against the skin of his forehead. It was as if the stone were a fingertip, rapidly tapping the head of a drum. *This is Gonthril. I'm in Hlondeth. I want to meet with you. Tell me where to find you.*

Tanju sat up, a startled look on his face. Surprise muted into a thoughtful expression, and he mumbled something—to someone else, since Arvin couldn't hear what was said. Fortunately, Tanju was equally unable to hear Arvin's chuckle. Arvin had baited his sending with something the tracker found irresistible: "Gonthril." And Tanju had just swallowed the hook.

I'm on the road to Mount Ugruth, Tanju answered. *Camped at the top of the first pass. I'll wait until evening for you, but no longer.*

The vibrations faded as the sending ended.

Arvin smiled. Perfect. Even allowing for a brief nap—which he badly needed—he could reach the pass by sunset. That would still give him four full days until the mind seed took over. He started to speak the command word that would cause the lapis lazuli to drop from his forehead when he realized something. Zelia had told him that the stone could be used to manifest a sending just once a day, but this was only partially true. The stone could be used several times per day—if a different person was contacted each time. If Naulg was still alive. . . .

Arvin summoned the familiar prickle of psionic energy back to the base of his scalp. Then he concentrated on Naulg's face: his easy grin, his dark hair, his distinctive eyebrows. . . .

Just as the image of Tanju had done, the mental picture of Naulg suddenly solidified in Arvin's mind. It was as if Arvin were staring at the rogue from a point somewhere behind Naulg. He was sitting, arms wrapped around his drawn-up legs, his head hanging down dejectedly, chin on chest.

Alive! Naulg was still alive!

Elated, Arvin tried to see more, hoping for some clue as to Naulg's whereabouts. But it was no use. All he could see was Naulg himself.

Naulg, he thought urgently. *It's Arvin. Answer me. Tell me where you are so I can rescue you.*

Abruptly, Naulg's head lifted. He whirled around, still in a seated position, searching for the source of the voice he'd just heard. Arvin, still linked by the sending, gasped as he saw the rogue's face. Naulg's cheeks were as sunken as those of a corpse, and his eyes were hollow pits under a scalp that was dotted with bald patches. Horrified by the change in his friend's appearance, Arvin nearly lost the connection. Then Naulg's reply came whispering back at him.

I am . . . unclean, he answered, his eyes gleaming with madness. A shiver passed through his body, and he wrapped his arms around his legs once more. *My body must . . . burn.*

"Unclean?" Arvin echoed. He wet his lips nervously.

Naulg, as if mimicking Arvin, wet his own lips. Arvin felt his face pale as he saw Naulg's tongue. The tip of it was forked, just like a yuan-ti's.

The rogue was still speaking telepathically to Arvin, still linked to him by the sending. He shook his head violently, and his eyes seemed to clear for just a moment. *Arvin?* he asked. *You escaped?*

"Yes, Naulg, I escaped. Where *are* you?" Arvin spoke out loud, despite the fact that Naulg wouldn't hear him. That was how a sending worked: the psion sent a brief message, and received one in return. Then it ended.

Fortunately, Naulg was still answering—though his eyes had resumed a wild, darting look. *The walls. . . . It's hot. They're burning.* The rogue paused, and his eyes cleared a little—though they were glazed with pain. *It hurts. Oh gods, my stomach feels like it's—*

Abruptly, the sending ended.

Arvin stood, shaken by what he'd just seen and heard. His friend was in the grip of a hideous transformation that seemed to be sapping both his strength and his sanity. And he was counting on Arvin to rescue him.

Arvin spoke the command word and the lapis lazuli fell from his forehead. As he tucked it back inside the false seam of his shirt pocket, he debated what to do. Tanju was well to the north of the city—it would take Arvin a full day to reach him and another to get back to the city. Could Naulg wait that long for rescue?

If Naulg had been able to say where he was, Arvin wouldn't be asking that question. But his reply to the sending had been baffling. Burning walls? The Pox could be hiding inside a foundry, or a pottery factory . . . or next to a building that was being cleansed of plague.

With a sinking heart, Arvin decided that Naulg would have to come second. Tanju would only wait one day for Arvin; Arvin couldn't let his only chance at dislodging the mind seed just walk away.

"Hang on, Naulg," Arvin whispered. "I'll come for you. Just hang on."

CHAPTER 13

ARVIN TRUDGED ONWARD, WEARY AND FOOTSORE AFTER A FULL day of walking in the hot sun along the road that wound its way into the foothills north of Hlondeth. Built centuries ago when the aqueduct was constructed, the road was little more than a track, its flagstones all but lost among the weeds. The aqueduct itself was still sound; Arvin could hear water gurgling through the enormous stone troughs overhead. Here and there water spurted out through a crack where two of the troughs joined, providing a cooling shower for the travelers trudging below.

Arvin had expected to be the only one on the road; summer was a grueling time to be undertaking a climb into the mountains north of the city. He was surprised by the number of people who were heading in the same direction that he was. They turned out to be devotees of Talos the Destroyer, on their way to Mount Ugruth to view the most recent venting of the volcano. Every so often—whenever they caught sight of the plume of smoke rising from the peak of the mountain—the pilgrims would fall to their knees, tear their shirts, and claw at the earth until their fingers bled. A few even went so far as to claw at their faces, opening bloody wounds they displayed proudly to one another, bragging that this would speed the flow of lava down the mountain's sides and the destruction of all in its path.

Arvin, reminded of the excesses of the priests who had run the orphanage, kept well away from these fanatics. What point was there in worshiping a god who offered only death and destruction as rewards for faithful service? Surely that was madness.

Yet it was madness that offered the perfect cover. As he drew nearer to the top of the first pass, Arvin stepped into the trees, out of sight from the road. When he emerged again, his shirt hung in tatters, his trouser knees were dirty and his hair and face were streaked with blood from a cut he'd opened on one finger. Raising his hands to the distant volcano, he continued up the road.

Up ahead on the left was a blocky cliff that had been cut into the forested hillside—one of the quarries that had provided the stone used to build the aqueduct. Chunks of partially squared stone littered the ground; travelers in years gone by had used these to create rough, unmortared shelters. Their crude walls were roofed with tree branches, hacked from the nearby forest. Many of the shelters had fallen to pieces, but at least two or three were currently in use, judging by the thin wavers of smoke that rose from them into the summer sky.

Arvin entered the old quarry and began going from one shelter to the next, mumbling nonsense about death and ashes under his breath. But every shelter that he looked inside held only pilgrims. They beamed at Arvin, waving him inside, then shrugged as he turned and stumbled away.

After peering inside the last of the shelters, Arvin slowed. Had Tanju already gone? The tracker had promised to wait until evening, but perhaps sunset had marked the end of his patience.

Arvin turned and stared back in the direction from which he'd come. Hlondeth lay far below, a dark spot at the edge of the vast expanse of blue that was the Vilhon Reach. Far away across the water, Arvin could just make out the opposite shore, where the Barony of Sespech lay. Clouds were gathering above the Reach, indicating that the muggy heat would soon break.

Wiping the sweat from his forehead with the back of a sleeve, Arvin wet his lips. He certainly could use a drink of water. Then again, he was equally drawn by the heat he could feel rising from the sun-warmed stone on which he stood. Exhausted after a full day of walking, he yearned to curl up on it and soak up the last few rays of the setting sun. Perhaps if he drowsed, the headache that had been plaguing him would finally ebb. Tilting his face up to the sun, he closed his eyes and stretched. . . .

He heard a faint tinkling, like the sound of chimes being stirred by the wind. An instant later pain lanced through his skull, staggering him. Gasping, he clutched his head. The pain was unbearable; it pierced his skull from temple to temple. He heard the familiar *thunk* of a crossbow shot. Something wrapped itself around his ankles, lashing them together. In that same instant, a second mental agony was added to the first. This time it slammed into the spot between his eyes and out through the base of his skull. Arvin would have screamed, but found himself unable to force a sound out through his gritted teeth. Opening his eyes seemed equally impossible, as was anything other than toppling over onto his side. A third bolt of agony pierced the crown of his head as he fell. This one seemed to explode within his mind, sparking out in all directions like a shattered coal and burning everything in its path. As it sizzled inside his skull, Arvin felt his mind dulling. Coherent thought was a struggle, and yet somehow a part of what remained of his consciousness—the part that held the mind seed—recognized the attack for what it was. A series of crippling mental thrusts.

Tanju was still at the quarry, after all.

He . . . dares . . . attack . . . me? thought the part of Arvin's mind that had been seeded.

Then he crumpled to the ground.

25 Kythorn, Evening

Arvin came to his senses suddenly, sputtering from the cold water that had just been dashed on his face. Blinking it out of his eyes, he saw that he was inside one of the crude shelters in the old quarry. Moonlight shone in through the loose lacing of branches that constituted the roof, revealing a shadowed form sitting cross-legged on the opposite side of the shelter: Tanju. The tracker stared silently at Arvin, his hands raised above his head and palms pressed together, his hairless chest visible through rips in his shirt. His eyes were filled with shifting points of colored light; it was as if hundreds of tiny candle flames of differing hues were flickering in their depths.

Standing next to Tanju was a young man with pale, close-cropped hair who held a dripping leather bucket in one hand. His shirt was also torn like those of the pilgrims; through the rents in his sleeve Arvin could see three chevrons on his left forearm. That, and the peculiarly rigged crossbow that hung from his belt, marked him as a militiaman. Arvin's backpack lay near his feet.

Arvin tried to rise but found that he was unable to move. Cool, wet tendrils of what looked like white mist encased his body from head to foot, leaving only his eyes and nose uncovered. They shifted back and forth across his body like drifting clouds, but though they left a damp film on Arvin's hair and skin, he was unable to slip out of them. When he strained against them, they held firm, as solid as any rope. The knowledge of what they were came to him out of one of Zelia's memories. They were strands of ectoplasm, drawn from the astral plane by force of will and twined around the victim with a quick twist of thought. The resulting "ectoplasmic cocoon" was almost impossible to escape. If cut, the strands would just regenerate.

Much like a length of trollgut, Arvin thought, his mind still groggy.

The flickering points of light disappeared from Tanju's eyes. He lowered his hands. "This isn't Gonthril," he told the other man. "His aura is wrong. Very wrong."

The militiaman frowned. "He looks like Gonthril."

"Gonthril wouldn't have allowed himself to be captured like this."

Arvin tried to speak, but the strands of ectoplasm pressed against his lips and held his jaw firmly shut. All he could manage was a muffled exhalation that sounded like a hiss.

Tanju waved a hand in front of Arvin's face, as if fanning a candle flame, and the strands shifted away from Arvin's mouth. "Who are you?" he asked.

Arvin wet his lips nervously. "My name's Arvin," he said. "I'm a rope maker from Hlondeth. Unfortunately, I look like this Gonthril fellow you're searching for. You mistook me for him in the Mortal Coil two mornings ago."

"That was you?" Tanju asked.

"Yes."

"Why did you flee?"

Arvin tried to gesture with his head, but could not. "Take a look at my left forearm," he suggested. "The militia were rounding up men for a galley. The thought of four years of pulling an oar didn't appeal to me."

"I see," Tanju said. He didn't bother to inspect Arvin's arm. "How do you know Gonthril's name?"

"I overheard one of the militia mention it when I was hiding in the pottery factory," Arvin said. "'There's a ten thousand gold piece bounty coming to the man who captures Gonthril," he said. "I figured that was the name of the person you were looking for."

"Why did you claim to be him?" Tanju asked.

"I didn't think you'd agree to meet with me otherwise." Arvin was uncomfortable inside the cocoon of ectoplasm. The slippery feel of the strands reminded him of the unpleasant cling of sewer muck. His clothes and hair were growing damper by the moment. At least the ectoplasm was odorless, the gods be thanked for small mercies.

The militiaman standing beside Tanju snorted as he placed the bucket back on the ground. "It's a trick, Tanju," he said. "The stormlord is trying to stall us—and we fell for it. We've already lost an entire day."

Tanju gave the militiaman a sharp look, as if the other man had just said something he shouldn't have. "Our quarry knows nothing about the rebels, least of all what their leader looks like."

"What if we were wrong?" the militiaman suggested. "Maybe the rogues were, in fact, rebels and the theft nothing more than a plot to draw you out of the city."

"The theft was real enough," Tanju said grimly. "And they *weren't* rebels. I know that much already."

The militiaman frowned. "But how does this man fit in?"

"I don't," Arvin interrupted, exasperated by their endless speculations about rogues and rebels and stormlords—whoever they were. "I'm here because I need Tanju's help. I need him to negate a psionic power that's been manifested on me."

Tanju tilted his head. "Why should I do this for you?"

"I can pay," Arvin continued. "Look in my backpack and you'll find a magical rope. It's yours, if you'll help."

The militiaman began to pick up Arvin's backpack, but Tanju held up a hand, cautioning him. Then Tanju waved his hand over the backpack and a faintly sweet smell filled the air. The scent was a little like the burnsticks Arvin's mother had burned when she was meditating—flower sweet, with sharp undertones of resin.

Tanju lowered his hand. "You can open it now," he told the militiaman.

The militiaman undid the buckles on the backpack and tipped it open. Arvin's clothes, extra pair of boots, blanket, and food spilled out, together with a neat coil of rope. Tanju stared at them, his eyes sparkling with multicolored fire a second time.

"It's braided from trollgut," Arvin explained. "I made it myself. A command word causes it to expand. The extra fifty paces worth of rope will eventually rot away, but it can be grown back over and over again. The rope is quite valuable; you can sell it for three thousand gold pieces or more to the right buyer." He paused then, when the tingle arose at the base of his scalp, and used his most persuasive voice. "Will you do it? Will you use your psionics to negate the power that's been manifested on me? If you do, I'll tell you the command word; the rope is useless without it."

Tanju fingered the rope, squeezing its rubbery strands between his fingers. He cocked his head as if listening to a distant sound— the secondary display of the charm Arvin was manifesting. When he turned back toward Arvin, he was smiling. Arvin peered at the psion, uncertain whether his charm had worked on the man or not. "Well, friend?" he ventured. "Will you help me?"

"I need to know what power has been manifested," Tanju said.

Arvin wet his lips. "A mind seed."

Tanju's eyes widened. He placed his hands on his knees then nodded. "That explains the aura."

"What aura?"

"The one that surrounds you. It was a strange mix. Dominated by yang—male energy—but streaked with yin. Mostly good but tainted with evil. It contained elements of both power and weakness, human and reptile. I assumed you were trying to alter your own aura . . . and not quite succeeding. But I see now that it must be the mind seed."

"Can you negate it?" Arvin asked.

"Excise it, you mean," Tanju said. He shook his head. "You really are a novice, aren't you? Despite the fact that you used a sending to contact me, you didn't mount even the simplest of defenses against my mind thrusts."

Arvin glanced down at the ectoplasm that held him. "If I'm so harmless, how about releasing me?"

Tanju considered Arvin for a moment, as if weighing the danger he posed. He took a deep breath then blew it out like a man extinguishing a lamp. The tendrils of ectoplasm vanished.

Arvin sat up, working the kinks out of his muscles. He ignored the militiaman, who had scooped up his crossbow and was aiming it at him. Pretending to stretch, he saw with satisfaction that his glove was still on his left hand, his braided leather bracelet still on his right wrist. So far, so good. The slick wetness the tendrils had left disappeared rapidly in the warm night air. Within the space of a few heartbeats, Arvin's hair and clothes were dry He turned to Tanju. "I know the name of the power, but not much about it. Tell me what a mind seed is."

"It's a psionic power that can be manifested only by the most powerful telepaths," Tanju answered. "It inserts a sliver of the psion's mental and spiritual essence in the mind of another—a seed. As it germinates, it slowly replaces the victim's own mind with that of the psion who manifested the seed. When it at last blooms, the victim is no longer himself, but an exact duplicate of the psion. In mind, but not in body. His thoughts, his emotions, his dreams—"

"I get the point," Arvin said, shuddering. He massaged his temples, which were throbbing again. "How do I get rid of it?"

"Your head aches?" Tanju asked. "That's to be expected. It's the seed, setting in roots. The pain will get worse each day, as the roots expand and—"

"Gods curse you!" Arvin shouted, shaking his fist at Tanju. This human was toying with him, being coy. Gloating as he withheld the very thing Arvin most needed. "I haven't got much time. Don't just sit there—*excise* it, you stupid, insolent—"

The *click-whiz* of a weighted wire from the crossbow cut off the rest of Arvin's shout. One of the paired lead weights slammed into his cheek, making him gasp with pain as the other yanked the wire tight, pinning his wrist against his neck. Almost unable to breathe with the wire around his throat, Arvin felt the amulet his mother had given him pressing into his throat. "Nine lives," he whispered to himself—a plea, this time. He raised his free hand, palm out, in a gesture of surrender. "I'm sorry," he gasped. "That wasn't me. I didn't mean to. . . ."

"I could see that," Tanju said, rising to a kneeling position. He carefully began to unwind the wire from Arvin's neck and wrist. He spoke over his shoulder to the militiaman. "That was unnecessary. Please wait outside."

The militiaman grumbled but did as he was told, flipping aside the blanket that served as the shelter's door and stalking out into the night. Tanju, meanwhile, coiled the weighted wire into a tight ball and placed it in a pocket. He must have realized it would make an ideal garrote.

"Who planted the mind seed?" Tanju asked.

Arvin hesitated. "Why do you want to know?"

"I'm curious," Tanju answered. "Judging by your mannerisms—and your aura—it was a yuan-ti. I didn't know that any of them were trained in psionics."

Arvin stared at Tanju; the tracker's curiosity seemed to be genuine. Arvin decided that he might as well answer. "Her name's Zelia."

Tanju's expression didn't change. Either he didn't know Zelia—or he was a master at hiding his emotions.

"Will you help me?" Arvin asked.

"To excise a mind seed, one must know how to perform psychic chirurgery," Tanju said. "Unfortunately, that is a power I have yet to acquire." He paused. "You asked if I could negate it. There is a chance—a very slim one, mind you—that a negation might work. I'll attempt it now, if only for my own peace of mind while we speak further. Sit quietly, and look into my eyes."

Arvin did as instructed. Tanju stared intently at him, his eyes once more glinting with sparks of multicolored light. An unusual secondary display, a part of Arvin's mind noted—the part that had access to Zelia's memories. Tanju must have trained in the East. . . .

The motes of color suddenly erupted out of Tanju's eyes like sparks leaping from a fire. They shot into the spot between Arvin's eyes, penetrating his third eye and spinning there for a brief instant, then rushed through the rest of his body, leaving swirls of tingles at the base of his scalp, his throat, his chest, and his naval. The tingling coiled for a moment around the base of his spine then erupted out through his arms and legs, leaving his fingers and toes numb.

"Did it work?" Arvin asked, flexing his fingers.

"Try to think of a question that you don't know the answer to—something only Zelia would be able to answer," Tanju suggested.

Arvin stared at the rough walls of the shelter. Zelia seemed to know a lot about gems and stones. Presumably, she would know what type of stone had gone into the making of these rough walls. It was a reddish color, the same as the stone used in the oldest buildings in Hlondeth. . . .

Marble. Rosy marble, a crystalline rock capable of taking a high polish. Useful in the creation of power stones that conveyed the power to dream travel.

Arvin hissed in alarm. "It didn't work," he told Tanju in a tense voice.

Tanju sighed. "I didn't think it would. The mind seed is too powerful a manifestation. I can't uproot it." He gestured at Arvin's backpack. "You can keep your rope."

Arvin felt panic rise in his chest. "Is there nothing else you can try?"

Tanju shook his head.

"The mind seed was planted around middark on the twenty-second of Kythorn," Arvin said, wetting his lips. "If it blooms after seven days, that means I've only got four days left—until middark of the twenty-ninth."

"Possibly."

Arvin caught his breath. "What do you mean?"

"It could bloom sooner than middark," Tanju said. "Any time on the twenty-ninth, in fact."

"But Zelia said it would take seven days to—"

"A mind seed is not like an hourglass," Tanju said. "It doesn't keep precise time. The seven-day period is somewhat . . . arbitrary."

Arvin swallowed nervously. "So I've really only got three days," he muttered. He shook his head. "Will I . . . be myself until then?"

"As much as you are now," Tanju said. "Not that this is much comfort to you, I'm sure."

"When will I be able to start manifesting the powers that Zelia knows?"

Tanju shook his head. "You won't. Not until it's her mind, not yours, in your body. If it worked any other way, the victim would be able to use the psion's talents against him."

"Is there *nothing* that can be done to stop it?" Arvin moaned.

"Nothing. Unless. . . ."

Arvin tensed. "Unless what?"

Tanju shrugged. "There is a prayer that I once saw a cleric use to cure a woman who had been driven insane by a wizard's spell. He called it a 'restorative blessing.' I asked him if it was a divine form of psychic chirurgery. He had never heard the term before, but his answer confirmed that the prayer was indeed similar. He said a restorative blessing could cure all forms of insanity, confusion, and similar mental ailments—that it could dispel the effects of any spell that affected the mind, whether the source of the spell was clerical magic or wizardry. Presumably, that included psionic powers, as well. If you could find a cleric with such a spell, perhaps he could—"

"I don't know any clerics," Arvin said in exasperation. "At least, I don't know any that would—" Here he paused. Nicco. Did Nicco know such a prayer? He'd known what a psion was. Perhaps he knew more about "mind magic" than he'd let on. But if Nicco did know the restorative prayer, would he agree to use it?

Thinking of Nicco put Arvin in mind of the promise he'd made to the cleric: to attempt vengeance upon Zelia. If Arvin actually succeeded—if he was somehow able to defeat Zelia—perhaps she could be forced to remove the mind seed. The only trouble was she was a powerful psion, and he, a mere novice.

But a master was sitting just across the room from him.

Zelia had taught Arvin, in a single evening, to uncoil the energy in his *muladhara* and reach out with it to snatch his glove from the air. Perhaps there was something that Tanju could teach him, too. Some power that would help him confront Zelia—or at the very least, to defend himself against whatever else she might throw at him.

"That 'mind thrust' you used on me when I first arrived," Arvin said. "Could you teach it to me?"

"I'm surprised you don't know it already," Tanju said. "The five attack forms—and their defenses—are among the first things a psion learns. What lamasery did you train at?"

"I didn't," Arvin said. "My mother was going to send me to the one she trained at—the Shou-zin Lamasery in Kara Tur. Unfortunately, she didn't live long enough to—"

Tanju's eyebrows lifted. "Your mother trained at Shou-zin?"

Arvin paused. "You've heard of it?"

Tanju chuckled. "I spent six years there."

Arvin's mouth dropped open. "Did you know my mother? Her name was Sassan. She was a seer."

Tanju shook his head. "She must have trained there after my time." He paused. "How old were you when she died?"

"Six," Arvin said, dropping his gaze to the floor. He didn't want to discuss the orphanage, or what had followed.

Tanju seemed to sense that. "And those who cared for you after her death never thought to send you to a lamasery," he said. He pressed his palms together and touched his fingertips to his forehead then lowered his hands again. "Yet you know how to manifest a charm."

Alvin's cheeks flushed. "It didn't work, did it?"

Tanju shook his head.

"Did it anger you?"

"No."

Arvin glanced up eagerly. "Will you teach me the attacks and defenses?" As he spoke, he stifled a yawn. The long walk had left him weary and exhausted; he was barely able to keep his eyes open.

"Tonight?" Tanju chuckled. "It's late—and I'm as tired as you are. And I have an . . . assignment I need to attend to. Perhaps in a tenday, when I return to Hlondeth."

Arvin hissed in frustration. "I haven't got that much time. The mind seed—"

"Ah, yes," Tanju said, his expression serious again, "the mind seed."

"I'll pay you," Arvin said. "The trollgut rope is yours, regardless of whether I learn anything or not."

Tanju stared at the rope. "For what you ask, it is hardly enough. The secrets of Shou-zin are living treasures and do not come cheaply."

"I know how to make other magical ropes. If you wanted one that could—"

"Your ropes are of less interest to me than your eyes," Tanju said. "You're Guild, aren't you?"

Arvin hesitated. "What if I am?"

"I may need a pair of eyes within that organization, some day," Tanju said. "If I agree to help you, can I call upon you for a favor in the future?"

Arvin paused. If he agreed, Tanju would be yet another person to whom he'd be beholden. Then again, in four days' time the promise might not matter, anyway. At last he nodded. "Agreed."

Tanju smiled. "Then in honor of your mother—may the gods send peace to her soul—I'll teach you what little I can. But not until tomorrow morning, when you're rested and your mind is clear."

"In the morning? But—"

Tanju folded his arms across his chest.

Grudgingly, Arvin nodded. He'd hoped to begin his walk back to the city at dawn's light. But Naulg had survived this long. An additional morning probably wouldn't make much difference. "All right. In the morning, then."

Tanju turned toward the doorway.

"Where are you going?" Arvin asked.

"To join my companion," Tanju answered. He paused, his palm against the blanket that was the shelter's doorway. "I'm reluctant to sleep in here with you. The mind seed. . . ." He shrugged.

Arvin hissed in frustration, but held his temper.

"Sleep well," Tanju said. He stepped out into the night, letting the blanket fall shut behind him.

CHAPTER 14

*26 Kythorn,
Sunrise*

I N HIS DREAM, ARVIN GASPED AS THE MENTAL BLAST SLAMMED AGAINST the shield he had thrown up, shattering it. The shield exploded into a bright nova of individual motes of thought, which swiftly vanished. Immediately, before he could manifest a fresh shield, a second mental blast slammed into him. The psionic attack targeted his mind, rather than his body, but even so it sent him staggering backward. The backs of his legs struck something—the low wall around the fountain—and he flailed backward into its pond.

Leaping to his feet, he was dimly aware of water streaming from his hair and the sodden fabric of his dress clinging to his breasts and thighs. But the vast majority of his awareness—which had lessened, thanks to that last blast of energy, which had stripped away several layers of his painstakingly constructed self-control—was focused on his attack. Summoning energy up from his *muladhara*, he formed it into a long, thin, deadly whip of thought and sent this lashing out at his opponent.

He heard a low thrumming noise—a sound like an enormous, low-timbral drum still vibrating long after it has been struck—and cursed, knowing his master had raised a defense just in time. Arvin's mental whip struck harmlessly against a barrier then vanished.

His master, standing several paces away, his bare feet hidden by the flowering bush he'd stumbled into, shook his bald head. His face was deeply lined, almost haggard looking. He'd aged—greatly—during the years in which he'd served as Arvin's tutor.

In one dark hand he held two thumb-sized crystals, bound together with silver wire, his capacitor. The golden glow that once blazed brightly in it was dimmer than it had been a moment ago, almost gone.

"Enough!" the master cried. "You've proved your point. You surpass me."

Arvin hissed with satisfaction, but sweet as his master's admission of defeat was, there was something more Arvin wanted. His tongue flickered out of his mouth, tasting defeat in the wind.

Then power surged, coiling and furious, into the spot at the base of his skull. Arvin lashed out with it, wrapping it tightly around his master's will. But in that same instant, his master's eyes flared, emitting a bright green light as pale as a new-grown leaf. One final blast of energy crashed into Arvin, shredding his confidence like a once-proud flag frayed by the wind. A shred of his mental fabric, however, held. Control, Arvin told himself, repeating the favorite motto of his master—this human who had been foolish enough to share his secrets.

His psychic crush held.

Arvin squeezed with it—and his master crumpled. First his face, which sagged into a look of utter despair, then his shoulders and his torso. His legs buckled under him and he folded to the ground. The crystal capacitor, drained by his last, feeble attempt at defense, fell to the ground beside him, darkened, drained of energy.

Swiftly, Arvin manifested one of his favorite powers—one that locked away the victim's higher mind, leaving him paralyzed and unable to react. As the flash of silver light died away from Arvin's vision, he saw that his manifestation had been successful. From the crown of his bald head to the pink soles of his feet, his master was covered in a thin sheen of ectoplasmic slime.

As the human lay there, unable to move, Arvin strode across the garden. He bent low over his defeated opponent and tasted the sweat on the man's brow. "Surpassing you wasn't enough," he whispered in his master's ear. "But this will be."

He reared back, opening his mouth wide, and sank his teeth into the old man's throat. . . .

Arvin gasped and sat up, heart pounding, horrified by what he'd just done. He'd just killed a man. By *biting* him. And the taste of the old man's blood had been so *sweet*.

For several moments all he could do was look wildly around. Where was he? Still in the garden of his family compound?

With an effort, he shook off the dream-memory. He saw that he was inside one of the crude huts in the ancient quarry. Early-morning sunlight was streaming in through its open doorway. He stared at it for several moments before realizing that the blanket that had served as its door was gone.

Tanju! Had the psion crept away in the night?

Leaping to his feet, Arvin scrambled outside, only to nearly run into the psion as he was coming in through the doorway.

Tanju chuckled. "Eager to begin, I see. Good. Once you've relieved yourself and washed, we can start."

A short time later, Arvin sat cross-legged in the crude stone shelter, hands resting on his knees and eyes closed, in the position he'd seen his mother adopt each morning at sunrise. He'd always assumed her morning meditations to be a form of dozing, but now he understood what she'd really been doing. The mental exercises Tanju was putting him through were every bit as strenuous as the *asanas* Zelia performed. They were not a flexing of muscle, though, but a flexing of mind.

Following Tanju's instructions, he relaxed his body, concentrating on letting his muscles loosen, starting with his forehead, his eyes, his jaw—and thus on down through his entire body. That done, he concentrated on his breathing, drawing air in through his nose, out through his mouth, in through his nose, out through his mouth. . . .

He was supposed to be aware only of his breathing—to clear his mind of all other thoughts—but this was a much more difficult task than it sounded. Like a small child running zigzags across an open field, spiting its parents' attempts to make it stand in one place and be still, Arvin's mind kept darting this way and that. To Zelia and the mind seed—if Tanju didn't help, whatever was Arvin going to do next? To the rebels—were Gonthril and the others still alive, or had they died in the assassination attempt? To the horrible rotted-flesh *thing*, and Kayla, and the sewers, and the Pox, and the flasks shaped like snake rattles, and the—

"Maintain your focus," Tanju snapped. "Concentrate! Clear your mind of stray thoughts."

With an effort, Arvin wrenched his mind back to the current moment. He breathed in through his nose, out through his mouth, in through his nose. . . . Dimly, he was aware of Tanju, seated beside him in the shelter. The psion's breathing matched his own. Slowly, Arvin's mind stilled.

"Better," Tanju said. "We can begin now."

Tanju took a deep breath and began his instruction. "Before he can master a power, a psion must master his own mind," he told Arvin. "He must explore every corner, every crevice. Especially those that he would rather remain in darkness. He must seek out the desires, fears, and memories that lie in darkness and bring them out into the light, one by one. Until you can prove yourself capable of doing this, it is pointless for me to try to teach you."

Arvin nodded, determined to try.

"In order for you to attempt to gain mastery over your fears, it will be necessary for me to guide you," Tanju continued. "To do this, I must join my mind with yours."

As he realized what Tanju was asking, Arvin's breath caught. Zelia had already trampled through his mind and left her deadly seed. Did he really want another person crowding in there, too? "Is there any other way?" he asked.

"Without my guidance, what you're about to attempt could take a tenday or more to master. It's your choice."

After a few moments, Arvin realized that's just what he didn't have: a choice. This might be his only chance to learn more about psionics before. . . . Shrugging the thought aside, he concentrated and found the breathing pattern again. In through his nose, out through his mouth; in through his nose. . . . "All right," he sighed. "Do it. Join."

Suddenly, Arvin's skin felt wet. A thin, slippery coating of ectoplasm coated his body. Then it was gone.

Good, Tanju said, his words slipping into Arvin's mind like a whisper. *Now we can begin.*

Tanju guided him, instructing Arvin to come up with a mental picture that represented his mind. Some object that Arvin could visualize—a network of roads, perhaps, or a system of streams and rivers down which his thoughts journeyed.

Arvin considered these examples and decided to visualize his thoughts like a flowing river. It proved to be a mistake. The river swiftly shifted into an image of snakes, slithering through his mind, trying to find each other so they could form a mating ball. Recognizing them as the tendrils of the mind seed, Arvin recoiled, his heart pounding.

What is it? Tanju asked.

The mind seed.

You fear it.

Yes. Arvin hesitated. *Must I . . . overcome this fear . . . before you will train me?*

Arvin felt rather than saw Tanju shake his head. *This fear is too great, and it is justified. We will choose something else, instead. But first you need to picture your mind—your mind, rather than the portion the mind seed has already claimed. Choose another image, one that has a resonance for you alone.*

Arvin, still struggling to keep his breathing even, considered. What could he picture his mind as that wouldn't trigger a sharper image from the mind seed? Then it came to him. *A net?* he ventured. His mind indeed felt like that: a series of strands of thought, knotted together by memory.

A net that Zelia was trying to unravel.

Tanju gave a mental nod. *A net. Good. Now explore that image. Send your mind ranging over the net and show me what you see.*

Arvin did as instructed. The net he visualized was made up of strands of every fiber he had ever worked with, from coarse hemp twine to silken threads woven from individual magical hairs, from leather cord to rubbery trollgut. A handful of these strands were green and scaly and writhing with life—the strands of the mind seed, gradually snaking their way into the weave. But the center of the net was still intact, still Arvin's own. The knots that held it together ranged from simple square knots to the most complicated knot he knew how to tie—the triple rose. The latter—a large, multilooped flowering of twine—was at the very center of his imaginary net, lurking like an ornate spider at the middle of its web.

That one, Tanju said, *The largest knot, the memory you've tied the tightest. Ease it open, just a little, and look inside.*

Arvin did as instructed, teasing one of the strands back . . . and saw his mother's face. She was smiling at him, leaning forward to tie a leather thong around his neck—the one that held the bead he'd worn since that day. "Nine lives," she said with a wink and tousled his hair.

With the memory came an emotion—one of overwhelming grief and loss. "Mother," he moaned aloud. The strands of thought that led to this memory seemed thin, frayed, ready to snap and recoil.

Tanju gave Arvin's hand a mental squeeze, steadying him. *Go deeper,* he urged, *As deep as you can. Learn to look upon your mother's death and not be afraid.*

Arvin shuddered. *I can't,* he thought back. *Not with you watching.*

But I need to guide—

No!

Very well.

All at once, Arvin felt Tanju withdraw. Relieved, Arvin steadied his breathing and returned to his task. He could do this on his own. He could confront this fear and master it. He loosened the memory knot a little more, forcing himself to revisit the day he'd learned that his mother was dead. Arvin continued reluctantly, like a man probing with his tongue at an aching tooth.

He remembered the words his uncle had spoken when breaking the news of his mother's death—how he'd callously answered Arvin's tearful questions about whether her body would be brought back to the city for cremation. "Are you mad, boy?" his uncle had asked scornfully. "She died of plague. Her body will have to be left where it lies. Nobody would be stupid enough to touch it. Besides, you wouldn't want to see it. She died of the Mussum plague. She'll be covered in abscesses."

Arvin hadn't known what an abscess was. He'd imagined his mother's skin erupting with maggots. That night, he'd had a nightmare—of his mother's face, her eyes replaced with two fat, white, squirming things.

It had been more than a tenday before he was able to sleep without the lantern illuminated. Every time his uncle had stormed in and angrily blown it out, Arvin had lain awake in darkness, imagining "abscesses" wiggling under his own skin. He sent his mind deep into that memory, remembering how he had felt to be a small boy lying awake all night long, too terrified to touch his own skin. It was just a nightmare, he told himself. Mother didn't actually look that way when she died.

No, she would have looked far worse. According to what Arvin had learned over the years since then, the Mussum plague turned the skin green and covered it in terrible boils.

He imagined her covered in pockmarks, like the Pox.

He immediately wrenched his mind away from the image. But after a moment, he forced himself to return to it. His mother was dead—she'd been dead twenty years. By now the marks of plague would be long gone. She'd be a skeleton . . .

A skeleton lying alone and forgotten, on the plains outside Mussum. . . .

Once again, his mind recoiled. He forced it to return to the thought, to make himself acknowledge the fact that his mother was indeed a corpse. Or perhaps, not even that—her body would have been consumed by time and the elements long ago.

She is dust, he told himself.

The thought comforted him. In his mind, he held the dust that was his mother close to his heart then extended his hand and let it trickle through his fingers to be borne away by the wind. His mother was at peace.

And so, he realized with some surprise, was he.

Tanju must have heard the change in Arvin's breathing. "Well done," he said, a hint of awe in his voice. "Perhaps I will be able to teach you something, after all. Are you ready to continue?"

Arvin gave a satisfied smile. "Yes."

"Good. Then, open your eyes."

Tanju rose to his feet and gestured for Arvin to do the same. "It's unlikely that you can learn a form in so short a space of time as a single morning, but I can introduce you to the concept of psionic combat," Tanju began. "We will begin with the defenses," he said. "There are five of them, each designed to counter a specific psionic attack but still useful, to a lesser extent, against the other attack forms. It is useful to picture each as a physical posture. This gives the mind something to visualize as it manifests the defense.

"The first form is Empty Mind," Tanju continued. "It is most useful against a psychic crush. It can be visualized like this." Raising his hands, Tanju held them on either side of his face, palms toward himself. For a moment he stood utterly still, eyes closed and face turned slightly up to the sunlight that shone down on him through gaps in the ceiling above. Then his hands began to move, sweeping through the air in front of his face as if he were washing it clean.

"The empty mind leaves the opponent with nothing to grip," Tanju continued. "The mind slips through the fingers of the psychic crush like an eel sliding through the hands of a fisher."

"Or a rat slipping out of the coils of a snake," Arvin said as a memory came to him—one of Zelia's, not his own. Of coiling her thoughts around the mind of a priest who had threatened her, of squeezing his mind until it was limp. When she was finished with him, the priest had been unable to understand even the simplest of symbols for several days. The snake-headed staff that was in his hand had seemed no more than a carved piece of wood. . . .

Arvin shuddered. "Zelia knows the psychic crush attack," he told Tanju.

The psion lowered his hands. "I suspected that she would. Empty Mind is also the most useful defense against a mind thrust—the attack I used to render you helpless—and against insinuation."

"What's insinuation?" Arvin asked.

"An attack form that forces tendrils of destructive energy into the opponent's mind," Tanju answered, raising a hand and wiggling his fingers. "They worm their way in deep and sap the mind's vitality—and with it, the body's strength. If the insinuation is repeated enough times, the opponent will be debilitated to the point where he cannot lift himself off the floor, let alone mount an attack."

Tanju settled into a stance like that of a barehanded brawler, feet firmly on the ground and hands balled into fists. "The second defense form is Shield, which can be visualized like this." He raised his left arm to forehead level, as if shielding his face from a blow and lifted his left leg, twisting it so his shin was parallel with the ground. He stood like this for a moment, perfectly balanced on one foot. Then he spun in place—whipping his body around to present the shield to imaginary opponents closing in from all sides.

"Shield is most useful against a mental lash," he told Arvin, returning to an easy standing position. "The lash cracks harmlessly against it and is unable to tear apart the energies that bind mind and body together. Without the shield, the opponent would become weak and unsteady, unable to coordinate his limbs."

Once again a memory bubbled unbidden to the surface of Arvin's mind. Zelia lashed out again and again with her mind, reveling in each strike. It was better than sinking your teeth into flesh—better because the mental lash didn't use up its venom, but could go on and on. . . .

Arvin shuddered. "Zelia knows that attack, too."

Tanju nodded. "The third form, Fortress, is also an effective defense against a mental lash," he continued. "Visualize a tower, erected by your own will." He dropped into a wide, crouching stance and raised his hands to head level, bending his elbows at right angles. His hands were stiff, fingers tight together, palms facing inward toward his head.

After a moment, he relaxed. "The Barrier form is similar," he continued, "but circular. Like so." Leaning to the side, he lifted his left leg until it was parallel with the floor, presenting the sole of his foot to Arvin. He drew his hands in tight against his chest, palms facing outward, then suddenly spun in a circle. Returning to an easy balance, he stood on both feet again. "Think of it as a wall. An impenetrable barrier constructed from determination, and strong as stone."

Arvin nodded, trying to imagine what that would feel like. It might be a second skin, perhaps, one with the toughness of scale mail. One that could be quickly donned then shed as soon as it had—

No. He was thinking like Zelia again. He massaged his temples, trying to ignore the ache that throbbed through his mind. He hissed angrily, wishing it would just go away.

Tanju paused, a wary look on his face.

"I'm fine," Arvin reassured him, lowering his hand. "Please go on. What is the fifth form? Did you save the best defense for last?"

Tanju's lips quirked into a brief smile. "The fifth form is known as the Tower of Iron Will. It can be used not only to protect oneself, but also one's allies—providing they are standing close by."

"Show me," Arvin said.

Tanju held his right hand out in front of him, palm up and fingers curled. "The will," he pronounced, staring at it. Then he clenched his fist. Slowly, he raised it above his head, turning his face to stare up at it as his hand ascended. He extended his left hand to the side, as if reaching for the hand of a companion, then clenched it, as well. "Walled inside the tower, the will can weather the stormy blasts of the opponent's mental attack. Imagine it as a secure place, as a home."

Arvin imagined his workshop, hidden at the top of the tower in his warehouse. It had been secure, safe . . .

Until Zelia had breached it. She hadn't come in with the fury of a storm, but instead had slithered in, silent as a snake. Any psionic attack she mounted would likely be the same, sneaky—and intimate.

From the brief taste he'd just had of her memories of psionic combat, Arvin knew which attack form was Zelia's favorite. It was the one that allowed her to wrap herself around her opponents mentally and savor their agonies face to face, or rather, mind to mind.

The psychic crush.

"Empty Mind," he told Tanju. "That's the form I want to learn."

Tanju inclined his head. "An interesting choice. Let us see if you are capable of learning it."

They worked together for some time, Arvin slowly learning how to "empty" his mind and at the same time maintain his focus and awareness. Under Tanju's guidance, he began by using the motions that Tanju had, "washing" his face with his hands as he visualized himself erasing his features. Slowly, he learned to imagine replacing his face—*himself*—with vacant space, hiding his mind from sight in shifting clouds of mist. He felt himself getting closer, closer . . . and a tingling began in his throat. Suddenly the shelter was filled with a low, droning noise—the same deep, bass tone that had accompanied his manifestation of the distract power. Arvin laughed out loud, realizing he'd done it—and was surprised to hear his laughter overlapping the droning noise. Abruptly, the droning stopped.

"I did it!" Arvin exclaimed. Then he noticed the expression on Tanju's face. The psion was nodding, as if in encouragement, but there was a wary look in his eyes.

"You learn remarkably fast," Tanju said, "quicker than any pupil I've ever taught—quicker than you should. Under the guidance of the right master. . . ."

Arvin waited for Tanju to finish the thought, but instead the psion turned and picked up the trollgut rope. "That's enough for now," he said, undoing the buckles of his backpack. "I must be going. What is the rope's command word?"

Arvin frowned. "But we only just—"

Tanju stared at him, the rope in his hands. "The command word?"

The lesson was definitely over. Sighing, Arvin told him.

As Tanju tucked the coil of rope into his pack, Arvin saw a glint inside the pack—a shiny surface that reflected the sunlight. It was the three finger-length quartz crystals—one a smoky gray, one clear, and one rosy—bound together with silver wire.

"That's a crystal capacitor, isn't it?" Arvin asked, pulling the words from Zelia's memories. As he stared at it, his upper lip lifted disdainfully, baring his teeth. The human who had tutored Zelia had used one of those to augment his abilities. It had allowed him to continue manifesting psionic powers long after his own internal supply of energy was depleted. Over time, the crystal capacitor had become a crutch—one that gave the tutor a false sense of security. It had been easy, once that crutch was kicked away, to defeat him. . . .

Arvin shook his head to clear it and realized that Tanju was staring warily at him.

"My mother carried a crystal with her," Arvin said. "Until . . . recently I didn't realize what it was."

"A single crystal?" Tanju asked, buckling his pack shut.

Arvin nodded, remembering. "An amethyst."

"How large was it?"

Arvin held his hands about three palm's widths apart.

"A dorje, then," Tanju said. "And not a power stone."

"What's the difference?"

Tanju rebuckled his backpack. "A dorje is like a wizard's wand. It contains a single power, and enough psionic energy to manifest that power up to fifty times. A power stone can contain more than one power—I've heard of some with as many as six inside them. But each power can be manifested only once."

"So a dorje is more valuable," Arvin guessed.

Tanju shook his head. "A dorje can hold only low-level powers," he said. "A power stone, on the other hand, can hold powers that could normally be manifested only by a master psion. Using a power stone, however, is dangerous. If the psion makes the slightest error during the manifestation, the result can be brain burn."

Arvin nodded. Whatever brain burn was, it didn't sound healthy.

"A power stone is smaller than a dorje, then?" he asked.

"Typically, about half the length of a finger," Tanju answered, slinging his backpack over one shoulder.

Arvin thought of the lapis lazuli in his pocket, wondering if it might be a variant on a power stone. If so, perhaps it would allow him to do more than merely manifest a sending. "How do you know what powers a stone contains?"

"The psion must hail it," Tanju said. "He must send his mind deep into the stone, address it by name, and link with it. Only then will the stone give up its secrets."

"But how——"

Tanju held up a hand. "I've taught you enough for this morning," he said. "And I must go. I've already tarried here too long. Look me up again, when I get back to Hlondeth, and I'll tell you more." He paused. "Unless. . . ."

"Yes," Arvin said softly. "The mind seed."

"Tymora's luck to you," Tanju said. "I hope you find a cleric who can help."

26 Kythorn, Highsun

Arvin stood and watched the psion and the militiaman trudge up the road, wondering if he'd see Tanju again. The pilgrims had departed from the quarry at dawn; Arvin would be the last to leave the crude stone huts baking under the intense, midday sun. Stepping back inside the hut in which he'd spent the night, Arvin touched a hand to his breast pocket, reassuring himself that the lapis lazuli was still there. He'd already decided what he'd do next. He would use it to send a message to Nicco, to ask the cleric if he did indeed know the restorative prayer that Tanju had mentioned. But first Arvin wanted to try something. If the lapis lazuli really was a power stone, perhaps it might hold other, even more useful powers.

Arvin pulled the lapis lazuli out of his pocket and stared at it, trying to penetrate its gold-flecked surface. Meanwhile, the morning grew hotter. Arvin hooked a finger under the collar of his shirt, fanning himself with it. For just an instant, his mind brushed against something cool and smooth—and multifaceted, like a crystal. But though he tried for some time to connect with it, he was unable to get beyond this point. Eventually, thirst—and the knowledge that time was sliding past—made him put an end to the experiment.

He touched the lapis lazuli to his forehead. *Atmiya*, he thought, and felt it adhere. Then he imagined Nicco's face. It took even less time to contact the cleric than it had to contact Naulg or Tanju—within heartbeats, Arvin felt a tingle of psionic energy at the base of his scalp as his visualization of Nicco solidified. Arvin was surprised to see the cleric's face twisted in a mixture of grief and barely controlled rage. Nicco was staring at something Arvin couldn't see. Whatever it was, it didn't seem to be an opportune time for Arvin to be asking a favor. Quickly, he amended the message he'd been about to send.

Nicco, it's Arvin. I'm a day's journey from Hlondeth. I need to meet with you—tonight. Where will you be at sunset? And . . . what's wrong?

Nicco startled. A moment later, however, his reply came back— terse and angry. *You want to meet? Then be at the execution pits at sunset—if you dare.*

Abruptly, the connection was broken.

"*Atmiya*," Arvin whispered. The lapis lazuli fell into his palm.

The execution pits? Arvin shuddered. That was what Nicco had been staring at with such a look of grief and loathing on his face. Someone was being publicly executed—and Arvin could guess who.

CHAPTER 15

26 Kythorn,
Fullday

Hot, footsore, and thirsty, Arvin hurried through the city. Hlondeth lay under a muggy torpor; the storm clouds that were gathering over the Reach had yet to break. The public fountains he passed tempted him with their cool, splashing water, but he passed them by, wary of drinking from them. Instead he wiped the sweat from his brow and trudged on.

Though Arvin had returned to the city as quickly as he could, it was almost sunset. But before he met Nicco, there were two stops Arvin had to make. The first was the bakery up the street from his warehouse.

As he drew near the warehouse, he noticed a half-dozen militia standing guard outside. At first, he thought they were looking for him—then he saw the yellow hand painted on the door. Someone had finally reported the stench of the dead cultist. A crowd of people stood across the street from the warehouse, murmuring fearfully to each other in low voices. From inside the building came the sound of a chanted prayer. Arvin found himself making an undulating motion with his right hand—the sign of Sseth. He jerked his hand back and thrust it in his pocket.

He circled around the block to the bakery. Kolim stood on the sidewalk, crumbling a stale loaf of bread for a cluster of tiny brown birds at his feet. They took flight as Arvin approached. The boy looked up, and a wary expression came over his face. He tossed the bread aside and backed up a pace.

"Hi, Kolim," Arvin said, halting a short distance from the boy. "What's wrong?"

"They found a dead guy in your warehouse."

"Really?" Arvin asked, rubbing his aching forehead.

"They say he died of plague."

Arvin looked suitably grim and glanced up the street. "That's bad. That means I can't go back to my warehouse. I wonder what he was doing in there." His breath caught as the militia turned in his direction. When they glanced away again, he hissed in relief.

Kolim stared up at him. "Why are you breathing funny?"

"It's nothing," Arvin hissed angrily. Then, seeing Kolim flinch, he hurriedly added, "I'm fine, Kolim, really. I'm just having trouble catching my breath. I've been walking all day. I'm hot and tired—and I'm sorry I snapped at you."

Kolim nodded, uncertain. "There's a cleric inside your warehouse," he continued. "They say everything in it has got to be burned."

Arvin nodded. He'd expected that. Fortunately he had cached his valuables well away from the warehouse—one of them, at this bakery. "Kolim, remember the 'monkey fist' I asked you to keep for me?"

Kolim nodded.

"I need it. Can you go and—"

"Kolim!" a shrill voice cried from within the bakery. "Get inside this instant!"

Kolim's mother, a dark-haired woman with a chin as sharp as a knife blade, stepped out of the bakery and grabbed Kolim by the ear, yanking him inside. Then she rounded on Arvin. "How dare you come here? Get away from my son." She glanced up the street and waved, trying to catch the eye of the militia.

Arvin took a step forward, wetting his lips. "I knew nothing about the dead man until just now, when Kolim told me about him," he said, holding up his hands. "I haven't been inside my warehouse in days. There's no danger of—"

Kolim's mother didn't wait to hear the rest. Abruptly stepping back inside the bakery, she slammed the door shut. A moment later, however, Arvin heard a noise from one of the windows above as a shutter opened. Kolim leaned out of the window, waved, and dropped a ball-shaped knot attached to a short length of twine. Arvin caught the monkey's fist and signed his thanks to Kolim in finger speech.

Easy going, Kolim signed back. The sound of his mother's harangue came from somewhere behind the boy, and Kolim ducked back inside.

Arvin hefted the monkey's fist. It looked identical to a nonmagical monkey's fist—a round knot, trailing a short length of line, used to weight the end of a ship's heaving line. But instead of having a lead ball at its center, this monkey's fist contained a surprise—a compressed ball of powder taken from the gland of a gloomwing. To release it, the correct command word had to be spoken as the monkey's fist was thrown. When it landed, the knot would immediately unravel, releasing the gloomwing's powerful scent.

Arvin tucked the monkey's fist into his pocket and glanced up at the sun, which was slowly sinking behind Hlondeth's towers. There was one more stop he had to make before meeting Nicco. Fortunately, Lorin's workshop was on the way to the execution pits. He hurried in that direction.

As he approached the locksmith's workshop, he heard the sound of a file rasping against metal. Entering the shop, he found Lorin hunched over a bench, filing the pin mechanism of a brass padlock. The locksmith was a tall, skinny man with a wide forehead from which his short dark hair was combed straight back. The hair was tarred flat against his scalp, like that of a sailor, to keep it out of his eyes. Faded chevrons marked Lorin's left forearm; he'd done his time in the militia years ago, serving as a guard in Hlondeth's prisons. Rumor had it that he'd been working for the Guild even then, slipping lockpicks to prisoners the Guild wanted freed.

Lorin looked up as Arvin entered the workshop. He immediately set the file aside and rose, but held up a warning hand as Arvin strode forward. "Stop right there," he said. "I heard about your warehouse. I'd rather not take any chances."

Arvin halted. "Word travels fast. Did you have a chance to look at the key?"

"Yes."

"And?" Arvin pulled ten gold pieces from his pocket and set them on the end of the workbench. Lorin made no move to pick them up.

"It was very interesting . . . but I don't appreciate objects tainted with plague being brought to my workshop."

Arvin placed ten more gold pieces on the bench. "Interesting in what way?"

"When I tossed it into the fire to cleanse the plague from it, an inscription appeared on the key." He folded his arms across his chest and eyed the coins Arvin had set out, waiting.

"I didn't know you could read," Arvin said.

"I can't. But there's those in the Guild who can. And their services cost. The lorekeeper I consulted was equally as expensive."

Arvin pulled his last eight gold pieces from his pocket and placed them with the others. "That's all the coin I have—aside from three silver pieces."

"It'll do," Lorin said. "With a consideration: a discount on the next thief catcher I buy from you of fifty gold pieces."

Arvin hissed in frustration. "That's an expensive rope," he protested. "Cave fisher filament isn't easy to come by—or to work with—and I go through at least a gallon of brandy stripping the stickiness from the ends. Then there's the spell that has to be cast on the middle third of the rope, to hide the sticky residue. . . ."

"Do you want to know what the inscription on the key said, or not?" Lorin asked.

Arvin sighed. "You'll get your discount. But with my warehouse currently being . . . cleansed I'm not sure when I'll be back in business."

Lorin waved the protest aside. "You'll manage." Left unspoken was an implied threat. If Arvin didn't supply a thief catcher in a reasonable amount of time, something unpleasant would happen. The Guild took a dim view of tardy deliveries.

Lorin turned and picked up a wooden tray that was slotted into several compartments, each holding a key. He pulled out the key Arvin had found in the cultist's pocket and laid it on the workbench then wiped soot from his fingers. "What's interesting is that you found this in the pocket of someone who died of plague," he began. "The inscription on it reads 'Keepers of the Flame.' That's a religious order—one that was active during the plague of '17."

"What god did they worship?" Arvin asked, certain the answer would be Talona.

Lorin laughed. "What god didn't they worship? They were clerics of Chauntea, of Ilmater, of Helm, even of Talos. . . ."

"So the key would have belonged to one of those clerics?"

Lorin nodded. "One of the duties the Keepers of the Flame were charged with was collecting and disposing of the corpses of those who died in the plague. They set up crematoriums all over the Reach."

Arvin smiled grimly. It all fit. The cultists were attracted to places associated with disease—their use of the slaughterhouse and sewers were prime examples. Naulg had said he was in a building with burning walls, and the cultist had bragged about Talona's faithful "rising from the ashes"—a boast he'd meant literally. No wonder he'd been smug. A crematorium, intended to put a stop to one plague, would serve as the starting point for another.

"Was one of those crematoriums in Hlondeth?" Arvin asked.

"Yes—and anyone who was living in the city in '17 can tell you where it is. But that key is probably for a crematorium in another city. The one in Hlondeth had walls of solid stone, without a door or window anywhere in them."

"Why would they build it like that?"

Lorin shook his head. "Nobody knows for sure, but the loremaster I consulted heard that the building contained a gate that opened onto the Plane of Fire. I suppose the clerics didn't want anyone messing with that."

"How did the clerics get inside?"

"They teleported—together with the corpses they were going to burn." He snapped his fingers. "Just like that. It eliminated the problem of having to haul bodies through the city in carts—and spreading the disease."

Arvin frowned at the key. The Hlondeth crematorium must have had a door—possibly one cloaked in illusion. That no one had sought this door in fifty-six years was no surprise. Only a madman would want to break into a building in which plague victims had been housed, however briefly.

A madman—or someone with a mind seed in his head.

Lorin nodded at the key. "If I were you, I wouldn't use it."

Arvin picked up the key and slipped it into his pocket. "Don't worry," he told Lorin. "If I do enter the crematorium, I'll be sure to take a cleric along."

26 Kythorn, Sunset

The Plaza of Justice was a wide, cobblestoned expanse, large enough to accommodate several thousand people and encircled by a viaduct supported by serpent-shaped columns. From his vantage point on a rooftop just above the viaduct, Arvin could see down into the execution pits—two circular holes, each as wide as a large building. Inside each pit was an enormous serpent, its body so thick that a man would barely be able to encircle it with his arms. One was an adder, its venomous fangs capable of imparting a swift death. To this serpent were thrown the condemned deemed worthy of "mercy." The other was a yellowish green constrictor, which squeezed the life out of its victims slowly. On rare occasions, it would skip this step and swallow its victims while they were still alive and thrashing.

Arching over each of the pits was a short stone ramp. Up these, the condemned were forced to march. Their final step was off the end of the ramp and into the pit below.

Both of the snakes had eaten recently. Arvin counted one bulge inside the adder, three inside the constrictor. He shuddered, wondering which of the rebels they were. Only one of the rebels had been shown "mercy," which made Arvin's choice easier. Nicco would show no mercy, either. He'd choose the punishment the majority of the Secession's raiders had suffered.

Slaves were still sweeping up the litter dropped by the crowd who had come to watch this morning's executions. The yuan-ti spectators were long gone from the viaduct that encircled the plaza, but a couple of dozen humans still lingered below—those who had been mesmerized by the serpents. They stood, staring into the pits and swaying slightly, as mindless as grass blown by a malodorous wind. The slaves swept around them.

One man stood, alone and rigid as an oak, at the western edge of the plaza. Nicco. He stared at the pits, scowling, arms folded across his chest. His shadow was a long column of black that slowly crept toward the pits as the sun sank. So unmoving and determined did he appear that Arvin wondered for a moment if Nicco had stood there since morning, plotting divine vengeance against the executioners.

And against Arvin.

Arvin waited, watching the cleric. Nicco finally turned and glanced at the setting sun, as if gauging the time of day, then stared out toward the Reach and the clouds that were building there. While he was thus occupied, Arvin rose to his knees and whirled the monkey's fist in a tight circle over his head. He spoke its command word as he let it fly—and hissed in satisfaction as it landed inside the constrictor's pit. The enormous snake didn't react to the sudden movement. Eating three condemned people in a single day must have sated it.

As Nicco returned his attention to the pits, Arvin climbed down onto the viaduct. He strode around it to the spot where Nicco stood. Only when he was directly above the cleric did Nicco look up. Nicco squinted and raised a gloved hand to shield his eyes from the sun; Arvin had the sun behind his back and would be no more than a silhouette. Then Nicco pointed an accusing finger. "Four people died this morning," he rumbled in a voice as low and threatening as thunder. "Their blood is on your lips. You betrayed them."

Arvin shook his head in protest. "I didn't say anything that—"

"You must have! How else do you explain the yuan-ti who surprised them just outside Osran's door—a yuan-ti with powers far beyond those normally manifested by her race—a psion. Deny that you serve her, if you dare!"

"I don't serve her. Not willingly. She—"

Nicco jerked his hand. A bolt of lightning erupted from his fingertip. It blasted into the viaduct at Arvin's feet, sending splinters of stone flying into the air. Several of them stung Arvin's legs. The edge of the viaduct abruptly crumbled and Arvin found himself falling. He managed to land on his feet and immediately let his knees buckle to turn the landing into a roll, but scraped his ungloved hand badly in the process. Blood began to seep from it as he stood, and from the numerous nicks in his legs that had been caused by the flying stone.

As the startled slaves fled the plaza—together with those spectators whose trances had been broken by the thunderclap—Arvin turned to face Nicco. Arvin was careful not to make any threatening moves. The cleric was angry enough already.

But at least he was still talking. All Arvin had to do was get him to listen—and to believe him.

"I didn't tell the yuan-ti psion anything," Arvin protested. "If I had, your geas would have killed me. She reached into my mind—she *violated* it—and plucked out Osran's name."

"You gave it to her willingly," Nicco accused. "That's why you fled the city. You feared Hoar's wrath."

"Then why would I have come back? Why would I seek you out? I needed help—I left the city to find it. But the person who tried to negate what Zelia had done to me wasn't able to—"

"Zelia." Nicco's eyes narrowed. "So that's the name of your master."

Arvin opened his mouth to explain further, but in that same moment Nicco barked out a quick prayer. "Walk," he commanded, the lightning bolts in his earring tinkling as he thrust out a hand, pointing at the execution pits.

Arvin felt the compulsion of the prayer grip him—and found himself turning smartly on his heel. Like a puppet, he marched toward the pits, guided by Nicco's pointing finger as the cleric strode along behind him. Arvin had an anxious moment when they passed the pit with the adder. He hissed with relief as Nicco directed him to the constrictor's pit, instead.

"Halt," Nicco ordered.

Arvin did. Stealing a glance down, he saw a strand of cord peeking out from under the serpent's body—the unraveled monkey's fist. A faint, powder-sweet odor rose from the pit, just detectable over the stink of the snake—the last of the gloomwing scent. Arvin took care not to inhale too deeply.

Nicco stared at him from the edge of the pit. "Any last words, condemned man?"

"Just this," Arvin answered. "If I'm guilty, then may Hoar punish me by allowing the serpent to crush and consume me. If I'm innocent, may Hoar let me survive unharmed."

"So be it," Nicco said. Then he gave a third command: "Walk."

Arvin did, not even bothering to try to fight the compulsion. He fell onto the serpent's back and tumbled to the floor of the pit. The constrictor had been placid about the monkey's fist landing beside it earlier, but at the touch of a large, living creature, it immediately responded. It whipped a coil around Arvin's upper chest and flexed, driving the air from Arvin's lungs. Another coil immediately fastened around Arvin's legs.

For one terrible moment, Arvin thought he had miscalculated. As the serpent squeezed, his vision went gray and stars began to swim before his eyes. . . .

Then he felt its coils loosening. The one around his legs slackened and fell away, followed by the one around his chest. Gasping his relief, Arvin staggered away from the constrictor. The gloomwing scent had done its work. The serpent had just expended what remained of its strength.

From above, he heard a sharp intake of breath. Glancing up, he saw Nicco staring down at him, a troubled expression on his face. "It seems that I accused you unjustly," he said. He reached down into the pit. "Take my hand. Climb."

Arvin did.

From the east side of the plaza came the sound of running footsteps. Looking in that direction, Arvin saw a dozen militia hurrying down one of the side streets toward the plaza. From one of them came a shout: "There he is!"

Arvin thought it was Nicco they were pointing at; then he realized it was him.

Nicco began murmuring a prayer that Arvin had heard once before and recognized. It was the one that would teleport him away. Realizing he was being left behind, Arvin spoke quickly. "I know where the Pox are hiding!" he cried. "Take me with you!"

A weighted line, fired from a crossbow, whizzed overhead.

Nicco smiled. "What makes you think I was going to leave you here?" Then he touched Arvin's shoulder. Arvin felt himself wrenched through the dimensions by a teleportation spell. The Plaza of Justice—and the militia who were raising their crossbows—all disappeared from sight.

26 Kythorn, Evening

Arvin and Nicco stood together in the alley the cleric had teleported them to, talking in low voices. A few paces away, the alley opened onto the courtyard of the Nesting Tower, an enormous pillar honeycombed with niches in which flying serpents made their nests. Every now and then, their dark shapes flitted across the moonlit sky toward the faintly glowing tower.

"Zelia's not my master," Arvin explained to Nicco. "I met her for the first time four nights ago. She negated the poison the Pox made me drink and tried to hire me to spy on them. She needed a human who would pretend to join their cult—someone who had survived one of their sacrifices. When I refused, she told me I was going to wind up working for her, like it or not. She'd planted a mind seed in my head."

Nicco's eyebrows rose.

"It's a psionic power," Arvin said. "In seven days, it—"

"I know what a mind seed is," Nicco answered.

Hope surged through Arvin. "Do you know the restorative prayer that will get rid of it?"

Instead of answering, Nicco stared into the distance. "Whether you meant to betray them or not, four members of the Secession are dead: Kiffen, Thrond, Nyls . . . and Kayla."

"Kayla?" Seeing the ache in Nicco's eyes, Arvin dropped his voice to a sympathetic murmur. "But she was so young. . . ."

"She died swiftly—and bravely. Her father would have been proud of her. Ironically, by now he will have turned into the very thing he fought against—one of the foul creatures who condemned his daughter to die—a yuan-ti."

"Kayla's father was among those handed over to Osran Extaminos by the Pox?" Arvin asked.

Nicco nodded sadly. "Kayla hoped to save him. In that endeavor, she failed. But she did succeed in exacting Hoar's retribution for what was done to her father. It was she who dispatched Osran with her knife."

"Osran's dead, then?" Arvin asked.

"Gonthril saw him die."

Arvin wet his lips nervously as Nicco continued his story. Zelia had surprised the assassins as they were preparing to leave Osran's chambers. Only Gonthril, thanks to one of his magical rings, had been able to escape. Hearing this, Arvin realized that Zelia had arrived too late to question Osran. She wouldn't have been able to learn if additional yuan-ti were involved with the cultists. Without this information, she wasn't going to remove the mind seed from Arvin's head any time soon . . .

If she had ever planned to at all.

Nicco stared at Arvin, his face dimly illuminated by the glow from the wall beside him. "You said you knew where Talona's clerics were hiding."

Arvin reached into his pocket with his left hand, at the same time whispering his glove's command word, and felt the key appear between his fingers. "Not only do I know what building they're in," he told Nicco, pulling his hand from his pocket. "I have a key that will get us inside." He held it up where Nicco could see it. "So what do you say? Is a chance at vengeance against the Pox worth a restorative prayer?" He held his breath, waiting for Nicco's answer.

Nicco stood in silence for several moments before answering. "It is . . ."

Arvin let out a hiss of relief. Nicco was going to save him, after all.

" . . . if that key leads where you say it does," Nicco concluded. "Shall we find out?"

"Now?"

Nicco scowled. "Have you given up on rescuing your friend?"

Arvin shook his head. "Not at all. I just thought that maybe you could say the restorative prayer first."

Nicco shook his head. "After," he said firmly.

Arvin hissed in frustration, but managed to hold his temper. At least the solution to his problem was in sight. He and Nicco would sneak into the crematorium, make certain the Pox were indeed there, and sneak out again. Then Nicco would remove the mind seed and Arvin could go on his way, leaving it up to the Secession to deal with the cultists.

Arvin reached for the bead at his throat for reassurance. "Nine—" He stopped abruptly as his fingertips brushed the bead. The clay he'd used to repair the crack was crumbling, falling out. The bead felt as if it was ready to break in two. Was it an omen that he'd used up the last of its luck?

He didn't want to think about that just then. Not when every moment that passed brought him closer to his doom. The throbbing ache of the mind seed was slowly, inexorably spreading throughout his head. The sooner they explored the crematorium, the better.

"Let's go," he told Nicco.

Chapter 16

26 Kythorn,
Middark

ARVIN AND NICCO STOOD IN A DOORWAY ACROSS THE STREET FROM the crematorium, staring at what appeared to be a blank stone wall. Earlier, Nicco had whispered a prayer, one that allowed him to see through the illusion that had been placed on the building. He'd assured Arvin that there was, indeed, a door—one with a lock. But instead of trying the key in it right away, Nicco had insisted upon waiting. And so they had stood, and waited, and watched, hoping to see one of the cultists enter or leave the building.

None had.

Nor had anyone walked down the street. And no wonder—all of the buildings in the area, including the one behind Arvin and Nicco, bore a faded yellow hand on their doors.

Arvin was getting impatient. The throbbing in his head wasn't helping. "This is useless," he griped. "We've got the key; let's use it."

Nicco nodded. "It looks as though we'll have to. But first, a precaution."

The cleric began a soft chant. When it ended, he vanished from sight. The only way Arvin could tell that Nicco was still standing beside him was by the sound of his breathing and the rustle of Nicco's kilt as the cleric shifted position.

"Your turn," Nicco said. "Ready?"

When Arvin nodded, Nicco repeated his prayer. Arvin felt a light touch on his shoulder—and suddenly couldn't see his body. It was an odd sensation. Being unable to see his own feet made Arvin feel as if he were floating in the air. He touched a hand to his chest, reassuring himself he was still corporeal.

"Is the key in your hand?" Nicco asked.

Arvin held it up. "Right here."

Instead of taking it, Nicco grasped Arvin's arm and steered him across the street. When they reached the crematorium, Nicco guided the jagged-toothed key up to what, to Arvin, appeared to be solid stone, and Arvin felt the key enter a keyhole. Nicco let go of his arm. The cleric was obviously wary about whatever traps might protect the door. Wetting his lips, Arvin turned the key in the lock and heard a faint click. With a hiss of relief—the poisoned needle he'd half-expected to emerge from the lock mechanism hadn't—he eased the door open. Then, pocketing the key, he whispered the command that materialized the dagger from his glove.

"You first, this time," he told Nicco. He waited until he had felt Nicco brush past him then closed the door behind them.

They stood in a round, empty room as large as the building itself. At its center was a circular platform, about ankle high. Around its circumference were dozens of tiny, finger-sized flames that filled the room with a flickering light. They burned with a faint hissing noise and seemed to be jetting out of holes in the platform.

Arvin hadn't known what to expect a crematorium to look like, but this certainly wasn't it.

Beside him, Nicco murmured the prayer that would allow him to see things as they truly were.

"Is there a way out of this room?" Arvin breathed.

The tinkling of Nicco's earring told Arvin the cleric was shaking his head. "My prayer would have revealed any hidden doors. It found none," he whispered. "I'm going to search the platform."

"Be careful," Arvin warned. "It might teleport you to the Plane of Fire."

"That would require a teleportation circle—something only a wizard can create," Nicco answered, his voice moving toward the platform. "We clerics must rely upon phase doors, which merely open an ethereal passage through stone."

Arvin saw the flames flicker as the cleric walked around the platform. "Are you certain the cultists use this place?" Nicco asked.

Arvin was starting to wonder the same thing. He fingered the key in his pocket. Then his eye fell on something—a small leather pouch that lay on the other side of the platform. He strode over to it and picked it up, and felt something inside it twitch. He raised the now-invisible pouch to his nose and caught a faint leafy smell he recognized at once—assassin vine.

"Nicco," he whispered. "The Pox were here—or at least, they kept their victims here. I've just found my friend's pouch."

There was no reply.

"Nicco?"

Worried that the cleric might have stepped onto the platform and been teleported away, Arvin tucked the pouch in a pocket and crossed the room. He stood beside the platform, listening, and heard what sounded like snoring over the hiss of the flames. It seemed to be coming from the center of the platform.

Wary of the flames, Arvin leaned across the platform. His hand brushed against tassels—one end of Nicco's sash. The cleric must have fallen victim to a spell that sent him into a magical slumber. Arvin grabbed the sash and tried to pull Nicco toward him, but when he yanked, the sash suddenly came free, sending him stumbling backward. Dropping it, Arvin made a circuit of the platform. He leaned over it as much as he dared, but his questing hands encountered only air. He could hear Nicco snoring but couldn't reach him. The platform was simply too wide. Nicco must be lying directly at its center.

Arvin paused, thinking. Whatever laid Nicco low hadn't taken effect immediately. Maybe if Arvin didn't venture too close to the center of the platform, he'd be safe. He couldn't just let the cleric lie there. If he did, Nicco might never wake up.

Arvin stepped up onto the platform.

As soon as he did, he felt a rush of vertigo. It was as if someone had grabbed hold of his trousers at the hip and yanked, sending him tumbling forward. Too late, he realized what had happened. The key in his trouser pocket must have triggered something—one of the phase doors that Nicco had spoken about. Like an anchor chained to Arvin, the key pulled him down into a patch of blurry, queasy nothingness.

Arvin landed facedown on a hard stone floor, knocking the air from his lungs. He felt a throbbing in his lip and tasted blood; his lip was split. Hissing with pain, he sat up and looked around and found that he was in utter darkness. He wet his lips and found them coated with a damp, gritty substance that tasted of ashes.

The remains of the cremated dead.

He spat several times, not stopping until his mouth was clean. Then he rose to his feet. Somewhere in the distance, he could hear a faint chanting—the voices of the cultists, raised in prayer to their loathsome god. As his eyes adjusted to the darkness, he saw, in the direction the chanting was coming from, a patch of faint reddish light, rectangular in shape—a hallway. As he stared at it, something small scurried across the floor nearby, making him hiss in alarm.

It's just a rat, he admonished himself angrily, embarrassed at having startled. Where's your self-control?

He raised a hand and found that the ceiling was just overhead. Its stonework felt solid. He tried prodding it with the key, but nothing happened. Whatever doorway Arvin had just passed through appeared to work only in one direction.

Somewhere above, Nicco lay in magical slumber. The cleric might as well have been in another city, for all the good he was going to be.

Arvin worked his way around the room, feeling the walls. He didn't find any other exits; there was only one way out.

Toward the chanting voices.

He shuddered at the thought of facing the cultists alone and raised a hand to touch the bead at his throat. "Nine—"

The bead wasn't there.

Hissing in alarm, Arvin dropped to his knees and scuffed around in the ash. Dust rose to his nostrils and he choked back a sneeze. Then he spotted something near the middle of the room—a faint blue glow. Brushing the ash away from it, he saw that it was coming from his bead. It was no longer smooth and round; fully half of the clay had crumbled away and something was protruding out of it—a slim length of crystal that glowed with a faint blue light.

A power stone.

Suddenly, his mother's last goodbye made sense. "Don't lose this bead," she'd told him as she tied the thong around his neck. "I made it myself. I had intended to give it to you when you're older but. . . ." She paused, eyes glistening, then stood. "One day, that bead may grant you nine lives, just like a cat. Remember that—and keep it safe. Don't ever take it off."

"Nine lives," Arvin repeated in an anguished whisper as he stared at the power stone. "And you gave them to me. Why didn't you use them to save yourself instead?" He knew the answer, of course. That his mother must have foreseen her death in the dream she had the night before—and, contrary to her assurances, believed it to be inevitable.

A tear trickled, unheeded, down Arvin's cheek.

Grasping what remained of the bead in both hands, he crumbled it apart. The crystal came away clean, unmarred by its years inside the bead. Holding it between his thumb and finger, he peered into its depths. The faint blue light inside it was the color of the summer sky and seemed equally as limitless. His mother had created this power stone. Somewhere, deep inside it, was a tiny piece of her soul. It whispered to Arvin in a voice just at the edge of hearing, as if calling his name. Allowing his mind to fall into the cool blue depths of the stone, he tried to answer.

Mother?

There was no reply—just a soft sighing, as impossible to grasp as the wind.

Staring at the power stone, Arvin drifted in that vast expanse of blue, no longer aware of his physical surroundings. What was it that Tanju had said? In order to hail a power stone, one had to know the proper name to use. If a stranger had created the stone, Arvin might guess for a thousand years and never come up with the right name. But it wasn't just anyone who had crafted this power stone. It was Arvin's mother.

This time, he used his mother's name: *Sassan?*

Still nothing, just an empty sighing.

Arvin drifted, trying to think what his mother might have named the stone. It would almost certainly be a name Arvin was familiar with—one his mother knew he would eventually guess. She wouldn't have given him the power stone if there were no hope of him ever using it.

He tried again, using the name of the lamasery: *Shou-zin?*

Nothing.

He thought back, again, to his mother's final words to him, wondering if they might have held a clue. But she hadn't said anything, really, after the cryptic message about the bead granting "nine lives." She'd simply given him one of her brief, formal hugs then turned to go, stopping only to shoo the cat away from the door so she could open it.

Suddenly Arvin realized the answer.

Cinders? Arvin tried, using the childish name he'd given the stray cat that had taken up residence with them, despite his mother's protests.

Who hails me?

The voice that answered sounded female—and slightly feline. It was braided together from several different voices, each with a different timbre and pitch. Though they all spoke at once, Arvin knew instantly how many they were—six. The maximum number of powers a power stone could hold.

Arvin hails you, he answered. *Show yourselves.*

Six twinkling stars suddenly appeared in the pale blue sky. They hung like ripe gems just waiting to be plucked, each burning with a light either bright or faint according to the amount of energy that fueled it. Arvin brushed his mental fingers against the closest of these stars—a medium-bright mote of light—drinking in the knowledge of the power it contained. By manifesting this power, he would be able to teleport, just as Nicco did, to any destination he could clearly visualize—the chamber above, for example.

Laughing, he touched another of the motes of light, its glow approximately equal to the first. This second power also conveyed the ability to teleport but was intended for use on another person or creature, rather than on the manifester himself. Strange, Arvin thought, that his mother had included a power that would only affect others. The ability to teleport someone else wasn't exactly a life-saving power. Giving a mental shrug, he moved on to the next.

He touched another of the gemlike stars and discovered it to be a power that would allow him to dominate another person, forcing him to do whatever he bid. He gave a mental hiss of satisfaction—then realized that was the mind seed, reacting to the extremes to which this power could be put. Even so, a part of him savored the idea of using it on Zelia. With it, he could force her to obey his—

Wrenching his thoughts off that path, he shifted his awareness to the next power, which had the brightest glow of any of them. It was also an offensive power, designed for use against other psions. By manifesting it, Arvin could strip a single power from another psion's mind. Permanently.

The fifth power would allow Arvin to produce, from one or both hands, sweat even more acidic than a yuan-ti's. It was a useful weapon—and one that would have the element of complete surprise.

The sixth and final power was an odd one: it would allow him to plant a false memory in someone's mind—but that "memory" could be only a few moments long. What good was that, he wondered. Surely, in order to be convincing, the false memory would have to span a period of days, or even tendays.

It was a strange mix of powers to have chosen. Arvin shrugged, wondering what his mother had been thinking. Perhaps she had been shown, in one of her visions, what Arvin would one day find useful. The teleport power, for example, was just what he needed at the moment. He'd use it to teleport to a spot *beside* the platform where Nicco lay then use the cleric's sash to drag Nicco from the platform. He hoped Nicco would then wake up, and Arvin wouldn't have to face the cultists alone.

Visualizing the chamber above, Arvin grasped the mote of light with his mind. He felt its energy rush into the third eye at the center of his forehead, filling his vision with bright sparkles of silver light. It started to paint the scene he held in his mind, limning it in silver, making it more solid and real. . . .

Then the motes of silver light came rushing back at Arvin, slamming into his mind. Pain exploded throughout his head then arced through the rest of his body, at last erupting out of his fingers and feet. The part of Arvin's mind still capable of coherent thought noted the power crystal slipping from numbed fingers, his legs buckling. Arvin's mind felt hot and ready to burst, like a melon left too long in the sun.

Brain burn.

Slowly, he sat up and shook his head then stared at the power stone that lay, glowing, in the ashes. He felt weak, shaky. He wasn't going to try *that* again any time soon.

Picking up the stone, he thrust it into his trouser pocket. Then he stood and contemplated his options. There was only one way out toward the chanting voices.

Moving quietly, he crept down the hallway. It was arrow straight, with a ceiling that was square, instead of curved—built by humans, rather than yuan-ti. It led to a heavy metal door with a palm-sized sliding panel, set at about eye level. The panel was open. Through it came a flickering red light—and the chanting.

After first making sure he was still invisible, Arvin tiptoed up to the door and peeked through the opening. In the room beyond the door were nearly two dozen people—men and women, judging by the blend of voices, though most had faces so heavily pockmarked it was difficult to recognize which were which. All wore the same shapeless, grayish green robes—and all stank of old, sour sweat. They stood in a loose circle around the wooden statue of Talona that stood, buried to its ankles, in the ashes and crumbled bone that covered the floor. Kneeling next to the statue was a naked man with unblemished skin, save for the chevrons on his arm. His arms were outstretched as if he were about to embrace the pitted stump of wood. For a moment, Arvin thought he must be captive—then he discarded this idea. The man was chanting along with the rest.

Glancing up, Arvin saw a dozen fist-sized balls of flame hovering just below the ceiling, next to the walls. They must have been magical, since there were no visible torches or lamps supplying them with fuel. They burned with a dull, red light, as if close to being extinguished. Something was climbing the wall directly beneath one of them—a rat with ash gray fur and glowing orange eyes. It paused just below one ball of flame and thrust its head inside it. Withdrawing its head a moment later, it scurried down the wall and disappeared into the ash that covered the floor.

Arvin dropped his gaze back down to the cultists. They blocked his view of the far wall, but by leaning to the left and right, he was able to see the side walls. The one to the right had a door. Like the one he was peering through, it was made of thick metal, with a small panel in it at eye level. The inner surface of the door was blackened, as if by fire.

It seemed to be the only way out.

It would be suicide, however, to make a move at this point—even invisible, Arvin couldn't hope to sneak past the cultists. The instant he opened the door, they'd be alerted to the presence of an intruder. All he could do was wait and hope that they would finish their ritual and exit through the second door.

One of the cultists stepped into the center of the circle. He was a large man with hair that grew only in patches. Arvin hissed in anger as he recognized him as the cultist who had forced him to drink the poisoned potion. As the man reached for a pouch on his belt and began untying its fastenings, Arvin held his breath, expecting to see one of the potion flasks. Instead the fellow pulled out two miniature silver daggers, each about the length of a finger and nearly black with tarnish. The tiny weapons were a type of dagger known to rogues as a "snaketooth." Their hollow stiletto blades usually held poison.

Was this some new kind of sacrifice? As the patch-haired cultist raised the daggers above his head—one in either fist—over the kneeling man, Arvin tensed.

The chanting stopped. The patch-haired man's arms swept down—but instead of stabbing the kneeling man, he presented the daggers to him, hilt first.

"Embrace Talona," the patch-haired cultist droned. "Endure her. Prove yourself worthy of the all-consuming love of the Mother of Death."

The kneeling man reached up and took the daggers. "Lady of Poison, Mistress of Disease, take me, torment me, teach me." Then he stabbed the tiny daggers into his flesh. Once, twice, three times . . . over and over again, he jabbed them into his arms, chest, thighs—even into his face—leaving his body riddled with a series of tiny punctures. Meanwhile, the cultists surrounding him chanted.

"Take him . . . torment him . . . teach him. Embrace him . . . enfold him . . . endure him."

The man continued to stab himself, though with each thrust of the daggers, he was visibly weakening. Rivulets of blood ran down his chest, arms, and face, dripping onto his wounded thighs. Even as Arvin watched, the punctures puckered and turned a sickly yellow-green.

Soon the blood that ran down his body was streaked with pus. At last the man dropped the daggers and fell forward into the ash. He clutched weakly at the image of Talona for a moment then his hand fell away, leaving a smear of blood on the pitted wood.

Sickened, Arvin looked away. The kneeling man had been healthy, handsome—but after this ritual, assuming he survived it, the fellow would be as disfigured as the rest of the misguided souls who served the goddess of plague. He was ruined in body, as he must have been in mind.

Arvin was glad that he'd refused Zelia's demand that he pose as an initiate. This would have been the result. This was why Zelia had sown the mind seed—no sane man would ever willingly go through the initiation rite Arvin had just witnessed. To infiltrate the Pox, what was needed was not just a human, but a human whose mind was not his own—a mere shell of a man, controlled by a yuan-ti who was as ruthless as she was determined. Or she could have used a man whose life was measured in days, desperate for a reprieve.

Rusted hinges squealed, breaking Arvin's train of thought. Peering into the room, he saw that the door in the wall to the right—which was indeed the only other exit from the room—was open. The cultists filed out through it. None so much as glanced at the man who lay trembling in the ashes beside the statue of Talona. As the last of them left, the door squealed again and grated shut.

Arvin waited, his eyes firmly on the other door. When he was certain the cultists weren't returning, he slowly eased open the door behind which he stood. Like the other, its hinges were rusted. Each time they began to squeal, Arvin paused, waited for several heartbeats, and resumed his task even more slowly than before. Eventually, the gap was wide enough for him to slip through it.

Hugging the wall, not daring to come any closer to the newly pockmarked man than he absolutely had to—those punctures were fresh, and weeping—Arvin made his way to the other door. The floor felt uneven under his feet; curious, he scuffed the ashes away and saw that it was made from a thick metal mesh. More ashes lay below this grate; he wondered how deep they went. As he stared at the floor, his legs and feet suddenly appeared. Nicco's prayer had at last worn off. The fact that he was visible again was going to make his escape more difficult—assuming the second door really did offer a way out.

As he reached for the handle of the door, he heard a voice behind him.

"You're not . . . one of them," it gasped. "Who—"

Whirling around, Arvin saw that the new convert had risen to his knees. He stared at Arvin, pressing a hand to his temple. His face was ghastly with streaks of ash, yet something about it was familiar.

"Did you bring . . . the potion?" the man asked, his eyes gleaming with hope.

Arvin had no idea what the man was talking about. As the fellow crawled toward him, he shrank against the door. "No," he answered. "And stay away from me."

The fellow sank back down into the ash, the hope in his eyes fading. "But I thought Zelia—"

"Zelia?" Arvin echoed. He stared at the fellow more closely, suddenly realizing where he'd seen him before—on the street near Zelia's tower, two nights ago. Suddenly he realized why the fellow had been holding a hand to his head.

"She did it to you, too, didn't she?" Arvin whispered. "She planted a mind seed in you."

The man nodded weakly. "Three . . . nights ago."

"Abyss take her," Arvin swore softly.

"Yes." The latter was no more than a faint sigh; the blood-streaked man was fading fast. A tremble coursed through his body and sweat beaded his forehead. Arvin stared at him, wondering what to do. If this fellow provided Zelia with the information she wanted, Arvin would become superfluous. Would Zelia remove the mind seed—or simply dispose of him? He fingered his dagger, wondering whether to use it. Would killing this man be a mercy—or a selfish act? It looked like a moot point, however. The fellow had his eyes closed and was lying prone in the ash, his body still except for the occasional tremor.

He was dying.

Of plague.

As quickly as he dared, Arvin eased the second door open. He was relieved to see only an empty hallway beyond it. The hallway ran a short distance, meeting up at a right angle with another, wider hallway.

As Arvin slipped through the door, something under the layer of ash brushed against his boot—another rat. Within heartbeats, his foot grew unbearably hot. The rat—as hot as an ember fresh out of the fire—was burning through the leather of his boot! Arvin kicked it away from him. The rat sailed down the hallway and thudded into the far wall. It shook itself, sat up—and stared at Arvin with its glowing orange eyes. Then it opened its mouth and squealed, shooting a gout of flame from its mouth that licked at Arvin's trousers, scorching them.

"By the gods," Arvin muttered. He'd never seen a creature anything like this. He whipped his dagger out of its sheath, but even as he prepared to throw, squeals immediately sounded from the room where the initiate lay. The layer of ash began to hump and move as dozens of rats scurried up through the grated floor and moved in a wave toward the door. Worried now, Arvin whirled and kicked the door. It slammed shut with a groan of rusted hinges. In that same moment, the first rat attacked. This time its gout of flame struck Arvin's chest, setting his shirt on fire. Tearing at the burning fabric with his free hand, Arvin simultaneously threw his dagger. He grunted in satisfaction as it sank into the rat's chest. The rat fell onto its side, twitched twice—then erupted into a ball of bright orange flame. An instant later, it crumbled into ash and the dagger clinked to the floor.

Summoning the hot dagger back into his hand, Arvin hurried down the corridor, slapping at the smoldering remains of his shirt. He peered quickly down the wider hallway in both directions. Behind him, the other rats scrabbled at the closed door. The wider hallway was completely dark; Arvin wished he'd thought to bring another of Drin's darkvision potions along. From the left came the sound of voices, raised in what sounded like anxious conference—no doubt the cultists, wondering what had caused the noise. From the right came only silence. Arvin hurried in that direction, his gloved hand tracing the wall, fearing that he'd tumble down an unseen flight of stairs at any moment. Behind him, he heard a door open. Clutching his dagger—and wincing as the heated metal blistered his palm and fingers—he hurried on.

The hallway turned a corner just in time to hide Arvin from the lantern light that suddenly filled the hallway behind him. The voices of the cultists grew louder. He heard one of them direct another to check on the initiate and the creak of hinges as the heavy metal door was opened. Meanwhile, the hallway Arvin was hurrying along brightened as whoever was holding the lantern drew nearer to the bend he'd just rounded. Two choices presented themselves: a flight of stairs, leading up, and a doorway in the wall to the left. Arvin immediately sprang for the stairs—then whirled and bolted down them again at the sound of footsteps rapidly descending. Hissing with fear, he rushed to the door instead. It was locked—but the key he still had in his pocket opened it. He wrenched the door open and hurried into the dimly lit room beyond. Closing the door as quickly and quietly as he could behind him, he locked it.

"Nine lives," he whispered, touching the place at his throat where the bead had hung.

He turned, trying to make out details of the room into which he'd blundered. The light was poor; the single oil lamp that hung against one wall had its wick trimmed so low that it cast only a dim red glow that left the corners in darkness. The air smelled bad—a mix of urine, sickness, and sweat. Arvin saw that, aside from the door behind him, the room had no exit. Worse yet, there was a body lying on the floor, next to the far wall. Another initiate—one who didn't survive whatever disease was in the poisoned fangs? No, this "body" was stirring.

Strike swiftly! a voice inside his mind shouted.

Arvin lifted his dagger, ready to throw it, but something made him pause. The creature that rose from its slump to stare at him was horrifying. Its eyes were sunken and bloodshot, its body misshapen and gaunt, its skin a diseased-looking yellow-green with the hair falling out in clumps . . . except for the heavy eyebrows, which met above the nose.

"Naulg?" Arvin whispered, lowering his dagger.

The creature wet its lips with a forked tongue. "Ar . . . vin?" it croaked.

The voices in the hallway drew level with the door. There were two of them—a man and a woman, arguing about whether the initiate had been the one to open the door of the "chamber of ashes," then slam it shut. "Something stirred up the ash rats," the woman insisted. The man at last concurred.

"Search the upper chamber," he shouted at someone down the hall.

Hearing that, Arvin prayed that Nicco wasn't slumbering there still. He reached for his breast pocket. Perhaps the lapis lazuli would allow him to contact Nicco before—

The pocket was gone—he must have torn it away with the rest of his burning shirtfront—and so was the lapis lazuli. Arvin cursed softly as he realized the stone must be lying in the hallway where he'd killed the rat.

Another voice joined the two outside the door. "What's happened?" It was male, and sibilant, the inflection that of a yuan-ti. The voice sounded vaguely familiar, but Arvin couldn't place where he might have heard it before.

Naulg, meanwhile, shuffled across the room to Arvin, his arms wrapped tightly around his stomach, his eyes glazed. "It hurts," he groaned, letting go of his stomach to pluck imploringly at Arvin's sleeve. His fingernails were long and yellow, almost claws. The stench that preceded him made Arvin's eyes water, but Arvin kept his face neutral. He remembered, from his days at the orphanage, how it felt to have a stench spell cast on him—how the children would pinch their noses and make faces as they passed. The crueler ones would throw stones.

Arvin might have lost the lapis lazuli, but he still had his power stone. He thrust a hand into his pocket, trying to decide whether he should teleport Naulg out of here. The rogue was obviously unstable; if Arvin tried to sneak him out, he'd probably give them both away. But brain burn wasn't something Arvin was willing to risk, not with a yuan-ti just outside the door.

Naulg's voice rose to a thin childlike wail. "It *hurts.* Help me, Ar . . . vin. Please?"

Arvin winced. Naulg's plea reminded him of how he'd felt during those long months in the orphanage before he'd finally found a friend: lost and alone—and frightened. He pressed a hand against the rogue's lips. "Quiet, Naulg," he whispered. "I'm going to get you out of here, but you have to be—"

The clicking of the lock's bolt was Arvin's only warning. He whirled as the door opened, whipping up his dagger. As the patch-haired cultist leaned in through the door with an oil lamp, flooding the room with light, Arvin hurled his dagger. The weapon whistled through the air and buried itself in the cultist's throat. The cultist fell, gurgling and clutching at his bloody neck, his lamp shattering on the floor. Arvin spoke the dagger's command word and his dagger flew back to his hand. He caught it easily, despite Naulg tugging on his sleeve.

"*Why?*" Naulg wailed. "Why did they—"

Arvin shook him off. "Not now!" From the hallway came the female cultist's voice, raised in rapid prayer. Arvin sprang toward the doorway, trying to line up a throw at her, but the yuan-ti whose voice Arvin had heard a moment ago stepped into the doorway, blocking it. He was a half blood with a human body and head, but with a snake growing out of each shoulder where his arms should have been. The lamp wick—still burning, feeding off the puddle of spilled oil—threw shadows that obscured the yuan-ti's face, but Arvin could see his snake arms clearly. They were banded with red, white, and black. The snake heads that were his hands were hissing, their fangs dripping venom. If either of them succeeded in striking Arvin, he'd be lucky to feel the sting of the puncture; a banded snake's venom was that swift.

Arvin took a quick step back. The yuan-ti followed him, his head weaving back and forth, his snake arms thrashing and hissing. Arvin wet his lips. Hitting a vital spot with his dagger was going to be difficult.

"Ar . . . vin!" Naulg wailed.

Arvin elbowed the rogue aside.

In that instant, the yuan-ti attacked—not with his venomous hands but with magic. A wave of fear as chilling as ice water crashed into Arvin's mind and sent shivers through his entire body. Gasping, Arvin staggered backward. Irrational fear gripped him, made him fling away his dagger, turn his back to the yuan-ti and scrabble at the wall like a rat. The yuan-ti was too powerful; Arvin would never defeat it. Crumpling to his knees, he began to sob.

A small portion of his mind, however, remembered the pouch he'd stuffed into his pocket—the one that held the assassin vine he'd sold to Naulg—and realized that this could be a weapon. But the main part of Arvin's mind was consumed with the magical fear that engulfed him as water does a drowning man.

Hissing, slit eyes gleaming, the yuan-ti walked slowly and deliberately toward him.

The fear increased, making it difficult even to sob. Arvin was going to die—he knew it. He . . . could . . . never—

Control. The word echoed faintly in Arvin's mind: a thin, distant cry. Then again, louder this time, a shout that throbbed through his mind, pounding like a fist against the fear. *Control! Master the fear. Move!*

Arvin screamed then—a scream of defiance, rather than fear. He yanked the pouch out of his pocket, ripped it open, and hurled the twine at the yuan-ti. The yuan-ti tried to slap the writhing twine aside, but it immediately wrapped itself around his wrist and swarmed up his arm. A heartbeat later it had coiled around his throat. The yuan-ti staggered backward, his snake hands trying to get a grip on the twine around his neck but only succeeding in tearing slashes in his throat with their fangs.

The fear that had nearly paralyzed Arvin fell away from him like an unpinned cloak.

Arvin scooped up his dagger and leaped to his feet. "Naulg!" he shouted, shoving the rogue toward the door. "Let's go!"

The yuan-ti had at last managed to grab the twine with one of his snake-headed hands and was pulling it away from his throat. He glanced wildly at Naulg then gestured at Arvin with his free arm.

"Kill him!" he cried.

Before Arvin could react, Naulg spun and leaped on him. Together, they tumbled to the floor. Naulg was weaker than Arvin, and slower, and Arvin had a dagger in his hand—but he was loath to use it, even though Naulg's eyes gleamed with crazed rage. Arvin vanished it into his glove instead. Seizing the opportunity, Naulg grabbed Arvin by the neck. Arvin was able to wrench one of Naulg's hands free, but the rogue continued to cling to Arvin. He snapped with his teeth at Arvin's shoulder, his neck, his arm. Only by writhing violently was Arvin able to avoid Naulg's furious attacks. Locked together, they rolled back and forth across the floor.

Out of the corner of his eye, Arvin saw the yuan-ti at last succeed in tearing the twine from his neck.

That brief glance was Arvin's undoing. Naulg reared up, lifting Arvin with him, then slammed Arvin's head into the floor.

Bright points of light danced before Arvin's eyes. They cleared just in time for him to see Naulg swoop down, mouth open wide. Arvin felt Naulg's teeth stab into his shoulder—and a hot numbness flashed through him.

Poison.

Naulg's spittle had turned poisonous, just as the old sailor's had.

Arvin tried to draw air into his lungs, but could not. His body was rigid; he was dying. His mind, however, was whirling. He was stupid to have tried to rescue Naulg. He should have listened to the mind seed's warning and killed the rogue the instant he saw him. Instead, the faint hope of aiding an old friend had been his undoing.

Arvin let out a final, hissing sigh. The room, the snake-armed yuan-ti, and Naulg all spun around him as he spiraled down into darkness.

CHAPTER 17

27 Kythorn,
Darkmorning

ARVIN HEARD A SOFT HISSING AND FELT BREATH STIR THE HAIR NEAR his left ear. Someone was bending over him, touching his cheek with something as soft as a feather. It tickled against beard stubble then was gone.

He opened his eyes and saw he was lying on the cold stone floor of the chamber in which he'd discovered Naulg. The transformed rogue was nowhere to be seen, but the yuan-ti was still there. The half blood was kneeling beside Arvin, one of his snake hands hovering just above Arvin's face. Its flickering tongue was what had brushed against Arvin's cheek a moment ago. Arvin wet his lips nervously. The eyes of the banded serpent were small, slit— and held just as much intelligence as the half blood's human eyes. Those serpent hands—like the yuan-ti's voice—seemed vaguely familiar to Arvin, yet he knew he'd never met this yuan-ti before. He decided that the sense of familiarity must have come from one of Zelia's memories.

The yuan-ti's face was illuminated by what was left of the lamp the patch-haired cultist had dropped. The wick was still burning, fueling itself from the patch of spilled oil. Arvin could feel the oil seeping into his hair. Instinctively he turned his head away from it and felt a sharp pain in his shoulder—the one Naulg had bitten. The venom in his spittle had come close to killing Arvin.

He stared up at the yuan-ti. "You neutralized the poison, didn't you?" He didn't bother to ask why; that much was obvious as soon as the yuan-ti spoke.

"Did you come here alone or with others?" it hissed.

"I. . . ." Arvin let his words trail off, pretending to be mesmerized by the venom beading at the tips of the snake hand's fangs and the head's slight swaying motion. All the while, he was thinking furiously. The yuan-ti must have heard Arvin and Naulg use each other's names and realized Arvin had been making a rescue attempt. If Arvin could convince the yuan-ti he was on his own, it might protect Nicco—but he'd doom himself. He needed to convince the yuan-ti that it was more than a rescue mission, that there was vital information only he could provide.

Which, fortunately, there was.

"Rescuing my friend was only one of my goals in coming here," Arvin answered. "I also wanted to learn more about the Pox. I was ordered to spy on them by a yuan-ti who goes by the name of Zelia." As he dropped the name, he searched the yuan-ti's eyes for a sign of recognition.

The yuan-ti's expression remained unchanged. "Describe her," it ordered.

"She looks human, but with green scales. There's nothing else, really, to distinguish her."

"Her scales had no pattern?"

Arvin shrugged. "Not that I noticed. They were just . . . green."

The yuan-ti considered this. Fortunately, it didn't ask about Zelia's one distinguishing feature—her hair. Hair color and length was something the scaly folk generally took no notice of; all human hair looked alike, to them. Even so, Arvin wasn't going to volunteer the information that Zelia was a redhead. Nor was he going to reveal that she was a psion. She'd be all too easy to track down if he did, and Arvin would become . . . superfluous. But he could whet the yuan-ti's appetite a little.

"I think Zelia works for House Extaminos," Arvin continued.

A sharp hiss from the yuan-ti told him he'd struck a nerve.

"Though that's just a guess on my part," Arvin continued quickly.

"Zelia only engaged my services a few days ago. And she did it in a fashion that hardly endeared me to her. She placed a . . . geas upon me. If I don't return with the information she wants in two days' time, I'll die."

"She's a cleric?"

Arvin nodded.

"Of Sseth?"

"I suppose," Arvin demurred. As he answered, a part of his mind was focused deep within himself, drawing energy up his spine and coiling it at the base of his skull. When he felt the familiar prickle in his scalp, he narrowed his eyes in what he hoped was a suitably sly expression. "If you remove the geas, I'll help you kill Zelia or capture her, whichever you prefer. Do we have a deal?"

The yuan-ti cocked his head as if listening to something then gave a thin-lipped smile. Arvin's hopes rose. His charm must have worked. Then he realized the yuan-ti had heard footsteps in the hall. Arvin heard a rustling in the doorway and turned his head. Slowly—he didn't want to give the snake hand an excuse to bite him.

The female cultist who had fled earlier entered the room. She held a flask in one hand. It was metal, and shaped like the rattle of a snake. She started to remove the cork that sealed it then glanced at the yuan-ti, as if seeking his permission.

Arvin wet his lips nervously. "The Pox have already made me drink from one of those flasks," he told the yuan-ti. "The potion didn't work on me. As you can see, I wasn't transformed into a—"

"Silence!" the yuan-ti hissed.

The cultist lowered the flask, a puzzled expression on her face. Seeing it, Arvin realized that the Pox still believed the flasks to contain poison or plague—and he had just come within a word of destroying that fiction. Had he just proved himself too dangerous to be allowed to live? He wet his lips nervously. His dagger was still inside his glove. There was a chance—a very slim chance—that he could kill the yuan-ti before the snake hand sank its venomous teeth into Arvin's throat.

The yuan-ti nodded at Arvin. "This man is dangerous," he hissed. "Why don't you let me feed him the plague, instead?" He held up his free hand, the jaws of its snake head open, imploring.

The cultist hesitated. "It should be a cleric who. . . ." Then her eyes softened, and she held out the flask.

Quicker than the blink of an eye, the yuan-ti's free hand shot out. The cultist gasped as fangs sank into her hand then she immediately stiffened. Unable to breathe, she purpled. Then she toppled sideways, crashing onto the floor like a felled tree.

The yuan-ti picked up the flask with one of its snake hands then turned its unblinking stare on Arvin. "You must be tired—why don't you sleep?" it hissed. "I have no reason to harm you. I *need* you. Sleep."

Arvin felt his eyelids begin to close. He mounted the only defense he could think of—the Empty Mind Tanju had taught him—pouring his awareness out in a flood. But it was no use. The suggestion felt as though it came from deep within; it wasn't something that grasped the mind from without. What the yuan-ti was saying just seemed so *reasonable.* Arvin was safe enough; the yuan-ti wasn't finished with him yet. And Arvin was exhausted, after all. . . .

His heavy eyelids closed as the last shred of his resistance fluttered away like a snake's discarded skin.

27 Kythorn, Fullday

In his dream, Arvin slithered across the floor of the cathedral between its forest of columns, each of which was carved into the form of two vipers twining around each other, one with its head up, the other with its head down. The columns supported an enormous domed ceiling of translucent green stone through which sunlight slanted, bathing everything in a cool light reminiscent of a shaded jungle. Water from the fountain that topped the cathedral dripped through holes in the roof, pattering onto the floor like rain.

Just ahead was one of the Stations of the Serpent—an enormous bronze statue of the god in winged serpent form, his body banded with glittering emeralds and his mouth open wide to reveal curved fangs of solid gold. The base of the statue was wreathed in writhing jets of orange-red fire, symbolic of Sseth's descent into the Peaks of Flame.

One day, Sseth would rise from them again.

A dozen other yuan-ti were weaving in prayer before the station, mesmerized by the slit eyes of Sseth. Arvin slithered closer, welcoming the warmth of the oil-fueled fire on his scales. Twisting himself into a coil, he raised his upper body and swayed before the statue then opened his mouth wide in a silent hiss. Feeling a drop of venom bead at the tip of each of his fangs, he lashed forward in a mock strike, spitting the venom forward onto the tray that stood just in front of the statue. The venom landed on the fire-warmed bronze and immediately sizzled as it boiled away.

Hearing the hiss of scales against stone behind him, Arvin turned and saw the priest he had come here to meet. The priest's serpent form was long and slender and narrow nosed, with black and white and red stripes running the length of his body. The part of Arvin's mind that was his own—the part that was observing the dream from a distance, like a spectator watching a dance and unable to resist swaying in time with the music—recognized the priest as the one he—no Zelia—would eventually reduce to a broken-minded heap. But that memory was months in the future.

The priest flickered a tongue in greeting and gestured with a weaving motion. "This way," he hissed.

Arvin followed him down a side corridor. The priest led him to one of the binding rooms. Inside it, on a low slab of stone, lay the body of a young man—a yuan-ti half blood. The head was that of a snake, with yellow-green scales and slit eyes, and each of the legs ended in snakelike tails, rather than feet. The body was naked. Arvin could see that a number of its bones were broken; one jagged bit of white protruded through the skin just below the shoulder. The left side of the face was crushed, caved in like a broken egg.

Two yuan-ti were working on the corpse, binding it in strips of linen. Both were male and both wore tunics that bore the Extaminos crest. They appeared human at first glance, save for slit eyes and brown scales that speckled their arms and legs. They worked quietly and efficiently—but carefully, giving the corpse the respect it was due as they wound the linen around it. When finished, the binding would be egg shaped, a symbol of the spirit's return to the cloaca of the World Serpent.

"Leave us," the priest said. The two servants exited the room, bowing.

The priest slithered up to the corpse and raised himself above it. Arvin slid around to the other side of the slab. He didn't recognize the dead man, but he knew who he was—a younger cousin of Lady Dediana. Arvin let his eyes range over the body. The corpse reminded him of prey that had been constricted then rejected as unfit to swallow.

"Keep your questions simple," the priest said. "The dead are easily confused. And remember, you may ask only a limited number of questions. No more than five."

Arvin nodded. The information he wanted was very specific. Five questions should do nicely.

The priest swayed above the body in a complicated pattern, tongue flickering in and out of his mouth as he hissed a prayer in Draconic. As the prayer concluded, the mouth of the corpse parted slightly, like that of a man about to speak. "Ask your questions," the priest told Arvin.

Arvin addressed the body. "Urshas Extaminos, how did you die?"

"I fell from a great height." Urshas's voice was a creaking echo, his words sounding as if they were rising out of a dark, distant tomb. Broken bones grated as his smashed jaw opened and closed.

Interesting. Urshas's body had been found late last night, lying on a road near the House Gestin compound. The tallest of the viaducts that spanned that road was only two stories above street level—and was three buildings distant from the spot where the body lay. "How did you reach that height?" Arvin asked.

"Sseth's avatar carried me. We flew."

The priest gave a surprised hiss. "How do you know it was Sseth's avatar?" he asked.

Arvin's head snapped around angrily. "*I* am asking the questions."

Urshas, however, was compelled to answer: "She told me so."

"She?" Arvin said aloud—then realized his error. His inflection had turned the word into a question.

"Sibyl," Urshas answered.

"Sibyl who?" Arvin asked.

"She has no house name," Urshas croaked. "She is just . . . Sibyl."

"Sibyl," a different voice—one that wasn't part of his dream—hissed from somewhere close at hand.

Roused to partial wakefulness, Arvin contemplated the dream. At the time of the memory he was reliving, the name Sibyl had meant nothing to Zelia. But it would, in the months to come. Arvin tried to cast his mind into Zelia's more recent memories, to conjure up an image of Sibyl, but he could not. Instead he made a momentary connection with one of his own memories—of the way Sibyl's name had popped into his head while Gonthril was questioning him. With it came a realization. It was desperately important that Zelia find out if Sibyl was involved in all of this. If she was, it would give Lady Dediana the excuse she needed to—

"Sibyl," the voice hissed again.

Fully awake at last, Arvin opened his eyes the merest of slits. He was lying, bound hand and foot, in a different room than the one in which he'd fallen asleep. Its walls were round, not square, and were made of green stone. By the hot, humid feel of the air, the room was above ground, and it was day. The floor was covered in a plush green carpet, on which stood a low table. A yuan-ti half blood—the one from the crematorium—was seated at the table, his back to Arvin. He stared at a wrought-iron statuette of a serpent that held in its upturned mouth a large crystal sphere. Sitting next to it on the table was the lamp that illuminated the room.

"Sibyl," the yuan-ti hissed again "It is your servant, Karshis."

Silently, Arvin took stock. His glove was still on his left hand, but the restraints that held him made it impossible to tell if his magical bracelet was still on his wrist. His wrists were bound together behind his back by something cold and hard; his ankles were similarly restrained. A length of what felt like a thin rod of metal connected these restraints. Glancing down, he saw that his ankles were bound by a coil of what looked like rope but felt like stone. He was hard-pressed to suppress a grin. He'd braided the cord himself from the thin, fine strands of humanlike hair that grow between a medusa's snaky tresses. The Guild and Secession weren't Arvin's only customers, it would seem.

Nine lives, he thought to himself, adding a silent prayer of thanks to Tymora.

The yuan-ti's attention was fully focused on the sphere, which was filled with what looked like a twisting filament of smoke. This slowly resolved into a solid form—a black serpent with the face of a woman, four humanlike arms and enormous wings folded against her back. As the winged serpent peered this way and that with eyes the color of dark red flame, tasting the air with her tongue, Arvin made sure he remained utterly still, his eyes open only to slits. Then the winged serpent turned her head toward Karshis, as if she'd suddenly spotted him. Her voice, sounding far away and thin, rose from the sphere. "Speak," she hissed.

Karshis wet his lips. "A problem has arisen," he said. "A human spy has discovered the hiding place of the clerics. Fortunately, we captured him."

"A human?" the black serpent asked scornfully. Her wings shifted, as if in irritation.

"He says he was sent by a yuan-ti who calls herself Zelia. She may be a *serphidian* of House Extaminos."

Though the word was foreign, Arvin recognized it as one of the titles used by the priests of Sseth. He suddenly realized that the entire conversation between Karshis and Sibyl was being conducted in Draconic—a language he didn't speak. Zelia spoke it, however. And the mind seed—a familiar throbbing behind Arvin's temples— allowed Arvin to understand it.

"Shall we abandon our plan?" Karshis asked.

The winged serpent inside the sphere fell silent for several moments. "No," she said at last. "We will move more swiftly. Tell the clerics to abandon the crematorium—"

"It has already been done. They have scattered into the sewers."

"—and to prepare to receive the potion tomorrow night."

"That soon?" Karshis exclaimed. "But surely it will take more time than that to replace Osran. We haven't—"

"You dare question your god?" the winged serpent spat, her voice low and menacing.

"Most assuredly not, oh Sibilant Death," Karshis groveled. Both of his secondary heads hissed as he twined his arms together. "This humble member of your blessed ones simply expresses aloud the confusion and uncertainty that inhabits his own worthless skin. Forgive me."

"Foolish one," she hissed back. "Sseth never forgives. But your soul will be spared a descent into the Abyss—for now. There's still work ahead. See that it is done well. The barrel will be delivered to the rotting field at middark. When it arrives, be sure the Pox save a little of the 'plague' for themselves. After tomorrow night, we'll have no further use for them."

"What of the spy?" Karshis asked.

"Kill it."

Arvin's heart thudded in his chest.

"But find the *serphidian* first," Sibyl continued. "If she has disappeared into some hole, use the human as bait to lure her out again."

"Yes, Great Serpent," Karshis answered, bending his flexible upper torso into a convoluted bow. "I will set our spies in motion. She will be found."

The image inside the sphere dissolved into a coil of dark mist then was gone.

As Karshis rose from the table and lifted the sphere out of the statuette's mouth, Arvin closed his eyes fully and made sure his breathing was even, slow, and deep. Soft footsteps approached. Karshis prodded him in the ribs with a foot then continued across the room. Arvin heard a key rattle in a lock, the groan of hinges as a door opened and closed, and a click as the door was locked again.

He waited for several moments then opened his eyes. He spoke a command word and the stone coils that bound his wrists and ankles turned back into braided hair and fell to the carpet. Arvin sat up, quickly coiled it, and stuffed it into a pocket.

Tymora willing, he would get out of here—wherever *here* was.

Crossing to the door, Arvin inspected it carefully. He didn't want to fall victim to another glyph like the one Nicco had used. This door, however, appeared unmarked. Reaching for his belt buckle, Arvin bent down and fitted its pick into the keyhole. One pin clicked into place, a second—

The door suddenly smashed into his face, sending him crashing to the floor. Blinking away the pain of a bloodied nose, Arvin realized Karshis had returned. The yuan-ti was trying to force the partially open door, which was blocked by Arvin's body.

One of Karshis's arms snaked in through the opening, its snake hand trying to sink its fangs into Arvin. He flung himself to the side, barely avoiding the bite. "*Shivis!*" he cried, summoning his dagger to his glove. He leaped to his feet in the same instant that Karshis lunged into the room. As the yuan-ti's snake hand lashed forward a second time, Arvin met it with his dagger, slicing cleanly through the snake hand's neck. The head dangled from a thread of flesh, its eyes glazing as blood pumped from the wound.

Karshis staggered back, hissing with pain, and grabbed at the door with his other snake hand to steady himself. Seizing his chance, Arvin leaped forward and slammed the door shut, crushing the second snake hand between the door and its frame. All that remained was the yuan-ti's main head—which, unfortunately, also had venomous fangs.

The yuan-ti writhed in pain then rallied. Suddenly, the room was plunged into darkness. Unable to see anything, surrounded by a darkness through which not even the faintest pinprick of light penetrated, Arvin backed up warily, his dagger at the ready. He could still hear the yuan-ti's labored breathing; Karshis was standing somewhere just ahead of him. Could the yuan-ti see in the dark? Would he use it as a screen for a retreat—or an attack? Taking aim by ear, Arvin readied his dagger for a throw.

Karshis slammed into Arvin, knocking him sprawling, facefirst, onto the carpet. Arvin slashed wildly with his dagger—only to feel a snake arm coil around his wrist, trapping it. A second snake arm coiled around Arvin's other wrist, but this snake arm was slippery with blood. Arvin wrenched one hand free and scrambled to his feet. He tried to leap away, but Karshis's grip on his other arm was too strong. Held fast, like an unwilling dance partner, all Arvin could do was flail in a circle around Karshis, blindly dodging the yuan-ti's attempts to bite him. Venom sprayed him each time the yuan-ti lunged and missed.

The dagger was still in Arvin's gloved hand, but that was the arm Karshis held. Despite the wounds Arvin had inflicted upon him, Karshis was still swift and strong; even if Arvin was somehow able to wrench his arm free, a dagger might not be enough to stop the yuan-ti.

The power stone, however, might.

If it didn't knock Arvin flat with brain burn.

Swiftly—between one desperate dodge and the next—Arvin cast his mind into the crystal. Linking with it took only a fraction of a heartbeat; finding the power he wanted among the five glittering gem stars that remained took only an instant more. Arvin felt its energies flow into his third eye, as before, and also into a spot on his spine directly behind his navel. Silver motes of light danced in his vision— and this time coalesced into a line of bright silver light that lanced out at Karshis through the magical darkness. In that same instant, Arvin felt Karshis's dry, scaly skin suddenly become slippery and wet with ectoplasm and knew that, this time, his manifestation had been a success. Strangely, though, he was unable to lock his mind on the spot to which he wanted to teleport Karshis. His mind remained unfocused, blank, *scattered.*

Karshis's body suddenly flexed, bringing his venomous fangs within a hair of Arvin's throat. Then it exploded. One moment Karshis was lunging at Arvin—the next, a fine spray of mist erupted from him, soaking Arvin, his clothes, and the carpet around him. What remained of the yuan-ti fell to the floor with a thump.

Hissing with relief, Arvin dragged the body out of the pool of darkness and stared at Karshis's corpse. Its flesh was dotted with thousands of tiny tunnels from which blood was starting to seep; it seemed as if miniscule portions of the yuan-ti had been teleported in all directions. Arvin shook his head in disgust and spat until the bloody, scale-flecked mist was gone from his lips. He wiped his face with a trembling arm then reached into his pocket and pulled out the power stone. The second teleport power had seemed so benign— had he used it improperly? Somehow, he didn't think so. He hadn't suffered brain burn, this time. He hissed in relief, glad he hadn't tried to use it to teleport Naulg.

Out of long habit, he raised a hand to his throat to touch his bead then remembered it wasn't there. "Nine lives," he whispered, shoving the stone back into his pocket.

Then he picked up his dagger and rose to his feet. The door was unlocked and open—and the hallway it opened onto was silent. No one, it seemed, had heard the sounds of the fight.

Arvin whispered a prayer of thanks to Tymora. He'd really have to fill her cup this time. But there was much he had to do, first. He had to rescue Naulg . . . and find Nicco.

But not necessarily in that order.

CHAPTER 18

*28 Kythorn,
Morning*

IN HIS DREAM, ARVIN STARED AT THE WEMIC WHO STOOD BEFORE HIM, flexing his muscles. The creature was magnificent, his body that of a lion and covered in lustrous golden fur, his upper torso that of a human. The wemic's face was a blend of both: human in overall appearance, but framed by a mane of coal black hair and with pupils that were vertical slits. His long tail swished back and forth behind him, fanning the grass that stretched in an unbroken plain to the distant mountains.

"How does it feel," Arvin asked, his forked tongue flickering in and out of his mouth as he spoke, "to occupy that body?"

In answer, the wemic threw back his head and roared then flexed his forepaws, rending the earth with his claws. "Powerful," he replied, throwing a low growl into the word.

"And your psionics?" Arvin asked.

The wemic squatted, placing his human hands on the ground, then slowly bent his human torso backward. He held the pose for a time then balanced awkwardly on his front paws and raised his hindquarters into the air, tail lashing wildly as he sought to maintain the *asana*. He went through the entire series of *asanas*—slowly and clumsily, making up in brute strength what he lacked in balance and flexibility—and was panting by the time he had finished.

"I've lost some of the powers you had when you created me," the wemic answered at last. "The more powerful ones are gone."

Arvin gave a soft hiss of satisfaction. "Keep that in mind," he told the wemic. "And remember what happened to the seed who tried to defy me with what she retained."

The wemic, which shared the memory of the first seed—the dwarf whose mind Arvin had squeezed into a pulp by a psychic crush—nodded slowly.

"Events have progressed swiftly over the past seven days," Arvin told the wemic. "Garrnau has been padding about, insisting that she be the delegate to the Three Cities. She felt that you have been too . . . preoccupied over the past few days to present the Ten-Paw tribe's case clearly. She will need to be dealt with. And there has been a communication from Lady Dediana. She thought it might be amusing if you were to be caught in the act of devouring one of Lord Quwen's horses—especially if it was the racing stallion she sent him two days ago, as a truce offering."

The wemic threw back his head and gave a roaring laugh. It was followed, incongruously enough, with a satisfied hiss. "All of Ormath will spring for their saddles and swords," he said. "To protect their precious herds from—"

"Yes," Arvin said. "And Hlondeth will have one less bothersome neighbor."

The wemic leveled a stare at Arvin. "And what of me . . . afterward?"

Arvin smiled. "Cast your memory back to the elf seed in Xorhun, and the lizardman seed in Surkh. Did I abandon them?"

The wemic shook his head. "No." A guarded look crept into his eyes. "As of seven days ago, you had not."

Arvin laid a palm against the wemic's broad chest and let his fingers slide seductively through the downy chest hair. "In fact," Arvin murmured, his flickering tongue tasting the lionlike musk that hung heavy in the air, "in the case of the elf seed, I continue to visit—frequently."

The wemic mirrored Arvin's lascivious smile. He wrapped muscular arms around Arvin, drawing him to his chest. Arvin felt claw tips poke with delicious pain into his back as the wemic lowered his head to kiss him. Surrounded by the wemic's mane and musky scent, Arvin met the kiss with a hunger of his own—

Suddenly, Arvin was awake—and gasping for air. He didn't know which was more disturbing, the image of Zelia twining herself about a creature that was half lion—or the thought of her making love to herself. A part of him, however, insisted on lingering on the memory. Zelia was a beautiful woman, after all. . . .

Shaking his head, Arvin pushed the thought from his mind. Control, he told himself.

Rising from his bed, he crossed the rented room and splashed lukewarm water on his face from a ceramic bowl that stood on a low table. Sunlight streamed in through the shutters on the room's only window; it was going to be another hot, humid day.

If he didn't find Nicco, it might also be his last.

Suddenly furious, he hurled the bowl across the room. It hit the far wall and shattered, leaving a spray of water on the wall. He manifested his dagger into his glove and stared at it. Maybe he should just end it, he told himself. Death was one way to prevent Zelia from claiming him, from *winning*. One quick stab and it would all be over. . . .

No. He was thinking like her again. It was doing him no good to rage. What he had to do was stay calm, try to find a way out of this mess. There was still time—though not much. He rubbed his temples and squeezed his eyes shut, forcing the anger aside. Then he disappeared the dagger back into his glove.

He sank into a cross-legged position on the floor and slowed his breathing then ran through the series of mental exercises Tanju had taught him. When he had finished, he assumed the *bhujanga asana*. It came even easier to him than it had before; his body seemed to adopt the pose of its own accord. As he held the *asana*, muscles straining, he cast his mind back over the events of the evening before.

After escaping from Karshis, he'd hurried back to the crematorium to search for Nicco and Naulg. He no longer had the key—Karshis must have taken it from him—but by fumbling at the blank stone wall, he'd found the door and its keyhole by feel and managed to pick the lock. He'd crept in, half expecting to find the Pox inside, but the room had been empty. So, too, was the platform where Nicco had fallen into magical slumber. Arvin had tossed a loop of rope onto the platform and pulled it back again and again, hoping that, by some miracle, Nicco might still be lying there, invisible. But the cleric was gone. Whether the cultists had found him or he had simply woken up and teleported away, Arvin had no idea.

Arvin had searched the room again—thoroughly—but the results were the same as before. The only way into the crematorium proper, it seemed, was through the platform. Without the key, Arvin was only going to wind up in magical slumber, as Nicco had. If Arvin was going to get in, he'd need Nicco's help.

Slipping out of the building again, Arvin had once more turned, reluctantly, to his Guild contacts. He put out the word that he was looking for a man of Nicco's description—or a man matching Gonthril's description, or even Chorl's. Someone, somewhere, had to have seen one of them. But without coin to pry open their lips, the Guild members weren't saying anything. "No," was the usual reply, "haven't seen anyone like that."

At last, exhausted, Arvin had rented a room above a tavern near the waterfront. The bed still stank of the tarred hair of the sailor who'd occupied it last, and the room was stiflingly hot, despite the window. Arvin had lain awake long into darkmorning, listening to the sounds of laughter and ribald singing from the tavern below. He'd tossed and turned, hissing with frustration at having come so close to salvation—only to lose Nicco. If only he knew where the rebels had holed up after abandoning the chambers under the garden. . . .

Ending the *asana*, Arvin rose to his feet and rubbed his forehead. The ache of the mind seed had grown worse, and was now a constant throbbing behind his eyes that filled the front of his head from temple to temple. Frustrated, he banged his hand against the shutters, sending them flying open. No wonder the room was so hot; the window faced north, away from the breeze that blew off the harbor.

Arvin stared up at the city. Though his room occupied the fifth floor of the tower, its window was barely level with the foundations of the buildings farther up the hill, those of the yuan-ti section of the city. Only by craning his neck could Arvin see the snake-shaped fountain that topped the cathedral dome, or the spires of the palace, or the Nesting Tower. . . .

Arvin frowned as he stared at the distant, flitting specks of flying snakes. It was odd that Nicco had chosen that location to teleport them to when they had fled from the Plaza of Justice. Why teleport into an area frequented by yuan-ti nobles? Arvin would have thought the cleric would have teleported them somewhere that, to Nicco, represented safety.

Maybe, Arvin mused, he had. What was it Kayla had said about Gonthril's choice of hiding places for the Secession? The rebel leader liked to use spots Lady Dediana would least suspect—a private garden of the Extaminos family, for example.

And perhaps, also, the Nesting Tower that housed many of the royal family's flying snakes.

Arvin nodded; it made sense. Gonthril had been so certain he and his fellow rebels would be able to slip into the royal palace undetected. What was it he'd told them? Closing his eyes, Arvin tried to recall the words he'd overheard, just before Nicco's glyph had frozen him in place. "One sip of this," Gonthril had said, and something about the royal family mistaking the rebels for "his little pets, out for a middark soar."

Arvin realized what he'd been talking about—a potion of polymorphing that would turn the rebels into flying snakes. And not just any flying snakes, but ones that Osran Extaminos would recognize: his pets. In order to polymorph that precisely, the drinker of the potion had to have seen the creature he wanted to polymorph into firsthand. That much Arvin knew from his conversations with Drin.

The rebels were using the Nesting Tower as one of the Secession's hiding places. Arvin was certain of it.

Tymora willing, they would be there.

And Nicco would be with them.

28 Kythorn, Highsun

Arvin stood at the base of the Nesting Tower, resisting the urge to pinch his nose against the smell of snake feces. The slave who tended the flying serpents was mucking out the holes, sluicing them out with water. It ran in stained torrents down the sides of the tower into drains in the courtyard below—which was unoccupied at the moment, due to the filthy spray. The flying snakes, meanwhile, wheeled in elegant circles overhead, their wings flashing green, red, and gold in the sun.

Stepping warily to avoid a rain of murky, stinking water, Arvin waved at the slave who was floating above. He was an older man with a shaved head, clad only in sandals and a filthy pair of trousers. His skin was as brown as a cobra.

"Slave!" Arvin shouted through cupped hands. "Descend. At once!"

The slave glanced down, hesitated, and hung the bucket he'd been holding on a hook on his belt. Slowly he began his descent. He halted several paces above Arvin and eyed him suspiciously—and for good reason. Flying snakes were expensive pets and there had been attempts to steal them in the past. For this reason, the outer walls of the tower had been bespelled with a magical grease to discourage climbing; it glistened in the sunlight. With a magical rope—like the one Chorl had used to help Arvin and Kayla climb down into the garden—Arvin might have bypassed the greased wall under cover of darkness. But he didn't have another climbing rope, and it was broad daylight. The only way up was via whatever magical item the slave was using to levitate.

"Yes?" the slave asked.

Arvin stood with hands on hips, swaying impatiently. Deliberately, he let his tongue flicker in and out of his mouth as he stared up at the slave. "A yuan-ti died three nights ago," Arvin told him. "He was killed by a flying snake—one with venom powerful enough to fell a yuan-ti. That snake is to be dispatched."

"Which one is it?" the slave asked. "I'll—"

"No you won't," Arvin said. "I will."

"But it's highsun," the slave protested. "The snakes are all away from the—"

"Don't question me, *slave*," Arvin spat, easily imitating Zelia's imperious tone. The throbbing in his head helped; it gave an edge to his impatience. "Come down here at once, or you will be punished." Arvin twitched his upper lip, as if about to bare his fangs. "I'll see to it myself."

The slave's face paled and he sank to the ground. As he landed, Arvin eyed his sandals. They were made from unblemished white leather—pegasus hide.

The slave stood, eyes obediently on the ground but with a wary look on his face. It was clear he didn't believe Arvin's story, yet at the same time he was frightened of disobeying a yuan-ti. Seeing this, Arvin drew upon his psionic talent. The base of his scalp prickling with energy, he spoke softly to the slave. "You've served the Extaminos family for many years, slave. You can be trusted to keep a secret. It wasn't just any yuan-ti that was killed, but Osran Extaminos, tenth in line for the throne."

The slave had been standing with his head tilted, as if listening not just to Arvin but also to a distant sound —the charm's secondary display. "I heard the palace slaves whispering about Osran," he confided. "I didn't believe it was true."

"I assure you, it is," Arvin said gravely, steering the slave into the shade of a nearby building. "We suspect the snake that killed him was a polymorphed assassin. I'm here to lay a trap for him. I need to take your place for the day. Give me your clothes and bucket . . . and those sandals."

The slave looked at him warily, "I can't. I'll be punished if they find out."

"They won't," Arvin snapped—a little more testily than he'd intended. "Nobody will know." He reached into his pocket, pulled out his last three silver pieces, and pressed them into the slave's hand. "Take the day off. Treat yourself to a bath—a long one. Don't come back until sunset. I'll leave the sandals in the bucket, under here." He gestured at the base of a nearby ramp. The shadowed hollow under it would make an excellent hiding place.

The slave stood, staring uncertainly at the silver coins on his palm. "I don't know. . . ."

Arvin rubbed his throbbing temples. The midday heat was making them pound worse than ever. "You don't know *what?*" he snapped, hissing angrily.

The human swallowed nervously. "Maybe we should speak to my master, first, before. . . ."

Arvin couldn't stand it any longer. Humans weren't supposed to question—they were meant to obey. His whole plan was about to come undone. He couldn't permit that to happen. His angry hiss turned into a whisper. *"Shivis!"*

Quick as thought, the dagger was in his gloved hand. He thrust forward and the blade bit deep into the slave's stomach. "You're not"—*stab*—"speaking"—*stab*—"to your master!" Arvin hissed.

The slave sank to the street, eyes wide and mouth making faint gasping sounds. His bucket clattered to the ground beside him, spilling its last dribble of water. Something warm and sticky coated Arvin's hand; he licked his fingers and was rewarded with the sweet taste of blood. "Insolent human," he muttered, the last word twisting his lips.

Only then did he realize what he'd done.

He stared down at the slave, horrified. Then he realized the man's blood was still on his lips. He spat and nearly threw up. He slammed his fist into the wall. "Gods curse you, Zelia."

Realizing he might be in trouble—big trouble—if any of the militia were nearby, Arvin looked wildly around. No one was in sight. Disappearing the dagger into his glove—he'd clean it later—he shoved the body under the ramp. He crouched for a moment in the cool shadow, and closed his eyes against the throbbing in his head, saying a prayer for the slave's soul. Then, hands shaking, he unfastened the man's sandals. He glanced at the bright red drops of blood on the white leather then at the body. "I didn't mean to . . . " he started to say. Then he sighed. What did it matter what he meant to do? The man was dead.

Arvin pulled off his boots and fastened the sandals to his feet then crawled out from under the ramp. The three silver pieces lay on the street, next to a smear of blood. He left them where they'd fallen. Picking up the empty bucket, he walked toward the tower.

The magical sandals proved surprisingly easy to use. Arvin merely visualized himself rising and up he went. The tower was six stories high, but fortunately, he had no fear of heights. He stared, unconcerned, as the ground seemed to fall away below him. He landed easily on the rooftop, which was bare aside from a single tap whose pipe rose out of the ceiling like an erect snake.

A trapdoor at the center was closed with a padlock. Using the picks in his belt buckle, Arvin quickly opened it. He lifted the trapdoor and saw a stone staircase that spiraled down. Sunlight slanted into it through holes that gave access to the niches in which the flying snakes nested. The air in the narrow stairway was dry, dusty, and hot—and stank of snake.

Arvin stepped down into the stairway then sat and pulled off the sandals. They were valuable, and he might need them to get out of the tower, but he didn't care. He didn't want them on his feet a moment longer than was absolutely necessary. He placed them, together with the padlock, inside the bucket and set it aside. Then he closed the trapdoor and tiptoed down the stairs, barefoot.

The stairs seemed to spiral down endlessly. After a while the air grew cooler as Arvin descended below the last of the beams of sunlight—and below ground level. At last, after several more turnings, they ended. The light at the bottom of the stairs was extremely poor, but Arvin had a sense that the staircase opened onto a large room. A new odor filled the air—rodent droppings. As his eyes adjusted to the gloom, Arvin saw that the walls of the room were lined with cages. Rats scrabbled within them, filling the air with their soft scurrying. Remembering the rat that had burst into flames, Arvin shuddered. But at the same time he wet his lips in anticipation and strained forward, half expecting to sense the rat's body warmth through the pits in his—

No. He was thinking like Zelia again. The rats were *not* food.

Not for him, at any rate.

He made a circuit of the room, inspecting the floor in front of the cages. Had he gone to all this trouble—even killed a man—for nothing? Then he spotted something that gave him hope—faint scrapes in the layer of grime that covered the floor. The cages had been moved recently. Peering at the wall behind them, he saw a faint line: a hidden doorway. Warily, he grasped the top cage and began to move it aside.

Pain exploded in his head as something smacked into the back of it. Staggered by the blow—and the jolt of magical energy it unleashed—Arvin fell against the cages, which crashed down on top of him. The rats inside them squealed furiously and nipped at his hands as he scrambled to knock the cages aside, to see who had attacked him.

"Wait!" Arvin gasped, flailing under the cages. "I'm a friend. I'm—"

"Arvin!" a harsh voice said, completing the sentence for him.

Chorl stood looking down at him. The balding rebel must have been invisible until his attack. He held the end of his staff level with Arvin's chest, ready to thrust it at him. Its tip crackled with magical energy, filling Arvin's nostrils with a sharp, burnt odor. With a sinking feeling, Arvin saw that it was poised over his heart. All that was holding Chorl back was righteous anger—and the need to tell Arvin off. "You dare come back here, you scaly bastard?" he spat. "This time, I'll see to it that—"

"Get Nicco," Arvin said. "He'll vouch for me."

"Nicco's busy."

Relief washed through Arvin. "He escaped?" He started to let out a slow hiss but abruptly covered it with a whispered prayer. "Tymora be praised. Tell him I've learned more about what the Pox are up to. They're taking delivery of the transformative potion tonight—a whole barrel of the stuff. It's going to be delivered to the cultists in a field, and I can tell you which one. Your people will need to move quickly, if you want to prevent them from tainting the public wells. They—"

"You want Gonthril to rush everyone out to some field," Chorl guessed. "Tonight."

Arvin nodded. "It will be your one chance to stop the cultists," he said then quickly added, "and to stop the yuan-ti who are really behind this."

"And you, of course, will lead us to this field."

"No. All I promised was information—which I've just delivered—in return for a . . . healing from Nicco. Saving Hlondeth—preventing its humans from being transformed into yuan-ti—is in the Secession's hands now."

Chorl scowled. "You yuan-ti," he growled. "You think you're so superior. Did you really think we'd fall for—"

Seeing what was coming, Arvin attacked—not with his dagger, but with the power stone. Linking with it was a matter of mere thought; manifesting the power he wanted came almost as swiftly. Even as Chorl thrust his staff at Arvin's chest, a rush of energy filled Arvin's third eye. He caught the head of the staff with his bare palm just before it struck his chest and heard it begin to sizzle. The staff's magical energies flared—then were snuffed out as the acid in Arvin's palm ate away at the staff. The wood crumbled back like a candle being melted by a blast of flame.

Shoving what remained of the staff—a mere stub that Chorl held in one hand—Arvin sent the rebel staggering backward. Arvin followed him, sending a stinging flick of acid at Chorl from his dripping hand. The rebel winced as it struck his cheek.

"Be thankful I chose to dissolve your staff," Arvin hissed angrily. "I could have chosen your hand—or your face."

Chorl gaped at the stub he held in his hand then threw it aside. "I *knew* you were a yuan-ti," he snarled.

Too late, Arvin realized he'd manifested a power that "proved," in Chorl's mind, that Arvin was a yuan-ti. As Chorl drew a dagger and moved forward, holding it low and ready, Arvin manifested his own dagger into his glove. He heard the scrape of stone—the hidden door behind him was opening. So filled with fury was he, that he ignored it. Hissing with rage, he drew back his arm for a throw at Chorl's throat even as Chorl tensed for a charge.

"Peace!" a man's voice shouted.

Calm flowed into Arvin, filling him with a warm, slow languor. Part of his mind recognized it as a magical effect, but he couldn't seem to find the energy to fight it. As his anger drained away, he lowered his dagger. His free hand rubbed his temple and he stared at Chorl, who stood, staring at his own weapon. Why had Arvin wanted to hurt the rebel? Oh yes, because they were fighting. He'd been angry about . . . something.

Nicco stepped forward, plucked the dagger from Arvin's hand, and shoved it into the sheath on Arvin's belt. "Arvin," he said, wrapping an arm around his shoulder. "I've been looking for you. Come with me." He turned. "You too, Chorl."

Feeling relaxed and content, Arvin walked with the cleric through the hidden door—not even caring that his back was to Chorl—and down a short corridor. It led to a wine cellar. Enormous barrels, split with age, lined the walls. A staircase that used to lead up to ground level was nearly buried under rubble from the Nesting Tower's construction. A dozen or so rebels were in the cellar, some sitting and conversing in low tones, others drowsing on blankets spread on the floor. They turned to stare at Nicco and Arvin as they entered the room. Several leaped to their feet, drawing swords. One of them— Gonthril—held up a hand, halting them. His intense blue eyes took Arvin's measure for a long time before he spoke.

"Four rebels are dead," he said, toying with one of the rings he wore. "Explain to me why we should let you live."

Wetting his lips nervously, Arvin glanced at Nicco. The cleric gave a nod that Arvin hoped was meant to be encouragement.

"Osran wasn't the only yuan-ti involved with the Pox," Arvin began. "There are at least two more. Karshis, who I killed—"

This brought a murmur of surprise from the rebels.

"—and the yuan-ti who is Karshis's superior: an abomination named Sibyl. She's delivering the transformative potion to the cultists tonight, and I know where that delivery is going to take place. All of the cultists will be together in one place. If you want to finish what you started, tonight may be your only chance."

Gonthril reached into his pocket and withdrew a silver ring—the one that compelled the truth. "Tell me how you know this," he said, handing it to Arvin.

Arvin put on the ring then recapped what had happened in the crematorium, reciting from memory the conversation he'd overheard between Karshis and Sibyl. "It took me a while to figure out which field they must have been talking about," he said. "The Pox like to use places associated with disease: the sewers, the closed slaughterhouse, the crematorium. The 'rotting' field is the one that lies trampled and burned. The field used for last year's Rotting Dance."

Chorl, standing beside Gonthril, listened with narrowed eyes. "An open field," he grumbled, "with no place to hide. If this is an ambush, we'll be cut down like ripe wheat."

The rebels muttered; Gonthril silenced them with a curt gesture. "Arvin has told us the truth," he told them. "Tonight may be our only chance to save our people. It's worth the risk; we'll send someone ahead to scout the field, and the rest of us will wait here until just before middark. In order to prevent information from . . . slipping out again, Arvin will remain here with us, under guard." He turned to Arvin. "Agreed?"

Arvin wet his lips. "Agreed," he said.

Gonthril held out a hand and the ring was suddenly loose on Arvin's finger. Arvin took it off and passed it back to him.

As the rebels clustered around Gonthril, talking, Nicco led Arvin aside. Arvin dropped his voice to a whisper, and spoke urgently to the cleric. "I've given the rebels what they need," he reminded Nicco. "Now how about that restorative prayer?"

Nicco shook his head. "I'm going to need all of the blessings Hoar has bestowed upon me for tonight's work. There are more than a dozen people who must be rendered invisible—not to mention bestowed with protective blessings—and other prayers will be needed. Once we have dealt with the cultists—"

"But that won't be until middark!" Arvin protested. "And tomorrow will be the seventh day since the mind seed was planted. It could blossom as soon as middark turns. By making me wait, you're condemning me to—"

"I condemn you to nothing," Nicco flared. "I have promised you a restorative prayer, and you shall receive it—when I am ready. Until then, you are in Hoar's hands. If it is his will that the mind seed blossom at the turn of middark, it may blossom. But I think that it will not. Hoar showed you mercy once, already, in the pit. He will surely continue to do so."

Arvin nodded glumly. His own clever trick was working against him. Nicco might be convinced that Hoar favored Arvin, but Arvin himself knew otherwise. He reached to touch the bead at his throat then remembered it wasn't there any more. He thrust a hand into his pocket instead, clenching the power stone in his fist.

"Nine lives," he muttered.

Then he stood and watched—and waited and fretted—as Nicco, Gonthril, and the rebels conferred with each other, laying plans for tonight's ambush.

28 Kythorn, Evening

Arvin squatted next to a low stone wall, staring at the field it enclosed. The Rotting Dance had been held eight months ago, at Highharvestide, but the field still had a ripe, rotten odor. Low, mushy mounds of what had once been piles of rotten fruit and vegetables dotted the ground, and a large patch of blackened earth near the center of the field marked the spot where the bonfire had raged. The field was fallow and tangled with weeds.

Like Arvin, Gonthril and the other rebels had been rendered invisible by Nicco's prayers. Nearly two dozen of them were waiting, positioned around the field, for the cultists to appear. Unlike Arvin, though, they were free to move about. At Chorl's insistence, Gonthril had ordered Nicco to use an additional prayer on Arvin, one that prevented him from moving. All Arvin could do was breathe and blink.

Was it middark yet? He had no idea. His temples pounded like drums. For the moment, however, his mind was still his own.

Sweat trickled down his sides as he waited in the darkness. Even though the sun had set long ago, the air was still muggy and hot. The heavy gray clouds that had been building over the Reach had at last moved inland over Hlondeth, and, judging by the low rumbles of thunder in the distance, would soon break. In the meantime, they obliterated the moon, throwing the vineyards and fields outside the city into utter darkness. Out of the corner of his eye, Arvin could see the green glow of Hlondeth's walls, several fields distant.

The rumble of wheels announced the approach of a cart. Though he strained to turn his head, he still could not move; he was only able to see the cart after it turned into the rotting field. It was being driven by a yuan-ti who sat balanced on a coiled serpent's tail. A cask the size of a wine barrel was lashed in the back. It was too dark to make out details of the yuan-ti's face, but Arvin could see his head snaking this way and that as he scanned the field. While the yuan-ti seemed at ease, his horse did not; it kept tossing its head and whickering, as if it had sensed the invisible rebels. When the yuan-ti reined it to a halt, the horse pawed at the ground with a hoof, digging a furrow into the stinking soil.

The yuan-ti glanced up at the sky, as if trying to tell what segment of the evening it was, then continued glancing around the field. As his head turned toward the spot where Arvin crouched, Arvin would have tensed—if he had been capable of it. Instead he let out a low hiss of relief as the yuan-ti's glance continued past him.

A moment later, the yuan-ti's head whipped around as something materialized on the far side of the cart. It happened in the blink of an eye. One moment the burned patch near the center of the field was bare of all but ashes, the next, a dozen cultists were standing there, holding hands. Their gray-green robes made them almost invisible in the darkness. Their pale, pox-spotted faces were faint white ovals.

Arvin felt something brush against him and heard the faint tinkle of Nicco's earring.

"At the signal, use your dagger," the cleric breathed, touching his arm. "Aim for the yuan-ti."

Suddenly, Arvin could move. Wary of making any noise, he rose slowly to his feet—only to find that his legs were numb from having remained in a crouch for so long. He winced at the hot tingling of blood returning to his feet, and nearly stumbled.

The attack began without him.

A shrill whistle sounded. A heartbeat later, from several points around the field, came the *thwap, thwap, thwap-thwap* of crossbow strings releasing. Several of the cultists staggered, clutching at the bolts that had suddenly appeared in their bodies. In that same instant, the rebels became visible. Arvin saw Gonthril, running at the cultists with his sword raised, and other rebels closing with spears and swords. Nicco had not yet become visible, but Arvin could hear him praying. The cleric's voice came from a spot near the cart.

The yuan-ti also heard the prayer. Hissing with anger, he turned to face the spot where Nicco must have been standing. A tangle of weeds next to the cart came alive and began wrapping themselves around an invisible form.

Belatedly, Arvin threw his dagger, but in that same moment, the yuan-ti reared up. The dagger plunged not into his throat but into his coiled body, well below any vital organs. Hissing in frustration, Arvin threw up his bare hand, summoning his dagger, which yanked free of the yuan-ti's scaly body. Arvin caught it—but the yuan-ti had seen him. The yuan-ti stared at Arvin, turning the full force of his magical fear on him.

Arvin staggered backward under a wave of magical fear. He had to flee, to get out of here, to *run*. The dagger forgotten in his fist, he whirled to look for an escape—

Something jerked him to a halt: the mind seed. The pain of it was excruciating. *No*, an inner voice shouted. Zelia's voice. *The driver must be captured. He's the proof I need that Sibyl is—*

"Get . . . out of . . . my . . . head!" Arvin raged.

Whatever else the mind seed might be saying, he didn't hear it. The compulsion to flee was gone—but his head felt as though it were about to explode from within. Each thought was a slow, sluggish step, like wading through tar.

Only dimly aware of the battle that was raging in the field, Arvin caught no more than brief glimpses of it. Despite the fact that they were outnumbered two to one, the cultists had magic on their side. One of them waved his hand in a circle, causing a greasy, roiling darkness to rise from the field and engulf the four rebels closest to him. Three staggered away, retching, while the fourth sank to his knees and disappeared from sight under the black cloud. Another rebel, trying to spear a cultist from a safe distance, was swarmed by a cloud of insects summoned by a cultist; the rebel dropped his spear and staggered away, screaming and slapping at the thousands of black dots that covered every bit of exposed skin. Chorl managed to take one of the clerics down with a well-thrown dagger, but then one of the Pox grabbed him from behind and drew a finger across Chorl's throat. The bare-handed attack opened a gushing wound; when the cultist released Chorl, the rebel fell to the ground.

Gonthril accounted for two of the Pox in quick succession, lopping the head off one and disemboweling the other. Then one of the cultists lunged past his sword and slapped a hand on the rebel leader's chest. Gonthril ran the cultist through, but the damage had been done. The rebel leader staggered, his arms shaking so violently that he nearly dropped his sword. A hideous cough that sounded like hiccupping laughter burst from his lips as he doubled over, chortling and gasping.

"Cackle fever!" one of the rebels closest to him shrieked—then turned and ran away.

Nicco, visible now, was frantically dodging as the yuan-ti lashed down at him from his seat on the cart, trying to sink his fangs into Nicco's neck. Unable to move, his feet entangled by the weeds, Nicco prayed loudly, one hand raised imploringly to the heavens. A glowing shield of magical energy sprang up in front of his hand, but even as Nicco swept it down between him and the yuan-ti, the driver lunged past it and sank his fangs into Nicco's shoulder. The cleric sagged to his knees as venom coursed through his blood.

"No!" Arvin cried.

Thunder boomed overhead once, twice, a third time—Hoar's death knell for his fallen cleric?

One hand clutching his pounding head, Arvin raised his dagger. The yuan-ti was still sitting on his cart, no more than a dozen paces away. An easy target, in daylight—but rain was falling in thick, splattering drops, further obscuring his aim. Arvin threw—and hissed in satisfaction as he saw the driver thrash once then crumple in a loose coil.

The rebels were faltering, more than one of them turning to run, but somehow Gonthril managed to pick up his sword and rise to his feet. "Finish them," he croaked, staggering weakly forward.

Amazingly, the rebels rallied. Weapons raised, they moved grimly forward.

The Pox seemed to have had enough. They stared, stricken, at the dead yuan-ti. Then one of the cultists leaped up onto the cart. "Form a circle!" she shouted. "Join hands with me."

They did and, a moment later, were gone.

So, too, was the barrel. It had been teleported away—right out of the straps that had bound it to the cart.

Arvin, nearly blinded by the falling rain that soaked him to the skin, staggered forward to the place where Nicco had fallen. The cleric, he saw to his infinite relief, was still alive. One of Nicco's hands gripped a deep puncture in his shoulder, which closed, healing itself, as he completed his prayer. As Nicco tore his feet out of the weeds that had entangled them, Gonthril staggered up to him, a stricken look on his face.

"We have . . . failed," the rebel leader gasped. "They took . . . the potion."

"Yes—Hoar be praised," Nicco said, a gleam in his eye.

Seeing Gonthril's mute question, Nicco explained. "Not only did I dispel the potion's magic and negate its poison; I also placed a blessing upon it. The 'potion' is harmless—to anyone but the Pox. When they drink what is now holy water, Hoar's vengeance will be complete."

Gonthril laughed then—a genuine laugh, if weak. Then a violent trembling shook his limbs and he sagged weakly.

As Nicco moved toward Gonthril, Arvin clutched at the cleric's rain-soaked shirt. Arvin didn't have much time left. He could feel the mind seed unfolding within his head, pushing aside his awareness, crowding out his thoughts with a fierce, gloating joy.

"The mind seed," Arvin gasped. "It's blossoming. Nicco, *please*, pray for me."

Nicco glanced at him, sympathy in his eyes, then turned away. "Gonthril first," the cleric said over his shoulder. "His need is more urgent."

"No!" Arvin wailed.

Too late. Nicco had already slipped out of Arvin's grasp. As the cleric prayed over Gonthril, healing him, Arvin sank to his knees under the weight of the crushing pain that filled his head. Moaning, he felt the mind seed expand and start to push his awareness aside. He saw Nicco finish his prayer and turn toward him, but then his vision dimmed. What remained of his consciousness began to slough away like a torn and tattered skin.

CHAPTER 19

Z ELIA CAST HER AWARENESS AHEAD TO THE TAVERN WHERE THE
human seed waited. He sat at a table near the far wall of the
room, at the same table where she herself had been seated seven nights
ago. As she watched, he paid for a mug of ale then tipped it back,
swallowing whole the small egg it contained. That—and his loose,
swaying body posture—convinced her. He had succumbed.

Her tongue flickered in anticipation. How delicious he looked.

Her lapis lazuli was affixed to his forehead. He must have used it
to manifest the sending Zelia had just received. The wording of his
brief message had been tantalizing. At long last she would have the
proof she needed that Sibyl was moving against House Extaminos.

She walked down the ramp and into the tavern, pausing to give the
half-dozen sailors who were drinking there a quick scan. Silver flashed
in her eyes as her power manifested, but it revealed nothing—all of
the sailors were exactly what they seemed. She crossed the room and
joined the human seed at the table. He rose and greeted her with a
passionate kiss that sent a fire through her, but she pushed him away
and indicated that he should resume his seat. There would be plenty
of time for pleasure, once this bit of business was concluded.

"Tell me what happened," she said.

"I found myself lying in a field," the human seed told her. "The signs of a recent battle were all around me. There were seven bodies—six clerics of Talona and one yuan-ti."

"Describe him."

"He was a half blood with a human upper torso. His scales were black, banded with purple. The bands had a faint diamond pattern within them."

Zelia nodded. The pattern was typical of the yuan-ti of the Serpent Hills. Interesting.

"There was no sign of whoever attacked the clerics. They must have hauled their dead and wounded away. I must have been fighting on the side of the clerics, since I was left for dead."

"The attackers were probably the humans who killed Osran," Zelia mused.

The human seed stared at her. "Osran is dead?"

Zelia smiled. "A lot has happened in the past seven days." She stared at the human seed, noting its strong resemblance to the one human who had escaped after Osran was assassinated—Gonthril, the rebel leader. The faction he led was little more than an annoyance, but perhaps it could be manipulated into providing a distraction, should Lady Dediana choose to move against Sibyl. All that would be required would be to replace Gonthril with the human seed.

Or perhaps, she mused, to seed Gonthril himself.

The barman approached with a mug of ale. Zelia glared at him, sending him scurrying away, then turned to the human seed. "You said you found proof that Sibyl is backing the Pox?"

The human seed nodded. "That's why I asked you to come here. I found a letter in a scroll tube the yuan-ti was carrying. It's addressed to Karshis, from Ssarmn. It makes reference to Talona's clerics—and to Sibyl." He placed a scroll tube on the table and pushed it toward Zelia. "It should prove quite . . . enlightening."

Zelia stared at the tube. "Read it to me."

The human seed showed no hesitation as he tipped the document out of the tube; perhaps her suspicions were unfounded. Unrolling the document, he began to read in a low voice. " 'Karshis,' it begins, 'Please relay, to Sibyl, a warning about the potion. If the clerics drink it and survive—and are not transformed—an unforeseen result may occur. Any psionic talents they have will be greatly enhanced. You may inadvertently produce an opponent capable of—"

"Give me that," Zelia said, thrusting out a hand. Anticipation filled her. Perhaps the letter would also contain proof that Sibyl was not the avatar she claimed to be, but mortal, like every other yuan-ti.

The human seed passed her the letter. She avidly began to read.

The letter flared with a sudden brilliance that left her blinking and unable to see. Too late, she realized it had been a trick, after all. The letter had contained a magical glyph—one that had blinded her. She could still hear the human seed, however, and could still pinpoint his position by his body heat. Immediately, she attacked. Wrapping mental coils around him, she flexed her mind, squeezing with crushing force—only to feel her target slip away. Suddenly his mind was gone—empty—and her coils were passing through insubstantial, vacuous emptiness. The human seed's mind had retreated into the distance, leaving her with nothing to grasp.

Expecting an attack in return, she threw up her own defense, raising a mental shield and interposing it between them. From behind it she lashed out with a mental whip—and hissed aloud, a vocalization that overlapped the hissing of her secondary display, as she felt it lash the human seed's ego. Surprisingly, he had maintained the same defense, instead of switching to a more effective one. Of course, he had only half of her powers. Gloating, Zelia drew back her mental whip to strike again.

She heard a sound that startled her: a faint tinkling, like the sound of distant bells. She recognized it in an instant as a secondary display and knew that it was coming from the human seed across the table from her, but something was somehow *wrong* about it. Then she realized what it was. The tone of the sound was subtly off. It wasn't *her* secondary display.

It wasn't a human seed who sat across the table from her, but Arvin.

She almost laughed aloud at the notion of a novice psion—a mere *human*—daring to attack her. Arvin, with his pathetic roster of powers, what was he trying to do, charm her? He didn't stand a chance of—

Her arrogance was nearly her undoing. Arvin's mind thrust into hers like a needle into flesh, forcing a link between them. Into this breach quested mental strings, seeking to knot themselves into the part of Zelia's mind that controlled her physical body. She recognized the power he was using at once. He was hoping to dominate her, to make her his puppet. Where had he learned to manifest that power? It should have been well beyond him.

No matter. Unwittingly, he'd played right into her hands. She'd half expected her seed to go rogue—it happened with disturbing regularity when she seeded a human. And so she'd manifested a turning upon herself. The strings of mental energy suddenly doubled back on themselves and needled their way into Arvin's mind instead.

There, they knotted.

"Stop fighting me," Zelia commanded.

Arvin did.

Zelia tasted the air with her tongue, savoring the odor of fearful sweat that clung to Arvin. This was going to be so much fun.

29 Kythorn, Highsun

Arvin trudged along the seawall, his footsteps as reluctant as a man going to the execution pits, with Zelia a step behind him. She was still blind, but it didn't matter. She had manifested a power that allowed her to "see" without eyes. She was taking a great delight in humiliating him; back at the Coil she'd forced him to order a second ale, and a third, and crack the eggs they contained over his head, much to the uproarious delight of sailors at a nearby table. The yolk was still in his hair and growing crustier by the moment in the highsun heat. Then, when they began walking along the seawall, she'd forced him to deliberately bump into a burly sailor who had flattened Arvin's nose when Arvin "refused" to apologize. Arvin's nose was still stinging from the punch and blood was dribbling down his lips and dripping off his chin. But none of the people they passed—even those who spared Arvin a sympathetic look—dared to question what was going on. They took one look at Zelia, lowered their eyes, and hurried past.

Arvin had tried to fight the domination Zelia had turned back on him, but to no avail. She controlled his body completely. All he could look forward to, once she was done playing with him, was a swift death—preferably a bite to the neck, like she'd given her tutor.

Arvin had been stupid to think he could defeat her, even with Nicco's help. The glyph the cleric had provided hadn't even slowed Zelia down. So much for the "nine lives" Arvin's mother had promised. The power stone was still in his pocket—Zelia had been too confident in her domination to bother searching him—but the two powers that remained weren't going to be any help. He wished the teleportation power he'd used to kill Karshis were still available. He could have used it when they first embraced in the tavern.

In the end, Arvin thought, he'd gone in a circle. Despite all of his efforts, he'd only succeeded in replacing one form of control with another. Nicco had managed to purge the mind seed even as it blossomed, but at the end of it all, Arvin had wound up back under Zelia's thumb. She couldn't force him to do anything truly self-destructive—to stab himself, for example—or else the domina tion might be broken. But she could certainly think up numerous lesser torments.

Smelling a foul odor, he glanced at the waves that gently lapped against the base of the seawall and shook his head. The sewage outflow—in this spot, seven nights ago, the circle had begun.

"Stop," Zelia ordered.

Arvin jerked to a halt, wondering what new instrument of torment Zelia had just spotted. Perhaps she was going to order him to flagellate himself with the coil of line that lay on the seawall, next to a bollard. The monkey's fist at the end of it would inflict some fine bruises. . . .

He glanced back at her and saw a malicious smile on her lips.

"Turn toward the harbor," she said.

Arvin did.

"Jump into the water."

Arvin's body tensed. No. He wouldn't. That was *sewage* down there—foul-smelling, filth-choked water, laden with disease. The stench of it brought back all of Arvin's worst memories of the orphanage and the cruel punishments Ilmater's priests had inflicted on him. Of being wrapped in magical stink that wouldn't wash off, that made him the subject of the other children's taunts and jeers, of—

"I said *jump!*" Zelia hissed.

Arvin couldn't. He *wouldn't*. . . .

Like a cloak falling from his shoulders, the domination fell away. In the split second that Arvin knew he was free of it, he realized something more. If he tried to attack Zelia directly, he wouldn't stand a chance. Zelia was swifter than he, more powerful. He needed a distraction.

He jumped.

Cold water engulfed him. He came up with his eyes and mouth screwed shut and heard Zelia's hissing laughter above him. Ignoring the disgusting slime on his lips, the feel of sewage on his skin and the sludge dripping from his hair, he forced his eyes open. Immediately, he spotted his weapon—the monkey's fist. Energy flowed up and into his third eye then streaked out in a flash of silver toward the monkey's fist, which rose into the air, spinning, as if twirled by an invisible hand.

Hissing in alarm, Zelia spun around—but too late. The monkey's fist shot through the air toward her, striking her temple with a loud thud. Eyelids fluttering, Zelia tried to turn back toward Arvin but only managed a half-turn before sagging at the knees—then suddenly collapsing.

Arvin, still treading water, was as surprised as Zelia by the result. Had he really felled a powerful psion with so simple a manifestation as a Far Hand? Quickly, he scrambled up the seawall. He stood, dripping, over Zelia, hardly daring to believe his eyes. Her chest still rose and fell, but she was definitely unconscious. Already a large red welt was swelling at one side of her forehead.

Arvin flicked his sodden hair back out of his eyes and shook his head. "You shouldn't have taught me that power," he told her. Then, seeing the curious onlookers who were starting to collect—including a militiaman who was striding briskly up the seawall—he knelt beside Zelia and pretended to pat her cheek, as if trying to revive her.

The militiaman shoved his way through the spectators and glared down at Arvin through the slit-eyed visor of his cobra-hooded helmet, his crossbow leveled at Arvin's chest. "What's going on here?" he demanded.

Arvin glanced up at the militiaman. "Thieves," he said quickly. "They shoved me off the seawall and knocked my mistress unconscious. They stole her coin pouch." He felt the familiar tingle of energy at the base of his scalp.

The militiaman cocked his head, as if listening to a distant sound, succumbing to the charm. But Zelia was beginning to stir. Arvin prayed she wasn't going to regain consciousness just yet.

"I'm a healer," Arvin continued. "I just have to lay hands on my mistress, and she'll be all right. We don't need your help. Why don't you try to catch the thieves, instead? There was a bald man and a little guy." He pointed. "They went that way."

The militiaman nodded and jogged away. Arvin, meanwhile, flourished his hands then laid them on Zelia's forehead. He linked with his power stone. Seizing one of the two remaining "stars" in its sky, he delved deep into Zelia's mind. It was as he'd visualized it when he'd first explored the mind seed under Tanju's guidance—a twisted nest of snakes. Her powers lay within this writhing mass. They looked, to Arvin, like a cluster of glowing eggs, some large, some small. He hefted them one by one, getting a sense of what each one was. The largest proved to be the one he was looking for. Lifting it from the nest, he crushed it.

Somewhere in the distance, he thought he heard a faint cry. Ignoring it, he linked with his power stone once more and manifested its final power, the one that would allow him to tailor memories. Reaching out with mental fingers, he began rearranging the snakelike strands of thought, braiding them into lines of his choosing.

Zelia's eyes fluttered open. Someone was touching her temple— Arvin! He had just manifested a psionic power on her, had reached deep into her mind and removed something that had taken her nearly a year to learn—the mind seed power. He was still rummaging around inside her head, manifesting a second power on her. Immediately, before he could throw up a defense, she attacked. A loud hissing filled the air as she manifested a power. An instant later it was joined by a sharp exhalation as the air was forced from Arvin's lungs.

Wisely, the other humans fled.

Arvin attempted a gasp, but was unable to inhale; Zelia's power had squeezed his lungs shut. She rose to her feet as he crumpled to his knees and watched, smiling, as his face turned first red, then purple. His eyes were wide, pleading—she would have loved to have heard him beg for his life, but the crisis of breath he was experiencing prevented that. Instead, she leaned forward and let her lips brush his ear as she whispered into it.

"Which was worse," she asked. "The mind seed . . . or this?"

It took all of her self-control to resist sinking her teeth into his throat. Instead, she stepped back and watched him fall to the seawall. He twitched for a time, mouth opening and closing like a landed fish. Eventually, he lay still.

Zelia placed a foot against his back and shoved. Arvin's body flopped over and fell, landing with a splash where it belonged.

In the sewage.

❧

As Zelia slowly regained consciousness, Arvin strode away down the road at a brisk pace, away from the harbor, pleased with the false memory he'd just planted. As he walked, he pulled the power stone from his pocket. Its powers spent, it had stopped glowing.

He tossed it into the air and caught it again then thrust it back into his pocket. "Nine lives," he chuckled.

29 Kythorn, Evening

Arvin paced back and forth across the room, unwilling to look at his friend. Naulg lay on the floor, writhing and gnashing his teeth, trying to strain his hands out of the twine that bound them. The twine—the same one Karshis had used to bind Arvin—was solid stone; Naulg didn't have a hope of slipping it. Even so, he'd continued to struggle long after his wrists were chafed and bloody.

Arvin turned to Nicco. "Isn't there anything we can do for him? There must be some way to reverse the effects of the potion, some healing prayer you could try."

Nicco's earring tinkled as he shook his head. "I've tried everything. Your friend is beyond help. Hoar grant that, one day, you'll find a way to avenge him. There is only one thing, now, to be done."

Arvin forced himself to stop pacing, to turn and look at Naulg. The rogue was barely recognizable. His body was emaciated and his skin was a yellowish green, like that of a plague victim. The last of his hair had fallen out and his distinctive eyebrows were gone. His eyes—which only days ago had still held a spark of sanity—were the eyes of a madman. Sensing that Arvin was looking at him, Naulg bared his teeth in an angry hiss. Venom dripped from his incisors.

Arvin squatted on the floor beside him. "Naulg," he said, touching the rogue's shoulder. "I'm sorry. If only I'd been less concerned with saving myself. . . ."

Swift as a snake, Naulg twisted his body and snapped at Arvin's hand. Arvin jerked it away just in time to avoid the bite. Rising to his feet, he stared down at the creature Naulg had become. Once, this had been a friend. Now, it was nothing but a monster—a dangerous one.

Why, then, were Arvin's eyes stinging?

"Do it," he croaked, turning away.

Nicco nodded. Quickly—perhaps wanting to complete the act before Arvin changed his mind—he chanted a prayer. Arvin heard a rustle of clothing as Nicco bent over Naulg and touched him. There was a choked gasp—then silence.

A tear trickled down Arvin's cheek. He felt Nicco's hand gently touch his shoulder.

"Will you avenge him?" the cleric asked.

Arvin shrugged the hand from his shoulder and angrily wiped the tear from his cheek. "There's no one left to take vengeance on," he said. "The Pox will have consumed the holy water by now; I doubt if any of them are still alive. Osran, too, is dead."

"You're forgetting Sibyl."

Arvin turned to face Nicco. "We know nothing about her," he said. "Where she is, *who* she is. . . . What if she's an avatar, as she claims?"

Nicco's eyes blazed with grim determination. "Even avatars may be defeated," he said. He placed a hand on Arvin's shoulder. "You've proved your worth to Gonthril. And Chorl—may Hoar weigh his soul well—is no longer here to oppose you. It's time for you to take a stand, to join us. Throw in your lot with the Secession." His eyes softened as he smiled. "It wouldn't be the first time a member of the Guild had secretly joined our ranks."

Arvin sighed. The offer was tempting. The Secession just might be his way out of the Guild. But old habits died hard.

"I'm sorry," he told Nicco. "I prefer to work alone. And I need time to hone my talent."

Nicco nodded, dropping his hand. "Hoar be with you, then." He turned and left.

Arvin stared at the door for a long time after it closed. Then he turned to the body of his friend. At least he could give Naulg a proper cremation—something the rogue wouldn't have had if he'd died back in the sewers—or if he'd starved to death in the locked room of the crematorium, where the Pox had left him. Arvin spoke the command word and the stone binding Naulg's wrists turned back into twine. Arvin knelt and gently unwound it from Naulg's wrists.

Slowly coiling it, he paused. Maybe, he decided, Nicco was right.

"I'll make Sibyl pay for what she did to you, Naulg," Arvin promised. "If the gods grant me the chance, I'll avenge you."

Somewhere out over the Vilhon Reach, thunder rumbled.

BOOK II

VIPER'S KISS

Prologue

T HE MAN ON THE SHIP'S FO'C'SLE WOULD HAVE GONE UNNOTICED IN other circumstances. Of average build and height, and with dark, shoulder-length hair drawn into a knot at the back of his neck like a sailor's tarred bun, he would have blended into any crowd. His ornaments were few: a slim chunk of clear crystal hanging on a leather thong at his neck; a bracelet of braided leather around his right wrist; and a thumbnail-sized dark blue stone, flecked with gold, that he wore on his forehead in the spot where the Learned painted their marks.

Two things, however, made him remarkable. The first was his pose. He lay facedown, his rigid arms holding his upper torso away from the wet fo'c'sle deck, his head bent back so that he appeared to be looking straight up at the spot where six sailors toiled above him, reefing the foresail. The second was the fact that he was unclothed, save for his tight-fitting breeches and a black leather glove on his left hand.

Unclothed—on a gusty, open deck in a winter far colder than was usual for the Vilhon Reach—the man seemed oblivious to the brisk wind that blew a spray so chilling that the sailors above worked with clumsy, cold-stiff fingers as they hauled up the canvas sail. He'd been there since dawn first paled the sky, unmoving, unblinking. And not shivering, even though the sun was only now just starting to shine on the gray waters of the Reach.

As the sun crested the horizon, limning the ship in a faint winter light, the man at last moved. He did not so much rise from the deck as flow up into a crouch, then into a standing position. A series of poses followed, joined one to the next like the steps of a flowing dance. The man moved as sinuously as a snake, even though he was human, without a hint of yuan-ti about him. The pupils of his dark brown eyes were round and his skin was smooth and not patterned. When he assumed the final pose, standing on one foot and staring up at the sky through hands that were slowly coming together, as if crushing something between them, the teeth that showed as he grimaced were square and white. Slowly, he lowered his foot to the deck and his arms returned to his sides. Then, his exercises complete, he reached for his shirt.

A wave caused the ship to roll. The man steadied himself by grabbing one of the rope ladders that led up to the mast. Suddenly his smile disappeared. His gaze became unfocused, as if he were staring out at something on the distant horizon. A moment later, he blinked. "The hemp in one of the ratlines is rotten," he called up to the sailors. "If you don't replace it, one of you will die."

He spoke with such certainty that the sailors above shivered. One of them began to whisper a prayer.

The man below dressed himself, pulling on his trousers, shirt, and boots, and belting on a knife so that its sheath was snug against the small of his back. Then, rubbing himself briskly and at last shivering, he strode along the rolling deck and disappeared down the hatch that led to the passengers' cabins.

CHAPTER 1

ARVIN LEANED ON THE SHIP'S RAIL, STARING ACROSS THE WATERS OF the broad bay the ship had just entered. Ahead lay the city of Mimph. Like Hlondeth, it was a port, its harbor crowded so thickly with ships that their masts resembled the bare trees of a winter forest. But there the resemblance ended. Hlondeth had been built by serpents—it was a city of round towers, gracefully arcing viaducts, and ramps that led to rounded doorways reminiscent of the entrance to a snake's burrow. The buildings of Mimph, in contrast, were squat, blocky, and square. The city was a series of sharp angles and edges, from its square windows and doors to the jagged-looking flights of stairs that led up from the piers that lined the waterfront. Where Hlondeth's buildings were of green stone that glowed by night with the residual energies of the magic used to shape them, Mimph's structures were of plain gray granite that had been hewn by hand.

By human hands.

As the ship sailed slowly into the harbor, making its way between the dozens of ships already at anchor, the only other passenger aboard her joined Arvin at the rail. He tasted the air with a flickering, forked tongue then gave a slight sniff. "Humans," he hissed under his breath.

Arvin glanced sideways at the other passenger—a yuan-ti half-breed with a distinctive diamond pattern on the scales of his face. The yuan-ti's head was bald and more snakelike than human, and his lower torso ended in a serpent's tail. He wore an expensive looking winter cloak, trimmed with white ermine fur, that draped all but the tip of his tightly coiled tail. He hugged a stove-warmed stone to his belly; his breath, unlike Arvin's, didn't fog in the winter air. His unblinking, slit-pupil eyes stared with open distaste at the city as he sluggishly turned his head to stare at it.

"How they stink," he hissed, completing his thought.

Arvin's eyes narrowed. He smelled nothing but clean sea air, wet canvas and hemp, and the tang of freshly cut pine drifting over the water from the dockyards, where dozens of naval vessels were being constructed to counter the threat from neighboring Chondath. Arvin said nothing, even though the yuan-ti's remark was designed to goad him. He was the only human aboard this ship who was not a slave; the sailors who toiled above, calling to one another as they furled the sails, all had an **S** brand on their left cheek. The yuan-ti obviously couldn't resist an opportunity to remind the one free human about his place in the world.

Arvin smiled. Enjoy it while you can, he thought. Here in the Barony of Sespech, it's the humans who run things.

Foremost among those humans was Baron Thuragar Foesmasher, the man who had wrested control of Sespech away from its former baron—a Chondathan lackey—nine years ago. The barony was now fully independent, a rising star among the states that lined the Vilhon Reach. It was a place where a man with the right skills and talent could go far.

Arvin, with his psionic talents, was just such a man. And this trip was going to give him the opportunity to prove himself to no less a person than the baron himself.

Six days ago, the baron's daughter Glisena, a headstrong young woman of eighteen years, had gone missing from the palace at Ormpetarr. The baron's spellcasters had been unable to find her; their clerical magic had failed to reveal even a hint of where she might have gone. With each passing day the baron's fears had increased. There had been no ransom demand, no boastful threats from his political enemies. Glisena had just . . . vanished.

Desperate, Baron Foesmasher had turned to his yuan-ti allies. Lady Dediana's militia, he knew, included a tracker said to be the best in all of the Vilhon Reach, a man with an extremely rare form of magic. Perhaps this "mind magic" could succeed where the other spellcasters had failed.

That tracker was Tanju, the psion who was Arvin's mentor.

Lady Dediana, however, was loath to loan Tanju to Baron Foesmasher. There was pressing business within Hlondeth for him to attend to, and he couldn't be spared. Yet a failure to respond to Baron Foesmasher's plea might fray the alliance that had recently been woven between the two states.

Tanju had proposed the solution. In recent months, he told Lady Dediana, he'd taken on an "apprentice," one with a quick mind and immense natural talent. This apprentice, he assured her, could do the job. Delighted at being presented with a solution that would swallow two birds in a single gulp, as the old expression went, Lady Dediana had readily agreed. And so, early yesterday morning, Arvin had set sail for Sespech.

If all went well, he'd never have to return to Hlondeth. Tanju had agreed that, when the job was done—assuming the baron approved— Arvin could remain in Sespech. From time to time, Tanju might contact him and ask for information on the barony, but otherwise, Arvin would be his own master.

Staying on in Sespech suited Arvin just fine. After months of constantly looking over his shoulder, wondering if Zelia was going to suddenly appear, he could at last relax. He felt more at ease already than he had since last summer, when the yuan-ti psion had tried to take over his body with a mind seed. Arvin had narrowly defeated her by planting a false memory of his own death in her mind. In order to maintain that deception, he'd had to remain in hiding since that time. It hadn't been easy.

A light snow began to fall. The yuan-ti beside him hissed once more, tasted a snowflake with a flicker of his tongue, and slithered back to the passengers' quarters. Arvin watched him go, wondering what urgent business had stirred the yuan-ti out of his winter torpor and sent him south across the Reach. This winter was colder than any Arvin could remember, and yet the yuan-ti were more energetic than ever. They seemed . . . restless.

As the ship drew closer to the spot where it was to unload its cargo of wine, sailors scrambled down to the deck where Arvin waited and stood ready with heaving lines. The gap between the ship and the pier narrowed and the sailors whirled the lines—each weighted at the end by a large "monkey fist" knot—above their heads. At the captain's order they let fly, and the lines, looking like white streamers, arced toward the pier. They were caught by dock workers, who hauled them in rapidly hand over hand, drawing toward them the thicker ropes to which the heaving lines were tied, then looping these over bollards on the pier. The sailors, meanwhile, scrambled to the ship's two capstans and grasped the wooden arms. The ship jerked abruptly to a halt as the mooring lines pulled tight. The capstans turned with rumbling squeals as the ship drew closer to the pier.

The hull snugged up against the large, ball-shaped fenders of woven rope that hung against the pier to protect the ship from scraping. One of the fenders tore apart with a wet ripping sound, and Arvin snorted disdainfully. Whoever had made it must have used substandard materials. Not only that, but the weave was sloppy and uneven.

He waited patiently while the ship was secured. Unlike the yuan-ti—who was lethargically directing the sailors hauling his numerous heavy trunks up onto the deck—Arvin was traveling light. A single backpack held his clothing, travel gear, and the handful of magical items he'd been able to make for himself without the Guild finding out about them. Collecting these from their various caches throughout the city had been tricky. If anyone in the Guild had realized that Arvin was thinking about leaving Hlondeth for good, the Guild would have seen to it that he was stopped. He owed them an enormous debt; it had been the Guild that had helped him hide from Zelia these past six months. And Arvin was a valuable resource—a source of magical ropes and nets at mere coppers on the gold piece. Too valuable to ever be let go. If they found out he was planning on running, they'd make sure he'd never do it again. They'd probably lop off a foot, this time.

He sighed and adjusted his pack into a more comfortable position on his shoulders. Inside it, carefully wrapped in cloth against breakage, was a magical item Tanju had given him—a crystalline wand called a dorje. Made from a length of clear quartz as narrow as Arvin's forefinger and twice as long, it pulsed with a soft purple light: the psionic energies Tanju had charged it with. Using it, Arvin would be able to view Glisena—and her current surroundings—as if he were standing next to her. All he need do was touch the dorje to something that had once been close to her. A dress she had worn or, better yet, a hairbrush with a strand of her hair in its bristles.

Once Glisena was located and returned home again, Arvin would, no doubt, be rewarded by a grateful baron. Coin would be involved. Much coin, since Baron Foesmasher was known to be a generous man. Arvin would use the coin to set up shop in Sespech—an independent shop, not one controlled by the Guild. He would at long last reap the full profits of his magical rope making and net weaving, without the Guild dipping a hand in the purse. He'd make a new home for himself far away from the demands of the Guild, the reminders of his years in the orphanage—and the constant slithering hiss of the City of Serpents.

When the ship was secure, one of the ship's officers—a muscular fellow whose braided beard hid most of the slave brand on his cheek—shouted directions. The other sailors unfastened the hatches and swung a crane into place, preparing to unload the barrels that filled the hold. Another officer—this one a yuan-ti with patches of yellow scales on his cheeks and forehead, slithered over to the rail and coiled himself there. He watched the crew with unblinking eyes, one hand gripping a wand whose tip was set with a hollow snake fang. The slaves glanced nervously at him over their shoulders as they worked. The yuan-ti officer did not speak, but his message was clear. Any human seeking his freedom ashore would meet a swift end.

Arvin ignored the yuan-ti officer, taking in the people on the pier instead. The dock workers all appeared to be free men—many were bearded, an affectation that was forbidden to all but the most trusted slaves. Four teenage boys stood on the pier next to them, jostling each other and waving up at the ship, trying to catch the eyes of its passengers. Their voices overlapped as they shouted up to those on deck.

"Come to the Bluefish Inn! Good food, good ale."

"Clean rooms, just five silver pieces a night at the Travelers' Rest!"

"Hey, Mister! Let me show you the way to the Tangled Net Tavern. It's close by."

"Cheap rooms! Cheap rooms at the Silver Sail."

A handful of women were also present. One walked behind a boy who trundled a wheelbarrow laden with a steaming pot of dark red liquid, a ladle in her hand. "Hot mulled wine!" she called. "Sweet and hot, six coppers a cup." The half dozen other women were all doxies in low-cut dresses that were too thin for the winter air, strolling back and forth across the pier in an effort to keep warm.

Arvin's eyes were immediately drawn to one of the doxies, a woman with high cheekbones and dark hair that fell in a long braid down her back. She was pretty, but what had caught his eye was the gesture she just used. She'd raised a hand to her face, pretending to rub her eyes with fingers that were spread in a **V**. As Arvin watched, she lowered her hand, rubbing her fingers against her thumb, then pointed at the ship on which Arvin stood, directing someone's attention toward its passengers.

Arvin nodded. So Mimph had a rogues' guild as well, did it? He supposed that was only to be expected. He glanced around the pier and easily spotted the weedy-looking boy lounging a short distance down the pier. The boy—who looked about fourteen, the age Arvin had been when he found himself on the streets and was forced to steal to survive—acknowledged the doxy with a quick nod of his right fist, then began making his way toward the ship.

Arvin was glad it wasn't the doxy who would be attempting the grab. That was how things had started, the last time around. He looked around, trying to spot the other rogues he suspected would be somewhere nearby. There would probably be three or four in total, all working together in a carefully choreographed routine that would see whatever was stolen passed from one hand to the next. But the others—assuming there were more than just the woman and boy—didn't tip their hands.

Arvin slipped his pack off his shoulders, checked to make sure its flaps were securely fastened, then put it back on. He made a show of nervously patting a trouser pocket, drawing the boy's eyes to it. The only thing in that pocket was the remainder of Arvin's breakfast—some nuts and a dried cheese, wrapped in waxed cloth. His coin pouch with its supply of the local currency—small silver and gold coins called "fists" and "plumes," respectively, after the symbols stamped onto them—was tucked safely inside his boot.

As the ship was made fast, Arvin's eye ranged over the waterfront. The businesses lining it were typical of any port city: warehouses, boat builders, sail and rope makers, taverns, and fish-salting houses. There were also a number of stables, judging by the whinnying coming from some larger buildings farther down the waterfront, buildings that were fronted by fences that led to ramps on the pier. From these, the swift-footed horses of Sespech's famed Golden Plains were loaded aboard ships.

Instead of fountains, which could be found everywhere in Hlondeth, the people of Mimph seemed to prefer religious sculpture. At the top of a short flight of steps leading up from the pier where Arvin's ship had tied up was a low stone dais that supported an enormous gauntlet as tall as a man—the symbol of the god Helm. The statue was brightly polished and appeared to be made of silver. The fingers were stiff and erect, as if the gauntlet were saying, "Halt!" It faced the harbor; on its palm was the symbol of an eye, outlined in blue. The pupil of the eye was an enormous gemstone. Judging by its rich blue color, it might have been a sapphire.

Arvin whistled softly under his breath. Even if the gauntlet were only coated with a thin layer of hammered silver, it would have been worth a fortune. It should have been locked away behind temple doors. Yet there it sat in plain view, unguarded. It might be too heavy to carry away, but surely thieves like the pair below would have found a way around whatever magical wards the statue bore to pluck out the gemstone at the center of that eye.

A horn sounded from somewhere near the center of the city. Once, twice, three times it blared. At the final note, all activity on the pier below stopped. Dock workers, vendors, doxies, the boys from the inns and taverns—even the two thieves—turned toward the sound and raised their left hands in a gesture that mimicked the gauntlet's, their lips moving in silent prayer.

Straining to see past the warehouses that lined the docks, Arvin caught a glimpse of a larger building topped with a square watch tower. Its crenellated battlements had led him to assume it was a keep or well-fortified noble home. He realized it must be a church—one devoted to Helm, the Vigilant One. Unlike the Chapel of Emerald

Scales in Hlondeth, which was topped by a spouting serpent, this church was devoid of any representation of its deity. Instead, its tower was capped by a curved object, also of brightly polished silver, that Arvin guessed must be the horn that had just sounded.

The midday genuflection was brief; moments later the dock workers were back at their tasks. Aboard the ship, two sailors brought out a gangplank, ran it over the side, and lashed it to the rail. Arvin moved toward it, then remembered the other passenger. He stepped back, eyes lowered, as the yuan-ti slowly made his way to the gangplank. The yuan-ti gave a smug hiss as he passed Arvin and slithered down the gangplank to the pier.

Arvin watched, amused, as the weedy-looking boy—pretending to be one of the cluster of touts for the inns and taverns—crowded around the bottom of the gangplank with the other boys. The gangplank suddenly tipped—one of the dock workers must have bumped it—and the yuan-ti stumbled. The boy jumped forward to steady him. As he caught the yuan-ti, his left hand darted into a pocket inside the yuan-ti's cloak. The yuan-ti bared his fangs in an irritated hiss, and the boy backed away, bowing and making a sweeping gesture with his right hand in order to draw onlookers' eyes away from the object he'd palmed with his left.

The yuan-ti wasn't fooled. His slit eyes narrowed, and he touched his pocket with slender fingers. "Thief!" he hissed.

Arvin, descending the gangplank, was surprised by the speed of the yuan-ti's reaction, given the fellow's earlier sluggishness. The yuan-ti lunged forward, grabbing for the boy's wrist.

The boy was faster. The yuan-ti's hand caught his shirt cuff, but he wrenched his arm free and danced back out of the way. His hands—now empty—were spread wide. "He's crazy!" he protested. "All I did was help when he stumbled."

The doxy moved into position at the base of the flight of steps. Arvin knew what would happen next. The rogue would turn and flee—only to run headlong into her. During this "accidental collision" whatever he'd just stolen would be exchanged. Eventually he would be caught, and searched, but by this time the doxy would be well on her way down the pier and out of sight, passing the object off to the next rogue.

The yuan-ti, however, wasn't playing along. Instead of calling out for the militia—or whoever patrolled this city—he used magic. No words were spoken, no gestures used, but suddenly the young rogue's face blanched and his hands started to tremble. Arvin knew just how he felt, having been the target of a yuan-ti's magical fear himself.

"You've . . . made a mistake, sir," he gasped.

The yuan-ti raised a hand and flicked his fingers. Acidic sweat sprayed from his fingertips, striking the boy in the face. The young rogue howled and clawed at his eyes.

"Give it back," the yuan-ti demanded.

The boy turned and ran—blindly, crashing into the dock workers and shoving them out of the way. As he neared the base of the steps, the doxy opened her mouth as if to call out to him then thought better of it and turned away. The rogue waved his arms around, feeling blindly for her, then staggered up the steps.

The yuan-ti turned to the officer on board the ship. "Use your wand," he hissed. "Stop him."

The officer shook his head . . . slowly.

Nearly spitting with anger, the first yuan-ti slithered after the blinded rogue. The stairs slowed him down somewhat—he slithered back and forth along them, humping his serpent's body up them one by one—but the boy's progress was even slower. He ran headlong into a pair of dock workers who were carrying a heavy sack between them and careened backward down the stairs. As he scrambled to his feet again, the yuan-ti lashed out, trying to bite him, and just missed. The yuan-ti's fangs caught the boy's collar, tearing it, and the boy shrieked. "He's trying to kill me! Stop him, somebody!"

Arvin strode down the gangplank and onto the pier. He caught the doxy's eye, made his left hand into a fist, placed it on his open right palm, and jerked his hands upward. *Help him.*

The doxy's eyes widened as she saw Arvin using silent speech. For a heartbeat, she hesitated. Then, as the young rogue on the steps screamed a second time, she shook her head and hurried away.

Arvin was furious. The doxy could easily have saved the boy by "accidentally" colliding with the yuan-ti. She still had eyes to see with, and could have run away, but she'd abandoned him instead. Muttering to himself—and wondering what in the Abyss he was thinking, getting involved in the local guild's business—Arvin ascended the steps. He slipped his gloved hand inside the back of his shirt and grasped the dagger that was sheathed there. With a whisper, he vanished the weapon into his glove; it would make a persuasive backup if his psionics failed. He readied himself to manifest a charm and felt the familiar prickle of energy coiling at the base of his scalp, waiting to be unleashed. But as he reached the top of the steps, he paused. Maybe—just maybe—this dispute would resolve itself.

The young rogue had backed up against the dais that held the statue of the gauntlet. He threw down whatever it was he'd stolen; Arvin heard a metallic clatter as the object hit the cobblestones. "Take it!" the boy screamed. "Take it, and let me be! You've blinded me—what more do you want?"

The yuan-ti slithered over to the object—a small silver jewelry case—and picked it up. He slipped the case back inside his pocket and smiled at the boy, baring his fangs. His long forked tongue flicked in and out of his mouth, tasting the young rogue's fear. "Your death," the yuan-ti answered belatedly. Then he slithered forward.

None of the people in the small plaza that surrounded the statue came to the aid of the blinded boy—thieves must have been as despised in this city as they were in Hlondeth. And yuan-ti must have been just as greatly feared. The humans had parted to let the angry yuan-ti pass, though Arvin noted they weren't lowering their gazes. Instead they stared at the yuan-ti, faint smiles quirking their lips, as if expecting something to happen.

They didn't have long to wait. The young rogue, hearing the rustle of the yuan-ti's tunic and cloak against the ground, spun in place then leaped. His jump carried him up onto the ankle-high dais, where he crashed into the gauntlet. He clung to it like a drowning man clutching a log as the yuan-ti reared above him, savoring his terror. A drop of venom fell from his fangs onto the boy's hair. Amazingly, though the young rogue flinched, he did not move.

Arvin manifested his charm.

The yuan-ti cocked his head, as if listening to a distant sound, then shook it.

"Master yuan-ti!" Arvin called in as obsequious a tone as he could manage, sorry that he hadn't bothered to ask the yuan-ti his name during their day-and-a-half-long voyage across the Reach. "You're needed back at the ship. The crew aren't certain which trunks are yours. Don't waste your time on this boy. You got your jewelry case back. All's well now, friend."

The yuan-ti stared at Arvin for several heartbeats while flakes of snow drifted down between them. His lips twitched in a sneer. "Friend?" he asked.

"Damn," Arvin muttered. Quickly, he spoke the command word that made the dagger reappear in his gloved fist. He started to raise it—but a man beside him caught his arm. The fellow—a large man in a food-stained apron, his lack of a cloak indicating he'd stepped out of a building to watch the fight—shook his head. "No need, stranger," he whispered. "The gauntlet will provide sanctuary."

While Arvin was still trying to get his arm free—the man beside him might have been stout, but he had a grip tight as a coiled serpent—the yuan-ti lashed out at the rogue, fangs bared.

Halfway through his lunge the yuan-ti jerked to a halt. He strained for several moments against an unseen force, his body quivering, then slowly drew back. He studied the rogue for a moment, swaying back and forth, and glanced at the gauntlet. Then he reached down to grab the young rogue's ankles.

It was clear to Arvin what the yuan-ti intended—to drag the boy away from the gauntlet, which obviously was providing some sort of magical protection. But once again, the yuan-ti jerked to a halt, his grasping fingers just shy of the rogue's ankle. The yuan-ti shook for a moment in silent rage, and his face flushed red where it was not covered by scales.

A woman in the crowd chuckled.

The yuan-ti spun and lashed out at her instead.

Screaming, she jerked away, clutching her shoulder. She tried to get to the gauntlet, but the yuan-ti slithered into her path, cutting her off. The crowd, suddenly fearful, broke apart. Several people shouted, and some ran.

The young rogue, still gripping the gauntlet, turned his head from side to side, trying to hear what was happening through all the commotion.

Arvin felt the hand fall away from his arm. He still held his dagger but was jostled by the panicked crowd and could not get a clear throw. Too many people were between him and the yuan-ti—but the crowd was quickly thinning.

The woman who had been bitten, her face pale, backed up until she was against a building then stared with wide eyes at the yuan-ti. "No!" she moaned, her hands clasped in front of her. "Please, no." The yuan-ti's first bite must have failed to penetrate her thick cloak, but his second one wouldn't. The yuan-ti's head wove back and forth, his eyes fixed on her bare hands. If Arvin didn't act swiftly, an innocent woman would die.

Just as the crowd thinned and Arvin raised his dagger, a deep male voice shouted from somewhere to the right. "Hold!" it cried.

Arvin caused the dagger to vanish back into his enchanted glove and turned, but the command wasn't for him. The two armored men who had appeared in the plaza from out of nowhere had their eyes firmly locked on the yuan-ti. Both wore breastplates of brightly polished steel, each emblazoned with the blue eye that marked them as clerics of Helm. Their helmets were without visors, leaving their faces bare. Crimson cloaks hung from their shoulders. Their gauntleted fists were empty; amazingly, neither seemed to be armed.

"You," one of the clerics ordered, pointing at the yuan-ti. "Step away from that woman."

The yuan-ti turned slowly. His lips twitched into a false smile, the effect of which was spoiled by the forked tongue that flickered in and out of his mouth. "I was robbed," he said. He pointed at the young rogue. "By that human."

The second cleric strode over to where the young rogue knelt and took hold of the boy's cloak, dragging him to his feet. "Did you steal from this. . . ." The cleric hesitated, then glanced at the yuan-ti as if uncertain what to call him. "From this gentleman?" he concluded.

The rogue shook his head, but the cleric raised his left hand, turning the eye on the palm of his gauntlet toward the boy. The boy nodded. "Yes," he said in a broken voice. "I stole from him. But I gave back what I took. And he *blinded* me."

The crowd, recovered from its earlier panic, drifted back into the plaza. The yuan-ti drew himself up, imperiously wrapping his cloak around himself. "Take the human away," he ordered, pointing at the rogue. "Throw him in the pit." He began to slither back to the ship.

"Not so fast," the first cleric said, stepping between the yuan-ti and the stairs. He turned to the woman the yuan-ti had been menacing. "Did he harm you, miss?"

Before the young woman could speak, the yuan-ti gave an irritated hiss. "Step aside," he told the cleric. "Step aside, human, or it will go badly for you. I am an important person. I will not be trifled with. Step . . . aside."

Arvin felt the hairs on his arms raise, as if he'd just shivered. Once again, the yuan-ti was using his innate magic—this time, in an attempt to bend the cleric to his will. In another moment the cleric would either step obediently aside—or would feel the sharp sting of the yuan-ti's bite.

Ignoring the yuan-ti's order, the cleric raised his gauntlet and turned its eye toward the woman. He stood, waiting for her answer.

"He bit me," she replied. "By Helm's grace, my cloak stopped his fangs. If it hadn't, I'd be. . . ." She shuddered, unable to say the word.

The spectators crowded forward, calling out to the two clerics.

"I saw the whole thing. . . ."

"The boy did give the jewelry case back. . . ."

"The yuan-ti spat in his eyes. . . ."

"It was a silver case. It's in the serpent man's pocket. . . ."

The yuan-ti's eyes darted right then left. Slowly he raised his hand. Acid trickled down his palm; he was about to use the same trick he'd used to blind the rogue. Arvin opened his mouth to call out a warning—

No need. The cleric neatly sidestepped the flick of acid. A weapon appeared in his fist—a translucent mace that glowed with an intense white light. He used it to knock the yuan-ti's hand aside. The blow was no more than a light tap, but as soon as the mace touched the yuan-ti, his body became rigid. He stood, paralyzed, his eyes wide, the tips of his forked tongue protruding from his mouth, so still and silent that Arvin wondered if he was still breathing.

The cleric's glowing mace disappeared.

"That'll teach him," the man beside Arvin said—the fellow who had grabbed his arm earlier.

"What will they do with him?" Arvin asked him.

"Throw him in prison."

Arvin's eyebrows rose. "But he's a yuan-ti."

The other man shrugged. "So?"

"But. . . ." At last it sank in. In Sespech, the yuan-ti were afforded no special status. Arvin had heard this—but witnessing it firsthand made his mind reel. It was as if sky and earth had switched places, leaving him dizzy. With the realization came a rush of satisfaction that bent his lips into a smile.

"Intention to kill," the stout man continued. "That's what they'll charge the yuan-ti with. If he pleads guilty and shows repentance, the Eyes of Helm may allow him to make atonement. If not, he'll be branded with a mark of justice. If he tries to bite or blind anyone again, he'll suffer a curse—as foul a curse as Helm can bestow."

Arvin whistled softly, glad the clerics hadn't seen his raised dagger. He watched as the second cleric placed a gauntleted hand on the rogue's head and chanted a prayer.

"And the boy?" Arvin asked.

The cleric's prayer ended. The rogue blinked, looked around with eyes that had been fully restored, and fell to his knees, weeping. His right hand raised above his head, he broke into fervent prayer.

Once again, the man beside him shrugged. "He'll probably be released, since he seems to have genuinely repented."

Arvin shook his head, incredulous. "But he's—" Then he thought better of what he'd been about to say. The young rogue could no more cast off his guild—and its obligations—than he could shed his own skin. But if Arvin said this aloud, the fellow next to him might think back to Arvin's earlier actions and draw some conclusions that could bode ill for Arvin. It was bad enough that Arvin had drawn his dagger. He should have been more careful and stuck to his psionics. "—a thief," he concluded.

"Yes," the man said. As he spoke, he scratched his left elbow with the first two fingers of his right hand—probably the local sign for guild.

Arvin pretended not to see the gesture. The last thing he needed was to get enmeshed in the web of the local rogues' guild. He clenched his left hand, and the ache of his abbreviated little finger—the one the Hlondeth Guild had cut the tip from—enforced his resolve. This time, he'd stay clean. The whole point in coming to Sespech was to make a fresh start.

"And the gauntlet?" Arvin asked. "Can anyone use it?"

"Anyone. Even thieves. It shields the petitionary from blows, weapons—even spells that cause harm. But not," the man added with a twinkle in his eye, "against justice. Use it carefully, if you've committed a crime."

"Sound advice," Arvin replied. "But I don't intend to commit any."

He watched as one of the clerics laid a hand on the paralyzed yuan-ti and spoke a prayer. An instant later they both vanished; snowflakes swirled in agitation in the spot their bodies had just occupied. The second cleric touched the young rogue gently on the shoulder then waved him away, dismissing him. Then he, too, teleported away.

The snow continued to fall, dusting the ground with a thin layer of white. The crowd began to disperse.

The man beside Arvin shivered. "Need a place to stay, friend?" he asked. "That's my inn over there: Lurgin's Lodgings."

Arvin shook his head. "Thanks, but no. I'm just passing through Mimph. I hope to catch a boat for Ormpetarr this afternoon."

The man placed a cupped hand over his heart. "As you wish."

Arvin turned and walked away, still awed by the treatment the yuan-ti had received.

He was going to like it in Sespech.

CHAPTER 2

ARVIN SQUINTED, TRYING TO PEER THROUGH THE FALLING SNOW. He'd never seen it fall so thickly; usually the lands surrounding the Vilhon Reach received no more than a sporadic, wet slush that quickly melted. This winter, however, had seen more than one snowfall like this one; the thick, fluffy snowflakes had piled up ankle-deep.

Despite the snow, the wagon in which Arvin rode was making good time as it crossed the frozen fields east of Mimph—though Arvin wondered how the driver could see where he was going. Arvin could see no more than a few paces in any direction; beyond that was only the occasional dark blur—thin and tall if it was a tree, short and squat if it was a cottage.

The driver, a dwarf with a thick red beard, stared resolutely ahead over the backs of the two horses that drew the wagon. He gave the reins an occasional flick or clucked to the animals, encouraging them to keep up their pace. The only other sounds were the crunch of wheels on snow and the tinkling of the tiny bells that hung from the horses' braided manes. Steam rose from their backs, mingling with the swirling snow.

Arvin tucked the heavy wool blanket tightly around his chest and legs and shivered. He was able to block out discomfort while performing his *asanas*, but not for a whole afternoon at a stretch. The cold bit at his ears and nose and caused a throbbing ache in his abbreviated little finger, and the snowflakes settling on his shoulders and drifting down into his collar chilled him further. He glanced across at the wagon's only other passenger, wondering how she could be so comfortable. Her own blanket was loosely draped about her knees, and she wasn't hugging herself, as Arvin was. Her winter cloak was open at the neck, and she hadn't bothered to brush away the snowflakes that dusted her long black hair. She stared over Arvin's shoulder at the snow-blurred landscape that fell away behind them. Judging by her dusky skin, she came from the warm lands to the south and shouldn't be used to cold. Her breath, like his, fogged the air. Yet she looked as comfortable as if she were sitting beside a crackling fire. Arvin decided she must have magic that helped her to endure the cold. Maybe that bulge under the glove on her right hand was a magical ring.

Envious though he was, Arvin couldn't help but glance at her. She was exquisite, with eyes so dark it was difficult to see where pupil ended and iris began, and long lashes that fluttered each time she blinked. Her cheekbones were high and wide, and the hair that framed her face was lustrous and thick, with a slight wave. Arvin imagined brushing it back from her face and letting his fingers linger on the soft skin of her cheek. The riverboat wouldn't be leaving until tomorrow morning; perhaps she could be persuaded to. . . .

She shifted on the wagon's hard wooden bench, at last shaking the snowflakes from her hair. Arvin caught a glimpse of an earring in her left ear—a finger-thick plug of jade, its rounded end carved in the shape of a stylized face with drooping, heavy lips. Then her hair covered it again.

Her eyes met Arvin's. Realizing he was still staring at her, he blushed. "Your earring," he stammered. "It's pretty."

She stared at him for several unnerving moments. Then her gaze shifted to his forehead. "That stone. Is it your clan?" She spoke in the clipped accent of the southern lands, each word slightly abbreviated.

"This?" Arvin touched the lapis lazuli on his forehead. The fingernail-sized chip of stone was a spot of warmth against his chilled skin, joined by magic with his flesh—and joined with his thoughts, when its command word was spoken. He'd put it on as soon as the ship was safely away from Hlondeth and had left it in place since. There didn't seem to be any reason to hide it anymore. Zelia—the stone's original owner—was far behind him now, gods be praised.

"It's just a decoration," he answered at last.

"I see." She glanced away, seemingly losing interest.

"You're from the south?" Arvin asked, hoping to continue the conversation.

She nodded.

"I'm from Hlondeth, myself."

That got her attention. She studied him a moment. "You are not a yuan-ti."

"No. My name's Vin," he said, using an abbreviation that was as common as cobblestones in Hlondeth. "And yours is . . . ?"

She paused, as if deciding whether to answer. "Karrell."

"You're going to Ormpetarr?" It was an unnecessary question, since the only reason anyone would be taking this wagon would be to reach the riverboats that plied the Lower Nagaflow.

She nodded.

"Me too," Arvin continued. He plunged into the carefully rehearsed story that would explain his presence in Sespech. "I'm an agent for Mariners' Mercantile. I hope to encourage Baron Foesmasher to buy from our rope factories. Those new ships he's building are going to require good strong hemp for their rigging." He patted the backpack on the seat beside him. "I've brought samples of our finest lines to show him."

Karrell raised an eyebrow. "You are meeting with the baron?" She glanced at his cloak—woven from coarse brown wool—and the worn boots that protruded from the blanket draped over his legs.

Behind her, the driver chuckled into his beard and flicked his reins.

"These are my traveling clothes," Arvin explained. She obviously thought he was a braggart, trying to impress her. He drew himself up straighter. "I'll change into something more suitable once I arrive in Ormpetarr, before going to the palace. Ambassador Extaminos has graciously agreed to introduce me to—"

"Dmetrio Extaminos?"

Arvin blinked. "You know him?"

"I know his work. He has a great love of architecture. He restored the Serpent Arch, the first Hall of Extaminos, and the Coiled Tower." She paused to stare at Arvin, as if expecting a reaction.

He shrugged. "Old buildings don't interest me."

It was the wrong thing to say. Karrell tossed her head. "They interest me," she said. "That is why I came north: to study architecture. The yuan-ti have a particularly graceful style, with their arches, spirals, and towers."

Arvin realized there might be more to the woman than just a pretty face. "Are you an architect?" He glanced at the bag at her feet. Like him, she was traveling light.

"Architecture interests me," she said. "I make sketches of buildings." She tilted her head. "Old buildings."

Arvin scrambled to salvage the conversation. He dredged up what little he knew about the subject, casting his mind back to the "lessons" the priests had given at the orphanage—lessons that were delivered to the backs of the children's heads while they worked. The lessons helped the priests convince themselves they were educating and instructing the children, not just profiting from their labors.

"The Coiled Tower was built in. . . ." Damn, the date had eluded him. Was it 641 or 614? He could never remember. "In the year of the city's independence," he continued, reciting what he remembered of his lessons. "The Extaminos Family erected it to honor the snakes that saved Hlondeth from the kobolds. The ones Lord Shevron summoned with his prayers. The snakes, that is—not the kobolds."

Karrell's lips twitched. A smile?

"The year was 614," she said. "Eighty-five years after your people and mine first made contact."

"Your people?" Arvin prompted.

"My father's tribe." Karrell made a dismissive gesture. "You will not know their name."

"I might," Arvin said. "Where did you say you were from?"

"The south."

She was right. He knew little of the people to the south and probably wouldn't have recognized the name of her tribe. But he wasn't completely ignorant of geography. "By your accent, I'd say you were from the Chultan Peninsula," he commented. "That's where the flying snakes come from, isn't it?"

She gave him a sharp look.

She obviously didn't like snakes—they had that much in common, at least. Arvin quickly changed the subject. "You must have been traveling a long time," he continued. "What places have you visited?"

"I was most recently in Hlondeth, sketching the buildings that Dmetrio Extaminos was restoring. I had hoped to meet him and talk to him about his project but learned he had returned to Sespech to take up the ambassador's post."

"Is that why you came to Sespech?" Arvin asked.

Karrell shook her head. "No. I came to sketch the palace at Ormpetarr. But I am glad to have met you." She leaned forward and rested a hand on Arvin's knee. "Will you introduce me to Dmetrio Extaminos?"

Arvin hesitated. Karrell's answers to his questions had been short and evasive. What if she was a spy, or even an assassin? Even if she was exactly what she claimed to be, he could think of a dozen reasons to say no. Dmetrio didn't know about Arvin's mission—to him, Arvin would be nothing more than a "rope merchant's agent" that he was to introduce to Baron Foesmasher. This would give Arvin an excuse to chat informally with Dmetrio, to find out—with a little prompting, in the form of a psionic manifestation—if Dmetrio knew anything about Glisena's disappearance. Dmetrio had been courting Glisena for several months; there was a chance that her disappearance was part of an illicit elopement. If it was, the alliance between Sespech and Hlondeth would unravel as quickly as a frayed rope.

Arvin didn't need a stranger hanging about while he asked Dmetrio delicate questions. Nor did he want her tagging along behind him in Ormpetarr. The next thing he knew, she'd be asking for an introduction to Baron Foesmasher and a tour of the palace.

On the other hand, Karrell was the most beautiful woman Arvin had ever met. And the touch of her hand on his knee—even through the thick wool blanket—was sending a welcome flush of warmth through him.

Karrell raised her free hand to her chest, making a brief, imploring gesture that reminded Arvin of the silent speech. She leaned closer still, whispering a plea in her own language, and Arvin caught a whiff of the scented oil she must have combed into her hair to make it shine so. She smelled of the exotic flowers of the south, of orchids underlaid with a hint of musk. A snowflake landed at the corner of her upper lip, and Arvin was filled with an urge to kiss it away.

"Please," she breathed. "It would mean so much to me to meet Ambassador Extaminos, to share my sketches with someone who appreciates the subject as much as I do."

Arvin swallowed. "I'd like to see your sketches, too."

Karrell's dark eyes shone. "So you'll introduce me?"

Arvin tugged at the neck of his cloak, loosening it. The snow was still falling thick and fast, and the air had chilled as the sun went down, but he was suddenly very warm. "I. . . ."

The wagon jerked to a halt. "We're here," the dwarf grunted— the first words he'd spoken since their journey began. "Riverboat Landing. The Eelgrass Inn." Bells tinkled as the horses shook their heads, taking advantage of the slack reins.

Arvin glanced around. The wagon had pulled up beside the largest of the half dozen inns that lined the bank of the Lower Nagaflow. Several piers splayed out into the river like fingers. Tied up to them were the riverboats—wide-hulled sailboats with tall masts, canvas sails furled tight against their yards. Snow had blown into drifts on the decks of most, but one had been swept clean. Aboard it, two men were fitting a repeating crossbow to the port rail amidships. A second repeating crossbow was already mounted on the starboard rail.

Arvin caught the eye of the dwarf, who had climbed down to tie the reins of the horses to a hitching post. "Why the crossbows?" he asked. "Are they expecting trouble?"

The dwarf's feet crunched in the snow as he walked back to open the door of the wagon. "Slavers," he said as Arvin climbed down from the wagon. "From Nimpeth." He pointed across the river at the far shore. "They have their own boats. Sleek and fast."

Arvin caught Karrell's eye as she rose and gathered up her bag. "Don't worry," he assured her. "If the slavers do attack, there will be more than just crossbows to stop them. I'm armed with a magical weapon—and I'm very capable in a fight."

Karrell gave him a bemused glance. She swept back her cloak, revealing an ironwood club, with a knobbed, fist-sized ball at one end, that hung from her belt. "So am I."

Arvin's eyebrows rose. "But you're—"

She stared down at him, eyes narrowed. "A woman?"

"No," Arvin said quickly. "I mean yes. You're *clearly* a woman." He realized he was staring not at her weapon, but at the curves the drawn-back cloak had revealed—at weapons of a different sort. "And there are lots of women in the Guil—" He caught himself just in time and took a deep breath. "I meant that you're . . . an artist," he finished lamely.

"And you, so you say, are a rope merchant's agent," she said, giving the final word a slight emphasis, as if to imply she thought he was an agent of a different sort.

Arvin swore to himself. What had he been thinking, bragging to this woman? To a complete stranger. She might have been anyone—even a spy from Chondath. She seemed to have guessed that he was more than he was pretending to be, but then, so was she. Arvin glanced at her bag. It didn't look big enough to hold an artist's ink pots, quills, and scroll tubes. Even so, he had a feeling he could trust her.

A gust of wind caught his cloak, and he shivered. The inn the wagon had stopped in front of was two stories tall, with walls made of roughly squared logs and a roof whose eaves were crusted with icicles. A signboard hanging above the front door was painted with a picture of a snakelike creature winding its way through submerged river grass. The door opened briefly as a man—one of the sailors from the riverboats, carrying a hand crossbow—exited the inn and headed for the piers. The smell of stew flavored with winter sage and onions drifted out in his wake.

The dwarf grunted and marched back to the hitching post, his feet crunching in the snow. "I need to rub down my animals," he grunted. "When you're done chatting." He untied the reins and stared pointedly at the stable that adjoined the inn.

Karrell nodded. "Of course." She stepped down from the wagon, glanced up at the inn's signboard, and picked her way gracefully toward the door.

Arvin trailed after her. "You're taking a room here?"

Karrell nodded.

"Maybe we could share it," he suggested. "To save some coin."

She paused, one hand on the door latch, and tilted her head. "We have only just met. Perhaps once you have introduced me to Ambassador Extaminos. . . ."

Arvin nodded eagerly. Then he realized something. Once he got to Ormpetarr, he was going to be busy with his mission. And he didn't think he could wait until then. Karrell was an amazing woman, as quick-witted as she was beautiful. If he didn't win her over now, someone else surely would.

Karrell opened the door, releasing a gust of warm, savory-scented air that was thick with conversation. At least two dozen people were inside. Several glanced up from their meals as the door opened. More than one man raised his eyebrows appreciatively or whistled under his breath at the sight of Karrell.

"Listen," Arvin said, desperate now. He dropped his voice to a low, confiding whisper. "I won't have time to spend with you once we reach Ormpetarr. I'll be too busy. You were right—I'm not really here to sell rope. I actually came to Sespech to find someone. She—"

The words froze in his throat as he saw who was seated at one of the tables. A woman with long red hair, slit eyes, and skin freckled with green scales. She lifted from her plate what looked like a raw egg that was still in its shell, swallowed it whole, and licked her lips with a forked blue tongue.

For the space of several heartbeats, Arvin stood rooted to the spot, unable to breathe. The chill that filled him was colder than the thickest ice.

Zelia—here?

She glanced up.

Arvin jerked back, putting the half-opened door between himself and Zelia. He stared at Karrell, who was hesitating in the doorway. Suddenly, Arvin saw her in a new light. The flame of desire that had almost driven him to confide his mission to her had been snuffed out the instant he'd spotted Zelia. He recognized it now for what it was—a magical compulsion.

He'd been charmed by Karrell. And she'd led him straight to Zelia.

Or . . . had she? Karrell glanced once at Arvin, then back through the open door, her eyes ranging over those within. She obviously realized that Arvin had spotted someone inside the inn who terrified him—but she'd made no move to force him inside. Instead she had a thoughtful expression on her face.

She *wasn't* in league with Zelia. But if Arvin didn't act quickly, she'd give him away.

"Go on," Arvin said, flicking his hands at Karrell, frantically motioning her inside. Sharing a room with her was the last thing on his mind now. "This place looks too expensive. I'll find a room somewhere else."

Karrell frowned. "Will I see you in the morning?"

"Perhaps," Arvin said. "If not, safe journey." He turned and walked swiftly away. Thank the gods that it was dark. The night's gloom hid his face—and, most important, the lapis lazuli on his forehead. He spoke the word that would loosen it and peeled it from his skin. Then he vanished it inside his magical glove. He ducked around the corner of the building, his heart still pounding at his narrow escape. Why hadn't the sixth sense that had been plaguing him, ever since he'd begun a serious study of psionics under Tanju, given him any warning that the person he most feared was lurking within the inn? All his premonitions could do, it seemed, was give him unsettling glimpses of the dangers that other people faced. The vision he'd had on the ship—of a sailor falling from the ratlines and snapping his neck on the deck below—was a prime example.

Keeping low to avoid being spotted through the inn's windows, he made his way to the rear of the building.

What now?

Every instinct screamed at him to flee, to put as much distance between himself and Zelia as possible. Should he steal a wagon and return to Mimph? Or maybe try for Fort Arran? He stared at the falling snow and realized he would only get lost in the darkness.

No, there were only two ways out: as a passenger on one of the wagons back to Mimph or on tomorrow morning's riverboat. Either way, he'd have to be careful not to be spotted. If by wagon, he could hide overnight in the stables then board at the last moment after making certain Zelia wasn't also catching a wagon back to Mimph. Bundled in a heavy blanket, he'd be indistinguishable from any other passenger. There was always the risk that some stable hand or driver would find him in the stables, but he could give the simple excuse of not having enough coin for an inn, and charm the fellow into agreeing to let him sleep in a stall.

If by riverboat, he'd also have to find a way to board without Zelia seeing him.

Two men were approaching—the sailors who had been mounting

the repeating crossbows on the boat earlier. Fortunately, the snow was still falling. Screened by its mottled white curtain, Arvin stepped into the shadows at the rear of the Eelgrass Inn and watched the men enter another of the inns. He glanced at the boat they'd just come from. Of the dozen tied up to the piers, it was the only one with a guard—Arvin could see him moving on the boat's raised stern, beside a dull red glow that must be a brazier. The guard obviously wasn't going anywhere, which meant the riverboat had cargo loaded on board. It was the one that would sail in the morning. It would be an easy matter for Arvin to use his psionics to distract the guard then slip into the hold and hide. That would ensure that Zelia wouldn't see him. Then, with Tymora's blessing, Arvin would be on his way to Ormpetarr. Zelia would never even know that he'd nearly blundered into the inn where she was staying.

Unless she, too, was planning on leaving by riverboat.

Arvin couldn't very well hide in the hold for the whole of the two-day journey to Ormpetarr. He had to know whether Zelia was planning on being aboard the riverboat tomorrow morning. More important, he needed to learn what she was doing here. Had she heard that Arvin was alive and on his way to Ormpetarr, then positioned herself at the one place he was sure to pass through on his way there?

In order to find the answers to his questions, Arvin had to take a risk.

A very big risk.

Taking a deep breath, he placed a hand on the rough wooden wall next to him. He withdrew into himself, drawing his consciousness first into the "third eye" at the center of his forehead and deeper, into the spot at the base of his throat. Tightly coiled swirls of energy were unleashed in each location; a heartbeat later he heard the low droning noise that accompanied his manifestations of this power. Silver motes of light sparkled in his vision then flared out around him, sputtering into invisibility as they moved away from him.

They penetrated the walls of the inn. Following them with his consciousness, Arvin quested about mentally, looking for the distinctive disturbances that accompanied the use of psionics. He found none. At the moment, Zelia was not manifesting any of her powers.

Thus reassured, Arvin shifted his consciousness away from his throat and into a spot at the base of his scalp. Energy awakened there with a prickling that raised the hairs on the back of his neck as he manifested a second psionic power. Once again, the silver sparkles erupted around him. He sent his consciousness into the inn a second time, searching, this time, for thoughts. He skipped lightly from one patron of the inn to the next. Strangely, he could not locate Karrell—had she left the inn without Arvin spotting her? But Zelia's mind, powerful as it was, rose above the others. Catching his breath, he listened.

She wasn't thinking about him. Instead her thoughts were focused, impatiently, on someone she was waiting for: a male—someone who couldn't come inside the inn, for some reason. This someone probably wouldn't arrive for another day or so, given the unusually snowy weather. She was stuck here until he arrived, and she wasn't happy about it. But all she could do was wait. He would send her a message as soon as he was in the vicinity of—

Arvin felt Zelia's thoughts jerk to a sudden halt. There was a faint tinkling noise at the edges of her awareness—the secondary display of the power Arvin was manifesting. Zelia focused on it. Someone was trying to contact her. Was it—?

Instantly, Arvin disengaged. He scrambled away from the Eelgrass Inn, putting as much distance between himself and Zelia as possible. The power that allowed a psion to detect manifestations in his or her vicinity had a limited range, typically no more than twenty paces. Likewise the power that allowed a psion to detect thoughts—a power Zelia also had.

Only after he'd slipped and staggered through the snow and put a hundred paces between himself and the inn did Arvin slow to a walk. Panting, he looked nervously around. That had been close. "Nine lives," he whispered, touching the crystal that hung at his throat. The power stone, a gift from his mother, was long since used up. He wore it on a thong about his throat for sentimental reasons only. But old habits died hard.

Listening in on Zelia's thoughts had nearly alerted her to his presence. It had been worth it, though. It seemed that Zelia's presence here was a coincidence. She wasn't looking for him. Not yet, anyway.

Unfortunately, Arvin had gleaned neither a name nor a description of the fellow Zelia was waiting for. Now he had to watch out not only for Zelia, but for her ally, as well. But at least it sounded as if the fellow wouldn't be here tonight. Arvin could take a room at an inn, wait until just before dawn, then slip aboard a riverboat and be out of here, leaving Zelia behind.

Of course, that didn't mean that she wouldn't drop whatever she was doing and come slithering after Arvin, once she learned that he wasn't dead, after all. Which she would quickly realize, if Karrell mentioned the name "Vin" and "rope" within earshot of Zelia.

If only Arvin knew which room Karrell was staying in, he might be able to prevent her from giving him away. One charm—let's see how *she* liked being on the receiving end—would see to that. Trouble was she didn't seem to be in the Eelgrass Inn. And he couldn't very well go around using his psionics to search for her. That would be certain to attract Zelia's attention. It would be like dangling a live mouse in front of a snake. No, it would be better to save his psionic energies in case he needed to mount a defense against Zelia—futile though that defense would be.

If Zelia did discover him, Arvin was a dead man. He knew Zelia nearly as well as she knew herself. The mind seed that had been lodged in his head for six days had seen to that. If there was one thing Zelia savored, it was vengeance. Exacting it upon a human who had thwarted her would be especially sweet. She'd stop at nothing to obtain it. Not to mention the fact that he knew more about her—and her secret dealings—than anyone else in Hlondeth, save perhaps, for Lady Dediana. Arvin knew a number of details that Zelia would kill to keep secret: the identities of several of the mind seeds that served as her spies, for example.

He toyed, for a brief moment, with the thought of sneaking into Zelia's room. He could lay in wait for her, attack her when and where she least expected it. But he quickly rejected that idea. The last time he'd tried to get the drop on Zelia, he'd failed miserably, even after springing several magical surprises on her—surprises he didn't have at his disposal, this time. No, he'd do better to sneak away, instead, and pray—pray hard—that Zelia would finish her business at Riverboat Landing and depart without ever knowing that their paths had crossed.

At least, Arvin thought, he had one thing in his favor if Zelia did find him: the power that Tanju had taught him, shortly before Arvin had departed for Sespech. Using it, Arvin could link the fates of any two individuals. While it was active, if one was injured, the other would be, too. If one died, so would the other. Or, at the very least—in the case of extremely powerful spellcasters or magical creatures—the other would be seriously reduced in power.

Knowing that Zelia would be severely debilitated or even die if she killed him was cold comfort, but it was the best he could do. Her powers were vastly superior to his; the defenses he'd learned would only hold her off for so long. But if he could link their fates, it would at least give him some bargaining time.

Keeping a wary eye on the Eelgrass Inn, Arvin made his way to the inn farthest from it to book a room for the night. He'd have to rise just before dawn in order to sneak aboard the riverboat, but he didn't think he was going to have any problem with that.

He doubted he was going to get much sleep.

CHAPTER 3

With a lurch that caused the hard, lumpy ingots of iron Arvin had been lying on to shift, the riverboat got under way. The cargo hold was nearly full; the deck was a mere palm's width above Arvin's face. Footsteps thudded across it, loud above the constant rush of water past the hull. Arvin, lying in darkness, shivered and tried to flex numbed fingers and toes. The temperature had hovered around the freezing point even after the sun came up, and he was chilled to the bone.

He lay just below one of the smaller hatches, its edges outlined with thin morning sunlight. As footsteps passed over him once more, making the deck creak, he awakened the energy that lay coiled at the base of his scalp and manifested the power he'd used the night before. Silver sparkles flared around him then disappeared. He sent his awareness upward, through the deck, and sent it questing through the minds of the people who were aboard the boat. He dipped briefly into the thoughts of a sailor who was gripping the riverboat's tiller—how much better it was, this fellow was thinking, to sail aboard a boat as a free man—and into those of a second sailor who was serving as lookout. Perched high on the mast, this second fellow was awed by the speed at which the riverboat was traveling. It was only his tenth trip south, and yet he'd been chosen as lookout, due to his keen eyesight. The thought filled him with pride.

There were also two guards on board—one half-asleep as he leaned on one of the deck-mounted crossbows, the second tense as a spring and gleefully visualizing sending a bolt into attacking slavers. Idly watching them was the captain, a man whose mind wasn't on his duties. Instead his thoughts were lingering on the woman he'd lain with last night as he tried to recall her name.

The thoughts of the next man were much more interesting. His mind was focused intently upon the wind that was driving the boat along. He was controlling its intensity with a spell. Unlike the others on board, he thought in terms of sound and tactile sensation. Though he was directing the wind against the sail, there was no accompanying picture in his mind. He thought of the sail in terms of a taught canvas under his hand, of the creak of its yard as it shifted under the wind. He must, Arvin realized with some surprise, be blind.

There were three passengers on board: a merchant who was fretting over a delay that had nearly caused him to miss the boat, and a husband and wife on their way to Ormpetarr to attend a relative's wedding. She was eagerly anticipating it; he was dreading the tedium of being cooped up in a room with her boring kinfolk.

Arvin continued searching, but found no sign of Karrell. He wondered why she wasn't on board. Had she chosen not to travel to Ormpetarr after all? The thought disappointed him. At the same time he felt relief to have found no sign of Zelia. There were only nine people aboard the riverboat, all of them strangers to Arvin. All were just what they seemed to be. None were mind seeds.

Arvin drew his awareness back inside himself, ending the manifestation. He slid a hand under the small of his back, grasped the dagger that was sheathed there, and vanished it into his glove. He wouldn't use his weapon unless he had to. For now, his plan was to present himself as a stowaway with good reasons for sneaking on board—the captain's thoughts had given him an idea—and offer to pay for his passage.

He shoved open the hatch and clambered up onto the deck, dragging his pack behind him. Two people who must have been the husband and wife—he a sour looking man with a heavy black beard, she a narrow-faced woman wearing a white fur hat, her hands shoved into a matching muff—had been standing next to the hatch. They started at Arvin's sudden appearance. The merchant, a portly, balding fellow in a gold-thread cloak, was a few paces away. As Arvin appeared from the hold, he blinked in surprise.

One of the guards—a wiry fellow with a hook nose and tangled black hair—whipped a glance over his shoulder, shouted, "Slaver!" and immediately tried to swing his crossbow around to point inboard, only to find that it wouldn't swivel that far. The other guard—the older, gray-haired man Arvin had distracted last night when he crept aboard—looked startled but wasn't yet awake enough to react.

Arvin glanced up at the raised rear deck, searching for the captain. Three men stood there: a dark-skinned human with short, dark hair tarred flat against his head and a shadow of stubble on his chin; a barrel-chested man with a beard that didn't quite hide the faded **S** brand on his cheek, holding the tiller; and an elf clad head to toe in white, his eyebrows furrowed in a **V** of concentration and his silver hair twisting in the magical wind like fluttering ribbons. The elf's eyes were unfocused, identifying him as the blind spellcaster.

Though both of the other men looked like ordinary sailors, the dark-skinned one was clearly in command. He stared a challenge at Arvin, fists on his hips.

Arvin gave the captain a grin and opened his mouth to begin his explanation, but before he could get a word out, he saw a motion out of the corner of his eye. The hook-nosed guard had yanked a sword from the sheath at his hip. He tensed, about to attack.

So much for explanations, Arvin thought. Quick as a blink, he summoned energy from points deep in his throat and his third eye and sent it down into his right foot. A droning noise filled the air as he stomped the deck, sending a flash of silver shooting through the planks toward the guard holding the sword. The deck below hook-nose's feet bucked, sending him staggering. He grabbed at the rail and managed to steady himself, but lost his weapon overboard. "My sword!" he shouted. Cursing, he stared at the dark water that had swallowed it.

The gray-haired guard by now had a hand crossbow leveled at Arvin's chest, but Arvin's chief worry was the spellcaster at the stern. The elf, however, seemed oblivious to what was happening on the main deck. His attention remained focused on the riverboat's main sail. By feel alone, he was directing the magical wind, his fingers moving in complicated patterns as if he were knotting a net.

Arvin bowed to the captain and manifested a second power—this one coercive rather than confrontational. "Sorry to have startled you, sir," he said. The base of his scalp prickled as energy coiled there. He let it uncoil in the direction of the captain and saw the fellow tilt his head as if listening to something as the power manifested. "I'm no slaver, but a simple stowaway. I snuck aboard to avoid a woman who . . . ah . . . thinks I should marry her."

The captain's lips quirked in a smile. "Got her in the family way, did you?" He walked down the short flight of steps to the main deck, motioning for the gray-haired guard to lower his crossbow.

As the guard complied, Arvin sighed with relief. His charm had worked. He reached into his boot, pulling out his coin pouch. "I'll gladly pay for my passage to Ormpetarr."

The hook-nosed guard stomped over to where the captain was standing, muttering under his breath. "What about my sword, then? Who's going to pay for that?"

"Do not worry," a female voice said from the bow. "This man is on his way to a meeting with Ambassador Extaminos. If he does not compensate you, the ambassador surely will."

Arvin whirled around. "Karrell!"

"Hello, Vin." She stood, smiling, a pace or two behind him. She'd obviously been aboard all along; she must have been wearing or carrying a magical device that protected her from mind-probing magic. That would explain how he'd missed her last night, when he sifted the thoughts of those at the inn. She'd been standing up on the bow until a moment or two ago, screened from view by the sail, which was why Arvin hadn't seen her. The wind of the boat's passage had tangled her hair. Somehow it made her even more beautiful.

The captain tilted his head slightly in her direction and spoke to Arvin in a low voice. "Is she the one you're—"

"No," Arvin said firmly. "She's not. We met on the wagon to Riverboat Landing. I got to know her during the journey."

The gray-haired guard smiled knowingly. "Lucky man," he said, a chuckle in his voice. "I can see why you wanted to slip the other woman."

The wife clucked her tongue in disapproval and tucked one of her hands possessively into the crook of her husband's arm. The merchant rolled his eyes.

"What about my sword?" the hook-nosed guard complained. "It was dwarven-forged steel."

The captain gave him a disdainful stare. "It was a standard trade sword, and cheaply made."

Hook-nose lowered his eyes.

"But I'm sure this man—Vin, his name was?—will pay for it," the captain continued. Then, to Arvin, in a low voice, "Five plumes is more than enough. And nine more, for your passage."

Arvin nodded, rummaged in his pouch for the gold coins, and handed them to the captain, who counted five of them into the hand of the guard.

Karrell, meanwhile, moved closer to Arvin. "I am glad you are aboard, Vin," she said, taking his arm. "Come. We will talk."

Arvin picked up his pack and followed her to the bow. As they passed the sail, the wind of the ship's passage hit them full force, whipping Arvin's cloak. They were traveling up the broad, open river at the speed of a galloping horse; already the cluster of inns that made up Riverboat Landing was far behind.

The windblown bow was empty; the closest person was the lookout, who sat on a swinglike perch that had been hoisted to the top of the mast. He was a teenager, judging by the cracking of his voice as he called out hazards on the river ahead. Cupping his hands to his mouth, he shouted back at the captain. "Snag! Snag dead ahead, two hundred paces!"

The yard creaked as the sail shifted, swinging the bow slightly to port. Arvin glanced over the bow and saw a submerged log, its tangled root mass just below the surface and barely visible. The roots were wound around something round and gray, probably a large stone that had been uprooted with the tree when the wind blew it over. Arvin heard a thump and scrape as the hull grazed the snag, and the riverboat continued on its way, having avoided the worst of the hazard thanks to the lookout's keen eyes.

Arvin set his pack at his feet and turned to Karrell. "I'm surprised to find you on the boat," he said. "I didn't, ah . . . see you come aboard."

Karrell's lips twitched. "I did not see you board, either."

"I slipped into the hold this morning, just before dawn," Arvin said. He lowered his voice so the sailors wouldn't overhear. "I told the guard the truth—there was a woman, back at the Eelgrass Inn, who I'm trying to avoid. A woman with red hair and green scales that look like freckles. And a blue forked tongue. Did you notice her?"

"So that is why you left so hastily." Karrell thought a moment. "She is yuan-ti?"

"Yes. But she can pass for human, at a distance."

"I saw her. Twice. Last night, when I first arrived at the inn, and this morning, when she was talking to the innkeeper."

Arvin leaned forward, tense. "You didn't say anything about me, did you? Anything she might have overheard?"

"No."

Arvin relaxed a little. "Did you hear what she said to the innkeeper?"

"That she would stay another night."

Arvin nodded, thankful that Zelia hadn't chosen to catch this morning's riverboat. He'd been terrified by the prospect of being trapped in the cargo hold, unable to emerge on deck, and slowly freezing to death during the long voyage. Even if she did set out for Ormpetarr on the next riverboat, he would reach that city a full day ahead of her.

Karrell stared at him. "Why do you fear her?"

Arvin swallowed. Was it that obvious? He gave Karrell a weak grin. "She dislikes me. A lot. She wants me dead. Fortunately, she believes I *am* dead. I'd prefer to keep it that way."

"Did you quicken her egg?" Karrell asked.

"Her what?"

"She is yuan-ti. The snake people lay eggs. And the captain said—"

"Oh," Arvin said, understanding at last. He laughed at the absurdity of it and shook his head vehemently. "We didn't have *that* kind of relationship. We were . . . close, for a time. But not that close. She's a. . . ." He paused, shuddering. He'd been about to tell Karrell that Zelia was a psion, but she probably wouldn't know what that was.

He saw that Karrell's lips were pressed together in displeasure and decided to change the subject. Like most humans, she was probably appalled at the thought of a yuan-ti and human mating. "What was it you wanted to talk to me about?" he asked.

The displeased look vanished instantly from Karrell's face. She leaned forward and placed her hand upon his arm. Her touch sent a thrill through him but nothing near the rush of desire he'd felt after she'd charmed him. "You never said whether you would introduce me to Dmetrio Extaminos."

Ah. So it was that again, was it? He wondered why she wanted to meet him so badly. Was she an assassin, after all?

Karrell reached for her cloak, one hand curling as if she were about to draw it closed at her neck. Odd—she didn't look cold. Suddenly Arvin remembered where he'd seen the gesture before. It was the same one she'd used yesterday when she'd charmed him. Even as her lips parted to whisper the spell, Arvin awoke the psionic energy at the base of his scalp and manifested a charm of his own. Karrell halted in midwhisper, her eyes shifting to the side as if she'd heard something in the distance, over the creak of the riverboat's rigging.

Arvin suppressed his smile. The shoe would be on the other foot, this time around.

Above them, the lookout shouted. "Disturbance in the water, one hand to port, three thousand paces ahead!"

The boat swung slightly to starboard and slowed.

Arvin glanced over the bow. The boat would soon be passing a small, rocky island near the center of the river; between this island and the boat was a circular patch of disturbed water about two paces wide. It looked as though a boulder had splashed into the river at that spot, sending out ripples. Arvin searched the island, but didn't see anything. The island was rocky and flat—devoid of vegetation that would offer concealment, and low enough that a ship wouldn't be able to hide behind it, which ruled out a catapult.

"What's causing it?" the captain called up at the lookout.

The young man at the top of the mast chewed his lip. "I don't know. Maybe a dragon turtle?" he asked nervously.

"Do you *see* a dragon turtle?" the captain asked in a tense voice. "No."

The gray-haired guard snorted. "It was probably air escaping from a wreck. Or a fish fart."

The lookout twisted around to glance down at him. "Do fish fart?"

The guard chuckled.

Red-faced, the young lookout went back to his duties.

Arvin turned back to Karrell. "I'll introduce you to Ambassador Extaminos," he told her. "But I'd like to know more about you, first." He lowered his voice and caught her eye. "You can trust me. Is it Chondath you serve?"

Karrell gave a slight frown. "Who?"

Arvin was surprised by her response. Chondath, directly to the east of Sespech, was a country, not a person. Either she was playing dumb—really dumb—or she was what she claimed, a traveler from the Chultan Peninsula. "Tell me," he urged. "What's the real reason you're going to Ormpetarr?"

Karrell's voice dropped to a whisper. "I'm looking for—"

"Disturbance three hands to starboard, two thousand four hundred paces ahead!" the lookout shouted, interrupting her. This time, his high-pitched voice had an edge to it.

The riverboat turned a few degrees back to port, and slowed still more. Karrell glanced in the direction the lookout was pointing, a slight frown on her face.

Arvin touched her arm—and felt her move into his touch. "What are you looking for?" he prompted.

"Something that was entrusted to the people of Hlondeth many years ago. It—"

"Disturbance one hand to starboard, one thousand paces ahead!" the sailor shouted.

The riverboat slowed momentarily then picked up speed and turned sharply to port.

"Yes?" Arvin prompted.

Karrell opened her mouth to speak but was interrupted a third time.

"Disturbance dead ahead, four hundred paces!"

Arvin glanced up as the lookout repeated his cry, his voice breaking. "Disturbance dead ahead!" he shouted at the guards. "Something's breaking the surface!"

Arvin glanced back at the guards. They stood tensely behind their crossbows, fingers on triggers as their eyes searched the river ahead.

The merchant, the husband, and the wife milled uncertainly on the main deck. At the stern, the elf and barrel-chested sailor awaited the captain's orders. The elf's hands were raised, ready to redirect the wind. The captain glanced back and forth between the low island—much closer now—and the bubbling patch of water, his face twisted with indecision. At last he gave an order; the sailor responded instantly, leaning into the tiller.

The boat heeled sharply to port, causing Karrell to stumble. She blinked, gave Arvin a sharp look, and took a quick step back from him, withdrawing her arm from his hand. The charm Arvin had manifested on her seemed to have broken. "What is happening?" she asked, glancing warily around.

"I don't know," Arvin answered. "But I don't think it's goo—"

"Naga!" the teenaged lookout shrilled. "Gods save us, it's a naga!"

"This far north?" the captain shouted. "Are you *sure*?"

The lookout mutely nodded, white-faced. Arvin stared at the spot he was pointing at—a frothing patch of water a few dozen paces to starboard. A serpentlike creature had risen from the center of it. The creature looked like an enormous green eel with blood-red spines running the length of its body. Its head was human-shaped, its face plastered with wet, kelp-green hair that hung dripping from its scalp. Its eyes were dark and malevolent as it stared at the riverboat.

"Shoot it!" the captain shouted.

Arvin heard a twang as the gray-haired guard loosed a crossbow bolt. In that same instant, the naga withdrew under the surface of the water with astonishing speed. Even as the bolt plunged into the river, the naga was gone, leaving only a spreading circle of lapping waves behind.

A moment later, over the shouting of the crew, Arvin heard a loud thud as something struck the underside of the hull. The boat canted sharply up, its stern leaving the water entirely, throwing Arvin and Karrell together into the point of the bow. Timbers groaned as the boat was forced upward by the naga rearing up beneath it; Arvin heard wood splintering as the tiller was torn away. Something splashed into the water near the stern, and someone amidships screamed— either the wife or the merchant, he wasn't sure. From above came the crack-voiced, terrified prayers of the lookout.

Then the stern slammed back down into the water. The riverboat rocked violently from side to side, water sloshing over the gunwales and its sail wildly flapping. A wave nearly carried Arvin's pack over the side. As he grabbed for it, he heard Karrell whispering urgently in her own language. From behind them came the shouts of the captain and the terrified screams of the other passengers.

A thud came from the starboard side as the naga rammed the boat a second time. The riverboat rolled sharply to port, a yardarm brushing the water. The lookout screamed as his swing-seat cracked like a whip, throwing him into the water. Clinging to the rail, Arvin heard thumps and curses as the other crew and passengers tumbled across the now-vertical deck, and a groan and cracking noises as the mast struck the water. Karrell flew past him and fell headlong into the river; Arvin shouted her name as she sank from sight. Then something hit him from behind, and he was underwater.

The first thing he noticed was the water's terrible chill; it would have taken his breath away had there been any air in his lungs. The second was the fact that the strap of his pack was loosely tangled around his left wrist. Clinging to it, he fought his way back to the surface in time to see the deck of the riverboat rushing down at him. It slammed into his face, tearing open his cheek and forcing him under again.

When he came up for the second time, he tasted blood on his lips; warm blood was flowing down his cheek. Karrell was treading water nearby. "Are you all right?" Arvin shouted.

Karrell grimly nodded, her wet hair plastered to her face. Like Arvin, she appeared to be unhurt, aside from a few scrapes and bruises. Her dark eyes mirrored Arvin's concern. "And you?" she asked, staring at the blood on his face.

Arvin took stock. He ached all over, but nothing seemed broken. "Fine." He touched the crystal at his neck, silently thanking Tymora for her mercy. "Nine lives," he whispered to himself.

The lookout floated facedown a short distance away. Arvin swam over to him and tried to flip him over then saw that the young crew-member's neck was broken.

The riverboat was turned completely over, its splintered keel pointing skyward. A tangle of lines surrounded it like a bed of kelp. Four people treaded water within this tangle: the gray-haired guard and the three passengers. The merchant was closest to the boat; he clambered onto the overturned hull, water streaming from his hair and sodden cloak, then clung to the broken keel, dazedly shaking his head. The gray-haired guard immediately followed, dragging a hand crossbow behind him, then turned to help the husband and wife out of the water. The wife was sobbing but seemed unhurt; the husband grunted with the effort of trying to kick his way out of the water with an injured leg.

There was no sign of the rest of the crew, save for the hook-nosed guard. He was swimming determinedly toward the tiny island without a backward glance.

Arvin heard a third thump as the naga struck the bottom of the overturned boat; it rocked violently, prompting a whimper from the merchant. Arvin turned to stare at the hook-nosed guard—the fellow had already reached the island, which was no more than a hundred paces away—then caught Karrell's eye. "Let's go," he told her.

She stared at the overturned boat. "But the passengers—"

"There's no room for us on the hull," Arvin said. "And we can do more on solid ground."

At last Karrell nodded. They swam.

Karrell reached the island first. Arvin was still dragging his pack; it slowed him down, but he couldn't afford to lose the dorje inside it. He nearly let it go when he heard a splashing noise behind him, but when he glanced over his shoulder, he saw it was the husband. The fellow had slipped back into the water and was trying to scramble out again.

Arvin reached the rocky shore and climbed out, gratefully accepting Karrell's hand. He'd only been in the river a short time but was shivering violently. Noticing this, Karrell chanted softly in her own language then touched his hand. Warmth flooded through Arvin, banishing the cold from his body. He nodded gratefully, understanding now why she hadn't needed the blanket during yesterday's wagon ride. Though a chill wind had started to blow, he felt as comfortable as if he were in a fire-warmed room. His abbreviated little finger didn't even ache. A useful spell, Arvin thought, wondering if there was a psionic power that might do the same.

"Hey," the hook-nosed guard protested, his teeth chattering. "What about me?"

Karrell was turning toward him when the wife's scream made her whirl toward the river instead. The naga had burst out of the water next to the boat, no more than a pace or two away from the battered hull. Its slit eyes ranged over the four humans who had taken refuge on top of the overturned boat: the merchant, cowering with a horrified expression on his face; the wife, trying to pull her husband out of the water; and the gray-haired guard, loudly cursing as he fumbled one-handed with his crossbow. The guard was injured, Arvin saw; the fingers of his other hand stuck out at odd angles and his face was drawn and pale.

The naga's eyes settled on the merchant. Its tongue flickered out of its mouth, tasting the man's fear. Then it opened its mouth, baring its fangs.

The merchant screamed.

The naga lashed forward. Its teeth sank into the merchant's shoulder, injecting a deadly dose of venom. Then it reared up. The merchant, hanging from its jaws, gave one feeble kick then slumped. The naga dropped his lifeless body. It splashed into the river then bobbed back to the surface facedown.

Arvin tossed down his pack and summoned his dagger into his glove. Before he could throw it, however, the gray-haired guard raised his crossbow and shot. The bolt struck the naga in the neck. The naga jerked and lashed its head from side to side, trying to shake the bolt loose. Then it glared at the guard. It opened its mouth and flicked its tongue four times in rapid succession. Four glowing darts of energy streaked toward the guard, striking him in the chest. He grunted, slumped down onto the deck, and slid into the river.

"Tymora help us," Arvin whispered. He'd heard tales of nagas. They were said to be as cunning as dragons and as slippery as snakes, with a bite as venomous as that of a yuan-ti. He hadn't realized they also were capable of magic.

Realizing his dagger would do little against such a fearsome monster, Arvin vanished it back into his glove. He glanced at the hook-nosed guard, hoping the fellow might also have a crossbow, but the fellow had lost his weapons during the swim to the island.

Karrell took a step toward the water's edge; it looked as though she were about to dive back into the river. "Don't," Arvin urged, catching her hand. "Wait."

"For what?" she said fiercely. "Someone else to die?"

Despite her angry rebuke, Karrell halted. She began chanting what sounded like a spell.

The naga, meanwhile, gave a loud hiss and turned its head back and forth, as if trying to decide who its next victim would be.

Arvin had to do something—and quickly, before the naga struck again.

Sending his awareness inward, he manifested one of the attack forms Tanju had taught him—the mind blast. A psion targeted by this attack would crumple emotionally as his self-esteem and confidence were flayed away by the blast of psionic energy. A creature incapable of psionics, like the naga, would only be briefly stunned. But perhaps it would be enough.

Arvin imagined the form as Tanju had taught it to him—a man standing braced and ready, his hands held out in front of him with forefingers and thumbs touching to form a circle. When the visualization was clear, Arvin imagined the man—himself—drawing the circle toward his forehead. As power coiled tightly behind his third eye, he threw it outward at the naga. Silver sparks spiraled out from this third eye as the energies contained in the blast swept toward the creature. As they struck, the naga swayed. Its eyes rolled back in its head.

"Swim for the island!" Arvin shouted at the couple. "It's stunned—now's your chance!"

The husband tried to get into the water, but his wife clung to him. "Lie still!" she cried. "Lie still, and it won't see us!" As they struggled together, the naga blinked and shook its head. It glared down at them, its tongue flickering in and out of its mouth as its jaws parted in anticipation.

Arvin swore. The naga had recovered from the mind blast with surprising speed. Arvin wished, belatedly, that he'd chosen a different power to manifest. If he'd linked the naga's fate with that of the merchant—or the guard—their deaths would have weakened the naga, perhaps even killed it. He could still manifest a fate link—but not until he knew for certain that another death was both imminent and unavoidable.

Arvin's eye was caught by a flash of white above his head; craning his neck, he saw that it was the elf, walking through the air as if on solid ground. He held his hands out in front of him, as if half expecting to bump into something. "What happened?" he shouted. "Where is everyone?"

The hook-nosed guard stood. "Over here!" he shouted, waving his arms.

The elf turned toward the sound of his voice and started to descend. Each step carried him forward several paces at a time. But he wasn't going to reach them in time. Not before someone else died.

Karrell finished her spell. She shouted at the naga it in a language Arvin didn't recognize. The naga whipped its head around, staring at her, and made a series of strangled cries that sounded almost like words. Then it gave a long, menacing hiss.

Arvin groaned. Karrell had distracted the naga's attention from the couple—but her spell seemed to have angered the monster. Would a glowing bolt of magical energy follow?

Just then, however, the husband at last wrenched himself away from his wife. He balanced unsteadily on the hull, preparing to dive, but then his injured leg slipped on the wet wood. Spotting the sudden movement, the naga lashed down, catching the husband's arm in its jaws. The wife screamed in horror. The husband cursed, striking the monster with his free hand. But his blows were feeble; the poison was swiftly sapping his strength.

That decided it.

Arvin sent his awareness deep into his chest, unlocking the energies stored there. As he exhaled through pursed lips, a faint scent filled the air—the power's secondary display. To Arvin, it smelled of ginger and saffron, spices his mother used to cook with, but each person catching a whiff of it would interpret it differently. To some, it might be the scent of a flower; to others, the tang of heated metal.

Arvin directed the energy first at the husband, then at the naga. The monster continued to hold the husband's arm in its jaws, oblivious to the fact its fate had just been linked with the human. The husband, meanwhile, grew increasingly weak. When his eyes began to glaze, the naga at last released him. The husband collapsed in a heap on the hull, next to his ashen-faced wife.

Arvin stared at the naga in anticipation. It shook its head and swayed loosely back and forth, part of its body sliding back under the water. It stared with dull eyes at the humans who were proving so much of an annoyance, and for one hope-filled moment Arvin thought the injuries the fate link had inflicted might cause it to retreat back into the river. But then it gave a loud, angry hiss. Whatever had prompted its attack on the riverboat, it wasn't giving up.

Arvin heard the sound of panting just above. Turning, he saw the elf had reached them at last.

"The naga's by the boat!" Arvin shouted at the elf. "Use your magic against it—quickly!"

"Where?" The elf cocked his head, trying to pinpoint the naga by sound alone. The monster, however, was no longer hissing. And the wife was wailing as she clutched her husband's lifeless body, masking any sounds the naga was making.

Arvin made a quick mental calculation. "About a hundred and fifteen paces away," he called over his shoulder. "And. . . ." He glanced at the naga and took a wild guess. It was slightly to the left. "And one hand to port?"

The elf immediately cast a spell. Pointing a finger at the sky, he shouted in his own lilting tongue, and whipped his hand down so that it was pointing at the naga. As he did, a bolt of lightning streaked down from the overcast above, momentarily blinding Arvin. Thunder exploded directly overhead.

When Arvin opened his eyes again—blinking them to clear away the white after-image of the lightning—he saw that the bolt had missed. Instead of striking the naga it had struck the overturned boat, tearing a huge hole in the riverboat's stern. Smoke rose from the blackened planks.

"Did I hit it?" the elf cried.

The naga gave a humanlike scream, which ended in a fierce hiss of anger. Then it retaliated. Its tongue flicked out, hurling a glowing dart of energy toward the elf. He gave a sharp cry as it struck him in the shoulder and he immediately tried to cast a counter spell. But even as his lips parted, a second magical missile struck him in the chest, then a third, and a fourth. The elf faltered, fell to his knees, and began sinking through the air toward the island.

Arvin tried to manifest a second fate link—this time, between elf and naga. The monster wouldn't suffer the effects of the damage the elf had already taken, but if it continued to attack, the pain it would suffer would give it pause for thought. Though he felt a slight tingle in his chest, nothing happened. His psionic energies were too depleted to manifest that power.

The wife's wails were increasing in volume. Releasing her husband's body at last, she rose unsteadily to her feet and shook her fist at the heavens, one hand gripping the keel. "Why him?" she screamed. "Why?"

The naga's head whipped around. It lunged down, sinking its teeth into her upraised arm. She gave a choked cry and staggered backward as the naga released her. She collapsed into a seated position, supporting herself with one hand.

"Stay where you are," Karrell called to the woman. "I am coming to help." Then, before Arvin could stop her, she dived into the water. What Karrell thought she could accomplish, Arvin had no idea. The woman would be dead within a few heartbeats from the naga's venom. Even if Karrell reached her in time to cast a preventive spell, she'd be the next to fall.

"Karrell, no!" Arvin cried. "Come back!"

She ignored him, swimming steadily on toward the boat.

He had to do something—but what? His energies were almost depleted, but there was one small thing he could do. Sending his awareness down into his throat, he chose one of his lesser powers— one that caused its target to become momentarily distracted by an imagined sight or sound. A low droning filled the air as it manifested. The naga had been lashing back and forth, but as the power manifested, its head turned sharply to stare at a distant spot on the river.

As Karrell at last reached the boat and climbed up to help the injured woman, Arvin used his power to distract the naga a second time. "Karrell!" he shouted. "Swim with her back to the island! Get away from there!"

Karrell, however, wasn't listening. She crouched beside the woman, touching her arm.

The naga glanced down at her and parted its jaws.

Arvin distracted it a third time.

"Hurry up," Arvin gritted under his breath. "Finish the spell."

The naga recovered—more quickly than before.

Arvin distracted it a fourth time.

Karrell still hadn't completed her spell.

The naga loomed above her, hissing furiously. It was almost as if the monster realized it was being hit with psionics—and blamed the attacks on the woman who was crouched on the overturned boat, within easy striking distance.

Arvin tried to distract the naga a fifth time.

Nothing happened. The energy stored in his *muladhara* had run dry. "Leave her!" he shouted at Karrell.

She ignored him.

"Where . . ." a faint voice asked, ". . . is it?"

Arvin glanced around. The elf was kneeling on the rocks behind him, his head drooping.

"Give me your hand," Arvin said. "I'll show you." He grabbed the elf's hand and aimed it at the spot where the naga was. "There," he said. "About. . . ."

Seeing that Karrell was also in a direct line with the elf's hand, he hesitated. If he judged the distance or angle incorrectly, she would die.

The naga bared its venomous fangs. Its eyes were locked on Karrell.

"One hundred and seventeen paces away!" Arvin urged. "Quick! Cast your spell."

The elf's lips drew together in a determined line. He pointed at the sky with his free hand and chanted the words of his spell. Guided by Arvin's hand, his arm swept down—

The naga lunged forward; Karrell jerked to one side. The naga reared back, preparing to lash out at Karrell a second time—

The lightning bolt struck. This time, the aim was true. The bolt lanced into the naga's head, exploding it. This time it was bits of skull and brain that splashed down into the water, rather than splinters of wood. The suddenly headless naga swayed back and forth for a moment longer then crumpled into the water. It disappeared from sight, leaving behind ripples that sloshed against the overturned boat, staining the river red.

The elf turned his head, listening. "Did I—"

"Yes," Arvin answered. "It's dead." Dropping the elf's hand, he dived into the water and swam rapidly toward Karrell. She was hunched over the injured woman, unmoving. But as he crawled up onto the hull, he saw Karrell straighten. Her movements seemed steady enough.

"Thank the gods it missed you," he started to say. "For a moment there, I thought——" As he climbed up onto the hull, his eyes fell on her trouser leg and the twin puncture marks in it. A dark stain surrounded each puncture: blood.

Karrell glanced at the wound. "Yes. It bit me. But the wound is small." As she turned back to comfort the injured woman, Arvin saw her wince.

"But the venom?" he asked. "Why didn't it kill you?"

"My magic halted it."

Her hands, Arvin noticed, were bare. She'd yanked off her gloves to lay hands on the injured woman. Arvin saw now what had caused the bulge under her glove—a wide gold ring, set with a large turquoise stone, on the little finger of her right hand. It was probably the source of the magic that shielded her thoughts.

"You're a cleric?" Arvin guessed.

Karrell nodded. She reached for her gloves and began pulling them on.

"Of what god?" Arvin continued.

"You will not have heard of him, this far north. He is a god of the jungle."

"Your wound is still bleeding," he told her. "We've got to staunch the blood." He reached for her leg.

"No," Karrell said sharply.

Arvin drew his hands back. "No need to take offense," he told her.

"I can heal it myself." She laid a palm over the punctures and chanted a brief spell in a language Arvin had never heard before—her native tongue, he guessed. The words were crisp and short, as abbreviated and staccato as her accent.

The riverboat creaked, listing slightly as it settled deeper into the river. Glancing down at the water, Arvin saw a dark-skinned body, surrounded by a stain of red, tangled in the submerged rigging. That explained where the captain had gone. The body of the husband floated nearby. The man's head had suffered the same fate as the naga's; it had ruptured like a smashed melon. Pinkish chunks floated in the river next to it.

Karrell, wisely, had turned the wife's head away from the gruesome sight.

The boat shifted, releasing a bubble of air half the size of a wagon. Arvin was forced to grab the keel as the boat tilted still further. "It's going to sink," he told Karrell. He glanced down at the injured woman. "Let's get her to the island."

The wife had fallen silent now; she stared straight ahead with dull eyes. Together, Arvin and Karrell eased her into the water and dragged her between them as they swam back to the island where the guard and elf waited.

Karrell immediately went to the elf, despite the guard's protests that he was "freezing to death" and in need of one of her warming spells. Kneeling beside the elf, she cast a healing spell. Arvin, meanwhile, stared at the riverboat. Its bow rose slowly into the air at an angle, and it sank, borne down by the weight of its cargo.

The injured woman sat up and stared at the spot where it had gone down, crying. Karrell's spell had saved her life, but the woman's heart was still wounded. "My husband," she keened. "Why . . . ?"

Karrell, meanwhile, cast a warming spell on the hook-nosed guard. Instead of thanking her, he spat. "So many dead—and for what? A few lousy ingots of iron."

The elf turned toward him. "The barony needs steel; that iron would have forged new shields, armor, and weapons to keep Chondath at bay." He turned blind eyes toward the water. "Did the boat sink? Was the cargo lost?"

"All but this pack, here," the guard muttered, giving Arvin's pack a kick. The pack rolled over, spilling a length of trollgut rope. Horrified, Arvin realized that the main flap had been torn. Had his dorje fallen out during his swim to the island?

The guard frowned. "That's a strange-looking rope."

Arvin hurried to his pack and began rummaging inside it, searching frantically for the dorje. He breathed a sigh of relief as his fingers brushed against the cloth-wrapped length of crystal.

"What I don't understand is what the naga was doing this far north," the guard continued, turning back to the elf. "Nagas *never* come north of the barrier. And why did it attack? We did nothing to provoke it."

"Yes, we did," Karrell said softly. "We crushed her nest."

The guard snapped his fingers. "That snag," he said. "The one we grazed."

Karrell nodded. "She had laid her eggs in its roots."

Startled, Arvin looked up at Karrell. He'd seen the "rock" in the snag—but Karrell hadn't. "How did you know that?"

"I asked her."

"*That* was the spell you cast?" he asked, incredulous.

Karrell shrugged. "I thought I could talk to her. But she was too angry."

Arvin shook his head. "You can't reason with a gods-cursed *serpent*," he told her. He gestured at the weapon that still hung from her belt. "Next time, use your club."

Karrell's face darkened, but before she could snap back at him, Arvin turned to the elf. "What now?" he asked. He wanted to pull the dorje out of his pack and check it, but not in front of the others. "Do we wait here for the next riverboat?"

"There won't be another until tomorrow morning," the elf said. "But I can air walk back. With a magical wind to push me, I'll be swift."

Arvin stared at the elf's unfocused eyes. "How will you find your way back?"

"Hulv will guide me," the elf said, gesturing in the general direction of the hook-nosed guard. "I can cast the spell on him, as well."

Karrell nodded down at the injured woman. "Can you take her with you?" she asked. "She needs more healing than I can provide."

The elf nodded. "Hulv will carry her."

"What about my husband?" the woman asked in a trembling voice. She stared at the spot where his headless body floated, next to that of the merchant. The lookout and gray-haired guard floated a short distance away, but the captain's body was nowhere to be seen; it must have been dragged below by the boat. As for the barrel-chested sailor, he had completely disappeared.

"Lady, your husband's body will be recovered later, together with the others who died," the elf told her. He tilted his face in the general direction of Arvin and Karrell. "I don't have enough magic to cast the spell on all of us, so you two will have to wait here. I will get them to send another riverboat—it should reach you by midday."

"Fine," Arvin said. He pulled his cloak tighter as a breeze started to blow—a natural wind, this time. Arvin squinted up at the overcast sky, hoping it wasn't going to start snowing again. If it did, the river-boat would have a hard time locating them.

The elf cast the spell on himself then on the sailor. Hulv picked up the injured woman and followed the elf into the air, as if climbing an invisible staircase. They walked swiftly away and soon were no more than specks in the distance.

Arvin glanced at Karrell, who had her back to him. She was staring at the bodies, which were slowly drifting away from the island, back in the direction of Riverboat Landing.

"We should recover them," she said. "Before the current carries them away."

"I suppose," Arvin agreed reluctantly. Despite the fact that the spell Karrell had cast on him was keeping him warm, he was nervous about entering the river again. "But what if another naga happens along?"

"None will come," Karrell said. "The naga was alone—an outcast, hiding from the others of her kind. She thought this would be a safer place to lay her eggs."

"Ah," Arvin said. He glanced again at the bodies. The river had only a sluggish current; it wasn't as if they were going to vanish in the next few moments. "I need to check something in my pack first. Just give me a moment; then I'll help."

Karrell didn't reply. She seemed to still be smarting from his critical remark about the spell she'd used on the naga. Arvin gave himself a mental kick for being so sharp with her—especially after she risked her own life to save that of the woman—and tried to stammer out an apology, but she dived into the water alone.

"Uh . . . I'll be right there," Arvin called to her.

He pulled the dorje out of his pack—then stiffened as he felt something shift inside the cloth in which it was wrapped. He tore the cloth open with fumbling fingers and groaned as he saw what lay within. The dorje had snapped cleanly in half. The lavender glow of psionic energy that had once filled it was gone.

Cursing, he slammed a fist against his leg. Now that the dorje was broken, Arvin would have to rely on his own, limited, psionic powers.

Finding Glisena wasn't going to be easy.

He shoved the broken crystal back into his pack, together with his ropes. As he tied the torn flap shut, he wondered how long it would take the second riverboat to reach them. Thinking about that, he realized the broken dorje wasn't his only problem. When the riverboat came to rescue them, it would also recover the bodies Karrell was so diligently recovering. Its crew wouldn't want to travel with these all the way to Ormpetarr. Instead they would return to the closest town—to Riverboat Landing . . .

Which was the last place Arvin wanted to go . . .

Especially if Zelia was still there.

Chapter 4

As the dark shape that had been moving upriver drew closer, resolving into a riverboat, Arvin waved his arms above his head. This boat had neither sail nor rudder. Instead it was drawn by a giant eagle whose talons gripped a crossbar attached to the end of the bowsprit. The bird was enormous, with a wingspan nearly as wide as the riverboat was long. The eagle let out a *skree* as it spotted the pair of humans on the island, and the boat slowly turned until its bow was pointed toward them.

"They've seen us," Arvin said, lowering his arms. Warming his back at the fire they'd built from wood salvaged from the wreck of the first riverboat, he watched as the boat draw nearer. He tried to pick out the figures on board, hoping he wasn't going to see an all-too-familiar face. He'd wrapped a scarf around his face so that only his eyes showed and had disappeared his dagger into his glove. If Zelia was on board, these crude preparations might give him a chance to catch her off guard. He just wished he hadn't used up his store of psionic energy. He couldn't even manifest a simple distraction, let alone shield himself from whatever Zelia might hurl at him.

Karrell stared at the approaching boat. "Is it dangerous?"

It took Arvin a moment to realize she was talking about the eagle. "I'm sure we'll be fine," he said. "They wouldn't use a bird that wasn't tame. They probably raised it from a hatchling."

Karrell seemed unconvinced. As the riverboat drew up to them, dropping anchor next to the island, she took a step back. The eagle—taller than a human and looming even larger from its perch on the bowsprit—flapped its massive wings in agitation, stirring up ripples in the water on either side of the boat. It must have sensed Karrell's uneasiness, for it snapped its beak in her direction. The driver—a human with close-cropped brown hair—gave the reins a quick yank, jerking the bird's head back. He stood on the bow, just behind the bowsprit.

"Sorry," he called out. "She usually isn't this skittish."

Arvin's mind was on other things. By now, the elf would have told everyone at Riverboat Landing about their narrow escape from the naga—and the role that "Vin" had played in it. The chances were slight that the sailor would have mentioned Arvin's pack and the "strange-looking rope" that had spilled from it. But if he had, and Zelia had overheard. . . .

Arvin glanced quickly over the boat's open deck. Besides the driver, the crew included two sailors—one working the tiller at the rear of the boat and one amidships—and two guards. As before, they were stationed at rail-mounted crossbows on either side of the boat. Their eyes ranged warily over the river.

Zelia wasn't on board. Arvin breathed a sigh of relief.

The sailor lifted a gangplank over the side of the boat; Arvin caught the end of it and placed it firmly on the island's rocky shore. Then he made his way across it. Karrell followed, keeping him between her and the eagle. "Don't worry," Arvin said over his shoulder. "I'm sure the driver will hold it in check."

The eagle turned, keeping a baleful eye on Karrell as she approached the boat.

Arvin climbed aboard and turned to help Karrell, but the sailor was there first, handing her a woolen blanket. She took it but ignored his urgings that she wrap it around her shoulders. Arvin, whose clothes were also still sodden, wasn't offered a blanket.

"Will we be continuing to Ormpetarr?" Arvin asked.

The sailor—a man with calloused hands and uncombed

hair—shook his head. "Nope. Back to Riverboat Landing to finish loading." His eyes lingered appreciatively on Karrell.

Arvin fought down his uneasiness. "But I need to get to Ormpetarr quickly," he protested. "I have important business there that mustn't be delayed."

The sailor grunted. "Where we go next depends on how much coin you've got. Speak to the captain." He jerked his head in the direction of the man on the bow. Then, together with the second sailor, he crossed the gangplank to the island and surveyed the five bodies Karrell and Arvin had recovered from the river. Karrell had laid them out in a neat row, arranging their arms at their sides and closing their eyes before the bodies stiffened.

Arvin approached the captain. The eagle had settled down, allowing him to slacken the reins. Arvin repeated his plea to journey directly to Ormpetarr, but the captain shook his head.

"She's only half loaded," he said, nodding at the deck beneath his feet. He glanced at the two sailors, who were carrying the first of the bodies to the ship. "It's not worth my while, unless. . . ."

Arvin took the hint. He dug his coin pouch out of his boot and jingled it. "How much?"

The captain gave the pouch a brief glance then shook his head. "More than that can hold, even if every coin in it is a plume."

Arvin lowered his pouch. Normally, he'd have manifested a charm to help things along, but he'd expended every bit of energy his *muladhara* could provide. Not until after tomorrow morning's meditations and *asanas* would he be able to manifest his powers. "When we reach Ormpetarr, I'll be meeting with Dmetrio Extaminos, prince of Hlondeth and ambassador to Sespech. He will reimburse you for your losses."

The captain thought about this. "I'd need some sort of security. Something of value. Do you have any magical devices?"

Arvin hesitated. He'd no sooner give up his glove, bracelet, or knife than he would another fingertip, and while he did have magical ropes, he didn't want word of them reaching Zelia's ears. If she was still at Riverboat Landing when this crew returned in a few days' time, she'd quickly realize who "Vin" was.

The captain grew impatient. He glanced at the sailors, who were struggling to lift the last of the bodies on board—that of the husband.

The headless corpse was as stiff as a beam of wood. They angled it down through a hatch and into the hold, on top of the other bodies, then closed the hatch and hauled up the rope ladder.

"Bodies stowed," one of the sailors reported. "We're ready to go."

"Right," the captain said, gathering up his reins. "Back to Riverboat Landing, then."

Arvin decided to take the chance. "I do have a magical device," he said, shrugging the pack from his shoulders. The captain of a riverboat would surely recognize the value of the trollgut rope. "It's a valuable one. Here, let me show you."

"Sure you do," the captain scoffed.

Karrell touched Arvin's arm, startling him—she'd come quietly up behind him during the conversation. "Allow me," she murmured. She said something in her own language then turned to the captain, making a pleading gesture. "I, too, must reach Ormpetarr quickly," she told him. "My mother is ill, and I have magic that can cure her. If I am delayed even one day. . . ."

Arvin was impressed with the quaver she managed to inject into her voice.

The captain gave a hesitant frown. "I don't know. I—"

"I can compensate you for your losses," Karrell said. She reached into the pouch at her belt and pulled from it a grape-sized, multifaceted gem the color of new grass. Normally, Arvin wouldn't have had the first idea of what it was—or its value. But a little of the knowledge he'd gleaned from Zelia's mind seed remained—enough to tell him it was a spinel, and valuable due to its unusual color.

"Please," Karrell continued. "Won't you accept this? It is all I have left—it cost me everything else I had to get this far. But if this will help me to reach my mother before it is too late, I will gladly give it to you."

"Keep it," the captain said gruffly. "You'll need it." He turned to Arvin and held out a hand. "You, on the other hand, can pay for your passage. Twenty plumes."

It was more than twice the amount normally charged, but Arvin handed over the coins without complaint.

The captain shouted down to his crew. "Make ready. We're making for Ormpetarr."

When the riverboat was underway, Arvin walked with Karrell to the stern, where they seated themselves on a raised hatch. "Nicely done," he said, nodding in the direction of the captain. "You're handy with a charm spell."

Karrell tilted her head. "As are you. But I would advise you not to cast one on me a second time."

"What makes you think I charmed you?" Arvin asked, feigning innocence.

Karrell just stared at him.

Arvin shrugged. "Well, you charmed me first, so that makes us even."

Karrell tossed her head. "I never——"

Arvin raised a finger. "Yes, you did. I wouldn't have . . . made such a fool of myself, otherwise."

"All men are fools," she said. Then, as Arvin drew himself up to protest, she smiled. "And so are some women, at times."

Arvin nodded. To a woman as beautiful as Karrell, the men constantly gaping at her must indeed seem fools. Drawn by the eagle, the riverboat traveled swiftly. The wind of its passage swept through Karrell's hair, drawing it back and revealing her jade earring and the smooth curve of her neck. Even without the charm spell, Arvin felt a rush of longing for her.

She leaned toward him. "When we get to Ormpetarr——"

"I know," Arvin said. "You want me to introduce you to Ambassador Extaminos." He folded his arms across his chest. "Tell me why you want to meet him so badly. The real reason. Is it connected with whatever it is you're looking for?"

Karrell was silent for several moments. The only sounds were the steady *whup-whup* of the eagle's wings and the creak of the hull timbers.

"Yes," she answered at last. "Dmetrio Extaminos may know where it is. I simply want to ask him a few questions."

"That's all?" Arvin asked.

Karrell met his eye. "That is all. I do not intend harm to the ambassador."

"I see." Arvin wanted to believe Karrell, but everything pointed to her being a rogue, out to steal something of Dmetrio's. A rogue armed with clerical magic, as well as natural beauty—but even so, she needed someone to help her earn Dmetrio's trust, to get her inside. Arvin sighed, wondering if he would ever be free of rogues and their schemes.

"You're going to charm Dmetrio," he said. It was an easy enough guess—that was the tactic Arvin had planned to use. "And get him to give you . . . whatever it is you're looking for."

Karrell's silence was answer enough.

Arvin pictured her luring the ambassador into her bed—once there, any man would gladly give her whatever it was she wanted. The image of the ambassador's scaly body coiled around hers repulsed Arvin.

"How about this," he offered. "I'll be meeting with the ambassador in his residence. Just tell me what it is you're looking for, and I'll try to find out where it is. I'm . . . pretty good at spotting things."

Karrell tilted her head. "You are asking me to trust you."

"Yes."

Her eyes narrowed. "What is it *you* are looking for? Or rather . . . who?"

"I can't tell you that."

Karrell stared at him, waiting.

Arvin sighed. "Point taken."

Karrell shifted her gaze to the captain. "I am helping you to reach Ormpetarr—and to avoid the woman you so fear. Without my assistance. . . ."

"Fine," Arvin sputtered. "I'll introduce you to the ambassador. But not until after my business in Ormpetarr is concluded."

He was hedging, of course. The last thing he needed was a member of House Extaminos's royal family linking him with a theft. One yuan-ti wanting him dead was trouble enough. But Karrell seemed to accept his offer; after giving him a long, measuring look, she nodded.

"In the meantime, no more charm spells," Arvin insisted. "Agreed?"

"Agreed." She touched a hand to her heart and looked sincere, but Arvin vowed to be careful, even so.

The rest of the journey passed too swiftly—and too slowly—for Arvin's liking. Too swiftly, because once they reached Ormpetarr, he would probably never see Karrell again. Too slowly, because, despite his best efforts to pass the time in conversation, he kept saying things that irritated her—that made him wish the journey were already over. When the riverboat stopped for the night at Halfway Station, a hamlet even smaller than Riverboat Landing, he'd struck up a conversation about Hlondeth over dinner, telling her how pleased he was to be away from the city of serpents. He cautioned her that the yuan-ti were a devious and cruel race that cared little for humans. It was merely intended as a warning that the members of House Extaminos were dangerous folk to anger, but she seemed to take this to imply that she couldn't take care of herself. After the meal, she curtly declined Arvin's offer of a mug of mulled wine and his invitation to linger at their table beside the fire, and turned in to bed.

The next day, when their journey resumed, she spoke little. She stared over the rail, watching the riverbank slide by. Arvin tried once more to engage her in conversation, asking if it ever snowed in the Chultan Peninsula, but though she smiled at him as they chatted, the smile never quite reached her eyes. After a while, he gave up on conversation and instead stared at the passing scenery, watching as the riverboat left the river behind and slid out onto a broad, open lake.

It was well after sunset before they caught sight of their destination. Like the other cities of the Vilhon Reach, Ormpetarr had been built centuries ago and had long since outgrown its walls. A scattering of buildings spread for some distance up and down the lake. Most appeared to be connected with the fishing industry; the small amount of moonlight that penetrated the clouds gave Arvin a view of racks used for drying fish, and a number of boats that had been drawn out of the water for the winter. The buildings themselves were little more than blocks of darkness from which squares of light shone—windows, Arvin realized after a moment, square, rather than round.

As the riverboat drew closer to the city proper, these squares of light became numerous and clustered closer together.

At last Ormpetarr's harbor came into view. The city was walled even on the side that fronted the lake; the stout stonework was punctuated by a series of heavy wooden gates, each lined up with a pier that ran out into the river. More than a dozen riverboats were tied up there. Most were empty, their sails furled, but a few were disembarking passengers and unloading freight.

The city seemed dark to Arvin, who was used to the constant glow of Hlondeth's magically quarried stone, but somehow he found that comforting. In Ormpetarr there would be plenty of shadows, plenty of places to hide from Zelia. And what light there was—the glow of street lanterns and the light that shone out of the windows—was warm and yellow and welcoming, rather than an eerie green.

The riverboat drew up to one of the piers. Once the sailors had tied the boat fast, Arvin gathered up his pack and climbed down onto the pier. Karrell immediately followed. The planks underfoot were treacherous with half-melted ice; at one point she slipped, and he caught her arm. She smiled her thanks to him and continued to cling to his arm as they walked up the pier.

"Which inn are you staying at?" she asked.

Arvin gave her a wry look. Was she going to suggest they share a room? "I won't be staying at an inn," he told her. "I have accommodation elsewhere."

"At the ambassador's home?" Karrell guessed. "Or perhaps at the palace?"

They reached the small group of people who were passing through the gate at the end of the pier. On either side of the gate was a watchful soldier. Each wore a brightly polished steel breastplate, embossed with the eye of Helm, over a padded leather coat that hung to his knees. Unlike the clerics in Mimph, these soldiers carried visible weapons—maces with knobbed heads. Their open-faced helms were decorated with purple plumes.

Each person passing through the gate was asked his or her business in Ormpetarr. Arvin and Karrell repeated the stories they'd told each other earlier: he saying he was a rope merchant's agent; she claiming to be an artist.

When they were through the gate, Arvin plucked Karrell's hand from his arm. "Well, goodnight," he told her.

Karrell raised an eyebrow. "Surely you do not think to be rid of me so easily?"

"I'm not trying to get rid of you," Arvin told her. "When my business here is done, I'll send for you. I'll introduce you to the ambassador then."

Karrell snorted. "You have not even asked what inn I am staying at."

"I was just about to."

"No you were not."

Arvin sighed in exasperation. "Goodnight," he said firmly. He strode up the street. The shops on either side were closing for the night, their merchants busy shuttering windows and locking doors. The roads ran in straight lines and were hundreds of paces long—a far cry from the mazelike streets of Hlondeth—and were illuminated along their length by lanterns. It would be more difficult to hide here—or to lose someone who was following you—than he'd expected.

He glanced over his shoulder. Karrell was a few paces behind him, following like a shadow.

Arvin picked up his pace, sidestepping the other people on the street.

Karrell did the same.

After several blocks, Arvin realized the futility of trying to leave her behind. He could hardly run through the streets. She'd only chase after him—and gods only knew what the local folk would think of that. At the middle of a wide square dominated by one of the silver gauntlet statues, he rounded on her. "Look," he said, irritated. "You'll just have to trust me, and wait until I send for you. Unless you back off, I'm going to warn the ambassador about you—tell him *not* to meet with you."

Karrell's eyes narrowed. "You think you can threaten me?" she asked. "That dagger cuts both ways. What if I were to tell that woman at Riverboat Landing about you?"

Arvin felt his face grow pale. With an effort, he steadied himself. "Riverboat Landing is two days downriver. By the time a message got there—"

Karrell smiled. "A spell can always be used to speed a message on its way."

Arvin shivered. She might be bluffing, but he didn't want to take the chance. "It seems we've reached a stalemate."

Karrell started to whisper something in her own language. Before she could finish, Arvin slapped a hand onto the gauntlet. The cold metal chilled his bare fingers, making him shiver. "Don't try to charm me," he warned her. "It won't work. Not here. This statue is magical. It will turn the charm back on you, instead."

He had no idea, of course, if the statue's magic would even

protect him from a spell that did no actual injury. But presumably, neither did Karrell.

She stared at him. "You will not stand here all night."

"I will if I have to," Arvin said.

"So will I."

They stared at each other for several moments. Then Arvin heard footsteps behind him. He turned—his hand still on the gauntlet—and saw one of the red-cloaked clerics approaching. The man hadn't been there a moment ago; the gauntlet seemed to have summoned him.

"Is there a problem?" the cleric asked, his eyes on Karrell. "Did this woman threaten you?"

Arvin let his hand fall away from the gauntlet and raised it to his lips, blowing on it to ward off the metal's chill. For a moment, he considered answering yes. Having Karrell detained was a tempting thought—it would keep her out of the way until he'd accomplished his mission. But subjecting her to the magical punishments the innkeeper in Mimph had described was something Arvin just couldn't do. He shook his head.

"No," he told the cleric. "I was just leaning against this statue while we talked. But she is pestering me—she keeps trying to solicit me and won't leave me alone. Do you have a law against that?"

The cleric scowled at Karrell. "Helm's Sanctuary is not a place for solicitation."

Karrell's face flushed. Her mouth opened then closed. "I apologize," she said at last. "It will not happen again." Chin in the air, she turned and strode away.

The cleric turned his scowl on Arvin. "The gauntlet is intended to be used only in times of true danger."

"Sorry," Arvin said. "I'm a stranger here. I've got a lot to learn about your customs." He paused. "Could you direct me to the home of Ambassador Extaminos? I came to Ormpetarr to meet with him."

The cleric gave Arvin a skeptical look. Then he raised his left hand and held it, palm out, toward Arvin. "State your business with the ambassador."

"I'm. . . ." Arvin started to say that he was a rope merchant's agent who hoped for a formal introduction to the baron, but other words spilled out of his mouth. "I'm here to question Dmetrio Extaminos about the disappearance of—" With an effort that brought beads of sweat to his brow, he choked off the rest of what he'd been about to say. The magical compulsion the cleric had just placed on Arvin was one he recognized; he had once been forced to wear a ring that compelled him to speak the truth.

The truth, fortunately, could be told selectively. "I'm here on state business," he told the cleric. "I'm meeting with the ambassador at the baron's request. Baron Foesmasher will not be pleased if you force me to reveal state secrets."

"Ah. My apologies." He lowered his hand, gave Arvin directions, and strode away.

After a quick glance in the direction Karrell had gone, Arvin started on his way. It took him a while to figure out what "blocks" were, but after he started walking, it became obvious. He was used to the directions they gave in Hlondeth—a series of "fork rights" and "fork lefts." Here in Ormpetarr, the intersections were composed of four streets, not three. Each intersection offered three choices—straight ahead, right or left, but instead of saying "fork straight" the people of Ormpetarr grouped all of the straights together and simply gave a total. Arvin lost his way more than once but eventually got himself pointed in the right direction. He peered over his shoulder several times, making sure that Karrell was not following. Though he did catch sight of the same man twice—a tall man with gaunt, beard-stubbled cheeks—he saw no sign of Karrell.

The tall man, however, was cause for concern. Arvin had noticed him down on the docks earlier; it seemed improbable that the fellow would have taken exactly the same route as Arvin through the city. Convinced the fellow was a rogue, out to tumble a newcomer to the city—and well aware that where there was one rogue, there might be others—Arvin took an abrupt turn into a side street and activated his magical bracelet. He scuttled up a wall like a lizard, jogged across the rooftop and climbed down the other side of the building. Peeking around the corner, he spotted the tall man hesitating at the side street Arvin had just vanished from. As the fellow started down the street, Arvin hurried back up the main thoroughfare then turned into another street two blocks from the one the tall fellow was searching.

He continued for several blocks, sometimes walking with his cloak hood up, other times with it down. On streets where others were walking, he positioned himself immediately beside or behind them, giving the appearance that he was part of a larger group. On streets that were empty, he turned into doorways, pretending to be opening the door with a key but all the while keeping an eye on the street, searching for the tall man—or anyone who might be one of his accomplices.

At last, satisfied he'd given the rogue the slip, he started again for the ambassador's residence.

It took him some time to find it, despite the cleric's directions. Losing the rogue had thrown Arvin off; he had to double back and recount the blocks. It was quite late before he found the right section of town; the darkened streets were empty, and the temperature had dropped below freezing, making the streets slippery with ice.

Eventually he located the building he was looking for: a three-story residence that stretched from one street to another, the length of one of Ormpetarr's blocks. He knew it must be the ambassador's residence when he saw two members of Hlondeth's militia—recognizable by their distinctive helmets, which were flared in the shape of a cobra's hood—standing just inside the wrought-iron fence that surrounded the building. Arvin hailed them and explained that he'd come to meet with the ambassador.

"This late at night?" one of the men asked from behind the gate. He was an older, stocky man with a neat gray beard and hands crisscrossed with faded white scars: a career soldier.

Arvin spread his hands apologetically. "I was delayed." He held up the letter of introduction Tanju had given him. Written by one of Lady Dediana's scribes, the folded letter bore a dab of wax impressed with the insignia of House Extaminos: a mason's chisel and a ship on either side of a wavy line that represented a serpent.

"Could you at least show Ambassador Extaminos this and ask if he'll see me?"

The bearded militiaman held out a scarred hand; Arvin passed the letter through the bars. As he carried the letter inside the building, the second militiaman—a thin, young man with a prominent nose that was red with cold—stood by the gate, waiting. Arvin heard his teeth chattering.

"An unpleasant night to be stuck outside," Arvin said. "I've never seen a winter this cold."

The militiaman nodded. "It's better than crewing a galley, though." He glanced at Arvin's face. "What happened to you?"

Arvin touched the wound on his cheek. The flesh was tender and bruised under the scab. He hadn't shaved this morning and probably wouldn't for the next few days, at least. "A riverboat accident," he answered. "We were attacked by a naga."

The young militiaman's eyes widened. "*That's* what delayed you?" Before he could comment further, however, the other militiaman returned. "The ambassador will see you in the morning," he announced, passing Arvin's letter back.

"But I've traveled far," Arvin protested. "And my business is urgent."

"In the morning," he said firmly.

Silently, Arvin cursed the thief who had delayed him. Baron Foesmasher was expecting Arvin to show up at the palace tomorrow morning, and—so Arvin had heard—the baron wasn't a man who liked to be kept waiting. Arvin had hoped to question Dmetrio this evening. If Dmetrio was sleepy, so much the better. It would be easier for Arvin to manifest a charm on him.

"I realize it's late," Arvin said, manifesting a charm on the bearded militiaman even as he spoke. "But I won't have time to come back in the morning. I just need a quick word with the ambassador, and I'll be on my way." He smiled and drew the coin pouch from his boot. "I realize he'll be angry at you for annoying him a second time, but I can make it worth your while. Please let me speak with him. Tonight."

The bearded militiaman tilted his head—then shook it, like a man shaking himself awake. "No," he said firmly.

Arvin swore under his breath. The bearded man's mind must have been as tough as the rest of him.

The younger man stared greedily at Arvin's coin pouch. "Sergeant," he said in a low voice. "Couldn't we just—"

"That's enough, Rillis," The sergeant placed a hand on his sword hilt and stared at Arvin through the gate. "The merchant can come back at a civilized hour of the morning . . . or not at all."

Arvin let his hand fall away from his pouch. "In the morning, then," he said with a sigh. Then, "Could you at least tell me where to find a reputable inn?"

CHAPTER 5

THE NEXT MORNING, ARVIN ROSE WELL BEFORE DAWN. HE DRESSED in his better clothes and ate a quick meal of fried cheese and thick-crusted bread. He waved away the ale the innkeeper offered; he wanted a clear head for this morning's work.

As he stepped outside the inn, the air bit at his lungs, crisp and cold. The sky to the east was turning a faint pink behind the clouds. It had snowed overnight; a few flakes were still falling from the sky. Snow crunched beneath Arvin's boots as he strode past merchants opening the shutters of their shops, boys kindling fires in the stoves of their mulled-wine carts, and men carrying heavy sacks on their backs as they made early-morning deliveries to the shops and homes in this part of the city. These men were doing the work of slaves, yet not one of them had an **S** brand on his cheek.

Arvin had heard that, while slavery existed in Sespech, it was an uncommon practice. Those slaves who did exist within the barony had been brought to Sespech by their masters. Hearing this and seeing it with his own eyes, however, were two different things. It felt odd to be walking along streets populated by free men. It was odder still to have no viaducts arching above—to be on a street that was open to the sky. For perhaps the first time in his life, Arvin walked without the slight hunch that a human in Hlondeth automatically adopted—the tensing of shoulders and neck that came with the constant awareness of the yuan-ti slithering along the viaducts overhead. He felt lighter, somehow, more sure of himself, relaxed.

He smiled.

The smile vanished as something sharp pricked through the fabric of his cloak and shirt, jabbing his back. A hand on his shoulder turned him toward a doorway.

"Inside," gritted the man behind him.

Arvin risked turning his head slightly. The tall rogue from last night had the hood of his cloak pulled up, but Arvin recognized him by his gaunt, stubbled cheeks. "My pouch is in my boot," Arvin told him, gesturing at his coin pouch; as soon as the fellow bent for it, Arvin would draw his dagger and stab backhanded through his cloak, giving the rogue a nasty surprise. He put a quaver in his voice. "Please don't hurt me. Just take my coin and go."

The rogue pressed the sharp object—most likely a dagger—into Arvin's back. The blade was icy cold; the flesh around the wound immediately began to ache.

"One thrust, and it will freeze your flesh," the man promised in a grim voice. "I don't think you'd survive long with your entrails turned to ice." He gave Arvin a slight shove. "Now . . . inside."

"Listen, friend," Arvin began, raising his hands so the rogue could see them. He'd use silent speech to show the fellow that he, too, was Guild, albeit from Hlondeth, then hit him with a charm. "I'm one of—"

The dagger pricked harder, drawing a gasp of pain from Arvin. It felt as though a needle of ice were being driven into his back.

"No tricks," the rogue gritted. "There's others watching—others with weapons who will take you down if I fall. One suspicious move, mind mage, and you're a dead man."

Arvin blinked. How did the rogue know he was a psion? Arvin knew better than to look around. The threat would be genuine; rogues almost never worked alone. "What do you want?" he asked.

"To talk," the rogue answered.

"All right," Arvin said. "Let's talk." He reached for the handle of the door and opened it.

As he stepped inside what turned out to be cooper's workshop, he braced himself for what was to come. Someone in the local rogues' guild must have heard that a member of the Hlondeth Guild was in Sespech. The locals probably wanted to learn what Arvin was doing here—to make sure he wasn't planning on thieving on their turf. Arvin balled his left hand into a fist and felt the familiar ache of his missing fingertip. He didn't intend to lose another.

The rogue removed the dagger from Arvin's back and stepped quickly away from him, closing the door. The weapon was an odd-looking one, made of metal as white as frost and with a spike-shaped blade that tapered to a point, like an icicle. The rogue sheathed it—a bad sign. It meant that the room held other, more potent threats.

Arvin glanced around. The workshop looked ordinary enough; half-finished barrels stood on the floor, next to loose piles of metal hoops. The smell of fresh-sawn wood lingered in the air, suggesting the workshop had been used recently. Chisels, saws, and mallets were scattered about; Arvin could have turned any one of them into a surprise weapon using the power that allowed him to move objects at a distance. He refrained, however, realizing that the tall man probably wasn't the only rogue in the room. His guess was confirmed a moment later when some sawdust on the floor shifted slightly; a second person, cloaked by invisibility, was also present. The tall man confirmed this a moment later, with two words in the silent speech, directed at his invisible companion: *None followed.*

Arvin shifted his eyes away from the spot where the invisible person stood, looking at the tall man instead. "What do you want to talk about?"

"We know the baron's daughter is missing and that you've come from Hlondeth to find her," the rogue said.

Only through years of practice did Arvin manage to prevent his eyes from widening. This wasn't what he'd expected.

"We want to make you an offer," the rogue continued.

Arvin raised an eyebrow. "One that's just too good to refuse?"

The rogue nodded. He pointed at one of the finished barrels; a small leather pouch sat on top of it. "Look inside."

Arvin stepped over to the pouch and loosened its ties. Something glittered inside: gems—dozens of them. Seeing the way they sparkled, even in the dim light of the shop, Arvin realized what they were: diamonds. Small, easily portable and immensely valuable, they were a currency that could be spent anywhere in Faerûn that Arvin might care to go.

Assuming they weren't just an illusion, which gave him an idea. "How do I know they're real?" he asked.

"Inspect them as closely as you like," the rogue offered.

"May I use magic to evaluate their worth?"

The rogue hesitated. "No tricks," he warned. "Or—"

"I know, I know. Or I'm a dead man," Arvin continued. "Don't worry. There will be no tricks."

He bent over the pouch and stirred the gems with a finger. They seemed real enough. Then he braced himself; it was now or never. He picked up the pouch and manifested the power that would allow him to listen to the thoughts of those in the room. Silver sparkles erupted from his third eye and streamed toward his hand, dissipating as they hit the gems; if his bluff held, the rogue would think the spell was targeting them. Out of the corner of his eye, Arvin saw the rogue frowning, as if listening to a distant, half-heard sound. Arvin wondered if the invisible person was doing the same thing.

An instant later, his question was answered. Two separate voices whispered into his mind: the thoughts of the rogue and the invisible person. Ignoring the former—he would be an expendable member of the guild, one who'd been told as little as possible—Arvin concentrated on the latter. The thoughts were those of a man who stood with his finger on the trigger of a crossbow, loaded with a bolt whose head was smeared with a poison more lethal than yuan-ti venom. Worse yet, the trigger was a dead man's switch: if the invisible man relaxed his finger, even a little, the crossbow would shoot.

Arvin hid his shudder and gestured at the gems. "What do I have to do to earn this?"

"The girl," the rogue answered. "When you find her, give her to us."

Arvin nodded, concentrating on the thoughts of the second man. The fellow was worried about the diamonds, which were real enough. If he killed the psion, they'd scatter on the floor, and some might be lost in the cracks. If even one went missing, someone named Haskar would have his head.

"What will you do with Glisena?" Arvin asked.

"Ransom her," the rogue answered. He gestured at the pouch.

"For a *lot* of coin. What we're going to demand from the baron will make that look like the contents of a beggar's cup."

Arvin nodded, still listening to the thoughts of the second man. The guild wasn't going to ransom Glisena to the baron. No, that would be too dangerous. They'd sell her, instead. Lord Wianar would pay well for the girl—and there would be no need for dangerous exchanges or worrying about those damn clerics.

Arvin nodded to himself. Alarmed though he was at the thought that the local rogues' guild knew who he was—they must have a spy in the baron's court—he was relieved to find that their plan was so simplistic. He let his manifestation end, satisfied he'd learned everything he could.

Somewhere outside, a horn sounded three times: the morning call to prayer for Helm's faithful. The rogue ignored it.

"How do I contact you?" Arvin asked.

"Enter any tavern and make this sign," the rogue instructed. With a finger, he rubbed first the inside corner of his right eye, then the outside corner.

Arvin smiled to himself. It was one of the first words in silent speech the Guild had taught him.

"When you see someone make this sign," the rogue continued, making a **V** with the first two fingers of his right hand and drawing them along his left forearm from elbow to wrist, "you'll know you've found us." He paused. "Do we have an agreement?"

Arvin nodded. "It's certainly a tempting offer," he said. "I'll let you know." He set the pouch back on the barrel—carefully, so none of the diamonds spilled. "May I go now?"

The rogue opened the door and stepped away from it. As Arvin walked past him, he moved his hand to the hilt of his dagger. "Just remember," he warned in a low voice. "We'll be watching you. Don't cross us."

Arvin nodded. The rogue wasn't telling him anything new. If Sespech's rogues' guild was anything like Hlondeth's, Arvin's every move would be marked.

It had been bad enough, finding Zelia in Sespech.

Now he had a second reason to watch his back.

☙

Arvin went directly to Dmetrio's residence. There was no need to be secretive about his destination—not when the local rogues' guild knew who he was. The meeting with its two representatives had taken only a short time; the sun had risen, painting the winter sky a dull white, but it was still early in the morning. The same two militiamen were still on guard duty outside the residence. The younger man was yawning widely—and being glared at by his sergeant.

"Good morning, Rillis," he called to him. "Don't they ever let you sleep?"

Rillis grinned through chattering teeth. "Soon, I hope. The watch change—"

The sergeant jabbed him with an elbow. "Quiet, soldier," he snapped. Then, to Arvin, "I suppose you expect to see the ambassador now?"

Arvin nodded and pulled out his letter of introduction.

The sergeant took it. "I'll let him know you're here."

After a few moments, he returned and opened the gate. "This way," he instructed.

As Arvin stepped through the gate, he heard rapid footsteps behind him.

"Vin! I am so sorry!"

Startled, Arvin turned and saw Karrell hurrying toward him. She slipped her hand under Arvin's arm, grasping him firmly by the elbow. "Please do not be angry with me, Vin," she said, tugging him toward the front door of the residence. "I did not mean to sleep so late. When I saw that you had left without me, I hurried here as quickly as I could." She tugged Arvin toward the residence.

The sergeant quickly blocked their way. Rillis was slower to react; he'd been gaping at Karrell. Belatedly, he stepped forward and held up a hand.

Karrell beamed a smile at him. "Was Ambassador Extaminos kept waiting?" She loosened her cloak, as if to cool down from her run.

Rillis's eyes lingered on her breasts, which rose and fell as she panted. "No, lady. He has only just been summoned."

Arvin glared at Karrell.

She gave him a coy smile. "Come, Vin. Be thankful it's me who is accompanying you, and not that blue-tongued she-demon. She'd only embarrass you in front of the ambassador."

Arvin tensed at the thinly veiled reference to Zelia. He wished he'd had the cleric lock Karrell up last night, when he had the chance. What now? If he protested, she would alert Zelia to his presence in Ormpetarr.

"It's all right," he told the sergeant. "She's with me." He pinched Karrell's arm, however, as they walked toward the door. "An introduction," he gritted under his breath. "No more. Then you go."

She nodded.

Rillis unlocked the front door with cold-stiffened fingers and ushered them through. He was about to close it again when the sergeant motioned him inside. "Go ahead, Rillis," he said. "Warm up a bit."

Rillis grinned then followed Arvin and Karrell inside. They stepped through the door into a wide, semicircular hall whose floor tiles glowed with a soft green light. A ramp, its stonework also glowing, curved up the wall on the right to doors on the building's second floor. The wall to the left had a fireplace in which a fire was roaring; a rolled-up carpet and several boxes lay against the wall next to it. The air in the hall was uncomfortably hot and stank of spice and snake. Arvin unfastened his cloak and wiped his face with a sleeve, blotting away the sweat that was beading on his forehead. Another member of the militia—this one with wide shoulders and watchful eyes—stood just inside the door, dressed in full armor. Arvin wondered how the fellow could stand the oppressive heat.

As Rillis warmed his back at the fire, sighing his relief, Karrell moved toward what Arvin had at first taken to be a painting that rested on the mantle. He saw that it was a hollow pane of glass, filled with viscous red, turquoise, and indigo liquids that rose and fell in a swirl of ever-changing patterns.

"It's a slitherglow," Rillis said. "I don't suppose you've seen one before."

"It is beautiful," Karrell answered. She held out her hands to the fire, warming them, and stared at the slitherglow as if mesmerized. Arvin shook his head. She certainly wasn't acting like a rogue casing the residence. Her eyes should have been darting around the room, noting the exits and appraising its contents. The larger boxes, for example, probably held breakables, judging by the sawdust packing that had trickled out of the corner of one of them—ceramics, perhaps, or statuettes. And the rug was bulged slightly; something was rolled inside it. Judging by the boxes and the bare appearance of the room, the ambassador was planning a move from the residence, probably in a few days' time. Arvin wondered where he was going.

A door at the top of the ramp opened. The militiaman standing next to Arvin stiffened, and Rillis ushered Karrell back to Arvin's side then stood flanking her. Neither had a weapon in hand, but Arvin didn't want to make any sudden moves. Rillis was probably new to the militia, but the second man looked tougher, more experienced—and the House Extaminos bodyguards were rumored to coat their weapons with yuan-ti venom.

A man in a red silk robe stepped through the door and began making his way down the ramp. He appeared human, at first glance. He had dark hair that swept back from a high forehead; a long, narrow nose; and a thin, muscular body. His walk, however, immediately gave him away as yuan-ti. Instead of stepping, as humans did, he turned each footstep into a slither, sliding his slippered feet along the stone. His body swayed as he walked, his head moving gently from side to side. As he drew closer, slit pupils and a flicker of a forked tongue confirmed his race. Despite these attributes, he was a handsome man, full of poise and self-confidence. No wonder the baron's daughter had fallen for him.

In one slender hand, he held Arvin's letter of introduction. The other hand was hidden by a silk sleeve that hung past his fingertips.

Arvin bowed. "Ambassador Extaminos."

Dmetrio stared at him. "Vin of Hlondeth," he hissed, his voice as devoid of emotion as dry leaves. "Agent of the Mariners' Mercantile House."

Dmetrio shifted his gaze to Karrell, who also bowed. He stepped closer to her as she rose, his tongue flickering in and out of his mouth as he drank in her scent. "And who is this?"

Arvin rose. "An . . . acquaintance of mine," he said slowly. Threat or no threat, he wasn't going to call Karrell more than that. "We met on the journey here, and she insisted on meeting you. Her name is Karrell. She—"

Out of the corner of his eye, Arvin saw that Karrell's hand had curled in what was, by now, a familiar gesture to him. She was whispering her charm spell. Arvin thought about grabbing her hand and putting a halt to the spell, but she finished it before he could react.

"I'd like to show you something," Karrell said to Dmetrio, reaching under her cloak.

"Guards!" Dmetrio hissed.

The militiaman behind Karrell reacted with the speed of a striking snake. He grabbed Karrell's arms, yanking her elbows behind her back.

Karrell yelped. She dropped a piece of parchment she'd been holding; it fluttered to the floor. It landed faceup, revealing a rendering, done in ink and charcoal, of the cathedral in Hlondeth.

Arvin stared at it. The drawing was good—really good. Maybe Karrell was an artist, after all.

That, or she'd stolen the picture.

Belatedly, Rillis reacted, yanking out his sword and stepping back to give himself room to swing it, if need be. He glanced between Arvin—who carefully stood with his hands open and away from his sides—and Karrell.

Karrell tossed her head. "I simply wanted to show you a drawing," she said. Her face was flushed—she was obviously angry that Dmetrio had not succumbed to her spell. She had to nod at the picture on the floor, since the militiaman held her arms. "A sample of my work. I also do portraits. I have drawn a number of members of noble yuan-ti houses."

Dmetrio stared at her, unblinking. "Name one."

"Mezral Ch'thon, *ssthaar* of the Se'sehen."

Dmetrio's eyebrows rose. "You are from Tashalar?"

Karrell nodded.

"Are you Se'sehen?" Dmetrio asked. He added something in a language filled with soft hisses.

"*N'hacsis*—no," Karrell said, shaking her head. "I speak only a little Draconic. The language is difficult for me. It requires a serpent's tongue."

"You are *human?*" Dmetrio asked, giving the word a derisive sneer. He flicked his fingers, and the militiaman holding Karrell released her. Rillis reacted a moment later, sheathing his sword.

Karrell gave a slight bow in Dmetrio's direction then gathered up the parchment. "It is true that I invited myself here today, but I could think of no other way to meet with you. I had hoped to do your portrait."

"And gain a healthy commission from House Extaminos, no doubt." Dmetrio gave a hiss of laughter. "Your trip to Ormpetarr was a waste of time. I'm leaving—and have no time for portraits."

Arvin raised his eyebrows. Dmetrio was leaving Ormpetarr? That was interesting. "Ambassador Extaminos," he said, wresting the conversation away from Karrell, "my letter of introduction included a request that you——"

Dmetrio's upper lip twitched, revealing just the points of his fangs, a subtle sign of irritation. "I have no time for meetings, either," he said. He thrust the letter of introduction in Arvin's direction.

Arvin caught it just before it fell. "But I was told you would introduce me to the baron," he protested. "My merchant house is counting on me to——"

"Introduce yourself," Dmetrio said curtly.

Karrell stepped forward. "Your Excellency, I——"

"Show them out," Dmetrio hissed.

As they were hustled back to the street, Arvin fumed. This wasn't the way it was supposed to have gone. If Karrell hadn't butted in, he would have been talking to Dmetrio still, subtly nudging the conversation around to Glisena as he talked about his "trade mission" to Sespech. Now, in order to question Dmetrio, Arvin would have to be blunt. He'd have to reveal his real reason for coming to Ormpetarr. If Dmetrio was involved in Glisena's disappearance, he would be on his guard. Charming him would be that much more difficult—maybe even impossible.

As the wrought-iron gate clanked shut behind them, Karrell turned to Arvin. "It seems you are a merchant's agent, after all, and I have ruined your chances to——"

"Not another word," Arvin said, a quiver in his voice. He pointed down the street. "Go."

Karrell opened her mouth to say something more then thought better of it. She turned and walked up the street.

Arvin closed his eyes and sighed. Karrell had really gotten under his skin. He wished he'd never started that conversation with her in the wagon in the first place. He'd been stupid—and had shown a pitiful lack of self-control.

When he opened his eyes, she was gone. He stared at her footprints, which were starting to fill with falling snow.

"All for the best."

Arvin turned. It had been Rillis who had spoken—he was still standing just on the other side of the wrought-iron gate. The sergeant was at the far corner of the building, making his rounds.

"You're better off not having the ambassador introduce you," Rillis added in a confiding tone.

Arvin turned. "What do you mean?"

Rillis rubbed a thumb and forefinger together. The gesture was the one word in silent speech that was understood even by those not in the Guild: coin.

Arvin nodded and pulled his pouch out of his boot. He counted two silver pieces into the militiaman's outstretched hand.

Rillis quickly pocketed them. "The ambassador and the baron had a falling out," he told Arvin. "It's been more than a month since Ambassador Extaminos visited the palace. I don't think they've even sent a message to one another, in all that time."

"Why is that?" Arvin asked. Carefully, he probed for information, under the pretense of sarcasm. "Did the baron's daughter pay him a visit and forget to go home one night?"

Rillis laughed. "You obviously haven't met her chaperones. She never sets foot outside the palace without them. Baron's orders." He winked. "He didn't want any little ones slithering out from under the woodpile. Not without a formal joining of the houses."

Arvin nodded. "Is a joining likely?"

"Not now that the ambassador's being withdrawn from Sespech." He paused to draw his cloak tighter across his chest.

"When is he leaving?"

Rillis stared pointedly at Arvin's pouch. Taking the hint, Arvin handed him another silver piece.

"As soon as the new ambassador arrives," Rillis continued. "Meanwhile, the house slaves can't seem to pack fast enough for Ambassador Extaminos. He's been hissing at them for nearly a tenday."

Arvin nodded. Interesting, that was roughly the amount of time that had elapsed since Glisena's disappearance. He glanced up at the windows of the ambassador's residence, saw slaves bustling about in each room, and wondered why Dmetrio was in such a hurry to leave. Was the baron's daughter hiding somewhere nearby, waiting to depart with him?

Arvin sighed and stared down the street, in the direction Karrell had gone. After what Rillis had just told him, Arvin realized that he probably wouldn't have gotten anything out of Dmetrio, anyway. The ambassador had shrugged off Karrell's charm like a duck shedding water. Arvin's attempt to charm Dmetrio probably would have been equally futile.

"Thanks for the information," Arvin told Rillis.

The militiaman patted his pocket. "My pleasure."

Bidding Rillis good day, Arvin set out for the palace.

CHAPTER 6

BARON THURAGAR FOESMASHER SAT AT ONE END OF THE COUNCIL chamber, his broad hands resting on the arms of the heavy wooden chair. The man exuded both power and confidence. He was large, with dark eyes, hair cut square just above his eyebrows, and a blockish chin framed by a neatly trimmed beard. He wore a purple silk shirt; black trousers tied at the ankle, knee, and groin; and leather slippers embroidered in gold thread with the Foesmasher crest: a clenched fist. A heavy gold ring adorned the forefinger of his right hand; a silver brooch in the shape of a beetle was pinned to his shirt front. Arvin had no doubt that both pieces of jewelry were magical.

On a table next to the baron sat a helmet chased with gold and set with a single purple plume. Foesmasher had entered the room wearing it, but had taken the helm off after Arvin submitted to a magical scan by the baron's chief advisor, a cleric named Marasa. She stood to the left of the baron's chair. She wore a knee-length blue tunic over trousers and fur boots with gold felt tassels. Her hair was steel-gray and hung in two shoulder-length braids, each capped with a silver bead shaped like a gauntlet. On each wrist was a thick bracelet of polished silver bearing the blue eye of Helm. A mace hung from her belt.

The baron had dismissed Marasa from the chamber earlier, when he'd sent the servants away, but she had refused to leave. She was obviously an old friend—a supporter, rather than a vassal.

"Both clerical magic and wizardry have failed to locate my daughter," the baron told Arvin. "But Lady Dediana has informed me that you can work a different kind of spell—one that requires neither spellbook nor holy symbol. She said it might circumvent whatever is preventing Glisena from being found."

Before Arvin could respond, Marasa interrupted. "I doubt a sorcerer can part a veil that Helm himself has failed to rend." She stared at Arvin, a challenge in her eyes. It was clear from the derisive way she'd used the term that she disapproved of sorcery.

Arvin met her eyes. "I'm not a sorcerer," he told her. "I'm a psion."

"What's the difference?" she asked.

"A sorcerer casts spells that draw upon magic that is woven into the world. A psion uses mind magic. We tap the energies of the mind itself. If the magic of the Weave were to unravel tomorrow, sorcerers and wizards would lose their spells, but psions would continue to manifest their powers."

Marasa nodded politely but appeared unconvinced.

"What spell will you cast?" the baron asked.

Arvin was acutely aware of the broken dorje in his pack. Without it, he had to rely on his wits—and the one psionic power that just *might* be of use—in order to find the baron's daughter. "We call them 'powers,' not 'spells,' Lord Foesmasher. There are many I could choose from," he continued, waving his hand breezily in the air, "but I'll need to know more about the circumstances of your daughter's disappearance in order to determine the best one to use. When was the last time you saw Glisena?"

The baron sighed heavily. He stared the length of the room, past the tapestries that commemorated his many skirmishes with Chondath, past the trophy shields and weapons that hung on the walls. His eye settled on a half dozen miniature ships that sat on a table near the far wall, models of the galleys Hlondeth was helping him build. For several moments, the only sound was the crackling of the fire in the hearth behind him.

"A tenday ago," he said at last. "We dined together, spent the evening listening to a harpist, and Glisena took her leave and retired to bed. The next morning, her chamber was empty. High Watcher Davinu was called in to recite a prayer that should have discerned her location but was unable to. It's as if Glisena was spirited away to another plane of existence." His voice crackled. "Either that, or she's. . . ."

Marasa touched his arm. "Glisena is still alive," she said. "Davinu's communion told us that much, at least." She turned to Arvin. "But she seems to be shielded by powerful magic, which leads me to believe she didn't leave willingly. She was kidnapped, most likely, by agents from Chondath. They—"

"There have been no demands," Foesmasher interrupted, "from Wianar, or anyone else. My daughter left here of her own accord." He stared broodingly at the wall.

The cleric gave an exasperated sigh. It was clear she had ventured this theory to the baron before—with the same result.

"Lady Marasa, I believe Baron Foesmasher is right," Arvin said, breaking the silence. "Lord Wianar does not have Glisena."

"How do you know this?" Marasa asked.

The baron, too, turned to stare at Arvin.

Arvin took a deep breath. "Does the name Haskar mean anything to you?"

The baron's eyes blazed. "Haskar!" he growled. "Is *that* who has my daughter? By Helm, I'll have his head."

Arvin raised a hand. "Haskar doesn't have Glisena. But he knows that she's missing. He'd like to find her so he can sell her to Lord Wianar." He turned to Marasa. "So you see, lady, it appears that Lord Wianar doesn't have Glisena. If he did, Haskar wouldn't have made him the offer."

"How do you know all this?" the baron asked.

Arvin told him about the events of that morning. He emphasized the reward he had been offered, adding that he'd rather receive "honest coin" for his work. He was careful, however, to avoid any mention of his ability to listen to others' thoughts, making it sound instead as though he had tricked the man into giving him the information. The baron seemed like a straightforward, honest man, but there might come a time when Arvin needed to know what he was really thinking.

Marasa listened carefully to Arvin's report then shook her head.

"The fact that Haskar's rogues want to offer Glisena to Chondath means nothing," she said. "Lord Wianar might have kidnapped her without the rogues' knowing it."

"The fact remains," the baron interrupted, "that there have been no demands. Chondath is silent." He turned to Arvin. "You've done a good morning's work, but now comes the true test. Can you find my daughter?"

Arvin took a deep breath. "Of course, Lord Foesmasher," he said in a confident voice. "But I need to know just a little more about what happened on the night of her disappearance. Did you entertain any guests that evening?"

The baron's eyes bored into Arvin's. "If you mean to ask if Ambassador Extaminos was here, the answer is no. Nor were any other guests present. It was a . . . quiet evening. Just Glisena and myself."

"And the harpist," Marasa noted. "She may have been a—"

"The harpist is a regular guest of this household and well trusted," the baron growled, "as are the servants who attended us that evening."

Arvin knew little of royal households, but he'd spent two months in the home of the wealthy uncle who had cared for Arvin briefly after his mother had died. There had been a constant flutter of servants around his uncle—servants to help him dress and undress, to carry his parcels, to turn down his bed and place a draught of fortified wine on his bed table each night. In summer a servant stood over his bed while he slept, waving a fan to keep him cool. Arvin's uncle had little privacy—a princess of a royal household would have even less.

"Have you questioned Glisena's servants?" Arvin asked. "The ones who attended her bedchamber that night?"

"No servants attended her on the evening she disappeared," Foesmasher said. "Glisena's head pained her. She said she could not bear even the slightest noise and dismissed them from her chamber."

"Her head pained her?" Arvin echoed. A wild notion occurred to him—that Zelia might have planted a mind seed in the baron's daughter. Arvin had stripped that power from Zelia six months ago, but she may have regained it since. That would explain what she was doing in Sespech—she may have been stopping at Riverboat Landing on her way *back* from Ormpetarr, rather than on her way to the city. It would also explain Glisena's sudden disappearance.

Then again, he reminded himself, it might be a simple elopement he was dealing with, after all. No need to jump to conclusions . . . yet. "Was this the first time your daughter complained of a head-ache?" he asked.

Foesmasher shook his head. "Glisena had been feeling unwell for several days."

"How many days?" Arvin asked sharply. A mind seed took time to blossom. If her headache had begun seven days before her disappearance . . .

"Several days," Foesmasher repeated. He gave an exasperated sigh. "What does it matter? Her illness had nothing to do with her disappearance."

"Glisena had been unwell for nearly a month," Marasa told Arvin. She turned to the baron, "You should have summoned me."

"Her illness was minor," Foesmasher said. There was a testy edge to his voice. It sounded, to Arvin, that the baron and his advisor had gone through this argument at least once before. "It was a slight upset of the stomach. Nothing that required magical healing."

"A stomach upset?" Arvin asked, confused. "I thought you said she had a headache."

Neither the baron nor Marasa was listening to him. Marasa bristled at Foesmasher. "A simple laying on of hands would have saved Glisena much discomfort."

"The headache was an excuse to dismiss the servants!" the baron growled. "Glisena *ran away.*"

Marasa glared right back at him. "How can you be so sure? Wianar's agents may have infiltrated the palace and kidnapped her. Whether the headache was feigned or not, if you'd summoned me that night—"

"That's enough, High Watcher Ferrentio!" Foesmasher shouted. He looked away, refusing to meet the cleric's eye. He glared at the far wall, visibly composing himself.

Marasa gently touched his hand. "You and Glisena were arguing again, weren't you?"

Foesmasher sighed. "Yes."

Arvin's eyebrows rose. A "quiet evening," the baron had said. Given the baron's propensity for shouting, it had probably been anything but. No wonder Glisena had fled to her chamber. "So the headache had only come on that evening?" he asked.

The baron turned to Arvin, a suspicious look in his eye. "Why are you so interested in my daughter's health?"

Arvin paused, considering whether to tell the baron about Zelia. Foesmasher was a powerful man, with an army at his disposal. That army included clerics of Helm—clerics who had proven themselves capable of dealing with the yuan-ti. They could arrest Zelia and throw her in prison. On the other hand, Zelia's presence in Sespech might be mere coincidence; she might not be searching for Arvin, after all. If she was hauled before the baron for questioning and was able to probe his thoughts, she'd be alerted to the fact that Arvin was alive, and in Sespech. If she later escaped. . . .

Arvin decided it was worth the risk. Perhaps Zelia would resist capture, and the clerics would kill her. The thought made Arvin smile.

"There is a power that psions can manifest," he told the baron, "one that plants a seed in the victim's mind that germinates slowly, over several days. During that time, the victim suffers head pains and experiences brief flashes of memory—the memories of the psion who planted the seed. On the seventh day. . . ." He paused, revisiting the dread he'd felt at slowly losing control of his mind. For six days and nights, Zelia's mind seed had warped his thoughts and slithered into his dreams, turning them into nightmares. Under its influence, Arvin had lashed out at people who tried to help him, had even killed an innocent man. Only on the seventh day, when he'd been within heartbeats of having his own consciousness utterly extinguished, had the mind seed at last been purged.

"On the seventh day?" the baron prompted.

Arvin chose his words carefully; he was about to impart what might be very bad news, indeed. "On that day," he said slowly, "the victim's own mind is destroyed, and replaced it with a copy of the psion's mind, instead."

Marasa's face paled. "Helm grant it is not so," she whispered.

The baron leaned forward, his eyes intent on Arvin. "You know someone who can cast this spell," he said. "Someone here, in Sespech."

Arvin met his eye. "Yes."

"Name him."

"It's her, not him," Arvin answered. "Her name is Zelia. I spotted her three days ago, at Riverboat Landing. She's a yuan-ti."

Arvin expected the baron to immediately demand a description, but Foesmasher seemed uninterested. Beside him, Marasa looked visibly relieved.

"Aren't you going to arrest Zelia?" Arvin asked. "If she planted a mind seed in your daughter—"

"She couldn't have," the baron said. "Glisena has had no contact with yuan-ti for . . . some time."

"How can you be so sure?" Arvin asked. "Yuan-ti can assume serpent form. Zelia could have slithered into the palace undetected and—"

Marasa interrupted him. "Tell him, Thuragar," she said, giving the baron a hard look.

Baron Foesmasher sighed. "You will, no doubt, have heard that I disapproved of Ambassador Extaminos's courtship of my daughter?" he said.

Arvin nodded.

"A little over a month ago, I forbade my daughter from seeing Ambassador Extaminos again. I took precautions against him . . . contacting her. It is no longer possible for a yuan-ti to enter certain sections of the palace. The hallways, doors, and windows   every possible entrance to those parts of the palace that Glisena would have any cause to enter—have been warded to prevent serpents from entering. All serpents. Even yuan-ti in human form."

He gave a heavy sigh before continuing. "Glisena has not . . . *had* not," he corrected himself, "set foot outside those sections of the palace since this was done. She's had no contact with serpents since that time. *That* is how I know this Zelia person could not have planted a mind seed in my daughter."

"I see," Arvin said. He understood, now, why the baron was so certain his daughter had run away. Anyone would, after being placed under what was, essentially, a prison sentence, however sumptuous and comfortable the prison might be. Arvin was starting to have second thoughts about the baron. If he ruled his own daughter with such a domineering hand, how did he treat his hirelings?

"You're certain the wards were effective?" Arvin asked.

It was Marasa who answered. "I oversaw their placement myself." The look she gave the baron suggested she'd been unhappy with this task.

Arvin nodded. Even if Zelia had relearned the mind seed power, it wouldn't have been possible for her to plant a seed in Glisena—she wouldn't have been able to get close enough to the princess.

Marasa leaned closer to the baron and spoke, interrupting Arvin's thoughts. "This 'mind seed' could be used to create the perfect spy," she told him in a voice that was pitched low—but not quite low enough that Arvin couldn't overhear.

"Yes," the baron agreed. "It could." He gave Arvin a level stare. "Is that why you told us about Zelia? Is this a warning from Lady Dediana—that she has ears within my court?"

Arvin met the baron's eyes. "I didn't come to Sespech to play at politics, Lord Foesmasher," he answered. "I'm here for one purpose only: to find your daughter. Whether Zelia has seeded anyone in your court is a question that's best put to her. But be careful; Zelia's dangerous. This I know, from personal experience."

"She's your enemy," the baron observed. "Yet you serve the same mistress."

Arvin took a deep breath. Now was the moment he'd been waiting for, the moment to make a commitment—one that would affect everything that was to follow in his life. He reminded himself that this wasn't like his incarceration in the orphanage, or his obligation to the Guild. He was *choosing* this alliance.

"I don't serve Lady Dediana," he told the baron. "I'm a free agent; I choose who I work for. It is my belief that working for a human—especially a man of your stature—will be much more . . . rewarding."

The baron gave a low chuckle. "I see." He exchanged a look with Marasa. "I think that, after Arvin has found my daughter, he and I will have a chat about mind seeds and spies . . . and rewards."

"Will you arrest Zelia?" Arvin asked.

"That wouldn't be expedient at the moment," Foesmasher replied. "There was an . . . unfortunate incident a few days ago. It seems that the new ambassador from Hlondeth had an altercation with one of the less reputable citizens of Mimph—an altercation that resulted in his arrest. If I simply order his release, it will appear that certain people are above Helm's law. Yet if I allow the Eyes to place Helm's mark on him, it may fracture the alliance. I have to tread carefully, where yuan-ti are concerned. I can't afford to ruffle any more scales."

Arvin realized at once who the baron was talking about: the yuan-ti who had attacked the young pickpocket. He shook his head in disbelief. The yuan-ti had a lot to learn about diplomacy.

Foesmasher continued speaking. "If you provide me with a description of Zelia, I will see to it that she is watched. If she comes to Ormpetarr, you'll be alerted."

Arvin murmured his thanks. It was time to get back to business. "You said that, on the night of Glisena's disappearance, she retired to her chambers and dismissed her servants. Presumably after that, she slipped out her door—"

"No," the baron said. "The guard in the hall was questioned under Helm's truth. He did not see her, and he was awake all night."

"Did she climb out a window?"

"Her chamber has no window."

Glisena was sounding more like a prisoner by the moment.

"Does your daughter know any magic?" Arvin asked.

Foesmasher shook his head. "Not so much as a cantrip. Yet she must have used magic to flee the palace. Someone aided her."

"Or kidnapped her," Marasa muttered under her breath.

Wanting to stave off another argument, Arvin interrupted. "I'm ready to manifest my power," he told them. "Could I see Glisena's chamber?"

"High Watcher Davinu already examined it," Marasa said. "There was nothing—"

"And now the psion will examine it—with mind magic," Foesmasher told her sternly. "Come," he said to Arvin, rising from his chair. "I'll take you there."

❦

Glisena's bedchamber was even more ornate than Arvin had imagined. The bed, side tables, and wardrobe were painted white and trimmed with gilt. The rug on the floor was also white, with a border of prancing centaurs. Arvin's feet sank into its softness as he entered the room. The windowless walls were divided into panels, painted with scenes of noblewomen waving silken favors at jousting knights. The ceiling was of molded white plaster, the pattern an ornate spray of bouquets and tree boughs.

The chamber gave the appearance of still being occupied. A fire crackled in the hearth, and a brazier filled with scented oil perfumed the air. A gown had been laid out on a clothing rack and fresh water stood in a pitcher beside a floral-print wash bowl. Next to these were a comb and brush. The bed was turned down for the night.

"I felt it wise to keep up appearances," the baron explained. "None of the servants know that Glisena is gone."

Marasa, standing a little behind him, shook her head sadly but made no comment. "What do you hope to find here?" she asked Arvin.

"There is a psionic power that allows me to view emotionally charged events that have occurred in this room," Arvin explained. "Whether Glisena ran away or was kidnapped, she's certain to have been highly emotional at the time. I hope to catch a glimpse of something that will provide some clue as to where she went." He glanced around the room, wondering where to begin. "The manifestation will take some time," he told them over his shoulder. "Please don't interrupt until—"

The baron placed a heavy hand on Arvin's shoulder and turned him around. "You said you were going to use mind magic to track her—not to spy on her private moments. What my daughter does in her chamber is her own affair."

"What are you so concerned about, Thuragar?" Marasa asked. "That he might catch a glimpse of Glisena undressing for bed?"

The baron's face flushed. "He will not cast that spell."

"Thuragar!" Marasa said in an exasperated voice. "Your daughter is missing. Surely a chance at finding her, no matter how slim it might be, is more important than—"

"Lord Foesmasher," Arvin interrupted. "Be at ease. I assure you that, whatever I might see, I will be . . . discreet."

"For Glisena's sake, Thuragar," Marasa said. "Let him cast the spell."

Arvin smiled to himself. Marasa, so doubtful of his powers at first, now seemed willing to believe in them.

The baron stood in silence for several moments, conflicting

emotions in his eye. At last, reluctantly, he nodded. "Very well." His hand fell away from Arvin's shoulder. "Begin."

Arvin looked around the chamber, sizing up its contents. Though the power could provide glimpses into the past of any event that happened in the immediate area—up to three dozen paces away from the manifester—it was most effective if it was concentrated on a specific item—a bed that an angry young woman might have flopped down onto after an argument with her father, for example.

Touching one of the lace-trimmed pillows, Arvin manifested the power. Psionic energy awoke within two of his power points: his throat vibrated, and a coil of energy slowly unwound within his abdomen, tickling the area around his navel. The baron and Marasa glanced uneasily at each other as a low droning filled the air—part of the secondary display. As the power manifested fully, Arvin felt the pillow dampen with ectoplasmic seepage where his fingertips touched it.

The vision came almost at once. Suddenly the bed was occupied by two people thrashing against one another—a man and a woman making love. The figures were transparent, almost ghostly, and seemed to be writhing on the neatly folded-down sheets without ever mussing them.

The woman was young and somewhat plain in appearance; her face was a little too square to ever be pretty, though her naked body was sensuously curved. Her head was thrown back in rapture, her long loose hair splayed against the pillow Arvin was touching. Arvin felt a blush warm his face as he realized he was looking at the baron's daughter, soon to peak in her passion.

The man on top of Glisena had his back to Arvin. His lower torso was hidden by the bedding. But when he tossed back his long, dark hair, Arvin caught a glimpse of slit pupils and snake scales, and a face he recognized at once. Dmetrio ran the forked tip of his tongue along Glisena's breast, and as her mouth fell open in a low, shuddering moan, he began to laugh. The look in his eyes was harsh, triumphant. He suddenly withdrew from her, levering himself up off her body, and spoke in a sneering hiss. "If you want more," he taunted, "you'll have to beg for it."

"Please," Glisena gasped, clutching at Dmetrio and trying to draw him back down to her. "I'd do anything for you. Please."

"That's a good start," Dmetrio said, a look of triumph in his slit eyes. His feet were visible now, protruding out of the bedding. They were rounded and scaly and looked like snake tails; each foot ended in a single large, blunt toe. Dmetrio wrenched himself free of Glisena and sat up in a kneeling position, then twined his fingers in Glisena's hair and yanked her forward. Dmetrio, like many yuan-ti males, had a slit at the groin, inside which his reproductive organs rested. Arvin, staring, was horrified to see emerging out of it not one, but two. . . .

With a shudder, Arvin yanked his fingers away from the pillow. He felt sullied by what he'd seen. If he did manage to find the baron's daughter, it would be hard to look her in the eye.

"Well?" the baron asked. "What did you see?"

Arvin hesitated. The baron had closed the gate long after the horse had bolted from the stable—or rather, into the stable, in this case. The wardings on the palace had been in vain, but how to tell the baron that diplomatically?

"Your daughter was quite . . . passionate about Dmetrio, wasn't she?" Arvin began.

The baron's face purpled as he realized what Arvin was implying. "Here? In this room?"

Marasa glanced sharply at the baron.

"I saw Glisena and Dmetrio kissing," Arvin said. "The vision must have been more than a month old—from before the wards were set. It wasn't the one I was hoping for. I'll try again."

Before the baron could reply, Arvin retreated into a second manifestation. As the droning of his secondary display filled the air once more, he looked around the room, this time trying to pick up general impressions. As he glanced at the baron, he once again saw a double image—a ghostly baron standing just behind the first, his face also twisted with rage. He was shouting something. Curious, Arvin extended his hand in that direction, willing the vision to come into focus.

It did, with a volume that startled him.

"You will never see him again!" the ghostly image roared.

Arvin heard the sound of weeping behind him. He turned and saw Glisena—fully clothed, this time, and sitting on a neatly made bed—wringing a lace-trimmed handkerchief in her hands. Tears were sliding down her cheeks and a strand of her dark hair had fallen out of the pearl-studded net that held her hair in a bun at the nape of her neck. "But we're in love," she sobbed.

The baron snorted. "*You're* in love. That . . . *snake* is as cold-hearted as any of his race. He cares nothing for you, girl. Nothing."

Glisena shook her head fiercely. "That's not true. You'll see. When I tell him about—"

"You'll tell him nothing." The baron strode forward and loomed over Glisena. "Nor will you tell anyone else what's happened. We're going to take care of this . . . quietly."

Anger blazed in Glisena's eyes and flushed her cheeks. "You only care about your stupid alliances. If Dmetrio marries me—"

"He won't."

"Yes, he will," Glisena shrilled. "And when he does, your hopes of an alliance with Turmish are over. You can't force me to marry Lord Herengar's son. He's as stupid as he is ugly."

"At least he's *human*," the baron spat back.

"What do you think I am?" Glisena wailed. "A child? I'm a grown woman. You can't do this to me."

The baron's voice dropped dangerously low. "You did this to yourself," he growled. "And now you'll face the consequences." Turning on his heel, he wrenched open the door, startling the guard who stood in the hallway outside. "Make sure she doesn't leave," he snapped at the guard then slammed the door behind himself.

The vision—and Glisena's faint sobbing—faded.

"What did you see this time?" the baron asked. His voice startled Arvin; it took a moment for Arvin to realize that he was back in the here and now. A fine sheen of ectoplasm shimmered in the baron's hair. He didn't seem to notice it.

Arvin swallowed nervously. The last thing he wanted to report was that he'd listened in on a family argument—a very private family argument.

"I didn't see much this time," he said, "just Glisena sitting on her bed, crying. But I think I'm getting closer to the night of her disappearance. I'll try again."

The baron gave a brief nod. His hands, Arvin noticed, were white-knuckled. What was it he was so afraid of?

Arvin manifested his power a third time, scanning the room,

and out of the corner of his eye saw a movement near the hearth. There were two ghostly women there, one standing, the other kneeling in front of her. Concentrating on these, he brought them into focus.

The standing woman was Glisena. She held her night robe slightly open, revealing her stomach. The look on her face was one of acute apprehension.

The woman who knelt in front of her touched Glisena's stomach with a forefinger and chanted in a language Arvin couldn't understand. Her finger moved back and forth across the bare flesh as if sketching, but left no visible marks. She was casting a spell of some description, but Arvin had no idea what its purpose might be.

This second woman had her back to Arvin; all he could tell was that she was large and was wearing a dark green cloak. He moved across the room—closer to the hearth, which began to sweat a sheen of ectoplasm—and got a view of her face.

The spellcaster had heavy jowls, a double chin, and brown hair with a streak of gray at one temple. Her small eyes were screwed shut as she concentrated on her magic. Arvin looked for a brooch or pendant that might be a cleric's holy symbol, but saw none. The only item of jewelry the woman wore was a ring, a band of brownish-red stone around her pudgy little finger. A band carved from amber, Arvin thought, identifying the stone from the lingering bits of gem lore Zelia's mind seed had left him with.

When the spell was done, the woman stood. Glisena closed her robe and stood with her palms lightly pressing against her belly. "When will it take effect?" she asked.

The spellcaster gave her a motherly smile. "Some time tomorrow." She tugged at the ring on her little finger. "This," she said, working it back and forth to pull it free. "Will convey you to me." She held the ring out to Glisena. "Use it as soon as you feel the magic of the spell begin."

Glisena took the ring with what looked like reluctance. A tear blossomed at the corner of one eye and trickled down her cheek. "Did he really tell you to end it?" she asked.

"He did." The spellcaster said in a grim voice. Then she patted Glisena's cheek. "But all's well now. We'll fool him." Glisena nodded and clenched her hand around the ring. "Yes."

"Now listen closely, and I'll tell you how the ring works," Naneth said.

The vision shifted then. The spellcaster disappeared, and Arvin had a palpable sense of leaping forward in time to a moment when Glisena stood in just the same spot in front of the hearth. As before, the moment was emotionally charged. Tears were streaming down her face. She wore clothes instead of a night robe, as well as a heavy cloak pinned at the shoulder and high leather boots. And her stomach was no longer flat. It bulged, visibly pregnant. *Very* pregnant.

Arvin whistled under his breath. No wonder Glisena and her father had argued. Glisena was carrying Dmetrio's child. A child that was only partly human. He watched as the ghostly Glisena toyed with something she held in her hands—the spellcaster's amber ring. A knock at the door caused her to startle, nearly dropping it.

"Glisena?" a muffled male voice called. "I'm sorry we argued. Can we talk?"

Glisena's eyes flew open wide. She glanced down at her belly then back at the door, and she drew her cloak around herself, as if to hide her pregnancy. Then her lips pressed together in a determined line. Tossing the ring on the floor, she spoke a word: *"Ossalur!"* As the ring hit the floor, it grew, expanding into a hoop fully two paces in diameter within the space of an eyeblink. Glisena jumped into the center of it—an awkward hop while holding her belly—and vanished. The ring contracted to its normal size then disappeared.

The door to her chamber opened. Baron Foesmasher poked his head tentatively into the room. "Glisena?" he called softly. He glanced at the empty bed—then looked wildly around the chamber. "Glisena!" he shouted. "Glisena!"

The vision faded.

Arvin let out a long, slow sigh and stood for several moments with his eyes closed. Then he turned to the baron. "I have news," he reported. "I've seen how Glisena esca—ah, that is, how she fled from the palace."

The baron ignored Arvin's slip of the tongue. "Tell me," he said.

"Your daughter was given a ring," Arvin said. "One that gave her the ability to teleport."

"Who gave it to her?" Marasa asked, her voice low and tense.

"A spellcaster," Arvin said. He started to describe the woman, but Marasa interrupted him after he'd barely begun.

"The midwife?" she asked. Then, to the baron, "What was she doing here, in the palace?"

Arvin was wondering the same thing. What *had* the spellcaster been doing to Glisena?

The baron stood rigid, his shoulders tense. The words jerked out of him. "Glisena was pregnant. By that . . . serpent. By Ambassador Extaminos."

Marasa's mouth dropped open. "Pregnant?" she whispered. Then she nodded to herself. "Was *that* why she'd been feeling unwell?"

The baron stared at the far wall, not answering.

"And Naneth?" Marasa prodded.

"She came to cast a spell," the baron began. "A spell that. . . ." His voice trembled. He sank onto the bed, head in his hands, unable or unwilling to say more.

Marasa's face paled. "Naneth came to end the pregnancy, didn't she?"

The baron refused to look up.

Marasa flushed with anger. "Killing an innocent is a grievous sin! And nothing is more innocent than an unborn child." She pointed a trembling finger at the baron. "Helm will never countenance this. Never! He will demand retribution. He—"

The baron looked up, his face twisted with remorse. "Helm has punished me already. Glisena is gone. *Gone.*"

Marasa lowered her accusing hand. "Oh, Thuragar," she said, her voice anguished. "What were you thinking?" She turned her back on him and paced across the room to stare at the hearth, shaking her head.

Arvin shifted uncomfortably, wishing he were someplace else. He stood in silence, debating whether to tell the baron what he'd seen in that last vision. The spell Naneth had cast on Glisena hadn't ended her pregnancy. Instead, it had hastened it to term. In that first vision, Glisena had not been visibly pregnant—she was at most two to three months along. And in the second vision, the one in which she'd used the ring, she'd been full-bellied, close to giving birth. Yet only a day had passed.

The spell must have taken effect on the evening that Glisena disappeared. That was why she'd dismissed her servants that night—she could feel the spell starting to work its magic. That was why she'd hidden her belly from view when her father knocked at her door.

The baron didn't know that Glisena was still pregnant.

But he would, once Arvin found her.

Sickened, Arvin stared at the carpet, unwilling to look at the baron. The last thing he wanted to do now was return Glisena to him.

Foesmasher balled his fist. "She's with Naneth," he said in a low voice. He sprang to his feet and crossed the room, wrenching the door open. "Stand aside," he shouted at someone as he stomped down the hall.

Marasa had whirled at the sudden motion. As the baron's heavy footsteps faded down the hall, she ran after him. "Thuragar! Wait!"

After a moment's hesitation, Arvin hurried after her. He caught up with Marasa as she was passing a guard who had a puzzled expression on his face. The baron was nowhere to be seen. Somewhere down the corridor, a door slammed.

Marasa grabbed Arvin's arm and dragged him down the hall with her. "He'll go to Naneth's house," she said in a low voice. "I'm worried. If he finds Glisena there. . . ."

Arvin nodded grimly. "Indeed. And when he learns she's still pregnant—"

Marasa jerked to a halt. "She's what?"

"Still pregnant. Naneth didn't end the pregnancy—she cast a spell that hurried it along instead. In that last vision, Glisena looked ready to give birth at any moment. She may even have had the child by now."

Marasa looked grim. "We must find her, then. Quickly, before Thuragar compounds his sin."

Arvin's eyes widened. "He wouldn't harm the child . . . would he?"

"No," Marasa said. "He wouldn't. Not *Thuragar*," she said, sounding as if she were trying to convince herself. "But I do fear for Naneth's safety."

"What can we do?"

"Does your mind magic allow you to teleport? Could you reach Naneth's house ahead of Thuragar?"

Arvin shook his head. "No. But I can send a warning to her"— shoving a hand into his pocket, he pulled out the lapis lazuli—"with this." He touched the fingernail-sized chip of stone to his forehead. It adhered at once as he spoke its command word. Drawing power from the magical stone, he manifested a sending. He imagined that he was looking at Naneth and felt a prickling at the base of his scalp. A heartbeat later her image solidified, and he was staring at the midwife. She was leaning over, placing a saucer filled with water inside something that Arvin couldn't see. As the connection between her and Arvin grew stronger, she jerked upright, spilling the water. Her mouth moved in a sharp question, but Arvin couldn't hear what she was saying.

"Naneth," he said, speaking the words aloud. "I know you have Glisena. If she's at your home, move her. Hide her. The baron is on his way there now. He knows what you did."

The sorcerer repeated her question; this time Arvin could hear it. "Who are you?" she said, staring intently at his face. Her eyes were narrow with suspicion. "I don't recognize you."

She paused, waiting for an answer, but Arvin couldn't give one. That was how the lapis lazuli worked—he could send a brief message, and receive one in return. A few heartbeats later, the sending reached the limits of its duration. Naneth faded from view.

"It's done," Arvin said. "What now?"

"Are you quick on your feet?" Marasa asked.

Arvin nodded.

"Then let's get moving. I know where Naneth lives."

CHAPTER 7

THEY ARRIVED AT NANETH'S RESIDENCE JUST AS THE BARON STORMED out the front door, sword in hand. "Glisena's not here," he gritted. "Neither is Naneth. But the Eyes will round her up, soon enough."

Two of Foesmasher's soldiers emerged from the building, one of them holding the arm of a frightened-looking woman whose long black hair was starting to gray at the temples. She looked vaguely familiar, but Arvin couldn't place her.

"I've done nothing wrong," she protested.

"We just want to question you," the soldier holding her arm said.

"I simply came to pay Naneth for her services," the woman continued, drawing her cloak protectively around herself with her free hand as the soldiers led her away. "I don't *know* where she is." She turned to the baron, a pleading look in her eyes. "Lord Foesmasher, please. Whatever quarrel you have with the midwife, I have no part in it."

Foesmasher ignored her. "Have one of the Eyes question her," he said. "Find out if she does know where Naneth is. And send a detail of soldiers to secure this house."

The soldiers nodded and led the woman away.

"Baron Foesmasher," she pleaded. "Please don't imprison me. I've done nothing wrong."

Foesmasher stood, hands on his hips, scowling as she was led away.

Marasa, still panting from the run through the streets—the residence was more than two dozen blocks from the palace—exchanged a look with Arvin then hurried after the baron. "Thuragar," she said in an ominous voice. "You face Helm's wrath for what you ordered Naneth to do. You must atone before he—"

"I have other matters to attend to, first," Foesmasher snapped. Turning on his heel, he strode away.

Marasa hurried after him. "Thuragar, wait! Hear me out."

Arvin, only half listening, stared at the residence. It was a narrow building, two stories tall and sharing a wall with the building on either side. All of the windows were shuttered against the cold. His eyes ranged from one window to the next as he calculated the distance between them. If there was a wall that was a little thicker than it should be—enough to conceal a person—he'd find it when he counted off the paces inside.

The front door was open. Arvin walked up the short flight of steps that led to it and knocked—loudly.

"Naneth?" he called out, hoping that, if she was still here, she might recognize his voice.

No one answered.

A long hallway ran the length of the first floor. On the left was a kitchen; on the right, a sitting room. A flight of stairs at the rear of the hall led to the second floor. He stepped inside and shut the door behind him.

The kitchen was warm and steamy; water boiled in a large pot on the stove. Bundles of drying herbs hung from the kitchen's ceiling beams, filling the air with their aromatic scents. Arvin moved the pot to the table, setting it beside a stack of neatly folded squares of white cloth, and the bubbling noise slowly calmed. He listened, but heard only the hiss of dried grain spilling from a sack that had slumped over inside a pantry cupboard. The doors of the pantry stood ajar, as if they'd been yanked open.

The sitting room also showed signs of the baron's intrusion. A tapestry lay on the floor beneath a broken curtain rod; a chair was on its side; and a shelf had been yanked away from one wall, spilling books onto the floor. One of them was on the hearth, its pages starting to curl from the heat of the fire. Arvin picked it up. Flipping idly through it, he saw that the book contained a number of illustrations: male and female pairs of various humanoid creatures—orcs, two-headed ettins, cloven-hoofed satyrs, lizardfolk, and several other races. Next to each figure was an enlarged drawing of that creature's genitals; the female illustrations were accompanied by a drawing showing a baby growing within the womb.

He had no idea what the text of the book said, but here and there he spotted a line that he recognized as Draconic. The spine of the book was deeply creased, as if it had been referred to many times, and one of the pages was marked with a ribbon. Flipping to it, Arvin saw an illustration of a male and female yuan-ti. Dmetrio Extaminos, it seemed, had been no aberration. It was common for a male yuan-ti to carry two swords in his scabbard . . . so to speak.

Closing the book, he set it back on the shelf.

A quick pacing of the first-floor rooms and a few knocks on walls determined that neither the kitchen nor the sitting room had any hiding places. There was a cupboard under the stairs at the back of the hall, but a glance inside revealed nothing but dust and cobwebs.

"Glisena?" Arvin called. "Are you here?"

There was, as he expected, no answer.

The stairs led to a landing with three doors. All were open. The one to Arvin's right looked as though it had been kicked open, splintering the door frame; it must have been locked when the baron arrived. Arvin glanced into the other two rooms first—a small washing-up room and a bedroom, its bed dragged to one side and its wardrobe open and spilling clothes—then turned his attention to the third room. He eased open the broken door.

"Glisena?" he called. "Naneth?"

As the door swung open, the stench struck him. Small and shuttered tight against the cold outside, the room reeked of snake. The walls were lined with tables; on these stood square containers made from panes of leaded glass, each with a wooden lid that had been drilled with holes. A different type of snake slithered around inside each container. One was a brown-scaled boa, coiled tight around a feebly twitching rat. Its body flexed, and the rat stopped moving. In the container next to it was a clutch of small green snakes, tangled together in a mating ball. Next to these was a flying snake from the southern lands, its body banded in light and dark green, its wings a vivid shade of turquoise. It fluttered inside its glass-walled container, hissing.

Arvin shook his head. Naneth certainly had odd taste in pets.

As he stepped into the room, a reddish-brown viper with a thick band of black at its throat reared up and spat a spray of venom onto the glass. Arvin eyed it warily, glad that the lid prevented it from getting out. The container next to it, however, was open; its lid sat on the table beside it. A saucer lay upside down inside the glass-walled cage, next to the gold-and-black-striped snake that was coiled there; this was where Naneth had been standing when Arvin contacted her with his sending.

Arvin picked up the lid and set it cautiously back in place, closing the cage. The snake inside, he saw now, was coiled on top of a clutch of eggs. Its body covered most of the small, leathery ovals, but as the snake shifted, Arvin caught a glimpse of something strange—it looked like a symbol, painted in red, on the egg that was closest to the glass. Squatting down for a closer look, Arvin saw he was right. The symbol was in Draconic. What it signified, he had no idea. He touched a hand to the glass the egg rested against, and it happened. Just as it had on the ship. For the space of several heartbeats, he stared, with naked eyes, into the future.

A pool of blood spread around someone's feet. And a finger-thin stream of red flowed away from the pool, toward a dark shape Arvin couldn't quite make out. Yet somehow he knew that it was something evil, something *monstrous.* The creature looked down then lifted the stream of blood from the ground with one hand—the hand of a woman—and began drawing the blood toward itself like a fisher hauling in a line.

Arvin's ears rang with an anguished scream—a woman's scream. Startled by it, he jerked his hand away. Only after his heart had pounded for several moments did he realize the sound had been part of his vision.

The snake shifted, covering its eggs once more. It looked at Arvin through the glass, tongue flickering in and out of its mouth, and gave a soft, menacing hiss.

Shaken by the premonition, Arvin stood.

Someone was going to die. Naneth?

He forced his mind back to the job at hand. Had Naneth still been in this room when the baron kicked the door in? If so, the room might hold a clue as to where she'd gone.

For the fourth time that evening, Arvin manifested the power that made him sensitive to psychic impressions. The snakes hissed as a low droning noise filled the air. Allowing the energy that lay just behind his navel to uncoil, Arvin held out a hand and turned in a slow circle, scanning the room. Ectoplasm blossomed in his wake on the containers that held the snakes, covering their glass with a translucent sheen.

Arvin focused on the saucer Naneth had dropped. A vision flashed before his eyes—of Naneth, startled, releasing it. The image was faint and ghostly, at first, but grew in detail and solidity as Naneth listened and responded to the warning Arvin had sent. By the end of the sending, the midwife was visibly agitated. She ran from the room, into the bedroom across the landing, and returned an instant later with something tucked in the crook of one arm. Slamming the door behind herself, she quickly locked it. She shoved aside one of the glass containers, ignoring the agitated hissing of her snakes, and placed the item on the tabletop. It turned out to be a wrought-iron statuette of a rearing serpent holding a fist-sized sphere of crystal in its mouth.

Arvin felt the blood drain from his cheeks. He'd seen a crystal ball identical to it once before. It had belonged to a yuan-ti named Karshis—a yuan-ti who had served Sibyl.

Sibyl, the abomination who had killed Naulg, Arvin's oldest friend.

Painful memories swam into Arvin's mind—of Naulg, barely recognizable as human, his body hideously transformed by the potion Sibyl's minions had forced him to consume. Driven insane by his transformation, Naulg had glared at Arvin after his rescue, frothing and snapping his teeth, not recognizing his friend. And Arvin, staring down at one of the few people to have shown him kindness without wanting something in return, had realized that there was only one thing he could do for his old friend, one final kindness.

He could still hear Naulg's final choked gasp as the cleric's prayer took effect . . . and the silence that followed.

Together with Nicco and the others in the Secession, Arvin had thwarted Sibyl's plan to turn the humans of Hlondeth into mindless semblances of yuan-ti. But the abomination herself was still at large. Though the Secession had been searching for her, these past six months, they'd turned up no trace of her. Arvin had bided his time, hiding from Zelia and slowly learning new psionic powers from Tanju. He'd told himself that, when Sibyl did rear up out of her hole again, he'd be ready to avenge himself on her. That was something he'd sworn to do—sworn in the presence of a cleric of Hoar, god of retribution.

The god must have been listening. Why else would he have placed another of Sibyl's followers in Arvin's path?

As if in answer, thunder grumbled somewhere outside, rattling the shutters of the windows.

Arvin swallowed and nervously touched the crystal that hung at his throat.

The vision his manifestation had conjured up was still unfolding. In it, Naneth raised a hand to her mouth and pointed her forefinger at the crystal ball. "Mistress," she said in a tight, urgent voice, one hand stroking the crystal. "Mistress, heed me."

A figure took shape within the sphere—a black serpent with the face of a woman, four humanlike arms, and enormous wings that fluttered above her shoulders. The abomination twisted to look at Naneth with eyes the color of dark red flame, her forked tongue flickering.

"Sibyl," Arvin said in an anguished whisper, speaking the name at the same time the ghostly figure of Naneth did.

"Speak," the abomination hissed.

Arvin watched, horrified.

"I have just received word, mistress," Naneth said, addressing the figure that stared at her from inside the sphere. "The baron has learned of our plan."

Sibyl's eyes narrowed. "Who told you this?"

"A man I've never met before. A spellcaster—he used magic to deliver his message."

"Describe him."

Arvin's breath caught.

"He was human. With collar-length brown hair, and. . . ."

Naneth paused, frowning. "And an oval of blue stone attached to his forehead."

"Do you have any idea who he might be?"

"None."

Arvin laughed with nervous relief. The description Naneth had just given was vague enough that it might have been anyone—aside from the lapis lazuli, which he'd be careful to keep out of sight from now on.

"What, precisely, did the spellcaster say?"

Naneth frowned. "Only this: 'He knows what you did.'" She paused. "It's a ruse, isn't it? One designed to get us to tip our hand."

"You humans are not always as stupid as you seem," Sibyl answered, her tongue flickering in and out through her smile.

From behind the closed door came the sounds of a man shouting. Then footsteps pounded up the stairs. For a moment, Arvin thought the baron had returned, but then he realized that this was part of the vision. To his eyes, the door was still closed and locked—and shuddering as the baron pounded on it and shouted at Naneth to open it.

The midwife gave a quick glance over her shoulder then turned back to the sphere. "The baron is here," she whispered in a tight voice. "Should I—"

Sibyl's wings flared. "Do nothing rash," she hissed. "Do not go to the girl; if this is a ruse, they will have a means of following you. Avoid the baron, for now. Continue your preparations."

Naneth bowed her head. "I am your servant, oh Sibilant Death."

As the baron shouted what sounded like a final warning, the image of Sibyl vanished from the sphere. Scooping up the crystal ball, Naneth spoke several words in a foreign language. Then she vanished, leaving only swirling dust motes behind.

A heartbeat later the door crashed open, propelled by the baron's boot. He stormed into the room and glared around it, nose crinkling as he caught the odor of snake. Then he whirled and stomped out of sight.

Devoid of emotion to feed it, the manifestation ended.

Arvin knocked a fist against his own forehead, chastising himself in the silent speech. Stupid. If only he hadn't sent that warning to Naneth, they might have learned where Glisena was—but now Naneth was gone.

It was no consolation to Arvin that, until a few moments ago, Naneth had seemed nothing more than a helpful midwife. Marasa had been right all along. Glisena *had* been kidnapped, albeit without her realizing it. The baron's daughter had unwittingly placed herself—and her unborn child—in the hands of servants of an utterly ruthless and evil abomination. What terrible scheme was Sibyl up to this time?

Whatever it was, it had to involve the child.

Six months ago, Sibyl had attempted to install Osran Extaminos, youngest brother of Lady Dediana, on Hlondeth's throne. She would have succeeded, had Arvin not thwarted her plan to turn Hlondeth's humans into Osran's private slave army. This time around, Sibyl must have been planning to use Lady Dediana's grandchild.

That this was a scheme of opportunity, Arvin had no doubt. There was no way for Sibyl to have known that Glisena was pregnant by Dmetrio, or that the baron would summon a midwife to the palace to end that pregnancy. That it had been Naneth the baron had chosen had been mere ill fortune.

Unless—and here was a chilling thought—Dmetrio was somehow involved. Had he gotten the baron's daughter pregnant on purpose?

Another talk with Ambassador Extaminos was in order. It would have to be a very private talk, one in which Arvin would listen both to what was said—and what wasn't being said.

In the meantime, he needed to send a warning. He stepped out into the hallway, pulled the lapis lazuli from his pocket, held it to his forehead, and spoke the command word. He concentrated, and the face of his mentor became clear in his mind—a deeply lined face framed by short gray hair, the eyes with a curious fold to the eyelid that marked Tanju as coming from the East.

Tanju blinked in surprise as the sending connected them then turned to listen to what Arvin had to say.

"Glisena is pregnant with Dmetrio's child," Arvin told him. "A midwife named Naneth helped Glisena hide. Naneth serves Sibyl. Sibyl hopes to use the child."

Tanju nodded thoughtfully. He ran a hand through his hair as he composed his reply. "Learn what Sibyl intends. I will warn Lady Dediana."

The connection faded. "*Atmiya*," Arvin said, letting the lapis lazuli fall into his palm. He tucked it carefully back into his pocket and turned toward the stairs. Just as he was about to descend, he heard a creaking noise from below: the front door opening. Then a male voice called out. "Naneth?" The voice sounded hesitant, uncertain. Something moved in the hallway downstairs. It sounded like the clomping of a horse, though softer, like the footsteps of a foal.

Remaining motionless, Arvin peered down the stairs. A short, slender man wearing a forest-green hooded cloak stood in the hallway, staring nervously into the kitchen. At first Arvin took him to be an elf, but then he realized that those weren't goat's-fleece trousers but the fellow's own thickly furred legs. Each ended in a black cloven hoof. As the man turned, Arvin saw his face. It was narrow and had pointed ears, like those of an elf, but a black horn curled from each temple. The chin was sharp and covered in a tuft of black hair.

A satyr.

What was a satyr doing in a city, far from any forest?

"Naneth?" the fellow called again. "Come now, woman, are you here?" He spoke with a high, soft voice, with a lilt that made it sound as if he were reciting poetry.

Was the satyr also one of Sibyl's servants? There was one way to find out by probing his thoughts. Slowly, Arvin drew back from the staircase, intending to manifest the power from hiding, but the satyr's senses were keen. His eyes darted to the spot where Arvin stood. He bleated in surprise then bolted.

He was out the door before Arvin could react. Cursing, Arvin pounded down the stairs and out the front door himself. He glanced right, left . . . and saw the satyr disappearing around a corner. Arvin charged after him, elbowing his way through the people on the street and summoning his dagger from his glove as he ran. If need be, he would use it, but only as a threat—he had less lethal ways of bringing the satyr down.

The satyr sprinted up the street, darting nervous glances behind himself as he ran. His hood had fallen away from his head, revealing his ramlike horns and dark, flowing hair. He skidded around a corner, slipping a little on the snow, and Arvin narrowed the gap between them. Arvin pelted around the corner.

A hoof lashed out, narrowly missing his groin. Pain shot through Arvin's thigh as the hoof gouged into it—and the satyr was off and running again, this time down an alley.

Biting his lip against the throbbing of his thigh, Arvin stumbled after him. He shoved his ungloved hand into his pocket and pulled from it a fist-sized knot. He skidded to a stop and threw the monkey's fist at the satyr, shouting the command word that activated its magic.

The ensorcelled knot unraveled in flight, splitting into four trailing strands. The main part of the monkey's fist struck the satyr in the side as he rounded another corner, and immediately two of the strands of twine wrapped around his waist. The others encircled his legs. The twine yanked his legs together, immobilizing them, and he tumbled to the ground.

Arvin approached cautiously, dagger in hand. He halted just outside the flailing arc of the satyr's bound legs. He glared down at the fellow, manifesting the power that would allow him to listen in on the satyr's thoughts. "Who . . . are you?" he panted, a spray of silver sparkles erupting from his forehead as the power manifested. He turned his dagger so that its blade caught the light. "Do you serve Sibyl?"

The satyr's ears twitched. He tossed his head. "Leave me be, thief. I carry no gems—not a single sparkle." Behind the words was a faint, panicky echo: his thoughts. They were in his own language, but Arvin heard them as if they'd been spoken in the common tongue. *What has he done to Naneth? If he has caused her harm. . . .*

"Sibyl," Arvin repeated sternly. "The abomination. Do you serve Sibyl?"

Who? The satyr struggled against the twine and tried to rise to his feet, but tripped and fell backward. His thoughts tumbled over one another. *What game does he play? What does he want of me?*

Arvin sighed and vanished the dagger back into his glove. "I made a mistake, it seems," he told the satyr. "I thought *you* were the thief."

The satyr paused in his struggles. "You were not the mischief-maker who trampled Naneth's home?" *Who is he, then?*

Arvin shook his head. "I came to consult Naneth," he said, answering the unspoken question. "I found her door open, her home disrupted."

"Ah." The satyr relaxed. *That is why he was there. His woman is with child.*

Arvin knelt beside the satyr and grasped the monkey's fist firmly. He repeated the command and the twine instantly unwound from the satyr's limbs and reknotted itself back into a monkey's fist.

A sorcerer, the satyr thought. *They are thick as brambles here.*

"Was that why you came to Naneth's house?" Arvin asked, extending a hand to help the satyr up. "Is your woman also pregnant?"

A troubled look crept into the satyr's eyes. *The female,* he thought. *She is unwell. If Naneth does not attend her, she may lose her child.* "Yes," he answered aloud.

Arvin barely masked his startle. The satyr was thinking in his own language, but the power Arvin was manifesting allowed him to understand the subtle nuances of each word. "Female," he'd said, not "woman." He wasn't referring to one of his own kind—he was talking about a woman of some other race.

Glisena?

"Is the birth not going well?" Arvin probed. "Is that why you came to fetch Naneth?"

The satyr nodded.

"Perhaps I could help. When my first child was born, I assisted the midwife. I know some healing spells—I used them to help my wife." He paused, pretending to think of something. "Of course, my wife is *human*. . . ."

Might he help? the satyr wondered. *He may have a spell that will banish fever from humanfolk.*

Arvin felt his heart quicken. The satyr *was* talking about Glisena. He was certain of it.

The satyr considered, for the briefest of moments, accepting Arvin's offer—then decided against it. "The midwife would be more suited," he said. "Do you know where she might be?"

"I wish I did," Arvin answered truthfully. He paused. "If I do see Naneth, where should I send her? Where is the woman who needs help?"

A brief thought flickered through the satyr's mind—a mental picture of a hut made from a mud-plastered lattice of woven branches, its bark-slab roof draped with brambles. It stood at the base of a tree in a snow-dappled forest.

"Is your forest far from here?" Arvin prompted.

"Why ask you this?" the satyr asked suspiciously.

"That is, I'm assuming you live in a forest," Arvin added hurriedly, realizing he'd almost given himself away. "For all I know you have a house here in Ormpetarr. If your woman was ill with a fever, you would naturally seek out the closest midwife who could—"

The satyr's eyes narrowed. *I never told him the female had a fever.*

Arvin had only the briefest flicker of a warning before the satyr leaped forward and up—just enough to let Arvin twist aside as horns slammed into his forehead. Hot sparks of pain exploded across Arvin's vision as he was knocked backward. Stunned, barely conscious, he dimly heard the satyr running away. He rolled over onto his stomach and pressed his face into the snow. The cold revived him a little, took away some of the sting. But when he sat up, the alley spun dizzily around him. By the time he was able to stagger to his feet, the satyr was long gone. Arvin stood, one hand against a wall, the other holding his pounding head. For the second time in a single evening, he'd seriously misjudged someone.

The monkey's fist lay in the snow near his feet. He picked it up, brushed it clean, and shoved it back into his pocket. His finger brushed against a small, hard object: the lapis lazuli, tucked safely inside a hidden seam. He considered using it to ask Tanju for advice, but he knew what the psion would say. He'd tell Arvin to use the dorje to track the satyr—and Arvin would be forced to admit that the magical item had broken. Hearing this, Tanju might insist on coming to Sespech and conducting the search for the baron's daughter himself. And Arvin would be out of a job.

There was, however, still a chance that the situation could be salvaged. If the satyr could be found and questioned, Arvin might yet learn where Glisena was.

Touching the stone to his forehead, he formed a mental image of Baron Foesmasher. It took only a moment for the baron to become solid in his mind's eye; he was leaning over a table, barking orders and gesturing at something that was spread out on the table before him. He started as Arvin interrupted whatever it was he'd just been saying.

The sending allowed Arvin only a few words. He chose them carefully. "A satyr knows where Glisena is. He just fled from

Naneth's house. He's wearing a green hooded cloak. We need to find him."

The baron regained his composure instantly. "Return to the palace," he ordered. "At *once.*"

Arvin nodded his acknowledgment then tucked the lapis lazuli back in his pocket. Now that he knew that Sibyl's minions were involved, he felt a newfound resolution. He would find Glisena. He wouldn't allow Sibyl to claim another victim.

Rubbing his aching forehead—a lump was already starting to rise over his right eye—he turned and trudged back to the palace.

CHAPTER 8

ARVIN LAY ON THE FLOOR OF THE PRACTICE HALL WITH HIS ARMS extended and upper torso bent back like that of a rearing snake. His palms, hips, and feet pressed against the floor as he craned his neck back to stare with unfocused eyes at the ceiling. He wore only his breeches, despite the chill in the hall. Snow fell outside the narrow leaded-glass windows that reached from floor to ceiling, muffling the sounds from the city.

His breathing was slow and deep, his mind focused entirely on his meditations. With each breath in through his nose, he drew in strength, courage, and confidence. With each breath out through his mouth, he blew away weakness, uncertainty, and doubt.

Picturing his mind as a net, he sent his consciousness down the strand that twined around his spine and located the *muladhara* that lay at the base of it. When he was ready, he activated his power points one by one, following this line. The "third eye" in his forehead emitted a flash of silver sparkles; a vibration deep in his throat filled the hall with a low droning noise; the base of his scalp prickled, causing the hair on the back of his neck to rise; his chest filled with crackling energy, which he exhaled in a breath scented with ginger and saffron; and a spiral of energy uncoiled from his navel, dewing the floor around him with a fine sheen of ectoplasm.

The energies coiled around his *muladhara.* The spiral grew tighter and stronger as Arvin wove strand after mental strand into it, replenishing it.

Arvin let out one last slow exhalation, ending his meditation. But he wasn't finished yet. Rising gracefully to his feet, he completed his morning routine, flowing through the motions that Tanju had taught him. The five combat and five defensive modes each had a pose associated with them, designed to focus the mind of the novice. Arvin had learned how to manifest just seven of them, but he ran through all ten poses, flowing from one to the next in what looked like one long, continuous motion.

When he was done, he yawned. He'd had very little sleep this past night; upon his return to the palace, Foesmasher had demanded a full report of what had transpired with the satyr. Arvin had been forced to admit that he could lift private thoughts from the minds of those around him, but the baron hadn't seemed alarmed by this revelation. Instead he'd been overjoyed to at last have some indication as to where his daughter had gone.

"So that's where she is," he said, "the Chondalwood." One heavy hand clapped Arvin's shoulder. "Well done. Now we just need to find that satyr and learn where his camp is." He paused. "You said the satyr was worried about Glisena's health. What was it, exactly, that he said?"

Arvin met the baron's eye. "That she was ill. He was worried she would lose her child."

"There is no child," the baron said with a catch in his voice. "Naneth saw to that, may Helm forgive me. You said that the satyr didn't actually use Glisena's name?"

"No, but—"

"Then it must have been someone else who needed the midwife's ministrations. Some other girl. Glisena is no longer with child."

"Yes, she is, Lord Foesmasher," Arvin said quietly. "Naneth didn't do as you ordered. She tricked you." Choosing his words carefully, he summed up what the visions had shown him—both in Glisena's chamber and at Naneth's house. He omitted any mention of the warning he'd given the midwife.

"When you charged into Naneth's home, she must have realized you'd learned of her treachery," Arvin concluded. "She teleported away."

"Gods willing, she'll have gone to wherever Glisena is," the baron said. His forehead puckered with worry. "I shudder to think of my daughter alone in the forest, giving birth in some dirt-floored shack with only *satyrs* to aid her. At least some good has come of my actions: I sped the midwife on her way."

"That . . . would not be a good thing," Arvin said.

"What do you mean?" the baron asked sharply.

Arvin took a deep breath then gave the baron the bad news. Naneth wasn't just a midwife. She served one of Lady Dediana's enemies—Sibyl. The yuan-ti abomination must be hoping to use Glisena's child as a playing piece in her bid for Hlondeth's throne. Once she had the child in hand. . . .

The baron's eyes widened. "After the child has been born, Glisena is no longer of any value to them," he said in a strained voice. "She will be . . . disposed of."

"There may still be hope," Arvin said. "The satyr said the child hadn't been born yet. Until Glisena gives birth, Naneth won't harm her. Sibyl *wants* this baby. And once the baby is born, they will need Glisena to nurse the child." He paused. "Have your clerics found any trace of Naneth yet?"

The baron shook his head. "She has shielded herself, it seems, with the same magic that is preventing us from finding my daughter." He sighed. "It all hinges, now, on finding the satyr."

That was when things had become awkward. Foesmasher had demanded that Arvin use his psionics to find the satyr, and Arvin had been forced to do some quick talking. He'd drained his energies, he told the baron. He needed to sleep, then to meditate, before he could manifest any more powers. Like a wizard consulting his spellbook, or a cleric praying to her god, he needed to restore his magic.

Grudgingly, the baron had agreed to the delay. Marasa and her clerics would search for the satyr while Arvin rested.

If only the dorje Tanju had given Arvin hadn't broken, finding the satyr would have been an easy matter, Arvin thought. Without it, he would be forced to rely on his own, limited, powers. The only one he had that might be of use was one that gave him an inkling of whether a given course of action was good or bad. By manifesting it, he might get a sense of whether it would be better to search *this* section of the city or *that* one for the satyr. But the inklings weren't always accurate, and the power could be manifested only so many times. And now it was morning, and his meditations were over—and the baron would expect him to perform a miracle.

Hunger grumbled in his stomach, reminding him that he hadn't eaten yet. He should get dressed and find some food. He lifted his belt from the rack that held wooden practice swords and buckled it around his waist, adjusting it so his dagger was snug at the small of his back. His trousers and shirt were draped over one of the battered wooden posts that served as man-sized targets; his boots lay on the floor nearby. He dressed then crossed the room to a table on which stood a bowl of cold water. He splashed some of it onto his hair, combing it away from his eyes with his fingers. He flexed his left hand—his abbreviated little finger always ached in cold weather—then pulled on his magical glove. Then, just to see if he could do it, he drew his dagger, closed his eyes, and suddenly spun and threw the weapon, relying on memory to guide his aim. He heard a *thunk* and a creaking noise and opened his eyes. The arm of the quintain was rotating slowly, the dagger stuck fast in the center of the small wooden shield that hung from one end of it. Arvin smiled.

Applause echoed from above. Glancing up, Arvin saw the baron standing on the spectator's gallery that ran along one side of the practice hall. He had entered it silently, his footsteps muffled by the gallery's thick carpet. Arvin wondered how long he'd been standing there. The baron had changed into fresh clothes, but his eyes were pouchy; he hadn't slept. A sword was at his hip, and he was wearing his helmet. Its purple plume swayed as he descended the stairs to the floor of the practice room.

"The satyr has been found," Foesmasher announced.

"Excellent!" Arvin exclaimed, relieved. "If we ask the right questions, his thoughts will tell us where. . . ." Belatedly, he noticed that the baron's lips were pressed together in a grim line. "What's wrong?"

"When I received your warning last night, I ordered the city's gates sealed," Foesmasher said. "The Eyes began a block-by-block search of Ormpetarr; their spells flushed the satyr out a short time ago. He scaled the city wall. One of my soldiers gave chase along the battlements. The satyr slipped and fell to his death."

"That's terrible news," Arvin said.

"Yes. The soldier responsible has been punished."

Hearing the grim tone in Foesmasher's voice, Arvin cringed, thankful he hadn't been the one to cause the satyr's death. He didn't want to ask what had been done to the soldier; his imagination already painted a vivid enough picture.

The baron walked over to the quintain and pulled Arvin's dagger from it. "You've rested and replenished your magic." It was a statement rather than a question.

Arvin gave what he hoped was a confident-looking nod.

"What will you do next?"

Arvin was wondering that, himself. Even with the dorje intact, he might not have been able to locate Glisena. Whatever was preventing her from being located by wizardry and clerical magic might very well block psionics, as well. There was one person, however, who wasn't shielded by magic.

"I'm going to pay a visit to Ambassador Extaminos," Arvin told the baron.

Foesmasher frowned. "To what end?"

"It's possible that Sibyl plans to use the child as a means to force Dmetrio to do her bidding," Arvin explained. "Demands may already have been made—and if they have, and it's Naneth who's making them, Dmetrio may be our way of finding her. And through her, Glisena."

"Excellent," the baron said. "Let's go there at once. If he doesn't tell us what we want to know—"

"That might not be such a good idea, Lord Foesmasher," Arvin said in a careful voice. "Your presence might . . . agitate the ambassador. And an agitated mind will be harder for my psionics to penetrate. The best chance we have of learning more is if I meet with the ambassador alone."

The baron toyed with Arvin's dagger, considering this. "Was it mind magic that allowed you to find the target with your eyes closed," he asked, testing the dagger's balance, "or the magic of this dagger?"

"Neither," Arvin said, surprised by the change of subject. "I've worked as a net weaver and rope maker since the age of six. It makes for nimble fingers—you learn to be quick with a knife. Target practice does the rest."

The baron handed him the dagger. "Helm grant that the questions you put to Ambassador Extaminos also find their mark."

☙

Arvin paced impatiently in the reception hall, angry at having been kept waiting an entire morning. Dmetrio's house slaves had provided him with wine and food—roasted red beetles the size of his fist, precracked and drizzled with herbed butter—but Arvin waved away the yuan-ti delicacy. He'd already blunted the worst of his hunger at the palace and was too restless to eat. He ignored the smooth stone platform the slaves urged him to recline on and instead paced back and forth across the tiled floor, staring at the locked door of the basking room. At last it opened and a slave, bent nearly double under the weight of the jug of oil he carried, stepped through. Arvin strode toward the door.

"Wait!" the slave cried through the scarf that covered his mouth. "There's *osssra* inside. You mustn't go in there!"

"Too late," Arvin muttered as he pushed past the slave. "I'm already in."

The air in the basking room was thick with smoke that smelled like a combination of mint tea, singed moss, and burning sap. It hit Arvin's nostrils like a slap across the face, leaving them watering. As he breathed in the smoke, the room swayed and his legs began to tremble. He staggered, catching himself on one of the pillars that held up the domed ceiling. He clung to it, shaking his head, fighting the waves of dizziness.

A low chuckle helped him focus. Still clutching at the pillar, he turned toward the sound.

Dmetrio Extaminos lay in a shallow pool in the floor a few paces away. His naked, scaled body was coiled under him; it gleamed from the oil that filled the pool. His upper torso rose from it, bending back like a snake's. He looked up at Arvin with a languid expression, slit eyes wide and staring, his dark hair slicked back from his high forehead. A forked tongue flickered out of his mouth, tasting the smoke-filled air.

"Ah," he said. "The rope merchant's agent. Are you really here . . . or just part of my dream?"

Smoke drifted slowly from the half dozen lidded pots that surrounded the pool, drawing Arvin's eye. He watched, fascinated, as amber-colored tendrils twisted toward the ceiling. Only when he heard the slither of Dmetrio shifting position was he able to wrench his eyes away from the smoke. He shook his head violently, trying to concentrate. The smoke, he thought. He should have listened to the servant's warning. He tried to manifest the power that would allow him to overhear Dmetrio's thoughts, but his own thoughts were too sluggish; they drifted like the smoke. A glint of silver sparked in his vision then was gone.

"Ambassador Extaminos," he said thickly, his words slurred. "Glisena is in danger. Her child—"

"What child?"

"The one you fathered," Arvin continued. "The midwife, she. . . ." He paused, blinking slowly. What was it he'd wanted to ask?

"Glisena is pregnant?" Dmetrio asked. A slow hiss of laughter escaped from his lips.

Arvin tried to shake a finger at him and nearly fell over. "She's also missing," he said when he'd righted himself. "She's been kidnapped."

"So?" Dmetrio curled into a new position in the oil, his scales leaving glistening streaks on the tiled edges of the pool.

"Do you know where she is?"

Dmetrio slowly arched his neck, stretching it. Oil trickled down one cheek. "No. I don't. Nor do I care."

"She's with child. *Your* child," Arvin protested. "She might die."

"Human women die in childbirth all the time," Dmetrio said. "Bearing live young is messy. Laying eggs is a much more efficient way of doing things." He rolled over in the oil, coating his scales with it. "Glisena has grown tiresome. I'll be glad to be away from here."

Arvin let go of the pillar. He meant to take a step toward Dmetrio, but he reeled sideways. "But the child," he said. "You must care about. . . ." His mind wandered. It was getting more difficult to concentrate by the moment. His thoughts were like bugs, caught in sap and struggling to get free. The smoke. . . . His gaze drifted up to the ceiling again. He wrenched his mind back.

"But the child," Arvin repeated. "Won't you take it . . . with you?"

Dmetrio let out a loud hiss of laughter. "Why would I want to do that?"

"Because it's *your* child. You can't just *abandon*—"

Dmetrio waved a hand. Someone seized Arvin's arms from behind—two someones, wearing armor and helmets flared like cobra hoods. "Rillis?" Arvin asked, peering at them through the smoke.

Neither was the guard Arvin had bribed for information the day before. They dragged him backward out of the basking room. A servant—the one who'd been carrying the jar of oil—closed and relocked the door behind them. Arvin found himself being dragged through the reception hall, down a corridor, out a door, and down a snow-covered ramp. His heels skidded through the snow, leaving two drag marks. He stared at them, fascinated. They were like the trails left by snakes. If he moved his feet from side to side, they slithered. . . .

A gate creaked open and the militiamen lifted him up. Then he was floating through the air. No, not floating . . . he'd been thrown, tossed out by the militiamen. He landed on his back in the snowy street. As people drifted past him, shrinking back from the spot where he lay, he stared, intrigued, at the snowflakes falling out of the sky. He watched them while the snow soaked through his cloak, trousers, and shirt. They started off so small and got so big. Like that one . . . it was *huge*.

No, that wasn't a snowflake. It was a woman's face, looking down at him. She had dark eyes, wide cheekbones, and black, wavy hair that reached toward him like snakes.

Heart pounding, Arvin tried to crawl backward through the snow, to escape the snakes. Then he spotted the frog hiding behind them. The notion of a frog sitting on a woman's earlobe seemed so *silly*, somehow, that he had to laugh. It came out like a croak.

"Vin?" the woman asked. "Are you all right?"

Arvin stared dreamily up at Karrell for several moments, tracing the curve of her lips with his eyes. He tried to raise a hand to touch them, but his arm flopped into the snow above his head. He needed to tell her something—that he'd breathed in something called *osssra*—but his lips wouldn't form the word. "Sssraaa," he slurred.

Karrell bent down and lifted his arm from the snow. "Vin," she said, her voice low and serious. "You need help. Please try to stand."

His arm drifted up around her shoulder, and his legs were scrabbling under him, messing up the snow. Yanked along the street by Karrell, he stumbled after her, staring at the pattern his feet made, oblivious to the people staring at them. There were so *many* footsteps . . . and not a one of them from a satyr's cloven hoof.

Why that mattered, he couldn't say.

❦

Arvin sat up, rubbing his head. His mind was his own again, but his head ached, and he felt shaky; it was difficult to coordinate his movements. He took it slow, swinging first one leg, then the other, off the side of the bed. When he stood, his legs trembled. He was naked, save for his breeches and the braided leather bracelet around his right wrist. And—he touched the crystal that hung at his throat—the now-depleted power stone his mother had given him, all those years ago.

He was in a small, simply furnished room with a door and one window. Through the shutters he could see that the snow had at last stopped falling; the street was three stories below. It was dark and a horn was sounding elsewhere in the city, signaling the evening prayer. He must have been unconscious for some time.

The room's furnishings included a bed, a narrow wardrobe by the fire, and a wooden table and chair. He was relieved to see his belt hanging on the back of the chair, his dagger still in its sheath. His magical glove lay on the table, next to a drawing of his sleeping face, rendered in charcoal on parchment. It was an amazingly good likeness; Karrell must have drawn it. A fire burned in the grate; his damp clothes and cloak hung, steaming slightly, on the fire screen in front of it. Noise wafted up from somewhere below—the overlapping sounds of voices, a stringed instrument, and the clatter of crockery. With it came the smell of food, a mouthwatering blend of stew and baking bread. Arvin's stomach growled.

He walked toward the fire—slowly, so he wouldn't stumble—and searched the pocket of his shirt. Inside the false seam was a familiar bulge: the lapis lazuli. Pulling it out, he affixed it to his forehead and tried to concentrate on Tanju, but the psion's face kept slipping out of focus. Realizing he was simply too tired to manifest a sending, Arvin removed the lapis lazuli and tucked it back inside his pocket. He'd contact Tanju later. All he really had to report, anyway, was that Dmetrio wasn't involved in Glisena's disappearance.

As he was making his way back to the bed, the door opened. Karrell came in, carrying a platter on which stood a bowl of stew, some bread, and a mug of ale. She set the platter down on the table then took Arvin's arm, guiding him toward the table. "You're still unwell," she said. "You should rest."

Arvin sank into the chair. "How long have I been here?" The savory odors of carrots, potatoes, and beef rose to his nostrils. He licked his lips and picked up a spoon from the platter. "And where am I?"

"I found you at midday, outside the ambassador's residence," Karrell answered, closing the door. "You are at the Fairwinds Inn, a short distance from there."

Arvin nodded and tore a chunk off the bread, following it up with some stew. As the flavors washed over his tongue, he closed his eyes and sighed. He took a drink of ale then tucked into the stew in earnest. "Thanks," he said, nodding at the bowl. "And thanks for helping me."

"You were fortunate," Karrell said. "*Osssra* can be fatal to humans."

"What is it?"

Karrell walked to the fire screen and lifted Arvin's cloak from it, turning it so the other side was to the heat. "*Osssra* are oils," she told him over her shoulder. "When burned, they have special properties. Some *osssra* clear the mind, while others heal the body. Some purge enchantments, while still others—like the one whose odor lingers on your hair and skin—stimulate dreams and memories."

"The only thing it stimulated in me was dizziness," Arvin said, talking around a mouthful of bread. The food was helping; he was starting to feel better already. "It made me as stupid as a slug."

"Be thankful it only enfeebled your mind. Some *osssra* are fatal to humans. They are intended for yuan-ti."

"You know a lot about these magical oils," Arvin noted between spoonfuls of stew.

Karrell shrugged and continued turning his clothing. "You came from the direction of the palace. Did you manage an audience with the baron, after all?"

"You were watching the ambassador's residence, weren't you?" Arvin asked between mouthfuls of food.

"Yes," she admitted. "Was he just as rude as before?"

Arvin's fist tightened on the spoon. "Worse. He's an arrogant, unfeeling bastard. Just like all the rest of—"

Karrell's eyes narrowed. "All the rest of *what?*"

Arvin shrugged. He might as well say it. This wasn't Hlondeth; he could say what he liked.

"House Extaminos."

"Ah." Karrell walked back across the room and sank onto the bed—the only other place to sit. She toyed with the collar of her dress, which was white and hemmed with intricate turquoise embroidery. The dress was made from a soft, thin fabric unsuited to a winter climate, a fabric that hugged her breasts. She tossed her hair with a flick of her head, revealing her jade earplug and the soft curve of her jaw and throat. Arvin found himself losing interest in his food. He really *was* feeling better—much better. Even without the benefits of a charm spell, Karrell looked amazing.

She smiled and said something in a low voice. Arvin leaned forward. "Excuse me?" he asked, sopping up the last of the stew with his bread. "What did you just—"

He realized that she'd slid one hand behind her, as if to lean back on it. He caught sight of her fingers moving in an all-too-familiar gesture. Before she could complete her spell, he manifested a charm of his own. The base of his scalp prickled as psionic energy rushed from it. Break her promise, would she? Well he wasn't about to let her get the better of him this time.

He saw Karrell tilt her head slightly.

Arvin felt a rush of warmth flow through him. He could see, by the sparkle in her dark eyes and the way she looked at him, that she cared for him—*really* cared for him—as much as he did for her. She'd just saved his life, hadn't she? Karrell was someone he could count on, trust in, confide in. Setting down the piece of bread, he turned toward her. "He doesn't care," he told her.

She gave a slight frown. "Who does not care—and about what?"

"Dmetrio Extaminos." Arvin shoved the empty bowl away. "I tried to tell him that the woman carrying his child might be in danger, and he just laughed. He's not even going to try to look for Glisena; he's just going to walk away. To abandon his own child. Just like. . . ."

He looked away.

Karrell laid a hand on his knee. "Just like what, Vin?"

"It's Arvin," he said.

"Just Arvin?" she asked. "No clan name?"

"My father didn't live long enough to marry my mother. He died before I was born. Or at least, that's what my mother told me."

"Some fathers are not worth knowing," Karrell said.

Arvin caught the look in her eye, and saw that it would be better not to pursue this comment. He tried to lighten the mood. "The yuan-ti have that advantage," he said. "Their women lay their eggs all together in a brood chamber. None of them know their fathers." He chuckled. "It's a wonder they know who their mothers are."

"The yuan-ti of Tashalar have a similar custom," said Karrell. "So I hear." She flipped her hair back, showing off her jade ear plug. "I am of the Tabaxi, of Clan Chex'en."

"Check . . . shen," Arvin repeated, trying to capture the same inflection. "Was that your father's clan?"

Karrell smiled. "My mother's. The humans of Chult, like the yuan-ti, pay little attention to who sired them." Her smile faded. "In most cases."

"The Tabaxi don't have husbands?" Arvin asked.

"We do not use that word. We call them *yaakuns*," She paused, searching for the translation. "Lovers."

Arvin nodded. "What about you? Do you have—"

"Brothers and sisters?" she interrupted. "No. And you?"

Arvin had a feeling she'd deliberately misinterpreted his question. He let it drop. "I was my mother's only child."

"Was?"

"My mother died of plague when I was six."

"You must have been very lonely afterward."

Arvin shrugged. "There were plenty of other kids in the orphanage." Only one of them, however, had been his friend: Naulg. And Naulg was dead.

"Orphanage?" Karrell repeated. The word was obviously unfamiliar to her.

"It's something like a brood chamber," Arvin said, "for human children who have no parents. The priests run it."

"Priests of what god?"

"Ilmater," Arvin said, his lips twisting as he spoke the name. "God of suffering. His priests made sure we got plenty of it."

"This orphanage of yours sounds . . . unpleasant."

"It was," Arvin agreed grimly.

Karrell stared into the distance. Her hand was still resting on his knee. Arvin glanced at the ring on her little finger. He'd love to know what she was thinking right now. Just as well that the ring was shielding her thoughts; otherwise he might be tempted to listen in on them.

She must have sensed his unwillingness to talk further about his childhood, for she changed the subject abruptly. "That woman you came to Sespech to find," she asked. "Was it Glisena Foesmasher?"

A tiny warning voice sounded in the back of Arvin's mind. One look into Karrell's dark eyes, and it was extinguished. Arvin nodded. "The baron's daughter ran away a tenday ago; I came to Sespech to help find her. A midwife helped her flee the palace. Glisena thinks the midwife was helping her, but Glisena is being used. They want her child—Dmetrio's the father. They hope to use it in a grab for Hlondeth's throne. Once it's born, the gods only know what Sibyl will do with—"

"Sibyl?" Karrell asked sharply. Her grip on Arvin's knee tightened.

"She's a yuan-ti," Arvin explained. "The midwife is one of her followers. They believe that Sibyl's an avatar of the god Sseth."

"She's no avatar," Karrell whispered.

Arvin blinked. "You know who I'm talking about?"

Karrell's eyes bored into his. "How do you know about Sibyl?"

Arvin's jaw clenched. "She killed my friend. I swore I'd do whatever I could to avenge his death. Even if it meant taking on an avatar."

Karrell took his measure for several moments before speaking. "Sibyl is mortal, though that was not always the case. For a time— during the Time of Troubles, when the gods walked Faerûn—her body was possessed by Sseth. But when the Time of Troubles ended, the god withdrew from her body. That was fifteen years ago; she has been mortal since. But she hopes to become a god, just as did Sseth, who himself was once no more than an avatar of Merrshaulk."

Arvin stared at Karrell. He had only the barest notion of what she was talking about. The only god he knew much about was Ilmater; the priests at the orphanage had drilled every painful, gory detail of the sufferings of the Crying God's martyrs into the children under their care. Arvin didn't even know Hoar's history, despite the fact that he had sworn an oath of vengeance to that god—an oath the Doombringer seemed bent on forcing Arvin to keep.

"How do you know all this stuff about Sibyl?" Arvin asked Karrell.

Karrell gave him a hard, level look. "To defeat an enemy, one must learn her ways."

Outside the window, thunder grumbled in the distance: the voice of Hoar. Arvin whistled softly. "I think the gods have thrown us together for a reason."

"I, too, believe this," Karrell said. She leaned closer and spoke in a confiding voice. "The yuan-ti of the south still believe Sibyl to be Sseth's avatar. Only a handful see her for what she really is—a power-mad mortal out to resurrect the empire of Serpentes at any cost."

Arvin had heard of Serpentes. It was an ancient yuan-ti empire that had stretched across the whole of the Chultan Peninsula—an empire that the yuan-ti still talked about, even though it had fallen nearly fourteen centuries ago. "I thought it was Hlondeth that Sibyl was after," he said.

"Only as a means to an end," Karrell said. "Nearly two years ago, Sibyl vanished from our lands. We were relieved to hear that she was gone, until we learned that she had traveled north. When we learned that she had gone to Hlondeth—"

"Who's we?" Arvin interrupted.

"The *K'aaxlaat*," Karrell said.

He gave her a blank look.

"Protectors of the jungle. We walk in the footsteps of Ubtao."

Arvin nodded, though he was no closer to understanding. It sounded like some sort of druidic sect.

"We realized," Karrell continued, "what Sibyl must be looking for: an artifact that had been given, long ago, to House Extaminos for safekeeping. It was hidden, then forgotten as the centuries went by. But Dmetrio Extaminos found it."

Despite himself, Arvin was intrigued. "And you came north to Hlondeth to find it. To steal it."

Karrell's eyes blazed. "No. To *recover* it. To prevent it from falling into Sibyl's hands. To ensure it would never be used again."

"What is it?"

"Do you know the Story of Sseth?" Karrell asked.

Arvin shrugged. "Not really. Those of us of the 'lesser race' aren't exactly encouraged to learn about the serpent god. I've never even set foot inside the Cathedral of Emerald Scales. Except once. By proxy."

The memory rose, unbidden, from those that lingered on from Zelia's mind seed. He'd seen the temple through her eyes as she genuflected before a statue of the god in winged serpent form. He nodded to himself; no wonder the yuan-ti believed Sibyl to be Sseth's avatar. She had the wings—even for an abomination, that was rare. And her eyes glowed red—they flickered like the flames that had surrounded Sseth's statue.

Arvin dredged up the last of Zelia's memory. "There's a prophecy about Sseth rising from the flames, isn't there?"

Karrell nodded, visibly impressed. "From the Peaks of Flame—volcanoes on the Chult Peninsula. There is a door there, one Sibyl hopes to open. She thinks it leads to Sseth's domain. She hopes to convince the god to claim her as his avatar once more. But the door does not lead to the Viper Pit. It leads to a cave on the Fugue Plane occupied by one of the eternal evils—Dendar the Night Serpent. Should the door be opened, and the Night Serpent escape, thousands will die—perhaps hundreds of thousands. A giant is a mere morsel to her; she can swallow an entire village in one gulp. Those she swallows are utterly destroyed; not a shred of their souls remains for the gods to claim. And the more souls she consumes, the larger she grows—and the more she feeds. According to the prophecies, if released and unchecked, she will grow until she is capable of swallowing the very sun—of plunging the world into eternal night. A night in which no plants will grow, all of the waters of Faerûn will freeze, and the gods themselves will fade as their last worshipers die."

Arvin felt his eyes widen. Normally he would have blown off such an exaggerated story. But to hear Karrell tell it—to hear the tremble in her voice as she spoke of the end of the world—shook him. "This thing you came north to find," he said. "It's a key, right?"

Karrell's eyes bored into his. "It is called the Circled Serpent. It is made of silver, in the shape of a serpent biting its own tail and has a diameter about so." She held her hands about two palms' widths apart. "It was fashioned in two halves—one with a head, the other with a tail—which must be fitted together for its magic to work."

She lowered her hands. "I know this much: that Dmetrio Extaminos found the Circled Serpent when he was restoring the old section of Hlondeth. I believe he may have brought it with him to Sespech, but I am unable to locate it with my magic. During your last visit to the ambassador's residence, did you see anything like I have just described?"

Arvin shook his head.

"I did not expect so," Karrell said. "He will have it hidden. He fears another attempt by Sibyl's followers to steal it."

"The Pox?" Arvin asked, alarmed. "Did some of them survive?"

"Who are The Pox?"

"Followers of Talona, goddess of plague and disease," Arvin's heart was beating quickly. "And servants of Sibyl. They're the ones who killed my friend."

Karrell frowned. "No. The ones I am speaking of worship a different deity: Talos, god of storms and destruction. They, too, have formed an alliance with Sibyl. At her bidding, they tried to steal the Circled Serpent after Dmetrio Extaminos discovered it inside the ancient tower."

Suddenly, Arvin realized what she was referring to. Last summer, a gang of rogues had attacked the workers who were restoring the Scaled Tower, killing the project's yuan-ti overseer. The attack had been the talk of Hlondeth's thieves' guild for tendays; the rogues had not belonged to the Guild, and retribution was called for. The theft had taken place while Arvin was busy battling The Pox, and so he had not paid it much attention. Even when he'd met Tanju, and the militiaman accompanying him had let slip that Tanju was tracking someone who had committed a theft, someone called the "stormlord," Arvin hadn't put the pieces together. But now he understood. And he had bad news for Karrell. According to Tanju, the "rogues" had succeeded in getting what they came for.

"You're too late," he told Karrell. "Sibyl already has the Circled Serpent." Quickly, he recounted for her the events of last summer, and what he'd overheard.

Karrell's face paled. After a long moment of strained silence, she shook her head fiercely. "That is not possible," she said. "The workers I questioned said that Dmetrio Extaminos still had the artifact they had dug up in his possession. They even described the container it was in: a round wooden box, coated with lead to prevent magic from revealing the contents."

"Perhaps they lied," Arvin suggested.

"That would not have been possible."

"You charmed them," Arvin concluded. He thought a moment. "The people I spoke with were equally certain that the followers of Talos *did* manage to steal whatever had been found in the tower. Maybe they only got half of it."

"Yes. That must be what happened." She twisted the ring on her finger, a worried look on her face. "Do you know where Sibyl is now?"

Arvin shook his head. "If I did, I would have tried to avenge my friend's death. I've been looking for her for the past six months, but even the Guild can't find her."

"It is more vital now than ever that I recover the second half of the Circled Serpent," Karrell said. "The half Dmetrio still has."

"Do you think he knows what it is?" Arvin asked. "Perhaps if we told him what was at stake. . . ." Remembering who he was talking about, Arvin shook his head. Dmetrio Extaminos was arrogant, cruel, and callous. He cared nothing for Glisena and even less for his own child. He wasn't the sort to be moved by the fate of hundreds of thousands of strangers.

"What's next?" Arvin asked. "Are you going to try to speak to Dmetrio a second time?"

"I have already questioned his house slaves," Karrell answered. "None of them have seen the Circled Serpent. Nor have they noticed a lead-coated box among the household goods they have been packing. I am starting to suspect that he did not bring the Circled Serpent with him, that he left it behind, in Hlondeth."

"Will you return there?" Arvin asked, starting to miss her already.

Karrell sat in silence for several moments. "Perhaps." Then she straightened, a look of determination in her eye. "No. I will search for Sibyl, instead. Finding her should prove easier than trying to locate a small box lined with lead."

Arvin leaned forward. "I can help you with your search," he said. "But I'll need your help in return. I've promised the baron that I'll find his daughter. She's somewhere in a forest called the Chondalwood. She can't be located using magic; she's shielded against all forms of detection. But you have a spell that might be able to help—the one that allowed you to communicate with the naga. If you used it to question the animals of the forest, we might find one who has seen Glisena. If we can find her, we stand a good chance of also locating Naneth; the midwife will certainly be on hand for the baby's birth. And once we have Naneth. . . ."

"We can force her to tell us where Sibyl is," Karrell said.

"Then I'll have my revenge. And you'll have a chance to recover the Circled Serpent. Or half of it, anyway." He extended a hand. "What do you say? Partners?"

Karrell stared into his eyes for several heartbeats, ignoring his hand. Then she leaned forward and kissed him—passionately. Her fingers twined in his hair; her lips pressed against his. Excitement coursed through his body with a fire so fierce it left him trembling. Karrell was everything he'd dreamed of, everything he'd ever hoped to find in a woman. Her kiss left him as dizzy as the *osssra* smoke—and it showed no sign of ending. She pulled him toward her and he tumbled, landing on top of her on the bed. His hands brushed against her waist, her breasts—then found their way inside her dress. Still kissing her fiercely, he tried to stroke her breast, but for some strange reason the dress had gotten in the way. Its fabric felt rough under his fingertips.

No, that wasn't the dress. It *was* her breast. That wasn't skin his fingertips were caressing, but . . .

Scales?

Her charm spell—which only now did he realize she'd been successful in casting—abruptly ended. He broke off the kiss, jerking his hand out of her dress. Suddenly, everything made sense. Her strange comments, her taking offense when he'd tried to warn her about the yuan-ti of House Extaminos.

Karrell was—

She sat up. "You have just realized that I am half yuan-ti," she said. Her expression was a strange mixture of hurt and defiance.

Arvin nodded, mute. "That's not why—" he stammered. "It's just. . . ." Conflicting emotions surged through him. He wanted Karrell, he *ached* for her, even without the benefit of her charm spell—but now she reminded him of Zelia.

Her cheeks flushed. With a quick, angry motion she jerked at her dress, straightening it. "I am used to it," she snapped. "It is just one of the barriers in the maze of life—a barrier that I must overcome, if I am to find my true path. But it is hard. People are always mistaking me for human. How do you think it feels, to hear their comments about how 'cold-hearted' and evil the yuan-ti are, knowing that it is you they are talking about? The yuan-ti, also, are unkind. To them I look too human to ever be considered. . . ." She glanced away.

"Beautiful?" Arvin asked. "Desirable?" He reached out with a hand and lifted her chin. "You are. Believe me." He sighed. "It's just that, for a moment, you reminded me of someone. Another yuan-ti woman—a psion. She used her psionics to plant a seed in my head. If it hadn't been removed, it would have stripped my mind from my body and left me an empty husk for her to fill with a copy of herself. She *used* me."

Karrell's eyes softened. "The woman at Riverboat Landing?"

Arvin nodded.

"Not all yuan-ti are so cruel."

"I realize that," Arvin said. "And now that I look at you—really look at you—I see that you're not like Zelia at all. Not one bit."

He leaned forward—slowly—and kissed her.

Karrell didn't resist. Instead, at first hesitantly, she kissed him back.

Arvin broke off the kiss. "How do you say it?" he asked. "'Kiss'—in your language."

"*Tsu.*"

Arvin smiled. The word puckered Karrell's lips beautifully as she spoke it. "And 'beautiful'? How do you say that?"

"*Kiichpan.*"

"'Woman?'"

She gave a slight frown, obviously wondering what he was up to. *"Chu'al."*

Arvin returned it with a frank stare. "Keech-pan choo-hal," he said haltingly. "May I be your *yaakun?*"

She tossed her hair, mischief dancing in her dark eyes. Then she slapped him—lightly—across the cheek. "You charmed me," she said in an accusing voice.

Arvin chuckled. "And you charmed me." He rubbed his cheek, pretending the slap had stung the cut on his face, and saw her eyes soften in apology. "But I'm not under your spell anymore. Not that one, anyway."

"Your spell, also, has ended," Karrell said. Then she smiled. "Yet somehow, I still find you . . . intriguing." She hesitated then began unlacing the front of her dress.

As Arvin unlaced his breeches, removing them, his eyes were drawn to her breasts. Her scales, he saw, were small and fine, and a delicate shade of reddish-brown that nearly matched her skin, giving it a flushed appearance. He was, he realized, about to find out if the stories about yuan-ti women were true.

When she let her dress fall to the bed and moved toward him, encircling him in one graceful motion, he decided they might be, after all.

CHAPTER 9

"WHERE HAVE YOU BEEN?" THE BARON GROWLED. "MY DAUGHTER is ill—she may be *dying*—and instead of finding her, you—"

Arvin bowed. "I apologize, Baron Foesmasher. I was poisoned."

The baron blinked. "Poisoned?"

"The ambassador kept me waiting all day. I decided to confront him in his basking chamber. I didn't realize it was filled with poisonous smoke. I only recovered from its effects a short time ago."

That wasn't strictly true, of course. His interlude with Karrell had followed. It had been brief—both of them felt the urgency of what was now a shared goal. But time had been lost; it was now nearly the middle of the night.

The room in which they stood—a chapel with one of the enormous, silver gauntlets of Helm standing on a dais near one wall—was lit by a single lantern. The baron had been standing in prayer, his left hand raised and head bowed, when Arvin was ushered in. Karrell had been detained outside the room by the soldiers who served as palace guards. She stood at the end of the hallway, waiting.

Baron Foesmasher glanced at her. "Who is the woman?"

"Another tracker," Arvin said. "She's going to help in the search for your daughter."

The baron's eyes narrowed. "You have told her Glisena is missing?"

"Yes," Arvin acknowledged.

"What else have you told her?"

Arvin met the baron's eye. "Only that Glisena has run away," he said. "And that she is most likely hiding in the Chondalwood, among the satyrs. *And* that her flight from the palace was aided by minions of Sibyl, who hope to exploit your daughter for their own, ill purposes."

"By the sound of her accent, she's from Chult," Foesmasher said. "Is she yuan-ti?"

Arvin met the baron's eye. "Yes."

The baron grunted and turned back to Arvin. "You promised to be discreet. And now I find you've told a complete stranger. Another *serpent.*"

"If you want me to find your daughter, Lord Foesmasher, you'll have to trust my judgment," Arvin told him. "I trust Karrell. It was a stroke of Tymora's fortune that she turned up here, in Sespech. Karrell knows a great deal about Sibyl; the abomination has had her people under her thrall for some time. Karrell was already investigating what Sibyl's minions are up to in Sespech. She would have learned, eventually, of your daughter's disappearance. By including her now, we gain some valuable assistance."

The baron glowered. "You assured me your mind magic would locate Glisena."

"It's already narrowed the search," Arvin countered. "We've learned she's in the Chondalwood."

"That tells us very little," the baron said. "The Chondalwood is enormous. It's nearly as wide as Sespech is long. Were I to send an entire garrison into it to search for Glisena, they could wander for a tenday and never meet a soul, let alone find a band of reclusive satyrs. And ordering in a garrison is something I can't do. Lord Wianar has laid claim to the Chondalwood; he hopes to cut off the supply of wood I need to build my navy. Sending troops into it would only give him the excuse he needs to invade." His eyes bored into Arvin's. "One man, however, would slip into the Chondalwood unnoticed. But that brings us back to the central problem—we don't know where to look."

Arvin thought a moment. "How close is the nearest edge of the Chondalwood to Ormpetarr?"

"Nearly two days' ride to the north, just across the river from Fort Arran."

"The satyrs seemed quite worried about Glisena's health," Arvin said. "They wouldn't have come to Ormpetarr to fetch Naneth unless their camp was a reasonable distance from the city."

"Naneth gave a teleportation ring to Glisena," the baron pointed out. "She may have also given one to the satyr."

"If she had," Arvin countered, "surely he would have used it to flee Ormpetarr, instead of trying to scale the walls."

"Indeed," the baron said, nodding in agreement. "But even if you are correct in your guess about what part of the forest the satyr came from, how do you propose to find his camp?" He nodded at Karrell. "And why do you need her help? Is your mind magic not up to the search?"

"It is," Arvin assured him. "But it won't be able to cover enough ground in the limited time we have left before Glisena . . . becomes more unwell. Karrell knows a spell that can help find the camp quickly. One that gives her the ability to communicate with animals."

The baron frowned. "Asking questions of a handful of animals in one tiny corner of the forest will accomplish nothing." He shook his head. "And I thought you were an expert tracker."

"We won't ask just *any* animals," Arvin countered. "We'll ask wolves. They're swift runners, capable of traveling a distance as far as that between Ormpetarr and Mimph in a single day. Their territories span even greater distances than that. And their sense of smell is keen enough to pick out the scent of a human from an entire camp of satyrs. If anyone can locate the satyr camp Glisena is staying in, it's wolves."

The baron nodded, grudgingly impressed.

"The only problem," Arvin continued, "will be in getting to the Chondalwood quickly enough."

The baron picked up his helmet, which had been sitting on the floor next to him. "You'll be in the Chondalwood tonight," he said, pulling it on. The purple plume bobbed as he spoke. "Naneth isn't the only one with a teleportation device."

"Can yours teleport two people at once?" Arvin asked.

"It can," the baron answered. "But that brings up an important question." He gestured at Karrell. "If it's her spell that will find my daughter, what further use are you?"

Arvin had anticipated that question. "In order for Karrell to use her spell, the wolves need to be close enough for her to speak with them," he said.

"Any hunter can find a wolf," the baron countered.

"I'm not just going to *find* wolves," Arvin said. "I'm going to call them to me. With this." He pulled the lapis lazuli from his pocket and displayed it on his palm. "This is what I used to send you the message about the satyr. With it, I can contact anyone. Human . . . or wolf. It has magic that only a psion can use."

Though he spoke with confidence, Arvin wasn't actually certain what he was proposing would work. He could definitely send a message that would catch a wolf's attention—the whine of an injured pup, for example—but a sending wasn't like a shout; it sounded inside the recipient's head. Arvin might be able to say "come here," but only by putting the sending to the test would he find out if he could convey where "here" was. But it was worth a try.

"The stone will also allow me to report to you—'at once'—the moment we find Glisena," Arvin added, deliberately using one of the baron's favorite phrases.

The baron nodded, satisfied. "You're a man who uses his head," he said. "I like that." He reached into a pouch that hung from his belt and pulled from it a shield-shaped brooch. It was made of polished steel and no larger than a coin, with Helm's blue eye on the front of it. Foesmasher handed it to Arvin.

"Pin this somewhere it won't be seen," he instructed.

"What is it?"

"Something that will assist me in locating you, once that message is sent," Foesmasher explained.

Arvin pinned the brooch to the inside of his shirt. "You'll come to the Chondalwood in person?" he asked, surprised.

"Yes." The baron stared at Arvin. "My teleportation magic is limited, so be certain that you are with Glisena—at her side—before you summon me."

"I will."

Foesmasher turned to the soldiers in the hall then paused, as if remembering something. "Oh yes, that yuan-ti you mentioned: Zelia."

Arvin tensed.

"She's in Ormpetarr. She arrived by riverboat last night."

Arvin gave a tight nod. Zelia in Ormpetarr was bad news. But he'd soon be out of the city. Tymora willing, Zelia would be gone by the time he got back. Or she'd do something that would give Foesmasher an excuse to arrest her.

Foesmasher gestured to the soldiers, indicating they should bring Karrell into the room.

Arvin caught her eye as she entered. "Lord Foesmasher has agreed," he told her. "You'll be joining the search."

Foesmasher waved his guards away then clapped one hand on Arvin's shoulder, the other on Karrell's. "Shall we go?"

"This teleportation device," Arvin asked "Is it a portal, or—"

The floor suddenly fell out from Arvin's feet, and the walls of the chapel spun crazily around him. He dropped about a palm's width through the air, landing unsteadily on the floor of a room with thick stone walls and arrow-slit windows. Two officers wearing armor bearing the baron's crest who were sitting at a table, deep in discussion, leaped to their feet, startled, then bowed deeply.

"Lord Foesmasher," one said. "Welcome."

Foesmasher removed his hands from Arvin's and Karrell's shoulders. "These two," he announced, "are en route to the Chondalwood. Make sure they reach it without Lord Wianar's patrols spotting them."

The officers exchanged a glance.

"Is there a problem?" Foesmasher demanded.

"We're not sure," one of the officers replied. "Wianar's men seem to have drawn back from the river. There hasn't been a sighting of them all day. But there may have been an incident."

Foesmasher frowned. "*May* have been?"

"One of the patrols we sent across the river this morning didn't return," the second officer said. "Nor did the one we sent to find it. Until we know what happened to them, it wouldn't be prudent to—"

"These two must reach Chondalwood," The baron growled. "Tonight."

The officer gave an obedient bow. "As you command, sir."

❧

They crossed the Arran River in a wagon drawn by a centaur. The wagon had no driver, nor was the centaur fitted with reins; he seemed to be draft animal and driver in one.

Arvin was amazed to see such a magnificent creature in harness. Centaurs were creatures of the wild, untamed and proud. This one was the size of a warhorse, his upper torso more muscular than any human's could ever be, his arms nearly as thick as a man's thighs. Coarse, almost woolly hair covered his lower torso, but his chest and arms were bare to the elements. He seemed not to mind the cold as he trotted on enormous hooves that thudded heavily on the massive timbered bridge that spanned the river. Every now and then he snorted, his breath fogging the night air, and tossed back his black, tangled mane, exposing pointed ears. Around his waist he wore a belt; from it hung a sheathed knife the size of a small sword. Hanging from the sheath was a purple feather, like the ones Foesmasher's soldiers wore on their helms.

Two of Foesmasher's soldiers had been assigned to accompany Arvin and Karrell; each man was armed with a crossbow and sword. The first—Burrian, a burly fellow with a black beard and enormous, calloused hands who said he had been a woodcutter before joining the militia—would serve as their guide in the Chondalwood. The second—Sergeant Dunnald, a man with a narrow face and long blond hair—would return to Fort Arran with the wagon. Burrian was watchful as they left the bridge, turned right off the main road, and started toward the Chondalwood. Dunnald, however, seemed confident, even a little bored. Arvin hoped that boded well for their journey. Perhaps the two officers they'd met earlier had been alarmists. There were any number of reasons that soldiers might fail to return from a patrol. Even so, Arvin found himself touching the crystal at his neck, for luck.

It didn't comfort him.

The forest lay some distance ahead, a dark, bumpy line against an even darker sky. Behind them, the bridge across the River Arran fell steadily away into the distance. Fort Arran dominated the far side of the bridge, its crenellated wooden towers keeping watch over the timbered arch that spanned the narrows and the road that led north from it to Arrabar. For now, this road was open, linking the two capitals of Chondath and Sespech. Come daylight, it would be dotted with merchant wagons and travelers. But if war broke out between the two states, Fort Arran would act as a gate, barring entry to any army that Lord Wianar might send marching south.

Arvin glanced up at the sky. The moon was half full, haloed by a thin layer of clouds. At least it wasn't snowing. The air was cold, but Karrell had cast another of her spells upon him, making him feel cozy and warm. He yawned, exhausted. It must have been well past middark by now. He leaned back, trying to make himself comfortable. Lulled by the thud of the centaur's hooves and the warmth of Karrell seated next to him at the rear of the wagon under a thick wool blanket, he dozed.

A while later, something poked Arvin's side—Karrell's hand. Instantly, he was awake. "What is it?" he asked.

Karrell pointed at something ahead. Arvin tried to peer past the centaur but could see only the dark line of the woods, drawing steadily closer. Between the forest and wagon was a flat expanse of snow-covered ground that sparkled in the moonlight.

"I don't see anything."

"Was it the movement near the woods you spotted?" Dunnald asked Karrell. "It's just a herd of wild centaurs, out for a moonlit trot. There's nothing to be frightened of."

Burrian called out to the centaur who drew the wagon. "Some of your old pals, Tanglemane?"

The centaur ignored him.

"I did not mean the centaurs," Karrell told the sergeant, an indignant edge in her voice. "And I am *not* frightened." She stood and pointed. "There is something up ahead. A dark line on the ground."

Dunnald continued to smile indulgently. "That's nothing to fret about, either," he told her. "Just the trail left by the centaurs through the snow."

Karrell sat down again and turned to Arvin. "Do they always travel in such complicated paths?"

Arvin stood and peered ahead. The line in the snow Karrell had spotted ran in a broad arc from left to right, paralleling the curve of the woods at a more or less constant distance from the forest. But instead of following a direct path, the centaurs seemed to have paused at several points along their journey to loop back upon their own trail. "Looks like they doubled back the way they came, criss-crossing their path," Arvin told Dunnald, who obviously didn't take anything a woman said seriously. "Several times. What would make them do that?"

Burrian looked to his sergeant for an answer, but Dunnald only shrugged. "Who knows? Maybe they were playing follow the leader."

"Tanglemane?" Arvin asked. "What do you think?"

The centaur shook his head. "It is unusual," he said in a voice as low as the wagon's rumble.

As the wagon drew closer to a spot where the hoofprints formed a loop, Arvin's frown deepened. Now that they were about to cross the trail through the snow, its complicated meanderings reminded him of something.

"Stop the wagon!" he shouted.

Startled, the centaur skidded to a stop, his four legs stiff and ears erect. The wagon jerked to an abrupt halt, jostling its passengers and causing Dunnald to drop his crossbow.

"What are you doing?" Dunnald snapped, picking up the weapon. "Why did you order the beast to halt?"

Arvin glanced over the side. He had called out a moment too late; the wagon was already inside one of the loops that had been stamped into the snow. "Don't move, Tanglemane," he instructed, reaching for his pack.

"What is wrong?" Karrell asked.

Burrian scanned the open ground around them, his crossbow at the ready. "Yes, what's the matter?" he echoed. "I don't see anything."

Arvin pulled a sylph-hair rope out of his pack. Soft as braided silk, it shimmered in the moonlight. "I'll know in a moment." He tossed the rope into the air, and smiled at the faint intake of breath he heard from Burrian as the rope streaked upward then hung, motionless, as if attached to thin air. He passed the lower end of it to Karrell. "Hold this, will you?"

Karrell took the rope, a curious look in her eye.

Arvin climbed. As he did, the meandering trail through the snow came increasingly into view. From a height, it was possible to see the intricate loops that had been stamped into the snow. The centaurs had not been wandering randomly; there was a design below—one that had been deliberately done. The wagon had halted inside one of its loops.

"The centaurs weren't playing follow the leader," he called out to the others. "They were making an arcane symbol in the snow."

The soldiers, Karrell, and the centaur all stared up at him.

"What kind of symbol?" Dunnald asked.

Arvin, studying the design below, shook his head grimly. "I think it's a death symbol."

Dunnald scowled. "You *think?* You're not sure?"

Beside him, Burrian looked nervous. "So *that's* what got our patrols."

Arvin slid down the rope. "I saw a symbol just like this one, years ago," he told the others as he recoiled his rope. "It was the central motif on an old, threadbare carpet from Calimshan. The carpet supposedly once had the power to fly; the noble who owned it thought that repairing it might restore its magic. He hired me to do the job. The day after I completed the work, he must have decided to try the carpet out. His servants found him sitting on it later that day, dead. He was slumped at the center of the carpet, without a mark on him. The spot he was sitting on was blank—the symbol I'd restored had vanished."

Karrell glanced nervously over the side of the wagon. "We are inside the symbol," she observed.

"Yes," Arvin answered.

"But not fully inside it?"

"We're not at the center of it, no," Arvin began. "But I'm not sure if that—"

Dunnald abruptly stood. "This is getting us nowhere," he said. "We can't just sit here all night." He clambered down from the wagon and walked toward the line in the snow, then squatted down next to it.

"Don't touch it!" Arvin warned.

Dunnald drew his sword and used it to prod at the symbol. "It's a trick," he announced. "A feint, to frighten us away from the woods. I'm touching it, and nothing's happening."

"You're touching it with your sword," Arvin noted, wondering if the sergeant would be stupid enough to touch a foot to the line.

He wasn't.

"If it is a magical symbol, it's not very effective, is it?" Dunnald commented as he straightened up. "It's narrow enough to step right over." He gave Burrian a meaningful glance. "If this *is* what waylaid our two patrols, we need to get a report back to the fort."

Burrian's eyes widened. He wet his lips. "Sir, I. . . ."

Dunnald cocked his head. "Are you refusing my order, Burrian?"

Burrian shook his head. "No, sir.. It's just. . . ."

Dunnald gestured at the track in the snow. "Tanglemane walked across it without harm. Look here—one of his hooves actually touched it."

"He's a centaur," Arvin interjected. "Perhaps centaurs are immune to it and humans aren't."

"*Humans* crossed the symbol once already," Dunnald countered. He glowered at Burrian. "Get down from that wagon, Burrian."

The soldier swallowed. "Yes, sir." He glanced at Arvin, lowering his voice to a whisper. "What do you think?"

"I don't know," Arvin said, less certain now. "The sergeant's right about one thing: we did pass across it once already in the wagon. But I'm no wizard. I don't know how these things—"

"Trooper Burrian!" the sergeant snapped. "Now!"

Reluctantly, Burrian climbed down from the wagon. He started to walk up to the track in the snow, then turned around again and came back to wrench a board off the wagon. He laid this across the track, visibly screwed up his courage, and took a long step across, taking care to keep both feet on the board. As his foot touched the board on the far side of the track, however, he crumpled to the ground.

Karrell gasped then leaped out of the wagon. Arvin shot to his feet, calling out a warning to her, but Karrell had the presence of mind to stay well back from the line in the snow. She dragged Burrian away from the dark line in the snow, lifted his arm, tugged up his sleeve, and pressed her fingers to the inside of his wrist. "He's dead," she announced, staring accusingly at Dunnald.

Dunnald's eyes narrowed. He wheeled on Arvin. "This is *your* fault. You said the center of the symbol was what killed, not the—"

Arvin leaped out of the wagon and caught Dunnald by the collar of his cloak. The sergeant tried to draw his sword, but Arvin batted his hand aside. "Not another word," Arvin growled. Shoving the sergeant aside, he stared at the dead man who lay facedown in the snow, feeling sick. Then he squatted to study the symbol. The line was darker than it should be—blacker than the shadows that filled it. Though both Burrian's body and the board he'd tried to use as a bridge had been drawn back across it, scuffing deep gouges in the snow, the line itself remained intact.

"Can you dispel it?" Arvin asked Karrell.

She looked doubtful as her eyes ranged up and down the symbol in the snow. "It is so large. But I can try."

Spreading her hands, she began to pray. As she did, Arvin watched the line in the snow. When Karrell completed her prayer, there was no visible change. The darkness was just as intense.

The sergeant, meanwhile, rotated his hand in a circle. "Tanglemane! Turn the wagon around and go back across the line. Return to the fort and fetch one of the clerics. We need someone who can dispel this thing."

The centaur snorted, his ears twitching.

"There's nothing to be afraid of," the sergeant said. "You crossed it once already. Go on— move! What's the matter—what are you afraid of?"

"Afraid?" the centaur snorted, his breath fogging the air. His eyes narrowed. "You're the one who's afraid, human. Cross it yourself."

Arvin was still staring thoughtfully at the line in the snow. He noted the ruts the wagon wheels had made as they traversed it and the spot where one of Tanglemane's hoofs had touched the symbol. Perhaps the captain was right about Tanglemane being immune to its magic. Then again, perhaps he wasn't.

Arvin stood and pulled out his lapis lazuli. "Sergeant, there's no need to send another person across. I can use mind magic to send a message back to the fort."

Dunnald wasn't listening. His face red, he glared at the centaur. "That's an order, Tanglemane," he said in a low voice. "Don't forget, you are one of the baron's soldiers now. Shall I report to Lord

Foesmasher that you broke your vow by failing to carry out your duties?"

Tanglemane shook his head, a pained look in his eye.

"Then return to the fort," Dunnald ordered, pointing back at the distant bridge.

"As you order . . . sergeant." Tanglemane began to turn the wagon.

Arvin rushed forward and grabbed the harness. "Tanglemane, wait." He turned to the sergeant. "We don't know how the symbol's magic works. Maybe trying to *leave* is what activates it."

"Leaving it is what we need to do," said Dunnald. He pointed. "And quickly. The centaurs are headed this way."

Arvin glanced in the direction the sergeant had just indicated. The herd that Karrell had spotted earlier had turned around and was moving toward them at a brisk trot. Arvin glanced at Tanglemane. "Are they hostile?"

"Of course they're hostile," Dunnald snapped. "They're wild things. Not like Tanglemane, here."

"They will be angry, if they see me in harness," the centaur said in a low voice. He started to unbuckle the straps across his chest. "Already they have drawn their bows."

"The centaur's right," Dunnald said. "We need to get moving." He offered Karrell his hand, as if to help her into the wagon. "We'll be right behind you, Tanglemane, in the wagon," he told the centaur. He gave Karrell a sly look. "Won't we?"

Karrell took a step back, folding her arms across her chest.

"We're not moving," Arvin said. "Nor is Tanglemane," he added. "We'll take our chances with the centaurs."

Dunnald climbed into the wagon, muttering under his breath. Then, louder, "You'll all see in a moment there's nothing to fear."

Tanglemane continued to unfasten his harness.

"Stop that," the captain ordered. "Get moving."

One of the harness straps fell away from the centaur's broad chest.

"Move!" Dunnald shouted, drawing a crossbow bolt and slapping it against the centaur's flank.

At the sting of the improvised whip, Tanglemane's eyes went wide and white. He slammed a hoof against the wagon, splintering its boards. The wagon shot backward, yanking the partially unfastened harness from his shoulder.

Dunnald sprawled onto the floor of the wagon as it rolled away. "You stupid beast!" he shouted from inside the wagon. "When we get back to the fort, I'll have you—"

As the wagon rumbled to a stop just beyond the line in the snow, Arvin suddenly realized the shouting had stopped. Karrell took a hesitant step forward. Arvin caught her arm, holding her back.

Beside them, Tanglemane whickered nervously. "I have killed him," the centaur said. "Killed the sergeant. When the baron hears of it. . . ."

"It was an accident," Karrell said softly. "You didn't mean to."

Behind them, Arvin heard the sound of pounding hooves. Glancing in that direction, he saw a dozen centaurs racing toward them across the open plain. They skidded to a stop just outside the symbol and aimed powerful composite bows at Arvin, Karrell, and Tanglemane.

One of the centaurs—a male with a white body and straw-colored mane—snorted loudly and stared at them. "Soldiers of Sespech," he said in heavily accented Common. "You yet live?" He tossed his mane then pulled a white feather from a leather pouch that hung at his hip and waved it over the line in the snow. The magical darkness that filled it seeped away and the trail through the snow became just that: an ordinary trail of hoofprints. The centaur put the feather away and gestured curtly. "Come you with us."

❦

"What are they saying?" Arvin whispered to Tanglemane.

The centaur swiveled an ear to listen to the combination of whinnies, snorts, and whickers that made up the centaur language. Thirteen centaurs surrounded Arvin, Karrell, and Tanglemane, herding them along through the ankle-deep snow north along the river, toward Ormpetarr. The Chondalwood lay to their right, but it was falling farther behind with each step. The forest was still close enough that they could have reached it by dawn at a walking pace, even hindered by the snow. But it might as well have been a continent away. Six of the centaurs had their bows in hand with arrows loosely nocked; if the prisoners tried to flee, they'd quickly be shot down.

When the centaurs had first captured them, they had confiscated Karrell's club and Tanglemane's knife, giving the centaur several swift kicks when he didn't surrender it quickly enough. They'd taken an intense dislike to Tanglemane, perhaps because he'd allowed himself to be harnessed to a wagon. Tanglemane, however, showed a stoic indifference to the kicks the other centaurs had aimed at him, bearing them with only the slightest of winces.

The centaurs had also forced Arvin to turn out the contents of his pack. They seemed to have an aversion to rope—they'd tossed aside his magical ropes and twines as if they were poisonous snakes, and declined to search the pack further. Fortunately, they'd made no protest when Arvin gathered the ropes up again and returned them to his pack. Nor had they confiscated his glove, which he'd managed to vanish his dagger into.

The centaurs finished speaking. Tanglemane bowed at the waist to speak in Arvin's ear. "They serve Lord Wianar," he said. "They will turn us over to his soldiers."

Arvin had been afraid of that. Chondath wasn't officially at war with Sespech . . . yet. But the larger state was overdue for another attempt to oust Baron Foesmasher and reclaim lands they had never given up title to. Lord Wianar would be keen to question "soldiers from Sespech" to learn the current strength of Fort Arran's defenses. The questioning would no doubt be brutal and long.

Arvin swallowed nervously. "Would you tell them we're not soldiers?" he asked Tanglemane.

Tanglemane's eyes blazed. "I *am* a soldier," he said. Then his voice softened. "I tried to convince them earlier that you and the female are not the baron's vassals, but it was no use. They say you are spies."

Arvin swallowed. "That's worse than being a soldier, right?"

Tanglemane nodded. He lowered his voice. "You are not the first spies to cross the river. Last night, our soldiers took another across. These centaurs spotted him as he slipped into the woods. They laid the symbol in retaliation; they claim the woods as their own."

Arvin blinked. Foesmasher, it seemed, hadn't been content to wait for Arvin to reappear. There were others searching the Chondalwood for Glisena. The search had become a race.

Arvin glanced at the big white centaur. "What's their leader's name?" he asked.

"You could not pronounce it."

"In Common," Arvin said. "What would it translate as?"

"Stonehoof."

Arvin caught Karrell's eye then tipped his head at the centaur leader. "We need to talk him into letting us go," he whispered. "Let's see how . . . persuasive we can be. If I don't manage to convince him, perhaps you can."

"I cannot help you," she whispered back. "That . . . ability comes to me only once a day."

"Looks like it's up to me, then," Arvin said. Leaving Karrell, he jogged ahead to a position closer to the centaur leader. Stonehoof was even more powerfully built than Tanglemane, his massive hooves hidden by a fringe of hair. His upper torso was as pale as the rest of his body, covered with the same short white hair. His eyes were ice-blue.

Stonehoof glared at Arvin. "Return you to center of herd," he said sternly.

Arvin spread his hands in a placating gesture. "Stonehoof," he said, feeling energy awaken at the base of his scalp as he spoke. "You've got the wrong people. We don't serve the baron—we're not even from Sespech."

"Came you across river in soldier wagon." Stonehoof said. One of his ears swiveled, as if he'd heard something in the distance.

"That's true," Arvin agreed. "But we were only getting a ride with the soldiers. We're actually from Hlondeth. We were just passing through Sespech on our way to—"

One of the centaurs let out a loud, startled whinny. Instantly, the herd halted. They formed a circle, facing outward with bows raised. Stonehoof planted one of his massive hooves in Arvin's chest and shoved. Arvin stumbled backward, landing on his back in the snow beside Karrell and Tanglemane. He sat up, rubbing his bruised chest.

"The charm did not work?" Karrell whispered as she helped him to his feet.

"Apparently not," Arvin said.

Tanglemane stood next to them, listening. He lifted his head, his nostrils flaring as he sampled the breeze, then snorted.

A moment later, Arvin's less sensitive ears picked up the sound the centaurs had reacted to: the thud of hooves.

"Who is it?" Arvin whispered to Tanglemane. "Soldiers?"

"No." Tanglemane said. "A lone centaur."

As the centaur loped into view, Stonehoof and his herd relaxed. Most lowered their bows—though two kept arrows loosely nocked as they returned their attention to their captives.

The newcomer slowed to a trot and tossed his head. He was black from mane to tail, save for a blaze of white on each of his front hooves. Unlike the other centaurs, whose manes flowed freely down their backs, this one wore his hair pulled back with a thong. A wide leather belt around his waist held his quiver and bow case, as well as a large pouch.

As the black centaur approached, Stonehoof charged out to meet him. When only a pace or two separated them, Stonehoof reared up on his hind legs, forelegs flailing in the air. It looked to Arvin like a challenge of some sort, but a moment later Stonehoof bowed his head, and the two powerful males were slapping each other's backs in greeting.

"Who is he?" Arvin asked.

"They greet him by the name Windswift," Tanglemane answered.

"Is he their leader?"

Tanglemane stared appraisingly at the newcomer. "No. But he *will* lead the herd, someday soon, judging by the way Stonehoof submitted to him."

Windswift turned and trotted toward them, followed by Stonehoof. The other centaurs parted to let him through their circle. Windswift said something to Tanglemane in the centaur language and received an answer, then turned his attention to Arvin and Karrell. After studying them a moment, he spoke. "You're not soldiers." His Common was flawless, save for a slight lisp on the final word. He swayed slightly, causing Arvin to wonder if the centaur was as exhausted as he was. Steam rose from Windswift's back; he must have traveled some distance.

"You're right: we're not soldiers," Arvin agreed, relieved to be speaking to someone who might prove sympathetic. He manifested his charm a second time. This time, Tymora willing, there would be nothing disrupt it. "We're from Hlondeth. I'm a rope merchant's agent, and this—" He reached for Karrell's hand. "Is my wife."

One of Windswift's ears twitched, as if to catch a distant sound, and Arvin smiled. But then Windswift tossed his mane, and his eyes cleared. Arvin's heart sank. Windswift had shaken off his charm.

The centaur's eyes narrowed. "A psion?" he said in a voice barely above a whisper.

As Arvin stood stupidly, blinking—how had Windswift known?— Karrell gave his hand a quick squeeze and pressed something into his hand: her ring. He hid his surprise and slipped a finger into it, using her hand to shield the action. And just in time. A heartbeat later Windswift manifested a psionic power. Shielded by Karrell's ring, Arvin no longer had cause to fear Windswift listening in on his thoughts. What did send a shiver of fear through him, however, was the power's secondary manifestation.

A hiss.

By the gods, Arvin thought, feeling his face grow chill and pale, Windswift isn't just any psion.

He's one of Zelia's mind seeds.

Arvin's hands trembled, and his thoughts stampeded in all directions. Should he throw up a defensive mental shield? Launch a psionic attack? Had the centaur-seed realized who he was yet? Arvin had just identified himself as a rope merchant from Hlondeth, and Windswift had heard Arvin's own, unique secondary manifestation, and yet the centaur-seed hadn't attacked him. He didn't seem to know who Arvin was.

Arvin's racing heart slowed—a little. Zelia must have planted the seed in Windswift more than six months ago, *before* she'd met Arvin.

The hissing of the centaur-seed's secondary display faded. One hoof pawed the snow-covered ground in irritation.

Arvin nodded to himself. Windswift must have been the person Zelia had been waiting to meet at Riverboat Landing; the centaur-seed must have been spying, on Hlondeth's behalf, on Chondath.

It all fit. The centaur-seed couldn't have come into the inn without giving himself away; his appearance was too distinctive. And the fact that he hadn't reacted to Arvin must mean one of two things. Either he hadn't made it to his meeting with Zelia—or Zelia *hadn't* come to Sespech in search of Arvin, after all.

If the latter, Arvin's secret was safe. Zelia still thought he was dead.

Arvin could see only one way out of his current predicament, and it involved taking a gamble—a big gamble. He caught the centaur-seed's eye and lowered his voice. "Zelia."

Windswift drew in air with a sharp hiss.

"I, too," Arvin said. "Three months ago." He nodded first in Karrell's direction, then toward Tanglemane, turning the motion into the sort of motion a yuan-ti would make: swaying, insinuative. The mannerisms came to him easily—disturbingly so. "We three," he continued in a low, conspiratorial voice, "must reach the Chondalwood."

Karrell, thankfully, kept her silence. The gods only knew what she was thinking about the odd turn the conversation had taken, but she had the good sense not to interrupt. Tanglemane also stood quietly, a puzzled frown on his face. The other centaurs, however, were getting restless. Stonehoof took a step closer to Arvin and Windswift, only to prance back when the centaur-seed launched a warning kick in his direction.

"Why was I not told?" Windswift hissed. "I was just. . . ." He glanced out of the corner of his eye at the other centaurs, whose ears were twitching as they strained to listen, and thought better of continuing.

Arvin smiled to himself. So Windswift *had* met with Zelia. "I was at Riverboat Landing recently, too," he answered in a low voice. "And I was not told about *you*, either. We like to play our pieces behind our hand, don't we?"

Windswift tossed his head. "That we do." He arched one eyebrow. "You're not as handsome as we usually pick," he chided.

Arvin gave a mental groan. What *was* Karrell thinking of all this? He returned the centaur-seed's coy look. "We needed someone less . . . distinctive for this mission, this time. A mission I should be attending to." He glanced pointedly at the Chondalwood. The sky was brightening over the forest; it was almost dawn.

"Yes. You've been delayed long enough." Windswift turned and addressed the other centaurs in their own language. There was more than one murmur of protest, and Stonehoof reared up, challenging the centaur-seed a second time, but an instant later he clapped Windswift on the back, as he had before.

This time, Arvin was close enough to the centaur seed to hear the hiss of the charm power's secondary display.

Stonehoof whinnied an order, and the centaurs lowered their bows. They handed Karrell's club back to her—and very pointedly ignored Tanglemane when he held out his hand for his knife—then allowed a gap to form in their ranks. Tanglemane stiffened then, eyes darting back and forth and tail lashing, trotted through it. Arvin and Karrell followed.

When they were well away from the centaur-seed, Arvin slipped the ring off his finger and pressed it back into Karrell's hand. "Thanks," he whispered. "Now let's get out of here before Stonehoof changes his mind."

CHAPTER 10

When they reached the edge of the Chondalwood, Arvin glanced back the way they'd come. Stonehoof and his herd of centaurs were disappearing around a bend in the river, headed south. Across the river to the west, smoke rose from the chimneys of Fort Arran, white against the gray winter sky, as the soldiers started their day. A patrol would no doubt soon be sent out; Arvin had used the lapis lazuli to send a message to one of the officers he'd met last night, warning about the death symbols in the snow. The bodies of Sergeant Dunnald and Burrian—and those of the missing patrols—would be recovered. And the centaurs—including Zelia's seed—would be tracked down and dealt with.

In the meantime, the centaurs wouldn't be laying out any more death symbols in the snow, which had been gradually melting as Arvin, Karrell, and Tanglemane had walked toward the wood. Soon there would be nothing on the ground but slush.

Tanglemane, who had been trudging along behind Arvin and Karrell, also turned to look at the departing herd.

"What now?" Arvin asked. "Will you return to the fort?"

Tanglemane shook his head. "You'll need a guide." He smiled. "It will be good to be out of harness, for a time."

Karrell tipped back her head, looking up at the trees. "It looks so odd," she said. "Trees, without leaves. This forest seems so . . . lifeless."

"I assure you, it is not," Tanglemane replied. "The Chondalwood is filled with life—though only the strongest will have survived this harsh winter."

Arvin stared at the forest. The Chondalwood was a gloomy place, indeed. Tendrils of withered, brown-leafed ivy clung to bare branches, and dark moss hugged the trees. The slushy ground was an impassible-looking tangle of fallen logs, wilted ferns, and bushes dotted with blackened lumps that had once been berries. Dead boughs, snapped by the previous night's cold and hanging by a thread of bark, groaned in the breeze. As Arvin glanced up, an icicle fell from a branch and plunged point-first into the slush at his feet. He hoped it wasn't an omen of things to come.

He touched the crystal at his throat for reassurance then turned to Tanglemane. "I need to find a landmark," he told the centaur. "One that would be easily recognized by the animals that live in this part of the forest. Is there one nearby?"

Tanglemane thought a moment. "There is Giant's Rest, a stone that looks like a slumbering giant. Everyone knows it, and it's no more than a morning's trot from here."

Arvin stared at the tangle on the forest floor. "Even through that?"

"I will carry you."

Arvin's eyebrows rose. From all he'd heard, a centaur would rather cut off a hoof than allow a rider on his back.

"You saved my life," Tanglemane said, answering Arvin's unspoken question. "Not once, but twice. I repay my debts. Both to you . . . and to the baron."

"What put you in the baron's debt?" Arvin asked.

Tanglemane snorted. "Nearly two years ago, he spared my son's life. I vowed to serve him until that debt had been repaid. To serve in harness, if need be." He spoke in a level voice, but his whisking tail gave away his agitation.

Arvin smiled. "Gods willing," he told Tanglemane, "you're finally going to get the chance to pay off that debt. We came to these woods to find something for the baron. Something he holds dear. It's in a satyr camp we believe is nearby."

"A worthy task, indeed," Tanglemane said. He flashed broad white teeth in a grin. "Much better than pulling a wagon." He knelt. "Climb aboard."

❦

During their ride through the forest, a wet snow began to fall. It lasted only a short time, but by the time they reached Giant's Rest, Arvin was both soaked to the skin and utterly exhausted. The only thing keeping him awake was the constant ache of his legs, spread too wide across Tanglemane's broad back. Arvin didn't see the massive stone at first—he was too busy wincing. Only when Karrell, seated behind him with her arms tight around his waist, pointed it out did he realize they'd arrived at the clearing.

Arvin studied the stone through the dripping branches. It did, indeed, look like a sleeping giant lying on his back with an arm draped over his eyes. Fully fifteen paces long, the enormous rock was a variety of hues. A darker patch of brownish-gray began at the "waist" of the giant and ended just short of the "feet," and the knob of stone that looked like a head bore veins of quartz that streaked the stone white, giving the impression of hair.

"That is no natural rock," Karrell said. "Nor even a fallen statue. Something turned a giant to stone." She glanced around nervously.

"Whatever happened here took place centuries ago," Arvin said. "Just look at how weathered he is."

Tanglemane knelt, and first Karrell, then Arvin, slid from his back. Arvin winced; it felt as if his legs would never straighten. The insides of his calves and thighs had been chafed raw by the wet fabric of his pants, and his lower back ached. It was already highsun, and he still hadn't performed his morning meditations. He needed them as much as he needed to rest, and to sleep. But Glisena was somewhere in these woods. The more time that passed, the less chance they had of finding her before she gave birth to her child—and became expendable.

Arvin lifted his arms above his head, stretching. He twisted first right, then left, trying to loosen tightly kinked muscles. Then he reached into his pocket for the lapis lazuli. "I should get started," he told Karrell. "If I manage to summon a wolf, it might be some time before it gets here."

Karrell nodded. "When it comes, I will be ready."

Tanglemane whickered. "You're summoning wolves?" he asked, his voice rising.

"Only one," Arvin reassured him. "That's how we'll find what we're looking for. Karrell will speak to the wolf. It can tell us if there's a satyr camp nearby."

Tanglemane's nostrils flared. "Wolves run in packs. How can you summon just one? It is winter, and they will be hungry. You must not do this. Summon an eagle, instead. Their eyes are keen."

"I can't summon an eagle," Arvin said. "I couldn't possibly imitate its cries, and it wouldn't be able to see through the trees. What we need is a keen sense of smell. If you're afraid of the wolves. . . ." Belatedly, he realized what he was saying; the lack of sleep had left him irritable. "Sorry," he told Tanglemane.

The centaur turned, his tail whisking angrily back and forth. Without another word, he trotted away into the forest. Arvin sighed, hoping Tanglemane would come back when his temper cooled.

He touched the lapis lazuli to his forehead. He spoke its command word and felt tendrils of magical energy fuse with his flesh. Then he walked to the head of the stone giant and knelt beside it on the muddy ground. Pressing his cheek against the cold, wet stone, letting the weathered face fill his vision, he linked his mind with the power inside the lapis lazuli. Psionic energy slowly awakened at the base of his scalp; the power point there was as sluggish as his thoughts. Eventually, it uncoiled. Arvin sent his mind out into the forest, questing, and slowly the creature he was seeking materialized in his mind's eye. For a heartbeat or two, several wolves blurred across his vision. He selected one of them: a lean, gray wolf with a muzzle white as frost, its ears erect and nostrils flaring. To this wolf, Arvin sent out not words, but a wolf's howl. He imitated it from memory, drawing upon his recollections of the wolf he'd spotted, years ago, while walking past a noble's garden in Hlondeth. The animal had been straining at the end of a short length of chain—a prisoner. Intrigued by its cries, Arvin had returned to the garden the next night to stare at the wolf through the wrought-iron fence. And the night after that saw him at the garden again. Moved to compassion, he had slipped into the garden to set it free. His reward had been a sharp bite on the arm; two tiny white scars remained where the wolf's teeth had broken the skin. But he'd smiled and bade the wolf Tymora's luck as it bolted into the night.

Now, in his mind, he repeated one of the howls that had prompted him to free the creature: a long, wavering, mournful cry.

The wolf cocked its head and gave Arvin a questioning look. It would see him for what he was: a human who had just howled like a wolf. Then it threw back its head. Its reply startled Arvin; it sounded as if the wolf were right next to him, howling in his ear. The cry ended, the wolf cocked its head a second time, following Arvin's gaze as if it, too, were looking at the stone. Arvin could hear it panting . . . and the sending ended.

Exhausted, Arvin rose to his feet.

"Did it work?" Karrell asked.

"I made contact with a wolf, but I don't know if it will come," Arvin said. "We'll have to wait and see." He left the lapis lazuli in place on his forehead. If a wolf didn't arrive in a reasonable amount of time, he'd try again.

Tanglemane returned then, carrying an armful of dead branches. He cleared a bare spot on the ground near the stone giant then dumped the branches onto it. "We need fire," he announced. "To keep warm. And to keep the wolves from coming too close."

Arvin nodded. Tanglemane needed something to drive away his fear of the wolves while they sat and waited. Arvin slipped his pack off his shoulders and rummaged inside it for the wooden box that held his flint and steel. The moss and shavings that were nestled inside were still dry, he was glad to see. He offered the fire kit to Tanglemane, who took it with a nod of his head.

The centaur soon had a small fire burning, despite the dampness of the wood he'd collected. He fed it until it blazed. Arvin felt its heat as no more than a dull warmth, thanks to Karrell's spell, but soon his wet clothes were steaming. He stripped down to his breeches and hung his shirt, pants, and cloak on sticks near the fire. He even pulled off his glove; it might be magical, but the leather had become as soaked as the rest of his clothes by the fall of sleet.

Karrell hesitated a moment—unlike other yuan-ti, she seemed to be shy about her body—then stripped off her own clothes. Something that glinted reddish-brown in the firelight fell to the ground: loose scales.

Arvin glanced at them, wondering if he should say anything. Curiosity won out. "Do you shed your skin?" he asked.

Karrell stared at the scales that lay on the ground at her feet. "Not normally at this time of year," she said. Then she shrugged. "Perhaps it is the change in the weather. Or perhaps the wet clothing chafed them off."

She settled cross-legged by the fire, naked, combing her long, dark hair with her fingers. Her breasts and hips were full and rounded, her mouth soft and inviting.

If Tanglemane hadn't been with them. . . .

Arvin decided to channel his energy elsewhere, into something productive. He stood and kicked away fallen branches and dead leaves, expanding the bare patch around the fire. "I need to meditate," he told Tanglemane and Karrell. "Let me know if the wolf shows up."

He lay prone on the cold, wet ground, assuming the *bhujanga asana*. He still found it the most effective pose for replenishing his *muladhara*; sitting cross-legged, as his mother had done, never worked quite as well. The rearing-serpent pose gave his meditations an edge that the comfortable, seated position did not.

When his *muladhara* was replenished, he rose and flowed through the ten forms Tanju had taught him. Tanglemane was still keeping a close eye on the surrounding woods, but Karrell watched Arvin, her eyes ranging up and down his body. Her frank interest distracted him, causing him to lose his concentration and falter slightly on the final pose.

He sank down beside her and held his hands out toward the fire, even though her spell had made warming them unnecessary.

Karrell reached out for his left hand and turned it, looking at his abbreviated little finger. "An accident?"

Arvin shook his head. "I was young and on my own and hungry. I made the mistake of stealing on someone else's turf. The Guild cut it off as a warning." He picked up his glove, which had dried, and started to pull the stiff leather over his hand, but Karrell stopped him. She raised his hand to her lips and kissed it.

"You have had a difficult life," she said.

Arvin eased his hand from hers. "No more difficult than some. I'm sure your life hasn't been easy."

"It became much more pleasant after I pledged myself to the

K'aaxlaat. They helped set my feet on the path I was to follow through the maze of life. They have become like broodmates to me."

"Do you miss your home?" Arvin asked.

"Often," Karrell said. Then she smiled. "But not at the moment."

Tanglemane stood suddenly.

"What's wrong?" Arvin asked, reaching for his dagger.

"All is well," Tanglemane assured them. "I simply go to find more firewood." Without another word, he trotted into the woods.

Karrell gave a soft laugh. "He realizes we would rather be alone."

"Does he think we want to—"

Before he could finish the question, she kissed him, answering it.

Arvin could hear the sound of Tanglemane's footsteps growing fainter. Collecting firewood, indeed. As the fire crackled beside them, filling the air with the sharp tang of smoke, he returned Karrell's kiss, wrapping his arms around her. Before his meditations, he'd been exhausted. But now. . . .

Easing her onto the ground, he kissed his way down her throat.

A rustling in the woods startled Arvin awake. It was dark, but the fire was burning brightly. Tanglemane must have stoked it while Arvin and Karrell slept. The centaur stood next to the fire, head lolling on his chest, fast asleep.

Karrell lay beside Arvin. Like him, she was still naked; they had fallen asleep, tangled together, after their lovemaking. She stirred, lost in a dream. It must have been an unpleasant one; she gasped and jerked her hand, as if trying to free it from something.

Arvin nudged her awake.

She blinked then sat up. "What is it?" she asked.

"I'm not sure," Arvin said. "I heard something in the woods. I think it's—"

Eyes glinted at him from the edge of the clearing—eyes that were low to the ground and shone red from reflected firelight.

"A wolf," Arvin finished.

Tanglemane must have heard the word in his sleep. That, or he caught the wolf's scent. Instantly, his head was up, nostrils flaring. Tail flicking back and forth, he started to reach toward the empty sheath at his hip then changed his mind and turned his hindquarters to the wolf, lifting one massive hoof in readiness to kick.

Karrell sat up, fully awake now. "Tanglemane, wait. I will speak to it." She murmured something in her own language then gave a series of yips, half-barks, and growls. She was answered in kind by the wolf, which padded into the clearing. It proved to be an older animal, with a white muzzle and a lean, hungry-looking face.

"Has the wolf seen any satyrs?" Arvin asked. "Is there a camp nearby?"

"She does not know. She will ask her pack."

"Are they——" Before Arvin could complete the question, the wolf threw back its head and howled. A second wolf answered it from just inside the forest on the opposite side of the clearing. Then a third answered, from slightly deeper in the forest. Within moments, howls came from the woods on every side, both from close at hand and from a great distance. There must have been a dozen voices or more. The chorus lasted for several moments, rising and falling like a song, then one by one the wolves fell silent.

Arvin glanced at Tanglemane, who stood stiff-legged and trembling. He placed what he hoped was a reassuring hand on the centaur's flank. "Steady, Tanglemane," he told the centaur. "You were right; they're afraid of the fire. They're not going to come any closer."

The wolf who had answered Arvin's sending stared at Karrell and gave a series of yips and barks.

"A satyr camp lies to the east of here," Karrell translated, her voice tight with excitement. "There is a human in it. A female human."

"Tymora be praised," Arvin whispered. Touching the crystal at his throat, he whispered a quick prayer of thanks to the goddess of luck, promising to throw a hefty handful of coins in her cup—coins that would come from the baron's reward. "Can the wolves lead us there?" he asked Karrell.

She translated his question and received a reply. "They can. But they are hungry; the winter has been hard. They want something in return: meat. They want our 'horse.'"

"Our horse?" Arvin echoed.

Tanglemane gave him a wild-eyed look.

"Tell them that's out of the question," Arvin said, placing a protective arm across Tanglemane's broad back. He glanced at the rock behind them then spoke in a low voice to Karrell. "Too bad we didn't have a way to turn the rock back into a giant. We'd have enough meat to feed a dozen packs of wolves."

"Could you summon another animal for them to eat?" Karrell asked. "An elk, or. . . ."

"Not without knowing how it 'talks,'" Arvin said. "A wolf's howl is the only animal sound I could imitate reliably. Other than a snake's hiss, of course."

Tanglemane's nostrils flared. His eyes were wide, with white showing around the edges as they darted back and forth, following the shapes that flitted through the darkness. "They're coming closer," he whinnied.

Arvin manifested his dagger into his glove. "Then we'll fight them," he said.

"Wait," Karrell said, laying a hand on Arvin's arm. "Let me try something else."

Abruptly, she transformed into her serpent form—a sleek reddish-brown snake with a band of gold scales around the tip of its tail. One moment she was standing in the firelight; the next, she was slithering along the ground, circling around the fire. Tanglemane startled, rearing up, and for several moments Arvin frantically tried to calm him, terrified that the centaur would crush Karrell under his hooves. By the time Arvin turned around, Karrell was between them and the wolves, swaying back and forth. She hissed softly, slit eyes turning to stare first at one patch of darkened forest, then another. Arvin found himself swaying slightly as he watched her and felt Tanglemane doing the same.

The first wolf—the one with the white muzzle—padded closer. It stopped several paces from Karrell and stared at her as if mesmerized. Then another wolf walked out of the woods, then two more. Within moments, six shaggy gray beasts were sitting in a circle, surrounding Karrell. All were thinner than they should have been: hungry.

Something flashed out of the darkness—a seventh wolf that hadn't succumbed to her trance. Releasing the near-panicked Tanglemane, Arvin raised his dagger, but before he could throw it, Karrell turned and confronted that wolf with a spitting hiss. The wolf immediately flattened on the ground, ears back and tail tucked between its legs. Whimpering, it crawled back to the woods. As soon as it reached the safety of the forest, it fled, crashing away through the undergrowth.

Karrell, meanwhile, had resumed her dance. The six remaining wolves continued to sit and stare at her, swaying in time with her motions. She drank in their scent with her flickering tongue then opened her mouth. What emerged wasn't a hiss, but a series of yips, followed by a long howl.

One by one, the wolves threw back their heads and howled with her.

Arvin felt a shiver run through him. It suddenly came home to him that Karrell was something utterly nonhuman. It hadn't fully struck him when he'd first seen her scales. But seeing her in serpent form—watching as she reduced one wolf to a quivering bundle of fear and ensnared the remaining wolves in her trance—was a different matter. He'd been thinking of her as a human with a hint of serpent about her. He'd refused to fully acknowledge that she was yuan-ti—and everything that came with it. Those charms she'd cast on him were only a small fraction of her powers.

The sight of her in serpent form terrified him. Yet he cared for her—even admired her. She could be kind, selfless, and brave. Just look at how she'd risked her own life to save the woman who had been bitten by the naga. These were qualities that simply didn't occur in a yuan-ti.

And yet she was yuan-ti.

Karrell twisted, still swaying, to face Arvin and Tanglemane. "They have agreed," she announced in her human voice—a strange thing, indeed, to hear coming out of a serpent's mouth. "They will lead us to the satyr camp *before* we give them the meat."

"What meat?" Tanglemane asked, his eyes rolling.

Karrell turned to Arvin. "You said that Foesmasher would teleport to us, once we have located—" She paused as Tanglemane gave her a sharp look. "Once we have found what we are searching for. He can bring meat with him."

Arvin nodded. It was a sound plan—as long as the wolves' hunger didn't make them impatient.

Tanglemane glanced back and forth between Arvin and Karrell. "Lord Foesmasher will teleport into the *Chondalwood?*" he asked, incredulous. "This . . . 'thing' that he holds dear. It must be very precious."

"It is," Arvin assured him.

"As precious as my son is to me?" Tanglemane guessed.

"Yes," Arvin said, meeting his eye.

The centaur nodded then slowly smiled. "I will pray to Skerrit, lord of the herds, that we find her, then."

Arvin glanced at the hungry wolves then spoke in a low voice to Karrell. "If Glisena isn't at the camp, we're in trouble."

"She will be there," Karrell said. "The wolves said so."

Unless, Arvin silently added, Glisena gave birth before they reached the satyr camp. If she had, all they would find would be her corpse—a report that wouldn't please the baron.

And the wolves *would* feed.

❦

They walked all night, following the white-muzzled wolf through the forest. Arvin and Karrell walked on either side of Tanglemane, soothing him with reassuring words. Yet when dawn brightened the sky to the east, illuminating the trees with wintry light, Arvin could see that fully two dozen wolves surrounded them. They padded through the forest, tongues lolling, casting hungry glances at Tanglemane. Occasionally one would veer closer, and White Muzzle would growl and bare her teeth, warning it away. As the sun rose, these challenges became more frequent. And now that Arvin could see the wolves clearly, he realized they weren't eyeing just the centaur. They were looking hungrily at him and Karrell, too.

For the last little while, they had been climbing a low hill. The top of it was crowned with a tangle of brambles that extended for several hundred paces to the left and right. The pack halted before reaching it and White Muzzle turned and gave a series of bark-yips. Karrell recast her spell and spoke to the wolf.

"The satyr camp lies upwind, at the heart of these brambles," Karrell said.

"Is the human female still in the camp?" Arvin asked.

Karrell translated. White Muzzle sniffed the air and yipped once.

"Yes," Karrell said.

Arvin started to move toward the brambles, but White Muzzle planted herself in front of him, blocking his path, and growled. Glancing around, Arvin saw wolves in every direction, hunkered down as if ready to charge. He looked to Karrell for the translation, even though he really didn't need one.

"She has done as she promised," Karrell said. "She led us to the satyr camp. Now she wants her meat."

"Tell her she'll have to wait just a little longer," Arvin said. "Tell her the meat is at the satyr camp; that we'll return in a little while with it."

Karrell did then listened to White Muzzle's reply. "They want their meat now," she translated. "They want Tanglemane."

Arvin flexed his gloved hand. He'd disappeared his dagger into it earlier; at a whisper it was back in his hand.

Karrell tensed and laid a hand on her club. "We will fight?" she whispered.

"No," Arvin answered. "I have something else in mind."

One of the wolves moved in closer. Tanglemane whinnied nervously. Arvin laid a hand on his back. "Don't run," he urged. "It's what they want you to do."

Tanglemane nodded but remained tense. Arvin could feel him trembling. "Tanglemane," he said. "I'm going to cast a spell on you. Don't resist it."

That said, Arvin awakened the psionic energies that lay deep inside his chest. The wolves sniffed as the scent of ginger and saffron filled the air, and White Muzzle's hackles rose. But a moment later, it was done: the fates of Tanglemane and the pack leader were linked.

Arvin manifested his dagger into his gloved hand and passed it to Tanglemane. "When I tell you to," he instructed, "use this to prick the palm of your hand."

Tanglemane hesitated for only a heartbeat then took the dagger. Arvin, meanwhile, spoke to White Muzzle while Karrell translated.

"I have just cast a spell," he told the pack leader. "Whatever happens to the centaur will also happen to you. If the centaur is wounded, you will suffer the same injury." He nodded at Tanglemane, cueing him, and the centaur poked the dagger into his palm.

White Muzzle yelped and started to lift a paw. The other wolves tensed, and she immediately lowered it again. She growled at them, her legs firmly braced to meet any challenge.

"If the centaur dies, then *you* will die," Arvin continued, taking his dagger back from Tanglemane. "Tell your pack to stand aside and let us enter the satyr camp. After we've finished our business there, you'll get your meat. As promised."

White Muzzle's eyes narrowed as she heard this, but she quickly turned and spoke to her pack in a series of threatening growls. One or two growled back at her, but when she bared her teeth, they parted, letting Arvin, Karrell, and Tanglemane through. For several paces, Arvin walked with tense shoulders, expecting an attack to come at any moment—but none did. By the time the three of them had reached the edge of the brambles, the wolves had melted away into the forest.

"Well done," Karrell said.

Arvin nodded his acknowledgment. His eyes were on the brambles; they formed a near-impenetrable mass. Clumps of mushy berries, blackened by the earlier frost, hung from a tangle of vines studded with finger-long thorns.

"What now?" Arvin asked.

"There will be a path through them, somewhere," Tanglemane answered. "Let's circle around."

Before long, Arvin spotted hoofprints in the snow. Squatting down, he saw a tunnel leading into the heart of the tangled vines.

"This must be the way in," he said. He glanced up at Tanglemane then down again at the hole. He and Karrell could follow the path on their hands and knees, but Tanglemane would never be able to fit.

Tanglemane nodded, as if hearing his thoughts. "I will have to wait here."

"What about the wolves?" Karrell asked.

Tanglemane held up his bloody palm. "I'll have to trust in Arvin's magic to hold them back."

"The fate link will last at least until sunset," Arvin said. "Tymora willing, we'll be back before then—with some meat for the wolves. And the baron can teleport us all away."

He turned to Karrell. "The next part is up to you," he told her. "We need to make sure Glisena is here—and that Naneth isn't. In your serpent form, you could slip in and out without being seen. Will you do it?"

Karrell nodded and started removing her shirt.

"Be careful," Arvin added. "I don't want to lose you."

Karrell dropped her shirt to the ground, gave Arvin a kiss that sent a rush of warmth through him, and shifted. She slithered away into the brambles.

Arvin waited. While Tanglemane kept a wary eye on the forest, watching for wolves, Arvin stared at the brambles. After what seemed like an eternity, Karrell returned. Still in her serpent form, she coiled her body at his feet and lifted her head. "Glisena is there," she said. Her tongue flickered in and out of her mouth, which was curved into a smile. "She is in one of the huts. There is no sign of Naneth."

Relief washed through Arvin. He touched the brooch that was still pinned to the inside of his shirt. "I need to get close to Glisena," he announced. "Close enough that Foesmasher can teleport in. I'm going to go openly into the camp; I'll charm the first satyr I meet and tell him that Naneth sent me. If that doesn't work, I might need a distraction." He stared down at Karrell. "Follow me, but stay out of sight. If I run into trouble, I'll use my stone to call you. Use your own judgment about whether to intervene."

He turned to the centaur. "Stand fast, Tanglemane. Don't let the wolves spook you."

Then he dropped to his hands and knees. As he crawled into the brambles, keeping low to avoid snagging his pack, he saw Karrell slither off to the right.

The tunnel through the brambles twisted this way and that, branching several times and coming back together again. Wary of getting lost in what was obviously a maze, Arvin consistently chose the left fork, hoping this would eventually lead him to the center of the tangle. Every now and then he saw what was probably a satyr's hoofprint in the slush, but the wet ground was too soft to hold a firm outline. There was no way to tell which direction the satyr had been traveling in. A thorn plucked at his cloak, snagging it and preventing him from going forward until he yanked it free. Other thorns jabbed at him through the fabric of his clothes. Soon his arms and legs were covered in tiny scratches. He crawled on, ignoring these pinpricks of pain.

At last the brambles thinned up ahead, and he was able to see a clearing. From it came the murmur of voices and the sounds of satyrs going about their daily chores. Unfortunately, the tunnel through the brambles at this point bent sharply to the right. Arvin followed it, but after going a short distance, it led back to another path. He'd just looped back the way he'd come. Frustrated at being so close yet so far from his goal, he tried another route, turning right, this time. He crawled quickly, angry at the waste of time. The next fork, if he remembered correctly, was just ahead.

Glancing up, he saw a satyr squatting in the tunnel, pan pipes raised to his lips. Startled, Arvin manifested a charm, but even as he did, the satyr blew into his pipes. Music swirled around Arvin like falling leaves, lulling him to sleep.

CHAPTER 11

ARVIN'S EYES FLUTTERED OPEN. HE LAY ON HIS BACK IN THE MIDDLE of a clearing, surrounded by at least a dozen satyrs. All were standing with their bows at full draw, arrows pointed at him. The satyr with the pan pipes—a fellow with eyebrows that formed a **V** over his nose, and a pointed tuft of beard on his chin—stood next to Arvin's pack, peering at something he held cupped in one hand. Arvin frowned, and pain lanced through his forehead. Something warm and sticky—blood—trickled down his temple, and his hair felt matted. Moving his hand slowly, so the satyrs wouldn't shoot him, he touched his forehead and felt an open wound the size of a thumbprint. Realization dawned: they had cut the lapis lazuli from his flesh. The charm he'd manifested when the satyr had first startled him obviously hadn't worked.

"Is this how you treat a friend?" Arvin asked.

The satyr with the pan pipes tipped the lapis lazuli into a leather pouch that hung from his belt and wiped his hand on his furry leg. "Friend?"

"Naneth sent me," Arvin said, watching for a reaction. A couple of satyrs holding bows glanced at each other; one said something in the satyr tongue. The other shrugged and slackened the draw of his bow, just a little.

Arvin eased himself into a sitting position, keeping a wary eye on them. Blood from his forehead trickled into his eye; he wiped it away with his hand. As he did this, he took stock. The satyrs had taken his pack—it lay on the ground a short distance away—but they'd overlooked the brooch Foesmasher had given him; Arvin could feel its cold metal against his chest. They'd also overlooked his magical bracelet and glove. He'd vanished his dagger into the latter, but it would do him little good at the moment, with a dozen arrows pointed at him.

He debated whether to attempt one of his psionic powers. He longed to know what the satyr with the pan pipes was thinking, but was hesitant to use the power that would allow him to read thoughts. As soon as the first sparkle of light erupted from his third eye, the satyrs would feather him with arrows.

"I'm one of Naneth's assistants," Arvin continued. "When your friend arrived with the news that the human woman was feverish and ill, Naneth asked me to take a look. She had urgent business elsewhere, and wasn't able to come herself."

As he spoke, Arvin wondered just where Naneth *had* gone. Three nights had passed since the baron had stormed into her home, causing her to flee.

As the satyrs talked in their own language Arvin glanced around. There were three tunnels through the brambles leading away from the clearing; drag marks through the slush showed the one they had hauled Arvin out of. Around the edges of the clearing stood a dozen huts like the one he had glimpsed while reading the thoughts of the satyr in Ormpetarr; it was impossible to tell which one Glisena was inside.

"Where *is* the human?" he asked. "I have healing magic that can help her."

The satyr with the pan pipes motioned with his hand; the others lowered their weapons. Then he tipped his horned head toward one of the huts—the only one that had smoke rising through the vent hole in its roof. "Follow me."

Arvin scrambled to his feet, wondering where Karrell had gone. There was no sign of her. Out of habit, he reached to touch the crystal that hung at his throat, to steady himself.

The crystal was gone; the satyrs must have taken it.

Arvin glared at the satyr who was leading him to the hut. Arvin's mother had given him the crystal just before she died; he'd worn it faithfully for two decades. Through the long years at the orphanage, it had been the one reminder that he'd once had a parent who loved him. Arvin was damned if he was going to let the satyrs keep it.

The satyr opened the door of the hut—an untanned hide hung from crude wooden pegs—and motioned for Arvin to enter. Arvin stepped inside and felt excitement course through him as he spotted the object of his search.

Glisena lay on a sheepskin near a fire pit. She stared up at the ceiling, hands on her enormous belly, her long hair damp with sweat. Even over the smell of wood smoke, Arvin caught the odor of sickness; a fly circled lazily in the air above her head. Glisena still wore the dress she'd had on when she used Naneth's ring to teleport away from the palace; her winter cloak and boots lay in a heap against the far wall. Through the fabric of the dress, Arvin saw Glisena's stomach bulge momentarily; the baby kicking. Glisena gave a faint groan.

At least mother and baby were both alive.

Arvin should have felt elation. Instead he felt sadness and a grim sense of foreboding.

The satyr gave Arvin a shove from behind. "Heal her."

Arvin stumbled forward. Kneeling beside Glisena, he saw that the object circling above her was not a fly, after all, but a small black-and-white stone, ellipsoid in shape. That it was magical, he had no doubt It was probably what had kept the spellcasters from finding Glisena. He left it alone; grabbing it would only alarm the satyr.

Gently, Arvin turned her face toward him. Her skin felt hot under his fingers. "Glisena?" he said. "Can you hear me?"

She blinked and tried to focus. "Dmetrio?"

Arvin's jaw clenched. Dmetrio Extaminos had cast this woman aside like spoiled fruit, long ago. Arvin longed to tell Glisena the truth—that Dmetrio was the last person she should expect. That he would soon be departing for Hlondeth without giving her a second thought. But that would hardly be a kindness.

"No," Arvin said gently. "It's not Dmetrio."

He snuck a glance at the satyr. The fellow stood near the door, scowling at Arvin, pan pipes still in hand.

"Naneth sent me," Arvin announced in a louder voice.

"Where . . . is she?" Glisena asked weakly. "Why hasn't she come?"

Once again, Arvin said nothing.

As she finally focused on him, Glisena's eyes widened in alarm. "Your face," she whispered. "It's bloody."

That one, Arvin had an answer for. "There was a misunderstanding," he said, glancing at the satyr as he spoke. "The satyrs didn't recognize me. Now be still. I need to figure out what's wrong with you."

He went through the motions of checking Glisena as a healer would, drawing upon his memories of how the priests at the orphanage had inspected children in the sick room. He held a finger to her throat, feeling her lifepulse; peered into her eyes; and sniffed her stale-smelling breath. Then he laid the back of his hand against her forehead as if measuring the heat of her fever. "When did you last see Naneth?" he asked.

"The night I . . . left," Glisena said. "She brought me here."

Arvin lifted each of Glisena's hands, pressing on the fingernails as if checking their color. Her fingers were bare; she no longer had Naneth's teleportation ring. Naneth must have taken it from her to prevent Glisena from leaving the satyr camp.

Glisena looked at Arvin with worried eyes. "Is it supposed to hurt so much? Naneth said the baby would be born soon after the spell. But it's been more than . . . a tenday. And still it won't come. Do you think my baby is. . . ?" Her words choked off and her hands tightened on her stomach protectively. Tears puddled at the corners of her eyes and trickled down her cheeks.

Arvin wiped them away. "I'll check," he told her.

He laid his hands on Glisena's distended stomach. It felt taut as a drum beneath his palms. Was the child in distress? There might be a way to find out . . . and to learn what the satyrs intended, as well.

"I'm going to cast a spell," Arvin told the satyr. "One that will tell me what is causing the fever."

The satyr stared suspiciously at him a moment then raised his pan pipes to his lips. "Cast your spell. But remember that the others outside will kill you, should I fall."

Arvin nodded. He sent his awareness deep into himself, awakening the power points at the base of his scalp and in his throat.

Silver sparkles erupted from his third eye as the power manifested, momentarily obscuring his vision. Then the thoughts of those inside the hut crowded into his mind. Glisena's were filled with anxious worry—she feared for her own life, as well as that of her child. She also clung to a desperate hope that Dmetrio would come for her. Naneth had promised to tell Dmetrio where she was. What could possibly have delayed him? Had something bad happened to him? Maybe he—

Unable to listen further, Arvin turned his attention to the satyr's thoughts.

The satyr—whose name turned out to be Theyron—didn't believe Arvin's story. Naneth had warned him that one of the baron's men might show up and try to fetch Glisena home. The baron's man might even use Naneth's name, in an attempt to trick the satyrs and take Glisena away—just as this human had done.

But maybe this human did have healing magic, as he claimed. If he *was* the baron's man, he would want to heal Glisena; a dead female wasn't worth stealing. And it was important that Glisena remain alive. Naneth had promised the satyrs much wealth, in return for watching over the female for a few days. As to why Naneth had asked them to hide the baron's daughter, Theyron didn't know—and didn't care. When Naneth returned to claim the female, his clan would reap its reward.

As for the human, well, as soon as the baron's man completed the healing, Theyron would kill him. One note from the pipes, and the human would slumber. And his throat could be slit.

Unsettled by the callousness of the satyr's thoughts, Arvin disengaged from his mind; he doubted he was going to learn much more, and his manifestation would end soon. He turned his attention to the third source of thoughts within the hut: the unborn child. He focused on them, letting the thoughts of Glisena and the satyr fade to the background. . . .

Rage.

Boiling, inarticulate, all-consuming rage.

The thoughts of the child pounded into Arvin's mind like a hammer smashing against his skull. *Out!* snarled a voice as deep and hollow and devoid of humanity as a bottomless chasm. *Release me!* The thing inside the womb began kicking, fists and feet pounding against Glisena's flesh, jolting Arvin's hand up and down. *Let . . . me . . . OUT!*

Shocked, Arvin jerked his hand away and ended the manifestation. He stared at Glisena in horror.

Whatever was inside her wasn't human.

It wasn't yuan-ti, either.

Naneth had changed the unborn child in Glisena's womb into something . . . else.

The thought sickened Arvin to the point where he felt physically ill. This was even more monstrous than what Zelia had done to him. This time, the victim had been an innocent babe. But it was an innocent babe no longer.

"Something's . . . wrong, isn't it?" Glisena asked in a trembling voice.

Belatedly, Arvin composed his expression. "I don't know yet," he said. Then, acting on a hunch, he added, "I'll need to take a look."

Easing Glisena's hands aside, he unfastened the lacings of her dress nearest her stomach. Even without opening her dress, he could feel the heat radiating from her belly. He lifted the fabric to glance at her stomach and saw something that disturbed him: a series of crisscrossing lines. They looked like the faint whitish scratches fingernails would leave on skin. Remembering his glimpse of Naneth casting her spell on Glisena, Arvin was certain that the midwife had drawn them. That certainty solidified when he recognized the symbol the lines formed. It was the same one he'd spotted on the egg that one of Naneth's pet serpents had been sitting on.

Arvin had no idea what the symbol signified. But he was certain it wasn't good.

He refastened the lacings of Glisena's dress and took her hand. "Something *is* wrong," he told her. "But I'm here to help."

Theyron tapped a hoof impatiently. "Well? Can you heal her?"

Still squatting beside Glisena, holding her hand, Arvin brought his gloved hand up to scratch his head—a gesture a man would make when thinking. "The fever has held her in its grip for many days," he said. "It won't be easy to break its hold." As he spoke, the power he was manifesting filled the air with a low droning noise: its secondary display. Theyron didn't notice it, however; he had already turned to stare at the distraction Arvin had just manifested. His eyebrows pulled into an even tighter **V** as he frowned, trying to figure out what had just caught his attention.

With a whisper, Arvin summoned the dagger from within his glove. It appeared in his hand as he had been holding it when he'd vanished it: point between his fingers, ready to throw. His hand whipped forward. At the last instant, Theyron turned his head back and tried to blow into his pipes, but before he could exhale, the dagger buried itself in his throat.

Arvin leaped to his feet, manifesting a second power. A glowing line of silver energy shot out of his forehead, wrapped itself around the pan pipes, and yanked. The pipes flew out of Theyron's hands. Arvin caught them in his gloved hand and vanished them into his glove. He spoke the word that sent the magical dagger back to his other hand then rushed forward, plunging the weapon to the hilt in the satyr's chest. Slowly, with a faint gurgling noise, Theyron slumped to the floor, pulling free of the dagger.

Arvin felt a twinge of remorse at having taken Theyron's life but shook it off; if the playing board had been turned, the satyr would have killed him without a moment's pity. He peeked outside the flap that covered the doorway. The other satyrs stood a few paces away. Some were staring at the hut, but they didn't seem to have heard anything. Two were rummaging through his pack. When one pulled out a piece of the broken dorje, the other made a grab for it. An argument broke out. The first satyr wrenched it out of the second one's hand and bellowed a challenge. The other satyr glared back and said something. The first nodded, and placed the broken dorje back in Arvin's pack. Then, slowly, each backed away from the other. Suddenly they charged forward, horns lowered. Their foreheads slammed together with a loud crack. Each staggered back then lowered his head a second time, like duelists bowing at each other, ready to repeat the charge. As the combatants pawed the earth with their cloven feet, the other satyrs cheered in anticipation.

Arvin breathed a sigh of relief. That should keep them busy for a while.

When he turned around, Glisena had forced herself up off the sheepskin. Eyes wide and terrified, she held herself in a seated position with trembling arms. As Arvin took a step toward her, she bleated and tried to crawl back, but only managed to collapse. She opened her mouth to scream.

Arvin leaped forward to clamp a hand against her mouth. "Don't," he said. "I'm not here to hurt you. I've come to rescue you."

Glisena's lips moved under Arvin's palm. Cautioning her with a look, he lifted them slightly, allowing her to speak.

"From what?" she gasped.

"Naneth tricked you," Arvin said. "Her spell didn't just hasten your pregnancy along. It affected the child inside you in other ways. The child was transformed into something . . . else."

"No," Glisena whispered.

Arvin couldn't tell if she was hearing his terrible news—and denying it—or simply reacting with horror to his words. "I'm afraid so," he said. As he spoke, he plucked the stone that was circling her head from the air. It resisted him for a moment, straining to free itself from his palm. Then it went still.

"Naneth wouldn't—"

"Yes she would," Arvin said, tossing the stone aside. "Naneth isn't just a midwife. She's an agent of a powerful yuan-ti who is an enemy of House Extaminos. Naneth used you; she only pretended to help you after your father asked her to—"

"To kill my child," she said in a flat voice. Her hands cradled her belly.

"Yes."

She stared at her stomach a moment, groaned as the thing within kicked, and gave Arvin a defiant look. "I won't let him hurt my baby."

Arvin sighed. She was forcing him to be blunt. "Whatever's inside you isn't your baby anymore. We need to get you back to Ormpetarr. Someone there will know what to do."

Glisena's jaw tightened. "I won't go back." Exhausted as she was, with dark circles under her eyes, she had the determination—and stubbornness—of her father. "Dmetrio—"

"Isn't coming," Arvin said, finishing the sentence for her. "He's leaving for Hlondeth. Without you."

"That's not true," she whispered again. "He loves me. He'll take me with him."

"He won't."

"He will." The determination was still in her eyes, but something else had joined it: exhaustion. Fresh beads of sweat broke out on her forehead. She sank back onto the sheepskin, trembling. "My *father* sent you . . . didn't he? You're lying. About Naneth. And Dmetrio. So I'll . . . go back."

"I'm telling you the truth," Arvin insisted. "Much as I hate to do it."

Glisena turned away, not listening to him. Even when she was down, she wouldn't admit to defeat. Arvin had to admire that.

He'd been naive, to think that he could convince Glisena of the truth. It was simply too much, too hard. He peeked outside again—the satyrs were still butting heads, Tymora be praised—then turned his attention to the dead satyr's belt pouch. Opening it, he found his mother's crystal inside. He tied it around his neck with a whispered, "Nine lives," then recovered his lapis lazuli, which still had a jagged, coin-sized flap of his skin clinging to it. He spoke the stone's command word, and the skin fell away. Then he touched the stone to the raw wound on his forehead and spoke the command a second time. The lapis lazuli sank into the wound, attaching itself to the lacerated flesh. Fresh blood trickled from the wound; he wiped it away from his eye.

Not knowing how much time he had before the satyrs ended their contest, he decided to manifest a sending. He started to imagine the baron's face then changed his mind. Instead he pictured Karrell.

Nothing happened.

Arvin's heart thudded in his chest. He could visualize Karrell's face clearly, but he couldn't contact her. Was she dead?

Then he realized what was wrong. He was visualizing her human face. He shifted his mental picture of her, imagining her snake form instead. Instantly, the image solidified.

I'm with Glisena, he told her. *I'm inside her hut. Slip in through the back, where the brambles touch the wall. I'll contact Foesmasher.*

Karrell stared back at him, tongue flickering in and out of her mouth. Arvin couldn't read her expression—it was impossible, with that unblinking stare—but he could hear the concern in her voice as she stared at his forehead. *You are wounded! I am sorry; I fell to a magical slumber. I will come.* Her mouth parted in what might have been a smile. *At once.*

Her image faded from his mind.

Immediately, Arvin concentrated on the baron's face. When it solidified in his mind, Foesmasher was talking to someone, emphasizing his words with a pointing fork; Arvin must have interrupted his midday meal. From the scowl on his face, he was issuing a reprimand, or arguing with Marasa again. He halted abruptly in mid-sentence as he recognized Arvin.

I found Glisena, Arvin told him.

Relief washed across the baron's face. His eyes closed a moment; when he opened them, he blinked rapidly, as if clearing away tears. He whispered something Arvin couldn't hear; probably a prayer of thanksgiving.

Arvin chose his next words carefully. Even with the brooch for Foesmasher to home in on, Arvin needed to pack as much information as possible into the brief message the lapis lazuli would allow. *I'm with her inside a hut. Satyrs armed with bows are outside. And wolves. Bring—*

I'm on my way, the baron said.

Arvin silently cursed. Now that Foesmasher had replied, there was no way for Arvin to interrupt, to tell him to bring meat for the wolves. Foesmasher continued speaking as he yanked on his helmet and drew his sword. *Tell Glisena I'll be there at . . .*

". . . once," said a low voice from Arvin's immediate left.

Arvin couldn't help but be startled, even though he'd been expecting the baron. He raised a finger to his lips. "Quietly, Lord Foesmasher," he cautioned. "The satyrs are just outside."

The baron immediately fell to his knees beside his daughter. "Glisena," he said in a choked voice. "Father's here. My little dove, I'm so sorry. May Helm forgive me for what I've done."

The thing inside Glisena kicked, bulging her stomach. She screwed her eyes shut and groaned.

"What's wrong?" the baron asked, looking up at Arvin. "Is the child coming?"

"It's . . . not a child," Arvin said. Quickly, he told the baron his suspicions. He expected the baron's face to blanch, but Foesmasher proved to have more mettle than that. "Why would Naneth do such a thing?" he asked in a pained voice.

Arvin didn't answer.

The baron stared at his daughter. "Marasa will tend to it," he said firmly. "Whatever it is."

Arvin nodded, relieved.

Outside, the satyrs had resolved their argument. One of the combatants lay unconscious on the ground; the others stared at him, shaking their heads disdainfully. One, however, was staring suspiciously at the hut, his ears perked forward, listening. He turned to the others and said something to them. Arvin, watching, tightened his grip on his dagger.

Foesmasher must have seen Arvin tense. He sheathed his sword, lifted Glisena into his arms, and stood. He gestured for Arvin to come closer.

Arvin was still staring outside. He'd spotted a movement across the clearing in the brambles, well behind the satyrs: a snake, slithering along the ground.

Karrell was circling around the clearing to reach the hut.

"Wait," Arvin said. "Karrell's coming. I don't want to leave her behind."

"I can teleport no more than three people at a time," the baron whispered back. "Myself, Glisena . . . and one other."

Arvin's jaw clenched. Foesmasher had neglected to tell him this important detail. "Teleport us just outside the brambles, then," Arvin whispered back. "There's a centaur waiting there for us: Tanglemane."

The baron's eyebrows rose at the name.

"He and I can watch over Glisena while you come back for Karrell," Arvin continued.

The baron shook his head. "I am also limited to teleporting no more than three times per day. If I return for you, it will be a day before I can get back to Ormpetarr." He nodded at Glisena. "My daughter needs me."

Arvin's eyes narrowed as he realized what Foesmasher was saying. "You won't be back."

"No."

"Send someone else then," Arvin insisted. "One of your clerics. I know they have teleportation magic; I've seen them use it."

"Only the most powerful of them can teleport without the gauntlets to aid them—and Glisena will need their prayers." He held out his hand. "Come with me—or stay. Choose."

Arvin folded his arms across his chest. There really was no choice. Arvin couldn't just abandon Karrell, or Tanglemane. "I'm staying."

"I'll send help as soon as I can," Foesmasher promised. "In the meantime, Helm be with you." Then he teleported away.

The other satyrs had started walking toward the hut. One of them called out—to Theyron, Arvin presumed—and nocked an arrow when he received no reply. The others did the same, fanning out and training their arrows on the doorway. Arvin, trapped inside a hut with only one exit, tried feverishly to decide what to do. There were too many satyrs for him to charm. And it would only take one arrow to kill him.

What was keeping Karrell?

Arvin moved to the side of the doorway, readying his dagger.

A hairy hand gripped the door flap. It started to open.

A new voice sounded outside the hut: a woman, speaking the satyr tongue. She barked what sounded like an angry question at the satyrs—one they answered with a babble of voices.

Arvin peeked outside. As he saw who the newcomer was, his mouth went dry.

Naneth.

Chapter 12

ARVIN'S HEART POUNDED AS HE STARED OUT OF THE SATYR HUT AT Naneth. For the moment, the satyrs were busy talking to her—which was bad. They'd be telling her about the human who claimed to be her assistant. Arvin had to act quickly. Energy awakened at the base of his neck, sending a prickling through his scalp as he manifested a charm. The midwife, however, didn't cock her head; the power seemed to have had no effect on her.

She turned toward the hut and gestured.

The inside of the hut filled with an explosion of color. Arvin was still staring at Naneth and saw the swirling colors only in his peripheral vision, but his eyes were drawn to them like moths to a flame. He turned to watch the rainbows that danced and rippled in the air then took a step closer. It was like standing inside the criss-crossing rays cast by a thousand prisms. "Beautiful," he whispered, reaching up to touch one of the rainbows. It twisted away through the air like a snake, leaving a blur of red-violet-blue in its wake. "So beautiful," he breathed.

Dimly, he was aware of the door flap opening and Naneth stepping inside. She glanced around the hut—at Theyron's body, the empty sheepskin where Glisena had lain, and Arvin—and her lips pressed together in a thin line that made her mouth all but disappear in her heavy jowls. Fear flickered in her eyes. It was clear what she was thinking: she'd lost Glisena, and now would have to face Sibyl's wrath. Whatever punishment Sibyl dreamed up would probably make the suffering Naulg had gone through look trivial.

A distant part of Arvin's mind screamed at him that this was the moment to throw the knife he held loosely at his side, to manifest a different psionic power, to *run*, but the colors held him. His gaze drifted back and forth, watching the rainbows.

Naneth ignored the shifting lights. Above and behind her, Arvin saw a snake peering in through a gap in the rear wall of the hut. It, too, was staring at the beautiful lights, tongue flickering in and out of its mouth as if it hoped to taste them. For some reason, that concerned Arvin, but only briefly. The lights were fascinating, scintillating, and *beautiful*.

More beautiful than any snake.

Naneth reached into a belt pouch at her hip and pulled out an egg painted with a blood-red symbol. She held it out toward Arvin, but he barely glanced at it; the shimmering colors still held his eye. Then she spoke a word in what sounded like Draconic.

The rainbows disappeared.

So did the hut.

Arvin found himself curled in a ball inside something smooth and leathery that pressed against him on every side. Warm, sticky fluid surrounded him, soaking his clothes and hair. With a start, he realized he was breathing it in and out like air; it felt thick and heavy in his lungs. His mind was his own again, but he was unable to move. He couldn't even lift his chin from his chest. Suddenly claustrophobic, he kicked at the wall of his prison. It didn't give. He jabbed it with his knife. The blade bounced off it without making a dent. Trapped—he was trapped in here! It took all of his will to keep himself from panicking.

Karrell was out there somewhere, he told himself, in the hut, with Naneth. She'd do something to rescue him.

Unless she was still staring at rainbows.

A muffled voice came from outside Arvin's prison. "Where is the girl?"

"Naneth!" Arvin exclaimed. "You got my warning. Let me out

of here, and I'll tell you what's going on." His voice sounded only slightly muffled, despite the fact that he was exhaling liquid. The cloying taste of raw egg lingered on his tongue.

The egg shook violently. Arvin, dizzy, tried not to throw up.

"Where's the girl?" Naneth repeated.

Arvin tried to manifest the power that would let him listen in on Naneth's thoughts, but though silver sparkles erupted from his third eye, briefly illuminating the liquid that surrounded him, the link could not be forged. Whatever magic had protected Naneth from being charmed was also preventing Arvin from reading her mind.

Arvin groaned. He'd have to rely on his wits alone to convince Naneth to let him out of this prison. He thought frantically, trying to come up with a story that would sound plausible. Should he drop Sibyl's name and claim to be working for one of the factions allied with her? Claim to be one of Talos's worshipers? Neither was likely to work. He had only the vaguest of ideas of what Sibyl was up to, he'd probably say something that would give him away.

Suddenly, he realized there was one story that would make sense— and that would throw Naneth off track, way off track.

"You're too late," he told Naneth. "Chondath has claimed Glisena."

"You're one of Lord Wianar's men?" Naneth asked.

Arvin smiled. She'd taken his hook. Now to set it.

"I'm Wianar's eyes and ears within the Sespech court. Three days ago, Baron Foesmasher captured a satyr who had come to Ormpetarr to fetch you; the satyr told him his daughter was in the Chondalwood. It wasn't in Chondath's best interests that Glisena be found, so I sent you the warning. Just in case you didn't heed it, I made my way here. I was surprised to find the girl had not been moved. I was ordered to take advantage of that oversight."

"Where is Glisena now?" Naneth asked. "In Arrabar?"

"All you need to know is that Wianar has her."

For several moments, Naneth was silent. Then she replied—in a strained voice that instantly told Arvin how desperate she was, and how willing to bargain. "Tell your master that keeping the girl would be a terrible mistake. One that could prove fatal for him."

"What do you mean?" Arvin asked.

There was a long pause. When Naneth at last spoke, her voice sounded reluctant. "The child in Glisena's womb is . . . dangerous," she began.

"Go on," Arvin prompted. He held his breath, praying that Naneth would expound upon what she'd done to the baron's daughter—that she'd reveal the nature of the *thing* she'd put in Glisena's womb. "What is it?"

"A demon."

"A demon?" Arvin gasped, horrified. "How—"

"Magic," Naneth said smugly. "A unique form of binding no other sorcerer can perform."

"But why?" Arvin asked, still struggling with his horror at what Naneth had done. He felt queasy, as though he were going to be sick.

A gloating smile crept into Naneth's voice. "Lady Dediana is anxious to see the birth of her first grandchild," she said. "What a surprise it will be when she sees the new heir. The shock alone will kill her—and if it doesn't, the 'child' will. *Now* do you understand why it's in Chondath's best interests not to keep the girl? Wianar has much more to gain by letting us place someone more . . . agreeable on Hlondeth's throne. Someone who would turn her back on Sespech, and instead form an alliance with Chondath."

Arvin's eyebrows rose. At last he understood what Sibyl had planned. The thing inside Glisena was part of an elaborate assassination attempt against Lady Dediana. Sibyl, once again, was making a bid for the throne—and this time, she was going to claim it herself, instead of merely installing a puppet. Naneth must have been in Hlondeth, these past three days, setting the whole thing up.

"Glisena will give birth soon," Naneth continued. "When she does, she'll need a midwife. One who knows how to deal with what's inside her. Lord Wianar's best interests lie in turning the girl over to me."

"Who do *you* serve?" Arvin asked, knowing full well what the answer would be.

"Sseth's avatar," Naneth answered. "In this incarnation, he is known as Sibyl."

"Where is this Sibyl?" Arvin asked, hoping that Karrell was listening. "In Hlondeth?"

"Why?" Naneth asked—suspiciously enough that Arvin's guess might have been on the mark.

"Lord Wianar will insist on dealing with her personally."

"That won't be necessary. Deliver the girl to me, and I'll convey her to Sibyl."

"Why should Lord Wianar trust you?" Arvin asked. "The hiding place you chose was compromised; be thankful that I found it before Foesmasher did. No, I think he will want to deal with Sibyl, in person."

There was a long pause. "What is it Wianar *wants?*" Naneth asked.

"What do you mean?" Arvin asked.

The egg shook, making Arvin dizzy. "Don't play with me," Naneth spat. "Wianar wants something from Sibyl, in return for the girl. But he doesn't realize the consequences of the delay he's causing—or of angering Sibyl. Only a fool would dare to blackmail a god. And you are a greater fool, to serve him."

"I may be a fool, but I know where Glisena is, and you don't," Arvin countered. "And unless you want to face the wrath of your god, you'll have to do something other than threaten me. What can *you* offer, in return for Glisena?"

"I'm not so foolish as you think," the midwife growled. "I held a playing piece back from Sibyl—one that will prove valuable, if Dediana survives. I'm willing to offer it in trade for the baron's daughter. But I'm obviously wasting my time with you. I'll talk to Lord Wianar myself."

Arvin's breath caught. Would she kill him now? Then he realized that Naneth was bluffing—trying to make Arvin sweat a little. As if being trapped in an egg wasn't doing that readily enough.

"Lord Wianar knows better than to trust you," he countered. "But he trusts me." He paused. "What can you offer *me*, if I help you?"

"Your life," Naneth said, relief evident in her voice, "and the gratitude of a god."

"That's a good start," Arvin agreed. He rapped on the inside of the egg with the hilt of his dagger. "But I'm not going to negotiate from inside an egg. Let me out of here, and we'll talk."

Arvin was jostled back and forth, and a seam of light shone in through a rip in the egg. He saw Naneth's pudgy fingers—impossibly large—tear the egg, widening the rip, and felt the liquid drain away. Suddenly he was breathing air once more. The egg parted into two halves, and he fell. The floor of the hut rushed up to meet him. . . .

Before it struck him, he returned to his full size. His feet hit the floor with a thud. He staggered then regained his balance. As he looked up, he saw that the rainbows were gone—and that Karrell was hanging from the ceiling, just behind Naneth. She was swaying back and forth, hissing softly. No, not hissing, whispering the words of her charm spell.

A spell that, Arvin knew, would have no effect whatsoever on Naneth.

Reacting to the hissing, Naneth whirled to face Karrell.

"Naneth," Karrell hissed. "I have an urgent message for Sibyl from the *ssthaar* of the Se'sehen. Where is she?"

Naneth's eyes narrowed. One hand was behind her back; with it, she began a complicated gesture that could only have been the start of a spell. Karrell, under the impression that Naneth had been charmed, didn't seem to have noticed. She just hung there, swaying, about to take the brunt of whatever spell Naneth was going to cast.

The time for bluffing was over.

Arvin leaped forward, seizing the midwife's hand and clamping a hand over her mouth, but Naneth twisted her head aside and spat out a one-word incantation. Electricity shot into Arvin's hands and surged through his body, throwing him backward. He landed heavily on the floor, heart rattling in his chest, gasping for breath.

Naneth turned away, ignoring him. "Tell me your message. I'll convey it."

Karrell's head swayed back and forth. "My message is for Sibyl's ears alone. Where is she?"

Arvin, listening, knew that Karrell's attempt to pry information from Naneth was doomed. Under the compulsion of a charm spell, the midwife might have overlooked the extremely coincidental arrival of a messenger from Tashalar, asking exactly the same question "Lord Wianar's spy" had just asked. Without the charm, everything Karrell said was an obvious lie. Naneth was toying with Karrell, buying time to cast a spell. Once again, her hand was behind her back, her fingers working.

Forcing himself up off the floor, Arvin threw his dagger. It spun through the air, striking Naneth in the back. But instead of penetrating, the weapon fell harmlessly to the floor, deflected by magic. The midwife spun and leveled a pointing finger at Arvin.

Karrell hissed sharply, glanced between Naneth and Arvin, and sank her teeth into Naneth's shoulder.

Naneth's eyes widened. She jerked away, clamping a hand to her injured shoulder. Barking out a two-word incantation, she vanished.

Arvin clambered to his feet.

Karrell dropped from the ceiling, shifted into human form, and rose gracefully to her feet. Despite the urgency of the moment, the sight of her, naked, took Arvin's breath away. Her words, however, were harsh. "Why did you do that? In another moment she would have told me where Sibyl was."

"No she wouldn't; your charm spell didn't work," Arvin said, rising to his feet. "Naneth is shielded against spells that affect the mind. She knew you were lying and was about to cast a spell on you. I was afraid you'd be killed."

Karrell's eyes softened. "I thought the same . . . about you."

"I know," Arvin said, touching her cheek. He let his hand fall. "I'm sure whatever spell Naneth was about to cast wouldn't have been very pleasant. But at least we won't have to worry about her anymore. Yuan-ti venom is . . . pretty potent stuff, right?"

"My bite is not venomous."

"Oh," Arvin said. He frowned. "We'd better get out of here, then. As soon as Naneth figures out she hasn't been poisoned, she'll be back. And she won't be happy—with either one of us." He peered outside the door. The satyrs had obeyed Naneth's instructions and were waiting outside, but they looked agitated. They were talking in low voices, and pointing toward the hut.

Arvin beckoned Karrell to the doorway. "Do you have all of a yuan-ti's usual magical abilities?" he whispered.

She nodded.

"We need to get out of here," Arvin continued. He pointed at his pack, which lay on the ground near the satyrs. "If you cast a magical darkness just outside the hut, I should be able to grab my pack. I'll make for the nearest tunnel and keep going. In the meantime, use your magical fear on the satyrs; I hope I'll be out of the maze before they've gathered enough courage to follow me. As soon as you've done that, assume snake form and get out yourself. We'll meet back where we left Tanglemane and figure out some other way of finding Sibyl. Agreed?"

"Agreed." She planted a kiss on his lips. "For luck."

"Thanks," he said, smiling. His lips tingled where she'd kissed them. Dagger in hand, he readied himself, calculating the number of paces it would take to reach his pack. "Do it."

As utter darkness filled the clearing outside the hut, Arvin flung the door flap aside. He sprinted for his pack, keeping low. From his left, he heard the thrum of a bow, followed by the hiss of an arrow over his head. The satyrs shouted at each other in confusion. Then Karrell loosed her second wave of magic, and the shouts turned to bleats of fear. Arvin scooped up his pack on the run, slinging it over a shoulder by one strap and praying that its contents weren't spilling out behind him. Then he reached the edge of the darkness. He burst into daylight a dozen paces or so from the edge of the brambles. The tunnel the satyrs had dragged him out of was to his left. He raced for it then flung himself prone and started to crawl. Behind him, he heard shouts and the *thrum-thrum* of a bow being shot twice in rapid succession; at least one of the satyrs had shaken off the magical fear. His shots, though aimed at random from inside the darkness, passed uncomfortably close to Arvin. One struck a vine just above his head.

Crawling rapidly, pack still slung awkwardly over one shoulder, Arvin followed the drag marks. They led to the spot where he'd been ambushed by the satyr with the pan pipes; from this point on he followed his own trail. All the while he prayed that the satyrs wouldn't figure out where he'd gone—that they wouldn't know a quicker route through the bramble maze. The fear seemed to have worn off; Arvin could hear them in the clearing, shouting at one another.

Tymora must have been with him, however; the satyrs didn't catch up. Soon he could see Tanglemane through the thicket of thorny vines. The centaur's ears were twitching; when he spotted Arvin, he gave a snort of delight. Arvin crawled out of the brambles, leaped to his feet, and was relieved to see Karrell slither out after him a moment later. As she shifted into human form, he turned to Tanglemane. "We need to get out of here fast," he told the centaur. "We've got a hornet's nest of angry satyrs behind us. Will you carry us?"

"I would," Tanglemane said. Then he glanced into the forest nervously. "But there's a problem. The wolves are still waiting for their meat."

Arvin turned and saw the wolves. They had been sitting, waiting, but when White Muzzle rose to her feet, the rest followed her lead. Tongues lolling, they stared at Arvin and Karrell. White Muzzle growled—and even without Karrell to translate, Arvin understood. The wolves were hungry.

And the satyrs' shouts were growing closer. They would be through the brambles at any moment.

Arvin glanced at Karrell. "Magical fear?" he asked.

She shook her head. "Not again. Not so soon."

An arrow careened out of the brambles behind them, narrowly missing Arvin. "What about darkness?" he asked Karrell.

"Not yet. But I have other magic that may help." Turning, she gestured at the brambles. As her fingers wove complicated patterns in the air, the vines constricted, closing off the tunnel like a net being pulled shut. The satyrs, trapped inside and pierced by thorns, bleated angrily.

Karrell cast a second spell, and their bows twisted into knots. No more arrows were fired.

"That's one problem down," Arvin said. The wolves, however, continued to pad closer to Arvin, Karrell, and Tanglemane. They were working up their courage with a series of low growls. Any moment now, they would rush forward and attack.

Arvin eyed the trees. He and Karrell could climb to safety, but not Tanglemane.

The centaur's ears twitched wildly. "We should run."

"No," Arvin said. "That's what they want." He glanced once more at the vine-trussed satyrs then turned to Karrell. "Speak to the wolves. Tell them we've brought their meat: the satyrs. The moment your spell wears off, the wolves can rush them. Then they'll have all the meat they like."

Karrell nodded then rapidly barked this out to White Muzzle. The wolf growled something at her pack then yipped a question back at Karrell, who answered it.

"I told her I broke the satyrs' bows, but she is still fearful," Karrell translated. "The satyrs are fierce fighters, even without weapons."

Arvin chuckled in reply. "Not when they're asleep." He spoke his glove's command word, and the pan pipes he'd vanished into it reappeared. "Plug your ears," he instructed. Tanglemane and Karrell did as instructed. Arvin, praying the pipes wouldn't affect the person playing them, lifted them to his lips and blew.

A shrill noise squealed from the pipes, but nothing happened. Neither the satyrs nor the wolves fell asleep. The nearest satyr, however, did twist around in the brambles, earning himself several scratches, to say something to his fellows. His voice sounded worried.

Arvin lowered the pipes. Only a satyr could evoke their magic, it seemed. But if that was the case, why did the satyrs sound concerned? He glanced closely at the pipes, noting for the first time that they were made from individual reeds, bound together with twine in a series of intricate knots.

Magical knots?

Grinning, Arvin slid the point of his dagger under one of the knots. He held the pan pipes out where the satyrs could see them. "Do as I say!" he shouted. "Or I'll destroy them."

A babble of voices broke out as the satyrs conversed in their own tongue. Then one of them shouted. "What want you?"

White Muzzle had begun to slink forward again, the rest of the pack following.

Arvin spoke quickly to Karrell. "Can you loosen just a few of the brambles?" he asked. "Enough to let one of the satyrs go?"

She nodded.

"Translate what I say for the wolves," Arvin told her. Then he turned his attention back to the satyrs. "We're going to release one of you," he shouted. "That one will go back to the clearing and fetch Theyron's body, and bring it to me."

Karrell translated, and White Muzzle gave a satisfied growl. The satyrs, however, seemed reluctant. Arvin held the pan pipes a little higher, and started to saw with his blade.

"Stop!" one cried. "We shall bring him."

Arvin smiled. He tipped his head in the direction of the satyr who had spoken. "That one," he told Karrell in a low voice. "Loosen the brambles around him."

As the vines untwined themselves from him, the satyr leaped to his feet. He gave Arvin a fierce glare, then trotted back in the direction of the satyr camp. While he was gone, the brambles around the other satyrs began to loosen. Karrell recast her spell.

The satyr returned a short while later, dragging Theyron's body. He paused just before leaving the brambles, catching his breath, then readjusted his grip on the body and continued dragging it toward Arvin. The wound in the dead satyr's neck was still leaking blood; it left a trail of red. The wolves moved forward, licking their lips in anticipation. Then, at a yip from White Muzzle, they moved forward in a rush. The satyr bleated and scurried back into the brambles. The wolves converged on the corpse, growling at one another as they tore bloody chunks from it.

"Let's get moving," Arvin said in a low voice, eyeing the wolves. "Before they finish eating and decide they're still hungry."

Tanglemane nodded and knelt, motioning for Arvin and Karrell to get on his back. Arvin started to climb on then heard the creak of a bow being drawn. He turned his head just in time to see one of the satyrs—the one who had dragged Theyron's body back—standing inside the brambles with a bow held at full draw. Arvin ducked as the satyr let his arrow fly.

The satyr wasn't aiming at Arvin however, but at the wolves. One of them yelped as the arrow struck it.

"Let's go," Arvin shouted, boosting Karrell onto Tanglemane's back.

Tanglemane, however, crumpled to his knees, spilling her to the ground. The centaur staggered to his feet a moment later, clutching his chest. A thin line of blood trickled out from beneath his hands.

"Tanglemane," Karrell said, alarmed. "What's wrong?"

Even as she asked the question, Arvin realized the answer. The arrow had struck White Muzzle, and the fate link had caused Tanglemane to suffer an identical wound.

The satyr shot another arrow. This one struck another wolf in the head, instantly killing it.

The pack bolted, White Muzzle in the rear, limping.

Arvin silently cursed his stupidity; he should have guessed that the satyr would pick up another bow when he returned to the camp.

The satyr nocked another arrow. This time, he turned toward Arvin as he drew his bow.

"Wait!" Arvin shouted. "If you shoot me, you'll never get these back." He flourished the pan pipes then vanished them into his glove.

"The pipes are inside my glove," he told the satyr, splaying his fingers wide to show that they had truly vanished. "And I'm the only one who can work the glove's magic. Kill me, and you'll lose the pipes forever." He paused to let that sink in then added, "Let us leave the forest, and I'll give the pipes back to you. They're useless to me—I have no interest in keeping them. I'll leave them at the forest's edge for you. Do we have an agreement?"

The satyr lowered his bow a fraction and turned to speak to his fellows. Low murmuring followed. As the satyrs conferred, Arvin glanced at Tanglemane. The centaur's face was pale; his legs trembled. Only a trickle of blood seeped from the wound; the arrow must have still been buried in White Muzzle's flesh. Given her limited, animal intelligence, she would probably flee from the pain until she dropped, until she died.

"Agreed!" the satyr shouted back. "You may leave."

Cautiously, Arvin and Karrell backed away from the brambles, leading the injured Tanglemane. The satyr held his fire.

Tanglemane was able to walk, but he gasped with each breath.

Arvin touched the crystal at his throat. "Nine lives," he pleaded.

Tanglemane was going to need them. Even if the satyrs kept their end of the bargain, the centaur was unlikely to make it out of the woods.

Chapter 13

ARVIN SQUATTED BESIDE TANGLEMANE, GENTLY REPOSITIONING THE blood-soaked bandage he'd made earlier from pieces torn from his shirt. The centaur had proved stronger than Arvin expected; he'd walked for some distance through the forest before crumpling to his knees. Karrell had cast a healing spell on him just after they'd left the satyr camp, but it had only helped a little bit. The wound in the side of his chest was still open, still seeping blood. It was a hollow hole that, on White Muzzle, would have been filled with an arrow shaft. It was a wonder the wolf had survived this long, with an arrow still in her. Every now and then the flesh around the puckered hole quivered; Arvin realized that White Muzzle must have been licking her wound, jostling the arrow around. He hoped that meant she had found somewhere safe to hole up—somewhere predators wouldn't find her.

"Hang on, Tanglemane," Arvin urged, one hand on the centaur's shoulder. "It's almost sunset. The fate link will end soon." For the hundredth time, he wished he could dispel the power, but once manifested, a fate link endured for its full duration.

The centaur's breathing was labored now. He sat with head bowed and eyes screwed shut, as if trying to block out the pain. Had he been human, Arvin and Karrell might have carried him, but the centaur must have weighed three times their combined weight.

Karrell beckoned Arvin to her and nodded at the darkening forest. "The satyrs are still following us."

"It's not the satyrs I'm worried about," Arvin said. "I keep wondering where Naneth is—why she hasn't teleported back to squeeze more information out of me."

"She would have to find us first."

Arvin jerked a thumb in the direction of the dark shapes flitting through the forest. "Easily done. She just has to ask them where we are."

"Perhaps," Karrell said in a low voice, "that is what she is doing. She must hope we will lead her to Glisena."

Arvin nodded. It made sense for Naneth to allow them to think they had escaped. While the satyrs kept an eye on them, she could check up on the story Arvin had told her. But for all Naneth knew, Arvin might have teleportation magic—magic he'd used to spirit Glisena away. She was taking a big risk—for all she knew, Arvin might just vanish from the forest.

He paused to rub his forehead; his wound was itching again. The lapis lazuli was still in place; he'd used it just after they left the satyr camp to let Tanju know that Glisena had been found, that there was a demon inside her—and that Sibyl's plans had been thwarted. Tanju had commended Arvin for a job well done. After speaking to his mentor, Arvin had left the lapis lazuli where it was; removing it would have meant tearing open the scab that had already formed over it. Now he wondered if that had been wise. On two other occasions during their flight through the forest he'd felt a peculiar sensation behind the stone, deep in his "third eye"—a soft fluttering, like an eyelid rapidly blinking. He felt it again now. It was almost as if his third eye were trying to focus on something it couldn't quite see.

Along with it came an uncomfortable sensation of being watched. Arvin had assumed this was because the satyrs were following them, but now he began to wonder if there was something more to it. Was someone trying to manifest a sending?

No, that wasn't quite right. A sending created, in the recipient's mind, a mental image of the person dispatching the image. A failed sending produced no sensation at all. It simply . . . failed. This was somewhere between the two. It was almost as if someone had manifested the link that made a sending possible . . . without conveying any message.

Suddenly, Arvin realized the cause: Naneth was using her crystal ball to spy on them.

A chill ran through him as he wondered what he'd already given away. Had he said anything that would indicate the baron had teleported Glisena back to Ormpetarr while Naneth had been scrying on them? He hoped not.

Karrell was staring at Arvin, her brow creased. "What's wrong?" she asked.

"The satyrs," Arvin told her in a low voice—one just loud enough for Naneth to also hear. "They're listening. Say nothing, or Wianar will have our heads. And keep up the pretense in front of the centaur. Pretend that we're headed for Ormpetarr; if the satyr lives, he'll help throw Foesmasher off the scent."

Karrell's frown deepened, and for a moment Arvin worried that she was going to blurt out something that would give the game away. Then she nodded—though there was still a hint of confusion in her eyes.

A moment later, Arvin felt the fluttering in his forehead fade away. He waited, making certain it was gone, then whispered urgently to Karrell. "Naneth was just scrying on us. I can sense when she's doing it. If it happens again, I'll signal you. If I do this"—he formed a V with the first two fingers of his right hand and touched his shoulder: the sign, in silent speech, that someone was spying—"it means Naneth is listening. Be careful what you say."

"I will."

Behind them, Tanglemane gave a loud groan and tried to rise to his feet. Arvin and Karrell hurried to his side.

"What's wrong?" Arvin asked.

Tanglemane's nostrils flared. "Giant," he gasped. "Coming this way."

Arvin's jaw clenched. That was all they needed—another hostile creature to contend with. No wonder humans avoided these woods. Already he could feel the ground trembling and hear the snap of branches.

He caught Karrell's eye. "Shift form," he urged her. "Hide."

Her dark eyes bored into his. "And you?" she asked. She gestured at Tanglemane. "And him?"

Arvin drew his dagger. "Tanglemane doesn't have that option—and I can't just leave him. Fortunately, a little of my psionic energy remains." He grinned. "Perhaps the giant will find me . . . charming."

"Be careful," Karrell urged. She shifted into snake form and slithered under a bush.

Arvin, meanwhile, laid a hand on Tanglemane's shoulder, steadying him, and turned toward the direction the crashing sounds were coming from. A moment later he spotted the giant lumbering through the woods. The giant was more than twice the height of a man and had skin as gray and pitted as stone. His head was nearly level with the tops of the trees, which he parted with massive hands as he shouldered his way through the forest. He wore a tunic that had been crudely stitched together from the skins of a dozen different animals, and a wide belt into which was tucked an enormous stone club. His bare feet crushed bushes and snapped deadfall branches with each step.

Arvin watched nervously. That club looked heavy enough to crush him with a single blow.

The giant spotted Arvin and Tanglemane and came to an abrupt halt.

"Hello!" Arvin called, waving up at him. Swiftly, he manifested a charm. "It's good to see you, friend."

The giant cocked his head. "Baron Foesmasher told you I was coming?" he asked.

Arvin's eyebrows rose. "The baron sent you?"

The giant shrugged. "One of his clerics sent word to find you. She said you might be having trouble with the satyrs, and by the smell of it, she was right." He glanced down at Tanglemane then rested massive fists on his hips. "What can I do to help?"

Karrell reassumed human form and rose to her feet, clothing in hand. She gestured at Tanglemane. "Can you carry him?" she asked. "Gently?"

The giant grinned, revealing teeth that glinted like quartz. "I can, snake-lady." He dropped to his knees, and the earth trembled. Slipping broad hands under Tanglemane, he lifted the centaur as easily—and gently—as a man lifting a kitten. "Where to?"

"Fort Arran," Tanglemane gasped. "There are healers there."

Arvin stared at the centaur and whispered a prayer that Tanglemane would be able to hold on that long.

☙

The fate link wore off just after darkness fell, as they were leaving the woods. Tanglemane gasped as his chest suddenly started to bleed again, and the giant lowered him to the ground. Arvin stripped off what remained of his shirt and tore it into pieces, tying a fresh bandage against the wound to staunch the bleeding and Karrell cast a healing spell that partially closed the wound. Then the giant picked the centaur up once more.

Before following, Arvin summoned the pan pipes into his gloved hand. The satyrs had kept their side of the bargain by not attacking—though the giant's presence probably had a lot to do with that decision—and now Arvin would keep his. He set the pipes down on a rock, where they would be easy to spot.

They walked toward the bridge that spanned the river, Arvin and Karrell leading, followed by the giant. Arvin kept looking nervously around, hoping the centaur herd wouldn't return. He didn't want to face the centaur-seed a second time. Even in proxy, Zelia was formidable.

Karrell took his hand and gave it a squeeze. "Stop worrying," she said. "We are nearly there."

They walked on, holding hands. The air had turned colder as night fell; here and there puddles of water had developed a thin skin of ice that crunched underfoot. Moonlight glinted off the broken shards, making them sparkle like a scattering of diamonds. "I had heard about ice before I came north," Karrell said. "But I never knew it could be so beautiful."

Arvin nodded. He snuck a glance at Karrell, remembering the serpent form that lay beneath her human skin, then fixed his eyes on the far shore. In the distance he could see a wagon setting out from Fort Arran. It was moving across the bridge; the two horses drawing it were running at a good clip. The giant cradled Tanglemane in the crook of one arm and waved at it. Figures in the wagon waved back.

"What will you do, once we reach the fort?" Karrell asked.

Arvin touched his forehead. "Contact the baron, as soon as I'm able. Find out how Glisena is doing. Hopefully, the clerics have been able to . . . purge . . . what's inside her."

Karrell gave him a startled look. "They will kill her child?"

"It's no child," Arvin said. There hadn't been time, until now, to tell Karrell everything he'd learned. When he did, her face paled.

"Helm's clerics will deal with the demon," Arvin reassured her. "Lord Foesmasher seemed confident that they could. And once they have, we won't have to worry about Naneth looking over our shoulders anymore. In fact, we can turn her scrying to our advantage. If we let it 'slip' that Glisena's womb is empty, Naneth will realize her scheme has failed. Glisena will be safe from her."

And, Arvin added silently, he would be able to collect his reward. The baron would no doubt be pleased with his work; Arvin had done everything he'd promised, and more. Not only had he located Glisena, he'd provided vital information that would help the clerics save her. The baron's emotions ran high when it came to his daughter. No doubt he would be as generous with those who had saved her as he was merciless against those who threatened her.

He realized that Karrell hadn't answered. She walked in silence, one arm wrapped protectively across her stomach. Arvin supposed it only natural; what had been done to Glisena would hit a woman harder.

"I too have been thinking about what we might say the next time Naneth scries on us," Karrell said at last. "I think it would be a mistake to reveal that Glisena is no longer pregnant. If we choose our words carefully—make her think that Glisena is in a location of our choosing—we can lure Naneth to us."

"Are you sure that's wise?" he asked. Naneth was a powerful sorcerer—he wasn't keen on facing her spells a second time.

"I must find Sibyl and recover the Circled Serpent," Karrell said. "Naneth is the one thread that will lead me through the maze. I must follow it." She leveled a challenging look at Arvin. "If, however, you no longer wish to help me. . . ."

Arvin stared at the approaching wagon, wishing he could just board it, return to Ormpetarr, and collect his reward. Then he thought of what Sibyl's minions had done to Naulg and to Glisena's unborn child. He met Karrell's eye. "You kept your end of the bargain," he told her. "I'll keep mine. Whatever I can do to thwart Sibyl, I will."

Karrell gave him a long look. "If we find that Sibyl is in Hlondeth, will you return there with me?"

"Hlondeth isn't a healthy place for me to be," Arvin said. He clenched his left hand, remembering. By now, the Guild would be wondering where he'd gone . . . and asking questions—questions that might lead them to a realization that he'd been feeding Tanju information on their activities over the past six months. Arvin had been forced to trade his mentor *something*, in return for the lessons in psionics. If the Guild found that out, they'd cut out Arvin's tongue. "I have enemies there."

"You have enemies here," Karrell said softly. "Zelia."

"True," Arvin agreed. Then he smiled. "And Zelia, according to the baron, is in Ormpetarr—which makes my decision easier."

He expected Karrell to smile at his faint attempt at humor, or to ask what his decision was, but her face had a distant look, as if she were lost in thought.

"The centaur Windswift," she said abruptly. "You addressed him as Zelia. Was he one of her seeds?"

Arvin's jaw clenched. "He was. Zelia must have created him to spy on Chondath."

"Zelia is an agent of Hlondeth?" Karrell asked.

Arvin nodded.

"She serves House Extaminos?"

"Yes," Arvin answered. "Why?"

Karrell countered with a question of her own. "Why did she try to seed you?"

Arvin gave a bitter laugh. "You'll appreciate the irony, I'm sure. Zelia hoped to use me to infiltrate The Pox—the clerics who were allied with Sibyl during her first attempt at Hlondeth's throne. Zelia needed a human who had. . . ." His voice faltered as he remembered the terrible transformation Naulg had undergone—and the final kindness Arvin had been forced to pay him. "Who'd had the misfortune of falling into their hands. They wouldn't have accepted anyone else into their ranks."

Arvin was thankful that Karrell didn't ask him to elaborate.

"What other psionic powers does Zelia have?" she asked.

Arvin gave her a sharp look. "Don't even think about it," he snapped. "Zelia's dangerous. And untrustworthy. She's as slippery as a—" He realized what he was saying, and stopped himself just in time.

Karrell's eyes narrowed. She yanked her hand out of his. "As what? A serpent?"

Arvin's face flushed. That was exactly what he'd been about to say.

The giant, seeing that they had stopped walking, halted. "Is something wrong?" he rumbled. Tanglemane lifted his head slightly; his face looked pale.

"It's nothing," Arvin said. He pointed at the wagon, only a few hundred paces from them now. Behind the driver sat two soldiers and a third man, identifiable as a cleric of Helm by his eye-emblazoned breastplate and deep red cloak. "Get Tanglemane to the wagon. We'll follow in a moment."

The giant shrugged then continued with heavy footsteps toward the wagon. It pulled to a halt as he drew near it, and the cleric hopped out. The giant lowered Tanglemane to the ground. The cleric crouched beside him and started removing the centaur's crude wound binding.

Arvin turned back to Karrell. "Zelia's dangerous," he repeated. "Perhaps as dangerous as Sibyl herself."

"And she is Sibyl's enemy. And she has mind magic beyond what you possess. Magic that may force Naneth to tell us where Sibyl is."

"True," Arvin agreed, bristling. "But she's the last person I'd ever ask for help from. As soon as she found out I'm alive, she'd kill me. Quick as spit. It's bad enough that Windswift knows what I look like. The next time he reports to Zelia. . . ." He shook his head, amazed at the complicated net he'd managed to weave around himself, hoping he could keep it from drawing any tighter.

"I was not suggesting that *you* speak with Zelia," Karrell said. She raised her right hand and nodded at the ring on her finger. "And she will not learn that you are alive. Not from me."

Arvin shook a finger at her. "Don't do it. Gods only know what Zelia will do to you. She's dangerous," he repeated again, grasping at straws. "She's—"

"A yuan-ti," Karrell said. "As am I." She glared at him. "And do not presume to give me orders. I am not human, and you are not my. . . ." She paused, searching for the word. "Not my husband. Even if you did quicken my eggs." Tossing her hair angrily, she turned her back.

Arvin's mouth gaped open. "Your *what?*"

She touched her stomach. "My eggs," she repeated softly.

Arvin stared at Karrell. "You're pregnant?" he asked in a strained whisper. "But it's only been"—he did a quick tally in his head—"two days—no, three—since we first. . . ." He shook his head. "How could you possibly know so soon?"

"My scales," she said. "They are shedding out of season—it is one of the early signs." She touched a hand to her belly. "And the way I . . . feel. I *know.*"

Arvin was stunned. He didn't know what to say. What to think. If Karrell was right, he was a father. Or soon would be. The thought terrified him; he knew nothing about children. "How long until. . . ." He swallowed hard, and rubbed his forehead. His wound was bothering him again.

Beside Arvin, someone cleared his throat hesitantly—the cleric. He had completed his healing; Tanglemane was back on his feet, his color restored. The cleric had walked over to where Arvin stood without Arvin even noticing.

"Are you Arvin?" he asked.

Arvin nodded. Eggs, Karrell had said. Plural. How *many* eggs?

"I'm to convey you to Ormpetarr at once," the cleric continued. "The baron needs your mind magic. There's someone at the palace who's . . . not well. Will you come? You must be willing, in order for me to teleport you."

"I don't have any healing powers," Arvin protested. Absently, he rubbed at his forehead. The itching was getting worse.

"The baron needs you to . . . listen to some thoughts," the cleric said.

"Whose?" Arvin asked absently. He stared at Karrell, realizing he hardly knew her. Yet she bore his child. His *children.*

"A . . . demon's," the cleric whispered, shooting a worried glance at Karrell.

Arvin rubbed his itching forehead. No, not itching. Tickling. The flutter was back—had been back, for some time.

Naneth was listening.

"It is all right," Karrell assured the cleric. "I know all about Glis—"

Arvin sprang forward and clapped a hand across her mouth. With his free hand he signaled frantically, jerking two **V**-splayed fingers over his shoulder.

Karrell's eyes widened.

Pretending that he was worried about the cleric overhearing, Arvin whispered fiercely at Karrell in a voice he hoped was loud enough for Naneth to hear. "The cleric isn't one of us. Don't say anything that will give the game away. Don't mention Lord Wianar. Or the fact that it's not . . . not really Glisena that Foesmasher has, but a . . . an illusion. If they find out Glisena is really in . . . in Arrabar, they might find her."

The tickling in his forehead faded. Arvin stared at Karrell, stricken by the knowledge that they had probably just given the game away, despite his feeble attempt to lay a false trail. He let his hand fall away from Karrell's mouth.

Her eyes asked a silent question.

"Too late," he croaked. "She heard all of it."

Karrell's mouth tightened.

As the cleric looked back and forth between Arvin and Karrell, obviously confused. "Are you willing to come?" he asked. "Can I teleport you?"

"Teleport both of us," Karrell said. "To wherever Glisena is. As quickly as you can."

She held out a hand for Arvin. He took it.

"Let's hope Naneth doesn't beat us there," he said.

Karrell nodded grimly. "Yes."

๑

When they arrived at the palace, the baron was waiting. His face was haggard as he strode across the reception hall to meet them. His hair was uncombed, and the odor of nervous sweat clung to him. There were dark circles under his eyes.

"You're here," he said, clasping Arvin's hand as the cleric who had teleported them there hurried away. "Helm be praised."

"Be careful what you say, Lord Foesmasher," Arvin warned. "Naneth has a crystal ball. She's using it to scry on me. I tried to mislead her, but it might not have worked. If she learns . . . what's going on . . . she may—"

"Don't worry about Naneth," Foesmasher assured Arvin. "Marasa has placed a dimensional lock on Glisena's room. Nobody is going to teleport into it—or out. The room has also been warded against scrying. Come."

Foesmasher shifted his grip to Arvin's elbow and steered him toward a door that was flanked by two soldiers. Karrell started to follow, but the soldiers blocked her way, one of them rudely thrusting a hand against her chest.

Arvin stood his ground as Foesmasher wrenched open the door. "Karrell's a healer," he told the baron. "Her spells—"

"Come from a serpent god," Foesmasher said in a low voice. "My daughter needs *human* healing."

Arvin gave Karrell an apologetic look. She returned it with a shrug, but he could see the bitterness in her eyes. "Go," she said. "I will wait."

The baron led Arvin through another reception hall; up a flight of stairs; and through a room in which several soldiers stood, armed and ready. Foesmasher gestured, and they stepped away from a locked door. Foesmasher placed his palm on the door; a heartbeat later, magical energy crackled around the lock. The door swung open, revealing a chamber in which nine of Helm's clerics stood. They were gathered in a circle, praying in low voices, their gauntleted hands extended toward a bed where Glisena lay. Nine shields, each embossed with Helm's eye, floated in the air behind their backs, forming a circle that turned slowly around them. Marasa sat on a stool next to the bed, holding Glisena's hand. She glanced up, kissed Glisena, and rose to her feet, motioning for the baron to take her hand. He crossed to the bed, a strained smile on his face as he kneeled at his daughter's side. "Little dove," he whispered. "Father is here."

Glisena turned her head away from him.

Marasa's face was grim as she approached Arvin. "Helm be praised," she said. "The giant found you."

Arvin stared at Glisena. She was still pregnant—and looked even worse than before. Despite the ministrations of the clerics, her face had a sickly yellow pallor. She had been bathed—a ceramic tub filled with scented water stood in a corner of the room—and was wearing fresh night robe, but the odor of vomit lingered in the room. She twisted restlessly on the bed, her free hand scrabbling at the blankets, shoving them aside. Her stomach was an ominous bulge.

Arvin swallowed nervously. There was a *demon* in there. He met Marasa's eye. "Does she know?" he asked. "About—"

"We told her," Marasa said. Her expression grew pained. "But I don't know if she believes us. Not after what her father tried to do." She sighed heavily, not looking at Foesmasher.

"The cleric who teleported us here said you wanted me to listen to the demon's thoughts," Arvin prompted. "Are you going to try to banish it?"

"We can't," Marasa said, her voice low. "It is linked to Glisena by the blood cord. If we banish it, Glisena will be drawn into the Abyss with it. We will have to try to kill it, instead."

Arvin, suddenly remembering the vision he'd had in Naneth's home—of a woman, linked by a thread of blood, to her own death— felt his face grow pale. "That might kill her," he whispered. Quickly, he told Marasa of his vision.

Marasa listened quietly, a strained look on her face. Then she gave a helpless shrug. "There is nothing else left to try," she said. She stared at Glisena. "The demon is small, and Helm willing, will succumb to High Watcher Davinu's holy word. It can then be birthed—or removed—in the same way as a stillborn child. But if the demon does not succumb—if it tries to trick us by feigning death—we need to know what it is thinking. Perhaps it will give us some clue that will tell us what *will* harm it."

"I see," Arvin said, not wholly convinced. His eyes remained locked on Glisena's distended belly. It was taut as a drum—one that might tear open at any moment.

"Prepare yourself," Marasa said. "And we will begin."

Arvin took off his cloak and draped it over a chair. Sending his awareness down into his *muladhara,* he was relieved to see that it contained enough energy to manifest the power Marasa had requested. He walked across the room, steeling himself for what he was about to experience. The thought of contacting the demon's mind a second time terrified him, but—he glanced at Glisena's pale face—if it would help, he would do it.

He crossed the room and stood at the foot of Glisena's bed. "I'm ready," he told Marasa.

She nodded at one of the clerics—an older man with pale blue eyes and hair so white and fine that the age spots on his scalp could clearly be seen through it. He seemed hale enough, however; he wore the suit of armor that was the priestly vestment of Helm's clerics with the upright posture and ease of a much younger man.

"Give High Watcher Davinu a signal, Arvin, when you have made contact," Marasa said. "Once you have, he will begin."

Arvin smiled to himself. Using the silent speech, he could have described, moment by moment, exactly what was happening as he manifested his power. But he didn't want anyone to know he was Guild . . . ex-Guild. "I'll raise my hand," he said.

As he prepared to manifest his power, Glisena caught his hand. Startled, Arvin looked down at her. She was straining to speak, her eyes imploring him. Concerned, he moved to the side of the bed and leaned over to hear what she was saying.

"Where did it go?" she whispered.

"Where did what go?" Arvin asked.

Glisena glanced warily at her father then continued to whisper in Arvin's ear. Her breath was fever-hot. "My baby," she said. "Naneth had to take my baby out before she put the demon in. She had to put her *somewhere*. Find my baby for me. Promise you will. Please?"

Arvin blinked. It hadn't occurred to him, until now, to wonder what had happened to the child Glisena had been carrying. He'd assumed it had died or been subsumed when Naneth summoned the demon into Glisena's womb. Either that, or teleported elsewhere—the Abyss, perhaps—and had died a swift death outside the womb.

But what if it had been teleported into *another* womb?

If it had, Glisena's unborn child might still be alive. And Naneth would have an extra playing piece to haggle with.

An extra playing piece she had offered to trade for Glisena earlier, when she thought Arvin was Lord Wianar's man.

Foesmasher leaned forward, stiff with tension. "What is Glisena saying?"

Arvin straightened, shaking his head. "She's delirious," he said, trying to ease his hand out of Glisena's. She clung to it with a grip tight as death. Her eyes begged a silent question of him.

He nodded. "I'll do it," he promised her.

Glisena's hands relaxed.

"Do what?" the baron growled.

Arvin didn't answer.

Glisena sighed and released his hand, closing her eyes. When she opened them again, she nodded at High Watcher Davinu. "I'm ready," she announced in a faint whisper. Then, in a stronger voice, she said, "You may begin."

Arvin smiled. Despite Glisena's faults, she was her father's daughter.

As Davinu prepared to cast his spell, Arvin sent his awareness down into the power points at the middle of his forehead and base of his scalp. Linking them, he manifested his power. Sparkles of silver erupted from his eyes and drifted gently down toward Glisena's stomach; as they settled there, vanishing, the thoughts of those in the room swam into his mind. Marasa was relieved that Arvin was finally here, and praying for Helm's mercy on the innocent Glisena. High Watcher Davinu was concentrating on the spell he was about to cast. He would channel Helm's glorious might into a single word so powerful that it would snuff out even a demon's life. The other clerics were focused on their prayers.

And the demon—dark, malevolent, seething, and gloating. *Soon,* it thought, the words reverberating like the growls of a dragon in its cave. *I will be free soon. The bindings . . . fade.*

Arvin shuddered. He raised his hand and signaled for Davinu to begin.

Davinu raised one gauntleted hand above his head. Praying now—evoking Helm in a low chant as the other clerics whispered their own prayers in the background—he slowly closed his hand into a fist. He caught Marasa's eye—she nodded—and that of the baron. Foesmasher squeezed Glisena's hand. His free hand was clenched in a white-knuckled fist and trembling.

Soon, the demon thought, its voice an evil chuckle.

"Do it," Foesmasher croaked.

Davinu's hand swept down toward Glisena's stomach, creating a sound like that of a sword sweeping through the air. *"Moritas!"* he cried.

Glisena's eyes flew open. She gasped, arching her back.

Foesmasher's eyes squeezed shut; his lips moved rapidly in silent prayer.

Soon, the demon whispered. *I will be——*

Arvin heard a wet thud—a sound like a blade striking flesh. For the space of a heartbeat, everyone in the room was silent, their minds blank with suspense. Even the demon was still. Arvin searched desperately for its mind, hope bubbling through him.

He found only silence. He closed his eyes in relief.

Stupid mortal, the demon suddenly roared. *You thought you could kill me?* Its mind erupted with laughter: a sound like thick, hot, bubbling blood.

Arvin opened his eyes. Davinu, Marasa, and Foesmasher were staring at him expectantly, their faces filled with cautious hope.

"It's . . . not . . . dead," he croaked.

Their faces crumpled into despair.

I hear you, the demon growled into Arvin's mind. *I will remember your voice.* It gave a mental shove . . . and the manifestation ended.

Arvin sagged.

Marasa caught his arm, steadying him. "Did you overhear anything?" she asked. "Anything that might help?"

"The demon is bound," Arvin said. "But the bindings that hold it are fading. It thinks it will be free. 'Soon' was the word it used."

Marasa looked grim. She stared at Glisena's distended stomach. "Does that mean it will be born?" she asked softly. "Or. . . ."

Foesmasher dropped his daughter's hand and rose to his feet. "Abyss take you!" he gritted at Davinu, his fists balled. "And you," he said, pointing at Marasa. "You assured me the prayer would work."

"I don't understand why it didn't, my lord," Davinu protested, backing away. "Something so small . . . yet so powerful? We expected a minor demon—a quasit, given the size—but it appears we were wrong. Naneth seems to have reduced a larger demon—many times over—without diminishing its vital energies in the slightest."

Marasa stood her ground before the baron's verbal onslaught. "Thuragar," she said, her voice dangerously low. "If Helm has forsaken your daughter, you have only yourself to blame."

Foesmasher glared. His hand dropped to the hilt of his sword.

Marasa glared back.

The other clerics glanced warily between baron and cleric, waiting for the storm to break.

When it did, it came as a flood of tears. They spilled down Foesmasher's cheeks as he stared at his daughter. His hand fell away from his sword. He turned away, his shoulders trembling with silent sobs.

Davinu turned to Marasa. "What now?" he asked in a weary voice.

Marasa sighed. She looked ready to collapse herself. One hand touched Glisena's forehead. "We wait," she announced at last, "until it is born. And banish it then."

"The birth will be . . . difficult," Davinu said, his voice a mere whisper.

Marasa's eyes glistened with anguish. "Yes."

Arvin shuffled his feet nervously.

Marasa turned to him. "Go," she said in a flat voice. "Rest and meditate—but do not leave the palace. We may have need of your mind magic later."

Arvin nodded. He wanted to wish Marasa and the other clerics luck, but if Helm had forsaken Glisena, so too might Tymora. His heart was heavy—could he do *nothing* to stop Sibyl's foul machinations? Giving Glisena one last sorrowful glance, he left the bed chamber and walked wearily down the corridor, back to the reception hall where he'd left Karrell.

She wasn't there.

Arvin turned to the soldiers. "The woman I came here with," he said. "Where did she go?"

The soldiers exchanged uncomfortable looks.

"What?" Arvin snapped.

"She left a message for you," one of them answered at last. "She said she had to talk to someone, and for you to stay here, at the palace. She'll return when she was done."

Arvin felt his face grow pale. "Did she mention a name?"

The second soldier chuckled. "Looks like he's been stood up," he whispered to his companion.

The first soldier nodded then answered. "It was Zeliar . . . or Zelias. Something like that."

Arvin barely heard him. A chasm seemed to have opened at his feet. Nodding his thanks for the message, he stumbled from the room.

Zelia.

CHAPTER 14

Arvin sat in Karrell's room at the Fairwinds Inn, staring at the cold ashes in the fireplace, exhausted in mind and body. His limbs were heavy with fatigue and his wounds ached; even thinking was as difficult as wading through deep water.

What was Karrell doing, speaking to Zelia? She was putting not only Arvin's life in danger by doing so, but her own life, as well. The two women might share the same goal—finding Sibyl—but Zelia was utterly ruthless in that pursuit. She'd allowed Arvin and Naulg to fall into the hands of The Pox then subjected Arvin to one of the cruelest psionic powers of all in order to achieve her goal. Why would Karrell ever want to ally herself with such a person?

Because, Arvin thought heavily, Karrell was also a yuan-ti. She didn't fear that race, the way a human would.

And because—and with this thought, Arvin sighed heavily—Zelia was a far more powerful psion than he was, far more capable.

Had Karrell decided to abandon him?

The drawing Karrell had done of him was still lying on the table. He picked it up. She'd drawn him as he lay sleeping; in the portrait, his face looked relaxed, at peace, which was hardly how he felt right now.

Everything had gone right, yet everything had gone wrong. He'd done what Tanju had demanded of him—found Foesmasher's daughter—even without using the dorje. But what good had it done? Glisena was about to give birth to a demon; her chances of survival weren't high. And once again, those who had committed this foul crime—Naneth and the abomination Sibyl—would go unpunished.

Thunder grumbled in the coal-dark sky, a distant echo to Arvin's thoughts.

If Glisena did die, Foesmasher would be devastated. The baron didn't think clearly where his daughter was concerned. He was bound to take his frustrations out on those who were "responsible," in however oblique a way, for any harm that came to her. He demonstrated that when he'd lashed out at the soldier after the death of the satyr. Arvin might be the next one on the chopping block—especially if his absence from the palace were discovered. Marasa had instructed him to stay close at hand, and he'd disobeyed her. That alone would be enough to rouse the baron's wrath.

Arvin clenched his gloved hand until his abbreviated little finger ached. It was like serving the Guild, all over again.

He'd been wrong to think he could make a new home for himself in Sespech; wrong in putting his faith in the baron; and most of all, wrong about Karrell.

He stared at the bed in which they'd made love—in which they'd conceived a child—then he looked back at the portrait, still in his hand. He crumpled it and tossed it onto the cold ashes in the fireplace.

He leaned forward and drummed his fingers on the table. If he knew where Zelia was, he might have tried to head Karrell off, to talk some sense into her. But the baron had been too preoccupied—to say the least—for Arvin to ask him where Zelia had been spotted. All Arvin knew was that she was somewhere in Ormpetarr . . .

. . . Which was all Karrell knew about Zelia, as well. And yet the message she'd left with the soldiers sounded as if she knew where Zelia was. How? Karrell was a stranger here; she knew less about Ormpetarr than even Arvin did. She'd have no idea which inn Zelia might have chosen to stay at—

Arvin stiffened. Zelia was an agent of House Extaminos, a trusted employee of Lady Dediana. She wouldn't stay at an inn.

She'd stay at the ambassador's residence.

That was where Karrell went.

His exhaustion suddenly forgotten, Arvin hurried from the room.

Arvin approached the ambassador's residence warily, his feet squelching on melting snow. If he was right in his guess that Zelia was staying here, he didn't want to run into her in the street. He pulled his hood up and tugged it down over his forehead to hide his wound. The lapis lazuli was still in place over his third eye; if Naneth scried on him again, he wanted to know it. Besides, removing the stone wouldn't accomplish much. Though the cut on his forehead had scabbed over completely, hiding the stone from view, Zelia would quickly realize what had prompted such a wound. Even with several days' worth of stubble shadowing Arvin's face, she'd recognize him.

He stared at the ambassador's residence from the shadow of an arched gate down the street. Several lights were on inside the building, and figures moved busily back and forth, their silhouettes passing across the draped windows. A large cargo wagon was pulled up in front of the main gate. The wagon was already half filled with boxes, rolled-up rugs, and furniture; slaves hurried back and forth from the residence, loading it.

It looked as though Ambassador Extaminos was beating a hasty retreat from Ormpetarr. Had he heard what was happening at the palace?

Four militiamen in cobra-hood helmets stood guard over the wagon. Arvin recognized one of them by his prominent nose. He touched the crystal at his neck, whispering a prayer of thanks to Tymora for sending him good fortune. He still had a little energy left in his *muladhara*, but he didn't want to spend it on a charm unless he had to. Rillis, fortunately, responded to more mundane prods.

Arvin fished two silver pieces out of his coin pouch then walked toward the front gate of the residence, hailing Rillis by name. "I'm looking for Karrell—the woman who was with me when I spoke with Ambassador Extaminos. Have you seen her?"

The young militiaman shook his head.

Relief filled Arvin. Maybe Karrell had second thoughts about talking to Zelia. Then again, maybe Rillis hadn't been in a position to spot her. "How long have you been on watch?"

"All night," Rillis said with a wry look. "As usual."

"Always at the front gate?"

"Mostly," he said. He kicked at the slush. "The snow might be melting, but it's still been a damp, chilly night," he added with a wink.

Arvin noticed that Rillis wasn't shivering. He'd obviously been inside at least part of his watch, warming himself at the fire.

Rillis stared at the wound on Arvin's forehead. "What happened this time?" he asked. "Another naga?"

Arvin shook his head. "Nothing so exciting as that," he lied. "A thief tried to grab my coin pouch. He cut me."

Rillis nodded sympathetically. "Good thing he wasn't aiming lower," he said, drawing a hand across his throat.

Arvin nodded gravely. He stepped closer and opened his hand just enough to reveal the two coins. "There's another woman I'm also looking for. A yuan-ti who serves House Extaminos, named Zelia. She has red hair, green scales, and a blue forked tongue. Have you seen her?"

Rillis arched an eyebrow. "One gorgeous woman isn't enough?" He started to laugh but faltered when he saw the glower in Arvin's eye. "The red-headed yuan-ti is here," he said quickly. "She's a guest of the ambassador."

Arvin glanced up at the residence. "Is she here now?"

Rillis rubbed his finger and thumb together. Arvin passed him the coins.

"Yes."

"Which room is she in?"

"Second floor. At the back. The second to last suite on the right." Rillis gave Arvin a tentative glance, his expression a mixture of greed and fear. "Do you . . . need me to get you inside?"

"That won't be necessary," Arvin answered.

Rillis looked relieved.

Arvin took two more coins from his pouch and passed them to Rillis. "If Karrell does show up and asks for Zelia," he instructed, "tell her that Zelia's *not* here. That she's somewhere else."

Rillis grinned as he took the coins. "Consider it done. But I'm only on duty until dawn. The ambassador has finally risen from his dream sleep, and he's in a hurry to leave; I'll be part of the escort accompanying him to the morning riverboat."

"Will Zelia be going with him?" Arvin asked. "Or will she be staying on at the residence?"

Rillis shrugged. "That's up to the new ambassador. He'll decide which slaves and militia—and which house guests—he wants to stay on."

"Thanks," Arvin said. "You've been a big help."

He walked down the street, turned a corner, and circled around the block to the street at the rear of the ambassador's residence. He walked the length of the building, glancing up at the residence only when the two militiamen who were standing out back weren't watching. The last two windows of the second floor were dark, but light glowed through the next two; that must have been Zelia's suite. The curtains on one of the windows had been drawn but not quite all the way; a slight gap remained. It was impossible, however, to see inside from this angle.

The militiamen watched Arvin as he walked the length of the block but lost interest in him as he turned the corner. Making his way to the rear of the building that was directly behind the ambassador's residence, he walked up a short flight of stairs to one of its doors. Pretending to be fitting a key into the lock, he glanced up and down the street. No one was watching. Then he activated the magic within his bracelet and climbed the wall.

Arvin swung himself up onto the roof. Crawling to the far side through patches of wet snow, he stared across the street at the window that had caught his attention a moment ago. Through the gap in its curtains he spotted Zelia. She was seated in a chair that had its side to the window. She was leaning forward in hungry anticipation, her forked tongue flickering through a smile that sent shivers through him. She'd smiled at Arvin in just the same way when she gloatingly told him about the seed she'd planted in his mind. She leaned forward more, gesturing at someone who sat opposite her.

A sudden dread filled him. Who was Zelia talking to?

He crawled farther along the rooftop, ignoring the discomfort of the slush that had soaked through his pants and shirt. No matter what angle he viewed the window from, however, he couldn't see the second person. Working his way back to his original position—a spot directly opposite the window—he sent his awareness into his third eye. He was taking an enormous chance by manifesting a power—if Zelia detected his psionics, he would give himself away—but he had to know if Karrell was inside.

As the energy stored in his third eye uncoiled, a thread of silver light spun out into the night, toward the window. It penetrated the glass and touched the curtain inside, weaving its way into the fabric. Then, one tiny tug at a time, it began to pull.

Slowly, the curtain eased back. After each tug, Arvin waited for several heartbeats, terrified that Zelia might hear the soft slide of the curtain on its rod or notice the gradually widening gap between the curtains. She didn't.

Finally, Arvin got a glimpse of the person she was talking to. It wasn't Karrell.

It was Naneth.

Arvin blinked in surprise. He'd expected Naneth to come to Ormpetarr in an attempt to recapture Glisena, but he'd also expected her to show up at the palace. He did not expect her to be here, inside the ambassador's home.

He had to find out what was going on.

With all that remained of the energy in his *muladhara*, he manifested one last power. Sparkles of light streamed out of the center of his forehead then curled around his head. With them came a heightened awareness. The lighted windows in the ambassador's residence became a babble of overlapping sounds; the lights elsewhere in the city, a distant hum. Even the stars in the night sky emitted a faint, crackling hiss.

Those, however, weren't the sounds Arvin was interested in.

He curled both of his hands into loose fists then held both of them up to his left eye, forming a tube. Through it, he peered at Zelia's window with his other eye shut. The waves of noise that had been pouring into his mind were stopped down to a trickle; now he "saw" only the sounds emanating from Zelia's room. He had to shift, slightly, to screen out the light from the hearth, which filled his mind with a sharp crackle. The fire had been well stoked; like all yuan-ti, Zelia liked her rooms at basking temperature. At last he managed to narrow his field of view to include just Zelia and Naneth. As he did, their voices sprang into focus.

". . . to be done tonight," the midwife said.

"Why?" Zelia asked.

"Because Foesmasher has summoned his clerics," Naneth said urgently. "He's convinced *them* to do his dirty work. This time, the child will be killed."

Zelia arched an eyebrow. "Surely he wouldn't slay his own grandchild?"

Naneth snorted. "He doesn't have the same respect for life that Lady Dediana does. To him, the child is just a serpent. I've heard it said that he refers to it as 'the demon.'" She shook her head in a parody of sadness, sending a ripple through her double chin.

Zelia lounged in her chair, her expression confident. "I'll get the girl out."

"How?" Naneth asked. "Glisena's chamber is warded against serpents."

Zelia smiled. "There are ways of getting around wards."

Naneth leaned forward, pudgy hands on her knees. "Just so long as you can do it. Remove her from the palace, and I'll teleport her to Hlondeth."

"Directly to the House Extaminos compound?" Zelia asked.

Naneth nodded. "Yes. Tell your mistress the girl will be delivered, as promised."

Arvin waited, tense with anticipation.

"I'll contact you as soon as I have her," Zelia promised.

"This needs to be done sooner, rather than later," Naneth urged. "As swiftly as you can."

"Swift as a striking serpent," Zelia agreed with a hiss of laughter. She leaned forward as she spoke, playing with a strand of her long red hair. It parted, revealing a finger-long chunk of crystal that hung from a silver hoop in her ear. Judging by its faint glow, it was a crystal capacitor or power stone—which was strange, since Zelia had always before scorned the use of psionic "crutches."

Something must have made Naneth nervous; the midwife raised a hand to her temple to wipe sweat from her forehead.

Zelia settled back into her chair, staring at Naneth through slit eyes. Her tongue flickered out of her mouth, as if she were savoring the midwife's discomfort.

Naneth wiped her temple, glanced in the direction of the hearth, and moved her chair a little farther from it. Arvin gave a mental nod; he felt the same discomfort in the yuan-ti's overheated rooms.

"Will you be staying on in Sespech once our business is concluded?" Naneth asked.

Zelia smiled. "Only for a few days," she said. "Then we really must leave."

"Who is 'we'?" Naneth asked.

Zelia smiled. "You'll find out—seven days from now." A soft, satisfied hiss of laughter followed.

Arvin's eyes widened as he realized what he'd just witnessed. Naneth hadn't been wiping sweat from her brow. She'd been wiping away a sheen of ectoplasm. Zelia had just seeded her. The earring—a power stone—must have contained a copy of the mind seed power.

The power that Arvin thought he had stripped from her for good, six months ago.

Arvin closed his eyes, blocking out both sight and sound. Bile rose in his throat; he swallowed it down. He could guess what must have happened. He'd relayed his warnings about Naneth being one of Sibyl's minions to Tanju, who in turn had conveyed them to Lady Dediana. And she, in turn, had passed the information along to Zelia, her agent in Sespech. Together, no doubt, with an order: that Zelia try, once again, to plant a spy within Sibyl's ranks.

Thunder grumbled from a clear sky: the laughter of Hoar. Naneth had placed a demon in Glisena's womb, and Zelia had just planted a mind seed in the midwife. The god of poetic justice was, beyond a doubt, pleased.

Arvin shuddered.

He watched as the two women in the room exchanged good-byes. Zelia promised to use another sending to contact Naneth the instant Glisena was out of the palace. Naneth nodded then teleported away.

Zelia turned and stared out the window, her eyes flashing silver as she manifested a power. Fearful that she would detect him, Arvin immediately ended his power. For several terrible moments he held his breath, bracing himself for her attack. Then he saw Zelia shiver.

An annoyed look on her face, she swayed to the window and yanked the curtains shut.

Slowly, Arvin let out his breath. Then he scrambled to the far side of the building and climbed back down to the street. He hurried up the road, casting several glances behind him, but saw no signs of pursuit. Relieved, he turned his steps toward the Fairwinds Inn.

As he walked, he pondered what he'd just seen and heard. He didn't believe for a moment that Zelia would attempt to remove Glisena from the palace—she'd just wanted to distract Naneth while she seeded her. That seed, however, would take seven days to blossom. And long before those seven days ended, Naneth would face Sibyl's wrath for having failed to deliver the pregnant Glisena to Hlondeth. What good would Zelia's mind seed be then?

He reached the inn and—after one more careful glance around— let himself in through the back door. He climbed the three flights of stairs that led to the attic room that Karrell had rented. As he reached the landing, he heard sounds of movement behind her door. Karrell had at last returned, it seemed. He prayed she'd been unsuccessful in finding Zelia. As he started to reach for the latch, he heard a wooden clatter that sounded like a chair falling over inside the room. It was immediately followed by a whispered oath, spoken by a male voice.

Arvin summoned his dagger into his glove and flattened himself against the wall beside the door. With his free hand, he reached into his pocket for the monkey's fist he'd used to waylay the satyr. A heartbeat later, the latch turned. The door eased open and a man started to back through it. Arvin recognized the fellow at once: the gaunt-faced rogue with the ice dagger who had waylaid him four days ago. The rogue was bent over, carrying something: an unconscious woman. A second man, still inside the room, held her feet. Even though both the room and hallway were in darkness, Arvin recognized their victim at once by her long hair and hugely pregnant belly.

Glisena. What in the Nine Hells was she doing *here?*

Arvin sprang forward, simultaneously slamming the hilt of his dagger into the temple of the rogue while hurling the monkey's fist in through the door at the second man. The intricate knot unraveled as it flew through the air, strands of it lashing the second man's arms against his sides. The skinny rogue, meanwhile, staggered sideways down the hall under the force of Arvin's blow. Both men dropped their burden at once; Glisena fell to the floor with a heavy thud.

There was no time to check if she was hurt. Arvin's blow had stunned the rogue instead of rendering him unconscious, and the second man—a beefy-looking fellow with a wind-reddened face and greasy hair—managed, despite his bonds, to twist up the loaded crossbow that hung from his belt. Arvin heard the trigger click and leaped aside from the doorway. The bolt snagged his cloak. The first rogue recovered and rushed down the hall, thrusting with his ice dagger. Arvin parried, and the point of the weapon scratched his left forearm. A shock of cold swept through his arm from his elbow to the tip of his abbreviated little finger. His hand went numb, and he dropped his dagger.

Greasy Hair was out of commission inside the room; the monkey's fist had wound its strands around his legs as well, and he'd fallen to the floor. But the first rogue had recovered enough to press home his attack. He feinted with his ice dagger, driving Arvin away from the weapon he'd just dropped. Arvin backed down the short hallway until the wall was at his back then put a deliberately worried look on his face.

The rogue lunged.

"*Redditio!*" Arvin cried, and his magical dagger flew up from the floor toward his ungloved hand. He caught it as the rogue completed his lunge; the ice dagger scored a line across Arvin's side as he twisted, tearing his shirt. Gasping from the sudden cold—it felt as though an ice-cold hand had clenched his guts—Arvin completed his twist and slammed his own weapon home. It sank to the hilt in the rogue's back.

The rogue went down. He fell to the floor, gurgling like a man whose lungs were filled with fever-fluid. Then he coughed a spray of blood. He wouldn't live long.

Arvin stood on the rogue's wrist and plucked the ice dagger out of his hand then glanced through the doorway at the second man. The fellow had strained against his magical bindings until the cords cut deep grooves into the flesh of his arms and legs, but the ensorcelled twine was holding.

Transferring both daggers to his gloved hand, Arvin touched his side. Crumbles of frozen blood came away from the wound, causing it to bleed slightly. Like the cut on his arm, it was no more than a scratch. "Nine lives," he whispered.

Inside the room, on the table, was a mug of ale. Arvin was tempted to take a hefty swallow but decided against it. He didn't want the rogues thinking his bravery needed a crutch. He glared down at the trussed man.

"It wasn't my idea," the fellow whined. He jerked his head at the rogue who lay dying in the hall. "Lewinn was the one who wanted to cut you out of the deal. He said we could keep the diamonds for ourselves. I said, 'No, Lewinn, we should deal fairly with the mind mage,' but he wouldn't listen. He—"

"Shut up," Arvin said.

Greasy Hair did.

The wounded rogue exhaled one last, gurgling breath then was still. Arvin grabbed his ankles and dragged him inside the room. He eased the door shut—so far, the other occupants of the inn hadn't reacted to the sounds of the fight, and he wanted to keep it that way—then knelt beside Glisena. Her eyes were closed, but her chest rose and fell evenly. Arvin lightly patted her cheek and called her name, but she didn't wake up.

"What have you done to her?" Arvin asked.

"She's drugged," Greasy Hair answered. His voice matched the mental voice Arvin had listened in on earlier, when the skinny rogue had forced him into the cooper's workshop.

Arvin frowned down at Glisena. "How did—"

"It was Lewinn's idea," Greasy Hair interrupted. "He posed as the innkeeper and brought her the ale, and—"

"How did you know she was here?" Arvin asked, glad he'd resisted the urge to drink.

"Lewinn spotted her, looking out the window. That's how we knew you had her." Greasy Hair paused. A too-innocent expression appeared on his face. "Listen, mind mage, the diamonds are in my pocket. Untie me, and I'll give them to you. The diamonds for the girl, just like we agreed, and our dealings will be over. All right?"

Arvin ignored him. He stood, thinking. Doubtless it had happened just the way Greasy Hair described. But how had Glisena wound up in Karrell's room?

It was possible—though it bordered on the miraculous—that

Zelia had found a way to spirit Glisena out of the palace in the time it had taken Arvin to walk back to the inn. Could she have found a way past the wards and plucked Glisena out from under the very eyes of nine powerful clerics—ten, counting Marasa—and a watchful baron?

Possible, but hardly likely.

Unless Karrell had been the one to get Glisena out.

Karrell looked human enough; maybe she'd fooled the wards. And she had access to the palace. She might have been able to charm the clerics, to steal Glisena away and bring her here, to the room at the inn.

Whatever was going on, Arvin needed to get Glisena out of here.

Scooping the mug of ale off the table, he grabbed the rogue's greasy hair and wrenched his head back. "Drink it," he growled.

Greasy Hair struggled to wrench his head aside. "The diamonds aren't really in my pocket," he gasped. "But I can get them for you. Let me—"

Arvin poured the ale down his throat.

The man sputtered then swallowed. His eyes glazed then rolled—and he went limp.

Arvin pricked the fellow's arm with his dagger: no response. Greasy Hair wasn't feigning unconsciousness. Arvin spoke the command word that re-knotted the monkey's fist and shoved it back in his pocket. Then he reached inside his shirt for the brooch the baron had given him. He pinned it to the front of the thin rogue's shirt, where it was sure to be spotted. That would give Naneth something to puzzle over, if she came to claim Glisena and found one of the "baron's men" dead on the floor, next to an unconscious rogue.

Arvin removed the ice dagger's sheath from the dead rogue's belt, slid the weapon into it, and tucked it into his boot. Then he bent down and carefully picked up Glisena.

She was lighter than he'd expected—and cooler; her body no longer radiated heat. The drug the rogues had tricked her into drinking must have dampened her fever. It also seemed to have quieted the demon. Glisena's bulging stomach pressed up against Arvin's; he could no longer feel the demon kicking.

Arvin crept down the stairs, Glisena in his arms. He eased open the door at the bottom and peered out into the street. The street was deserted, except for a lone figure far down the block, walking toward the inn. Something about the person made Arvin uneasy; a second glance told him he'd been right to trust his instincts. The person moved with a swaying motion that instantly told Arvin her race: yuan-ti.

Zelia.

And she was moving toward the inn. Had she spotted him?

Arvin closed the door and hurried in the only other direction available: through the inn's common room, which had closed for the night. With Glisena in his arms, he wound his way between the tables, toward the inn's front door. Once again he looked cautiously outside. This time the street was empty.

Arvin hurried up the street. As he ran, slipping on patches of slush, he activated the lapis lazuli and visualized the one person he'd not yet contacted with it today who might be able to help: Marasa. Her face came into focus in his mind at once: drawn, worried-looking, and pale. Her left hand was raised, evoking Helm; her lips moved in prayer. Her eyes widened as a mental image of Arvin formed in her mind's eye.

Marasa, he thought, hailing her. *I found Glisena. She's unconscious; I'm carrying her back to the palace from the Fairwinds Inn. Send help. Hurry!*

Marasa's eyes widened in surprise. She glanced down then up at Arvin. *That's not possible*, she thought. *Glisena's here. I've been by her side all. . . .* Suddenly, her expression grew wary. One last thought—only half-directed at Arvin, but it came through anyway—drifted through her mind: *Is this a trick?* Then the sending was broken.

Arvin slowed and stared down at the woman in his arms. Glisena was still at the palace? If this wasn't Glisena, who *was* it? He glanced around, spotted a sheltered doorway up the street, and stepped into it. With one hand, he undid the fastenings of his cloak, letting it fall to the ground. He spread it out with his foot then lowered the unconscious woman onto it. Then, closing his eyes so he could concentrate, he ran his fingertips across her face.

It took several moments of intense concentration for him to feel what was truly there. The face felt broader than Glisena's, and flatter. And the hair, when he ran it through his fingers, was wavy, not straight. And the ears. . . .

Yes. There it was. The woman's left earlobe was pierced, the piercing filled with an earring of carved stone.

"Karrell," Arvin said in a stunned whisper.

She'd done an amazing job of transforming her appearance. She hadn't polymorphed herself—that would have fooled Arvin's fingers, as well as his eyes. She must have used some sort of illusion. He touched her hair a second time and felt what he'd expected: a gritty powder. Back in Hlondeth, one of the assassins who had commissioned a magical rope from Arvin had used a similar magical powder. By sprinkling a pinch of it on his head, he could change his appearance to that of anyone he liked. He'd actually gloated about how he'd used the powder to assume the appearance of a woman's husband then stabbed the woman in front of her own daughter. The husband had been charged with the crime—and executed in the pits with his daughter watching and cursing his name.

Arvin was glad he wasn't working for the Guild anymore.

He stared down at Karrell, shaking his head. Whatever game she'd been playing had been a dangerous one. The rogues had interrupted it, Tymora be praised.

Arvin idly scratched his forehead. The scab was starting to itch again.

His hand froze in mid-scratch as he realized it wasn't the wound. That tickling sensation was Naneth scrying on him.

And if she could see him, she could see Karrell. Who still looked like Glisena.

Arvin cursed his ill luck. Why had Naneth chosen this precise moment to scry on him? If she recognized the spot where he was crouching, she might appear at any moment.

He glanced wildly around. Just a short distance up the street, in the intersection, was one of the statues of Helm's gauntlet. Maybe, if he was quick enough. . . .

Arvin scooped Karrell up and ran toward the gauntlet. Naneth's scrying ended when he was partway there. He scrambled up onto the dais and slapped his bare hand against the gauntlet. "Come on," he gasped, looking around for one of the clerics who was supposed to materialize when the gauntlet's protection was invoked. "Come *on*."

He heard a faint pop behind him: air being displaced as a person teleported. He turned, expecting to see one of the Eyes.

It was Naneth, standing perhaps a hundred paces away, beside the doorway Arvin had just bolted from.

Then Zelia appeared from around a corner, holding a piece of parchment in one hand.

With a sinking heart, Arvin recognized it as the drawing Karrell had made of him. The one he'd crumpled up, thrown into the fireplace, and forgotten.

Zelia had found it.

"Arvin," she said as she walked with slithering steps toward Arvin. "We meet again. You look unusually healthy . . . for a dead man." Laughter hissed softly from her lips.

No, not laughter. That hissing meant she was manifesting a power: a psionic attack. And Arvin had no energy left in his *muladhara* to counter it.

He tensed, but the mental agony he was bracing against didn't manifest. Then he realized that the gauntlet was protecting him. Zelia couldn't attack him. Not here.

He shifted Karrell in his arms so that her limp hand also touched the gauntlet. They were protected, for the moment, against spells. But if Naneth used a spell that wasn't directly hostile—if she got close enough to touch Karrell and teleport away with her, for example—they'd be in trouble.

"There you are," Zelia said to Naneth, gesturing at Arvin and Karrell. "The girl. As promised."

Naneth thanked her with a silent nod then walked briskly toward them.

A second faint pop sounded, right next to Arvin. Relief swept through him as he saw the newcomer's red cloak and brightly polished breastplate, emblazoned with the eye of Helm.

"The baron's daughter!" Arvin gasped, shifting Karrell so the cleric could see her face. "She's in danger."

Out of the corner of his eye, he saw Naneth break into a run. For a large woman, she moved surprisingly fast. "Detain that man!" she screamed. "He's an agent of Chondath. He's kidnapping the baron's daughter."

The cleric frowned then raised his gauntlet, turning the eye on its palm toward Arvin.

Arvin answered the question before the cleric even asked it. "I serve

Lord Foesmasher," he said. As he spoke, a tingle swept through him: the gauntlet's truth-enforcing magic. He jerked his head at Naneth. "That woman's a sorcerer—an enemy of Foesmasher."

Naneth's hands were up, her fingers weaving a spell.

"Teleport us to the palace," Arvin shouted. "Now!"

The cleric had been summoning his weapon—a mace-shaped glow that had half-materialized in his fist. The glow vanished, and he clamped a hand on Arvin's wrist.

As he did, Naneth completed her spell. In the area next to the dais, up suddenly became down. Arvin fell into the air, legs flailing. Karrell tumbled from his arms. The cleric was still holding onto Arvin's wrist and was praying—a prayer Arvin recognized, though he'd heard it only once before, when the yuan-ti ambassador had been teleported away by the clerics in Mimph.

"Wait!" Arvin shouted. With his free hand, he twisted violently, trying to catch Karrell. He caught hold of her ankle as he had a dizzying glimpse of Naneth on the dais below, casting another spell while Zelia hissed furiously, manifesting a power.

Tendrils of thought wiggled their way into his mind like tiny serpents. Hissing, they slithered through his mind, tearing with their fangs at his thoughts. He felt his mind begin to fray, and with each strand that parted, his body became weaker. One leg went limp, his left arm suddenly stopped responding to his thoughts, his head lolled back on a weakened neck—and the fingers of his right hand, the one that was gripping Karrell's ankle, grew limp as severed strings. He tried to keep hold of her, but felt his fingers slipping, slipping. . . .

Naneth gloated up at him, reaching for Karrell with her pudgy fingers, while Zelia hissed with laughter.

"No," Arvin gasped. With his last bit of strength, he forced his thumb and one finger to close around Karrell's ankle—just as Zelia hit him with a massive thrust of psionic energy that smashed into his mind like a fist. Reeling, still falling upward, he caught a glimpse of her savoring his defeat with her forked tongue.

And the street vanished as the cleric teleported Arvin away.

❧

Arvin groaned and rolled over. He ached in several places, there were sharp pains in his side and along his left arm, and his mind felt as though it were full of holes—the aftermath of Zelia's psionic attack.

The memory jolted him fully awake.

Karrell! Had she—

He looked wildly around. He was in the same chapel in which he had spoken to Foesmasher two nights ago—inside the palace. Relief rushed through him as he spotted Karrell farther along the bench he was lying on, just beyond his feet. The effects of the magical powder had worn off; she looked like herself again. She'd been teleported back with him. She was safe.

He touched the crystal at his neck. "Nine lives," he whispered. He glanced around, but saw they were alone in the room. Oddly, the cleric who had teleported them here had just left them. Or perhaps it was not so odd, given the events that were unfolding elsewhere in the palace. Arvin wondered if Glisena had given birth yet.

Karrell's chin was on her chest, her body slumped with exhaustion. She seemed to be sleeping, albeit restlessly. Her fingers twitched, as if plucking at something. Then she groaned in her sleep.

Fear swept through Arvin then, chilling him like an icy wind. Was Karrell having a nightmare—one drawn from the dark pit of Zelia's memories? Fingers trembling, he nudged her awake.

Karrell's eyes flew open. "Arvin! You have recovered. The cleric assured me you would, but I was worried, even so. He told me that I had been drugged, that Naneth had attacked you and—"

Arvin pulled her closer to him and anxiously ran his fingers over her temples, her hair, searching for traces of ectoplasm. He found none, but that meant nothing. If she had been seeded, it had been done some time ago.

"What are you doing?" Karrell asked.

"Did you meet with Zelia?"

Karrell pulled away, a wary expression on her face. "I said nothing that would give you away. My ring prevented her from learning about you."

"That doesn't matter—not now," Arvin said. He laughed bitterly. "Zelia knows I'm alive. She showed up at the inn, just as I was carrying you out. She saw me." He winced and rubbed his aching head. "She nearly killed me."

Karrell glanced away. She was silent for several moments. "I am sorry," she said at last.

"'Sorry' isn't going to help me now," Arvin said. He shook his head. "What in the Abyss were you *thinking?*"

Karrell met his eye. "That Zelia might know where Sibyl is hiding. And I was right. She—"

"Damn it, Karrell," Arvin exploded. "Zelia might have seeded you."

"Yes," Karrell said gravely. "I know. But it was a calculated risk. You found a way to root out a mind seed once before; I was confident in your ability to do it again, if need be." Then her voice lowered. "I just wish you had an equal confidence in me."

Arvin sighed and ran his hands through his hair. "Were you dreaming just now?"

"Yes." She frowned. "Why?"

"Was the dream. . . ." He searched for the right word. He had found Zelia's memories foreign, disturbing—but perhaps Karrell wouldn't. She was a yuan-ti, after all, and female. "Did it seem to be a memory from someone else's life?"

"Ah. You are still worried about the mind seed. No, it was not Zelia's dream. It was one I have been having for many months. A troubling dream, in which I am bound tightly and cannot escape."

"Your own dream, then," Arvin said, feeling slightly relieved.

"No, not mine. Not mine alone."

"What do you mean?" Arvin asked sharply.

Karrell tilted her head and stared at the window. Pale winter sunlight shone through the stained glass, causing the blue-and-gold eye of Helm to glow. "I have talked to other yuan-ti. Many of us have been having troubling dreams. Dreams of someone who is embracing us who will not let go, or of being bound by ropes, or even—most strange, for a yuan-ti—of being a mouse, held tight by a serpent. No one knows what they mean. Not even Zelia."

Arvin nodded, completely at a loss. Whatever the dreams meant, they had little to do with their immediate problem. "If you start having strange thoughts while you're awake, tell me," he said. "Or strange dreams—stranger than the ones you've just described, I mean."

"I will," Karrell said with a grave nod. Then she said, "Tell me what happened. How did I come to be drugged?"

Arvin told her about the two rogues who hoped to sell "Glisena" to Chondath, about finding her unconscious in the room at the inn, and about trying to carry "Glisena" back to the palace, only to be confronted by Naneth. He also told her about their narrow escape, thanks to the cleric.

She listened, nodding.

Arvin paused. "So what were you doing, disguised as Glisena?"

"It was Zelia's idea," Karrell said.

Arvin waited, arms folded across his chest. He could tell, already, that he wasn't going to like the explanation. "Start from the beginning. Tell me all about your meeting. Don't leave out any details."

"I met with Zelia at the ambassador's residence," Karrell said. "I told her I was an agent of Yranil Suzur, *ssthaar* of the Jennestas—a ruler who, like Dediana Extaminos, is wary of Sibyl's rise to power. Zelia agreed to speak with me."

"She agreed to meet with a complete stranger?"

Karrell's eyes lighted mischievously. "I think she found me . . . charming."

Arvin's eyebrows rose. "You charmed Zelia? I'm impressed."

"We spoke about Sibyl —about how dangerous she is. And yes, Zelia *does* know where Sibyl is hiding," Karrell continued. "As you guessed, she in Hlondeth. Sibyl has denned in an ancient temple beneath the city—a temple that was erected at the peak of the Serpentes Empire to honor the beast lord Varae, an aspect of Sseth. The temple was abandoned and forgotten long before Hlondeth was even built, but nobles of House Extaminos rediscovered it two years after Lord Shevron's death. They briefly worshiped there, and it was abandoned again. Sibyl, together with her followers, has turned it into a fully fledged temple once more."

"How did Zelia discover this?" Arvin asked.

Karrell gave a graceful shrug. "One of House Extaminos's spies learned it."

Arvin wondered if it had been another of Zelia's mind seeds. "Zelia might have been lying to you."

"She might have," Karrell agreed. "But to what end? She would have been foolish to throw away the opportunity I offered—an alliance with a group that is also working against Sibyl."

"Zelia breaks alliances as quickly as she makes them," Arvin countered. "Still, go on. You haven't explained why you were impersonating Glisena."

"To lure Naneth to me," Karrell said. "Zelia gave me the powder, and suggested I play the part of Glisena. She said she would contact Naneth and promise to deliver 'Glisena' to her—and ensure that Naneth teleported me to the Extaminos palace in Hlondeth. There, House Extaminos's spellcasters would subdue Naneth. And I would use a second pinch of the powder to change my appearance to match Naneth's. Then I would infiltrate the temple where Sibyl lairs, and—"

"Did Zelia give you a second pinch of powder?" Arvin asked.

"No."

"You *trusted* her? After what she did to me?"

Karrell winced. "I had to take the chance. The lives of thousands of people—"

"What about this person?" Arvin asked, thumping a hand against his chest. It felt hollow. "You were going to leave without even saying good-bye."

"There was no time," Karrell said, her dark eyes flashing. "And I would have returned. Once I had secured the Circled Serpent and carried it to a place of safety, I would have come back to you."

"If you'd lived," Arvin said bitterly. "And if you didn't, I'd never have known what had happened to you."

She lifted a hand to his face. "You would have contacted me," she said. Her fingers lightly touched the scab on his forehead. "With your stone. I would have told you, then, where I was."

Arvin turned away from her touch.

"Do you want the truth?" she asked.

Arvin glanced reluctantly back at her.

"I feared that you would try to talk me out of it," she said. She sighed. "And that you would succeed. I could not run that risk. Too much is at stake."

Arvin nodded. He stared at Helm's gauntlet for several long moments then turned to Karrell. "Zelia played you for a fool," he told her. "When she told you that you would be the one to infiltrate Sibyl's lair, she was lying."

Karrell tossed her head. "Of course you would say that."

"I'm not just *saying* that," Arvin told her. "I know that. I spied on Zelia, earlier tonight. Probably just after you met with her. When she was talking to Naneth."

"And?" Karrell prompted.

"Zelia planted a mind seed in her."

Karrell absorbed this news without reacting. "I thought Zelia might do that," she said evenly. "And I knew it would anger you, if you found out. What I do not understand is why you feel any sympathy for the midwife. After what she did to the baron's daughter—"

"I *don't* feel sympathy for her," Arvin said. "Naneth deserves what's coming to her." He shuddered, remembering the terrible headaches, the nightmarish dreams, the impulses that were not his own—impulses that had, just before the mind seed was due to blossom, driven him to kill an innocent man. "The point is that Zelia was using you to further her own ends."

"Zelia no more used me than I used her," Karrell countered. "I sought her out. I asked her to help me get close to Sibyl, and that is what she did." She frowned. "Or rather, what she tried to do. Our plan would have worked, if the rogues had not interfered."

"You're lucky they did," Arvin said. "Zelia never would have let you impersonate Naneth."

Karrell's eyes narrowed. "Why are you so certain of that?"

"Zelia planted a mind seed in me—remember?" He tapped his temple. "I know how her mind works. Zelia doesn't delegate—she does the job herself. Or rather, her mind seeds do. She probably would have let Naneth teleport you to the House Extaminos compound—but that's as far as your part in it would go. She'd let Naneth report to Sibyl that 'Glisena' had been delivered—thus ensuring that Naneth remained in Sibyl's good graces—then would have found a way, somehow, to stall the midwife for seven days, until the mind seed blossomed. You, meanwhile, would become superfluous—and would be disposed of."

"It is a convincing argument," Karrell said. "Except for one point. Why would Zelia kill me? Why throw away a valuable ally?"

"She wouldn't have thrown you away," Arvin said grimly. "She'd have seeded you."

"Ah." Karrell remained silent for several moments. She stared out through the chapel's stained-glass window. Outside, a light snow had begun to fall. "Thank you for risking your life to save me," she said at last. "If I had listened to your warnings. . . ." A tear slid down her cheek. She brushed it angrily away. "It is just that so many lives are at stake. So much is resting on my shoulders. If Sibyl finds the second half of the Circled Serpent and uses it to unlock the door, the Night Serpent will escape."

"And the world will come to an end," Arvin whispered—believing it, this time. He held out his arms questioningly. Karrell nodded, and he embraced her. They kissed.

Several moments later she broke off the kiss and squared her shoulders. "At least Zelia has given me a starting point," she said. "The location of Sibyl's den. That is where the stolen half of the Circled Serpent must be." She met Arvin's eye. "I will go there," she said. "Alone, if need be. Unless. . . ."

Arvin hesitated. Recovering ancient artifacts wasn't what he'd signed on for, and the people Karrell hoped to save were strangers from a distant land. Whether they lived or died meant nothing to him personally. But the fact that they would die to further Sibyl's plans did.

"I'll do it," he said, taking her hand. "I'll come with you to Hlondeth, and help you find the Circled Serpent. But before we go anywhere, I need to meditate and restore my energies." He heard Karrell's stomach growl and gave her a brief smile. "And it sounds as though you need to eat." He laid a hand gently on her stomach. "Or as though someone does."

Karrell lifted his hand to her lips and kissed it then rose to her feet. "I will find a servant," she said. "Someone who can bring us food."

Arvin nodded and watched her leave. Then he stripped off his shirt and pants, preparing himself for his meditations. He lowered himself to the floor and assumed the *bhujanga asana.* The stone tiles were cold against his bare legs and palms; the sensation helped him ignore his aches and pains, helped him focus.

Toward the end of his meditations, he heard hurried foot-steps in the corridor outside the chapel. He rose to his feet as a soldier strode into the room. The soldier was one of those who had been standing vigil outside Glisena's chamber earlier—a man with short black hair and eyes as gray as steel. His eyes were wide and worried.

"The baron demands your presence," he announced. "At once."

Arvin looked around. "Where is Karrell? Have you seen her? She—"

"There is no time," the soldier said, gesturing impatiently. "High Watcher Davinu needs you."

Arvin nodded as he pulled on his shirt and pants. He told himself not to worry—Karrell was probably eating in the kitchen or somewhere else in the palace. She wouldn't abandon him a second time. Not after he'd promised to help her. He'd find her later, after the clerics had dealt with the demon.

As he followed the soldier from the room, he wondered what it would be like to listen in on a demon's thoughts as it was being born.

He shuddered. He was certain the experience wasn't going to be a pleasant one.

CHAPTER 15

As Arvin strode along behind the soldier, he glanced this way and that, looking for Karrell. He didn't think she'd desert him a second time, especially after he'd at last convinced her how dangerous Zelia was, but a lingering worry still nagged at him.

They passed the practice hall where servants were busy oiling and cleaning the equipment, and several rooms in which still more servants cleaned fireplaces, swept the floors, and dusted furniture. Arvin was amazed to see life at the palace apparently carrying on as if nothing untoward was happening. Only the clerics, it seemed, knew of the life-and-death struggle Glisena was facing.

They passed the council chamber where Arvin had first spoken to Foesmasher, following his arrival in Ormpetarr. Arvin glanced inside and saw two women polishing the many shields that hung on the wall. One of them caught his eye at once: a middle-aged woman with graying hair. It took Arvin a moment to remember where he had seen her before, but when he did, he halted abruptly.

The woman had been at Naneth's house, the night Foesmasher had burst into it, searching for the midwife—she'd been the one the soldiers had taken away for questioning. It seemed just a little coincidental that she should turn out to be one of the palace servants.

"I need to speak to someone," Arvin told the soldier. "It won't take long—no more than a moment."

The soldier grabbed Arvin's elbow. "There's no time. Lord Foesmasher—"

"Will want to hear what I'm about to find out," Arvin finished for him. "That servant," he said, nodding into the room, "is somehow involved in what's happened to Glisena. I intend to find out what she knows."

The soldier stared at him a moment, indecision in his eyes. Then his hand fell away. "Just be quick," he said.

"I will."

Arvin entered the council chamber and walked to the far end of the room, pretending to be admiring the model ships that stood on the table. As he passed the two servants, he manifested the power that would let him listen in on their thoughts. Silver sparkles erupted from his forehead, vanishing even as the woman with the graying hair turned around. Her eyes had a distant expression, as if she were listening to some half-heard sound. When they focused on Arvin, she nodded and bobbed a curtsey.

The other servant—a girl in her teens, glanced over her shoulder then continued with her work. Her thoughts were superficial: musings about one of the stable hands—how handsome he was—and a slight irritation that the baron's guest had trod on her clean floor. Arvin focused instead on the thoughts of the older woman, the one he suspected of being Naneth's spy. She was worried about something, but not clearly articulating her fears.

Arvin would help her along.

He gestured for her to approach. She did, holding a rag that smelled of beeswax. So far, her thoughts were a mix of annoyance at having been interrupted and puzzlement about what Arvin could possibly want. She didn't remember him.

He leaned toward her and spoke in a low voice. "I know who you serve," he said.

The woman frowned. Of course he did, she thought. She served the baron. What did this man *really* want with her?

Arvin was impressed. If the servant was a spy, she was a good one. "I know why you were at Naneth's home, the other night," he continued. "About your . . . arrangement with her."

That made her eyes widen. And her thoughts begin to flow. Who was this man, and how did he know about Naneth? Would he tell her husband? She prayed to Helm that he wouldn't. Ewainn was so proud—he would crumble if he knew the fault had been his, all along. She'd thought he'd find out, when she'd been hauled before the Eyes for questioning four nights ago, but all they'd wanted to know, it turned out, was where the midwife was. And just as well, that Naneth had disappeared. Now she wouldn't have to pay the midwife—coin Ewainn would notice was missing, sooner or later. If he'd pressed her, she might have had to explain to Ewainn that he wasn't the one who quickened a child in her—that the midwife had used magic to do it.

Arvin struggled to keep his expression neutral. This woman was pregnant? He'd assumed, when he'd overheard her protest to the baron's soldiers that she was just one of Naneth's customers, that she had gone to the midwife's home to arrange for Naneth to deliver a daughter's child. With her graying hair, he'd taken her to be a pending grandmother.

"I don't know what you're talking about, my lord," she choked out at last.

"Yes, you do," Arvin said, more gently, this time. He glanced pointedly down at her stomach; it had a slight but unmistakable bulge. "When did Naneth cast the spell?"

Her hands twisted the rag. "A tenday and a hand ago."

Arvin glanced once more at her stomach. She was three months along, at least. "What date?" he asked.

"The fifth."

Arvin nodded. The same night the demon had been bound into Glisena's womb. The night Glisena, thinking her pregnancy merely hastened along, had fled the palace.

Arvin stared at the servant, thinking furiously. Should he tell her that the child in her womb was really that of Glisena and Dmetrio? Seven days from now, Naneth would be as good as dead. No one except Arvin would ever know the baby wasn't the serving woman's.

Until the first time it turned into a serpent.

How would the woman's husband react to that, Arvin wondered.

In the doorway, the soldier cleared his throat impatiently. "'At *once*,' the baron said. Not a tenday from now."

Arvin touched the servant's hand. "Your name?" he asked gently.

Why does he want to know? she thought in a panicky voice. But she answered obediently, as her years of servitude dictated. "Belinna."

"We'll talk again, Belinna. Later. In private. There's something about your child that you need to know. In the meantime, your secret is safe with me." Ending his manifestation, he strode back to the soldier.

As he once more followed the soldier down the hall, he wondered whether he should tell Glisena he'd located her child. It would certainly bolster her for the ordeal she was about to face, but it would result in anguish for Belinna when Glisena reclaimed her child. Belinna had already come to regard the infant inside her as her own, to love it. That much Arvin had seen in her eyes and heard in her thoughts.

But would she love it still when it turned out to be half serpent?

They reached Glisena's chamber, and the soldier rapped on the door. Magical energy sparkled around the lock. It was opened a moment later by a haggard-looking Foesmasher. He ushered Arvin into the room then closed the door.

Glisena no longer lay on her bed; now she was seated on a birthing chair. Davinu and the other clerics still stood in a circle around her, praying with voices that were nearly hoarse; Arvin wondered how long they could continue without sleep. The shields still floated in a circle, surrounding them, but they were moving more slowly. Every now and then one would bob toward the ground like the head of a horse that had run too far and too long then rise again.

Marasa sat on a stool next to the birthing chair, holding Glisena's hand. A knife lay on a low, cloth-draped table beside her. To cut the cord once the demon was born, Arvin supposed. The room smelled of blood; rags under the birthing chair were stained a bright red.

The baron began to pace back and forth behind them, thumping a fist against his thigh. Each time his daughter groaned, his jaw clenched. "Can't you do something for her pain?" he growled at Marasa.

"I already have," the cleric said in an exhausted voice.

As Glisena bore down, panting, Marasa's face grew pale. Her free hand pressed against her own stomach, and she shuddered. Arvin, watching, realized that she must have cast a spell that allowed her to draw Glisena's hurts into her own body. There was a psionic power that did something similar—it operated on the same principles as the fate link that Tanju had taught Arvin, except that the damage and pain could only be channeled to the psion, himself. Arvin had declined it as something he didn't really want to learn. At the time, he couldn't think of anyone he cared enough about to want to inflict that kind of pain on himself.

Marasa exhaled through clenched teeth then gestured at one of the clerics. He stepped out of the circle and held his left hand out, palm toward her. Magical energy crackled faintly in the air as he cast a spell. Marasa shook her head, like a dog shaking off water. Her shoulders straightened, and her face resumed its natural color.

The baron continued pacing.

Davinu turned as Arvin approached. "The demon is a breach birth," he said. "We will need to cut it free. But before we begin, I need to know what it's thinking. Use your mind magic."

Glisena groaned, and Marasa shuddered. Another cleric stepped forward and healed her. As Glisena panted, blood trickled down onto the rags beneath the birthing chair. She looked up at Arvin, her face glistening with sweat. There was terror in her eyes—she was afraid of dying—but also something more: a question.

Arvin squatted beside her. The words came unbidden to his lips. "I found the person you asked me about," he said quietly. "She—or he—is safe."

The lines of strain on Glisena's face eased, just a little. "She," she panted, a mother's certainty burning in her eyes. "Take . . . care of . . . her."

"No need," Arvin whispered fiercely. "You'll make it through this."

Glisena shook her head. "Promise. That you'll . . . take care . . ." she gasped.

Arvin touched her shoulder. "I promise."

The clerics gently lifted Glisena onto the bed, reforming their circle there. Marasa pulled her stool up next to the bed. Davinu opened Glisena's night robe, exposing her stomach. The lines Naneth had drawn on it were almost gone; only the faintest traces of white remained. Davinu picked up the knife. It was silver, the blade inlaid with gold in the shape of a staring eye: Helm's symbol.

Davinu held the knife out, and one of the clerics poured water over it from a silver chalice that also bore a stylized eye. Then he held it ready, waiting.

Arvin manifested his power. Sparkles of silver erupted from his third eye and drifted down onto Glisena. The thoughts of those in the room crowded in on him: Glisena's relief that Arvin had located her child, Marasa's fierce love for Glisena and grim determination to bear her pain, Davinu steeling himself for the surgery he was about to perform, and the other clerics' fervent prayers, all overlaid with a tight clench of fear. Davinu had given them careful instructions about what was to happen; the moment the blood cord was severed, he would banish the demon. Arvin expected to hear Foesmasher's thoughts as well—his anguish at seeing his "little dove" in such pain was clear for all to see—but something was shielding his thoughts. Was it a magical item, like Karrell's ring? Briefly, Arvin wondered where Karrell was—he hoped far from this part of the palace—then turned his mind back to the task at hand. Blotting out the overlapping babble of mental voices, he sent his consciousness deeper, and found the voice he'd dreaded hearing.

So tight, so confined . . . but I will be free soon. If only I had my swords, I would slash my way out.

Arvin shuddered. "It's wishing it had its sword," he reported. "No, swords," he corrected. "Plural."

Distantly, he heard the clerics murmuring to each other.

"A balor, then?" one asked.

"Too large," another answered. "And the horns—they would have torn—"

Ah. That's better. I can turn.

"It's turning," Arvin said.

Glisena screamed as her stomach bulged. Something flickered between her legs then drew inside her again; it looked like the tip of a tail.

Foesmasher whirled, one hand on his sword hilt, his face twisted with anguish. Marasa clapped a hand on Glisena's stomach, drawing the pain into herself. "Do it," she gritted up at Davinu. "Now. Before it—" Her face paled as another spasm of pain rushed into her.

Davinu touched Glisena's forehead with a fingertip. "Hold," he commanded.

Glisena's body stiffened. Her chest, however, still rose and fell. And her stomach heaved.

Davinu lowered the point of the knife to her belly then took a deep breath. He began to cut.

Foesmasher stood rigid, eyes locked on Glisena, barely breathing. One fist was white-knuckled on his sword hilt; the other was pressed against his mouth.

The other clerics crowded around the bed, hands extended toward Glisena, chanting. "Guardian of the innocent, lord of the unsleeping eye, watch and protect this girl in her time of need. . . ."

Blood sprayed onto Davinu's breastplate as he cut. The knife parted muscle, and something that glistened, and a layer of darker flesh that smelled of seared meat. Then came a rush of sulfurous-smelling liquid, and something could be seen writhing within. Arvin caught a glimpse of flailing arms and a long, serpentine tail.

Marasa groaned and swayed, nearly falling from her stool. One of the clerics steadied her.

I am wounded! It burns!

"You've cut the demon," Arvin said. "You've injured it."

Him again! Where is he? He will pay for this!

Arvin felt a chill run through him. He swallowed nervously. "It thinks . . . that I'm the one who hurt—"

Davinu passed the knife to one of the clerics and grabbed the edges of the gaping hole he'd just cut in Glisena's bloody flesh. "Now," he shouted. "Pull it free."

One of the clerics plunged his hand into the wound and seized hold of the demon. He pulled, his free hand braced against Glisena's pelvis, and the demon suddenly came free. It was tiny, the size of a newborn child—but instead of legs, it had a thrashing tail fully twice the length of its body. It had six arms, a full head of sulfur-yellow hair and an upper body like that of a mature woman, with full, round breasts.

"A marilith?" the cleric holding it gasped. He had grabbed it by one of its arms and fought to maintain his grip on the blood-slicked flesh. The demon twisted violently, its tail lashing and flicking blood. A twisted pink cord spiraled down from its naval into Glisena's stomach.

Davinu seized the cord and motioned for the other cleric to cut it with the knife.

The demon twisted, knocking the knife out of the cleric's hand. As the cleric scrambled after the knife, the demon wrapped its tail around Davinu's neck. "You annoy me," it said in a voice deeper and more malevolent than any mortal man's. Then it constricted.

Davinu clawed at the tail that was choking him. "Cut . . . cut. . . ."

Behind him, the shields that had been circling through the air clunked to the floor.

Foesmasher drew his sword and lunged forward, slashing at the cord, but missed. His blade whistled through the air, narrowly missing the cleric who was holding the demon.

The demon slithered out of the cleric's grip, then thrust all six of its hands out at once, as if fending off foes. Tendrils of shadowy darkness sprang into being around it and coiled themselves around its body. Foesmasher shoved the cleric aside and thrust at the demon, but the tendrils coiled around the weapon, halting it. The darkness slithered up the blade and licked at Foesmasher's bare hand, and the baron dropped his sword. Foesmasher backed away, his fingers moving creakily as he tried to force his hands to obey him.

These mortals want to play with swords? the demon mused, tightening its grip on Davinu's neck.

Davinu's face purpled.

Then swords they shall have.

"Swords!" Arvin shouted. "The demon's going to use magic to—"

A loud whirring noise filled the air as thousands of tiny blades sprang into existence, forming a curtain of steel around the bed and enclosing Glisena, Marasa, Arvin, and Davinu inside it. The remaining clerics screamed as the blades slashed into them. The whirling weapons clattered off their breastplates but sliced into exposed arms, legs, faces, and throats; five of the clerics fell, mortally wounded. The remaining three staggered back, screaming, bloody but still on their feet. Foesmasher, well behind them, was still struggling to pick up his sword; the demon's magic seemed to have sapped the strength from his arms.

Outside the chamber, fists pounded on the magic-locked door. Arvin could hear the muffled shouting of the soldiers.

The demon, its tail still wrapped around Davinu's throat, glanced around the room. *Which one*, it mused, *was I supposed to kill?* It gave a mental sigh. *All of them, I suppose.*

Davinu leaned back—dangerously close to the whirling blades—pulling the birthing cord taught. "Cord . . ." he choked. "C-c-c. . . ."

"You cannot banish me," the demon gloated in a voice like thick, bubbling blood. *Not while I am bound by—*

"*Shivis*," Arvin shouted, summoning his dagger into his glove and leaping forward. The demon tried to twist aside but failed. With a clean stroke, Arvin severed the birthing cord.

Davinu staggered, the demon still wrapped around his throat. Blades clattered against the armor that shielded his back; one sliced through an unprotected spot near his shoulder, leaving a deep slash. He recoiled from the whirling curtain of steel and struggled to speak the words of the prayer that would banish the demon—Arvin could hear them echoing in Davinu's thoughts —but there was no air in his lungs.

"Marasa," Arvin shouted. "Banish the demon!"

Marasa, busy with Glisena, ignored him. She threw something to the floor—the afterbirth she had just pulled out of Glisena's wound—and pressed the two edges of the wound together, chanting a healing spell. She realized the danger—Arvin could hear it in her thoughts—but without a restorative spell, *now*, Glisena would bleed to death. Just a moment more, and Marasa would cast the banishing spell.

A moment they didn't have.

Davinu collapsed, unconscious. The demon released him and coiled its tail under itself, rising like a rearing snake, the lowermost pair of its six hands resting on its hips.

Outside the barrier of whirling blades, the three clerics who still stood were casting spells. One shouted commands at the demon while holding out a gauntleted hand; another had summoned a shimmering mace into his hand. The third chanted a prayer that caused a glowing sword to rush toward the demon, but the weapon broke apart before reaching its target, scattering into shimmers of light. Foesmasher, meanwhile, had finally picked up his sword and a shield and was trying to force his way through the barrier of blades. They thudded into the shield with a loud clatter, driving him back.

The demon eyed them scornfully. *Time to even the odds*, it thought. It cocked its head to the side. *Should it be dretches, or hezrou?*

Marasa continued to chant her prayer, running a finger along Glisena's wound. Slowly, the flesh knit itself back together.

"Marasa!" Arvin screamed. "The demon's going to summon—"

The demon stared at Arvin with slit eyes. "So it was you whose voice I heard."

An invisible force yanked Arvin's dagger from his hand.

Let's play.

The dagger reversed itself and drove, point-first, at Arvin's chest, forcing him to twist aside. He shouted the command word that should have caused it to fly back to his hand, but the demon's magic was stronger. The knife refused to obey. The demon, meanwhile, had begun the spell that would summon others of its kind; Arvin could hear the words of its summoning whispering through its mind. He glanced wildly at Marasa—she still hadn't finished healing Glisena—and the dagger thrust at him, slicing a nick out of his left ear.

No time.

The demon would finish its summoning before Marasa could banish it.

The dagger flew toward him again; he batted it away with his left hand. The blade sliced a line through the ensorcelled leather glove.

His glove.

Leaping toward the demon, he slapped his gloved hand down on its tail. "*Shivis!*" he cried.

The demon disappeared into the glove.

For several moments, no one spoke. A muffled pounding continued on the door—the soldiers outside, trying to break in—while the blades continued to whir through the air. Then, all at once, they clattered to the floor, together with Arvin's dagger. The three clerics hurried toward Davinu. Foesmasher stood gaping, his sword hanging limply from his fist.

Arvin held up his gloved hand, turning it slowly back and forth. "It worked."

Marasa uttered the final word of her prayer, sealing the wound shut. She started to turn toward Arvin but then suddenly tensed. She leaned over Glisena, pressing one hand to the girl's throat. Glisena's chest was no longer moving. Her eyes stared glassily at the ceiling. "No," she howled. "By Helm's mercy, *no!*"

A distant voice whispered into Arvin's mind. *The binding ends. I am free!*

The glove bulged. One of its seams split.

Ah. An exit.

The palm of the glove humped upward.

Terrified, Arvin yanked the glove from his hand and hurled it to the floor. "Marasa!" he shouted, allowing his manifestation to end. Too much was happening too fast. "The demon's breaking free!"

Foesmasher stared at his daughter. A pained look on his face, he caught Marasa's eye. "Is she . . .?"

Marasa hung her head. Foesmasher gave a grief-stricken sob.

The glove tore open with a loud ripping sound as the demon erupted from it. In the space of a heartbeat, the demon expanded to its full size. Even coiled on its tail, it loomed over Arvin; his head was barely level with its chest. The tail was as thick as a man's waist, and each of the demon's arms was twice the length of a human's. Each hand held a long sword that was utterly black, save for a glowing line of red that edged its wavy blade. Where the weapons had come from, Arvin had no idea. Tendrils of darkness still wreathed the demon: the magic it had used to sap the baron's strength earlier.

The demon stared at Arvin, chuckling. A forked tongue, black as the swords, flickered out of its mouth, savoring his fear.

Arvin backed slowly away. "Marasa," he croaked. "The demon—"

The cleric with the glowing mace rushed the demon, swinging his weapon, and shouted Helm's name.

Swifter than the eye could follow, the demon flicked one of its hands. Its sword sliced through the cleric's neck. The cleric fell to the floor in an expanding pool of blood, his head hanging by a thread of flesh. The other two clerics exchanged nervous glances. Behind them, the door finally burst open. One of the soldiers rushed into the room, three others crowding behind him. His eyes widened at the sight of the demon.

As if awakened from a nightmare, Marasa sprang into action. "By

Helm's all-seeing might," she shouted, thrusting her palm out at the demon, "I order you to return to—"

The demon disappeared.

Arvin blinked. "Did you—"

The flat of a sword blade tapped him on the shoulder. He whirled.

The demon was behind him.

The four soldiers rushed it. With a whirlwind of motion, the demon cut them down.

Marasa spun on her heel, trying to bring her palm into line with the demon. "To return to the—"

This time the demon teleported behind her. Its tail lashed out, coiling around the cleric's torso like a whip. Then it squeezed.

"To—" Marasa grunted as the air was forced from her lungs.

The demon squeezed.

Roaring, Foesmasher slashed at the demon's tail with his sword. Once again, the tendrils of darkness blocked the weapon and slithered up it. This time, they sent Foesmasher staggering. He stumbled back on wobbly legs then fell.

Marasa struggled to draw air into her lungs, to finish her spell.

The demon squeezed tighter, hissing.

Arvin opened his suddenly dry mouth, closed it, opened it again, and—fighting down the fear that washed through him in chilling waves—at last found his voice. "Hey, demon!" he shouted. He reached down for the ice dagger that was still sheathed in his boot. He watched the tendrils of darkness that coiled around the demon as they shifted, seeking a pattern. "*I'm* the one you were supposed to kill."

He whipped his hand forward, throwing the dagger. Swift as thought, it flew toward the demon and caught it square in the chest. Cold exploded outward from the weapon, etching crackling lines of frost across the demon's bare skin.

The demon glanced down at the dagger that had buried itself to the hilt between its breasts. It laughed and plucked it out. "A pinprick," it rumbled. It snapped the blade in two and tossed the pieces aside. Then its eyes met Arvin's. "But even pinpricks annoy me."

Suddenly releasing Marasa, the demon slithered forward.

Marasa sagged, facedown, onto the floor.

Terrified, Arvin backed away from the approaching demon. Then he turned and ran. Leaping over the mangled remains of the soldiers, he sprinted out through the adjoining room and into the hall. Behind him, he heard the hiss of scales on stone. Soldiers ran toward him up the hall; he dodged around them, shouting at them to get out of the way. Metal clashed against metal and wet *thunks* sounded as the soldiers rushed up to attack the demon—and died. Arvin ran past the council chamber, past other rooms in which servants startled then screamed as they saw what was slithering after him, and past the practice hall.

As he ran, he manifested a sending. The image of Marasa formed in his mind's eye. She was being helped to her feet by someone Arvin couldn't see. She was shaky and unsteady—but alive. She startled as Arvin's face appeared in her mind.

I'm leading the demon to the chapel, Arvin sent, praying that the demon wasn't also capable of reading thoughts. *Get Foesmasher to teleport you there. I'll keep it busy until you can banish it.*

Arvin, she croaked. Even her mental voice sounded awful; absorbing Glisena's hurts had taken its toll. *I'll come as quickly as I can.*

"Little mouse," the demon taunted from behind Arvin. "I can smell your fear. What a tasty little morsel you will be."

A blade swished through the air just over Arvin's head. A second blade *thunked* into the doorframe next to him as he pelted into the chapel. He raced for the gauntlet at the far end of the room, his breathing ragged and heart pounding. Leaping onto the dais, he slapped both palms against the gauntlet. He skittered around behind it, both hands still on the polished silver, placing the statue between himself and the demon.

The demon halted at the edge of the dais. Lazily regarding him through slit eyes, it coiled its scaly tail under itself. "Little morsel," it hissed. "Come down from there."

"Make me," he said, staring defiantly into its eyes.

The demon bared its teeth, hissing. Its incisors were long and curved, like a snake's. Arvin wondered if they held venom.

Footsteps sounded in the hallway: Marasa?

The demon's head started to turn.

One palm still pressed tight to the gauntlet, Arvin plunged his other hand into his pocket and found the monkey's fist. "Here," he said to the demon, hurling the knot of twine. "Catch."

Even as the monkey's fist unknotted, the demon raised its swords. Six blades flashed through the air, chopping the magical twine to pieces. The frayed remains fell at its feet. The demon cocked its head then frowned. "I grow weary of this."

"So do I," Arvin said in a loud voice, hoping to cover the sound of footsteps in the hall. Marasa would have a better chance if she was able to surprise the demon. She could banish it before it got a chance to teleport out of the spell's path.

"But I've got one more trick up my sleeve," Arvin bluffed. "One that's bound to—"

He faltered as he saw who was coming down the hall. Not Marasa, as he had desperately hoped, but Karrell.

"Arvin!" she called. "What is happening? Are you—" She jerked to a halt just inside the room as she saw the demon. Her eyes widened.

The demon turned.

Karrell immediately began to cast a spell, but even as she raised her hands, the demon lashed out with one of its swords. Karrell twisted out of its path, but the blade caught her raised right hand. Blood sprayed and fingers flew to the floor. Karrell gasped and clutched her wounded hand.

The demon snaked its tail across the doorway, blocking it, and prodded Karrell with one of its swords. "Go ahead," it hissed with malicious delight. "Try to flee."

Arvin tried to manifest a distraction, but though a loud droning filled the air, the demon's eyes remained locked on Karrell. He leaned out from the dais and kicked the demon in the back. A shock of weakness flowed up his leg as his foot struck one of the black tendrils that coiled around the demon's body. Ignoring the numbness it caused, he shouted at the demon's back and kicked it a second time. "Hey, scale-face! Behind you!"

Almost absent-mindedly, the demon turned its head and slashed backhanded at him with one of its swords. Arvin flinched as the blade came to a jerking halt a palm's width from his head, halted by the magic of the gauntlet. A heartbeat later, a whirling circle of blades appeared, this time surrounding the gauntlet and trapping Arvin inside. Cursing, he shrank back from them, his sweaty palms still on the statue. A moment ago, the gauntlet had provided sanctuary. The demon had turned it into a prison.

The momentary distraction, however, gave Karrell the time she needed. The far end of the chapel was suddenly plunged into darkness, hiding her from sight.

The demon frowned then twisted, whipping its tail through the patch of darkness. Arvin heard Karrell gasp—and the tail yanked her back into the light. Caught within the demon's coils, Karrell fought to free herself, her wounded hand leaving smears of blood on the demon's scaly tail. The demon lapped at the blood with its long black tongue then smiled. "A yuan-ti?" it said. "*You* must be the one I'm supposed to kill." It tail squeezed—and Karrell exhaled in pain. Arvin heard a dull crack that sounded like a rib breaking.

Footsteps sounded in the hallway—more than one person, and running this time—and a woman's voice was shouting orders: Marasa?

Arvin looked wildly around the chapel. He was weaponless, and the monkey's fist—the last of his ensorcelled items—was lying on the floor in tatters. If he let go of the gauntlet, he'd be cut down before he took a single step. But Marasa was at last on her way. He and Karrell only needed to survive for a few moments more.

"Helm," he croaked. "Help us now. Do something."

The skies outside lightened. Dusk-red sunlight slanted in through the chapel's stained-glass windows, turning the blue eyes at their centers an eerie purple. The light beamed in, limning the image of Helm's eye on the chapel floor.

With a hiss, the demon thrust its sword at the nearest window, smashing a hole through the eye. Glass exploded outward. The skies outside darkened again as the sun continued its descent.

As a loose pane of glass fell from the broken window to shatter on the floor, Arvin realized there was a weapon he could use, after all. He reached out with his mind, sending a thread-thin line of glowing silver toward the broken window. With it, he seized one of the panes of glass and threw it at the demon's face. The demon batted it away with a sword, smashing it into bright blue shards, but Arvin hurled another pane of glass at it, and another, keeping up the distraction.

Four of the baron's soldiers—three men and a woman—charged into the chapel, swords in hand. The woman shouted a command,

and Arvin's heart sank as he realized it hadn't been Marasa's voice he'd heard, after all. The soldiers leaped forward, engaging the demon.

The demon, however, needed only four swords to meet their attack. One of the men went down even before he'd managed to close with it, his throat slashed. With its fifth sword, the demon continued to knock away the panes of glass Arvin hurled at it. That left one more sword. This one it thrust at Karrell; it *thunked* into the wooden floor beside her head as she desperately twisted aside.

Karrell's face was purple now and her movements were jerky. The demon—still fighting the soldiers with three of its arms—yanked the sword free and flexed its tail, dragging Karrell across the floor.

The female soldier pressed the demon, shouting Helm's name. The demon thrust a sword through her stomach, spitting her, then flicked her limp body away. One of the two remaining soldiers turned to run; with a flash of steel, the demon lopped off his head. The other grimly continued to attack but met the same end.

Its opponents dead, the demon glanced down at Karrell, tongue flickering through its hissing smile.

Karrell's fear-filled eyes sought Arvin's. He could see that she realized she was about to die. Her lips tried to form a word, but there was no breath left in her body.

Arvin ended his manifestation; the pane of glass he'd been about to throw fell to the floor and shattered. Reaching deep inside himself, he manifested a different power—one whose secondary display filled the air with the scents of saffron and ginger. Then, for a heartbeat, he hesitated. He didn't want to make the same mistake he'd made with Tanglemane. If the demon died. . . .

It was a gamble he had to take. Spells and steel hadn't defeated the demon; he doubted anything would. And if he didn't manifest his power, Karrell would die.

Guiding the energies with his mind, he coiled one loop around the demon, another around Karrell. Then he tied them together and yanked the knot tight.

"Demon!" he shouted. "I've just bound your fate to the yuan-ti woman. Kill her, and you'll die!"

It was a desperate lie. Karrell's death would mean little to the demon. She might cause it a slight wound, but no more.

Ignoring Arvin, the demon slashed at Karrell with its sword. This time, Karrell's reaction was slower; the sword sliced a line down her cheek as she wrenched her head aside. The demon grunted—then hissed and touched its own cheek with the back of a hand. The hand came away slick with green blood.

The demon turned to face Arvin and tried to speak, but no words came from its mouth. It seemed to be having trouble breathing. It frowned down at Karrell, who lay gasping on the floor, then uncoiled its tail from her. Then it stared, its eyes slit with malevolence, at Arvin. "Unbind me, sorcerer," it commanded.

Relief washed through Arvin. He glanced at Karrell.

Her lips formed silent words: "Thank you."

Arvin gave her a grim smile. Just a few moments more, and Marasa would surely appear and banish the demon. He stared back at it through the whirling blades that still surrounded the dais. "No," he told the demon. "You will remain bound."

The demon flicked a hand, and the blades disappeared. It cocked its head to the side and considered Arvin. "Mortal," it hissed. "Surely you can be persuaded." Its hand opened, revealing a glitter of gems. The demon tipped its hand, letting them spill from its palm onto the floor. "The yuan-ti means nothing to me; she may go. Unbind me from her, and these are yours."

Arvin smiled grimly. "A rogue tried to entice me with a similar offer a few days ago," he said. "He's dead now."

The demon clenched its fist—causing the swords to reappear—and pointed one of them at Arvin. "Unbind me!" it roared.

Arvin gripped the gauntlet with sweaty hands. "No."

"We seem to have reached an impasse," the demon hissed.

Outside the chapel, just beyond the spot where one of the soldier's bodies lay, Arvin saw a flash of silver: light, glinting off a polished breastplate. Marasa stepped into view in the doorway, her lips moving as she whispered a spell, her left hand—clad in a silver gauntlet whose palm was set with an enormous, glittering sapphire—extended toward the demon.

"Yes," Arvin answered. "It seems we have." He shrugged, a gesture that removed his hands for no more than a fraction of a heartbeat from the gauntlet. It had the desired effect; the demon lashed out with a sword, but before the blade connected, Arvin's hands were back on the gauntlet.

The demon glared at him, oblivious to Karrell, who had risen to her hands and knees and was crawling away, her wounded hand leaving a smear of blood on the floor, and to Marasa, who was casting her spell. Marasa swept her hand down toward the demon, the sapphire in her gauntlet glinting. "By Helm's all-seeing might, I order you, demon, back to the place from whence you came!" she shouted.

The demon rose from the floor, roaring, slashing wildly with its swords. A rent appeared in the air next to it; an angry boil that burst open, emitting a sulfurous stench. Dark shapes writhed inside the tear in the fabric of the planes, howling and thrashing. The demon tumbled toward them.

Karrell fell onto her side—had she slipped on her own blood? As she rose again, blood from her wounded hand streamed toward the hole in a thin red ribbon—a ribbon the demon grabbed in one clawed hand.

Arvin reeled, realizing he'd seen this once before: in the vision at Naneth's home.

Still roaring, the demon disappeared through the gap between the planes. Karrell was yanked after it, screaming.

The gap closed.

For a heartbeat, Arvin stood rooted to the spot, Karrell's scream echoing in his mind. Then he hurled himself across the chapel toward the spot where she'd disappeared. "Karrell!" he cried desperately. Tears streaming down his face, he clutched at empty air. He sagged to the ground and beat his fists against the floor. A fate link wasn't supposed to work that way; it transferred pain, wounds, even fatal injury from one individual to the next, but that was all.

What had gone wrong?

He felt a hand on his shoulder. He looked up and saw Marasa staring down at him. Her face was deeply lined and streaked with tears; her hair seemed even grayer than it had been before. "I'm sorry," she whispered. "I didn't realize. . . ."

Arvin looked up at her through tear-blurred eyes. "Karrell was still alive when she went into the Abyss. Is there any way she could still be—"

Marasa shook her head grimly. "No. She would never survive."

Arvin's shoulders slumped.

"She was pregnant," he whispered, "with my child." He shook his head and corrected himself. "With my *children*. They're all. . . ." His throat caught, preventing him from speaking further.

Marasa nodded but seemed too weary to offer any further comfort. Her hand fell away from his shoulder.

Outside, the skies darkened and a wet snow began to fall. A chill wind blew flakes of white in through the shattered window. A shard of blue—all that remained of Helm's eye—fell to the floor like a tear and broke, tinkling.

Arvin spotted Karrell's ring, lying on the floor in a pool of blood. Two severed fingers lay next to it. He picked the ring up and wiped it clean on his shirt, then stared for a long moment at the turquoise stone. Then he pressed the ring to his lips. "Forgive me," he whispered.

He slipped the ring onto the little finger of his left hand then clenched his hand shut, savoring the pain of his abbreviated little finger.

Karrell was dead.

So was Glisena.

Arvin had failed them both.

But Sibyl was still alive. And if she managed to get her hands on the second half of the Circled Serpent, many more would die.

He stared down at the ring on his finger. "I'll do it," he vowed. "Finish what you started. See to it that Sibyl never gets a chance to use the Circled Serpent."

In the darkening skies outside, thunder rumbled.

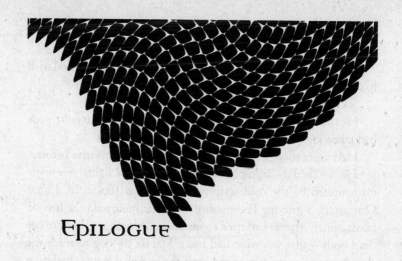

Epilogue

ARVIN STOOD NEAR THE STERN OF THE SHIP, WATCHING THE shoreline of Sespech fall away behind. Already the square buildings of Mimph were no more than tiny squares on the horizon, their lights slowly fading. The waters of the Vilhon Reach were as dark as the overcast evening sky above, a perfect counterpoint to his grim mood.

Seven days had passed since Karrell had disappeared into the Abyss. His eyes still teared whenever he thought of her. Her life had entwined with his only briefly, yet he still felt frayed by her loss. He thought back to what she'd told him on the day he'd discovered she was a yuan-ti. After they'd made love, she'd told him more about the beliefs of her religion. Every person's life was a maze, hedged with pain, disappointment, suffering, and self-doubt, she'd said. To find one's way through this jungle, one had to keep one's eyes on the "true path"—the course the gods had cleared for one through the thorny undergrowth.

Arvin had joked that he still hadn't found his true path—that he kept fumbling his way from one near-disaster to the next. Karrell had just smiled and told him he would find it, one day, by following his heart.

Arvin sighed. He *had* followed his heart—to Karrell—only to lose her.

On the day she disappeared—and every day after that—he'd tried to contact her with his lapis lazuli, but she'd never answered.

She was dead. And it was his fault.

He touched the chunk of crystal at his throat, wishing the gods had taken him instead. "Nine lives," he muttered.

He'd never thought of his continued survival as a curse before.

He watched as Mimph sank from sight, its lights seemingly extinguished by the cold waters of the Vilhon Reach. In distant Ormpetarr, a grieving Foesmasher would be mourning the loss of his daughter. Marasa had tried to summon Glisena's soul back to her dead body—that was what had taken Marasa so long to reach the chapel—but her attempt to resurrect the baron's daughter had been in vain. Glisena's death had been magical in nature, and irreversible— the contingency that allowed the binding to end and the demon to assume its full size.

At least Foesmasher still had his grandchild. He'd reacted amazingly well to the news that Belinna was carrying it. Instead of denouncing the "serpent," he'd begun to weep. "It's all I have left of her now," he'd moaned. Then, wiping away his tears, he'd summoned Belinna to his council chamber. Belinna, forewarned by Arvin that the child in her womb was not only half yuan-ti, but of royal blood, had responded hesitantly to the summons. That hesitancy had turned to amazement and joy when the baron announced she would be elevated to the position of royal nursemaid. That her child would, from the moment it was born, have everything it needed—as would she and her husband.

Despite his daughter's death, Foesmasher had also been generous to Arvin—very generous. With his coin pouch filled with gems and coins, Arvin would have no difficulty making a new life for himself anywhere he chose. But that could wait. For the moment, there were more pressing matters he had to attend to.

As for Naneth, there had been no sign of the midwife, despite the baron's soldiers having searched every corner of Ormpetarr. Arvin wondered where she was. Or rather, where the mind seed was that, even now, would be taking over her body. The seed would, no doubt, soon be on its way to infiltrate Sibyl's lair. There, Arvin was certain, it would face an unpleasant reception from Sibyl, who must by now have known that her plan to assassinate Dediana Extaminos had failed.

Nor had the baron's men been able to locate Zelia. Would she follow Dmetrio and the mind seed back to Hlondeth? If so, Arvin would have to tread carefully, starting the moment his ship docked there. Tymora willing, he would spot Zelia before she spotted him.

The ship rose and fell, its rigging creaked, and tie-lines fluttered against the taut canvas above. Arvin could no longer see Mimph; the gloom had swallowed it. "Farewell, Sespech," he said. "I doubt I'll see you again."

Then he turned to stare across the water at the dark line that was the north shore of the Vilhon Reach—at the faint green glow on the horizon that was Hlondeth. Somewhere beneath its streets, Sibyl was laired in an ancient temple, with her half of the Circled Serpent.

Somewhere in the city above, Dmetrio had his half.

Somehow, Arvin would have to find one or the other, before the two halves were joined.

BOOK III
VANITY's BROOD

PROLOGUE

THE AIR WAS HOT, LADEN WITH THE HEAVY SCENTS OF DECAY AND mold. Black clouds of insects—tiny as gnats, but with a sting that made Karrell gasp—swarmed around her face, drawn by the sweat that trickled down her temples. She pulled a fold of her cloak across her mouth and nose to screen herself from the insects, but the fabric tore away in her hand. The acidic rains had rotted it, leaving it thin as pockmarked gauze. She cast the scrap of fabric aside, too weary from her trudge through the jungle to care if it was found by the demon that was searching for her.

She glanced up through foliage so thick it was almost impossible to see the mottled purple sky above. Vines wove through the branches overhead, giving the jungle canopy the appearance of a vast net. The stems of the vines coiled down the scabrous tree trunks like snakes, past clumps of gaggingly sweet-scented black orchids whose roots curled like shriveled white fingers.

Things moved through the jungle canopy above: dark, flitting shapes that startled her, then disappeared before her eye had a chance to fully register them. Their muted cries and sibilant hisses filled the air.

How long had she been fighting her way through the jungle? She had slept five times since escaping the cage the demon had kept her in since drawing her into the Abyss, but "nights" that strange plane were artificial ones. The sky was unchanging. It brooded, neither fully dark nor fully light, but somewhere in between, a perpetual almost-dusk.

Where *was* she? Whatever layer of the Abyss it was, she had been there several months, long enough for her pregnancy to make her slow and heavy, long enough for her to be dangerously close to the time when she would give birth. When those first labor pains struck, the demon would discover the truth—that it didn't need to keep her alive after all.

Karrell was no longer its prisoner, and she had to fend for herself. She was hungry all the time—the children were growing bigger inside her each day—but it was hard to find food she was certain was safe. The fruits that grew there were overripe, soft with bruises and rot, and the lizards she'd been able to catch had flesh that stung the tongue with its acidity. She worried, with each mouthful, whether she was doing harm to her unborn children. The only other option, however, was starvation. She had tried to summon a creature of her homeland—some small animal that she could kill and eat—but her prayer had failed. Wherever she was, it had no connection with her native plane.

She pushed her way through ferns that dusted her hands and arms with pale yellow spores, and vines whose curved, fang-sharp thorns left scratches in her flesh. With each step her feet crushed wide-leafed plants sticky with foul-smelling sap. The ground underfoot squelched as she walked. Spongy and soft, it was made up of layer after layer of dead and rotting vegetation, dotted with puddles of putrid water. In a normal jungle, she could pass without leaving any trace, but the Abyssal vegetation conspired against her, leaving behind a trail of footprints and broken branches that even the most unskilled tracker could follow.

She stopped at a pool ringed by foul-smelling yellow plants whose stalks were papery with peeling skin. Picking a wide leaf, she curled it into a cone and used it to scoop up a little of the scummy green water. A pass of her hand over the makeshift cup and a quick, whispered prayer turned the water clear. She drank thirstily, closing her eyes and wishing she could blot out the oppressive odor of decay that pervaded the place. Another scoop of water, another quick prayer, another drink—it still wasn't enough to quite slake her thirst, but she dare not cast the spell a third time—not there.

The jungle reacted to her prayers. A vine snaked toward her along the ground, brushing against her ankle with feather-soft tendrils. She jerked her foot away, tearing free of the vine, then rose to her feet and continued on her way.

She glanced around. Which way? Did it really matter? The jungle looked the same no matter which direction she went in. There were no landmarks, no trails, no bodies of water large enough to be called a lake. Months before—the first time she'd escaped—she had climbed as high as she could up a tree and bent back its branches so she could see out over the jungle. The view hadn't been encouraging. As far as she could see in any direction, there was nothing but unbroken jungle, green and matted from horizon to horizon—nothing that suggested a way out.

As she walked, something tripped her: a root that had humped up out of the spongy ground like a living snare. She stumbled forward, landing on hands and knees with her fingers in a brackish pool of water. The acid in it stung her skin; she wiped her hands furiously on what remained of her cloak. Then, hearing a slurping noise just ahead, she froze.

At the far side of the pool, no more than a half-dozen paces from her, through a screen of vegetation that hung like mottled green lace from the trees, a pale-skinned creature the size of a large dog lifted its head from the surface of the pool and sucked a purple tongue back into its small, sharp-fanged mouth. Squat and hairless save for a strip of matted black hair down its bulbous belly, the dretch had a round, bald head set on a thick, blubbery neck. It blinked tiny eyes, listening. Then, slowly, its head began to turn toward her.

With a whisper, she cast a spell. Her arms became branches, her legs roots, her cloak-shrouded body the trunk of a gnarled log. Her bulging stomach took the appearance of a burl on the trunk, and her long hair transformed into green-leafed vines. As the dretch loped toward her through the pool, its knuckles dragging through the water, she saw it out of peripheral vision only, unable to turn her head. It moved in close, pushing its head forward to snuffle in her scent through mucous-clogged nostrils. Then it sat back and cocked its head to one side. Extending a misshapen hand, it flexed a finger, revealing a dirty claw. With this, it scratched the bark of the "tree" it had just sniffed.

The scratch sent a spasm of pain through her; sap oozed like blood from the wound in her thigh. She remained motionless, trusting to her spell. The demon that was hunting her had sent dozens of small, stupid creatures out into the jungle to search for her, and she'd managed to avoid them all. Never before had any of them come close enough to touch her.

The dretch sat a moment longer, staring at her, sucking its claw. Its nostrils twitched. Lowering its nose to the trail she'd made, it loped away through the jungle, back the way she'd come.

When she could no longer hear it, she let the spell end, transforming back into human form once more. Blood trickled from the scratch in her thigh. She laid a hand on it, started whispering a healing spell, then thought better of it. Already the orchids above were reacting to the spell she'd just cast, sending a shower of tiny, waxy balls of pollen down on her. The pollen stuck to her hair, shoulders, and arms like a coating of pale soot, drawing first one buzzing insect away from the pool, then a dozen, then a swarm. Batting them away, she waded across the pond to mask her scent then fled into the jungle.

Some time later—long enough for her sweat to wash away the orchid pollen and leave behind a crusting of salt—she realized there was an opening in the trees ahead. Slowing to a walk, she approached it cautiously. The clear spot turned out to be a wide area of toppled trees and crushed undergrowth. It was almost as if a giant had stamped the jungle flat. Curious, she climbed over a fallen tree and moved cautiously forward. Something had happened there— something momentous.

At the center of the smashed jungle she saw a large structure, entirely covered in vines. It looked like a rounded wall of black stone, its sinuous curves reminiscent of a snake. She stood for several moments, staring at it, trying to decide whether it was safe to approach. The wall was the only structure she had seen in this wilderness of swamp and jungle—perhaps it enclosed something significant, a portal out, for example.

Cautiously, she walked toward the wall, trying to peer through the foliage that covered it. Vines had grown up through the toppled trees on either side of the wall, knitting together across its rounded top. Once again, she was reminded of a net—a living net—each strand as thick as her thigh and deeply rooted in the spongy soil. As she drew closer, she could see that the wall was made from a shiny black stone—obsidian, perhaps. Curved lines had been carved into it that resembled the scales of a serpent.

She followed the wall, ducking under fallen trunks and tearing her way through the ferns and spike-leafed plants that had grown up since the jungle here was felled. She came, at last, to the place where the wall ended in a blunt wedge, the head of the snake. There was a circular patch of smooth stone on the side of the wedge, nearly as wide across as Karrell was tall. A door? Heart beating with excitement, she tried to shift the vines that covered it. She succeeded in tearing off a few leaves, exposing the circle on the wall, but the vines themselves were as rigid as steel bars and did not yield, even when she planted a foot on the wall and yanked with all of her strength. Panting, exhausted by her efforts and the oppressive heat, she contented herself with tearing away the rest of the leaves. It was difficult work, especially with the last two fingers of her right hand missing—a legacy of her battle with the marilith—but she persevered. When a large space was clear, she pressed her palm against the stone, praying that it would open.

It did, revealing an enormous, slitted eye.

Startled, she jerked her hand back. "Ubtao protect me!" she gasped.

Even as the name left her lips, an angry hissing filled the air. Vines creaked as the mouth of the "wall" parted slightly, revealing the bases of curved fangs. A forked tongue strained to escape but could not, and the hissing intensified.

Realizing that she had just awakened an enormous serpent—its wedge-shaped head alone the size of a small building—Karrell staggered backward, stumbling over a fallen tree that sent her sprawling. The serpent blinked and strained against the vines that bound it, causing the ground to tremble, but it could not pull free. Its eye fixed her with a look of such utter malevolence that for several moments she was unable to breathe. Suffocated by a blanket of fear, she felt as if she were about to faint. Even bound, the serpent exuded power: raw, violent, untamed. It could consume her with less effort than a thought, could squeeze her between its coils until not even a smear of her remained. It hated her with a loathing deeper than death itself and equally cruel.

At the same time, Karrell sensed a terrible *need*, one that caused the serpent to plead, silently, with the one person who had responded to its call, even though that person served a god that was its sworn enemy.

Sobbing in a lungful of air at last, Karrell turned and ran, back into the jungle and the dangers it held. She didn't care if the dretches found her, and delivered her to their mistress.

Anything was better than facing Sseth.

Chapter 1

ARVIN STARED DOWN INTO THE BOWL OF WATER THAT SERVED AS HIS makeshift mirror, concentrating. Energy prickled through two of his body's five power points; he could feel it swirling in tight circles around his navel and flowing outward in ripples that concentrated again at the center of his chest. The air filled with the scents of ginger and saffron, the smells growing stronger with each long, slow exhalation.

A sheen of ectoplasm blossomed on his skin like glistening sweat as he manifested his power. Studying his reflection, he watched as snake scales erupted on his skin. With a thought he turned them from flesh-pink to black, banded with thin stripes of gray. His collar-length, dark brown hair also turned black and melded itself against his head, as did his ears, giving him a more serpentine appearance. Hornlike ridges of scale appeared above each eye—the distinctive trait of the adder he was impersonating. His mouth widened; opening his loosely hinged jaw, he watched as his eye teeth elongated into curved fangs. Bulges formed below each ear: poison glands. A gleaming drop of venom beaded at the tip of one fang. He flicked it away with a tongue that tingled fiercely; as he concentrated, his tongue lengthened, its tip splitting into a fork.

He turned his head, searching for any hint of the human he had been a moment ago. His sandals and clothes remained unchanged, though the loose cotton shirt and pants he wore caught slightly on his rough scales. Karrell's ring—a wide gold band, set with a large turquoise stone—was still on the little finger of his left hand. Seeing it there, he blinked away a sudden sting of tears. Then he concentrated on that finger, which had been severed, years ago, at the joint closest to its tip. Flesh tingled as the finger elongated and sprouted a new fingernail. It felt odd, having a little finger that was whole again. Odder still to see a layer of small black scales on his hands and forearms and on his face. The musky odor of snake rose from his skin.

He curled his lip at the smell.

His body had slimmed as it morphed, the belt around his waist loosening. He lifted his shirt and tightened it and felt his dagger sheath snug up against the small of his back. Then he raised a hand to his cheek and scratched the still-tingling skin. The scales were as itchy and rough as a new beard.

Satisfied that no one would recognize him, he bent and picked up his pack. His body felt loose, supple, and he swayed into the motion as if he had been born a yuan-ti. A satisfied hiss slid from his lips. It was the perfect disguise.

It wouldn't last long, and before it ended, he had a score to settle.

That very night, Sibyl would die.

He stepped out of the hut he'd ducked into to undergo his metamorphosis—one of the huts the city slaves stored their tools in—and walked up a narrow street hemmed in by high walls, a section of Hlondeth that was one of the oldest parts of the city. Several of its buildings were made of dull red stone, instead of the glowing green marble that had later become the city's trademark. Most were noble residences—coiling towers and domed mansions that mimicked the city's most famous landmark, the Cathedral of Emerald Scales. Behind the walls lay private gardens; Arvin could hear the fountains in them gurgling. He wet dry lips. It had been another sweltering summer day, one that left him feeling drained. Even though the sun was setting, the air was still sticky-hot. He'd love a drink of cool water but couldn't stop to slake his thirst.

The streets were narrow and shadowed, mere paths between the high, curved walls. They were used primarily by human slaves. Their masters—the yuan-ti—slithered along the viaducts that arched gracefully overhead.

As Arvin started to turn into a side street, he heard something behind him. A premonition of danger came to him. He whirled, fangs bared, ready to defend himself—only to see a small, scruffy-looking dog with golden fur. It stood about knee-high and had large, upright ears that gave it a foxlike appearance. It stared at Arvin, tongue lolling, probably hoping for a handout. Arvin hissed, and it scampered away.

The street dead-ended after a dozen paces at a simple, one-room shrine whose roof had long since fallen in. The walls on either side of the building pressed against it, squeezing it like the coils of a serpent. The door was gone, as if burst from its hinges under the strain.

The shrine had been built nearly thirteen centuries ago, shortly after the first great plague swept the city. It commemorated Saint Aganna, a cleric and healer who had lost her fingers to the rot caused by what came to be known as the clinging death. An icon of the saint was attached to the rear wall of the shrine, above the altar stone, its oils almost faded to the color of the wood it had been painted on. It showed the saint offering up her fingers on a platter to Ilmater. Despite the loss of her fingers, Saint Aganna had remained in the city, using her prayers to heal the sick. The clinging death had eventually taken her, but until it did she labored without pause, tending the sick until she was too weak to heal herself. Those whose lives she had saved kept her memory alive by building the shrine.

Hlondeth had been a human city in those days. In the centuries since, the yuan-ti had become dominant, and the yuan-ti worshiped the serpent god Sseth. Shrines like the one to Saint Aganna were all but forgotten, known only to the handful of humans who still worshiped the Crying God. Arvin, placed under the care of those priests in an orphanage, had been taken, years ago, to visit Saint Aganna's shrine as a "reward" for having knotted the most nets in a month. The sight of shriveled fingers on a platter, however, had terrified him, as had the faint rotten-egg smell that lingered within the shrine—an odor he had been certain was the lingering taint of plague. The priest, however, had explained to the near-panicked boy that the smell came from the shrine's cellar, which the yuan-ti had tunneled into and turned into a brood chamber. When Arvin had worried about the yuan-ti bursting out of the cellar to defend their eggs, the priest had chuckled. The cellar had been abandoned, he explained, many years ago. The yuan-ti no longer defiled it.

Arvin thanked Tymora, goddess of luck, for having woven that vital piece of information into his lifepath.

For the past six months, since returning from Sespech, Arvin had been gathering information about the ancient temple in which Sibyl had made her lair. He knew it had been built to honor the beast lord Varae, an aspect of Sseth, and that it lay somewhere beneath the city at the heart of an even older network of catacombs. Abandoned long before Hlondeth was even built, the temple had been rediscovered by the Extaminos family in the sixth century and used for several years as a place of worship by that House. It had been abandoned a second time after the Cathedral of Emerald Scales was completed. Over the intervening three and a half centuries, it had largely been forgotten. Nobody in Hlondeth—save for Sibyl's followers—knew exactly where it was or how to get to it.

There was a text, however—one of several obtained by Arvin at great expense through his guild connections—that described a way in. It had been written by a man named Villim Extaminos in the late sixth century DR. In it, Villim had made a veiled reference to a trap door that led directly to the temple catacombs—a door that could only be opened by "the lady without fingers."

Saint Aganna. The entrance to the shrine's "cellar" was probably behind the icon.

The altar, Arvin saw, had sunk into the floor in the eighteen years since his visit with the priest; any offerings placed on it today would slide off its steeply canted surface. He climbed onto it and stood, studying the icon. It was even more faded than he remembered. He could barely make out the white, wormlike fingers on the platter Saint Aganna held.

Arvin grasped one edge of the icon and gently tugged. As he'd expected, the painting was mounted on the wall with hinges—hinges that tore free, leaving Arvin with the heavy wooden panel in his arms. He staggered back and nearly fell from the altar. Once he'd recovered his balance, he lowered the icon to the floor and studied the portion of the wall it had concealed. A close inspection revealed five faint circular marks—slight depressions in the stone. Pushing them in the wrong order might spring a trap. A poisoned needle, perhaps, or a sprung blade that would sever a finger.

Arvin wrenched a splinter of wood from the top of the icon and used it to push each of the depressions in turn. He tried several sequences—left to right, right to left, every other depression—but nothing worked. Frustrated, he stared at them, thinking. They were arranged, he saw, in a slight arc. As if . . .

He lifted a hand, fingers splayed, then smiled. One depression lay under the tip of each finger and thumb. The solution, he realized, was to push all of them at once.

He did.

He felt movement under his forefinger and little finger—each sank into the stone up to the first joint. Then they abruptly stopped. Flakes of red drifted out of the holes when he pulled his fingers out.

The mechanism was rusted solid.

Arvin braced a shoulder against the wall and shoved, but nothing happened. He shoved again—then gasped as the altar teetered with a grinding of stone on stone. Realizing his weight was about to send it crashing into the chamber below, he leaped off.

"Nine lives," he whispered, touching the crystal that hung from a leather thong around his neck. Then he smiled. The secret door behind the icon wasn't the only way into the catacombs.

Placing his hands on the lower end of the altar, he shoved. The slab of stone moved downward—then slipped and fell. As it tumbled into the chamber below, Arvin manifested a power, wrapping the block of stone in a muffle of psionic energy. Though the crash of the altar against the floor below sent a tremble through the shrine, the only sound was a soft rustle, no louder than a silk scarf landing gently on the floor.

Dust rose through the opening as Arvin peered down into it. Sunlight slanting through the hole dimly illuminated the chamber below. The floor was littered with what looked like deflated leather balls: the remains of yuan-ti eggs. All had hatched long ago; what remained was brown and withered. The walls bore some sort of plaster work, done in relief—knobby sculptural elements that Arvin couldn't make out from above.

He pulled a rope from his pack and laid it out on the floor, doubling the rope back on itself to form a **T**-shape. He tied a knot, then stretched the short bar of the **T** from one edge of the hole to the other, letting the longer piece dangle down inside.

"*Saxum*," he whispered. The rope turned to stone. He slid down what had become a pole, then whispered a second command word: "*Restis.*" The rope returned to its original form and slithered down into his hands.

He looked around as he untied the knot and stowed the rope away. The walls and ceiling of the chamber were decorated not with plaster reliefs but with human bones. On one wall, individual vertebrae and ribs had been arranged in floral patterns around a skull flanked by two shoulder blades that gave the appearance of wings. On another, leg and arm bones by the hundreds formed borders around still more skulls, arranged in circular rosettes. On the ceiling, thousands of finger bones were arranged in a starlike motif. A chandelier made from curved ribs and yet more vertebrae, wired together, creaked as it rocked slowly back and forth, disturbed by the fall of the altar.

On yet another wall was a gruesome parody of a sundial, arm bones dividing a circle of tiny skulls into the four quarters of morning, fullday, evening and darkmorning. Arvin's mouth twisted in disgust as he realized the skulls were from human infants. Stepping closer, he saw that the skulls were cracked, in some cases smashed in on one side; they must have been sacrificial victims. He touched one of the tiny skulls and it crumbled under the slight pressure of his fingertip, the fragments sifting down onto the floor like ash. The skulls were a poignant contrast with the hatched eggs that littered the floor—death and birth. The ones who had done the dying, of course, were human.

So were the ones who had done the killing. The Temple of Varae—and the catacombs—had been built long before the yuan-ti came to the Vilhon Reach.

There was one exit from the chamber, a doorway whose arch was framed in bones. It led to a flight of stairs that descended into darkness.

Arvin pulled a glass vial out of his pocket, pulled out its cork stopper, and drank the potion it contained. The liquid slid down his throat, leaving a honey-sweet aftertaste of night-blooming flowers and loam. The inky blackness that filled the staircase lightened as walls, stairs, and ceiling resolved into shades of gray and black.

He walked cautiously down the stairs, at several points having to duck to avoid decorative elements in the rounded ceiling where bones had been used to create mock arches. They gave the staircase an unnerving similarity to the gullet of a snake—something Villim had commented on in his text. Arvin shivered as a dangling finger bone brushed against the top of his head and clattered to the ground. He tensed, expecting one of Sibyl's followers to appear at any moment.

None did.

The air was cool and clammy, like cold sweat. He found himself missing the stifling heat he'd left behind.

The staircase should have ended in a hallway that led, according to Villim's text, to the temple. Instead, it ended in a jumble of fallen stone. In the eight centuries since Villim had penned his text, the ceiling must have collapsed.

Arvin swore softly and kicked at a loose stone. It rolled—farther than it should have. Bending down, he discovered a narrow gap, beyond which lay a wider passage. Clearing away the rubble that blocked it, Arvin realized it must be the tunnel the yuan-ti had used to reach the chamber in which they'd laid their eggs. It was too low to crawl through with a backpack on; he'd have to drag the pack behind him. He tied it by a short length of rope to one ankle then lay prone and wormed his way into the tunnel.

The narrow passage wound its way through the collapsed masonry, up and over sharp bits of stone that scraped Arvin's arms and legs and under jutting blocks that he would have banged his head against, had he not been able to see in the dark. Being in yuan-ti form helped. His increased flexibility enabled him to slither around corners a human would have been unable to negotiate.

At one point the tunnel constricted, forcing him to wriggle forward on his belly with arms extended in front of him. Claustrophobia gripped him a moment later when his pack got caught in the narrow section, jerking him to a halt like an anchor. He was trapped! He would lie there, entombed with Varae's victims, until he starved to death. He scraped at the rope around his ankle with his other foot, trying to free himself from it—then realized what he was doing. If he left the pack behind, he'd lose his chance to settle his score with Sibyl the abomination who had killed both his best friend and the woman he loved.

"Control," he whispered.

He blinked away the sweat that trickled down into his eyes and licked his lips with a long, forked tongue. The sweat tasted slightly acidic, reminding him that he was in yuan-ti form. The serpent folk had wriggled through that narrow spot to reach their brood chamber, and Arvin should be able to do the same. It was just a matter of freeing his pack.

He worked it back and forth, prodding it with a foot, then jerked against the rope tied to it. Eventually the pack came free. Relieved, he crawled on.

The tunnel ended a short distance ahead, opening into a chamber illuminated with flickering red light that washed out Arvin's dark-vision. A hissing noise filled the chamber: the soft, slow exhalations of serpents.

Dozens of them.

Arvin sent his mind deep into his *muladhara*, the source of psionic energy that lay at the base of his spine, then summoned energy up through the base of his scalp and into his forehead. He sent his aware-ness down the tunnel ahead of him, into the chamber beyond. The thoughts of the yuan-ti inside it, however, were not what he'd expected. He'd been prepared for guards, alert and suspicious. The thoughts of these yuan-ti were languid, jumbled, confused. As if . . . yes, that was it; they were dreaming. The mind of one was filled with images of a jungle, of a tree whose snake-headed branches had become tangled in a hopeless knot. Another dreamed that the viaducts that arched over Hlondeth were growing together, forming a stone lattice overhead. A third dreamed she was basking on a stone that had suddenly grown unbearably hot, but someone held her tail, preventing her from slith-ering away. Others dreamed of gardens that had become choked with weeds, of hatchlings that struggled to tear open the leathery eggs that enclosed them, and of ropes that turned into snakes and slithered into a mating ball that could not be untangled. All of the dreams were different, yet all had one thing in common: a restlessness—a need to *do* something—and a frustrating inability to grasp what that something might be.

Arvin withdrew his awareness from the dreamers, wondering what to do next. He'd planned to pass himself off as one of Sibyl's worshipers, bearing tribute for the avatar. He'd spent months studying the practices of Sseth's faithful, learning the gestures of propitiation and the hisses of praise. Sunset was one of the chief times of worship, the time when the yuan-ti ended the day's heat-induced lethargy with feasting and praise.

He hadn't expected to find Sibyl's worshipers deep in slumber.

He couldn't wait for them to awaken, however. His metamorphosis would wear off soon. He crawled forward, determined to either find someone who was awake or to find Sibyl on his own.

As Arvin drew nearer to the chamber, a wisp of amber-colored smoke curled down the tunnel toward him, bearing an odor he recognized: a combination of mint, burning moss, and sap. *Osssra!* The flickering light, he saw, came from flames dancing across a bowl of the burning oil—the same oil whose fumes had nearly poisoned him when he'd forced his way into an audience with Dmetrio Extaminos, royal prince of Hlondeth. In morphed form, Arvin would be immune to the worst of its toxic effects—but that didn't mean he wouldn't wind up drowsy and dreaming, like the yuan-ti in the chamber, if he inhaled it. Worried, he crawled out of the tunnel and untied his pack from his ankle. If he moved quickly, he might make his way through the chamber before he breathed in too much of the smoke.

The yuan-ti were sprawled together in loose-limbed heaps on the floor around the burning bowls of *osssra*, heads lolling in slumber. Breathing as shallowly as he could, Arvin stepped quickly across them, making for the chamber's only door. This chamber, like the previous one, was decorated with human bones. Here, however, complete skeletons had been used. They were wired together and attached to the walls inside arches made of vertebrae. One of the skeletons, just to the right of the door, was that of a woman, the tiny skeleton of an unborn child arranged within her pelvic bones.

A wave of nausea swept over Arvin. Karrell had been pregnant when she died, pregnant with his children. Eyes stinging, he reached for the handle of the door, but before he could open it, something twined around his ankle. Startled, he gasped—then realized he'd inhaled a deep lungful of smoke.

Looking down, he saw the snake-headed arm of one of the sleepers, coiled around his leg. "Stay," it hissed while the rest of the yuan-ti's body slept. "Dream with us."

Made drowsy by the smoke, Arvin yawned, inadvertently drawing in another lungful of it. He shook his head, but it couldn't dislodge the cobwebs of dream that clung to the edges of his thoughts. In that dream, he ran through a jungle, trying to escape from a slit-pupilled eye the size of the sun. It stared down at him from above, then suddenly became a mouth, which opened, drooling blood. Out of it fluttered a brown, withered egg shell. It landed on the ground next to him, staring up at him with Karrell's face. Long black hair splayed around her severed head like the rays of an extinguished sun. Her eyes were flat and dead in the wrinkled brown face. The jade earring in her left ear wriggled free, and the small green frog opened its mouth and gave a squeaking croak—a baby's shrill cry of need.

Arvin shook his head, purging the nightmare from his mind by sheer force of will. Shaking the snake-arm off his leg, he wrenched open the door and stumbled into a brightly lit hallway. He slammed the door behind him and took in several deep lungsful of cool, clean air. How long had he been standing there, lost in the dream? However long it had been, it had cost him precious time. His body was already starting to tingle. His metamorphosis would end soon.

"Well?" a soft voice beside him asked.

A yuan-ti holding a parchment and quill sat a short distance away, her limbless lower body coiled on a bench against one wall. Long red hair framed an angular face, and for a moment Arvin was reminded of Zelia, the woman who had become his nemesis, but this yuan-ti had red scales, instead of green. She raised her quill, an expectant look on her face.

"Your dreams?" she hissed—softly, as if not wanting to break the tenuous thread that connected dreaming and wakefulness.

Arvin wet his lips—a gesture that sent his long forked tongue flicking out toward her, sending a drop of spittle onto the parchment she held. Her upper lip twitched, baring the tips of her fangs—a gesture that often preceded a bite.

Arvin started to flinch, then remembered that he was supposed to be a yuan-ti. No, he *was* yuan-ti, at least for the duration of his metamorphosis. Drawing himself up imperiously—yuan-ti never apologized, even to another yuan-ti—he bared the tips of his own fangs. He and the scribe locked eyes for a moment—and the scribe was the first to look away. As she did, Arvin manifested the power that would allow him to listen in on her thoughts. She swayed slightly, tipping her head as if listening to a distant sound, and her thoughts tumbled into Arvin's mind.

She was annoyed at him—how dare he threaten her! The mistress had given her a sacred task to fulfill, and she would not let a petty annoyance get in the way. Later, perhaps, she might exact her revenge, but for now, the important thing was to record whatever dreams the *osssra* had induced.

Arvin decided to get that part over with, then ask where Sibyl was.

"In my dream, I was in a jungle," he told the scribe.

She dipped her quill in the pot of ink that sat on the bench beside her and started scribbling. The script was narrow and flowing, a series of lines that looked like elaborately looped scratch marks, punctuated by blots of ink. Draconic.

Wary that his own nightmare might reveal some hidden human quality, Arvin repeated a dream Karrell had related to him just before she was killed: of being a mouse, struggling within the grip of a serpent. His voice cracked a little on the final words. He remembered how vulnerable Karrell had looked as she lay on the bench in Helm's chapel, her expression pinched and her fingers twitching as she fought, in her dream, to free herself. Seeing that, he'd been worried that Zelia had seeded her—that Zelia had used her psionics to plant, deep within Karrell's mind, a tiny seed of psionic energy that would eventually grow, choking out Karrell's own consciousness like a weed and replacing it with a copy of Zelia.

That hadn't been the case. The dream Karrell had been having was just a simple nightmare, rather than a dream-taste of Zelia's thoughts.

The real nightmare had come later, when Karrell was yanked into the Abyss by a marilith.

Arvin's awareness was still hooked deep inside the scribe's mind. She was disappointed by what he'd told her; it offered nothing new.

"That wasn't very helpful, was it?" Arvin asked.

"No," she agreed, blowing on the parchment to dry the ink. "It wasn't." Certainly not worth bothering Mistress Sibyl with, her thoughts silently added, especially in the middle of the welcoming ceremony.

Arvin's heart quickened. The scribe knew where Sibyl was. He needed to convince her that he must be conveyed to her mistress at once, but how?

He thought quickly. Slumber—and dream—were important parts of Sseth's worship. In midwinter, a select few of the serpent god's priests underwent the Sagacious Slumber, a month-long hibernation during which they communed with their god, gaining new spells, but that didn't seem to be what was going on here. It sounded as thought Sibyl was looking for something in the dreams of her worshipers.

Arvin had an idea what it might be: a clue to the whereabouts of the Circled Serpent, an artifact Dmetrio Extaminos had found during his restoration of the Scaled Tower one year ago. Sibyl's minions had managed to get their hands on half of the Circled Serpent, but the other half was still in Dmetrio's possession. He'd hidden it so well, even Karrell hadn't been able to find it.

If Arvin's guess was right, he would be conveyed directly to Sibyl, welcoming ceremony or not. If not . . .

He decided he'd take the risk. He stared up at the ceiling as if lost in thought. "There was more," he told the scribe, "a second part to my dream."

"Yes?" she said, dipping her quill in the pot of ink that sat on the bench next to her. She gave a soft, hissing sigh. Her thoughts—which Arvin was still reading—held a note of bored indulgence. He was attracted to her—most males were—and he wanted to keep talking. He was probably making the second part up, she decided.

"There was a serpent," Arvin continued. "A silver serpent. Its body was coiled back upon itself in a circle." He sketched a circle in the air with his hands. "It was swallowing its own tail."

Arvin fought to contain his smile as he listened to the scribe's thoughts race. She scribbled furiously. It was *exactly* what she'd been waiting to hear. Mistress Sibyl had instructed her—personally instructed her!—to pay close attention to any mention of circled serpents.

"Go on," she prompted.

"A man was holding the silver serpent—a yuan-ti," Arvin continued, "a man with a high forehead, narrow nose, and dark, swept-back hair."

The scribe frowned as she wrote that down. Arvin had neglected to mention scale color and pattern, the first thing a yuan-ti typically mentioned, when describing another of his race.

"Oh yes," Arvin said, as if suddenly remembering. "There was something odd about him. He didn't have any scales. His skin was almost . . . *human*."

He managed to inject a shudder of disgust into the word that satisfied the scribe. "Did you recognize him?" she asked.

"I think it was Dmetrio Extaminos," Arvin answered.

While she recognized the name, it didn't trigger the sudden rush of excitement Arvin had expected. The scribe, he decided, had been told only so much.

"Where was he?" she asked. "In your dream."

"He was in . . ." Arvin said that much then deliberately halted.

He didn't know where the royal prince was. Nobody else in the city did either—at least, nobody the guild had been able to question. After being recalled from Sespech six months ago, Hlondeth's former ambassador had made a brief appearance at the palace then simply disappeared. Arvin had tried to contact Dmetrio with a sending, but it had met with the same lack of success as his attempts to contact Karrell. Dmetrio was either dead or shielded by powerful magic.

"Yes?" the scribe prompted.

Arvin drew himself up in a stiff pose and looked down his nose at her. "That, I think, is something for the ears of our mistress alone, hatchling." He used the diminutive term, despite the fact that he had assumed an appearance that wasn't much older than the scribe.

She hissed softly at the verbal bite. How dare he, she thought. She, a *ssethssar* of the temple, and he a mere lay worshiper! She started to bare her fangs then remembered the task she had been charged with. The mistress would be displeased, indeed, if this impertinent male died before his dream was recorded.

"Mistress Sibyl is too busy to meet with you," she began. "Tell *me* your dream. I will ensure—"

"Yes, yes, I know," Arvin said, waving a hand. It was tingling fiercely, the scales on it starting to shrink. Already the belt around his waist felt tighter. "The welcoming ceremony. I was supposed to be part of it but chose to dream instead. Take me to Sibyl—immediately."

That made her blink. He dared address the mistress by name alone? Perhaps she'd misjudged him. A few of the high serphidians had attended Dreamings in the past, but he wasn't one she recognized. She took careful note of his face—then blinked as she noticed it was changing. The black-and-gray scales were melting away into human flesh . . .

A spy! her mind shrieked. I must—

The scribe raised her hands to cast a spell. As she began reciting her prayer, Arvin manifested a power. He was already inside her mind, which made it easier, but in order for his deception to work he needed to manifest two powers at once.

He peeled back her layers of memory, starting with the sound she was currently hearing: the tinkling noise that was his power's secondary manifestation. Working backward from there, he erased the moment of realization that he was a not yuan-ti, but human—a spy—and the memory of his scales disappearing and human features emerging. At the same time, he remanifested his metamorphosis, restoring his body to serpent form.

In the middle of his mental labors, the scribe's spell went off and a snakelike whip of glowing red energy lashed out from her hand. It slapped across his shoulder, burning through the fabric of his shirt and sending a hot wave of pain through the flesh below. Arvin gasped, fighting to maintain his concentration. For a moment, it almost slipped away—scales stopped blossoming on his body, and the scribe managed to lay down another layer of memory: an image of Arvin as he shuddered under her mystic lash.

Then he regained control. He stripped this memory away, together with several others, peeling her memories down to the point just before his metamorphosis had ended, leaving her with the memory of him ordering her to take him to Sibyl. At the same time, he completed his transformation, forcing his body back into yuan-ti form.

When it was over, he was no longer listening to her thoughts, but he could guess what they were. She would wonder why he was suddenly panting and sweaty, why he was turning his shoulder away from her, as if hiding something.

"You're . . . unwell?" she asked, her voice uncertain.

"Uneasy," he corrected. "The dream left me . . . uneasy. It is sure to unsettle Si—Mistress Sibyl—as well. The sooner I describe it to her, the better." He waved a hand, as if dismissing her. "Take me to her now. I will follow."

"Yes, High Serphidian," she said.

Laying down her quill and parchment, she slid off the bench and slithered up the hallway. Arvin followed, shifting the strap of his back-pack to cover the bright red stripe of burned flesh on his shoulder.

She led him for some distance through the catacombs along a route so convoluted Arvin became lost. He doubted he'd be able to find the dreaming chamber again, then laughed grimly as he realized that it probably wouldn't matter. He'd accepted the fact that killing Sibyl would probably be the last thing he ever did. With Karrell gone, his own life no longer mattered. What he needed to focus on was making sure the attack was successful.

After a while, the bone decorations were replaced by bare stone walls that had been carved in a pattern that resembled scales. Arvin's heart quickened as he realized they were approaching Sibyl's lair. Villim's text had described Varae's temple as having walls like these. Several times the scribe led Arvin through arches that had arcane symbols graven into their stonework. Arvin's skin tingled as he passed through their magical fields. Though his heart raced each time he felt the wash of magical energy, no alarm sounded. Karrell's ring protected him, shielding his thoughts and suppressing any auras that might have given him away as an enemy of Sibyl.

The ancient temple, a veritable stronghold, was crowded with yuan-ti. The scribe led Arvin past an egg-filled brood chamber that was warmed by crackling braziers and a great hall in which dozens of yuan-ti feasted on an enormous millipede whose head and tail had been staked to either end of a long dining table. The diners tore out chunks of the still-wriggling insect, and washed it down with blood-tinged wine.

Along the way, they passed several guards: grotesque, hulking blends of human and reptile that bore an unsettling resemblance to the hideous creature Arvin's best friend Naulg had become, after being forced to drink the Pox's transformative poison. Arvin gave a mental shudder as he passed them and had to work hard to keep his expression neutral.

Eventually they came to a chapel in which clerics coiled in reverent prayer before a statue, carved from gold-veined black marble, of a winged serpent with four arms and enormous rubies for eyes.

A statue of Sibyl.

One of the clerics turned to watch Arvin and the scribe as they passed—then hurried out of the chapel to clap a hand on Arvin's shoulder—his burned shoulder. With an effort, Arvin prevented himself from wincing. A sheen of acidic sweat broke out on his face.

"Where are you going?" the cleric hissed.

The cobra hood that surrounded his otherwise human looking face flared as he spoke. A forked red tongue flickered out of his mouth, tasting the air next to Arvin's cheek.

Arvin knew that his morphed body would smell as yuan-ti as the real thing, yet he was hard-pressed to damp down the unease he felt. The yuan-ti was a cleric, a serphidian of Sseth, and a powerful one, judging by the elaborate cape he wore. The scales sewn onto the garment had been fashioned of fingernail-thin slivers of precious gems, which glittered in the lanternlight that filled the corridor. The cleric would know dozens of spells, perhaps one powerful enough to strip Arvin of his disguise.

"We are going to the altar room," the scribe answered. "This one dreamed of the Circled Serpent. I am taking him to the mistress."

"The Se'sehen are arriving," the cleric said. "The mistress is busy welcoming them." He turned to Arvin. "Your dream can wait."

"That's true," Arvin said, shrugging his backpack off his shoulders, "but this can't."

As he spoke, he manifested a power that would allow him to falsify one of the cleric's senses—in this case, the sense of sight. The cleric was a difficult subject. Arvin had to force his way into the man's mind with a mental shove that he worried might give him away. The cleric shook his head, as if trying to clear his ears of an annoying ringing.

As Arvin opened his pack, allowing the cleric to inspect its contents, he shaped what the other man saw. The pack actually held a net Arvin had spent the past three months weaving from yellow musk creeper vines—a net ensorcelled with the ability to entangle its victim upon a spoken command—but what the cleric "saw" as he opened the pack was something entirely different:

A gleaming half-circle of silver.

Half of the Circled Serpent.

Arvin closed the pack and withdrew from the man's mind. When he looked up, the high serphidian had an eager look on his face.

Arvin could guess what the man was thinking—that he, rather than a lowly scribe, should be the one to deliver the Circled Serpent half to Sibyl. He was probably also weighing his chances of overpowering

Arvin and taking the backpack from him. The cleric glanced at the distinctive ridges above Arvin's eyes then looked away, obviously deciding not to take on an opponent whose venom was more potent than his own.

"Who are you?" he demanded.

"Sithis," Arvin answered, giving a common yuan-ti name—one that was much more pronounceable with a forked tongue. "I'm one of Ssarmn's men," he added.

He waited, tense, wondering if his ploy would work. Ssarmn was the slaver from Skullport who had supplied Sibyl with the potion that would have turned the humans of Hlondeth into her slaves, had Arvin not thwarted her plan. That had been a year ago, but with luck—Arvin resisted the urge to touch the crystal at his neck—Ssarmn was still involved in Sibyl's operation.

"Ah," the high serphidian hissed. He waved the scribe away. "You may leave," he ordered. "Return to the dreaming chamber."

"But—"

The protest died on her lips at the look the high serphidian gave her. Cowed, she turned back the way she had come, but not without taking a good, long, quizzical look at Arvin's burned shoulder, revealed since he'd removed his pack. Arvin tried to manifest the power that would erase that glimpse from her memory, but before he could she had slithered out of range.

Motioning for Arvin to follow, the cleric led Arvin to a corridor that curved downward. The inside wall of the spiraling ramp was punctuated with vertical slits, and through these Arvin heard a sound like the hissing of waves on a beach. Glancing through one of the slits, he caught sight of a circular room, far below, bathed in lanternlight. Its floor was covered in thousands of snakes of every size and color imaginable. They slithered in a steady flow around a raised dais of glossy black obsidian.

Several times during their descent toward that room, Arvin heard a popping noise over the hissing of the snakes. He saw what was causing the sound when they reached the bottom of the ramplike corridor. One moment, the dais was bare; the next, a yuan-ti materialized on it. The dais must have been a portal, linked with some distant place.

The yuan-ti who had appeared on the portal was dressed in a white loincloth, high laced sandals, and a cape made from the pelt—complete with head—of a jungle cat whose golden fur was spotted with black. A necklace of heavy gold beads hung against his scaled chest, and on his head was perched an elaborate headdress decorated with circles of jade.

Arvin winced at the irony. The noble was from the Se'sehen tribe—Karrell's tribe—the people she'd come north in an effort to save.

Even though they were allies of Sibyl.

A cobra rose from the slithering mass and obediently presented its flared hood for use as a stepping stone. The noble stepped onto it. Other cobras did the same. Moving from one head to the next, the yuan-ti crossed the tangle of serpents that surrounded the dais, making his way toward a doorway whose frame was the gaping mouth of the beast lord's face. The cleric, meanwhile, led Arvin around the edge of the room—the snakes parted to clear a path for them—toward the same exit.

"Remain silent," he hissed. "I will announce you."

Arvin followed, tense with the knowledge that he was so close to his goal. Acidic-smelling sweat trickled down his temple, and he brushed it away. Ahead—down the curved corridor that connected the portal room to the one beyond—he could hear murmuring voices. Not one but dozens of Se'sehen must have come through the portal. In the chamber ahead, Arvin could see a large cluster of similarly garbed nobles. Moving among them were gem-caped high serphidians like the one Arvin followed, as well as a handful of yuan-ti in finery common to the Vilhon Reach: nobles from Hlondeth.

One of the high clerics, a woman, had hair that consisted of dozens of tiny, intertwined serpents. He knew her by reputation—everyone who lived in Hlondeth did—but had never expected to meet her face to face. She was Medusanna of House Mhairdaul, elder serpent of the Cathedral of Emerald Scales, high cleric of Hlondeth's most prominent temple, a yuan-ti abomination who was rumored to be able to petrify with a mere glance.

As the cleric led Arvin into the chamber, Medusanna turned to stare at them. She had been talking in the language of the Se'sehen with one of the nobles. Arvin's heart lurched as he heard a word he recognized—one that Karrell had taught him. *Kiichpan.* Beautiful. Swallowing his emotion, Arvin met Medusanna's eyes with a steady look and silently prayed that his disguise would hold—and that the rumors were wrong.

It did, and they were.

Instead of resuming her conversation, Medusanna continued to stare at Arvin as the cleric led him deeper into the gathering.

The chamber in which the Se'sehen and clerics had assembled had a ceiling whose stonework was set with a profusion of metal blades that hung, point down, giving the appearance of fangs. All were rusted and some had fallen out like rotten teeth, leaving holes behind. The walls to the right and left were carved with depictions of the beast lord in his various animal forms, each with a serpent draped around its shoulders and whispering in his ear. Between them were arched corridors that led off into darkness, five on either wall.

At the far end of the room stood a broad stone altar, carved to resemble a serpent coiled upon a clutch of eggs and flanked by two stone pillars—the twin tails of the serpent. Between these swirled a cloud of darkness that even Arvin's potion-enhanced vision didn't quite penetrate. Just in front of the altar, a rusted iron serpent statue held an enormous sphere of crystal in its jaws. Arvin swallowed, worried. If Sibyl appeared to her followers inside the crystal ball, instead of in person, all his efforts of the past six months would have been for nothing.

The darkness between the pillars began to swirl, as if an invisible fan stirred it. As it did, the yuan-ti assembled in the chamber fell silent. Then they began to chant. "Ssssi-byl. Ssssi-byl. Ssssi-byl." Arvin found himself swaying in time with the others. With an effort, he wrenched his mind away. Filling it with the memory of Karrell being yanked into the Abyss helped.

An enormous abomination burst out of the darkness. Ink black and nearly three times the height of a human, she hovered above the altar, lazily flapping her leathery wings. Two of her clawed hands held a spiked chain that glowed red as burning coal; the other two were empty. They rose into the air, drawing out the hissing adulation—then swept down.

A wave of shimmering energy swept from those hands, fanning out in front of her as it struck the floor. Arvin heard the nobles and clerics in front of him cry out in terror as it swept past them, saw them writhe and roll their eyes—and the magical fear crashed over him like an icy surf. Screaming, he sank to his knees, fighting for control and dimly noticing that others around him were doing the same. Even Medusanna had been driven to her knees, the snakes that made up her hair thrashing and spitting.

"Control," he whispered.

He threw up a psionic barrier, pressing with mental hands against the waves of magical fear emanating from the altar. The need to scream, to grovel, lessened a little, enough for him to glance in the direction of the altar where Sibyl sat coiled. Hatred helped him focus, but still a tiny part of his mind whimpered in fear.

Was Sibyl *really* the avatar of a god?

No, he told himself. Magical fear was something any yuan-ti could produce with a mere thought. Sibyl's was just more potent than the rest, potent enough to leave him gasping.

As the fear of those assembled in the chamber subsided to a subservient hiss, they slowly rose to their feet. Arvin rose with them. Sibyl stared with glowing red eyes down at her followers then smiled, revealing the tips of her fangs.

"Nobles of Se'sehen," she hissed in a voice that echoed throughout the chamber. "Welcome."

A lengthy speech followed: praise for the worthy and the faithful and a promise that they would soon reap their reward in Hlondeth as well as threats of swift and terrible vengeance against the unfaithful and unworthy. Arvin concentrated on calming his rapidly beating heart, on trying not to show his nervousness. The cleric who had led him there motioned for Arvin to give him the pack. Arvin nodded and started to slip it off his shoulders. The high serphidian obviously planned to present its contents to Sibyl himself—another of Tymora's blessings, since Sibyl was more likely to take it from the hands of someone she recognized. As long as Arvin was close enough when the pack was opened, he would be able to speak the net's command word and direct its attack. Doing so would instantly give him away, of course, but that was something he'd planned for. As soon as the net struck and began its deadly work, he would bite his own arm, injecting a deadly dose of yuan-ti venom, then end his metamorphosis. The instant he returned to human form, he would die and be forever beyond Sibyl's coils.

He touched the crystal at his throat. The last of his "nine lives" was about to end. In another moment, his soul would be joining

Karrell's on the Plain of the Dead. He only hoped she would still be there to greet him—that her god hadn't already summoned her up to his domain.

Sibyl was still talking to the assembled yuan-ti, praising their efforts and making promises to the Se'sehen. Arvin didn't bother listening. In a few moments, it wouldn't matter anyway. He passed the pack to the cleric, wary of a sudden bite to the hand. He didn't want to die quite yet.

The cleric grasped the pack—equally cautiously. As he did, a loud rattling boomed out from the altar. The cleric and Arvin turned in that direction, both still holding the pack. The sound came from the pillars on either side of the altar. Their tails shook violently, filling the chamber with a noise that vibrated the floor beneath Arvin's feet.

When it stopped, a face appeared inside the crystal ball: one of the high serphidians. "Mistress," he hissed in alarm, "a spy has been detected within your sanctum."

Heart pounding, Arvin realized the scribe must have noticed the gap in her memories, realized that the burn on Arvin's shoulder was of her own making, and come to the correct conclusion, which meant that Arvin could no longer afford to wait for the cleric who had led him there to present the pack to Sibyl. Wrenching it out of his hands with a curt, "I'll present it to her myself," Arvin started to force his way to the front of the crowd.

Sibyl, meanwhile, hissed an angry rebuke at the crystal ball. The cleric inside it gave an urgent reply—"No, Mistress, within the temple itself!"

Sibyl's eyes blazed. She pointed at Medusanna. "Seal the temple. Find the spy."

Arvin elbowed the Se'sehen nobles aside as he desperately struggled to reach the altar, the cleric following in his wake.

"Mistress!" Arvin called out. "I found the—"

Before he could complete the sentence, Sibyl thrust herself backward with a mighty beat of her wings. The darkness closed like a curtain around her.

"No!" Arvin groaned, his voice lost in the murmur of confusion that swept through the chamber.

Rage and despair filled him in equal measure. He'd prepared for *six months*—had come up with the perfect weapon with which to kill Sibyl and been ready to sacrifice his own life, only to have the opportunity snatched away at the last instant.

His body tingled, and started to lose its shape. In another moment, his metamorphosis would end. He could restore it a heartbeat later—but not before the dozens of yuan-ti closest to him saw his human form. He couldn't alter that many memories.

If he was going to survive long enough to get a second chance to kill Sibyl, he needed to think of something else. And fast.

CHAPTER 2

ARVIN WITHDREW HIS AWARENESS DEEP INTO HIMSELF. PLUNGING it deep into his *muladhara*, he imagined the color leaching from his body, imagined his body fading, then disappearing altogether. At the same time he leaped to the side, vacating the spot he'd just occupied.

I was never there, he broadcast to the yuan-ti around him. You did not see me. You do not see me now.

He knew the manifestation was successful when one of the Se'sehen nearly walked into him. The power had clouded the senses of those in the altar room. Though Arvin could see and hear himself, he was invisible to them, impossible to detect even by sound or scent, and just in time. Looking down at his arms, he saw that the black scales were gone. His metamorphosis had ended. Putting his pack back on, he glanced around.

The altar room was in turmoil. The Se'sehen babbled at each other in their own language while the nobles from Hlondeth milled about in confusion. Clerics ran for the doors, shouting orders. The high serphidian who had led Arvin through the temple stood with hands on hips, searching the room—his gaze passed over Arvin without stopping—and began elbowing his way through the crowd toward Medusanna.

Arvin started toward the exit that led back to the portal room, then remembered the snakes that surrounded the portal. Several were venomous, and he no longer had the yuan-ti's natural resistance to poison he'd gained by assuming yuan-ti form. He could manifest another metamorphosis, but the concentration necessary to reshape his body would result in the loss of his invisibility.

Whispering an oath under his breath, Arvin looked for another way out. The altar room had ten other exits: the five arched corridors along each side wall, between the statues of Varae, but which to choose?

Even as he tried to decide, Medusanna cast a spell, her arms moving in sinuous gestures as she prayed. Malevolent glyphs sprang into view at the top of each exit and the corridors beyond filled with a swirling mist. A whiff of it drifted out to where Arvin stood and stung his nose: acid.

His heart pounded. There was no escape. Then he laughed at himself; escape had never been part of his plan. Killing Sibyl had been, and Sibyl had disappeared into the dark cloud that still hung above the altar like a curtain—a curtain that Arvin's potion-enhanced vision allowed him to see through. Barely.

Through it, he saw the dim outline of the large corridor down which Sibyl must have flown. That it was also warded he had no doubt. The spells those wards contained would be fatal, he was certain, but he had to try and soon. Medusanna was casting another spell.

Swiftly, Arvin manifested one of his powers he'd only recently learned—a power that summoned ectoplasm from the Astral Plane. It was a risky choice. Psionic energy concentrated itself above and between his eyes then burst from his forehead in a spray of tiny silver sparkles that threatened to give his position away. The yuan-ti closest to him—all Se'sehen—were too busy to notice, talking together in slightly indignant voices. One of the them, a male with green scales and fingers that ended in snake heads, was close enough that Arvin's secondary display drifted down onto him like falling snow—fortunately, onto his back. The Se'sehen didn't notice them; he was intent upon some spell, holding the first two fingers out in a **V** and slowly turning.

Arvin's heart lurched as he realized the yuan-ti was casting a detection spell.

He sidestepped behind the snake-fingered yuan-ti as the fellow rotated, avoiding those splayed fingers. As he did, he completed his manifestation. He shaped the translucent, gooey ectoplasm he'd drawn into a vaguely human form and sent it running toward the portal room, roughly shouldering yuan-ti out of its way.

Medusanna took the bait, casting a spell at the construct. The spell had no visible effect, and Medusanna hissed in anger.

The snake-fingered yuan-ti, meanwhile, completed his spell and stared at the altar. He glanced over his shoulder—directly at Arvin—as he whispered something. For a terrible moment, Arvin thought he had been detected, but the Se'sehen's eyes were focused on something well behind Arvin in the rear corner of the chamber, something that, an instant later, made a loud, groaning noise.

Arvin turned just in time to see one of the statues of Varae tear itself away from the wall. With great, lumbering strides the beast-headed statue thumped forward, its heavy feet sending tremors through the stone floor. The vibrations rattled a sword loose from the ceiling, and the rusted blade clattered down amid the yuan-ti. One or two threw themselves to the floor, prostrating themselves before the statue. It strode right over them, crushing them to a bloody pulp.

Medusanna continued to direct her attacks at Arvin's construct. Whipping a hand forward, she sent a snakelike stream of energy toward it. The crackling line of force looped around the running figure like a constricting snake, but the construct passed right through it.

The statue lumbered forward, its body shedding chunks of stone as its joints ground against one another. Behind it, more stone fell from the ceiling above the spot it had just torn itself out of. Then one of the corridors next to where it had stood collapsed with a thunderous crash.

Arvin didn't wait to watch the rest. Making the most of the distraction, he hurried toward the altar. So did the snake-fingered yuan-ti. The Se'sehen was fast; he clambered up onto the altar a heartbeat or two ahead of Arvin, heading for the corridor at the rear of it. As Arvin followed, he realized that the Se'sehen might have been the one who had been detected; he was certainly acting like a spy. He'd animated the statue that was wreaking havoc at the back of the chamber, and praise Tymora, it looked as though he was going to clear a path to Sibyl.

Arvin touched the crystal at his throat and grinned.

Snake-fingers stepped into the darkness that shrouded the back of the altar. To Arvin, his vision still enhanced by the darkvision potion, it seemed as though the yuan-ti shifted from color to shades of black and gray. He watched as Snake-fingers took a deep breath and blew into the corridor. Inside it, on one wall, something glowed a faint blue. As soon as it did, the yuan-ti hurried into the corridor.

Arvin followed close on his heels. He tensed as he passed the blue glow—a symbol in Draconic that set his teeth on edge and made his eyes ache, even though he only saw it in his peripheral vision. Then he was beyond it.

The walls of the corridor were carved in a scale pattern, so he knew he was still within the ancient temple. It was enormous, with a rounded ceiling, easily large enough for Sibyl to have flown through it. After a short distance, the corridor forked. Snake-fingers hesitated and extended the first two fingers of each hand then pointed each down a different fork. A moment later, he continued up the left corridor. Arvin followed. As he did, he heard a thunderous crash from the altar room. Dust rushed up the corridor and the floor trembled. Glancing back, Arvin saw that the tunnel was blocked. The ceiling of the altar room had collapsed.

Snake-fingers glanced back and grunted in satisfaction then continued up the corridor, which grew steadily darker. Arvin followed, silent as a ghost, his psionics keeping him hidden. Soon he was relying entirely on his magical darkvision. The Se'sehen also seemed able to see in the dark, since he moved forward without hesitation.

Arvin wondered what the spy was up to. It would be the height of irony, indeed, if Snake-fingers had also come to kill Sibyl and had been given away by Arvin's blunder with the scribe. Curious to know if that was the case, Arvin tried to skim the spy's surface thoughts. He was surprised to receive nothing at all—not the faintest whisper of a thought. The Se'sehen didn't react at all; it was as if Arvin had never manifested the power. Snake-fingers must have had an amazingly strong will. Either that, or . . .

Arvin touched the ring on his left little finger—Karrell's ring. Was the Se'sehen protected by a similar device or by some spell?

The corridor forked a second time. Once again, the Se'sehen used magic to choose his course—and to reveal a nasty looking symbol positioned just inside the left fork. The Se'sehen disarmed it as he had the first, by pursing his lips and blowing. Arvin was close enough to hear the incantation he used. It didn't sound anything like Karrell's language, but perhaps that was because the yuan-ti's voice was lower, almost guttural—and strangely devoid of a hiss, which made Arvin wonder if all was as it seemed.

Once they were both beyond the symbol, Arvin risked another manifestation. Silver sparkles erupted from his forehead and his vision momentarily shimmered. When it cleared, he saw the person he'd been following for what he truly was.

He wasn't a yuan-ti at all.

He was a dwarf—but unlike any Arvin had seen before. His skin was so brown it was almost black, and his long, wiry black hair fell in what looked like matted braids across his shoulders. He was barefoot and wore only a loincloth made from a spotted animal pelt and two pieces of jewelry: a necklace of mismatched teeth and claws, and a band of gold set with a turquoise stone on his upper right arm. Faint white tattoos covered his body: the snarling faces of stylized animals. A small pouch hung from his belt. Next to it, tucked into the belt, was a hollow reed that might have been a wand. Aside from that, he seemed to be unarmed.

Arvin's secondary manifestation didn't go unnoticed. The dwarf whirled, blinked in surprise, then cast a spell of his own. Arvin felt no appreciable difference but could tell by the dwarf's widening eyes—and the way the shorter man glanced up to meet his eye—that he was no longer invisible. In that same instant, Arvin's manifestation ended. The dwarf's illusion returned, cloaking him in the image of a snake-fingered yuan-ti.

The dwarf raised his hands and snarled. A pulsing nimbus of red surrounded his body, washing out Arvin's darkvision.

"Wait!" Arvin said. "I'm a friend—an enemy of Sibyl."

Frantically, he tried to manifest a charm. Before he could, the illusion-cloaked dwarf launched his attack. Arvin twisted aside, but it was hard to tell where the dwarf's limbs really were. Arvin's attempt to parry passed through empty air. Something that felt like a hooked dagger—or a claw—caught at Arvin's belt and raked across his hip, opening a painful gash.

Dancing backward, Arvin reached for the dagger sheathed at the small of his back. He drew it but didn't use it. Instead he manifested another power, stamping his foot down on the floor.

More sparkles erupted from Arvin's forehead, and a low droning filled the air as the stomp sent the dwarf staggering sideways. He caught himself against the wall. His illusionary fingers looked like snakes but scritched against the stone. Claws?

Wincing against the pain of the wound in his hip—the slash was deep, soaking his pants with blood—Arvin at last was able to manifest his charm. He was thankful to see the dwarf frown as if listening to a distant, half-heard sound. The fellow could hear the power's secondary display.

"I'm an enemy of Sibyl," Arvin continued, backing away and still holding his dagger out to the side. "I came here to kill her."

The dwarf looked at him with a blank expression.

"Friend," Arvin repeated, tapping his chest. He was worried the dwarf didn't seem to speak his language. His charm wouldn't be any help if the dwarf couldn't understand him. Arvin spoke slowly, raising his dagger to make a violent cutting motion. "I want to kill Sibyl. Kill." With his free hand, he mimed a wing flapping, then a snake, as he repeated the cutting gestures, pretending to stab his own hand.

The dwarf shook his head like a dog throwing off water. His long, ropy hair whipped back and forth across his face. Then he charged.

Arvin dodged, still not using his dagger. He stared at the nimbus of red that continued to surround the dwarf, flickering like an angry flame. By concentrating, he could see where it was most prominent: around the smaller shape that was the dwarf's actual body. Arvin pretended to stumble, and as the dwarf leaped forward, caught him by the hair. Arvin touched the point of the dagger to the dwarf's throat, held it there for a heartbeat, then leaped away. Backstepping again, holding his left hand in a "wait" gesture, he returned the dagger to its sheath.

"Friend," he said again, in as loud a voice as he dared. He prayed that Sibyl wasn't just down the corridor, close enough to hear.

The dwarf halted, frowning. He said something in his own language and pointed at Arvin's extended hand.

Arvin spread his hands and shrugged. "I don't understand you."

The dwarf whispered something, raising his hands to his lips. Arvin tensed, but the spell produced no harmful effect. Instead the dwarf's words became intelligible. His illusion vanished—but the nimbus of red that had surrounded him didn't.

He grabbed Arvin's left hand and asked, "Where did you get this ring?"

"It belonged to a woman named Karrell."

The dwarf's grip on his hand tightened, and his claws pricked Arvin's flesh. "Where is she now?"

"She's—" the word stuck in Arvin's throat—"dead."

The dwarf's eyes blazed. In them, Arvin saw a mirror of his own grief.

"You *knew* her?" Arvin asked, incredulous. He thought quickly back over what Karrell had told him of her past—and her affiliations. "Are you one of the *K'aaxlaat?*"

The dwarf's eyes shifted at the question—answer enough. "Do you know what the ring does?"

Arvin nodded. "It shields thoughts."

The dwarf stared a challenge at him. "Take it off. Then tell me how you know Karrell—and how she died."

Arvin glanced warily around. "Here? Right now? What if Sibyl—"

"She is not that close. Speak quickly; there is still time."

Reluctantly, Arvin eased the ring off his finger. It felt like a part of Karrell—a part of him now. Speaking in a quick whisper, Arvin told the dwarf how he'd met Karrell, how they'd decided to join forces to fight Sibyl, and about how one of Sibyl's minions—the marilith—had yanked Karrell into the Abyss when it had been banished.

"It was my fault," he concluded. "I manifested the power that did it."

"Did what?" the dwarf asked.

Throughout Arvin's explanation, the red glow surrounding the dwarf faded. The hand that gripped Arvin's was normal again, without claws.

Arvin frowned. "I linked Karrell's fate with the demon's—but you should have been able to tell that from listening to my thoughts."

The dwarf shook his head. "My god has not granted me that ability."

"But—"

The dwarf nodded at Karrell's ring. "You were willing to remove it. I knew you were telling the truth."

"Then you believe me when I say that I came here with the same goal as you." Arvin shifted the backpack away from his injured hip. It was still bleeding. He took off his shirt, wadded it into a ball, and pressed it against the wound. He only needed to stay alive long enough to throw his net. "Lead the way."

The dwarf nodded at the blood that soaked Arvin's shirt. "First, there is something you need." He held out broad hands, as if in question.

Arvin nodded—then winced as the dwarf pinched the wound in his leg shut with his fingers. For several heartbeats, the pain was intense, but Arvin gritted his teeth against it. When the dwarf finished whispering, Arvin looked down at his hip and saw a threadlike vine, dotted with tiny leaves, holding the two edges of the cut together. The vine had a scent that reminded Arvin of a healing potion he'd once drunk. He flexed his leg. The muscle in his hip felt whole, and the pain was gone.

"Thank you, ah . . ."

The dwarf bowed, then supplied his name. "Pakal. Of the *K'aaxlaat*, as you guessed."

"I'm Arvin, of . . . no particular affiliation. My motive for wanting to kill Sibyl is strictly personal: to avenge Karrell."

"Thard Harr grant that your wish is fulfilled, some day."

"Today will be just fine," Arvin said. "Just lead me to Sibyl."

Pakal pointed back the way they had come. "Sibyl went in the opposite direction. She took the right passage when the tunnel first forked."

Arvin blinked. "You're not here to kill Sibyl? But I thought—" Then he guessed why the dwarf had disguised himself and come to the temple: for the same reason Karrell had come north to Hlondeth. "You're looking for the Circled Serpent."

Pakal nodded, and Arvin wondered if Pakal knew that Sibyl only had half of it.

"You can tell where it is?" Arvin asked.

"Yes." Pakal raised his hand and extended the first two fingers in a **V** shape. "With these." He pointed in the direction he'd been going. "The Circled Serpent lies in that direction."

"Is that so?" Arvin mused under his breath.

He remembered what Karrell had told him—that her search for the half of the Circled Serpent that Dmetrio had retained had been thwarted by something as simple as a lead-lined box. Surely Sibyl would have used a similar protection. Pakal had extremely powerful magic—he'd demonstrated that by getting past the wards Sibyl used to protect her lair—but even so . . .

"Doesn't this seem a little *too* easy?" Arvin asked. "We're deep in Sibyl's lair, yet there's been no sign of her minions."

"Any that might have pursued were squished like worms."

"That doesn't explain the lack of guards in these corridors," Arvin said. "It's almost as if Sibyl *wants* the Circled Serpent to be found. The easiest way to catch a mouse, they say, is to set out bait."

The dwarf grinned. "I am one mouse the serpent's coils cannot catch."

Arvin started to protest further then realized that if he was right—if Sibyl appeared in person to spring her trap—he'd get a second chance to snare her with his net, and Pakal seemed pretty confident of his own escape. The dwarf might have been deluding himself, but it was his decision. He'd been warned.

"You've got a way out, then," Arvin said. "Good."

Pakal stared up at him. "Don't you?"

Arvin shrugged. "That doesn't matter. Killing Sibyl does. Now that Karrell's . . ."

Arvin's eyes stung. He blinked.

"You loved her," Pakal said.

"Very much," Arvin agreed. Then he squared his shoulders. "I'm coming with you," he told the dwarf. "I've learned a few tricks from the guild. If there are traps guarding the Circled Serpent, I may be able to disarm them."

Pakal smiled. "Did you think I would come so ill prepared? I, too, can neutralize traps, but come. We have wasted enough time."

The dwarf led Arvin deeper into Sibyl's inner sanctum. The passage forked three more times, and each time, the dwarf paused to determine their direction and disarm another protective glyph. The corridors they followed continued to be empty, heightening Arvin's suspicions that it was a trap. At last the tunnel turned a corner and dead-ended in a massive stone, carved in the shape of a snarling, bestial face, that filled the corridor like a plug.

"It's here," Pakal said, "behind this door."

"How do we open it?" Arvin asked.

"With a spell, but first. . . ."

Whispering a prayer, Pakal moved his hands over the face, his palms not quite touching the stone. The mouth began to glow a dull red. For a terrible moment, Arvin thought the dwarf had activated a magical trap, but Pakal merely nodded.

"Trapped, as I suspected," he said. He stepped back and whispered a prayer, raking the air with curved fingers. Then his shoulders slumped. "The magic is too strong," he said as the glow faded. "I can not dispel it." He turned to Arvin. "I can still open the door, but without knowing what the trap does, it will be risky."

"I might be able to help," Arvin said.

Turning his palm in the direction of the massive stone face, he tapped the energy that swirled around his navel, drawing it up into his throat. A low droning filled the air and a thin sheen of ectoplasm glistened on the stone face as his power manifested. A psychic echo of the past flowed into his mind: a vision of a yuan-ti in old-fashioned clothing, carrying a lantern, who approached the face and cast a spell. The mouth yawned open, giving a brief glimpse of a chamber beyond, and the yuan-ti bent to slither through. As he entered, rubbery black tentacles erupted from the mouth, filling it like a nest of snakes. They lashed out at the intruder, wrapping around his arms, legs, and neck. Then they yanked, each in a different direction. The yuan-ti was literally torn to pieces; his limbs and head wrenched from his body with wet tearing noises. The tentacles released what remained of him and retreated. Then the mouth slammed shut.

Arvin shuddered as the vision ended.

"I know how the trap works," he told Pakal. "The doorway is the mouth. The trap is inside." He described what he'd just seen. "I have a rope that might be able to entangle those tentacles long enough for us to get through."

Pakal shook his head. "I have a better idea. Even tentacles cannot grasp the wind." He glanced up at Arvin. "With your permission, I will turn your body to air. When the mouth opens, float through it. I will make you solid again once we are safely inside."

Arvin hesitated. "What about my pack?" he asked. "And the things inside it?"

"They will become air also," Pakal assured him, "and will return to solid form after."

"All right," Arvin said. "Do it."

The dwarf uttered a prayer, moving his hands in a fluttering pattern. He started at Arvin's feet and moved up his body, standing on tiptoe to finish. Arvin felt a prickling numbness spread upward as Pakal cast the spell. Looking down, he saw his feet, legs, hips, and hands dissolve into individual motes of matter, then disappear. His body did not fall to the floor but remained standing upright. His heart lurched, however, as his arms and torso became fully gaseous. He felt a moment of panic as he realized he could no longer feel his heart beating. His breathing, too, had halted. Then his head became insubstantial as well. He floated, a detached awareness inside a swirl of air, somehow still able to see and hear but unable to feel. The only time he had ever come close to such a sensation was when he was deep in meditation—so deep, he feared he would lose his sense of self.

Beside him, Pakal cast another spell. He raised a fist and rapped once, smartly, on the stone face, then stepped quickly back. As the mouth groaned open, he rendered himself gaseous as well.

Follow me, a voice whispered.

Arvin felt the air next to him shift. It flowed toward the gaping mouth, leaving a swirling void where Pakal had been a moment ago. Arvin strained to follow it, but his legs wouldn't move—and he remembered he no longer had legs. Fighting down his fear, he concentrated on where he wanted to go—through the mouth—and felt himself drift in that direction.

Pakal hovered next to him, a swirl of coherency that Arvin could sense but not touch. They entered the mouth one after the other. As they did, the trap sprang to life. Tentacles uncoiled violently and lashed out at them, thrashing through the space that Arvin and Pakal occupied. Arvin instinctively recoiled as one of the tentacles whipped around his face, but the tentacle passed right through his gaseous form. His thoughts spun crazily as the gas that was his head swirled in its wake, then became coherent again. He concentrated on his objective—the chamber beyond—and drifted in that direction.

Once inside, his body solidified the same way that it had become gaseous: from the feet up. Blood rushed through his veins, sending a fierce tingle through his body from feet to head. He gasped and fought to keep his balance. As soon as the dizziness cleared, he reached over his shoulder to touch his pack. It was still there, the net inside it still weighing it down. Arvin heaved a sigh of relief.

The chamber was circular, its walls carved in the by-now familiar scale pattern. Against one wall lay the skeleton of an enormous snake, coiled in a neat loop where it had died.

"More bones," Arvin muttered.

He nudged the tail of the long-dead guardian with his foot, but the skeleton didn't react.

A simple wooden box sat on the floor; its hinged lid didn't appear to have a lock. Pakal materialized beside it—his feet, legs, torso, then head coalescing from air—then squatted to study the box. He pointed forked fingers at it, whispered something under his breath, and said, "The Circled Serpent is inside."

He reached for the lid.

"Careful," Arvin warned. "It's certain to be trapped."

"I sense no traps," Pakal said. He lifted the lid.

Arvin winced, but nothing happened.

The box was lined with black velvet. Inside was a silver tube twice the thickness of Arvin's thumb, bent in a half-circle. At one end of the half circle was a snake's head, its fanged mouth open wide and its eyes set with gems. The other end was tapered slightly; that would be where the other half of the Circled Serpent would join with it. Arvin held his breath, waiting for something to happen—for the mouth-door to close, for an alarm to sound, even for the snake skeleton to suddenly rear up and attack. Nothing did.

Pakal looked up at Arvin, a concerned expression on his face. "Only half? We thought that Sibyl had both pieces."

"Perhaps she does," Arvin said, thinking of Dmetrio's disappearance. "Perhaps that's why she decided that leaving this half in an easy-to-find location would be worth the risk; whoever found it would be tempted to waste time searching for the other half. Sibyl knows there's a spy in her lair; this is obviously part of a trap to catch that spy." He shrugged the backpack off his shoulders and began unfastening the straps that held it shut. He nodded at the door; the writhing tentacles that had filled the mouth were gone, but the mouth was still open. "Odd, don't you think, that the door hasn't shut yet."

Pakal tapped the half-circle of silver with a fingernail, making the metal ring faintly—probably making sure it was real and not an illusion—then closed the lid. He picked up the box and rose to his feet. "The other half of the Circled Serpent—"

"Will still be inside its lead-lined box, where your magic can't locate it," Arvin said. He rose to his feet as well, holding his pack, ready to toss the net inside it at the door the moment Sibyl came through it. A musky floral smell rose from its fibres. "Go," he told Pakal, "while you still can. You've got half of the Circled Serpent; be content with that."

"You are not—?"

"No," Arvin said. "I'm staying. Sibyl's bound to arrive soon."

Pakal nodded and said, "May Thard Harr guide your—"

The dwarf grunted and staggered forward, crashing into Arvin. The box tumbled from his hands as he fell, spilling Sibyl's half of the Circled Serpent onto the floor. Arvin heard a rattling noise: the sound of bones moving swiftly across the floor.

He swore and leaped backward. The skeleton—animated after all—reared up with its mouth open, ready to strike again. It had already bitten Pakal, and the back of the dwarf's left arm leaked blood. Empty eye sockets stared at Arvin across the dwarf's rigid body. Then the serpent began to sway.

Arvin dropped his pack and flung his hands outward toward the skeleton. Silver sparkles danced in the air between them as long strands of glistening ectoplasm shot from Arvin's fingers, coiling themselves about the undead snake. They looped through the ribs, and with a twist of his fingers Arvin knotted them there. Another yank pulled the cords of ectoplasm tight, cinching together the coils of the skeleton's body. Its head and neck, however, continued to sway.

A fog crept into Arvin's mind. He stared at the snake across Pakal's body, unconcerned about whether the dwarf was alive or dead. He felt dazed, thick-headed, as if he'd drunk too much wine. He could feel his body moving in time with the serpent's swaying motion.

The skeleton opened its mouth wide to bring curved fangs into play. Head and neck still swaying, it hunched toward Arvin, awkwardly dragging its ectoplasm-bound body behind it.

Arvin meant to take a step back but took a step forward instead. His foot struck something that skidded across the floor with a metallic rasp. Glancing down, he saw it was the upper half of the Circled Serpent.

The interruption gave him a heartbeat's respite from the skeleton's mesmerizing motion. Arvin sank into one of the poses Tanju had taught him, raising his left arm as if to fend off a blow. He imagined himself in the Shield form, whirling to protect himself on all sides. As he did, energy exploded outward from the power point in his throat in a loud drone. It formed a protective barrier around him—one that helped him fend off the effects of the skeleton's swaying dance. His mind cleared.

Knowing that most of his psionic powers would be useless—the skeleton had no mind to attack—Arvin yanked the stone rope out of his backpack. Whipping it through the air, he shouted its command word. The rope stiffened into a pole of stone. It struck the skeleton just below the head, shattering the uppermost vertebrae. The head clattered to the floor, followed by the rest of the bones. Whirling a loop of the stone rope up and over his head, Arvin brought it crashing down into the serpent's skull. Bone exploded across the floor as the head shattered. The stone rope smashed as it struck the floor, and pieces skittered across the room.

Panting, Arvin looked down at what remained of the creature. Already the ectoplasm that bound it was evaporating. The skeleton, however, did not move. It appeared to be dead. Arvin touched the crystal that hung at his throat.

"Nine lives," he croaked.

He crouched beside Pakal and pressed fingers against the dwarf's neck. Pakal's blood-pulse beat faintly beneath his leathery skin. His eyes were open and staring, his breathing shallow. The skeleton's bite had paralyzed him.

Arvin stared at his pack, wondering what to do next. Sibyl still hadn't come to investigate. What was keeping her?

Arvin heard a noise on the other side of the door; it sounded like the scuff of leather on stone or the slither of scales. Scooping up his backpack, he flattened himself against one wall. His heart pounded as he heard a woman's voice whispering an oath in the language of the yuan-ti. Certain it was Sibyl, he tried to yank the net from his pack. It wouldn't come free. He yanked harder, but it still wouldn't budge. He cursed silently as he realized what had happened: the yellow musk creeper vines he'd woven the net from had rooted in the soft leather.

Arvin yanked his dagger from its sheath, determined to cut the net free. As he drew it, he heard a furious thrashing sound from inside the mouth-door as the tentacles inside it were activated. Realizing it wasn't Sibyl but someone else coming through the door—or trying to—Arvin reversed his dagger, holding it by the blade, ready to throw. Whoever the intruder was, he was likely to be dangerous. Arvin reached deep into his *muladhara*, preparing to tap its energy.

Something stepped through the doorway—something that looked like the silhouette of a woman. In the blink of an eye, it expanded, becoming three-dimensional. The woman was a heavyset human with a double chin and brown hair with a streak of gray at one temple. Arvin's mouth dropped open as he recognized her. Naneth—the sorceress who had summoned the demon that had killed Karrell.

Or rather, he amended as he saw the sway in her body as she found her feet again and stared down at Pakal, a mind seed. The mind in that body was no longer Naneth's. It was Zelia's.

Arvin manifested the power that would cloud her mind, hiding him from her, and not a moment too soon. The wary Naneth-seed looked around the room then chuckled as her eyes fell upon the upper half of the Circled Serpent, lying next to Pakal's body. She bent to pick it up.

Knowing he was unlikely to surprise her with psionics—his secondary display would give her the instant's warning she needed to retaliate in kind—Arvin resorted to cruder methods. While she was distracted, he hurled his dagger. It struck home, burying itself between her shoulders. The blade would have killed someone with less fat padding her body, but the Naneth-seed merely grunted with pain.

She whirled around, her small eyes searching the room. Arvin gasped aloud as pain shot through his own back. It felt as though a dagger was embedded there. Something wet oozed down his back: not blood, but ectoplasm. The Naneth-seed must have manifested a power that transferred the pain of her wound to him.

The pain shattered Arvin's concentration, giving the Naneth-seed a brief glimpse of him. Her second psionic attack followed the first, swift as thought. Arvin tried to throw up a shield against it but wasn't quick enough.

Air exploded from his lungs in a rush as an invisible band of psionic energy looped around his chest then tightened. His own psionic power faltered as he fought for breath—and failed. He was visible.

"You again," the Naneth-seed said, the hissing of her secondary display overlapping her words.

Arvin struggled to draw a breath. He tried raising a mental fortress, but the Naneth-seed beat it down. He started to form a construct out of ectoplasm to attack her, but before it was fully shaped she usurped control of it and ran it headlong into a wall, splattering ectoplasm everywhere. He would have tried charming her, but there was no breath left in his lungs. He couldn't speak, couldn't even beg. He did manage the most tenuous of links with her mind and found a faint source of hope: she was debating ending the power that was preventing him from breathing and replacing it with one that would force him to take his own life. That would draw out his death, allowing her to savor it.

Then she changed her mind. No, she would end Arvin's life more quickly. Returning with the upper half of the Circled Serpent was more important, especially since Sibyl had been alerted.

When the Naneth-seed finally noticed Arvin listening in on her thoughts, she gave a brutal mental shove, propelling him from her mind. Then she squeezed harder.

Arvin sagged to his knees as darkness clouded the edges of his vision. He blinked furiously, trying to find the force of will to resist the Naneth-seed's manifestation. As he struggled, he thought he saw Pakal's arm move. A moment later, despite the dark spots that clouded his vision and the roaring in his ears, he was certain of it. The paralysis the skeleton had inflicted was wearing off.

Pakal's eyes fluttered, then opened to stare at the Naneth-seed. One hand crept toward his hollow reed while the other fumbled open the pouch at his belt.

The reed scraped against the floor. The Naneth-seed turned toward the sound.

With the last bit of his consciousness, Arvin manifested a power—one of the first he'd ever learned. A faint droning filled the air. Instead of completing her turn toward Pakal, the Naneth-seed glanced at the doorway, distracted.

The last thing Arvin saw before losing consciousness was the dwarf raising the hollow reed to his lips.

The next thing Arvin knew, Pakal was slapping him awake. Groggily, Arvin pushed him away and drew a shaking breath. He sat up—and had to wait for the room to stop spinning before he could speak. He felt as though he was going to be ill.

"What happened?" he asked.

Pakal pointed at the Naneth-seed, who lay face-down on the floor. She'd landed with one arm stretched out above her head, pudgy fingers splayed. One of her fingers, Arvin noticed, was encircled with a band of amber: the teleportation ring she'd used to spirit Glisena out of her father's palace. A tiny feathered dart protruded from the back of the Naneth-seed's neck, just above Arvin's dagger. He stared, not believing his eyes, at his defeated foe.

"Is she—"

"Dead." Pakal offered Arvin his hand.

Arvin sighed with relief. The fact that the dwarf had saved him was a sobering thought. Arvin should have, with his increased powers, been able to deal with the seed on his own. He took the dwarf's hand and climbed to his feet.

"Nice shot," he said.

He nudged the big woman's body with a toe. He half expected it to rise from death, as the skeletal serpent had.

Pakal picked up the Circled Serpent and placed it back inside the box, then pointed forked fingers at the room's only exit. His face paled as he lowered his hand.

"Sibyl comes this way," said the dwarf. "Are you certain you will not come? I can turn your body to air once more."

Arvin picked up his backpack and glanced inside. The net had indeed knotted itself into the pack, but a few quick strokes of his knife would cut it loose.

"I'm not leaving until I kill Sibyl," Arvin replied.

He yanked his dagger from the Naneth-seed's back and got to work.

The dwarf shook his head. "I will be gone before then. Even if you succeed, you may be trapped here."

"No, I won't," Arvin said. He tilted his head at the Naneth-seed's hand. "Her ring is magical. It can teleport me out of here. Assuming, that is, that I survive."

As he spoke, he continued working to free his net. It was tricky work; one slip and he'd sever a strand of the net itself, ruining it. He could hear the *whuff-whuff-whuff* of wings in the corridor beyond the chamber, as well as running footsteps and the slither of scaly bodies. Sibyl and her clerics drew closer.

Pakal laid a broad hand on Arvin's shoulder. "You are a braver man than I. Thard Harr grant you strength." He began the prayer that would turn his body to air.

It was cut short by an angry hiss from the corridor outside. "Naneth!" Sibyl shouted. "You will regret betraying me."

A heartbeat later, a wave of magical fear boiled into the room, even stronger than before. Panic filled Arvin's mind as he whirled, searching for a way out of the chamber. There was only one exit, and it led straight to Sibyl. He was trapped . . .

No. There was another way out. Shoving his way past Pakal, who cringed on the floor, Arvin grabbed the Naneth-seed's hand. He sobbed in relief as he located the band of amber on one of her pudgy fingers. Yanking it free, he threw it onto the floor.

"*Ossalur!*" he cried.

The ring expanded.

Waves of magical fear lashed Arvin toward the circle of amber, which had grown to nearly two paces wide. Safety lay just a step or two away. Outside the chamber, he could hear Sibyl's furious hissing, could feel the rush of air from her wings as she approached.

No! he thought, fighting the compulsion to flee.

Rallying, he turned and scooped up his pack. The moment he'd been waiting for, planning for six months, was at hand. Sweat erupting on his brow from the strain, he plunged a hand into the pack. He'd almost freed the net. One good yank and it would be in his hands, ready to throw.

Then another wave of fear struck. Pakal leaped to his feet, wide-eyed. He clutched the box tight against his chest in white-knuckled fingers, trembling like a mouse about to be consumed by a serpent.

Arvin, fighting against the icy blasts of fear that threatened to sweep him off his feet like a hurricane, turned toward the doorway and saw Sibyl, her wings folded against her back, slithering through the hole. He started to yank the net from his pack . . .

Then Sibyl looked at him. *Saw* him. As a third wave of magical fear struck, the courage Arvin had found a moment before melted to slush in his veins. Screaming, his pack dragging behind, he darted for the ring. He grabbed Pakal as he ran past, yanking the dwarf with him into the circle of amber.

The scaled halls of the Temple of Varae vanished.

So did the magical fear.

Arvin cursed. Six months of planning and preparation, ruined. Despite the fact that his terror had been magically induced, he was disgusted with himself. He was a psion, a master of mind magic. His will should have been stronger than that. He ground his teeth together then reminded himself that all was not lost. At least he'd had the presence of mind to pull the dwarf to safety and to bring his pack with him. Maybe, gods willing, he'd get a second chance to throw his net at Sibyl.

Still trembling from the after effects of the magical fear, Arvin extricated himself from Pakal and looked around. The ring—shrunk back to its normal size—had teleported them to a rooftop garden under an open, starry sky. A fountain tinkled, spraying the nearby potted plants with a cool mist. Arvin took a closer look at the plants, each fashioned into a topiary of a coiled serpent. He'd seen them before. Even as the realization struck him, he heard a gate creak open. A woman swayed into view from the staircase leading to the railing-enclosed rooftop—a woman with long red hair, and a freckling of green scales.

Zelia.

"Arvin!" she hissed. She glanced down at Naneth's ring. "What have you done with my seed?"

CHAPTER 3

ARVIN STARED BACK AT ZELIA FOR A HEARTBEAT—THEN THREW up a mental tower around himself. A loud droning burst from his throat as he imagined himself in the form Tanju had taught him: one hand clenched above his head, a wall of iron around his will. With a thought, he expanded the walls of his mental tower outward to include Pakal, imagining his free hand extended to the dwarf behind him. Zelia was certain to attack their minds, but she wouldn't kill them before finding out what they were doing with Naneth's ring. Arvin's psionic tower would shield them from the worst of it.

The attack came immediately. Arvin heard the distant, tinkling-bell sound of Zelia's secondary display and felt her try to force her awareness into his body. Her will slithered around the defense he'd thrown up like a tide of snakes trying to find cracks in a tower wall. One forced its way through and entered his right hand. His fingers spasmed open, no longer under his control, and the backpack he held fell to the floor. The tendril of will wormed its way upward inside his arm, its scales rasping against bone; Arvin shoved it down and out with a mental push.

"Pakal!" he shouted. "Your darts!"

Instead of reaching for his blowpipe, the dwarf grunted a prayer and fluttered his hands. Pakal's body began disappearing as it turned to air. Arvin groaned, realizing Pakal was about to abandon him.

Zelia, meanwhile, had managed to find another chink in Arvin's defenses. Her mental snake slid inside his neck. It wrenched his head to the side, forcing him to look away from her. Two more tendrils of will forced their way into his legs. Zelia swayed forward, eyes triumphant.

"Kneel," she ordered. "Submit to me."

Arvin's knees buckled under him. Zelia smiled. Arvin tensed, terrified that she was about to seed him.

Her attention, however, was divided. She turned toward Pakal, a frown of concentration on her face. Pakal, however, continued his transformation. He stared at Arvin with eyes that held a hint of remorse and said something in his own language then vanished from sight. A breeze stirred the top of the nearest plant, then rippled away across the topiaries and over the wall.

Zelia cursed.

Her hold on Arvin lessened a little—enough for Arvin to manifest another power. Summoning energy into a power point at the base of his scalp, he created an illusionary image of himself prostrated at Zelia's feet. At the same time, his real self vanished from sight. Zelia frowned at the spot where the illusionary Arvin lay, probably wondering why he had capitulated so easily.

Arvin began drawing ectoplasm from the Astral Plane, shaping it into a vaguely human-shaped blob. Sparkles of silver light burst from his forehead as he worked, giving his position away. Zelia's head whipped up—but in that same moment the construct's fist slammed into her temple, snapping her head to the side. She collapsed in a boneless heap, crashing into the side of the fountain as she fell. Mist drifted down on her splayed body and closed eyelids.

Its chill didn't revive her.

Arvin ended his manifestation, and the construct disappeared. Shaking, he rose to his feet. He couldn't believe it. A year ago, he'd felled Zelia with a similar trick, using a simple psychokinetic power to levitate a knot of rope and knock her unconscious. Shaking his head in wonder, he touched the crystal at his throat.

"Nine—"

A hiss of laughter sounded behind him. Whirling, Arvin saw a second Zelia enter the garden.

"Surely you didn't think it would be that easy?" she said, closing the gate behind her.

She cocked a finger at him, as if inviting him to try something. Arvin heard a sound like the tinkling of tiny bells.

He stomped his foot. Zelia staggered but did not fall, nor, strangely, did she hurl an attack back at him. Arvin used the respite to yank ectoplasm from the Astral and braid it into the massive construct he hoped would overpower Zelia.

As he did, he felt a curious, hollow sensation at the base of his spine. The construct was taking far longer to manifest than it should have—and was drawing power at an incredible rate from his *muladhara*. Arvin tried cutting the manifestation short in mid-flow but couldn't. Energy spiraled out of his *muladhara* at a faster and faster rate, spilling into the air around him like water from a torn wineskin. He tried fighting it, tried sending his awareness deep into his *muladhara*, only to have his consciousness nearly shredded by the violent whirlpool he found there. A moment later, the last of his psionic energies spilled out and were gone.

Zelia smiled. "I see you've learned a thing or two since we last met," she said, "so have I."

Terrified, Arvin whipped a hand around his back. Before he could draw his dagger, Zelia's eyes flashed silver as if reflecting the moonlight. Her hand shot out and slapped his cheek. Arvin stumbled backward, unbalanced. His forearm was stuck to the small of his back. When he tried to wrench it free, it felt as if the skin was ripping. His free hand brushed against his hip—and stuck there, the cloth of his pants melting away as flesh fused with flesh. He stumbled, one knee knocking against the other. They stuck fast as well.

Completely unbalanced, he crashed to the floor. Clothing melted away from his body like paper in the rain as his calves were forced up against his thighs, his arms stuck to his sides, and his chin to his chest, the flesh fusing together like clay being smoothed by an invisible hand. He crumpled down into a fetal ball. As he blinked, his eyelids tried to fuse shut. With an immense effort, he managed to tear one of them open again. Even as he did, his ears closed over, blocking out the sound of his own ragged breathing.

Terror gripped him. He prayed to Tymora, to Hoar, to Ilmater—to any god or goddess who would listen. He could feel the crystal his mother had given him pressing into his throat. The flesh had grown over it, sealing it inside.

He watched with his one open eye—not daring to blink, lest the eyelid seal itself shut—as Zelia stepped out of view behind him. The dagger at the small of his back had likewise been buried inside folds of fused flesh—or rather, its sheath had. Arvin felt the blade slide out of the sheath as Zelia drew it. His heart beat with faint hope. Was she going to end his suffering? Would she truly show mercy?

She stepped in front of him again, holding the dagger. She jabbed its point into first one ear, then the other, cutting the flaps of skin that had grown over them. Then she sliced open his lips. Arvin gasped at the pain and began to choke on the blood he'd inhaled. When he was able to speak again, he told Zelia what she wanted to hear.

"You've beaten me," he said, blood dribbling from his lips onto the floor. He stared up at her with his one good eye. "What now?"

Instead of answering, she stepped over to the first Zelia—the one that lay either unconscious or dead. She laid a hand gently on that Zelia's neck, as though checking for a life pulse. Instead of continuing to rest gently on the neck, however, her fingers sank deep into it, as if into soft dough. Then the first Zelia began to shrink. Head and legs and arms shriveled into the torso, and the torso itself collapsed around the second Zelia's hand.

Zelia closed her hand around the last vestiges of the body it as it flowed into her palm and closed her eyes, taking a deep breath. She shivered and her head lolled back—and groaned in pleasure. Her fist fell open, empty. She opened her eyes and bent down to pick up Naneth's ring.

"How did you come to have this?" she asked.

Arvin stared defiantly up at her. Maybe she wasn't going to seed him after all. His lips were raw with pain, and he spat out the blood that had puddled in his mouth.

"Abyss take you," he swore.

Zelia swayed closer, tossing her long red hair. "You *will* tell me," she said, "one way or the other. When you've finished telling me, I'll end your suffering." She smirked. "Perhaps by compelling you to kill yourself."

Her eyes flashed and a soft tinkling filled the air as she manifested another power. Arvin felt it brush against his mind as softly as a cobweb—then tear apart, as if it were equally fragile.

Zelia frowned, then grabbed his hair and used it to roll his body back and forth like a ball as she examined him. Her eyes flashed a second time and a soft hissing filled the air as she concentrated on her manifestation. Her hand paused briefly over the braided leather bracelet on his right wrist, and hesitated a second time over the lump that had been Arvin's left hand. She probed with her fingers.

Arvin realized she had found Karrell's ring.

With quick, deft slices that sent fresh spasms of pain lancing through his hand and up his arm, Zelia cut Arvin's little finger apart from the rest, then yanked the ring from it. She held the ring in the fountain until the blood was gone from it, then gave it an appraising look.

A tear welled in Arvin's open eye. He said nothing, however. Zelia would have enjoyed listening to him plead for Karrell's ring. He stared at the backpack, lying no more than a pace away. He'd never be able to kill Sibyl. Zelia would no doubt claim the net inside it, as well . .

His breath caught as he realized there might be a way out. If he could trick Zelia into speaking the net's command word while still holding it, the magical net would kill her. Arvin would be free once the manifestation she'd used to fuse his flesh together ended.

Assuming it ever did end.

Zelia's eyes flashed silver a third time as she manifested the power that would allow her to listen in on Arvin's thoughts. Without Karrell's ring or his own psionics to counter it, he had only his own raw will to defend himself with—and Zelia tore through that like a knife through cloth. Arvin pretended to panic, filling his mind with thoughts of his backpack. He prayed—falsely—to Tymora that his luck would hold, that Zelia wouldn't take the net inside it, that she wouldn't speak its command word—*pullulios*—and toss it on him. That would inflict a terrible agony, one that would cause him to crumple and succumb to whatever she wanted.

Arvin felt Zelia push deeper into his mind. She chuckled. "Try that trick on someone who's going to fall for it." Then she continued to sift through his thoughts.

Arvin's mind reeled as his thoughts were peeled back, layer by layer.

Memories flashed before his eyes, terrible memories of confronting the marilith and watching in horror as the fate link he'd manifested yanked Karrell into the Abyss with it when the demon was banished. And wonderful memories of making love to Karrell—just a flash of that, and a long sequence, replayed more slowly, of the conversation they'd had just before.

Zelia rifled through his memories of everything Karrell had told him about the Circled Serpent, then through more recent memories of sneaking into the temple and getting close—but not quite close enough—to exact his revenge on Sibyl. She saw him meet Pakal, get past the tentacled mouth and undead snake to claim half of the Circled Serpent, confront the Naneth-seed and defeat it, and she saw them found by Sibyl then teleporting to the rooftop . . .

"The Circled Serpent was *here?*" Zelia hissed, releasing his mind at last. She glanced around, wary, then kicked Arvin. "Where did the dwarf go?"

Arvin slumped, exhausted in both mind and body. "I don't know," he answered at last. He stared, unseeing, at the fountain. He'd been violated. Used.

Zelia swore under her breath. She sputtered for several moments, her fangs bared, then got control of herself again. She turned back to Arvin.

"You are certain the Naneth-seed is dead?"

Arvin supposed she would kill him for that, especially since she'd learned all that his memories could tell her. He tried to nod, but his fused body just rocked back and forth on the floor.

"She's dead," he answered.

Zelia gave a false-sounding chuckle. "Just as well. I was growing tired of her. Mind seeds can be so . . . infuriating . . . at times. Naneth was constantly complaining about the body I chose for her. And she was getting . . . defiant. They all do, given enough time—" she stared down at Arvin—"some of them even before their seed has blossomed."

Arvin met her unblinking stare with his one good eye. "What do you expect?" he said. "They're all just as self-centered and vain as you are." Blood pooled in his mouth again, and he spat. "Now shut up and kill me."

Zelia's eyes widened in mock surprise. "Kill you?" She tilted her head. "Oh, no. I never waste anything I can still use."

Swaying into a crouch, she brushed a hand against his cheek. A shiver rushed through Arvin's body and a thin sheen of ectoplasm blossomed on his skin, forcing its way into the folds of fused flesh. His arms and legs sprang apart and his eyelid fluttered open. He rose, shaking, to his feet. Blood still dripped from his lips, his ears, and his left hand. He stared down at the latter, and saw that the little finger and the one next to it were sliced open along their lengths. He picked up one of the scraps of cloth that remained from his shirt and wrapped the fingers together, debating whether or not he should attack Zelia. He glanced at his backpack. It was within reach, but the net had probably rooted itself back into the leather again.

Zelia saw his glance and bared her fangs: a warning not to try anything. She held up Karrell's ring. "You think she's dead, don't you?"

Arvin stared at the floor. "The demon drew her into the Abyss. Nobody can survive there."

"It drew her into Smaragd, you mean."

Arvin glanced up. "What are you talking about?"

"Smaragd is a layer of Abyss, the layer where Sseth dwells. That's where Karrell would have wound up."

"How do you know that?"

"Mariliths range throughout the Abyss, but this one was summoned by a servant of Sseth. It's the most likely place for the demon to have come from, and its banishment would have returned it there."

Arvin pressed his damaged lips together. The sting of cut flesh helped blot out the ache in his heart. "Even if she did get dragged into . . . there, she's still—"

"Dead?" Zelia gave a hiss of derisive laughter. "You humans know so little. Smaragd is dangerous but not completely inhospitable to mortals, especially if the mortal is yuan-ti. Your precious Karrell may still be alive."

Arvin felt a surge of hope. Karrell—alive? Zelia knew more about the Abyss than he did. Maybe she was right about this Smaragd layer being survivable, except that Karrell's god, Ubtao, was an enemy of Sseth. The serpent god would have immediately killed any cleric of Ubtao's that showed up in his realm. Zelia was toying with him, tempting him with the one possibility that she *knew*—now that she'd raped his memories—would most torment him.

He walked over to the fountain and splashed water onto his face, washing away the blood. "Quit lying to me," he told her, "and let's get this over with. Tell me what you want." He turned to her, his face dripping. "Why am I so 'useful?' Because I have something that can kill Sibyl?"

Zelia laughed. "That too," she said, her eyes glinting, "but also because you have eyes in Smaragd."

"Eyes?" Arvin echoed. He'd expected Zelia to send him on his way, to either order him back into the temple to make another attempt on Sibyl or to chase after Pakal and retrieve the Circled Serpent—perhaps after seeding him first, though he was starting to suspect she might have used her last power stone when she seeded Naneth.

"Eyes," Zelia repeated. "Karrell's eyes."

"She's dead." Arvin touched the lapis lazuli embedded in his forehead under a layer of scar tissue. "I tried sending to her, every day for more than a month."

"You kept my stone? How touching," she mocked. Her voice grew serious again. "A sending doesn't always penetrate to another plane. Smaragd lies deep in the Abyss—more than seventy layers shield it from this plane. There is another power, however, which can be used to view a mortal on another plane, even one as remote as Smaragd. And by viewing that mortal, to get a glimpse of what is happening on that layer of the Abyss."

Arvin's head came up. His breath caught as hope blossomed a second time in his chest. "You really do think Karrell's alive, don't you?"

Zelia gave a slow serpent nod.

Arvin hesitated, wondering if she'd just tricked him somehow. "What . . . is it, exactly, that you hope to see? Sseth?"

Zelia smiled. "Aren't you the smart little monkey?" She passed Arvin back his dagger then sank down, cross-legged, and patted the floor next to her. "Sit."

Arvin sheathed the dagger, hesitated, then did as she'd ordered. Aside from tatters of his clothing he was naked, and the stone floor felt cool against his skin. The only sound was that of water tinkling into the fountain. He glanced across the city's rooftops, glowing green against the night sky. He couldn't believe that he was sitting in that rooftop garden, talking to the woman he most feared. It was as if he'd stepped back in time to the night when Zelia taught him to master his psionic powers. But if there was a chance that Karrell was alive—even a small chance—he wanted to hear what Zelia had to say.

"For some time now—more than a decade—Sseth has been . . . strangely muted," she began. "His clerics are still granted spells, and the god still answers their prayers, but the voice of Sseth has changed in subtle ways. They say it has deepened, become somehow drier, more whispery . . ."

"Drier?" Arvin asked.

Zelia shrugged. "I am not a cleric." She toyed with the ring in her hands. "But I do serve House Extaminos, and that noble House controls the Cathedral of Emerald Scales. Anything that is of concern to its clerics disturbs Lady Dediana, and that, in turn, disturbs *me*."

"The clerics think something's happened to Sseth?" Arvin asked.

Zelia nodded. "A little over two years ago, I had a troubling dream, a dream of a larger serpent swallowing a smaller serpent, tail first. As the smaller serpent started to disappear into the larger one's jaws, it twisted and took the larger serpent's tail in its own mouth, and started consuming it in turn. Each serpent choked the other down, until both disappeared."

She paused to flick away the venom that had beaded on her fangs with a blue forked tongue. "I wasn't the only one to have this dream," she continued. "Dozens of other yuan-ti shared it—or one similar to it." She nodded at the ring. "Karrell was one of them. She told me of her dream when we spoke in Ormpetarr. She was one of the few to recognize the snakes in the dream for what they were: the two halves of the Circled Serpent."

Zelia obviously expected a startled reaction. Arvin didn't grant her one.

"Go on," he said.

"That same winter, a restlessness gripped the yuan-ti. Dmetrio Extaminos began his restoration of the ancient city, and Sibyl arrived in Hlondeth. Lady Dediana, deep in winter torpor, didn't recognize the danger Sibyl posed at first, not until Sibyl had killed her cousin Urshas and lured half of the cathedral's clergy away by claiming to be Sseth's avatar. By then it was almost too late."

"What's this got to do with . . . Smaragd?" Arvin asked, stumbling over the unfamiliar word. "And with Karrell?"

"That's what I hope to find out," Zelia said. "Why has Sseth not struck down an imposter? Does he condone what Sibyl is doing? Or is he merely . . . keeping silent?"

Arvin frowned. "You hope to find that out just by looking at Karrell? Why not look in on Sseth himself, or *ask* him?"

"Because I can't," Zelia hissed. "No one can—not even his clerics. Something is preventing it, but that same something may not prevent us from viewing a mortal in Sseth's realm. Your Karrell may be the crack in the wall that will allow us a glimpse into Smaragd."

"Why do you need me?" Arvin asked.

"If I tried to contact her, Karrell would resist, but she won't resist you. She trusts you."

"Why should I trust *you?* Given the way your mind seeds scheme behind your back, it looks as though you can't even trust yourself."

Zelia's lip twitched, revealing the tips of her fangs. Arvin's taunt had struck home. He knew, thanks to the dreams he'd had while seeded, that at least one of Zelia's seeds—a dwarf—had turned on her. He wondered how many others had betrayed her over the years.

With a visible effort, Zelia composed herself. "Don't you want to find out if Karrell is alive?"

Arvin stared back at her for a long moment. At last he nodded and said, "There's just one problem. I don't know the power that will let me view someone at a distance."

"That's easily remedied."

Silver flashed in Zelia's eyes. She sat silent, staring out over the wrought iron railing that enclosed the rooftop garden. After several moments, a finger-sized crystal rose into view and floated toward her. She caught it then passed it to Arvin.

He glanced at the crystal. It was deep blue and blade-shaped: thin, with a chisel-like point at one end. Azurite.

"A power stone," he said.

Zelia nodded.

Arvin closed his hand around it. "You trust me to tell you what I see?" he asked.

Zelia laughed. "No. That's why I'm going to look through your eyes."

Arvin shuddered. He'd had Zelia inside his head—or rather, a fragment of her—a year ago when she planted her mind seed. Having her coiled around his thoughts wasn't an experience he wanted to repeat, even briefly, but it was something he had to do. If Karrell *was* alive. . . .

"Let's do it," he said through gritted teeth.

Zelia stared into his eyes. Silver flashed across her pupils, then was gone. An instant later Arvin felt a soft fluttering under the scar on his forehead, the lapis lazuli silently alerting him to the fact that someone was watching him—from inside his own skull. As Zelia settled in behind his eyes, he saw her as she viewed herself: confident, poised, powerful—desirable. Then it was gone.

"How do I hail the crystal?" he asked.

"By its name," Zelia said. "Gergorissa."

Arvin whispered the name. He sent his awareness deep into the crystal and felt it awaken.

Yes? a female voice hissed as a mote of pale green light bloomed in the darkness. The voice was unsettlingly close to Zelia's own, and for a moment, Arvin thought Zelia had spoken to him. She must have created the power stone.

Arvin grasped the mote of light with his mind. He felt its energy rush into the base of his skull, filling the power point there. Suddenly he *knew* how to view Karrell anywhere on any plane of existence.

Assuming she was still alive.

Holding his breath, he manifested that power—and gasped as Karrell appeared in his mind's eye.

She sat slumped on the floor of a dripping jungle, arms clasped around her round, protruding belly. She was still pregnant, but otherwise she looked terrible. Her cheeks were hollow, her eyes dark, her hair tangled. The dress she wore was in rags and her arms and legs were covered in angry red scratches. The scar on her cheek from the sword wound the marilith had inflicted was barely visible under the dried mud that smudged her face. A tear trickled down her cheek, eroding a furrow through the grime. Despite her condition and the desperate, exhausted look in her eye, she was beautiful. Arvin's breath caught in his throat. He ached to reach out and touch her, to hold her.

To save her.

Karrell glanced up, startled.

"Karrell," Arvin whispered in a choked voice. "It's me."

Her eyes widened. "Arvin?" she gasped. "You're alive?"

Arvin almost laughed. Six months in the Abyss, and she was worried about *him*. "It's me, *kiichpan chu'al*. I'm alive."

Karrell's image blurred as tears formed in his eyes. Suddenly, they blinked rapidly: Zelia, trying to clear them. Arvin tried to push her from his mind.

Don't, she cautioned, shoving back hard enough to make his eyes bulge. *Talk to her, before the manifestation ends. Ask her what's happened to Sseth.*

Karrell continued to stare at Arvin. "Where are you?"

"In Hlondeth." He shook his head, still not quite willing to believe his eyes. "How did you survive?" he asked. "It's been so long."

Karrell gave him a weary smile. "By Ubtao's will," she said, "and through my own resourcefulness." She laid a hand gently on her stomach. "Because I had to."

Zelia gave him a mental jab that made his mind ache.

"Where are you?" Arvin continued. "In Smaragd? With Sseth?"

Karrell didn't seem to find his question odd. "Yes. The serpent god is stuck fast. His jungle has bound him. I escaped from the marilith, and now it's searching for me. It still thinks our fates are linked. It's been protecting me, but when I start to give birth, and it doesn't feel my pain . . ." she shuddered. "I can't let it find me."

Ask her more about Sseth, Zelia interrupted. *Is the god asleep? Awake?*

Arvin ignored her. He stared at Karrell's stomach. "The children. Are they still . . . ?"

Karrell smiled. "Alive? Yes. And kicking—at least one of them has feet, and not a tail." She bit her lip. A haunted look crept into her eyes. "It won't be long now. When my time comes, I won't be able to run any more. The marilith—"

"I'll get you out of there," Arvin promised. "I don't know how, but I will. I'll find a way."

"Find Ts'ikil," Karrell said. "She'll know what to do."

Sseth, Zelia insisted. *Tell her to go to where Sseth is.*

Karrell looked warily around. "Arvin! Did you hear a hissing noise?"

"It's nothing," Arvin lied, mentally shoving Zelia back as he spoke. "Who is Ts'ikil? Where is she?"

"She's—"

Their connection broke. Arvin found himself staring at Zelia across the rooftop garden. He leaped to his feet, furious. "What did you do that for?" he shouted.

Zelia gave him a long, unblinking stare. "You were supposed to make her go to where Sseth is."

Arvin almost laughed. "Karrell? I can't *make* her do anything." He sighed. "You got what you wanted—you heard Karrell. If she says Sseth is bound, he is."

Zelia thought about this for several moments, her eyes narrowed. Then she lounged back against the fountain, a lazy smile on her lips. She looked like a serpent that had just swallowed a juicy, squirming morsel.

"Karrell's pregnant?" she hissed. She gave him a withering look. "By you—a *human?*"

"You can hardly talk, given what *you* like to sleep with," Arvin shot back at her, "and Karrell's pregnancy is none of your business."

"Oh but it is," Zelia said, rising smoothly to her feet. "It makes you so much more . . . motivated."

"To do what?" Arvin asked, his voice tense.

"To rescue her." She let the silence stretch out between them for several heartbeats, then added, "Wouldn't you like to know how? Or would you rather let your children be born in the Abyss? I don't think they'd last long. Karrell couldn't possibly protect them. They'd be no more than a soft, squishy mouthful for any passing—"

"Get on with it," Arvin snapped. "How do I rescue her?" His hands balled into tight fists.

"By using the Circled Serpent. It can open a door to Smaragd."

"You lie," Arvin said in a low voice. "It opens a door to the Fugue Plain, to the lair of Dendar, the Night Serpent. If that door opens and Dendar is released, thousands will die."

"That's true," Zelia said, "but the Circled Serpent opens more than one door. There is a second—the door that Sseth used nearly fourteen centuries ago, when he vanished from this plane and became a god, a door that leads directly to Smaragd . . . and to Karrell."

Arvin stood rigid, stunned. "You're . . . making this up," he said. "It's a trick." He thought back to the little he had learned of the serpent god's lore from the dreams he'd had after Zelia seeded him. "Sseth left the realm of mortals by flying into a volcano," he told her, "one of the Peaks of Flame in Chult. Your own memories of the Cathedral of Emerald Scales told me that much."

Zelia hissed with laughter. "You believed them?" she taunted. Then the mocking smile fell away from her lips. "That's the official version," she said, "the one the clergy teach the laity. The clerics themselves know that Sseth left his plane of existence through a door, not an erupting volcano. The trouble is, nobody remembers where that door is, save that it is somewhere on the Chultan Peninsula. Over the centuries, the legends became intertwined. Some—Sibyl, for example—mistakenly conclude that Sseth entered Dendar's lair and somehow slipped from the Fugue Plain into Smaragd, though this is a ridiculous notion." She paused to shake her head, as if disappointed in Sibyl. Then her eyes glittered. "Using the Circled Serpent, you can open a door to Smaragd and rescue Karrell."

"There's just one problem," Arvin said. "I only know where half of the Circled Serpent is—with Pakal—and I don't know where he is."

"You'll find him," Zelia said.

"Maybe," Arvin countered, "but then what?"

"Dmetrio Extaminos still has the second half."

"I don't know where *he* is, either."

"I do," Zelia said. "His mind has been dulled lately by too much *osssra*, but he's still perfectly capable." She pointed at the scar on Arvin's forehead. "When you retrieve the first half from the dwarf, use my stone to contact me. I'll tell you where Dmetrio is—and where the door to Smaragd is. Together, you and Dmetrio can open it."

Arvin hesitated. He knew he couldn't trust Zelia, but what if the Circled Serpent *would* allow him to rescue Karrell? It was the only shard of hope he'd found. He clung to it, even though it cut deeply.

He met Zelia's eye. "You know I'll try to take Dmetrio's half of the Circled Serpent and open the door myself."

"Yes," Zelia answered, a gleam in her eye.

"Then why trust me?"

"I don't," she hissed, "but if you don't do exactly as I say, I'll tell the marilith that its fate is no longer linked with Karrell's. When the demon catches her—and it will—Karrell will die . . . and so will your children."

Arvin felt the blood drain from his face. He should have expected as much. Zelia always made sure she had something to threaten him with—and Karrell herself had handed Zelia just the weapon she needed.

"I'll need Karrell's ring back," he said at last.

Zelia tossed it to him—an offhanded gesture, as if the ring meant nothing to her. Arvin caught it and squeezed it tight in his hand. He stared at Zelia.

"What's in it for you?"

"The eternal gratitude of Lady Dediana Extaminos," she answered, "when it is her son—not Sibyl—who enters Smaragd, frees Sseth, and reaps the rewards of service to a god."

Arvin let out a long, slow breath. Dmetrio also wanted to become Sseth's avatar? For a year, Arvin had struggled against one arrogant yuan-ti who wanted to become a god, and Zelia was proposing that he join forces with another—with a man who had callously used then abandoned a woman who had been pregnant with his child, a man who had the backing of Arvin's most feared enemy.

Arvin rubbed his temples. It was a dangerous game he was about to play. In order to rescue Karrell—and not release an evil god in the process—he would need to find a way to defeat Zelia.

"Well?" she asked.

He closed his eyes and shuddered. Zelia still controlled his destiny, as certainly as if she'd seeded him. She liked watching him squirm.

"I'll do it," he whispered, "for Karrell and our children."

Chapter 4

ARVIN WINCED AS THE FLESHMENDER TURNED HIS HAND OVER, studying his lacerated fingers.

"Strange wound," she said.

Arvin merely nodded. "Can you heal it?"

The cleric was a young, blonde-haired woman who might have been pretty save for the deep lines in her forehead, the price to be paid for taking on the suffering of others. She returned his nod.

"The Crying God feels your pain, my son," she intoned.

Dressed in ash-gray tunic, trousers, and matching gray skullcap, she had Ilmater's symbol—a pair of bound hands—pinned over her heart.

Arvin remembered that symbol well from his childhood. The severed hands—he always thought of them that way—and the other symbols of martyrdom had decorated the orphanage. Ilmater's martyred clerics were painted in vivid glory, spotted with plague sores, being torn apart by wolves, or covered in open, weeping wounds. All had their faces turned toward Shurrock, a savage domain of broken hills, torrential rains, howling winds, and wild beasts. Ilmater's dwelling place—the domain where his faithful would reap their reward of eternal suffering.

Arvin could have gone to a guild healer, but that would have meant answering unwanted questions. The guild frowned upon members taking on "outside work." But in the Chapel of Healing that catered to the humans of Hlondeth, the only demand made was a coin or two—whatever the petitioner could afford—in the wooden donation box.

Darkmorning had almost ended, and outside the chapel, the streets were quiet. Only Arvin sought healing. Come sunrise, however, the chapel's stone benches would be filled with petitioners.

The cleric murmured a prayer—one that Arvin could recite from memory, even though healing prayers had been used infrequently at the orphanage; the clerics believed that suffering built character in children. The wounds on his fingers slowly closed. She touched his mouth and ears, and the sting of each wound faded. When she was finished, she held his left hand in hers and touched his abbreviated little finger.

"This," she said, lifting his hand slightly, "is too old a wound for me to heal. It requires a Painbearer's touch."

"That's all right," Arvin said. He had no desire to meet any of the senior clerics. The only reason he'd come to the chapel was that it was run by the order's most junior clerics—men and women who weren't old enough to dredge up unpleasant memories. "I'm used to it," he told her.

He didn't bother to explain what the guild would do to him if they found he'd removed their mark. One day, perhaps, when he was finally clear of Hlondeth, he might seek out a cleric who could regenerate his finger, but. . . .

She released his hand. "You have the face of someone who has seen much suffering. Ilmater bless you and help you to bear your load."

Arvin stood. He was grateful for Ilmater's healing, but that was as far as it went. The last thing he needed was another god meddling in his life.

As he dropped coins in the donation box, a disheveled woman rushed through the door, an infant lying limp in her arms.

"She's been bitten!" the woman shrieked. "There was a snake! A snake in her swaddling basket! She started to cry—it woke me—and I saw she had its tail in her fist. It bit her. Please, oh please, can you save her?"

The cleric turned her attention to the baby, touching its tiny hand and intoning a spell. Arvin watched a moment—the mother was panting from her run, and it was probably already too late for the poison to be neutralized—then he slipped out the door. He really didn't want to see the outcome. As he walked away from the chapel, he heard the cleric murmur condolences and the mother break into loud sobs. At least, he thought grimly, the woman had known the joy of holding her child in her arms, if only for a short time.

He wondered if Karrell would live to do the same.

As he walked the narrow, curving street, awash in the faint green glow from the buildings on either side, he struggled with his conscience. Karrell would be wary of his forced alliance with Zelia—she'd made the same mistake herself, six months before, with near-disastrous results. She would certainly condemn any plan that ran the risk of both halves of the Circled Serpent falling into the hands of one of Sseth's devotees. Arvin ached to speak to Karrell again, but the sending he'd attempted after leaving Zelia's rooftop garden had failed, just like the rest of them.

He still couldn't quite believe that Zelia had let him go. She'd tossed a blanket at him when he requested something to hide his nakedness—he'd since retrieved a change of clothes and tossed the blanket on a garbage heap—then escorted him out of her garden and down the ramp to the street. He'd followed her warily, expecting her to seed him, but she hadn't. Perhaps she thought recovering Pakal's half of the Circled Serpent would take more than seven days.

He paused beside one of the city's public fountains and scooped up a drink of water in his hands. A line of scar tissue ran down the finger the cleric had just healed, wavy as a snake. He wiped his fingers dry on his trousers. Zelia had drained his *muladhara*, but he still had his lapis lazuli. If he was going to steal the Circled Serpent from Pakal, he'd better get on with it.

He closed his eyes, concentrating on the dwarf's face. The scar tissue on his forehead tingled as the lapis lazuli activated, and Pakal's image solidified in his mind. The dwarf was awake, sweat trickling down his face as he walked through the darkness. Arvin couldn't see Pakal's surroundings—a sending only showed the person contacted—but it looked as though the dwarf was trudging up a steep incline.

Choosing his words carefully, Arvin spoke directly to Pakal's mind.

He'd already decided to tell the truth—part of it, anyway. *Karrell's alive*, he said, *in trouble. She told me to find Ts'ikil. Where are you? I need your help. Use few words; this spell is brief.*

Pakal halted, his eyes wide. He stared straight ahead for a moment—he would be seeing, in his mind's eye, a faint image of Arvin's face. Delight, then caution played across the dwarf's face. At last his expression settled into a look of contrition, and he spoke. Though the words were into the dwarf's own language, Arvin understood them as they flowed into his mind. *I will take you to Ts'ikil. Meet me at the temple on Mount Ugruth. I will wait there.* He paused, then added, *I am sorry I fled, but duty—*

Pakal's image vanished as the sending ended. Arvin frowned, wondering why Pakal would be heading for another god's temple, especially one dedicated to Talos, god of destruction. Arvin wouldn't be able to ask him, however, until the next night. The lapis lazuli would only allow him to contact any given individual once per day. He stared over the city, toward Mount Ugruth. A smudge of black smoke wafted from the volcanic peak up into the gradually brightening sky.

Arvin realized he was exhausted. He'd been awake for a day and a night, but he was too keyed up to sleep. He had to get moving to rescue Karrell.

As he turned away from the fountain, something brushed against his foot. He glanced down and nearly jumped as he saw a slender orange snake with large, bulging eyes slither out of a crack at the base of the fountain. The snake met his gaze and hissed a warning. Slowly, Arvin backed away from the fountain. Whether it was a natural snake or a yuan-ti in serpent form, he didn't want to make any sudden moves, not with its fangs bared and ready to strike.

The snake turned away and slithered up the street. With dawn approaching and the shadows lifting from the street, Arvin saw dozens of snakes emerge from cracks between buildings and holes in the ground. They slithered uphill, toward the section of Hlondeth where the nobles lived. Several of the snakes had scale patterns he'd never seen before: checkered beige-and-black with a circle of white crowning the head; jet black with a creamy pink belly; and cream-and-black bands with large red dots on each cream band. He was reminded of the legend of how Lord Shevron had summoned snakes to defeat the kobolds that crept through Hlondeth's sewers in the Year of Tatters to attack the city, except that these snakes slithered up from the sewers, not down into them. They were headed for the palace, rather than emerging from it.

Something was up—and Arvin was certain Sibyl was behind it. A fragment of her welcoming speech to the Se'sehen in the altar room came back to him then, her promises that those loyal to her would soon reap their reward . . . in Hlondeth. The oddly patterned snakes must have been yuan-ti from the south—the Se'sehen, breaking their longstanding alliance with Hlondeth. With that realization, a rush of anger filled him. One of those serpents must have been responsible for the death of the infant in the chapel.

A door opened to Arvin's left, and he waved back the sleepy-looking girl who emerged with a water jug.

"Bar your door!" Arvin shouted at the her. "The city is under attack."

Startled, the girl fled back into her home.

Arvin activated his lapis lazuli a second time. He paused, wondering who to send his warning to. He had never spoken with Hlondeth's ruler face to face, but he had seen her from a distance. He could visualize Lady Dediana well enough to contact her, but she wouldn't know who he was and might not heed his warning. Instead, with great reluctance, he visualized Zelia.

She was sleeping, but her eyes sprang open at Arvin's mental shout: *Zelia—wake up! Sibyl and the Se'sehen are attacking the city. They're moving toward the palace in serpent form, even as I speak.*

Zelia didn't even bother to reply. She merely nodded then with a brusque mental push, broke off the sending. Arvin shrugged; it was exactly what he'd expected. He'd acted instinctively in sending the warning. Hlondeth had been his home for too many years for him to ignore a threat to it, especially one that came from Sibyl. But did it really matter, to the humans who lived there which faction of serpents ruled them?

A gong sounded from somewhere up the hill, followed by another, farther in the distance. A bright flash of yellow seared the air above the section where the nobles lived, followed a heartbeat later by a thunderous boom. There were cries close by—humans, no doubt startled to find so many serpents slithering along the streets. Hlondeth's yuan-ti traditionally kept to the viaducts that arched overhead.

Arvin could hear shouted questions as people asked what was going on in the nobles' section, where a pillar of vivid green flame had just whooshed down out of a clear sky. Some cried that Mount Ugruth was erupting, while others, feeling the rumbling tremors under their feet, shouted back that no, it was an earthquake.

Arvin's part in this battle over—he'd passed on his message, and it was up to Zelia to relay it. He ran for the nearest city gate. People spilled out of doorways on either side as he ran past, some frightened, some clutching children or valuables to their chests, all looking confused. A half-elf holding his unlaced trousers up with one hand glanced sharply at Arvin as if he'd recognized him, then flicked his free hand to get Arvin's attention and gave a quick gesture in the silent speech: *What's happening?*

War, Arvin signed back as he ran past.

The guild member broke into a grin and grabbed an empty leather sack that had been hanging just inside the door. Then he ran toward the sound of the fighting.

Arvin turned into a wider street with shops on either side. Though none were yet open for business, the shuttered windows on their upper stories had been flung wide. People leaned out of them and called to each other across the street. Several shouted down at him, asking what was happening. Arvin ignored them; he needed his breath for running. He felt a tickle under the scar on his forehead. Zelia, looking in on him psionically? He slowed to a trot, expecting her to manifest some communication with him, but nothing happened. The tickling sensation continued. Someone, he realized, was scrying him.

An unpleasant possibility occurred to him. If Sibyl's crystal ball had survived the collapse of the altar room, it might be the abomination observing him. She'd gotten a good look at both Arvin and Pakal just before they'd teleported away with her half of the Circled Serpent; she'd be able to home in on him.

Fortunately, Arvin still had the net he'd created to kill her inside the backpack that bounced up and down against his shoulders.

He started to run into a circular plaza with streets radiating from it in five directions. At its center was a wrought-iron streetlight in the form of a rearing cobra. Something about it caught his eye, and he skidded to a stop. The streetlight was smaller than usual and of brightly burnished metal, rather than a dull black. It didn't have a glowing white stone in its mouth—and it was *swaying*.

As the metal snake turned and fastened glowing red eyes on Arvin, the sensation in his forehead intensified. This creature—whatever it was—had been using divination magic to search for him.

One of Sibyl's creatures!

With a scrape of metal on stone, the iron cobra slithered toward Arvin.

Unable to manifest his psionics due to his depleted *muladhara* and certain his dagger would be useless, Arvin turned and ran. Behind him, the scraping sound quickened. The iron cobra hissed like hot steam escaping from a boiling kettle. Panting, Arvin turned down a narrow alley, only to find that it dead-ended against the city wall. He leaped, activating the magic of his bracelet as he hurtled through the air. He slammed into the wall, knocking the air from his lungs, but his fingers and toes found a grip. The iron cobra lunged, and Arvin heard a *clang* as it struck the wall just below his foot. Venom splattered onto his boot. He scrambled up the wall, praying that the metal serpent wasn't capable of following.

It wasn't. As Arvin climbed, it remained coiled at the base of the wall, hissing softly, bathed in a faint green light from the glowing stones. It flared its hood and watched with ember-red eyes as Arvin climbed to the top of the wall and hauled himself onto the battlements. Then it turned and slithered back up the alley.

Arvin stood, panting, hands on knees. "Nine lives," he whispered, touching the crystal at his neck.

From inside the city came distant screams and more explosions. A militia member ran toward him along the wall, sword in hand. The soldier's flared helmet and scale armor reminded Arvin of the serpent he'd narrowly escaped.

"Out of the way!" the soldier shouted as he shoved past Arvin.

He clattered down a staircase a short distance beyond. Then he cried out in alarm. Arvin heard the clash of metal on metal—a single *clang*—then a *thud* as something heavy hit the street below. He straightened, wary. A heartbeat later, a metal head rose from the staircase and looked around. The iron cobra.

Cursing, Arvin clambered over the far side of the wall. He climbed down as quickly as he could, but the smooth green stones had been designed to offer little to grip, even to someone with a magical bracelet.

Above him, Arvin heard a rasping noise as the iron cobra slithered through a slit in the battlements. Realizing it was about to drop on him, Arvin shoved off the wall, twisting as he fell. He landed awkwardly, crashing down onto hands and knees in a tangle of gourd vines. As he scrambled to his feet, nearly tripping over one of the large, rock-hard gourds, he heard a *thump* behind him and a soft, metallic hiss.

Arvin looked around. The sun was rising—it was finally light enough to see clearly—but the iron cobra was screened by the vines. It was somewhere between Arvin and the wall. If he ran right or left it would merely change course and outflank him. Arvin wished he had a magical entangling rope—the net in his backpack would work only on living flesh—or even a sturdy club or a tree to climb, but the field he'd landed in offered none of those.

As he turned, the tingle in his forehead intensified. He smiled as he realized which direction the attack would come from. He started to sling his backpack around to the front, thinking he might be able to shove it at the serpent like a shield. Then he had a better idea. Yanking out his dagger, he slashed one of the vines and lifted the yellow gourd, holding it like a morningstar.

"Come on, you scaly bastard," he breathed, turning in the direction the magical tingling came from. "Come on . . ."

A gleam—morning sunlight on burnished iron scales—gave him a moment's warning. The iron cobra lunged up from the vines in a lightning-fast strike. Arvin whipped the gourd forward, slamming it into the serpent's head, but it was like hitting a solid metal door. The iron cobra's aim was knocked off only slightly—just enough that its teeth snagged and tore the hem of Arvin's shirt—but the blow itself didn't harm the cobra in the least. It reared back, body coiled beneath it, glowing red eyes watching the gourd, then lashed out again.

Arvin started to swing the gourd—but checked its motion, pulling the vine through his hand until the gourd was against his fist. He punched it into the cobra's gaping mouth, forcing the gourd down its throat. Metal fangs scraped along the gourd, then hooked fast. The vine was yanked through Arvin's fingers as the cobra tore its head away.

The iron cobra hissed and shook its head back and forth, trying to fling the plug from its mouth. It tried to gulp down the gourd, but couldn't swallow it. The metal bands that made up its body wouldn't expand enough. It lashed its tail in fury, ripping the vines around it into a tangle.

Arvin didn't wait around to see how long it would take to get the gourd out. He plunged through the field, tripping over gourds and falling several times as vines snagged his ankles. Ahead lay the road from the city's northern gate. People streamed out of Hlondeth, fleeing the fighting that echoed within the walls.

Arvin ran toward a cart being pulled by a horse. As he closed the gap, an elegantly painted ceramic jug spilled out the back and smashed on the road in a spray of dark red wine. The driver continued whipping his horse, trying to force it through the crowd, heedless of the missing cargo. Arvin vaulted up onto the cart and tried to find a place to stand among the rolling jugs.

The driver started to glance in Arvin's direction, then stared at something beyond him and gasped. Arvin glanced over his shoulder and saw the cobra rearing, its head level with the cart, its mouth clear. It lashed out, its fangs missing Arvin's hand by a hair's breadth. Then the cart veered off the road and into a fallow field. The horse broke into a trot, leaving the cobra behind. It followed, but the cart was moving too quickly for it to catch.

The driver of the cart turned again, met Arvin's eye, then broke into laughter. Arvin, taking a better look at him, was equally bemused. The driver was the half-elf Arvin had warned earlier, the one with the unlaced trousers. His long black hair was tangled and dusty, and one of his eyes was starting to purple. Someone must have thrown a punch at him. His trousers were laced and belted, and a thin black wand was tucked into the belt. A leather bag sat between his feet, bulging with something that clinked as the cart jostled along. Passing the whip into the hand that held the reins, he extended his left hand. Arvin took it and clambered onto the seat beside him.

"Good haul, hey?" the half-elf grinned, tipping his head at the dozens of jugs the cart held.

Arvin nodded, still panting from his mad scramble across the field.

"Was that a yuan-ti chasing you?" the driver asked.

"It was a——" Arvin paused, not really sure what it was. Better not to say too much. "Yes," he lied. "I think so."

Once they were ahead of the refugees the half-elf tugged on the reins, steering the horse back onto the road. "I just hope whatever you got was worth it."

"My life," Arvin muttered, touching a finger to his crystal.

The driver grunted. "You can call me Darris," he said, holding out a hand.

Arvin clasped it. "Call me Vin, and thanks for the ride."

Darris made a circle with forefinger and thumb and flicked it open, then tapped his index fingers lightly together: *It's nothing, friend.*

"Where are you headed?" Arvin asked.

Darris glanced back at the city. A mansion in the noble section burned, throwing a plume of dirty gray smoke into the air. Figures struggled in combat on the viaducts. Arvin saw two tiny shapes fall, snake tails flailing, into the street below.

"Away from that," the half-elf said at last. "Somewhere I can stash this until things cool down." He glanced at Arvin's abbreviated little finger and added. "Somewhere the guild won't take their cut."

Arvin nodded at the road that switchbacked up into the hills, toward Mount Ugruth. "There's an old quarry about a day's journey up the aqueduct road," he said. "Lots of broken rock, lots of places to hide things. The Talos worshipers use it as a stopping place on their way up the mountain, and they've built some huts out of the rubble."

"Sounds like as good a place as any," Darris said, flicking the reins.

Arvin whispered a prayer to Tymora, thanking her for sending Darris his way. Riding in a cart, he stood an excellent chance of catching up to Pakal.

He glanced back at the city one last time. Sunlight glinted off an object that slithered along the road, causing the refugees to draw away from it in fear. It was the iron cobra, still following him, and still producing a tickling sensation in the scar on Arvin's forehead.

"What's wrong?" Darris asked.

"It's the . . . yuan-ti," Arvin said. "He's following us."

Darris flicked the reins again. "Don't worry. He won't catch us, not unless he sprouts wings."

Arvin nodded, uneasy. The metal construct might not have wings, but Sibyl did. The battle of Hlondeth was keeping her busy for the moment, but when it was over, the iron cobra would lead her straight to him.

The cart jolted to a stop. Shaken awake, Arvin rose from the space he'd cleared for himself between the jugs of wine and looked around. By the slant of the sun, it was late afternoon. They had reached the quarry. Arvin recognized the cliff that had been cut into the forested hillside, the large blocks of broken stone that littered the ground, and the crude shelters that had been built out of unmortared stone and tree branches. When he'd been there a year ago, the place had been crawling with Talos worshipers. It had since been deserted.

Arvin rubbed the scar on his forehead. The tickling sensation was gone. The iron cobra had either given up its search, or they'd left it far behind.

"Looks like we've got the place to ourselves," he observed.

"Not for long," Darris said as he climbed down from the cart. "We passed a gaggle of doomsayers on the way up here. They wanted me to stop and sell them wine, but I told them they'd have to wait until they reached the quarry." He looped the reins of the horse around a tree branch and lifted the leather sack down from the driver's seat. It must have been heavy; he staggered slightly as he stepped back from the cart. "I wanted a chance to dispose of this first."

The cart had pulled up under the aqueduct that ran alongside the road. Mist drifted down from above, a welcome respite from the heat. Arvin turned his face toward it and closed his eyes, savoring the spray.

"Go ahead," he told Darris. "I won't look."

"That's right," Darris said, his tone changing. "You won't."

Arvin opened his eyes and saw Darris point the wand at him.

"Darris! Don't—"

A thin line of black crackled out of the tip of the wand and struck Arvin in the face.

He was blind.

"Stay where you are," Darris said. "I'll be right back."

"Darris, wait!" Arvin shouted. "I won't . . ." His voice trailed off as he realized the futility of pleading. Guild members didn't trust each other at the best of times, and they certainly didn't trust those who had "robbed" from the guild—as Arvin's amputated finger announced for all the world to see—which was ironic, because Darris was doing exactly the same thing: betraying the guild by denying them their share of his loot.

Arvin sighed. He'd just have to wait it out and pray that the wand's effects weren't permanent.

He heard the horse whickering, the splatter of water dripping from the aqueduct above, and the distant grumble of thunder as storm clouds built over the Vilhon Reach. Somewhere in that direction, the rulership of Hlondeth was being contested. Serpent versus serpent—a battle that needn't concern him. He said a prayer for the few people he actually cared about in that city, though there weren't many. Tanju was away for the summer, off on another mission for House Extaminos, and so would be safe. Gonthril and his followers had gone to ground, and Arvin hadn't seen the rebel leader in a year. Nicco had wandered off about four months past, summoned by his perpetually angry god on another mission of vengeance, but Drin, the potion seller, was still in town. So was little Kollim, eight years old and chafing under his mother's heavy hand. Tymora grant both of them luck.

The nap in the back of the cart had been uncomfortable, but it had refreshed him somewhat. He felt strong enough to perform his meditations. Arvin felt his way down from the cart, placed his pack on the ground next to him, then stripped off his shirt and tossed it aside. He lay down on his belly on the road, then levered his upper torso into an arch by extending his arms. Stretched out in the *bhujang asana*, his neck craned back and sightless eyes staring up into the sky, he pulled his awareness deep inside himself. It was even easier without sight to distract him, or it would have been, had he been certain that his eyesight *would* return. His mind was crowded with worries. There was no guarantee that Pakal would wait for him at the temple. The dwarf had abandoned Arvin once already, and there was also the iron cobra to worry about.

Arvin took a deep breath and pushed these thoughts from his mind with the exhalation.

"Control," he breathed.

It was Zelia's expression, but it served. In order to get through what lay ahead, he'd need nerves as steady as hers. He breathed in through one nostril, out through his mouth, in through the other nostril, out through his mouth, slow and deep, savoring the smell of sap from the pine trees nearby, restoring his *muladhara* with each long, extended breath.

When it was full, he rose gracefully to his feet and began the five poses of defense and five poses of attack that Tanju had taught him, alternating one with the other. He raised his hands and tilted his face back, then swept his hands through the air in front of his face, as if scrubbing his mind clean. Then he brought both hands to his forehead and thrust them forward, feet braced like a man shoving against a boulder, picturing his thrust shattering the rock that was an opponent's mind. He spun in a circle with hands extended and one leg parallel to the ground, forming an imagined barrier with both palms and the sole of his foot, then whipped his arms forward, one after another, imagining himself lashing an enemy's confidence to shreds and so on, through each of the ten poses, one flowing gracefully into the next.

When he was done, sweat covered his body. By sound, he found his way to one of the trickles that fell from the aqueduct above and caught the water in cupped hands. As he drank, he listened for Darris. The thief should have been back by then. Arvin hoped nothing had happened to him—especially if that wand was required to restore his eyesight. Already he could feel the air cooling slightly as evening approached.

The sound of footsteps caught his attention.

"Darris?" Arvin called.

More footsteps. Voices. Men and women, weary. Then a cry: "Smoke! The Stormlord speaks!"

The cry was followed by a rush of excited shouts and the sound of people—several dozen of them, by the sound of it—thudding to their knees. Arvin knew, from his experiences the previous summer, what they would be doing: tearing at their clothes and faces. His guess was confirmed by the sound of ripping cloth.

Above the commotion, he heard someone speak. "Wine!" the voice cried. "The wine merchant stopped here, just as he promised."

Arvin heard the people moving toward him. His nose crinkled as he caught the smell of hot, unwashed bodies and fresh blood.

"How much for a jug?" a woman's voice asked.

Arvin heard the clink of a coin pouch. He turned his head, trying to figure out where she was, and heard a male voice whisper: "He's blind."

Then a second man added, in a smirking whisper, "Pay him in coppers; he won't know the difference."

Arvin nudged his pack with one foot, making sure it was still there.

"Silence," the woman's voice hissed. "I will buy the wine, and you will drink only as much of it as I serve you. We must reach the temple tonight."

"Yes, Stormmistress," the second man said, contrite.

A hand touched his cheek, turning his face—a woman's hand, by the soft feel of the skin and the sweet-smelling, almost overpowering perfume she wore.

"I'm over here," the Stormmistress said in a silky, sensuous voice, "and I'd like to buy some wine for my fellow pilgrims. How much?"

"Five pythons a jug," Arvin answered, naming the price of the most expensive bottle of wine he'd ever seen ordered at the Mortal Coil. Judging by the fine ceramic jugs, Darris had stolen the stuff from a noble household, and it was probably worth that much or even more.

"Done," the woman said, not even bothering to haggle. "I'll take three." She caught Arvin's hand and pressed coins into it. He rubbed one of them. There was a snake embossed on one side of it, and what felt like the House Extaminos crest on the other. Judging by its weight, it was gold, not copper.

The woman leaned past him to lift a jug of wine from the cart. As she did, Arvin caught a whiff of what the perfume was hiding: the musky odor of snake.

That startled him. The clergy of Talos were all human as far as he knew. Yuan-ti scorned the Raging God as one of the lesser Powers, inferior to their serpent deity. To the yuan-ti, Sseth was the only god worth worshiping.

That brought up an unpleasant possibility—that the woman who'd just purchased wine for her "followers" had some ulterior motive for being there.

A moment later, when he listened in on her thoughts—hiding his secondary display by kneeling on the ground and pretending to search for his shirt—he discovered that it was even worse than he'd thought.

She was indeed a worshiper of Sseth.

One of the clerics who served Sibyl.

CHAPTER 5

ARVIN PATTED THE GROUND, PRETENDING TO SEARCH FOR HIS
shirt, as he probed the mind of the "Stormmistress." She was
delighted to have stumbled across the wine; that would make her job
all the easier. She planned to mix something into it before serving it
to the Talos worshipers. A word drifted through her mind: *hassaael*.
Arvin wasn't sure if it was the name of a potion, a poison, or the
yuan-ti word for blood. All three concepts seemed to be braided
into the word. She'd been given it by a yuan-ti in Skullport named
Ssarm—the same man who had provided the Pox with their deadly
transformative potion.

He probed deeper, worming his way into her memories of Sibyl.
He was relieved, somewhat, to find that her most recent meeting with
the abomination was more than a tenday in the past, and that she had
no knowledge of the events unfolding in Hlondeth or Arvin's role in
them. The cleric—Thessania, her name was—had been on the road
with the latest batch of worshipers, who had come all the way from
Ormath on the Shining Plains. Her instructions had been to herd
them to the temple, where they would be killed. If they didn't die that
night, Sibyl would be displeased.

An image of what Thessania intended flickered through her mind, swift as a snake's darting tongue: Men and women, piled in a heap, their faces bright red and eyeballs bulging.

Arvin shuddered. The followers of the Raging God might be crazy—they had to be, to view volcanic eruptions, hurricanes, and lightning-strike wildfires as something to celebrate—but that didn't mean they deserved to die.

Once again, Sibyl was taking advantage of human gullibility. The first time, it had been the Pox then it was the pilgrims. If Arvin could stop whatever was happening, he would.

He heard another grumble of thunder, out over the Reach. A natural storm? Or the voice of Hoar, god of vengeance?

Arvin cracked a wry smile.

"Vin!" a familiar voice cried out. "I told you not to sell any wine until I got back."

Arvin turned in that direction. Daris had said nothing about the wine. He was up to something, and Arvin decided to play along for the moment.

Suddenly, Arvin could see again. Darris strode toward him, the leather sack gone. He had one hand behind his back, inside his collar, as if scratching his neck. It was an old guild trick, a way of dropping something you'd palmed into your shirt. Probably the wand he'd just used to restore Arvin's eyesight.

Pretending to still be blind, Arvin held his hands out in front of him. *Play along*, he signed. Aloud, he added, "Darris? Is that you?"

Meanwhile, he studied Thessania. The surprise of his eyesight returning had broken the link with her mind, but he'd learned what he needed already. He committed her appearance to memory as he stared "blindly" past her. She was one of those yuan-ti who could pass for human. Her pupils were round and there was no sign of a tail under her robe. Ash-gray gloves covered her hands, which were human-shaped, and the only skin showing—her face, framed by a tight-fitting black cowl—was devoid of scales. Arvin noticed, however, that she kept her teeth clenched when she spoke, giving her words a tense, clipped sound. She probably had a forked tongue.

She was dressed as a cleric of Talos, in a long-sleeved black robe that reached to her ankles. Lightning bolts were embroidered on it in gold thread, and the sleeves ended in jagged hems, braided with more thread of gold. The front of the cowl bore the god's symbol: three lightning bolts in brown, red and blue, radiating out from a central point, representing the destructive powers of earthquake, fire, and flood. A black patch covered her left eye—another symbol of the one-eyed god she pretended to worship. Her face, Arvin noted, was unscratched, unlike those of the real worshipers.

She held the three jugs of wine she'd purchased in the crook of one arm, a traveling pack in the other. The worshipers clamored for the wine, insisting their throats were dry from the long march up into the hills. She rebuked them sharply, telling them to quench their thirst with water instead. The wine, she said, would be served with dinner.

"Start preparing our meal," she ordered.

The worshipers crossed their arms over their chests and bowed, then scurried away.

Darris, meanwhile, strode up to Arvin. "How much did you charge her for the wine?" he demanded.

"Five vipers a jug." Arvin held out the gold coins while staring slightly to one side of Darius.

"Five?" Darris asked, his voice rising. Pretending to scold Arvin, he waggled a forefinger at him, then brushed the front of his nose. *Pretend.* "I told you to charge six!" He slapped the forefinger into an open palm. *Fight.* Glowering, he shouted, "What did you do? Pocket the balance? Up to your old tricks again, are you?"

He grabbed Arvin by the shoulder and shook him. The gold spilled from Arvin's hand onto the ground. Arvin knew what Darris had in mind; the mock argument was an old guild trick. Arvin was supposed to shove Darris toward Thessania, who watched the two humans with a bemused look on her face. The rogue would stagger into her, grasp at her robe in an effort to keep from falling—and in the process, slip a quick hand into a pocket. A neat trick—if you were dealing with a human and not with someone who could kill with a single bite.

"You never said six," Arvin said in an even tone. "You told me five, and that's what I charged." *No,* he signed.

A bored look in her eyes, the yuan-ti turned away to follow the worshipers.

Darris raised his palm and jerked it forward—*Push!*—then slapped Arvin. Hard.

Arvin took the blow like a blind man, without ducking; the

worshipers still watched the fight. He lifted his hand to his mouth, as if to wipe away the blood from his split lip. Two fingers curled like fangs, he turned the wipe into a flowing motion while nodding in the direction of the fake cleric. *She's yuan-ti.*

That stopped Darris cold. "Ah," he said. Then, loudly, "I remember now. You're right; this *is* the five-viper wine. Sorry for the misunderstanding, Vin." He clapped an arm around Arvin's shoulder, using the gesture to whisper in Arvin's ear. "A yuan-ti *Stormmistress?* Are you sure?"

Arvin nodded.

"What's in her bag?" Darris breathed.

"Poison," Arvin whispered back. "She plans to mix it into the wine."

"I see," Darris said. He gave the worshipers a long, appraising look. "They look skinny as slaves," he said, using an old guild expression for someone with nothing worth stealing. Then he shrugged. "No sense hanging around, if you ask me. If the doomsayer really is yuan-ti, she'll demand first pickings."

Arvin, disgusted, realized that Darris thought he was suggesting they stay behind to loot the bodies once the poison had done its work.

"That's not what I meant," he said. "We've got to stop her from poisoning them."

Darris removed his arm from Arvin's shoulder and stepped back. "What she does is none of my business," he said. He watched the yuan-ti as she walked with swaying steps to the spot where the worshipers piled branches for a cooking fire. "What makes it yours?"

"Those people will die," Arvin answered.

"So?" Darris asked. "Sooner or later, one of the floods or fires they keep praying for will kill them, anyway." He tapped his temple. *Crazy.*

Arvin scooped up his pack and glanced at the worshipers out of the corner of his eye. One was a boy not yet in his teens who was being ordered about by an older, gray-haired man—probably his grandfather, given the resemblance between the two. Like the rest of them, the boy had ripped his shirt and gouged scratches in his face. He kept touching his cheeks however and wincing, giving his grandfather rueful looks.

"That one's just a boy," Arvin whispered. "He deserves a chance to grow up, to make his own decisions about which god to worship."

Darris listened, eyebrows raised. Then he nodded, as if enlightenment had suddenly come to him. He lowered his voice once more.

"You won't find my stash."

Arvin sighed. "I don't plan on looking for it."

The rogue chuckled. "Strangely enough, I believe you." He picked up the five coins and shoved them in a pocket, then clambered up into the cart. "People will be leaving the city—and they'll be thirsty. I'll have the rest of this wine sold in no time. Give me a hand, and I'll split the profits." He lifted the reins. "Last chance. Coming?"

Arvin shook his head. Thessania had disappeared inside one of the huts; she was probably lacing the wine with poison even as they spoke. Arvin was tempted to tell Darris what he thought of him but knew his words wouldn't change anything. The half-elf was a typical rogue; all he cared about was himself.

Darris released the wagon's brake, then paused. "If the doomsayer really is yuan-ti, you'd better watch yourself."

"I've dealt with them before."

Darris grinned. "I'll bet you have, and . . . thanks for the warning." He touched a thumb to his temple, then closed his other fist around it. *I'll remember you.*

He flicked the reins. The cart rumbled off down the hill, back in the direction of Hlondeth.

Arvin could feel, once more, the faint tickle in his forehead that warned him that magic was being used to search for him. The iron serpent must have been drawing nearer. He'd wasted too much time already.

But before he left, there was something he needed to do.

He sent his awareness deep into his *muladhara*. You don't see me, he mentally told the Talos worshipers. I'm invisible.

They continued going about their evening tasks, pulling food from their packs, tending the cooking fire and gathering water from the aqueduct in worn-looking iron pots. One or two turned to watch the cart as it left. As they did Arvin slipped an image into each of their minds of himself, seated next to Darris. Meanwhile, he picked his way carefully over the uneven ground toward the hut the yuan-ti had disappeared into.

She had hung a cloth over the entrance of the hut, preventing him from simply looking inside. The hut itself proved to be of better construction than the rest. Arvin couldn't find any gaps between the stones to peer through. That didn't matter, however. Retreating to a spot where the trees screened him from sight—he didn't need to be close to manifest the power he had in mind—he allowed himself to become visible again and imagined the interior of the hut. Psionic energy spiraled into the power points in his throat and forehead and a low droning filled the air around him as silver sparkled out of his "third eye." He sent his awareness drifting with it in the direction of the hut.

Slowly, its interior came into focus.

Thessania was pouring one of the jugs of wine into a wooden bowl. The other two jugs lay empty on the ground beside her. She must have been certain none of the worshipers would disturb her; she'd pushed her cowl back, revealing a hairless scalp covered in vivid orange and yellow scales. She had no ears, just holes in the side of her head. She had also removed her gloves; the scales covered her hands and fingers as well.

She set the empty jug down and rummaged inside her travel bag, then pulled out a glass vial containing an ink-black liquid. Unstoppering it, she poured a drop onto her finger, then stroked it along her wrist like a woman applying perfume. After repeating the application on her other wrist, she poured a few drops of the liquid into the wine. That done, she raised first one wrist to her mouth then the other.

At first, Arvin thought she was sniffing her perfume. Then he saw a drop of blood fall into the wine and realized she'd bitten herself. Thessania squeezed each wrist, milking herself of blood. As it dribbled into the bowl, the wine turned a vivid green. Thessania bent low, sniffing it, and licked her wrists clean. Then she spat into whatever the wine had become.

She pushed the stopper back into the vial—very little of the black liquid had been used—then pulled on her gloves. As she adjusted her cowl, Arvin skimmed quickly through the thoughts of the worshipers, searching for those who already had doubts about the stormmistress. From these he gleaned their names and a handful of recent experiences he hoped might be useful. By the time Thessania emerged from the hut, holding the bowl of wine, Arvin was ready. He stepped out of the forest and drew a mental shield between himself and the yuan-ti—who immediately turned in his direction as soon as she heard the droning of his secondary display.

"Worshipers of Talos," Arvin shouted. "You have been deceived."

Thessania bared her teeth in what would have been a hiss, had she not checked herself in time. She sent a wave of magical fear rushing toward Arvin, but his psionic shield deflected it.

"Thessania is no stormmistress," Arvin continued.

Thessania's charm spell hit him next. "Poor man," she said. "The sun has addled your wits. You don't know me; we've never met before. You have mistaken my voice for that of someone else. Come and drink wine with us."

Arvin's mental shield held. He needed to speak quickly. Once Tessalia realized her charm had failed, she would start tossing clerical spells at him.

"I may be blind," Arvin said, "blind as Talos's left eye, but by the god's magic I can still see." Silver sparkles—bright as the stars reputed to whirl in the empty space behind the Storm Lord's eyepatch—erupted from Arvin's forehead as he sent a thread of his awareness inside the hut. He pointed at one of the men, a tall fellow with bright red hair. "You wonder, Menzin, what Thessania was doing in the hut."

Arvin wrapped the invisible thread around the vial and lifted it into the air. With a yank, he pulled it out of the hut.

"She was adding poison to your wine."

Thessania whirled and spotted the vial. Bright green wine slopped over the edge of the bowl, staining her glove. Arvin sent the vial crashing against the wall of the hut, shattering it. Poison dribbled down the stonework like black blood.

The worshipers stared at it. Menzin muttered something to the man next to him.

"Ridiculous!" Thessania said. "Smell it—that's my perfume."

They did, and turned, glowering, toward Arvin.

Thessania pointed a slender finger at him. "This man has been sent by the Prince of Lies to stir up mistrust and strife among us. Don't listen to him."

"Cyric didn't send me," Arvin said, naming the god he'd frequently been warned about by the priests at the orphanage. He wove the name of Ilmater's chief ally into the lie: "Tyr did. The god of justice has allied himself with Talos to expose Thessania's trickery."

"The Raging God stands alone," said Thessania. "He allies with no one."

"Save for Auril, Malar, and Umberlee," Arvin said, hurling back the deity names he'd plucked from one of the worshiper's thoughts. "Though Malar would turn on the other Gods of Fury if he could— would send one of his beast minions sneaking like a serpent into Talos's tower to slay the Storm Lord, if he dared."

"Deceit!" Thessania cried. "More lies!"

She spat, and the glob of poisonous spittle hurtled through the air toward Arvin.

He imposed a psionic hand in front of it just before it struck, and smiled as it splattered on the leaves behind him. Thessania had moved precisely the playing piece he'd hoped she would.

He addressed one of the female worshipers—a thin woman who stared at him with narrowed eyes. "You've been wondering, Yivril, why your stormmistress didn't smite the blasphemer in Ormath with a lightning bolt."

The worshiper's eyes widened.

"Odd, isn't it, that she's not hurling one at me now," Arvin continued. "Instead she's spitting at me . . . like a snake."

With that, he used his manifestation to yank back Thessania's cowl.

Some of the worshipers gasped; others gaped in open-mouthed silence.

"It's an illusion," Thessania cried, yanking at her cowl. "Pay it no heed!"

Several of the worshipers began babbling at once.

"So that's why she refused to—"

"I thought it was strange that—"

"We've been tricked!" Menzin shouted, lunging at Thessania and knocking the bowl from her hands. "She's a yuan-ti!"

Spitting with fury, Thessania bit him.

Menzin collapsed, gasping, his lips already blue. The other worshipers, however, were not easily cowed. A handful were driven back by Thessania's magical fear, but the rest mobbed her. Arvin caught a glimpse of Thessania shifting to snake form in an attempt to get away, but then Yivril rushed forward, a chunk of broken stone in her hand. She smashed it down on Thessania's clothes. Even from where he stood, Arvin could hear the crunch of bones breaking.

Satisfied, he slipped away into the woods. As he did, he touched the crystal at his throat. "Nine lives," he breathed, thankful that none of the gods he'd falsely invoked had seen fit to take notice of the fact.

He circled through the woods, putting some distance between himself and the quarry before returning to the road. The tickling in his forehead grew stronger; the iron cobra was getting closer. Though Arvin was still tired—it hadn't been a very restful sleep, being jostled about in the cart—he needed to get moving again. Talos's temple was still a day's journey distant, and he doubted the cobra needed to rest or sleep.

Fortunately, his meditations had replenished his *muladhara*. If the iron cobra did catch up to him, he'd have mind magic to fight back with. He doubted the thing had a mind to affect, and it was probably immune to ordinary weapons, but there were one or two manifestations he might use to at least slow it down a little.

A branch rustled in the forest. Arvin whirled, then saw it was just a small bird that had flown from a tree. The tickling in his forehead was starting to get to him. He needed to get moving, to cover a lot more ground than his human legs were capable of. He decided to use his psionics to morph his body into something speedier, perhaps into a giant like the one he'd met the previous winter, or . . .

Watching the bird climb into the evening sky, he had an inspiration. He would morph into something with wings. A flying snake, perhaps—he'd seen enough of them in Hlondeth. He made sure his backpack was snug against his shoulders, then began drawing energy up from his navel and into his chest. He held his arms out, imagining they were wings.

Something sharp touched Arvin's throat—a curved sword blade— as a hand grabbed his hair from behind. A high-pitched male voice panted into his ear. "Where is it?"

"Where is what?" Arvin gasped, his heart pounding. "Listen, friend," he said, attempting a charm. "I don't know what—"

"None of that!"

The blade pressed against his throat, opening a hair-thin cut. Arvin didn't dare swallow. The charm obviously hadn't worked, so it was time for something less subtle. Raising his open hands in mock surrender, he imaged a third hand grasping his dagger. As the energy built he felt it begin to slide out of its sheath.

"Please, don't kill me," he pleaded, feigning fear.

At the same time he jostled the person behind him to cover the movement of the dagger. He guided it behind his attacker and turned it so the point was toward the man's back. Then he nudged it forward, manifesting a voice behind the man the instant he felt the dagger point poke flesh.

"Release him," it said, "or die."

The scimitar was gone from Arvin's throat as his attacker whirled to meet the illusionary threat. Arvin flung himself forward, wincing at the pain in his scalp as his hair was yanked out of the man's fist. As he tumbled away, he caught a brief glimpse of his attacker: a small, skinny humanoid with a doglike head, wearing a starched white kilt. The dog-man swung his scimitar through the space where an invisible dagger wielder would be. Still directing his dagger with his mind, Arvin slashed at the stranger's sword arm, opening a deep wound. The dog-man emitted a high-pitched yip and slashed once more through empty air, then backstepped to a spot where he could see both Arvin and the dagger.

It also gave Arvin a better look at him. The fellow stood only as tall as Arvin's shoulder and had a humanlike body but with thick golden fur on his neck, shoulders, and arms. Atop his lean body was a doglike head with a slender muzzle and large, upright ears. Those ears looked familiar—the fellow had the same face as the dog that had startled him near Saint Aganna's shrine. The dog-man must have been a lycanthrope of some sort, of a species that Arvin had never seen or even heard of before.

"Why are you following me?" Arvin asked. "What do you want?"

The dog-man merely stared at him. "You should learn," he said in a high, quick voice like that of a yapping dog, "to let sleeping serpents lie!" Then his eyes began to glow.

"I . . ." That was all Arvin managed before his gaze was locked by those large, golden eyes.

He dimly realized the dog-man was unleashing magic that didn't require words or gestures—just as a sorcerer or psion would. Arvin tried to mount a defense, but even as energy flowed into the power point at his throat his eyes closed. He felt himself falling . . .

When awareness returned, he found himself lying on the road in the spot where he'd been waylaid. Sunlight slanted through the forest as the sun slowly moved toward the horizon. Not much time had passed then. He sat up, rubbing an arm that must have banged against a rock when he fell. He blinked, yawned, and shook his head, willing himself to come fully awake.

The dog-man was gone. Blood marked the spot where he'd stood.

Arvin yawned again and rubbed his eyes.

More blood was on Arvin's dagger, which lay next to his pack. The pack was open.

Arvin scrambled toward it. He turned it over, inspecting it. The musk-creeper net was still inside—it looked as though the dog-man had the presence of mind to leave it alone but the contents of the side pouches had been pulled out. Arvin's magical ropes and twines were scattered about, as were the mundane bits of equipment he'd gathered together after leaving Zelia's rooftop garden. There were smears of blood on several of them. The dog-man hadn't stopped to bind his wound before rifling through the pack.

Stuffing the items back into their pouches, Arvin wondered what the dog-man had been looking for. Had he, like Pakal and the Naneth-seed, also been searching for the Circled Serpent? He didn't look—or act—like one of Sibyl's minions, which meant that some other faction must be involved, but who?

Arvin didn't know much about ordinary tracking, but it was clear from the drops of blood on the road which way the dog-man had gone. Uphill, toward the temple. Toward Pakal. A faint paw print in the dust marked the spot where he'd shifted back into a dog then started to run.

Arvin turned in the other direction and felt the tickle in his forehead intensify. The iron cobra was close—very close. He'd better get moving.

He slung his backpack onto his shoulder and drew deep from his *muladhara*. Ectoplasm sweated out of his pores and the scents of saffron and ginger filled the air around him as he began his metamorphosis. He pressed his legs together and spread his arms, and willed his body into a tiny, slender, snakelike form. It unnerved him, a little, feeling his legs join together to form a tail—it was a little too close to what Zelia had just put him through—but he clamped down on his trepidation and forced himself to concentrate.

Arms feathered into wings, his tongue split into a fork, and his pupils became slits. He felt his body shrinking, contracting, becoming sinuous and light-boned. He flapped his arms experimentally—and found himself hovering, his tail dangling just above the road. By concentrating, he was able to rise a little farther, but it was awkward; the form was so alien to his own. It was difficult to control, difficult to find his balance.

From behind him came the scrape of metal on stone. Glancing back, he saw the iron cobra slithering up the road toward him. Red eyes gleamed in the dusk as it spotted him and gave a malevolent hiss.

Silver burst from Arvin's forehead and coalesced as a sheen of ectoplasm on the cobra's body as Arvin manifested another of his powers. The ectoplasm solidified into transluscent ropes, and he gave them a mental yank, binding the cobra up in a tight ball. It thrashed, and two of the coils of rope burst apart, spraying ectoplasm, but the rest held.

Before the entangling net he'd created evaporated, Arvin drew still more ectoplasm from the Astral Plane and gave it human form. It was difficult work, manifesting yet another power while hovering in mid-air with unfamiliar wings, but by concentrating fiercely he managed it. He was still a beginner when it came to creating astral constructs—he couldn't yet imbue them with the ability to discharge electricity or do extra damage with a chilling or fiery touch—but the constructs he created could punch and stomp. The one he manifested then did just that, pummelling the cobra with massive fists and feet. The cobra's iron body rang with each blow, and several of the metal bands that made up its body were dented. The astral construct gave it a final kick, and the iron cobra's metal head snapped back, its neck bent at a sharp angle. It clattered to the ground.

The ropes of ectoplasm faded then disappeared. Still the iron cobra didn't move. Arvin hovered just in front of it, waiting. Even given that invitation, it didn't attack, and the tickling sensation in Arvin's forehead was gone. Satisfied, he let his astral construct fade.

He climbed into the air. He rose above the treetops and began winging his way above the road to the distant temple. It lay higher up Mount Ugruth, on a bare area with burned trees to either side. Higher still, the peak of the volcano smoldered, a dim red glow that rivaled the setting sun.

Arvin flew toward it, hoping that Pakal still waited for him.

❦

It was middark by the time Arvin reached the temple. He spotted it by the red glow in its central courtyard. The building had been built in a square surrounding a deep fissure in the ground, one that plunged like a knife wound all the way down to Mount Ugruth's molten heart. The white marble tiles surrounding the fissure were splattered with glossy black stone: lava that had cooled and hardened. Heat hazed the air above the crack, carrying with it the smell of sulfur. The inside wall of the building surrounding the courtyard had a wide portico supported by massive pillars that glowed a dusky red, like tree trunks in a burning forest. The rest of the building lay in shadow.

Farther up the mountain, Arvin spotted movement. He flew in that direction and saw a large group of people—about a hundred or so—climbing a narrow path that led toward the peak. Arvin swooped down lower and saw that they were Talos worshipers following a cleric—one who walked with a swaying gait. Suspicious, Arvin dipped into the cleric's thoughts.

The cleric—another yuan-ti in disguise—was leading an even larger group of worshipers to their deaths.

Not too much farther up the mountain was a large fissure, one that vented ash and poisonous fumes. The worshipers would be told to walk to its lip and breathe deeply. By breathing the fumes, they would "embrace" Talos and prove themselves worthy of him. If any of them dared to question their cleric's orders or realized what was happening and tried to run away, the wand would take care of them, just as it had taken care of the lower-ranked clerics. One way or another, they would die.

Arvin skimmed the thoughts of the worshipers closest to the cleric, hoping to find some spark of resistance. There was none. What their god had instructed them to do, they would do, no matter how odd his command seemed. Their thoughts were sluggish, as if they had been drugged.

The cleric glanced up at Arvin. *Strange*, he thought. *I didn't know Thessania kept a pet.*

Arvin broke contact. He wheeled back in the direction of the temple, searching for Pakal along the way. There was no sign of the dwarf, just as there had been no sign of him on the road leading to the temple. Nor did Arvin see anyone else. The temple seemed to be abandoned.

No, not quite. As Arvin circled over its roof, he spotted a solitary figure standing between two columns of the portico. Behind him was an arch that must have been the temple's main entrance. He was a tall man, his hair and beard as black as his clerical robes. Arvin might not have noticed him save for the javelin the man held. Its point, jagged as a lightning bolt, gave off a faint shimmer of electrical energy that illuminated his face. He leaned on the weapon, using it like a staff, staring into the courtyard with an unfocused gaze.

Arvin circled overhead, once again manifesting the power that allowed him to read minds, wondering if he'd discovered another yuan-ti. He was surprised to find nothing serpentlike at all about the man's thoughts. They were very human—and very troubled. The man wondered if he'd done the right thing. Did Talos truly demand more sacrifices? Already the clergy were gone, and they were forced to use lay worshipers from distant cities. The signs were all there, it was true—the smoke that rose from Mount Ugruth's peak, the lava that had bubbled up into the courtyard, the fire that had broken out on the hillside after the lighting strike—but was *sacrifice* what was truly required? And of the entire flock? Talos only seemed to be getting angrier with each passing day, yet if the high stormherald himself had sent word that sacrifice was necessary, it must be so.

He couldn't help but wonder, however, if he shouldn't have communed with Talos himself, just to be sure. If only his furies hadn't insisted on being the first to die, he might have consulted with them. Perhaps he should go after Siskin, ask the newly arrived cleric to wait until . . .

Arvin withdrew from the man's thoughts. The cleric—the storm-lord of the temple, Arvin guessed—had been duped by the yuan-ti, but his mind was still his own. If Arvin could convince him to listen, perhaps the slaughter that was about to happen on the hillside above could be stopped. The worshipers would surely listen to their stormlord.

Arvin landed outside the temple's entrance and allowed his metamorphosis to end. His tail sprang apart and became two legs again, and his body grew as it took on human form. He flexed his muscles, getting reacquainted with the feeling of arms and legs, then used his psionics to alter his appearance slightly, creating the illusion of deep red scratches in each of his cheeks. The stormlord would be more willing to listen to a warning if it came from one of his own followers.

Arvin strode through the entrance into the courtyard, he formed a cross with his arms against his chest as he'd seen the Talos worshipers do.

"Stormlord," he said, bowing, "I bring urgent news. May I speak with you?"

The brooding man turned. Close up, Arvin could see more details of his appearance. The stormlord's nose was long and sharp, his forehead creased with deep lines. Heavy black eyebrows were drawn together in what looked like a perpetual scowl. The right side of his face was puckered with white scar tissue and his hairline on that side was slightly higher. It looked as though he'd suffered a burn some time in the past. A wide metal bracer embossed with silver lightning bolts encircled each forearm.

"Approach," he said, "and speak."

Arvin rose from his bow and stepped closer. He had no idea what the protocol was for a lay worshiper addressing a cleric of this faith. He was taking a big chance. If he angered the stormlord, the man might strike him down with a lighting bolt. But he couldn't just let those people die—not when there was someone who might be able to do something about it.

"Stormlord," Arvin said, "I've just come from Hlondeth. I learned something there—something terrible. The cleric who just left the temple . . . Siskin. He isn't human. He's a yuan-ti."

"Nonsense," the stormlord said. "Siskin has been touched by Talos. I saw the burn mark myself."

Arvin was about to counter that the burn had probably been an illusion when he realized something. The stormlord's breath had a sweet odor to it. He'd been drinking wine.

Wine that smelled like Thessania's perfume.

Arvin had been certain, back at the quarry, that the black liquid was poison, but he started to wonder. Perhaps it was something else, something more insidious. Something that would bend a person's thoughts along paths they wouldn't ordinarily follow, until even the most horrific suggestions sounded perfectly reasonable.

"Siskin served you wine earlier tonight, didn't he?" Arvin asked. "And he insisted that all of your flock drink, as well."

The stormlord nodded. The furrow in his brow deepened. "What of it?"

"Did the wine taste unusual?"

"It was sweeter. Flavored. It came from the east, he said."

"After drinking the wine, you talked," Arvin said. "Siskin suggested that the lay worshipers be sacrificed. Tonight. It sounded reasonable at the time, but less reasonable now that you've had a chance to think about it."

The stormlord started to nod, but just then, the ground trembled. Deep in the fissure that split the courtyard, something rumbled. Arvin heard a wet *splat* as lava shot out of the crack. He could feel its heat through his shirt.

The stormlord stared at the cooling rock, which was already losing its glow. "It is . . . necessary," he said. "Talos demands a sacrifice. Without it, he will level Mount Ugruth. Thousands will die. Hlondeth itself may be wiped out. We cannot allow that to happen. The sacrifice is . . . necessary."

Arvin blinked. For a moment, the stormlord had sounded like Karrell. He'd sounded as though he cared about Hlondeth and its people. Arvin, like most folks in Hlondeth, had been taught that the clerics of Talos reveled in destruction and death, but the stormlord's comments gave him cause for thought.

"You *don't* want the mountain to erupt?" Arvin asked.

The stormlord glared at him. "You're not one of us," he rumbled.

"No," Arvin admitted. "I'm not. Nor is Siskin. I'll bet that when he arrived here, he was as much a stranger to you as I am." He spread his hands, entreating the cleric to listen. "Think about it—of the two strangers, who gives you more cause for concern? The one who is asking you to listen to your own doubts before it's too late—or a 'cleric' who got you drunk on a strange-tasting wine, then suggested you kill off all of your worshipers?"

The stormlord blinked and blinked again. A shudder ran through him. He shook his head like a man trying to throw off a dream. When he looked at Arvin again, his eyes were clear and hard. "Thank you—friend—for the warning. May Talos's fist never strike you."

Then he wheeled, javelin in hand, and ran through the temple, out into the night.

Arvin activated his lapis lazuli. It was time to find Pakal. He imagined the dwarf's face, but though he could picture it clearly—dark, tattooed skin framed by ropy hair—Pakal refused to come into focus. Arvin, worried, wondered if Pakal had decided not to wait for him. Even if the dwarf had moved on from the temple, a sending still should have been able to reach him.

Unless . . .

A terrible thought occurred to Arvin. Maybe the dog-man had caught up to Pakal, killed him, and taken the Circled Serpent.

Then again, Arvin realized, Pakal could just be in another form, as he had been in Sibyl's temple, cloaked in an illusion that fooled the sending—an illusion, for example, that would help him blend in at Talos's temple.

"Pakal!" Arvin shouted. "Are you here? Pakal!"

Arvin heard what he expected—silence. He could guess where Pakal was: on the footpath above the temple, somewhere among the hundred or so others who were walking to their deaths.

He bolted in the direction the stormlord had gone.

The path up the mountain was a steep one, made treacherous by loose volcanic rock that skittered away with each step. Arvin slipped repeatedly, scraping his hands and knees. The night was overcast, and Mount Ugruth lent an ugly red glow to the clouds above. Smoke and ash rose into the sky from its peak. Perhaps the mountain really was about to erupt. Arvin ran until his lungs ached, but instead of stopping to catch his breath, he pressed on.

The air was hotter than it had been below. Here and there beside the path, heat waves danced in the night air over a crack in the ground. Glancing down into one of them, Arvin saw glowing lava. It bubbled out onto the trunk of a dead tree. The bark smoldered, then burst into flame. A thin stream of molten rock oozed out of the hole and flowed downhill, cutting across the path.

From above, past a point where the path rounded a knoll that hid what lay above from view, came confused shouts then screams.

As Arvin reached the knoll, a bolt of lightning lanced out of the sky, then forked horizontally just before striking the ground, as if it had been deflected by something. One bolt hit a rocky outcropping just a few paces away from Arvin. He threw up his hand to shield his face as splinters of rock rained down on him. He scrambled up the path, manifesting the power that would allow him to see through illusions as he ran. Sparkles flashed into the night in front of his forehead then were gone.

As he rounded the knoll, he saw the stormlord locked in magical combat with the yuan-ti—and it didn't look good for the stormlord. The yuan-ti menaced the worshipers with bared fangs, using his magical fear to drive them toward a stream of flowing lava. The stormlord was several paces back, caught in a dead tree that had wrapped its branches around him like a magical entangling rope. One of the cleric's hands was free, and he swept it up and down as he shouted a prayer. A pillar of lava burst from the flow, arced toward the yuan-ti in a streak of red, then plunged down.

The yuan-ti raised a hand above his head, magically deflecting the molten rock. It shot back toward the stormlord then veered aside and splashed onto the ground in front of him, splattering the worshipers. At least a dozen were badly burned, and they fell to the ground screaming.

The yuan-ti retaliated with a flick of his hand that engulfed the stormlord in a cloud of magical darkness. Then he turned his attention back to the remaining worshipers with an angry hiss. They recoiled and stumbled backward, screaming and weeping. At least a dozen ran blindly into the lava and were killed, their hair and clothes bursting into flame and their flesh sizzling as it roasted from their bones. One or two managed to resist the fear and tried to run back down the hill past the yuan-ti, but the false cleric was faster. Whipping a wand out of his belt, he pointed it at them. A pea-sized mote of fire burst from the wand, growing as it streaked through the night. It struck the back of one of the worshipers and exploded into an enormous ball of white-hot flame. In the blink of an eye, all that remained of those who had fled were twisted, blackened corpses.

The yuan-ti turned back toward the remaining worshipers and

began swaying toward them, driving them like cattle with its magical fear. Behind him, lightning bolts arced out of the darkness that surrounded the dead tree where the stormlord hung, entangled. None came close to the yuan-ti. One struck a worshiper, blowing the man into the air.

Arvin searched the crowd, looking for Pakal. It took him a moment, even with his psionically clarified vision, to spot the dwarf under the illusionary human body he'd created for himself. Pakal tried to lift his blowpipe to his lips but kept getting jostled by the worshipers who ran toward the lava, lashed on by the yuan-ti's magical fear. The dwarf also suffered the compulsion's effects. The blowpipe trembled in his hand as he fought against the desperate desire to flee. He took one step back, then another—then someone ran into him, knocking the blowpipe from his hands.

Arvin needed to do something. Fast. He tried tossing a psionic distraction at the yuan-ti—only to hear Pakal scream his name from somewhere behind him. Arvin whirled then realized his distraction had bounced back at him. Whatever shield the yuan-ti had thrown up against the stormlord's magic also worked against psionics.

That must have been why Pakal had been trying to shoot the yuan-ti with a poisoned dart instead of using his spells. The dart lay beside the blowgun, useless, while Pakal was driven back toward the bubbling lava by the other worshipers. The man just behind him stumbled, weeping, into the lava. Pakal looked wildly around. His eyes locked on Arvin's. They were desperate, pleading . . .

Suddenly, Arvin realized he *could* use his psionics. He drew energy into the third eye in his forehead and sent it whipping forward in a thin, silver thread. He wrapped it around the dart then yanked. The dart flew from the ground and buried itself in the yuan-ti's neck.

The yuan-ti staggered backward then turned. Unblinking, wrath-filled eyes stared at Arvin and magical fear punched into his gut, making him want to vomit. Then it was gone. The yuan-ti crumpled slowly to the ground, dead.

The worshipers, freed from the effects of the yuan-ti's fear aura, let out a collective sob of relief. Several started to pray. Others turned to the tree, calling to their stormlord as the darkness seeped away from it into the ground. Arvin ran forward, toward Pakal.

The dwarf clasped his arms and said something in his own

language. It sounded like a thank you, and possibly an apology. Hearing it, Arvin felt guilty at the wave of relief he'd felt upon seeing the cloth sack Pakal carried—a sack that had something square inside it.

"Do you still have the Circled Serpent?" Arvin asked.

Pakal frowned, said something in his own language, then intoned what sounded like a prayer. "What do you ask?" he repeated.

Arvin repeated his question.

"I have it." Pakal glanced at the stormlord. Talos's worshipers were breaking off tree branches, freeing him. Other worshipers tore the clerical robes off the yuan-ti and pummeled his lifeless body with feet and fists. "We should go," Pakal added, "before my illusion wears off. I would not want them to think that I, too, am an enemy."

They moved quickly through the crowd, Pakal leading the way. They headed uphill, following the path. Soon the Talassan were well below them.

"Where are we going?" Arvin asked.

Pakal gestured at the peak. "Up there. To a portal that leads home."

"Where's home?"

"A jungle, far to the south. It is where Ts'ikil dwells."

"On the Chultan Peninsula?"

Pakal nodded. He glanced back at Arvin as they climbed. "Is Karrell truly alive? When we met in Sibyl's lair, you told me she was dead."

"I know," Arvin admitted, "but since then, I've been able to contact her. This time, for whatever reason, my sending worked. That's how I got Ts'ikil's name. From Karrell."

"Gods be praised," Pakal whispered. There was a catch to his voice; he must have cared deeply about Karrell, as well.

"Indeed," Arvin agreed, touching the crystal at his neck in silent thanks, "but Karrell's in deep trouble. She's still in the Abyss. In Smaragd."

"Sseth's domain," Pakal said.

"Yes." Arvin shuddered, imagining Karrell alone there. Giving birth. Vulnerable. "This Ts'ikil person will know how to get her out, right?"

The dwarf shook his head. "There is no escape from Smaragd."

"That's not true," Arvin countered. "I've learned there's a door that leads directly to Smaragd from this plane, a door that can be opened with the Circled Serpent. We can use it to reach Karrell, to rescue her, and we won't have to worry about the serpent god getting free. He's apparently been bound by his own jungle."

Pakal stopped. He turned to face Arvin, a wary look in his eye. "Who told you this?"

Arvin decided to tell only part of the truth. Pakal didn't need to know the details of what Zelia had forced upon him. "The woman in the rooftop garden—the one who attacked us after we escaped from Sibyl's lair. Her name is Zelia; she's a yuan-ti. Her agent—the human woman you killed with the dart—had also snuck into Sibyl's lair to look for the Circled Serpent. Zelia hopes to use it to open the second door, the one that leads to Smaragd. Like Sibyl, she hopes to free the serpent god."

Pakal's eyes narrowed. "Why would she tell you all this?"

"She didn't *tell* me," Arvin said. "I used mind magic to pull the information directly from her thoughts, after I defeated her."

"Where is this 'second door?'"

Arvin shook his head. "She didn't know."

"This Zelia recognized you," Pakal continued. "Why is that?"

Arvin smiled. That one he could answer with the truth. "Our paths have crossed before. She's an old enemy. She tried to kill Karrell and me when we were in Ormpetarr."

Pakal considered that.

"When I contacted Karrell, she told me to find Ts'ikil," Arvin continued. "She said that Ts'ikil would know what to do. I assumed that meant that Ts'ikil would help us use the Circled Serpent to open the door to Smaragd and free her."

Pakal folded his arms across his chest. "The Circled Serpent must not be used. Dendar must not be set free."

"We won't be opening *that* door," Arvin protested.

"If there *is* a second door, the Circled Serpent may cause both it and the one that would free Dendar to open at once."

"What if that isn't the case? What if the Circled Serpent only opens one door at a time?"

Pakal gave a firm shake of his head. "Ts'ikil will not allow it to be used. We cannot run the risk of Sseth emerging as an avatar. That would be as perilous as allowing Dendar to escape. The Circled Serpent must be destroyed. That is why we have been searching for it. Why *Karrell* was searching for it. Karrell herself would insist that this be done."

Arvin didn't like the sound of the word "destroyed." Maybe getting Pakal to take him to Ts'ikil wasn't such a good idea. He threw up his hands, exasperated.

"I thought you cared about Karrell, that you'd want to help rescue her."

"I do care about her," Pakal said, an intense look in his dark eyes, "and I would like to rescue her, but the life of one woman—even one to whom you owe your own life—does not negate the risk opening that door poses." He sighed and spread his hands. "This is an empty argument. We only have half of the Circled Serpent, and half cannot be used to open any door." He gave Arvin a level stare, as if warning him not to try anything.

"I know who's got the other half," Arvin said. "Dmetrio Extaminos."

Pakal's eyebrows shot up. "The yuan-ti prince from Hlondeth?"

It was Arvin's turn to be surprised. "You know him?"

"He claims to be on our side—to want to destroy the Circled Serpent. Why would he not tell us that he has—"

"Dmetrio is in Chult?" Arvin guessed.

Pakal gave him a look that made Arvin wonder if he'd spoken a little too enthusiastically.

"It's just that he disappeared from Hlondeth nearly six months ago," Arvin continued. "No one's heard from him since. I'm truly surprised to hear he's still alive. Everyone in Hlondeth thought he was dead."

"He's not dead," Pakal answered. He paused. "When we reach Ts'ikil, you must tell her what you have just told me."

"I will," Arvin agreed, uncertain whether he'd be able to keep that promise.

If Pakal was right about Ts'ikil not wanting the Circled Serpent to be used, maybe Arvin should grab Pakal's half and try to get to Dmetrio before the dwarf and Ts'ikil did. He was suddenly very glad of Karrell's ring. If the dwarf did turn out to have the ability to read thoughts, he wouldn't like what was going through Arvin's mind.

Arvin glanced up the path. "The portal is somewhere up above us, right?"

Pakal nodded. "Only a short distance ahead, but there is no hurry. The Talos worshipers are not following us."

"They're not what I'm worried about," Arvin said. He rubbed the scar on his forehead. It tingled again. "When I left Hlondeth, one of Sibyl's constructs was following me: a cobra, made of iron. I killed it, but my mind magic is warning me that Sibyl may have more than one of these constructs. If we don't get to the portal right away, it may lead Sibyl straight to us."

Pakal just stared at him.

"What?" Arvin asked.

"There is a problem," Pakal answered. "The portal can only be used at sunrise."

"Ah." Arvin thought for a moment. "We'll stay awake in turns until then and keep an eye out for the cobra. Maybe you can turn us to gas once we reach the portal. It may not be able to find us then."

"That I cannot do."

"Why not?"

Pakal sighed and spread his hands. "Thard Harr grants me only so many blessings each day. I can gain no more until I have prayed."

"Can't you pray now?"

"If I did, Thard Harr would not hear me," Pakal said. "The prayers must be said in daylight. The traditional time is when dawn first breaks."

"That's unfortunate," Arvin said.

He knew how Pakal felt. Arvin too was close to the limit of his own powers, already. His *muladhara* felt flat, a hair's breadth away from being utterly depleted. He needed to meditate.

He turned and stared down the mountainside. The stormlord and his worshipers were walking back to their temple, carrying the injured. Beyond the temple, the road vanished into darkness. Somewhere below, he was certain, another iron cobra slithered toward them.

CHAPTER 6

ARVIN BOLTED AWAKE, HIS HEART POUNDING.
"Karrell!" he shouted. "No!"

It took him several moments to realize that it had been a dream. A nightmare. Not real.

He could remember every detail. Sibyl, sending out waves of magical fear that turned into lava and burned the flesh from his bones, leaving him a walking skeleton that reeked of seared meat. Zelia, cracking open enormous eggs and slurping out the screaming infants they contained, her neck bulging grotesquely as she swallowed them down. The marilith demon, hacking open Karrell's pregnant belly with its swords—inside was a nest of dead snakes tied in an intricate knot.

Sweat trickled down Arvin's temples, and he wiped it away with a shaking hand. The nightmare had been so vivid, so *clear*. Usually, in dreams, some of the senses were blurred, but in this dream every detail of smell, sound, touch, and taste had been present. Even though Arvin was wide awake, the dream wasn't fading. It hung in his mind's eye like a gruesome painting.

He closed his eyes and concentrated on Karrell's face, trying to contact her, but nothing happened. As before, his sending was blocked.

The nightmare had left him more worried than ever—had the marilith found Karrell? Killed her? He remembered the prophetic dreams that had woken his mother, screaming, in the middle of the night. Was this what they had been like?

A hand touched his shoulder—Pakal's. The dwarf had been standing watch while Arvin slept.

Pakal muttered something, then spoke. Halfway through, his spell took hold and his words became intelligible. "—you dream?" he asked.

Arvin shivered. It was still dark, though the sky to the east was growing lighter. Almost dawn. "A nightmare," he answered.

Pakal grunted. "I, too. Earlier, when I slept." His face was difficult to see in the gloom, but the shudder that ran through his body made his feelings clear. "I dreamed of the jungle reduced to ash, like this place." He waved a hand, indicating a blackened tree that stood like gaunt shadow a few paces away.

They were almost at the peak of Mount Ugruth. The mountain-side was bare black rock, freshly spewed from the volcano. Gray ash and chunks of porous rock covered the ground where they sat. Hot, sulfurous gases vented from a deep crack in the ground a few paces away. The landscape was desolate, like something out of the Abyss.

Nearby, at the bottom of a crater in the loose volcanic rubble, was a stone dais, much like the one in Sibyl's lair. It too was of glossy obsidian—red obsidian. Glyphs, carved in Draconic script, encircled its rim. When the sun rose, they would activate.

According to Pakal, the portal was ancient. It dated to the height of the Serpentes Empire. Despite its incredible antiquity and the recent eruptions that must have pelted it with hot ash and chunks of falling stone, the dais looked almost new. Its edges were sword-sharp. Not a single chip had been knocked from them in all the centuries since its creation.

Arvin turned to Pakal. "Do you ever dream the future?"

The dwarf tossed back his braids. "No."

"My mother did. She dreamed of her own death—she couldn't prevent it." Arvin took a deep, steadying breath. "I dreamed about Karrell, and about our children. It was . . . terrible."

"Something has happened," Pakal said. "Dendar is not doing her job."

For a moment, Arvin wondered if the spell was translating Pakal's words incorrectly. "Her job?" he echoed. "I thought the Night Serpent was a monster who fed on mortal souls."

"Should she ever be released, that is what she would feed upon," Pakal said. "For now, she sustains herself on our nightmares. The dream fragments we remember upon waking are the crumbs she has left behind. Last night, for some reason, she did not feed."

Arvin sat up a little straighter. "Does that mean Dendar is dead?" he asked. If she was, he wouldn't need to worry about the door to her lair opening.

Pakal held up a hand. "I know what you are thinking," he said. "The answer is still no. The Circled Serpent must be destroyed."

Arvin nodded, feigning acceptance. He noted Pakal's wary look and the way the dwarf shifted his sack to his far hand. Arvin had been about to charm him but decided against it. He needed Pakal to show him how to use the portal. If the charm failed, Pakal would have even less reason to trust Arvin. As soon as they had stepped through the portal into the jungle, however, a charm would do the trick. If it failed, Arvin would take the Circled Serpent by force and amend Pakal's memory to erase any knowledge of the event.

Arvin glanced at the eastern sky. There was still some time before the sun rose. "Do I have time to meditate?" he asked the dwarf. "I need to restore my magic."

At Pakal's nod, Arvin adopted the *bhujan asana* and began his meditations. It felt good to slow his mind; it helped push the terrible images of his nightmare away. When he was done, the sun was peeping out from behind Mount Aclor. Slowly, it climbed higher in the sky.

Pakal climbed down into the crater, sending small avalanches of loose rock and dust toward the dais. Arvin forced himself to wait a moment before rising—casually—to his feet and following. The dais was knee-high on the dwarf but came only midway up Arvin's calves. One quick step would put him on top of it.

Together, they watched as sunlight crept across the dais, illuminating it like a waxing moon. As it did, the ash that had settled on that half of the dais vanished.

"What do we do?" Arvin asked. "Step onto it once it's fully in sunlight?"

Pakal nodded.

"Will Ts'ikil be waiting for us on the other side?"

"She will come once I call her."

Good. That would give Arvin some time. As the sunlight crept toward the western edge of the dais, the symbols that were already illuminated began to glow with a ruddy light. It looked, Arvin thought, as though their grooves had suddenly filled with lava. He passed a hand above one of the symbols but felt no heat.

"Does the dais work like the amber ring?" he asked. "Do we need to be touching to go through together?"

The dwarf eased himself to the side, slightly increasing the distance between them. "No. Once activated, it will transport anyone who steps onto it, but only for a brief time. Be ready."

"I will."

Arvin was glad the portal was almost ready. The tingling in his forehead had grown strong. If it was an iron cobra, it was getting closer by the moment. He risked a glance up at the lip of the crater but saw no sign of a snake, iron or otherwise.

As he started to turn back to the portal, something in the sky caught his attention. A creature flew toward Mount Ugruth from the direction of Hlondeth. It was big, with a serpent's body and four arms. With a sinking heart, Arvin realized who it must be.

"Sibyl's coming!" he warned. "She's headed straight for us!"

Pakal glanced in the direction Arvin had pointed then back at the dais. "She is still far enough away," he said. "We will be in the jungle, with the portal closed behind us, before she can reach us. The portal will not reactivate until tomorrow's sunrise."

Arvin nodded, only partially reassured. Sibyl a day behind them was all well and good if the Circled Serpent was destroyed by then, but destroying it wasn't Arvin's goal. A day wouldn't give him much time to trick Zelia into telling him where Dmetrio was, steal the second half of the Circled Serpent, and rescue Karrell.

"There," Pakal continued. "You see? It is ready."

He was right. The entire inscription glowed. Pakal placed a foot onto the dais. Arvin did the same. The tingling in his forehead turned into a steady burn . . .

A loud hiss and clatter of loose rock startled Pakal. One foot on the dais, one foot on the ground, the dwarf stared up at the source of the noise and cursed. Arvin, realizing it must be the cobra, grabbed the dwarf by the arm and boosted him onto the dais, leaping up after him. As the world beyond the inscription began to shimmer, Arvin saw the iron cobra he thought he'd defeated come skittering down the slope. Its hood was bent flat against its head and several of the iron bands that made up its body were jammed together, but it was moving again. Fast. With a screech of metal it heaved itself up onto the dais with them and bared bent fangs.

"Watch out!" Arvin yelled, yanking Pakal back. "It's going to—"

The mountainside vanished. For a heartbeat there was nothing under Arvin's feet as he fell sideways through the dimensions, still holding tight to Pakal's arm. Then his feet landed on something solid. A roaring filled the air: water. It slammed into Arvin's calves, knocking him prone. He had just enough time to register the fact that the portal had transported them to the bottom of a narrow, cliff-walled canyon filled with a rushing river before the force of the water dragged him off the submerged portal they'd materialized on. Then the river swept them away.

ʊ

Karrell heard something moving through the jungle off to her left. She froze. Rain pattered on the slab of bark she held over her head like a shield, making it difficult to hear. Already the bark felt spongy; the acidic downpour was eating through it.

Whatever was moving through the jungle, it was big, larger than the dretches the marilith had sent to search for her.

Karrell touched her belly, soothing the children inside her. They could sense her fear and were kicking. She began to whisper the prayer that would disguise her as a tree but realized the sounds of branches breaking and sodden vegetation squelching were moving away. She sighed in relief.

The sounds stopped. A voice she recognized grated out guttural words—the marilith, casting a spell.

Karrell croaked out a prayer. "Ubtao, hide me in my time of need. Protect me from my enemies; obscure me from their sight and do not let them find me."

The jungle reacted to her, just as it did each time she cast a spell. Thorny branches slashed at her bare arms and the ground underfoot became soggier, causing her to lose her footing. Gnats erupted from a nearby pool in a belch of foul-smelling air and swarmed her face. She squinted and waved them away.

Somewhere in the jungle to Karrell's left, the marilith continued to chant. Something that flashed silver rose into the sky. After a moment, she realized the flashes were coming from the marilith's swords, which circled above the treetops. Just as it had done in Baron Foesmasher's palace, the demon had summoned a barrier of blades.

Perhaps the demon was under attack, but if so, why had it flung the blades into the sky?

Karrell's heart beat faster. Perhaps, she thought, the blades had been driven there by some unseen adversary. Had Arvin done as he'd promised and found a way into Smaragd?

Tossing her makeshift rain shield aside—she could move more quickly without it, and the rain was slowing anyway—she pushed her way through the jungle toward the spot the swords circled above. She caught only glimpses of them through the thick vegetation— brief glimpses, for though the acidic rain had no effect on her skin, it stung her eyes.

As she got closer, she spotted the marilith. Its tail was coiled beneath it as it stared up at the circle of blades. All six arms were raised above its head, directing the whirling blades. Squatting next to it were two dozen dretches, drooling and idly scratching their bulging, hairless heads. The marilith guided the swords down through the trees, tilting the circle so that it was perpendicular to the ground.

In the middle of the circle, Karrell could see a flat gray plain with a walled city in the distance. The wall that surrounded the city had a greenish glow. Hlondeth? No, the landscape was wrong. The walled city wasn't a port; the gray plain continued behind it as far as the eye could see. Her heart beat faster as she realized the demon had opened a gate to another plane. Which one, Karrell had no idea, but it looked habitable. Somewhere on the prime material plane? Wherever it was, it had to be safer than Smaragd.

Moving as close as she dared, Karrell readied herself. Leaping through the gate with a bulging belly would be difficult, but it might be her only chance at escape.

The view through the gate shifted as the link between planes adjusted itself. With a rush that dizzied her to look at it, the view zoomed in toward the city. When it stopped, it was focused on a field of rubble. Huge blocks of masonry lay jumbled together with rusted bits of twisted metal and splintered wood. It looked as though a giant had trampled on whatever buildings had once stood there. A crowd of people milled around the rubble—humans in torn clothing. Several had scratches on their cheeks. All looked terrified, and all cried out. Karrell could not hear what they were saying, but she could guess—their actions made it clear that they were praying to their gods.

Behind them was a river of bubbling black water; beyond that, a stalagmite-encrused cave.

The marilith pointed at the gate. The dretches grunted then leaped through it, all but one of them making it through the circle of whirling steel. That one was instantly sliced to pieces. Blood sprayed outward in a circle and chunks of flesh were hurled into the jungle. A hand landed next to Karrell.

The other dretches seemed to rapidly shrink, and Karrell had to strain her eyes to see where they'd gone. She spotted them next to the milling crowd. The dretches drove the crowd forward like cattle, toward the cave.

The marilith, meanwhile, concentrated on keeping the gate open. Karrell edged closer, making sure she kept behind the demon. The prayer she'd uttered earlier had only hidden her from scrying and other divination spells. If the marilith looked in her direction, it would see her. She would have to time her escape just right. Slowly, glancing between the gate above her and the demon, she crept forward.

In the place beyond the gate, the dretches used magical fear and clouds of nauseating smoke to drive the crowd toward the cave. The humans screamed and wept as they stumbled into the water then into the cave. Karrell's heart ached for them, for they were clearly in torment. She eased closer still . . .

Her foot slipped on a wet branch and splashed into a pool of stagnant water. She halted, ready to chant a prayer. The marilith, however, didn't seem to have heard. It was intent on the gate. It watched, chuckling, as the first few ranks of the crowd disappeared into the cave.

Screaming erupted from inside it—the anguished cries of those within. Karrell pressed her lips together in a grim line, wishing she could do something for them, but realized she could do nothing until she was through the gate. She moved cautiously forward, taking a careful step, then pausing, then easing forward through the branches, then pausing again, all the while with one eye on the demon. Just a few steps more . . .

The last of the humans had been driven into the cave, and the field of rubble was empty again, save for the dretches. They loped back toward the hole, knuckles scuffing on the ground. Karrell, realizing the marilith would close the gate once they'd returned, quickened her pace, no longer caring if the movement of a branch betrayed her.

Behind the dretches, a head emerged from the cave. The head of an enormous serpent with midnight-black scales, its neck was as thick as the cave it emerged from. The serpent stared past the departing dretches at the gate, its tongue flickering in and out of its mouth.

"More," it hissed.

Karrell felt an icy cold settle in her stomach as she recognized the serpent and realized where the gate led.

To the City of Judgement and the lair of Dendar—grown large enough that she barely fit inside her cave. To the Fugue Plain.

A plane that could only be entered by demons, and the souls of the dead.

Karrell, still living, would be unable to pass through the gate the marilith had opened, even if she wanted to.

The dretches had driven the souls of the freshly dead—those whose gods had not yet claimed them from the Fugue Plane—into Dendar's gullet. Why?

The shock of this realization was Karrell's undoing. One of the dretches pointed and gabbled out a cry of glee. The marilith spun, spotting her. The gate slammed shut, slicing three dretches to bloody pieces.

The marilith lunged at Karrell, seizing her.

⟡

Arvin fought for breath as the river tumbled him away from the portal. He was above water, submerged, broke the surface, then was under water again. Choking, sputtering, he tried to fight his way back to the surface, but it was impossible to swim while clutching Pakal's arm and with a pack that had filled with water weighing him down. The dwarf thrashed about, kicking Arvin in the stomach, either trying to swim or just trying to get away from him. Arvin's head broke through the foaming water just as he and Pakal were slammed against the side of the canyon. Arvin lost his grip on the dwarf's arm. Pakal lost hold of the sack. As it swirled away in the current, the dwarf shouted and flailed toward it. Arvin was quicker. He kicked off the wall and lunged forward.

His hands closed around the sack.

Pakal grabbed him by the shoulders an instant later. The dwarf shouted something at Arvin, but his words were lost in the thunder of water. They struggled, Pakal clambering over Arvin—and nearly drowning him in the process—and at last grabbing the sack. The river swept them into a whirlpool, which spun them crazily around then out again. Arvin caught a glimpse of a tree that had fallen from the cliff above. It lay in the river at an angle, partially submerged, just ahead. The river was going to carry them right into the tree—and Pakal's back was to it. Arvin shouted and gestured frantically with his free hand then submerged, still clutching the sack. Pakal fought back, kicking up toward the surface.

Then, suddenly, Arvin was the only one holding the sack.

He burst from the water just in time to see the dwarf caught on the tree, his limp body draped across its trunk. Then the river turned a bend in the canyon, sweeping Arvin away. Cursing, he tried to fight his way back upriver, but it was no use. Even if he'd had both hands free and wasn't wearing a backpack, he would never be able to make headway against the current. It took all of his efforts just to keep his head above water. Kicking furiously, he quickly felt the sack to make sure the box that held the Circled Serpent was still inside. It was.

He began searching for a way out. It was some time, however, before he found one. By the time he battled his way over to a ledge that he could climb onto without being smashed against the wall of the canyon, Pakal was far behind.

Dripping wet, exhausted, Arvin opened the sack and took out the box. He opened it and saw a crescent-shaped object wrapped in crumpled lead foil resting on a bed of soggy black velvet. Carefully, he peeled back one edge of the foil, revealing the object it had been wrapped around. Gems glinted in a silver serpent face. The upper half of the Circled Serpent was in his hands.

He smoothed over foil and closed the box then touched the crystal at his neck. "Nine lives," he whispered. Then he tucked the box securely inside his pack.

Using his magical bracelet made the climb out of the canyon an easy one, but above the cliff, the jungle was thick and deeply shadowed. Something orange flashed through the trees. Instinctively, Arvin ducked and reached for his dagger, but it was only a tiny flying snake, its wings no larger than Arvin's hands. Its coloration made it stand out vividly against the jungle foliage, most of which was a green so dark it bordered on black. He wondered whose pet it was, but a moment later, when a second flying snake flitted past, he realized the creatures must be wild.

The jungle was filled with life, despite the fact that a thick canopy of trees blocked most of the light, throwing what lay below into shadow. Birds with bright turquoise, yellow, and red feathers cawed at him from the branches above; a centipede the length of his arm scurried out of his path; and tiny monkeys with bright orange fur leaped from tree to tree, chattering to each other. He saw at least a dozen more of the tiny flying snakes. Each would be worth a hundred gold pieces or more in Hlondeth, a fortune on the wing.

Despite the river that frothed through the canyon below, the air was oppressively hot. His clothes quickly went from being soggy and wet to just damp with sweat. Arvin combed his hair back with a hand. It was as hot in the jungle as the inside of Hlondeth's Solarium, but with the added discomfort of oppressive humidity that left him feeling slightly lightheaded. He was used to a dry heat and air that smelled of hot stone and snake musk.

He stood, debating what to do. He had the upper half of the Circled Serpent, and so he needed to find out where Dmetrio was and trick him into giving up his half.

Easier said than done, however. Arvin had no idea where Dmetrio was—no idea where *he* was, either. Pakal had seemed confident that the portal would convey them to his homeland but had seemed surprised to be deposited in a river. Had the portal malfunctioned and sent them somewhere else?

Pakal would know the answer to that question—but Pakal was draped, unconscious, over a log in the middle of a raging river, maybe even dead by now, if the river had swept his body away.

There was an easy way to find out.

Arvin started to summon energy into his lapis lazuli then hesitated. If Pakal was alive, a sending would allow him to see Arvin as well, and Arvin didn't want to give too much away. He took off his backpack and hid it behind a nearby tree. Then he resumed the sending.

Closing his eyes, he pictured the dwarf's face in his mind. A moment later, it came into focus. Pakal was bedraggled, his wet braids plastered against a bloody scalp, but alive. Both hands were gripping tightly to something and one foot was braced while the other was searching for a foothold. He'd not only survived but was trying to climb out of the canyon.

Pakal! Arvin said. *You're alive! I tried to swim back to you, but . . .* He paused, realizing that was eleven words, wasted. *Where are we? Did we reach your homeland?*

Yes, but we did not arrive where I expected. The portal must be—

He stopped, looked closely at each of Arvin's empty hands, then leaned to the side as if trying to see Arvin's back. Arvin turned slightly—a casual looking gesture designed to let Pakal see that his pack was gone.

Pakal's expression turned grim. Arvin could guess what he was thinking: that the box had been swept away by the river. The lead foil around the Circled Serpent would make it impossible to find.

Return to the fallen tree, the dwarf replied. *I will tell Ts'ikil to meet us—*

Having reached its limit, the sending ended.

Arvin grinned. Tymora must have been smiling on him; everything had worked out perfectly. All he had left to do was trick Pakal—or Ts'ikil—into telling him where Dmetrio was. First, however, he needed to hide the Circled Serpent.

Where?

He needed to get a good look around. The best way to do that would be by morphing into a flying snake again, much as Arvin hated the idea. The musky smell that clung to him even after he'd morphed back again was as bad as a dunking in Hlondeth's sewers. Sighing, he picked up his pack and put it on.

A scream made him jump—a bad thing to do so close to a cliff. One of his feet slipped off the edge, sending a stone clattering down toward the river. Arvin recovered quickly and reached for his dagger. The scream had come from somewhere close—no more than a few paces away—and it had sounded like a woman.

She screamed again, but her cry choked off suddenly. Arvin hesitated. Did he really want to get involved? Then he thought of Karrell. She, too, was alone and in trouble.

He plunged into the jungle toward the spot where the scream had come from. The vegetation was thick, and he was forced to push his way through a tangle of vines and bushes that blocked his way. When he was certain he was at the spot the screams had come from, he stopped. He searched the ground for tracks but saw none. The air smelled of dark soil and growing things, of sweet-scented flowers— and an acidic smell, like yuan-ti sweat.

Belatedly, he realized the jungle around him was silent. The monkeys, birds, and flying snakes were gone. A sharp smell hung in the air, one that stung his nostrils. He glanced down and saw tendrils of yellowish fog whisping out from under a waxy-leafed bush to his right. Then, with a loud hissing, the fog billowed out full force, enveloping him.

It became difficult to breathe or to see. The acidic fog tore at his lungs and throat with each breath. He doubled over, coughing. He could see no more than a pace or two in any direction. He tried to run but tripped over a vine.

It wrapped itself around his ankle. Then it tugged, sending him sprawling, and began dragging him along the ground.

He slashed at the vine, but three more came snaking out of the jungle after it. Coughing so hard he began to retch, he tried to crawl away, but his limbs moved at only a fraction of their normal speed. It was as if the air around him had turned to thick mud. The vines had wound around both legs and pulled him steadily along. He threw his body in the direction they dragged him, causing them to go slack, and slashed through another of the vines. But more came snaking through the air toward him—a dozen at least. Four more wrapped around him.

The vines belonged to an enormous plant. Yellow mist spewed out of the base of its trunk, and waxy green leaves fluttered like feathers around four flower buds that were each the size of a horse. One of these buds gaped open, revealing a mouth lined with row upon row of thornlike teeth. Another was clenched firmly upon the body of a monkey; the animal's limp leg and tail dangled from it. Arvin cursed as he realized it must have been the monkey that had screamed. The open bud swayed in Arvin's direction as the vines pulled him toward it.

Arvin cast his awareness toward the thing, trying to connect with its mind, but its thoughts were slow and ponderous, as impossible to grasp as the eye-stinging yellow fog that surrounded him. The plant would not respond to a distraction or to an illusion. An astral construct might be able to tear apart one of the buds, but not before the other three—all gaping open and turning hungrily in Arvin's direction—gobbled him up.

Instinctively, Arvin tried to slash at one of the vines that quested toward him, but his arm, like the rest of his body, moved too slowly. The vine wrapped around his wrist, immobilizing his weapon hand. If only, he thought feverishly, his body would move as quickly as his mind. . . .

That gave him an idea. He summoned energy into his third eye and sent out a streak of silver that wrapped itself around the vine. Rotating it swiftly, he uncoiled the vine from his wrist. Another line of silver burst from Arvin's forehead as he repeated the manifestation. He used it to grab his dagger and slash at the vines that held his legs. He manifested the power a third time, and a fourth, and a fifth, yanking back the vines that were still snaking toward him. He grabbed the end of each, then moved his energy-hands back and forth, over and under, tying the vines into a knot. Meanwhile, the dagger slashed through the last of the vines holding his legs. Slowly, sweat pouring from his body, Arvin crawled backward, moving at the pace of a slug.

Vines kept snaking through the jungle toward him, but he caught each one with a psionic hand, knotting it around the branch of a nearby tree. Coughing, his throat and lungs raw, he at last found the edge of the cloud of fog. He crawled into clean, clear air—and moved at his normal pace again. His pent-up muscles were sent leaping forward, and his shoulder slammed into the trunk of a tree.

In the branches above, a monkey screeched angrily—again, a very human-sounding cry—then swung away through the jungle. A piece of half-eaten fruit landed at Arvin's feet.

He rose, still coughing, and stared at the chewed-up fruit, its pulpy red seeds spilling out of its torn skin. "Nine lives," he whispered, touching the crystal at his throat.

Standing there, staring, he felt a tingle awaken in his forehead.

The iron cobra. It must have passed through the portal as well. It was still looking for him.

Arvin needed to get out of there. He drew energy into his navel and chest and manifested the power that would alter his body. It was disturbingly easy to morph into a flying snake; after his long flight to the temple, the wings that sprouted out of his arms felt familiar. Even feeling his legs meld together into a tail didn't bother him. He had an anxious moment as his backpack flattened into a brown patch of scales on his back, but the Circled Serpent in its box, like everything else in his pack, as well as his clothing, melded with his body. Exhaling the scent of saffron and ginger, he rose into the air, his snake tail lashing with each stroke of his wings.

He rose above the treetops and hovered, getting his bearings. Assuming no time had passed during their passage through the portal, the direction where the sun hung just above the horizon was east. The river snaked through the jungle in a roughly north-south direction. Its headwaters sprang from the slopes of a volcanic peak that resembled a broken serpent's fang. The river emptied, far to the south, into an ocean that stretched to the horizon. Another large body of water, a lake, lay to the east. To the west, about an equal distance away across thick jungle, was a range of mountains. Another chain of mountains lay to the north beyond the volcano.

Between these features, the jungle extended, unbroken, in every direction save one. About halfway between the river and the mountains to the west, enormous pyramids rose above the treetops. Arvin expected to see a city surrounding them but the jungle seemed to grow right up to their bases. Staring at the pyramids, he could see that their tops were jagged and broken—a ruined city.

He decided to follow the river; that way, he wouldn't get lost. Pakal was somewhere upriver, so the opposite direction was the way to go. He flew downriver along the canyon, looking for a place to hide the Circled Serpent.

CHAPTER 7

ARVIN DESCENDED TOWARD THE LIMESTONE BLUFF HE'D SPOTTED from the air. It was one of the few landmarks in the vast sea of dark green, rising above the jungle canopy at a spot where the river made a **U**-shaped bend. There were a number of small caves in the bluff, any of which would make an ideal hiding place, assuming the caves weren't inhabited.

Dozens of flying snakes swooped in and out of the caves like swallows; they probably nested inside. Arvin joined them. He paused above the bluff, listening, but heard only the rush of the river in the canyon below and birds calling to one another in the jungle. Somewhere in the distance, a larger creature roared, and Arvin could see the treetops shake as something big moved between them. He was doubly glad just then that he'd chosen not to make his way through the jungle on foot.

He chose a cave that was apart from the others, about halfway up the bluff, and sent his awareness drifting into it. Ectoplasm shimmered in the cave mouth as he probed for thoughts. The only ones he detected were those of the flying snakes, including some that appeared to be coiled up, sleeping, deep within the cave. Otherwise, the cave was empty.

He fluttered inside. The off-white walls had a wrinkled appearance. Here and there, a mounded stalagmite rose from the floor like a sagging column of dough. They were, however—as Arvin discovered a moment later when he accidentally brushed a wingtip against one—as hard as any other stone.

He glanced around, looking for a place to hide the Circled Serpent. There were no obvious choices, no convenient cracks into which the box could be wedged. Then a flying snake flew past him, toward the rear of the cave, and disappeared behind a natural column of stone that stood close to the rear wall. It didn't return. Curious, Arvin flew in that direction. Behind the column, he discovered a passage that had been sealed with clay bricks. Two of the bricks had fallen, leaving a small hole. The passage beyond the wall led up at an angle from the cave, worming its way deeper into the bluff.

It looked like the perfect hiding place. He flew into the gloomy passage, deciding that he would go only as far as the sunlight penetrated. After a short distance, the tunnel opened up into a second cavern. He gasped, barely remembering to flap his wings. For several terrible moments he thought he was staring down at Sibyl.

The abomination nearly filled the cavern, its serpent body a tight coil on the smooth floor. Its wedge-shaped head rested, eyes closed, on arms that were folded beneath it like a pillow. Its scales were black and shiny as obsidian, like Sibyl's, but it had no wings. It was dead, and the body had shrunk like a drumhead around the skeleton; every rib stood out in sharp relief.

There was no odor of rot. The air was only slightly less hot and humid than the steaming jungle below. Surely a body would decompose quickly, yet—Arvin sniffed—the only smell was that of herbs or perhaps flowers, a sweet, pleasant scent.

The cavern it lay in wasn't natural. Its walls were perfectly circular and smooth, with an equally smooth ceiling and floor, a tomb.

As Arvin's eyes adjusted to the gloom, he made out more details. Several of the yuan-ti's scales had nut-sized gems embedded in them. Though Arvin couldn't make out their colors, he was certain, given their size, that they were extremely valuable. Any one of them would probably feed, clothe, and house him for a year.

The flying snake he'd followed into the tomb flitted around the chamber. After several circuits of the tomb it fluttered past Arvin, back the way it had come.

Arvin landed on the floor and morphed back into human form, braced and wary. He waited several moments. If the tomb had any magical protections, they so far hadn't activated. He shrugged off his pack and unfastened its flaps, then pulled out the box that held the upper half of the Circled Serpent. After a moment's thought, he realized that the best place to hide it would be inside the corpse. Wary of touching the dead abomination—especially after facing the skeletal serpent in Sibyl's lair—he used a psionic hand to pry open its mouth. It was a struggle—the shriveled sinews of the jaw were tough as old leather—but slowly the mouth creaked open. A second sparkle of silver briefly illuminated the gloomy cavern as he used his psionics to lift the box into the air. He nudged it inside the mouth, cushioning it between the forks of the rotted tongue. Then he pushed the jaw shut. Fang clicked against fang like the closing of a lock.

He put on his pack and started to turn away. Then he turned back to the abomination again, unable to resist temptation. Drawing his dagger, he pried the largest gem from the body—one with a unique, star-shaped cut that would double its value—and caught it in his free hand when it fell. He stood, waiting. Nothing happened. Breathing a sigh of relief, he slipped the gem into his pocket and walked back to the tunnel that was the tomb's only exit. Steadying himself on the wall with one hand, he prepared to morph into a flying snake.

A soft hiss, just ahead of him, made him jerk his hand back.

A snake poked its head out of the wall near the spot where his hand had just been, out of solid stone. Then it was gone.

A second hiss, soft as the first, came from the ceiling just above his head. Arvin ducked as a swift-moving ripple of shadow flashed past his face. He caught a glimpse of curved fangs. Then that serpent, like the first, disappeared.

He glanced around, his heart beating rapidly, trying to see where the serpents had gone. There was a faint smudge on the wall where the first serpent had appeared—a wavy line that might have been a ripple in the limestone or a shadow cast by one of the columns at the far end of the tunnel. From somewhere deep inside the stone came an eerie hissing.

The tomb was protected, after all—by shadow asps.

Arvin had once had a close brush with one such creature of the Plane of Shadow many years past. A wizard the guild had paired him up with had the bright idea of making a "robe of shadows" from the shed skin of one of the magical serpents. The experiment, however, had fatal results. When Arvin had arrived at the wizard's workshop, he'd been met not with a living wizard, but the shadow creature the man had become. The shadow asp had escaped its bindings and bitten the poor wretch.

Arvin decided that one gem, no matter how valuable, wasn't worth dying for.

As a shadowy head emerged once more from the wall, Arvin yanked the gem from his pocket and rolled it across the chamber, back to the abomination. It worked; the shadow asp slithered after it. As it did, Arvin morphed into a flying snake. Wings flapping as rapidly as his heart beat, he streaked down the tunnel. A shadow asp emerged from a wall to watch as he dived through the hole into the first cavern, but it did not attack.

Back in sunlight again, safe from the shadow asps, Arvin morphed once more into human form. He touched his abbreviated little finger, thankful for his time in the guild. If he hadn't seen what had happened to the wizard, he never would have recognized the shadow asps.

The upper half of the Circled Serpent was safely concealed, but one more thing was required to ensure that it stayed hidden. Arvin took off his backpack and pulled out a few items he thought might come in handy in the next little while, including his trollgut rope, then placed the pack behind a stalagmite near the cave mouth—an easy hiding place to find. Pulling out a few items more, he arranged them around the pack to make it look as though someone had rifled through its contents.

His shirt was torn. He stripped it off and changed into the spare shirt he'd been carrying in his pack. He used his dagger to cut a length of fabric from the old shirt and wound it around his head like a loosely wrapped turban; it would keep the worst of the sun off. He cut the remainder of the fabric into long, thin strips.

Those he braided into a thin cord. At several points along its length, he worked intricate knots into the braid. When he was done, he dropped the cord next to the pack.

Then he manifested a psionic power—one he'd never used on himself before to the best of his knowledge. It was odd, hearing his own secondary display. The tinkling noise sounded just like the tiny silver bells, shaped like hollow snake teeth, that had decorated the hem of one of his mother's dresses. It was odder still, feeling the power take hold of his own mind and reshape it. Sharp as a dagger, it sliced away neat chunks of memory, excising everything from his finding of the tunnel to his narrow escape from the shadow asps. He left in the memory of himself hiding the pack behind the stalagmite but removed the part where he'd knotted the cord. He felt the remaining memories braid themselves together again and—

Arvin stood near the mouth of the cave, staring at the spot where he'd just hidden his pack. It wasn't possible to see the pack from the entrance, but still he wondered if he'd chosen the best hiding place. He glanced at the back of the cave, wondering if there might be a better spot there, but no, that cave was one of dozens in the bluff and was one of the less accessible. The chances of someone stumbling across Arvin's pack were slim.

He morphed back into a flying snake; the transformation was even easier than it had been before. He launched himself into the air and flew upriver again, toward the spot where he'd agreed to meet Pakal.

When he reached it, the dwarf wasn't there.

Perhaps Pakal was trying to find him. Arvin flew back downriver to the spot where he'd climbed the cliff. Worried that Pakal might have fallen victim to the carnivorous plant, Arvin circled above that spot. The plant had torn apart the knots he'd tied in its vines, but its bud-mouths were open. It didn't look as though it had swallowed anything lately, at least nothing dwarf-sized. Pakal, being native to the jungle, would surely know how to avoid the danger it posed.

He flew back along the other side of the river, back to the spot where he'd last seen Pakal, and continued on upriver, searching its banks, but saw no sign of the dwarf or of anyone who might be Ts'ikil.

Worried, Arvin hovered above the canyon. He wouldn't be able to sustain his metamorphosis much longer. He needed to find a safe place to land and somewhere he could spend the night, since he wouldn't be able to use a sending to contact Pakal again until the next day. The lapis lazuli only allowed him to contact a particular person once each day.

A short distance from the river was a place that looked suitable: a roughly circular clearing in the jungle. He flew toward it and saw that it was the plaza of what must have been a small city. A dozen low hills encircled the plaza: ruined buildings the jungle had long since grown over. Each structure was topped with an enormous serpent head carved from stone. It looked as if some ancient foe had decapitated a nest of serpents then set each of their heads upon a leafy green cushion. Their sightless stone eyes stared at the plaza like brooding serpents plotting their revenge.

Arvin landed on top of one of the heads, whose upper surface was as wide as a feast table. It afforded an excellent view of the plaza. The open area was paved with enormous red flagstones; bushes had thrust their way between them at several points, giving the stones the appearance of flotsam on a heaving sea. He morphed back into human form and stood. The sun beat down from above, and the weathered stone was uncomfortably hot, even through his boots. His feet were sweltering, but he didn't dare take the boots off. The jungle was full of strange insects, bristling with spines and pincers.

He wished, belatedly, that he'd filled his water skin from the river. It felt as though the heat had wrung every drop of moisture from his pores. Sunlight glinted off water that had collected in a murky green puddle in a hollow in one of the flagstones, and he decided to climb down and see if it was drinkable.

As he looked for the best way down, a movement at the edge of the jungle caught his eye. Something—or someone—was moving toward the plaza. At first, Arvin took it to be a human child or perhaps, given its short-limbed, heavy build and childlike face, a halfling. Its naked body, however, was covered in patches of what looked like green scales and it had a tail, not long and serpentine, like that of a yuan-ti, but thick and stubby, like a lizard's, and entirely covered in green scales. It moved with a bow-legged gait. When the half-man, half-lizard turned, Arvin could see that he held a crude spear.

Slowly, wary of any sudden movement that might catch the half-lizard's eye, Arvin settled into a crouch on the stone head then slid down beside it, out of sight. He watched, trying to decide whether to venture closer. The half-lizard was probably native to the jungle. He might know where Pakal was—might even know where Dmetrio was.

If Arvin could get close enough, he could read the strange creature's thoughts.

The half-lizard walked more or less upright, but as he approached the water, he dropped to all fours and scuttled. He scooped up water with a cupped hand then drank, his eyes ranging warily across the plaza. Then, as if sensing Arvin's eyes upon him, the half-lizard looked up, startled. A bright orange flap of skin shot out just under his chin, expanding into a half circle like a fan, as his head bobbed up and down several times in rapid succession.

Something moved through the jungle toward the plaza, something big—something that sent birds screeching out of the trees in flocks as it shouldered the trees aside like a man moving through a field of corn. It had to be as large as a dragon.

The monster smashed its way into the plaza a heartbeat later, knocking over a tree that slammed down onto the flagstones. It was an enormous reptile, its head level with the treetops. It stood on its hind legs, tiny forelegs scrabbling at the air, as if still tearing jungle vines out of the way. Slowly, it tilted its head from side to side. One eye fixed on the half lizard. The giant reptile threw back its head and roared. Its mouth was filled with rows of teeth that looked easily as long as Arvin's dagger.

The half-lizard grabbed his spear and fled into the jungle. The gigantic reptile charged after him, its clawed feet gouging flagstones out of the plaza with each step. It smashed into the jungle and disappeared from sight. Only after it was gone did Arvin realize that there had been what looked like a saddle on its back.

He watched the rippling wake it left in the jungle, thankful that he'd chosen somewhere elevated to land. His eyes ranged over the jungle. Dmetrio was out there somewhere—but where?

Something occurred to Arvin then, that perhaps he didn't need Pakal to tell him where Dmetrio was. Maybe a sending to Dmetrio would work, since Arvin was on the Chultan Peninsula himself. It was certainly worth a try.

He activated the lapis lazuli and pictured Dmetrio in his mind. The yuan-ti noble's features were easy enough to remember: high forehead, dark, swept-back hair, narrow nose, slit-pupil eyes, and flickering forked tongue. The connection wouldn't come, no matter how vehemently Arvin mentally whispered Dmetrio's name.

Dmetrio had either shielded himself—or he was dead.

Then Arvin realized there was a third possibility: that Dmetrio *was* dead in a manner of speaking, dead at Zelia's hands.

Zelia claimed to serve House Extaminos, but the mind seed she'd planted in Arvin had given him an intimate knowledge of where her loyalties truly lay. She thought of herself not as a subject of Lady Dediana but as working for herself, and she craved power. If the opportunity presented itself for her to become Sseth's avatar, she would have seized it.

The Naneth-seed had been Zelia's ticket into Sibyl's lair. With Naneth in place, there was a good possibility of both halves of the Circled Serpent falling into Zelia's hands if she could also control Dmetrio. Seeding the son of Hlondeth's ruler would have been a dangerous move for Zelia to make, but the fact that Dmetrio was headed south, where few knew him, made it slightly less risky. A seeded Dmetrio would explain why none of Arvin's sendings to the prince those past few months had been successful.

Still holding the image of Dmetrio's face in his mind, Arvin shifted his thoughts slightly. He imagined an identical body that housed a mind that went by a different name.

Zelia.

Immediately, his mental image of Dmetrio animated. The mind seed was lounging, his predominantly human body bent backward in an approximation of a coiled serpent. He was holding a languid conversation with someone Arvin couldn't see, but he broke that off immediately as the sending manifested. Slit-pupil eyes stared at Arvin for a long, appraising moment. Then the Dmetrio-seed's tongue flickered out of an anticipatory smile. Its mouth hissed a silent word: "Arvin."

Arvin took a deep breath. *Dmetrio,* he began, *Zelia sent me. I have the upper half of the serpent. Tell me where you are, and I'll bring it to you.*

The Dmetrio-seed smiled. A heartbeat later, Arvin felt a familiar tingling in his forehead. *Stay where you are,* the seed answered. *The jungle is dangerous. I'll come to you.*

"I'll bet you will," Arvin muttered as the sending ended. It had been just the response he'd hoped for. He had no doubt that the Dmetrio-seed had just scryed him. The stone head would be a familiar landmark, and the seed would be there soon.

He glanced again at the water the strange creature had drunk from then decided not to chance it. Quenching his thirst would wait. He needed to get ready.

☜

It was early evening, and still the Dmetrio-seed hadn't shown up. Arvin wondered if he'd guessed wrong. Maybe he wasn't in Chult, but some other, even more distant place. He'd finished his meditations long ago and sat, hidden in the foliage a few paces distant from the stone head, but still there was no sign of the seed.

Finally, low in the sky to the west, Arvin spotted something. At first he took it to be a soaring bird, but the movement and proportions were all wrong. It was, instead, a person seated on a carpet.

He was reminded of the magical carpets of Calimshan. He'd once been hired to repair one—though it had turned out to have a more deadly purpose than flying. As the person on the carpet drew closer, Arvin rendered himself invisible and created an illusionary image of himself sitting cross-legged on the stone head. Ectoplasm shimmered on the stone then swiftly evaporated in the heat. He toyed with the ring on his finger—he was counting on it to hide his thoughts from any probe the seed might do of the general area around the stone head—and watched as the flying carpet approached. As soon as it was close enough for its passenger to manifest a power against him, Arvin threw up a psionic shield.

On the carpet sat a yuan-ti, not Dmetrio, but a female. She was dressed as the Se'sehen had been, in a cape—hers made of overlapping "scales" of turquoise feathers—and a clinging, gauzy tunic that ended just below her waist, where her snake tail began. Both her skin and her scales were a dark brown. A band of gold encircled her left wrist, and a round plug of jade as wide as Arvin's thumb pierced the skin between her lower lip and chin. Instead of hair, a ruff of scales framed her face.

Wary that she might be yet another of Zelia's seeds—or the Dmetrio-seed itself, cloaked in illusion—Arvin probed her mind as soon as she was within range. To his surprise, he encountered no resistance. If she saw the silver that sparkled out of thin air when he manifested the power, she gave no sign.

She studied the illusion, mentally comparing it to the description

Hlondeth's prince had given her. She was surprised by how human Arvin looked. Dmetrio had led her to believe the person she'd been sent to fetch was a halfblood.

She spoke. Arvin, inside her mind, understood the words, even though they were spoken in Draconic. She asked if he was the one she'd been sent to fetch. He made the illusion nod.

Meanwhile, he probed deeper. The yuan-ti's name was Hrishniss, and she was a noble of House Jennestaa. She was one of those who had greeted Dmetrio when the prince had come to her tribe nearly six months before on a highly secret mission from Hlondeth. House Extaminos was poised to turn against its former allies, and assisted by the Jennestaa and Eselemaa, it would conquer the Se'sehen in a surprise attack.

She obviously had no idea what was going on in Hlondeth.

Hrishniss had no psionic powers, no clerical spells, also no attack or defense forms, aside from those native to the yuan-ti race. She had come alone and knew nothing about Arvin save that she was to fetch him back to Ss'yin, the ruined city he'd spotted in the distance. Her thoughts gave Arvin the city's full name—Ss'yin'tia'saminass—a word Arvin knew he'd never have a hope of pronouncing without a serpent's forked tongue.

Arvin's attempt to lure the Dmetrio-seed to him had failed. It looked as though Arvin would have to go to the seed instead—to place his head inside the serpent's mouth, so to speak.

Still wary but seeing no reason why he should continue to hide, Arvin ended the illusion and allowed himself to become visible. Hrishniss blinked but otherwise didn't react. Yuan-ti didn't startle easily, and she was no exception. She hissed something at him—an invitation for him to climb onto the carpet with her.

Arvin took a closer look at it. The "carpet" was a section of shed snakeskin with dozens of wings from the tiny flying snakes sewn into its hem. The translucent skin looked fragile, as if it would tear if too much weight were placed upon it. He climbed onto it—the skin gave slightly but seemed strong enough—and seated himself facing the yuan-ti. She turned her back to him and stared to the west, and the carpet moved in that direction.

As they flew toward the ruined city, Arvin wondered what was going on. It wasn't like Zelia to delegate a task, especially one as important as retrieving someone who claimed to have half of the Circled Serpent. She didn't trust anyone but her seeds—if indeed she trusted them. Arvin worried that Hrishniss might be part of some elaborate scheme but couldn't for the life of him figure out what it might be.

With a growing sense of unease, he rode the carpet toward Ss'yin.

The ruined city was even larger than Arvin expected—three times the size of Hlondeth at least. It stretched through the jungle for a vast distance. Tree-covered mounds that had once been buildings gave the jungle canopy a bumpy appearance. Here and there Arvin could see the jagged remains of a partially collapsed arch or viaduct rising above the treetops. Circular patches of lighter-colored vegetation marked the spots where plazas had once been. In the center of some of these were the lower coils of enormous serpent sculptures.

The setting sun filled the spaces between the ruins with ominous shadows. Dozens of yuan-ti slithered and strode those shadows.

As the carpet descended, a depression in the ground caught Arvin's eye—it looked like the remains of an enormous cistern. The rim of it was lined with hundreds of needle-like spikes that faced inward and down. It looked as though there were people inside it, and as the carpet passed over the cistern, Arvin got a better look. He was stunned to see a dozen halflings in ragged clothing, huddled in a group. One was smaller than the rest, probably a child. Two of them looked up listlessly as the carpet flew overhead. The rest stared at the floor.

Arvin once again manifested the power that would allow him to read Hrishniss's thoughts, then tapped the yuan-ti on the shoulder and pointed down. She spoke in her own language, but Arvin heard the words as they formed in her mind just before each was spoken.

"Monkey-men," she said. "Soon to join the other slaves, once we have altered them."

The word she'd used—"altered"—had several other meanings rolled into one. It was also the word for "improved" and "magically changed," and strangely enough, the word for "fed"—specifically, for feeding a liquid to someone.

With a growing horror, Arvin realized what Hrishniss meant. The halflings below were going to suffer a similar fate to his friend Naulg.

They would be fed a potion that would transform them into lizard creatures, just like the half-lizard Arvin had spotted in the plaza.

Arvin swallowed down the bile rising in his throat. His best chance at doing anything for the wretches below lay in feigning indifference. He stared back at Hrishniss, his face impassive, and nodded his approval.

They landed, as the sun was setting, in the deep shadow of a pyramid. It was shaped like a coiled serpent but was missing its head—this lay in the jungle nearby, blank eyes peering out of an overgrowth of vines. The broken neck was hollow. The serpent's mouth must have been the pyramid's original entrance.

As Hrishniss and Arvin stepped off the carpet, one of the half-lizards scuttled out of the shadows to retrieve it—a female with dull brown hair that had fallen out on the left side of her head to be replaced by scales. She smelled as if she had not bathed in several tendays and her clothes hung in rags. There were twin punctures in her left arm—bite marks—each surrounded by a nasty looking patch of red. Her eyes had a tortured, half-mad look that reminded Arvin of the way Naulg had looked just before he died.

Hrishniss hissed an order. The half-lizard flinched.

Arvin balled his fists. He exhaled, long and slow, breathing out his anger. He couldn't offer the transformed halfling so much as a sympathetic glance. He turned away and followed Hrishniss up the pyramid.

They entered the neck of the snake and descended through the pyramid's spiraling interior. For several circuits, they moved through darkness. Arvin had to listen for the sound of Hrishniss' footsteps as her feet slid along the stone. He walked with one hand brushing the wall, sliding his own feet forward to feel out any debris or sudden gaps, but he didn't encounter any. Despite the great age of the pyramid, its interior was clean and smooth.

The spiraling corridor lightened, and a yellow light flickered up ahead. The air felt drier. Arvin could smell sweet-scented smoke. Rounding the last bend, they entered a circular room illuminated by a enormous metal brazier, filled with oil, that occupied the center of the room. Yellow flames rippled across its surface, occasionally crackling as one of the chunks of resin floating on the surface burst into flame. Shadows danced on the walls, which were pierced around the circumference of the room with eight circular tunnels, including the one Hrishniss and Arvin had just emerged from. Each had been carved to resemble the open mouth of a serpent, and was framed by elongated, stylized fangs that stretched from roof to floor like curved pillars.

Inside one of those tunnels—the one directly opposite where Arvin stood—the Dmetrio-seed lounged, naked. His back was against one wall, his feet propped up on the other. His tongue flickered in and out of his mouth as he stared up at Arvin through the brazier's dancing flames. One hand made a lazy gesture.

"Leave us," he hissed.

Hrishniss bowed then backed out of the chamber.

Something tickled Arvin's forehead: his lapis lazuli, warning him that someone was using detection magic. Someone was scrying him.

There was nothing he could do about that now. Ignoring the tingling, he mentally braced himself. He stared at the Dmetrio-seed, ready for the psionic attack he was certain was coming, one thread of his awareness deep in his *muladhara*, touching the energy it contained. Worried that the burning oil might contain *osssra*, he breathed as shallowly as he could. He felt clear-headed, however. Sharp. Ready. He had defeated one of Zelia's mind seeds already, and he would match another, blow for blow, and beat it down, too—but not until he absolutely had to. For the time being, he'd play the game, pretending he didn't know it was Zelia.

The Dmetrio-seed rose to his feet and moved toward Arvin. The body might be male, but the swaying walk was feminine, seductive. Arvin wondered if the seed realized he was doing it. Arvin kept his eyes firmly on the Dmetrio-seed's face, deliberately not looking down at the spot in the yuan-ti's groin where his genitals were hidden.

"Lord Extaminos," Arvin said, bowing.

"Arvin." The answer was in a higher, softer tone than Dmetrio had used. "Zelia told me to expect you. Did you bring it?"

"No," Arvin said. "It's hidden. When the time comes, I'll go get it."

He felt a finger-light tickle touch his mind and heard the tinkling of Zelia's secondary display. A surge of magical energy tingled up his arm from Karrell's ring, sweeping away the seed's attempt to read Arvin's thoughts. Arvin drew energy up through his navel, into his forehead, preparing to manifest a defense against whatever the seed hurled at him next.

The Dmetrio-seed merely smiled.

Sweat trickled down Arvin's temples. This was unlike Zelia. He had to know what was going on. Taking a big risk, he redirected the energy that swirled around his navel and third eye into the base of his scalp instead. The Dmetrio-seed frowned slightly and turned his head, as if a distant sound had caught his attention.

Then, amazingly, Arvin was in.

It was Zelia's mind, all right. She stared at Arvin with tightly controlled loathing. He was a human—a member of a lesser race. An insect. Like an annoying gnat, he kept coming back to pester her over and over again. She ached to manifest a catapsi and watch his psionic energies bleed from him, then kill him. Slowly. For the moment, he was a gnat she dared not swat, not after all of the work the original Zelia had done to set things up. Of course Arvin hadn't been foolish enough to bring the other half of the Circled Serpent with him; Juz'la had said to expect that. Juz'la would worm the secret of where it was hidden out of Arvin. Yes, the seed would leave that to her.

Arvin blinked. Who was Juz'la? Whoever she was, the Dmetrio-seed was deferring to her like a subordinate. Arvin was shocked to hear even a seed of Zelia admitting that someone else was more powerful and capable. It was inconceivable.

He dug deeper and was surprised at the ease with which he read the Dmetrio-seed's thoughts. It was as if he were walking a well-worn path. The seed offered no resistance. Was he playing some sort of game—one that involved luring Arvin deeper into his mind? Arvin pushed on warily.

In a matter of moments, he had learned where the Dmetrio-seed had hidden the lower half of the Circled Serpent: inside a ceramic statue of Sseth that had been part of the tribute he had presented to the Jennestaa upon his arrival at Ss'yin, a statue that now sat in a place of honor on one of their altars. Bound up with that information was a much more recent memory—from five nights before— of the Dmetrio-seed bragging to Juz'la, over a glass of wine, how clever the hiding place was. No yuan-ti would dare smash open a statue of the god.

Arvin frowned. Juz'la again.

He found a picture of her in the Dmetrio-seed's memories: a dark-skinned yuan-ti woman with a bald head covered in orange and yellow snake scales that dipped down onto her forehead in a widow's peak. The image was nested amid a memory of the Dmetrio-seed seducing Juz'la. Memories of that seduction drifted to the surface of the seed's thoughts: Juz'la straddling the seed, naked, her muscular body glistening with acidic sweat, an indifferent look on her face. Skirting those images—which were fuzzy and incomplete, like the memories of a drunken man—Arvin explored the connection between the two. Zelia and Juz'la were old friends. They had known each other, long ago, in the city of Skullport.

The Dmetrio-seed had been surprised to learn that Juz'la had left Skullport, but he'd accepted Juz'la's explanation of needing to leave the city quickly, something about having run afoul of a slaver there. As for how Juz'la had wound up in the Black Jungles, that was simple. She had taken passage on a ship that had sailed through one of Skullport's many portals—one that led to the Lapal Sea—then made her way west. The seed thought it odd that Juz'la had wound up here in Ss'yin shortly after he did, but life was like that—people's lives entwined in the strangest of ways.

Stranger still was the fact that Juz'la, once human, now appeared to be yuan-ti. That part, too, Juz'la had explained. She'd drunk a potion, one that had transformed her into a yuan-ti. It was something she'd always wanted. Venom is power, she'd said.

All of this had the ring of truth—or at least, the truth as the Dmetrio-seed believed it to be. Something still didn't sit right, however. Zelia never accepted stories at face value, and one of her seeds would *never* look up to a human—even one who had since been transformed into a yuan-ti—with the kind of admiration and respect, even awe, that Arvin heard echoing through the seed's thoughts.

The Dmetrio-seed stared idly at the flaming oil—again, a most uncharacteristic behavior for one of Zelia's seeds. "Beautiful, isn't it?" he hissed. "Just like a slitherglow."

Arvin looked around, pretending to study the chamber. "This city must be ancient," he said, stalling as he tried to think what to do next.

"It was built centuries ago," the seed answered, "at the height of the Serpentes Empire."

"It's very remote."

"Yes."

"Why did you come here?" Arvin asked. He already knew the answer, but he wanted to hear what the seed thought about Dmetrio's mission.

"To forge an alliance," the seed answered. "House Se'sehen has turned its back on House Extaminos. We need new allies in the south."

That much was the truth. Dmetrio—the real Dmetrio, before Zelia had seeded him—had been ordered south by Lady Dediana on a secret mission to build up the Jennestaa forces in preparation for an attack on the Se'sehen. That, it was hoped, would draw Sibyl south. If all went well, Sibyl would be killed in the resulting battle, thus removing the thorn that had festered in Hlondeth's side those past two years. With Sibyl dead, Dmetrio could claim her half of the Circled Serpent, use it to free his god, and become Sseth's avatar.

Zelia, of course, had no intention of letting this happen, nor did she intend to let her seed become an avatar—that much was clear in the seed's thoughts. The Dmetrio-seed had been given strict orders to get the second half of the Circled Serpent from Arvin, kill him, and hand both halves over to Zelia.

The seed, of course, had his own thoughts on that matter. The idea of becoming Sseth's avatar—of gaining powers far beyond those the original Zelia possessed—was a tempting one, but also one that gave the seed pause. Zelia was a more powerful psion and a dangerous woman to cross. Seeds who had attempted betrayal before had all met a swift death.

Arvin pressed deeper. Had the Dmetrio-seed learned where the door was? Arvin couldn't find it anywhere in the seed's thoughts. That was disappointing, but there was still more to be learned. Whether the seed had told Zelia that Arvin had contacted him, for example.

"Was that why the Se'sehen attacked Hlondeth?" Arvin continued. "Because of the new alliance?"

The Dmetrio-seed blinked. He'd had no idea Hlondeth was under attack.

"You didn't know?" Arvin continued, even though he'd already heard the answer in the Dmetrio-seed's thoughts. "Zelia didn't tell you?"

The seed, he learned, hadn't been in touch with Zelia since receiving the message that Arvin would get in touch with him soon. The seed had wanted to alert Zelia to the fact that Arvin had just contacted him with a sending—that Arvin had the other half of the Circled Serpent—but Juz'la had advised against it. Amazingly, the seed had acquiesced.

"When did this attack take place?" the Dmetrio-seed asked.

"Two days ago."

The seed hissed. An attack on Hlondeth, he was thinking, might mean an attack on Ss'yin was imminent. The Jennestaa had been working hard to create an army, but they were nowhere near ready yet. After a moment, however, his agitation eased. He'd ask Juz'la for advice; she'd know what to do.

"War makes odd bedfellows," Arvin prompted, hoping to hear more about Juz'la.

The Dmetrio-seed didn't take the bait. His lips quirked into a smile. "That it does. The Jennestaa are wild and uncivilized—they find beauty in the power of the jungle to break apart even the largest stone. They'd like to see every city laid waste and reclaimed by the jungle."

"Even Hlondeth?"

The Dmetrio-seed touched Arvin's arm, drew him closer. "Even Hlondeth," he breathed in Arvin's ear. "Fortunately, they'll never get that far."

Arvin started to draw away—then stopped, as he smelled a faint but unmistakable odor. A perfume sweet scent, overlaid with wine.

Hassaael.

That was what was muddying the Dmetrio-seed's thoughts and making Zelia as passive as a slurring drunk. Like the Talassan on Mount Ugruth, she had fallen entirely under the sway of whoever had fed her *hassaael*.

Arvin could guess who that was.

Juz'la.

It all fit. Juz'la had run afoul of a yuan-ti slaver in Skullport, and she'd drunk a magic potion that transformed her—a potion that sounded hauntingly familiar to the one the Pox had used to transform Naulg. That potion had come from a slaver named Ssarm, a man who was also a supplier of *hassaael* to Sibyl's minions.

Juz'la was one of them, a minion powerful enough to have

conquered Zelia—or rather, one of Zelia's mind seeds. Zelia, Arvin was certain, didn't know that yet. She'd noticed the "dulling" of her seed's mind but had put it down to his *osssra* use.

A slithering footstep drew Arvin's attention to one of the tunnels. He glanced up in time to see Juz'la step into the chamber. She held a wine glass made of delicate green crystal in her hand.

"Ah," she hissed. "Our guest has arrived." She held the glass out to Arvin. "You must be thirsty after your journey. Here, drink."

Chapter 8

"THANK YOU," ARVIN SAID, TAKING THE WINE GLASS. HE PRETENDED not to notice the twin puncture marks on the inside of Juz'la's wrist. "I am indeed thirsty. This is the hottest place I've ever been."

He swept the improvised turban off his head and mopped his brow with it, then pretended to stuff it into his pocket. When he removed his hand, the fabric was inside his sleeve. He transferred the glass to this hand and raised it to his lips. He was tempted to manifest a distraction but was wary of alerting Juz'la with a secondary display. If she'd associated with Zelia in the past, she'd certainly know all about psions. He'd already noted the glance she'd given the crystal that hung at his neck.

The Dmetrio-seed stood slightly behind Juz'la. Arvin glanced in his direction and gave his head the slightest of shakes—just enough so Juz'la would notice. As he'd hoped, she glanced behind her to see what the seed was up to. Arvin used the opportunity to turn slightly to the right, to screen what he was doing from the seed, and tip the wine down his sleeve. The fabric inside it soaked it up, and any that bled through to his shirt would blend in with the sweat that already dampened it. He allowed the dregs of the wine to wet his tightly closed lips. As Juz'la turned back toward him, frowning, he wiped his mouth with the back of his free hand. If she saw any wine stains on his sleeve, she'd likely attribute them to that; few people could remember which hand, exactly, had been used in such a casual gesture.

"Unusual taste," he commented.

Juz'la glanced at the burning oil—probably making sure he hadn't poured the wine into it—and smiled. Her eye teeth were slender and curved, like a snake's. Scales covered her hairless scalp, her neck, and her arms, which were quite muscular. She wore a tight-fitting dress of a gauzy material that did nothing to hide her breasts or the darker patch of scales at her groin. If she'd been fed the same potion that Naulg had, it had left her mind remarkably unscathed; her eyes shone with a keen intelligence.

A black bracelet encircled her left wrist. Only when it lifted its head did Arvin realize it was a tiny viper. Juz'la lifted it to her lips and kissed it, then whispered an endearment to it as the tiny serpent twined around her fingers.

"Who are you?" Arvin asked, putting just a hint of suspicion into his voice.

"An old friend of Dmetrio's."

Arvin gave a mental nod. Juz'la was keeping up the pretense that Dmetrio was still himself. The Dmetrio-seed himself probably hadn't realized that Arvin knew his secret.

"What's your part in this?" Arvin continued.

"The same as yours. To help Dmetrio accomplish his goal."

"I see."

Arvin glanced at the seed, who followed their conversation with a passive look on his face. He wondered how much Sibyl's spy had been able to glean from the seed. "Dmetrio" would have all of Zelia's memories up to the time the seed was planted; if Juz'la had been rifling through those, she might know as much about Arvin as Zelia did. Presumably, she'd lifted more recent information from the seed, as well. Arvin had to assume Juz'la knew about the deal he'd struck with Zelia, and about Karrell. She would know that Karrell served Ubtao, a god that was Sseth's enemy, and that Karrell was in Smaragd.

Arvin was suddenly very glad that Sseth's worshipers were no longer in communication with their god.

"Where have you hidden the Circled Serpent?" Juz'la asked.

Arvin was surprised by the blunt demand. It had obviously been intended to startle. Juz'la whispered something to her viper again as she played with it, disguising the words and gestures of a spell. Arvin felt energy flow up his arm: Karrell's ring, blocking what must have been an attempt to listen in on his thoughts.

He manifested a power of his own. If she heard its secondary display, she might think it was because he was blocking her spell. His attempt to charm her, however, was met by a force that pushed his awareness back so hard it made his head ache. Either Juz'la had an amazingly strong mind, or magic shielded her.

"How about this," Arvin said, meeting her gaze with a challenging look. "You show me your half of the Circled Serpent, and I'll show you mine."

If Juz'la was disappointed by her spell's lack of success, she didn't show it. "You've made a mistake," she said. "It's not me you need to bargain with. I'm only Dmetrio's . . . assistant."

The Dmetrio-seed stepped forward. "I realize you don't trust me, Arvin," he hissed. "You're no more likely to hand me your half than I am to give you mine. Juz'la is our compromise. When the time comes to open the door, she can put the two halves together and wield the key."

Arvin wondered how much the *hassaael* would have affected him had he drunk it. It was probably safe to express a few lingering doubts. He glanced at Juz'la.

"Why should I trust *her?* We've only just met."

The Dmetrio-seed smiled —a slight upturn of the lips that was all Zelia. "Talk to her," he suggested. "Get to know her. Then decide." The smile widened. "Take your time. From what Zelia told me, I'm sure Karrell can wait."

Hissing with laughter, the Dmetrio-seed transformed into a serpent and slithered from the chamber.

Juz'la turned to Arvin. "Hungry?"

Arvin quickly considered whether Juz'la might drug any food he was served then decided that she probably wouldn't bother after having plied him with *hassaael*. Besides, he needed to show that he was starting to trust her.

"Famished," he answered. "I haven't eaten since yesterday."

Juz'la smiled. She turned and hissed something; a moment later, one of the mutated halflings—a male—carried in a platter bearing a selection of bright orange and green fruits. The half-lizard had a stubby tail and a scattering of yellow scales across his face, back, and chest. Four horns that looked as if they had only recently budded rose from his forehead, and his elbows and knees were scabbed over with what looked like fresh scales. He walked erect, however, still more halfling than lizard.

Kneeling, the half-lizard placed the platter on the floor. He started to back out of the chamber on his knees, but Juz'la flicked a hand at him.

"No need for that, Porvar," she said.

The half-lizard hesitated.

Arvin hid his frown just in time. Juz'la's attempt to show him that she treated the slaves well was failing miserably.

"You may go," she hissed.

Porvar turned and scurried away.

Juz'la indicated the platter with a wave of her hand. "Please eat," she said.

Arvin did. The fruit was thirst-quenching and tasted sweeter than any he'd eaten before. He licked the juice from his fingers.

Juz'la watched him in silence. Then, abruptly, she spoke. "Dmetrio told me about the bargain you struck with him," she said. "You want to enter Smaragd to rescue your woman—Karrell."

"Yes," Arvin said.

Juz'la gave him a conspiratorial smile. "You don't need Dmetrio for that."

Arvin played along. "Yes, I do. He has half of the Circled Serpent, remember?"

Juz'la gave him an unblinking stare. "So what? I know where it is."

"Ah," Arvin said, stroking his chin thoughtfully. "I see how it is, now." He used the gesture to hide his breath, which should have smelled strongly of the drug. His back was against the dish of flaming oil. Pretending its heat made him uncomfortable, he stepped away from it, putting more distance between himself and Juz'la. "Why betray Dmetrio?" he asked her. "What's in it for you?"

"It's not Dmetrio I'm betraying. It's Zelia."

Despite his years of hiding his reactions from the guild, that one made Arvin blink. "I don't understand."

"Yes, you do. You know who Dmetrio really is—why do you think I left you alone with him so long? I know about your powers. You can listen in on other people's thoughts, sift through their memories." She held up a hand when he started to protest. "You tried to do that with me a few moments ago."

Arvin shook his head. "I merely—"

"Here's what you would have learned, had you been able to probe my mind, as well," Juz'la continued. "I discovered, shortly after my arrival in Ss'yin, that Dmetrio is one of Zelia's seeds, and I decided to take my revenge upon her by thwarting whatever the seed hoped to accomplish."

"Revenge for what?" Arvin asked.

"Years ago, Zelia and I both worked for the Hall of Mental Splendor in Skullport, an organization similar to a rogues' guild that offered spies for hire. We became . . . friends.

"A few years ago, I was assigned the task of gathering information on one of Skullport's slavers, a man named Ssarm. Around the time of that assignment, Zelia announced that she was leaving Skullport. She told me she was setting out on her own—she'd just learned how to plant mind seeds, and meant to build up an organization similar to the Hall—but there was more to her departure than that.

"The day after Zelia left, Ssarm learned I'd been selling his secrets. To say that he was furious about this would be an understatement. He . . . punished me."

For several moments, her eyes shone with a fierce hatred. Then she smiled. "I know what you're thinking—even without my spells. Ssarm is Sibyl's man, but no, I'm not one of the abomination's followers."

For a heartbeat or two, Arvin actually believed her. Juz'la was that good. A strand of truth ran through everything she'd just said, but the end of the braid was frayed in two places.

Back at the portal, Pakal had said that the Dmetrio-seed had been in contact with Karrell's organization, the *K'aaxlaat*. Juz'la must have known this. If all she wanted to do was thwart Sibyl's plans, she could have handed the Dmetrio-seed's half of the Circled Serpent over to them for eventual destruction.

Zelia couldn't have been the one who betrayed Juz'la to Ssarm. Zelia had only heard the slaver's name for the first time a year before, when Arvin told it to her. Juz'la was faking her vengeful anger.

All of the threads came neatly together in a tight knot, however, if Juz'la was working for Sibyl.

Juz'la stared with unblinking eyes at Arvin as he considered his answer. Once again, Arvin was glad that Karrell's ring was on his finger.

"It sounds like we have a mutual enemy," Arvin said at last.

Juz'la smiled like a snake that had just swallowed a mouse. "Zelia's seed was wary of me, at first," she continued, "but she was also arrogant—and just as blinded by vanity as Zelia herself. The seed thought I was fooled by the body it wore. When I cast my domination spell, she never even noticed."

Arvin knew exactly what Juz'la was up to by claiming to have used a spell on the seed: trying to provide an explanation for the effects of the *hassaael*. He resisted the urge to touch the crystal at his neck. Tymora herself must have placed Thessania, the false stormmistress, in his path. If she hadn't, he'd never have known what *hassaael* was. He pretended to scowl.

"Don't try that on me," he warned. "My psionics—"

"Are a match for my sorcery, I'm sure," Juz'la said. A flicker of forked tongue appeared between her teeth as she laughed. Then her smile was gone. "Here's what I propose. Go and get your half from wherever you've hidden it. Contact me with a sending, and I'll tell you where the door to Smaragd is. I'll steal Zelia's half and meet you there." She paused, measuring him with her eyes. "Agreed?"

Arvin stared back at her, pretending to consider the offer. According to the Dmetrio-seed's memories, it had been five nights since Juz'la had learned where "Dmetrio's" half of the Circled Serpent was—two full days before Arvin and Pakal had snuck into Sibyl's lair and stolen her half of the Circled Serpent. If Sibyl had known where the door was, she would have opened it during the time that both halves were in her possession, but she hadn't known where it was. *That* was what her dreaming minions had been searching for: the location of the door. They hoped their god would tell them.

It also explained why the Dmetrio-seed hadn't been killed already. Sibyl had probably hoped that Zelia would learn the door's location and relay it to her seed, allowing Juz'la to intercept the information.

There was the slim possibility, however, that Sibyl had learned the door's location in the two days since Arvin and Pakal had stolen her half of the Circled Serpent, and—an even slimmer possibility—that she had told Juz'la where it was. Before he killed Juz'la, Arvin needed to rule that out.

"Agreed," Arvin lied. "I'll go and get my half at once."

Juz'la gave a satisfied hiss and stroked the head of her viper. "Excellent. I'll summon Hrishniss. She can fly you back to wherever—"

Arvin didn't give her a chance to finish. Silver flashed from his forehead as he hurled a stream of ectoplasm at her. It struck exactly where he'd intended: the hand that was stroking the viper. Strands of shimmering ectoplasm wound themselves around both her hand and face, immobilizing and gagging her, and preventing her from casting any spells. As he cinched them tight, Arvin manifested a mental shield between them. If Juz'la used her magical fear on him, the shield would deflect at least part of it.

He drew his dagger and spoke over the droning of his secondary display, "If you want to live," he threatened, "you're going to answer some quest—"

Juz'la was no longer standing in front of him. She'd transformed into an orange-and-yellow snake and fallen to the floor. The entangling ectoplasm, loosened, lay in a heap, together with her dress. Juz'la stared out from its folds and hissed something at him in Draconic. Then she flicked her tail.

The ice-white ray that shot from it streaked through Arvin's shield, striking his dagger hand. Frost blossomed on the blade and his hand went numb. He tried to release the dagger but his fingers wouldn't unbend. At least she'd used a spell that wasn't fatal. She needed him alive as much as he did her.

Arvin drew more ectoplasm from the Astral Plane and shaped it into a construct. Still half-formed, it lunged forward, seizing Juz'la by the neck and tail. Her eyes bulged as it squeezed. Her serpent body writhed furiously, but she couldn't slither free.

"Release me," Juz'la hissed.

Deep inside his mind, Arvin heard a groan as his mental shield intercepted whatever spell she had cast at him; it nearly buckled under the strain. With a thought, he directed the construct to clamp its hand over Juz'la's mouth, gagging her.

"Where is the door?" Arvin asked.

He let the shield dissipate and transferred his energy to a different power point. Silver sparkled from his forehead as he slipped inside Juz'la's thoughts. She put up a good fight—getting inside felt like battering down a stone wall with his forehead—but the instant he was in, he had his answer. She didn't know where the door was, and she was, indeed, Sibyl's minion.

Arvin heard a hiss. The construct, neglected by Arvin for those few moments, must have allowed its grip to loosen. Juz'la spat out the words of a spell and touched it with her tail. Electricity flashed through the astral construct in jagged streaks. It exploded into a mist of ectoplasm.

Juz'la, freed, fell to the floor.

Arvin hurled his dagger, but the metal of the hilt guard stuck to his skin, tearing it and throwing his aim off. The dagger missed, burying itself in the heaped-up dress next to her.

Juz'la's tail flicked forward. A second lightning bolt crackled out of it, striking Arvin square in the chest. The smell of burning flesh filled his nostrils as every muscle in his body wrenched into a painful cramp. His heart faltered and his vision swam with jagged streaks of light. He sagged to his knees. Only by force of will was he able to prevent himself from blacking out.

"If you kill me," he croaked, "you'll never get the other half."

He heard a hiss of laughter. "Corpses can be made to talk."

She was bluffing. She had to be. Otherwise she'd have killed him when they first met. Full mobility had already returned to his fingers, though they felt as though they were on fire. Beside him, he could hear the crackling of incense in the burning oil. With an effort, he lifted his head, stared at Juz'la. She was still in serpent form.

"Tell me where it is," she hissed, "and I'll spare you."

Arvin felt a spell slither into his mind. He wanted to live. He *needed* to live; he was Karrell's only hope. He heard those thoughts aloud at the same time he thought them—but in a woman's voice. Karrell's?

"It's in a cave," he whispered. "In a bluff where the river bends. Where the flying snakes nest."

Equally strangely, he was calm when he said it. As if it didn't matter at all that he had just revealed the hiding place of the one thing that would allow him to save Karrell.

He heard a hiss of triumph. Then something stung his hand.

Glancing down, he saw Juz'la's tiny black viper and twin specks of red on the back of his left hand. He'd been bitten.

The shock of it snapped him out of the spell Juz'la had snared him with. "No!" he roared.

Lunging to his feet, he slammed a shoulder into the brazier. It crashed to the floor, sending a wave of flaming oil racing toward Juz'la. She screamed as it engulfed her and shifted back into her yuan-ti form, but sticky smears of melted resin remained stuck to her, burning her skin. From head to foot, her body was a mass of seared red flesh. The burning oil, spread thinly across the floor and wicking into Juz'la's abandoned dress, illuminated her from below, throwing ghastly shadows across her face.

Arvin summoned his dagger and it flew out of the burning dress toward him. Catching it by the point, he hurled it at Juz'la. The blade buried itself in her throat. She fell to the floor, dead. The smell of burned flesh lingered in the air.

Arvin glanced down, found the viper, which was trying to slither away, and slammed a heel onto it. The tiny serpent died with a satisfying crunch.

It was cold comfort, however; Arvin could feel the viper's poison taking hold of his body. His left hand was already swelling; Karrell's ring was a tight, painful band around his little finger. He felt dizzy and weak; his heartbeat light and fast. He leaned over and vomited; it splattered onto his boots. He stared at it, shivering.

So this is how I die, he thought. Of a snake bite? After everything I've been through . . .

"I'm sorry, Karrell," he said aloud.

"Master?"

Arvin looked up. The half-lizard who had brought them the platter of fruit stood in one of the tunnels, staring at him, uncertain. He glanced at Juz'la, who lay face-down amid the burning oil. The scales on her head blackened and curled from the heat, peeling from her scalp like dry skin. Smoke thickened the air, making Arvin cough.

Arvin had stopped being ill, and his stomach started to uncramp. His hand still felt like all of the demons of the Abyss were tormenting it, but his heartbeat was slowing, becoming more steady. Amazed, he shook his head.

Maybe he would live.

"There's been . . ." he glanced at Juz'la, saw that the dagger that had taken her in the throat was hidden by the way her body had fallen.

"An accident," he concluded. He held up his grossly swollen hand. "Juz'la's viper bit me. I bumped into the brazier, and it toppled. The oil spilled out, and Juz'la was burned."

Realizing he should feign some concern, he moved to where Juz'la lay. The sudden motion, combined with his dizziness, made him reel. He turned the motion into a less-than-graceful squat, ignoring the tiny flames that licked at his boots, and pretended to be feeling for a pulse. As he did, he slipped the dagger up his sleeve. It was a clumsy palming, but if the half-lizard noticed anything, he made no comment.

"She's dead," Arvin concluded.

He started to stand, then noticed something that lay beside the body in the flaming oil: a tiny vial that must have been secreted somewhere inside Juz'la's dress. The dark liquid inside it bubbled from the heat, the cork that sealed the vial starting to char. Arvin picked up the vial before it burst and he blew on it, trying to cool it.

The half-lizard puffed out his throat, clearly agitated. He shifted uneasily on bowed legs, looking as though he'd like nothing better than to scurry away. "Master," he croaked. "What—"

Arvin stood, fought off another wave of dizziness. He stared down at the half-lizard. "Your name's Porvar, isn't it?" he asked.

The half-lizard nodded. There was fear in his eyes but also intelligence. He wasn't as far gone as the slave who had met Arvin upon his arrival.

Arvin smiled and manifested a charm. "I'd like to help you, Porvar."

The half-lizard blinked rapidly. His posture became a little less subservient.

"The Jennestaa forced you to drink a potion, didn't they?"

The half-lizard's throat puffed out in alarm.

"A good friend of mine was forced to drink a similar potion," Arvin said.

Porvar looked doubtful.

"It's all right," Arvin assured him. "You can trust me. I'm not yuan-ti. I'm human."

Porvar glanced down at Arvin's swollen hand. The flesh around the punctures was purple. "When vipers bite, humans die."

"Not this human," Arvin assured him, and it was true.

The dizziness ebbed, leaving him more certain on his feet. His left hand was in agony, though. He tried to flex his fingers and nearly cried out from the pain.

"There's a statue," Arvin said. "Dmetrio Extaminos brought it with him when he came to Ss'yin'tia'saminass. Take me to it, and I'll help you escape."

The half-lizard laughed. "Where to? The jungle extends to the horizon."

"Better free in the jungle than a slave here," Arvin countered.

The half-lizard blinked. Once. Twice. "Why do you want the statue?"

Arvin smiled. "I plan on smashing it."

The half-lizard considered this. "And the others?" he asked.

"There's more than one statue?" Arvin asked.

Porvar shook his head. "The ones in the pit. The halflings who are still . . . whole. Will you help them, too?"

"I'll do what I can," Arvin promised.

Porvar's lips twitched. He turned. "Come. I will show you where Juz'la moved it to."

The corridor was only chest-high; Arvin had to walk bent over to follow. While the half-lizard's back was turned, he shook the dagger out of his sleeve and sheathed it and placed the vial in a pocket. Then he looped the wine-soaked cloth around his neck as an improvised sling for his swollen hand. He wished, belatedly, that he'd gotten Tanju to teach him one of the powers that stabilized and helped heal the body. Instead, he'd focused, those past six months, on powers he thought he might need in his battle with Sibyl. He hadn't expected to live long enough to require healing.

It soon became too dark to see, so Arvin followed Porvar with one hand on the half-lizard's shoulder. The corridor they followed ran in sinuous curves for some distance, and Arvin was certain they were no longer under the pyramid. Every so often, they passed through another of the circular, multi-exited chambers. Most of them were filled with rubble, Arvin discovered after painfully stubbing his toe on a piece of broken stone.

Eventually, they drew near an illuminated chamber filled with yuan-ti. Arvin let go of Porvar and assumed a sliding, more fluid gait.

He filled the minds of the yuan-ti with the illusion of scales on his body and slit-pupilled eyes. He wet his lips with his tongue, adding a serpent's forked flicker. Porvar glanced back at him, perhaps wondering why Arvin shuffled his feet, but the illusion wasn't directed at the half-lizard's mind. Arvin gave him an encouraging nod and gestured for him to lead on.

Soon Arvin smelled earth and mold and saw a dim light up ahead. Porvar halted a few moments later at the entrance to an enormous circular chamber. Easily fifty paces across, it was illuminated by moonlight that shone in through a portion of the ceiling that had collapsed. The moldy smell probably came from the rotted timbers that had tumbled into the room. Vines trailed in through the hole, brushing the spot where they'd fallen. Arvin noted the leaves, shaped vaguely like human hands, and the berries that were clustered in bunches like grapes. Assassin vine.

The chamber was crowded with pieces of weathered statuary that had, presumably, been scavenged from the ruins above. Stone snake heads with jagged, broken necks lay here and there on the floor. Some were no larger than Arvin's own head; others were chest-high. All had once been painted in bright colors, but the paint was flaked from them like shedding skin. Empty eye sockets had probably once held gems.

There were also a number of broken slabs of squared-off stone: stelae, covered with inscriptions in Draconic. The chamber also included a more-or-less intact statue that Arvin recognized from Zelia's childhood memories: the World Serpent, progenitor of all the reptile races. Lizard folk, yuan-ti, nagas, and a host of other scaly folk stared up at her from below, paying the goddess homage. They stood on the bent backs of humans and other two-legged races who crouched, like slaves, in perpetual submission.

Sounds drifted down the corridor behind them. Somewhere in the distance, a yuan-ti voice shouted. That couldn't be good.

"Where is the statue Prince Dmetrio brought with him from Hlondeth?" Arvin asked.

Porvar pointed at the far side of the room. "There."

Arvin sighted along the pointing finger. The statue stood against the far wall. It was small, no more than knee-high, with a gray-green body and wings that were covered in gilt. Pale yellow gems glittered in its eye sockets: yellow sapphires. Its hands were raised above its head, forming the circle that symbolized birth. Sseth reborn—the perfect hiding place for the Circled Serpent.

Arvin took a step forward but Porvan caught his arm, preventing him from entering the chamber. He nodded at the vines that trailed in through the ceiling.

"Stranglevine," he whispered, as if afraid his voice might awaken it.

Arvin smiled. "I know. I've worked with the stuff often enough."

Silver sparkled from his forehead, lengthening into a long, thin rope. Quick as thought, it wound itself around the assassin vines, binding them together. The plant, sensing it was under attack, began writhing like a snake. Arvin wrapped the far end of the shimmering rope around one of the larger serpent heads, stretching the assassin vine as tight as a lyre string.

"Wait here," he told Porvar.

He jogged over to the statue. A quick glance noted a slight discoloration; a sniff told Arvin that it was contact poison. He slipped off his improvised sling, wound it around his good hand, and lifted the statue with that. He didn't feel or hear anything shifting inside the statue when he picked it up. That worried him—Juz'la might already have removed its contents, and if she'd hidden Dmetrio's half of the Circled Serpent somewhere else, he might never find it.

Fortunately there was an easy way to find out if there was anything inside. Raising the statue above his head, Arvin slammed it down onto the floor.

Out of the shattered remains fell the lower half of the Circled Serpent. It glinted silver in the moonlight, the tiny scales carved onto its surface made a netlike pattern on the gleaming metal.

Arvin closed his eyes and heaved a huge sigh of relief. He'd done it! Both halves were his. Now all he had to do was find the door.

One thing worried him, however. Dmetrio hadn't kept the lead-lined box the Circled Serpent had been found in, which meant that something else had been hiding it from divination magic. The gray-green glaze on the ceramic statue must have had lead in it—but Arvin had smashed the statue, so that protection was no longer in place.

Arvin wished he still had his magical glove; vanished inside it, the Circled Serpent would probably escape detection. Without it, all Sibyl had to do was cast a location spell to find it.

A rustling noise behind him warned him that the ectoplasm that bound the assassin vine was starting to fade. He renewed it with a fresh manifestation, tying several loops into the rope he bound it with. Then he scooped up the Circled Serpent and tucked it inside his shirt, using his sling to tie it in place. He turned and motioned Porvar forward.

"Come on," he said, placing a foot in the lowermost loop of his improvised ladder. "Let's get out of here."

The half-lizard glanced nervously at the vine.

Arvin nodded toward the corridor. The shouting he'd heard grew louder. "We may have been found out," he said. "Do you *really* want to go back the way we came?"

Porvar shook his head.

"Then climb," Arvin instructed. "Follow me."

The climb wasn't an easy one for Arvin, despite his magical bracelet. He could use only one hand, and Porvar, below him, kept jostling the rope. Halfway up, Arvin's feet slipped and he nearly fell. Feet flailing, he clung to the vine with his good hand, trying to twist himself back around. As his feet found the vine again, something tickled the small of his back—a tendril of assassin vine, worming its way up inside his shirt. Cursing, he fumbled at it with his injured hand, but the vine curled around his waist and spiraled its way up his body. Within heartbeats, it tightened around his throat. Arvin hooked his arm around the vine and tried to pull the tendril off with his good hand but couldn't get his fingers under it. He traded arms, hooking the left one around the rope, and reached for his knife. The tendril tightened.

The vine jerked as Porvar shifted below. Arvin tried to shout at him to back off but the vine had already cut off his breath. He felt hands grasping his ankles, then his legs—what was the half-lizard trying to do, climb past him and escape? He tried to kick Porvar off, but the half-lizard gripped his legs too tightly.

"No!" Porvar hissed.

Arvin heard a chewing noise. Porvar grunted then wrenched his head to one side. The pressure on Arvin's throat eased. Glancing down, Arvin saw Porvar spit out a length of tendril. The half-lizard grinned up at him.

"You can stop kicking me now."

Unwinding the limp tendril from his throat, Arvin breathed his thanks.

The rest of the climb went smoothly. Getting out of the hole was tricky, but Porvar gave Arvin a boost from below. Arvin scrambled out and secured the Circled Serpent inside his shirt again. That done, he extended his good hand to Porvar, helping him clamber out. He backed Porvar away from the hole. When the ectoplasmic bonds evaporated, the entire assassin vine would come snaking up out of it.

They had emerged into dense jungle. The weathered remains of stone buildings loomed nearby, smothered in a thick layer of leafy vegetation. A few paces away, an enormous stone snake head stared with sightless eyes into the jungle. Trees stood like living pillars, their branches forming a dark canopy overhead.

Off in the distance to their right, something crashed through the jungle—several things, judging by the sound of it. From the opposite direction—the center of the ruined city—came yet more shouting. One of the creatures moving through the jungle was headed their way. The ground trembled as it drew closer. Arvin heard the crack of branches and saw trees moving. As it broke through the trees, he dragged Porvar into the shadow of the serpent head. An enormous reptile like the one he'd seen earlier lumbered past, a yuan-ti perched on a saddle on its back. The yuan-ti brandished a spear in each fist, and a feathered cape fluttered out behind him.

"The Se'sehen," Porvar breathed. "Ss'yin'tia'saminass is under attack."

"That's good," Arvin said. "In the confusion, you can escape."

Porvar gave him a level stare. "Not without my son."

"He's in the pit, isn't he?"

Porvar nodded.

Arvin struggled with his conscience. He'd retrieved the second half of the Circled Serpent—the only sane thing to do was shift into the form of a flying snake and get out. Now Karrell was counting on him. Arvin's *own* children would die if he failed to save them. Porvar was a stranger, trying to hold Arvin to a promise he couldn't afford to keep.

"Please," Porvar begged.

His whisper was all but lost in the crashing that surrounded them. Dozens of the giant lizards were thundering through the jungle toward the center of Ss'yin'tia'saminass.

Arvin sighed. "Which way is the pit?"

Porvar grinned, revealing a jagged set of teeth. "This way."

They hurried through the jungle, moving at right angles to the attack. More than once they had to stop and hide from other Se'sehen, also mounted on lizards. Eventually, the jungle opened up, and Arvin could see the cistern just ahead. He heard cries coming from inside it: the halflings. One of them was dead, impaled on the needle-like spikes. His face, level with the rim of the cistern, had turned a faint blue and was so swollen it was impossible to see his eyes.

Porvar stared, transfixed, at the corpse. "Poison," he croaked.

"Is your son good at climbing?" Arvin asked.

The half-lizard startled, then nodded.

"Tell the halflings to be ready to catch a rope."

Without wasting any more words, Arvin uncoiled the braided leather cord he'd fastened around his waist and began to climb a nearby tree. When he was high enough to look down into the pit, he tied one end of the cord to a tree branch and tossed the other down into the cistern, shouting its command word as he did so. The trollgut rope expanded, more than doubling in length. One of the halflings caught the other end.

"Is there something you can tie it to?" Arvin shouted.

The halflings looked around then shook their heads. The floor of the cistern was rough with broken stone, but none of the chunks was large enough to serve as an anchor for the rope. Arvin was just about to break the unpleasant news that one of them would have to hold it while the others climbed out when another of the enormous lizards hurtled toward them through the jungle. It smashed through the trees mere paces away from Arvin, sending the tree he was in whipping back and forth, and skirted the cistern, the yuan-ti on its back clinging grimly to its saddle. Arvin clung equally grimly to a branch with his one good hand.

As the giant lizard thundered away, Arvin heard a cheer go up from the halflings below. Glancing down, he saw that the lizard had knocked over a tree, which had fallen into the pit. Its trunk formed a ramp up to the rim. Already the halflings were scrambling up, Porvar's son in the lead. The half-lizard moved forward to embrace him, but the boy shrank back, frightened. Then, visibly screwing up his courage, he hugged his father. Porvar looked up at Arvin, waved his thanks, then hurried away with the others into the jungle.

"Nine lives," Arvin whispered.

He added a silent prayer that Tymora keep sending the halflings luck. To escape in the middle of a full-scale assault, they would need it.

Arvin, fortunately, would be out of there as soon as he could morph into a flying snake.

He cut the new growth from his trollgut rope and looped what remained over his shoulder. Then he started to draw energy up through his navel and into his chest. Only then did he think to touch his chest and make certain the lower half of the Circled Serpent was still there.

It wasn't. It must have fallen when the lizard brushed the tree.

A chill ran through him. His heart stopped racing a moment later, however, when he spotted it on the ground near the base of the tree. Aborting his manifestation, he scrambled down to grab it. He secured the Circled Serpent back inside his shirt and resumed his manifestation.

He tried to draw energy up through his navel, but all that came was a trickle. Only the tiniest amount of energy remained in his *muladhara*. He'd been spending it wantonly, neglecting to check how much remained. There wasn't enough to morph himself into a flying snake.

He'd have to walk out of Ss'yin'tia'saminass on foot.

He turned, trying to figure out which way the river was. It was somewhere to the east, but under the trees, in moonlight, it was impossible to figure out which way that might be. He decided to find a place to hole up, sleep, and replenish his *muladhara*.

He walked for some time through the ruins of Ss'yin, leaving the sounds of battle farther and farther behind. Enormous stone snake heads and low mounds that had once been buildings loomed out of the darkness on either side. He paused under a tree, looking for a sheltered place to perform his meditations. After a moment, he found a good spot: a circle of darkness in the side of a ruined building that was overgrown with vines—a doorway.

Dagger in hand, he pulled aside the vines and crawled into a corridor. He was taking a risk. Something else might have already claimed it as its lair. The corridor, however, ended in a pile of collapsed rubble only two or three paces into the building. It smelled of mold, and its floor was littered with dead leaves and other debris but it was otherwise empty.

Arvin collapsed, exhausted. He would sleep only a short time, he told himself, just long enough to refresh his mind so that he could perform his meditations.

He lay down, pillowing his head on his arms. No more than a quick nap, and . . .

☀

A rustling noise snapped Arvin awake. He sat up, dagger already in hand. He'd slept for longer than he'd intended. Outside his hiding place, twilight was already filtering through the jungle. The air was steamy and hot.

The swelling in his left hand had gone down; he was able to move it again. The twin punctures on the back of it were still an angry red, but the agony had ebbed. The hand just felt stiff and sore.

He paused, listening carefully, and heard monkeys chatter to each other over the rasping *caw-caw-caw* of a jungle bird. The rustling noise had probably been the monkeys, swinging through the trees. Other than that, the jungle was quiet. Whatever the outcome of the Se'sehen attack on Ss'yin, the battle was over.

He considered performing his meditations inside his refuge but decided to take advantage of the animals outside. A quick dagger throw, and he'd have fresh meat. Then he'd restore his *muladhara*.

He crawled outside and stood, stretching out the kinks that came from sleeping on a stone floor.

A slight rustle of the leaves above his head was all the warning he got. A heartbeat later, a snake-tailed yuan-ti with green scales the exact color of the leaves around him swung down from the branch above him and yanked Arvin off his feet.

CHAPTER 9

ARVIN GASPED AS HE WAS YANKED SIDEWAYS BY THE YUAN-TI. ITS serpent tail coiled around the branch above, it swung like a pendulum, slamming Arvin against the trunk of the tree. An explosion of stars filled Arvin's vision; as he blinked them away he heard the yuan-ti land on the ground next to him. Something heavy coiled around his chest and squeezed: the yuan-ti's serpent tail. The lower half of the Circled Serpent dug into Arvin's ribs. The yuan-ti, a male with leaf-shaped scales whose raised tips feathered out from his face, squeezed tighter, driving the air from Arvin's lungs, then eased up just a little. He bared his fangs and hissed something in Draconic.

Arvin stared back into unblinking eyes. "I don't understand you," he gasped.

As he spoke, he reached deep inside himself and connected with the small amount of energy that remained in his *muladhara*. He manifested a charm and saw the yuan-ti blink. Sunlight slanted down through a gap in the forest canopy. The sun was rising, and the jungle was getting even hotter.

The yuan-ti hissed again in Draconic. Sweat blossomed on his body, stinging Arvin's skin. Unable to move his arms—the yuan-ti's tail held them fast—Arvin gestured with his chin instead.

"Se'sehen?" he asked.

The yuan-ti's head swayed from side to side. In a human, it would have been denial, but the gesture was accompanied by a gloating smile and bared his fangs. His tongue flickered against Arvin's face, savoring his fear.

Arvin decided to take a gamble. "Sibyl?" he asked. His good hand was pressed against his chest but still visible. Arvin tapped a finger against his chest. "Sibyl," he repeated. "I'm one of her followers, too."

The yuan-ti relaxed his coils. His face was triangular with slit-pupiled eyes, not the slightest bit human. He had human arms, however, though they too were covered in green scales. His forked tongue flickered against Arvin's chest. "Sybil?" he repeated.

Arvin nodded. "Yes. Yes. We're on the same side."

The yuan-ti smiled and released Arvin. "Sibyl," he hissed again.

A shadow flickered across the yuan-ti. Something big had momentarily blocked the sunlight. The yuan-ti looked up.

Arvin followed his glance and saw an enormous winged serpent silhouetted against the sky. He felt the blood drain from his face as he realized who it must be. With the arrival of dawn, the portal had once again activated. Sibyl had slipped through.

The yuan-ti said something to Arvin in a tense, urgent voice. He glanced up again at the winged serpent that circled above them. Then his tail uncoiled, releasing Arvin. He said something more, gesturing urgently at the jungle, then slithered rapidly away.

Arvin stared, surprised. It was almost as if the yuan-ti had been frightened off by Sibyl. Maybe he'd been Jennestaa, after all.

Time for Arvin to get out of here as well.

As he turned to go, he heard a sharp fluttering noise: air passing swiftly over massive wings. Glancing up, he saw the winged serpent hurtling down toward him. He ran, hoping to lose himself beneath the trees, and cursed. He had nothing to fight Sibyl with; he'd left the musk creeper net in the cave. He tripped over a vine, stumbled, then recovered and ran on. He—

Couldn't move.

Couldn't even blink as he crashed, still frozen in a running pose, to the ground. As he lay on the jungle floor, the only thing that was moving—swiftly enough to make him dizzy—was the blood rushing through his veins. Over the thudding of his heart, loud in his ears, he heard the rustle of wings and the prolonged thud of a serpent body settling on the ground.

A tic of despair tugged at the corner of Arvin's eye. He waited for Sibyl's fangs to strike.

"Arvin?" a familiar voice said. It sounded surprised.

Arvin could move again. He scrambled to his feet. When he turned around, he saw Pakal. The dwarf had an odd expression on his face. It looked as though he was trying to decide whether he was glad—or angry—to see Arvin again.

Coiled on the ground beside Pakal was the winged serpent Arvin had mistaken for Sibyl. Arvin saw that it was no abomination—or at least, unlike any abomination he'd ever seen before. From its wedge-shaped head to the tip of its tail, the serpent was covered in feathers that glowed at the touch of sunlight. Midnight blue shaded into indigo, then into red, orange, yellow, and green. It had wings white and lacy as fresh frost, each feather tipped with vivid turquoise. Its face, though that of a serpent, was set in a kindly expression. Its smile was neither sly nor gloating but serene.

A rosy glow emanated from Pakal's body, turning his skin a ruddy brown. He had one hand raised, two fingers extended in a forked position; claws were visible at their tips. He'd lost his blowgun, probably to the river, but his dart pouch was still attached to his belt. Pakal had obviously homed in on the Circled Serpent just as he had in Sibyl's lair. Smashing the statue had been a big mistake.

The winged serpent next to him stared at Arvin with eyes like twin moons. Without opening its mouth, it spoke to Arvin, mind to mind. Its voice was a soft female trill. *Which half of the Circled Serpent do you carry?*

Denial would have been pointless. The winged serpent radiated power. Even with a chance to perform his meditations, Arvin doubted he could counter it.

"The lower half," he said. "The one Dmetrio had."

Show me.

Compelled, Arvin's hand slipped inside his shirt. It pulled out the lower half of the Circled Serpent. The serpent nodded.

Arvin stared up at the feathered head. "What . . . are you?"

A couatl, the voice trilled. *One of those Ubtao called home again. To the people of the jungles, I am known as Ts'ikil.*

Karrell's friend. Supposedly. "Are you an avatar?" Arvin asked.

Laugher rippled into his mind. *No. A servant of the god, nothing more.* The couatl nodded at the artifact in Arvin's hand. *Where is the other half?*

"It was lost in the river."

Was it? The voice sounded bemused. *Let us see.*

Arvin felt the couatl sifting through his thoughts, like a finger idly stirring sand. He clenched his hand around Karrell's ring. Without any energy to fuel his psionics, it was his only defence. The familiar rush of magical energy up his arm didn't come.

It does not block me because I made it, the couatl said.

The couatl rummaged a little longer in Arvin's mind then withdrew.

Arvin felt sick. He knew the couatl must have found what she was looking for: a memory of the cave where he'd hidden his backpack.

Pakal nodded in response to an unheard command and stepped forward. He held out a claw-tipped hand.

"Don't make her force you," he warned.

Reluctantly, Arvin handed the Circled Serpent to him. The dwarf tucked it into his belt pouch.

"Please," Arvin said, his eyes locked on Ts'ikil's. "I need to rescue Karrell. She's in Smaragd, pregnant, and about to give birth. I have to get her out of there. Just open the door that leads to Smaragd long enough for me to slip inside; I'll find my own way out."

For a moment, Pakal looked sorrowful. Then he snorted. "You really expect us to trust you?" The ruddy glow that surrounded his body intensified. The claws on the hand that held the lower half of the Circled Serpent lengthened.

Arvin tensed, ready to counter the attack he knew was coming.

The dwarf, however, turned toward Ts'ikil. "No," he said. "He might tell the Se'sehen where—"

The couatl must have given him a silent rebuke; Pakal backed down.

Ts'ikil turned to Arvin. *Karrell's plight fills me with great sorrow,* she said. *If I could shift to the layer of the Abyss she occupies, I would have attempted a rescue myself, but it's just not possible to reach her.*

Arvin's heart beat a little faster. His eyes were locked on Pakal's pouch. "It is possible. Now that we have both halves, we could—"

The risk is too great.

Pakal gave Arvin one last glare then climbed obediently onto the couatl's back. Ts'ikil coiled her body beneath her, unfurled her wings, and sprang into the air.

"Wait!" Arvin called. "Take me with you!"

Too late. Ts'ikil burst through the trees into the open sky and flew away.

Arvin didn't waste his breath cursing. Instead he threw himself into the *bhujang asana*. It took all the willpower he possessed to still his mind and enter a meditative state. Frantic thoughts of Karrell filled his head.

He had to hurry—

Stay calm! he growled at himself.

To fill his *muladhara* and morph into a flying snake—

Breathe in through the left nostril, out through the right.

To beat the couatl back to the cave where he'd hidden his backpack—

Breathe! Draw in energy. Force it down. Coil it into the *muladhara*.

Before Ts'ikil got there. Before she found the other half and destroyed —

Stop it! Still your mind! Control!

He completed his meditation then whirled through the five defence poses and five attack poses like a manic dancer. Sweat flew from his body as he thrust with his hands, twirled and kicked. At last he was done.

He yanked a mental fistful of energy into his navel—nearly making himself sick in the process—then up into his chest. The scent of saffron and ginger exploded into the air as he morphed. He did it clumsily, not caring that his serpent tail ended in two human feet or that his head, though tiny, was still human. What mattered were the wings. He thrust them out and muscled his way into the air, bursting out of the treetops like an arrow loosed from a bow. He wheeled, getting his bearings, then flew toward the rising sun. Ts'ikil was a black dot, silhouetted against its bright yellow glare.

Despite having learned how to extend his metamorphosis well beyond its normal duration, Arvin had to land several times and remanifest the power. Each time he rose from the treetops, Ts'ikil was farther away. An ache clutched at his throat as he saw Ts'ikil dive down toward the sinuous break in the jungle that was the river. The couatl would recover the other half of the Circled Serpent long before Arvin would reach the bluff himself.

Even though he knew it was hopeless, Arvin flew on. It seemed to take forever before he could see the river, let alone the bluff. Eventually, however, he saw the dark spots in it that were the caves and could pick out the one where he'd hidden the backpack. He spotted Ts'ikil coiled at the base of the bluff on a ledge beside the river. She was too big to enter the cave herself—she would have sent Pakal in to recover the other half of the Circled Serpent. There was no sign of the dwarf, however. Hope fluttered in Arvin's chest. Maybe he hadn't arrived too late, after all. Perhaps something had delayed Pakal and the Circled Serpent had not yet been destroyed.

Arvin was just about to descend toward the cave when something in his peripheral vision caused him to turn his head. Something big raced downriver. Another winged serpent, flying almost at treetop level, its dark coloration blending with the jungle below. There was no mistaking its black body and batlike wings.

Sibyl.

She was almost at the bluff.

Arvin activated his lapis lazuli. He didn't need to picture Ts'ikil in his mind, not when he could see her just ahead of him. *Ts'ikil!* he cried. *Sibyl is flying toward you from the north. She's almost at the bluffs.*

The couatl reacted at once. Her white wings unfurled like sails and she sprang into the air. As she rose, a turquoise glow began at her wingtips and spread swiftly to cover her entire body—some sort of protective spell, Arvin guessed.

As Ts'ikil rose above the bluff, Sibyl wheeled sharply. Her tail flicked forward, hurling a lightning bolt. It ripped through the air, striking the couatl in the chest. The turquoise glow surrounding her exploded into a haze of bright blue sparks as it absorbed the bolt's energy. A heartbeat later, the thunderclap reached Arvin, rattling his wing feathers. He dived toward the bluff, praying that neither of the combatants would notice him.

Ts'ikil retaliated with a flicker of her tongue that sent twin rays of golden fire crackling toward Sibyl. So intensely bright were they that they left streaks of white across Arvin's vision. When he blinked them away, Sibyl was surrounded by a roiling cloud of black that lingered at treetop level. Arvin at first thought it was the aftermath of the couatl's attack, then remembered the yuan-ti's ability to shroud herself in darkness. Sibyl's attempt to make herself a more difficult target, however, did nothing to forestall Ts'ikil's second attack. The couatl swooped down toward the patch of darkness with an eagle's cry. The trees around and below the darkness shuddered, as if caught in an earthquake. Arvin's ears rang from the sound of Ts'ikil's scream.

The darkness surrounding Sibyl started to dissipate, Sibyl's form slowly becoming visible. It looked as though she was struggling to stay aloft. Her wing beats were ragged and her head drooped. Ts'ikil swooped lower, closing in for the kill. Her wingtips brushed the uppermost branches of the trees.

One of them came to life. Whipping its branches upward, it hurled a tangle of vines into the air that wrapped around Ts'ikil's tail, snagging it and jerking the couatl to a halt. She tore free an instant later, leaving a scattering of brightly colored feathers behind, but the momentary reprieve gave Sibyl the time she needed to mount another attack. She sent a tide of darkness toward the couatl—a boiling cloud that had a greasy, greenish tinge. Some of it touched the jungle below, and leaves fell away from the treetops like scraps of rotted cloth. Then it engulfed Ts'ikil. For the space of several heartbeats, all Arvin could see of the couatl were a handful of dull feathers falling out of the cloud. Then Ts'ikil emerged. Ugly brown patches marred her rainbow body.

Sibyl had been using two of her hands to direct her spells; the other two held a glowing length of spiked chain, which burst into flame. She whirled it above her head and dived on Ts'ikil. One spiked end caught the couatl in the chest, knocking her sideways through the air, but not before the couatl twisted, lashing Sibyl's side with her tail.

Sibyl recovered swiftly and swung her chain in a second attack. It passed through empty space as the couatl vanished, her body disappearing from tail to nose. Sibyl hissed and flailed with her chain, but her effort was futile. Just as Pakal had in Sibyl's lair, Ts'ikil had turned her body to air.

She rematerialized a moment later behind Sibyl. Her tail lashed forward, knocking the chain from Sibyl's hands. It fell, still flaming, to the jungle below. Ts'ikil's tail flicked out again, coiling around Sibyl's waist. With a mighty backward thrust of her wings Ts'ikil jerked the abomination toward her and bit Sibyl's neck. Sibyl, however, twisted in her grip and bit back, her teeth ripping feathers from Ts'ikil's shoulder. Locked together, wings beating and tails thrashing, the pair of winged serpents crashed down into the jungle below.

By then, Arvin was approaching the cave where his pack was hidden. He felt a familiar tickle in his forehead. The iron cobra, it seemed, was still searching for him. It didn't matter; he could always outfly it. The battered minion was the least of his worries, at the moment.

As he entered the cave, his wings tingled. A moment later, his serpent body sprang apart into legs and his wings shrank in upon themselves, becoming arms once more. He landed awkwardly, his body expanding and resuming human form. He was glad the transformation hadn't occurred in mid air.

He spotted his backpack immediately at the side of the cave. It had been hauled out of its hiding place and opened, though the musk creeper net was still inside it. Arvin plunged his hand into the pack and felt around, searching each of its side pockets twice, then a third time. The box that held the upper half of the Circled Serpent was gone.

Kneeling, Arvin balled his fists. Pakal had found the second half of the Circled Serpent and made off with it. The dwarf could have been anywhere.

Outside, Arvin could hear the two winged serpents thrashing in the jungle. A moment later, he heard wing beats and the sharp whistles and dull explosions of spells being cast. A breeze wafted in through the cave mouth, carrying with it the moist smell of the jungle—and of burned feathers. Ts'ikil was in trouble.

Maybe Arvin could even the odds. He still had the musk creeper net. He rubbed the scar on his forehead that hid the lapis lazuli. He wouldn't be able to contact Ts'ikil a second time that day, but if he could lure Sibyl close to the cave mouth with a carefully worded sending, he might be able to hurl the net on her.

Two shapes streaked across the sky, just above the treetops on the opposite side of the canyon: Sibyl, with Ts'ikil in close pursuit. The abomination had a number of deep gouges down the length of her body, but Ts'ikil didn't look much better. She flew raggedly, favoring one of her wings. Arvin rushed to the mouth of the cave with his pack and leaned out, trying to see where they went, but the two winged serpents were already behind the bluff. He heard

Ts'ikil's eagle cry and clapped his hands over his ears as her sonic attack struck the bluff, sending a shower of broken stone into the river below.

As he turned, his eye fell on something that must have fallen out of his pack: a thin strip of fabric that had been tied into a series of intricate knots. He recognized it at once as something he must have made, but when he tried to remember when, he felt a curious, hollow sensation.

He scooped it up and examined the knots. They were a code—one he'd invented himself, years ago—that was based on the silent speech used by rogues. Each knot, like a hand signal, represented a different letter of the alphabet. Quickly running them through his fingers, he deciphered the message:

R.E.A.R.C.A.V.E.T.U.N.N.E.L.H.I.D.D.E.N.I.N.M.O.U.T.H. S.H.A.D.O.W.A.S.P.S

"Hidden in mouth?" he whispered aloud. What did *that* mean?

The first part of the message was clear enough: there must be a tunnel, somewhere in the back of the cave. He had obviously hidden something inside it, then erased all memory of having done so. There was only one thing valuable enough to merit such a drastic step.

The Circled Serpent.

Arvin grinned. That explained why Pakal wasn't there. The dwarf had must have gone through the pack, reported to Ts'ikil that the other half of the Circled Serpent had been taken by someone, and been sent on a futile errand to track down the supposed thief.

Pocketing the cord, Arvin hurried to the back of the cave. He had to clamber up a slope to find the tunnel; it was hidden behind a column of rock and was bricked shut except for a small opening where two bricks had fallen out. Touching it dislodged still more bricks; the entire wall seemed loose. He'd expected to see the box containing the Circled Serpent just inside the tunnel's mouth, but it wasn't there. It was probably deeper inside the tunnel, but it was difficult to make anything out in the shadows. He'd have to wait for his eyes to adjust. A breeze passed over his shoulder; air flowing into the hole in the bricks. The tunnel must have a second exit.

The knotted cord had mentioned shadow asps. Heeding his own warning, Arvin sent his awareness down the tunnel in a sparkle of silver. If there were asps lurking in those shadows, he'd be able to detect their thoughts. The tunnel, however, seemed clear. He yanked at the bricks, clearing a large enough hole for him to enter. Then, dagger in hand, he crawled into the tunnel. His eyes slowly adjusted to the dim light.

A second cavern lay a short distance ahead. As he started to move toward it, his manifestation at last picked up the three serpent minds. Their thoughts were focused on moving forward, on the sensation of their insubstantial bodies slithering through stone. They were intent upon something that had entered the second cavern—that had just *appeared* there without warning a few moments before. They were dimly aware of a second intruder behind them—Arvin—but it was the one in the cavern they wanted.

Arvin had halted the instant he detected the asps, but he hurried forward. Belatedly, he realized the source of the breeze he'd felt when he first peered into the tunnel: Pakal's body in gaseous form. The dwarf must have been lingering in the cavern, watching Arvin the whole time. Protected by the armband that was the equivalent of Karrell's ring, his thoughts had gone undetected.

Arvin didn't bother moving quietly. Pakal would have heard the tumbling bricks and be expecting him to show up. He did, however, send his awareness on ahead of himself to observe what the dwarf was up to. A low droning filled the air as Arvin concentrated on the second cavern.

It was deeply shadowed, but Arvin was still able to make out a few details. At the center of the second cavern was an enormous serpent, its body coiled in a tight ball. Surprisingly, it had not stirred, despite the fact that Pakal stood with one foot on the serpent's jaw while forcing the mouth open with his hands. The mouth slowly creaked open, revealing a square object that rested against the serpent's tongue. Pakal kicked it, knocking it out of the serpent's mouth, then let the head drop. As he bent to pick up the box, three shadowy heads reared up out of the floor behind him.

Arvin couldn't bring himself to just stand by and watch Pakal die. Besides, if the dwarf was busy fighting snakes, Arvin could make a grab for the box.

"Pakal!" he shouted. "Behind you. Three snakes!"

Even as he spoke, he reached the end of the tunnel and could see what was happening with his own eyes. He manifested another power, and a thread of silver shot out from his forehead. One end of it wrapped around the box.

Pakal ignored Arvin's warning. He shouted in a deep, throaty voice that sounded like an animal's growl and gestured. Five glowing red claws detached themselves from the tips of his fingers and thumb and streaked through the air toward Arvin.

Arvin ducked, but the claws found his shoulder and raked through flesh. He gasped in pain and the power he'd been manifesting faltered. The thread of silver flickered and the box thudded to the floor.

The claws pulled back for another swipe—then disappeared.

Pakal was having problems of his own now. While his back was turned, the shadow asps had attacked. Pakal stood with one hand pressed against his leg, his teeth bared in a grimace. He ground out a prayer and swept his hand across the seemingly empty space in front of him. A heartbeat later the three asps were outlined in glittering gold dust. Pakal growled a second time and raked the air with one hand. Glowing red claws streaked toward the nearest of the asps. As they tore into it, black shadowstuff oozed out through the glitter that coated its body. With a flick of his hand, Pakal's claws tossed the body to the side.

Two more asps remained, however. They flanked him, slithered in close, and struck.

Pakal howled as their fangs sank into his bare legs. He managed to kill another with his glowing claws, but the third asp reared back and struck him again. The dwarf fell to his knees.

Arvin, meanwhile, steeled himself against the pain of his wounded shoulder. As blood dribbled down his right arm, he concentrated on the task at hand. He remanifested his power and used it to pluck the box from the floor. It sailed back into his hand. He caught it, then sent the thread of psionic energy back into the room and used it to yank open the pouch that hung from Pakal's belt. A crescent-shaped object fell out. It was wrapped in crumpled lead foil.

The other half of the Circled Serpent.

Pakal lunged for it, grabbed it with both hands, and fell heavily on top of it.

Arvin cursed. His psionic hand wasn't strong enough to lift a body.

The last of the shadow asps was still outlined in glittering dust, making it an easy target. Arvin leaned into the cavern just enough to give his arm some play, raised his dagger, then hurled it. He was almost surprised when the blade pierced the asp's head. Even though the dagger was magical, he'd half-expected it to pass right through the creature. The asp thrashed for a moment then stilled.

Arvin called his dagger back to his hand and waited. No more shadow asps appeared. He picked up the box that held the upper half of the Circled Serpent and stepped down into the cavern. Just to make sure there weren't any more guardians lurking within the stone, he sent his awareness sweeping in a circle around him. Nothing.

Still holding his dagger, Arvin hurried to where Pakal lay. He glanced warily at the enormous serpent that loomed over them. No wonder it hadn't moved; it looked as though it had been dead for many years. Its body was studded with gems, one of the largest of which—a stone that had been cut in a star shape—had fallen out. Arvin picked it up and smiled, realizing that the gem-studded body of the abomination was a fortune, ripe for the plucking with the shadow asps gone. That could wait, however. There were more important things to attend to.

He tucked the gem into a pocket, then bent and turned Pakal over. The dwarf's face was as gray as the stone floor on which he lay. His lips were an even darker shade and his eyes were closed.

"I'm sorry," Arvin told the corpse. "I tried to warn you, but . . ."

Arvin pushed any thoughts of remorse firmly aside. Pakal could have helped him rescue Karrell. Instead he'd chosen to oppose Arvin. The bloody wounds in Arvin's shoulder were testimony to that. Even so, Arvin felt a twinge of guilt. He told himself that Karrell was what mattered, that the dwarf was the one who had started the fight, but it didn't help.

As he picked up the lower half of the Circled Serpent, tears of relief welled in his eyes. At last he had both halves of the key that would open the door to Smaragd. He could rescue Karrell.

If only he knew where the door was.

Or how to use the Circled Serpent, for that matter.

He'd worry about that later. For now, he had to focus on getting out of the cave and away from there, before whichever of the flying serpents won the fight—Ts'ikil or Sibyl—returned. He smoothed the foil back into place and picked up the box. It looked large enough to hold both halves. As he nested them together inside it, he heard a faint whisper.

Pakal's eyes were open. He was casting a spell. Arvin startled, nearly dropping the box.

" . . . together," the dwarf whispered.

Arvin started to summon energy in preparation for a manifestation, but stopped when he realized Pakal had merely cast the spell that allowed what he said to be understood.

"Put . . . together," the dwarf repeated. Sweat blossomed on his forehead as he fought the effects of the shadow serpents' poison, straining to rise. His words were faint. "Push tail . . . into head. That's how . . . destroy . . ."

His eyelids fluttered, then closed. His body went slack.

Arvin touched a finger to the dwarf's throat. A pulse still flickered there. Faintly.

Relief washed through Arvin. Despite the wound in his shoulder, he hadn't wanted the dwarf to die. "I will destroy it," he promised. Then, under his breath, he added, "Once I've rescued Karrell." That said, he stood. He looked down at Pakal, hesitated, then decided. If he left the dwarf there, Pakal would die.

He tucked the box inside his shirt, then bent and hooked his hands under Pakal's shoulders. Grunting, he hauled the dwarf into the tunnel. It was a struggle, crawling backward down the tunnel while hauling the limp body. His left hand was still sore where Juz'la's viper had bitten it. Eventually, however, he reached the first cavern. He paused for a moment before entering it, listening, but heard only the rush of the river below and the cries of monkeys in the jungle on the far side of the canyon. He realized his forehead had stopped tingling—a good thing, since it meant the iron cobra wouldn't be showing up. Maybe the dunking in the river had finally caused it to seize up.

He lifted Pakal out of the tunnel and took a moment to find his footing on the steep slope. He would set the dwarf down near the mouth of the cave, where Ts'ikil could spot him, then stuff the box into his pack, morph into a flying snake, and get out of there. He edged his way around the column that hid the entrance of the tunnel.

Standing on the other side of it was the dog-headed man. Arvin barely had time to blink in surprise before large golden eyes bored into his. Arvin turned his head to the side and tried to manifest a psionic shield, but he was too late. His eyes rolled back in his head, his body went slack, and his mouth opened wide in an involuntary yawn. He felt Pakal slip from his arms, then his own body crumpled into a heap on top of the dwarf's.

❦

Arvin awoke with a jerk, his heart pounding. The dog-man—

Arvin leaped to his feet and drew his dagger. He shook his head violently, trying to throw off the cobwebs of sleep that clung to it. He looked around the cavern. The first thing he saw was Pakal, lying on the floor at his feet. The next was the dog-man, lying on his back. Bright red blood stained the golden fur of his face; it looked as though something had slammed into his forehead, hard enough to cave in his skull. More blood was splattered on the top of the stalagmite he lay next to.

Arvin slapped a hand against his chest. The box he'd tucked into his shirt was gone. His backpack still lay in a corner. Whoever had killed the dog-man had taken only the Circled Serpent. Arvin was close to weeping. He'd actually had the key to Smaragd in his hands, only to have it stolen from him again.

By whom? How had the dog-man known where to find him?

Arvin touched a finger to Pakal's throat and felt a faint pulse. The dwarf was still alive, though just barely. If it had been Sibyl who had returned, surely she would have finished both Arvin and Pakal off. What had happened?

There was one way for Arvin to find out. He drew energy up through his navel, into his chest, and exhaled slowly. The scents of saffron and ginger filled the air, and ectoplasm shimmered briefly on the walls of the cavern before evaporating in the jungle heat. The cavern blurred, shifted slightly . . .

Arvin stared down at a ghostly reflection of himself. The dog-man stood over him, his mouth open in a grin, tongue lolling as he panted with silent laughter. He rolled Arvin over and tore open his shirt. The box fell out. Panting harder, the dog-man picked it up.

A second source of powerful emotion drew Arvin's eyes to the entrance of the cave. The dog-man's back was turned, so he didn't see the snakeskin carpet that drifted to a halt at the cavern's mouth, its fringe of tiny wings fluttering. A serpent that had been coiled on it slithered into the cavern.

The dog-man, at last alerted to danger, whirled. He visibly relaxed—then his body tensed up again. As if turned by an invisible hand, his head was wrenched to the side. He stared at the wall for a heartbeat or two, then exploded into a run toward it. As he reached the wall, he flung himself forward, smashing his forehead into the rounded top of a stalagmite in a spray of blood. Then his body crumpled into a heap beside the stalagmite.

The serpent regarded him for a moment with unblinking eyes. Then it shifted into yuan-ti form. It was, as Arvin had half suspected, the Dmetrio-seed. The seed strode forward, lifted the box the dog-man had dropped, examined it briefly, then opened it. Seeing both halves of the Circled Serpent, he hissed in delight. Triumph shone in his slitted eyes.

The seed gestured and the flying carpet floated into the cavern. He placed the box on it. Then he bent to examine Arvin and Pakal. He lifted the dwarf's leg and flicked his tongue over a patch of black that spread outward from the twin puncture marks left by one of the shadow snake's bites. Hissing softly, he dropped the leg. He turned to Arvin and lifted Arvin's hand. Unblinking eyes stared down at the bite marks on the back of it—punctures surrounded by a dark bruise. The Dmetrio-seed looked disappointed—he probably assumed Arvin was dead and was rueing not having killed Arvin himself—and let Arvin's hand fall. Then he stepped onto the carpet. He shifted into serpent form and coiled tightly around the box. With a flutter of wings, the carpet lifted from the ground and flew out of the cavern.

The last impression Arvin's manifestation gave him was the Dmetrio-seed's triumphant hiss. Then the vision ended.

Arvin stood for several moments, staring at the body of the dog-man. The Dmetrio-seed had acted with the decisive brutality Arvin had come to expect from Zelia; the seed had seemed fully aware, powerful and in control. The death of Juz'la must have broken the lethargy he had been languishing under. Arvin shuddered as he contemplated what the dog-man had been forced to do. He had seen Zelia dominate someone before—he'd experienced her psionic compulsions first-hand—but had never dreamed they could be so strong. His tutor, Tanju, had hinted that there were powers that could compel a person to take his own life, but this was the first time Arvin had seen them in action, and Dmetrio was merely one of Zelia's seeds. Arvin would be doubly wary from then on of any version of Zelia.

Especially the one that had both halves of the Circled Serpent.

Arvin rubbed his forehead, realizing that the tickling he'd felt in his forehead as he descended toward the cave must have been the Dmetrio-seed using his psionics to view Arvin at a distance. Arvin had shown the seed exactly where the cave was.

His left hand still throbbed where the viper had punctured it, his right shoulder was crusted with dried blood from Pakal's attack, and his chest felt bruised from the crushing the yuan-ti who had swept him into the tree had given him.

The deepest ache, however, was inside him. For a few brief moments, he had held the key to Karrell's prison in his hands, then it was gone again.

He took a deep breath and pushed the melancholy thought firmly aside. He reminded himself that it could have been worse. It could have been Sibyl who had claimed the Circled Serpent. At least Arvin knew how the Dmetrio-seed's mind worked. There was a chance that the seed would dutifully carry the Circled Serpent back to Zelia in Hlondeth—but only a slim chance. More than likely, the seed had decided to betray Zelia—all Arvin needed to do was find the door. If Arvin could find a way to locate the Dmetrio-seed before the seed learned where the door was, then perhaps . . .

The *whuff-whuff-whuff* of wings startled him out of his reverie. A shadow—large and serpent-shaped—passed across the mouth of the cave. A flying serpent, landing at the base of the bluff. Was it Ts'ikil returning? Or Sibyl?

Arvin scrambled across the cavern toward his pack. Plunging a hand inside, he seized the musk creeper net. He used his dagger to slash the rootlets that had grown into the pack, at the same time manifesting the power that would render him invisible. Then, cautious, he crept to the mouth of the cave.

CHAPTER 10

THE MARILITH LOWERED ITS FACE TO KARRELL'S AND GLARED INTO her eyes.

"Naughty mortal," it scolded. "Don't you dare run away again."

Karrell, her legs held by a twist of the demon's tail, met the marilith's eye with a defiant look.

"Or what?" she countered. "You'll kill me? Go ahead."

The demon hissed. Its tail tightened. As it did, Karrell whispered Ubtao's name under her breath and brushed a hand against the marilith's mottled green scales. The wounding spell took effect, sending a jolt of pain through the marilith's body. The demon gasped and its coils loosened again.

Karrell felt the ground beneath her feet grow soggy. The foul smell of rot drifted up from the ground—the jungle reacting to her spell. She distracted the demon by speaking again.

"By killing me, you'll only kill yourself," she reminded it.

The demon's eyes narrowed.

"Let go of me," Karrell demanded. She nodded down at her belly. "You know I can't run."

The demon tilted its head, considering. One of its six hands toyed with a strand of sulfur-yellow hair. A half-dozen dretches surrounded it. One of them scratched at its belly, setting the blubber there to jiggling.

"Mistress," it croaked. "Should *we* kill it?" Drool dribbled from its mouth as it gave a fang-toothed smile.

"Silence, idiot!"

A sword appeared in the marilith's hand. Without even looking at the dretch, it slashed backward, neatly slicing through its neck. The head landed in a tangle of ferns, surprised eyes staring blankly up at the sky as the body crumpled, its neck fountaining red. The other dretches sniffed the splatters, then dropped to all fours and began lapping up the flowing blood with their tongues.

The marilith ignored them. It gestured with the point of its sword at Karrell's distended belly. "Soon your young will emerge," it observed.

Karrell eyed the sword point and readied another prayer. If the sword pricked her, she'd need to inflict yet another jab of pain to convince the demon that the fate link still held.

"I'll need a healer to tend me," she told the marilith, "someone who can take away the pain and staunch my blood if too much of it flows, someone who can keep me alive if the birth doesn't go well." She gestured at the circle of slashed and trampled vegetation where the marilith's swords had whirled. "Open another gate; send me home. The odds of survival—for both of us—will be much greater then."

"No."

"If I die—"

"Then your soul will wind up on the Fugue Plain, even without a gate," the demon said, "where, instead of being claimed by Ubtao and taken to the Outlands, it will be consumed by Dendar." The marilith smiled, revealing yellowed teeth. "As I'm sure you noticed, the Night Serpent has developed a taste for the faithful."

Karrell blanched at that but managed to keep her voice steady. "All the more reason to keep me alive," she argued, "since your soul will also be consumed."

"All the more reason to keep you close," the marilith answered.

Karrell gestured at the dretches. They had peeled back the skin of the dead one's neck and fought over the right to suck the spinal cord.

"You sent them in to herd the faithful into Dendar's mouth," Karrell said. "Why?"

The demon gloated. "You haven't figured that out?" it *tsk-tsked*. "You're not as clever as I thought, halfblood. Perhaps there's too much human in you."

"Then pity me. Tell me why you want Dendar to grow so big. Is it so she'll be stuck inside her cave?"

The demon frowned. "What purpose would that serve?"

"It would prevent the Night Serpent from escaping when Sibyl opens the door to her lair."

"Why should we care if Dendar escapes?"

"Because . . ." Karrell was at a loss.

The marilith was right. Why indeed? For all the demons cared, the entire world beyond the Abyss—and all of the souls it contained—could disappear.

"Why should Sibyl want to open that door?" the marilith continued. "Hmm?"

"To reach Smaragd," she said. She waved her hand in a circle. "Through your gate."

The marilith gave a throaty laugh. "You truly are as stupid as you seem, mortal. Nothing living can enter the Fugue Plane."

Karrell knew that, of course, just as she knew that Sibyl was very much alive—and as mortal as she was. If she could keep the marilith talking, perhaps she could learn what was really going on.

"Sibyl could enter it by dying," she said.

The marilith sighed. "Who would claim her soul?"

Karrell deliberately blinked. "Why . . . Sseth, of course."

The marilith started to say something, then bent until its lips brushed Karrell's ear. "You look tired. Rest. Sleep." It gave Karrell a wicked smile. "Dream."

Karrell flinched away from the demon's touch. The marilith's last comment had been an odd one. Since being dragged into Smaragd, Karrell had slept fitfully, one ear always open for the sounds of the marilith and its dretches. Her dreams had been troubled. With Dendar feeding on the souls of the faithful, any dreams Karrell had were certain to be full-blown nightmares, perhaps more than her mind could stand. Why would the demon want Karrell to do something that might harm her—and thus it?

With a suddenness that left her dizzy, Karrell realized what was happening. Sseth communicated with his worshipers through whispers and dreams, and Sseth was bound. The dreams he was sending had turned into a writhing nest of nightmares. *That* was why Karrell—why all of the yuan-ti—had been having such troubling dreams for the past several months, dreams that disturbed their sleep enough to cause them to wake up, hissing in alarm. Dreams of being bound, of feeling trapped, of being prey rather than predator, dreams that were terrifying in their imagery but not quite substantial enough or clear enough to convey whatever message Sseth was so urgently trying to send.

If Dendar gorged herself on the faithful—if she stopped eating nightmares—those dreams would come through, not in a trickle, as they had for the past several months, but in a terrible, mind-drowning rush.

Sibyl wasn't planning to enter Smaragd through Dendar's cave. Dendar was only the solution to her immediate problem. There had to be another entrance to Smaragd, one that Sseth knew—one that he was trying to send to his faithful through dreams that had become nightmares.

Whatever that route was, the Circled Serpent was the key. Of that Karrell was certain. She closed her eyes, praying that key didn't fall into the wrong hands.

Something stroked her hair—the marilith's claw-tipped fingers. "A copper for your thoughts," it hissed.

Karrell pressed her lips grimly shut. Inside her belly, her children kicked. They could feel her tension, her anxiety. Forcing herself to remain calm, she placed a hand on her stomach.

The demon stared thoughtfully at it. "Is it your time?" it asked. "Has it begun?"

One of the dretches rose from its feast and sniffed Karrell, its blood-smeared nostrils twitching. Karrell smacked its hand away.

"Not yet," she told the demon, meeting its eye.

It was a lie. Karrell's water had just broken; she could feel its warmth trickling down her legs. Her stomach cramped—a hint of the contractions that would follow.

She smiled up at the demon, hiding her fear behind a mask. "Don't worry," she told the marilith. "When my labor does begin, you'll feel it."

As she spoke, she sent out a silent plea. Arvin, she thought, if you're listening, come quickly. I'm running out of time.

Arvin eased his head out of the cave and stared down. He'd had the net ready to throw, but lowered it again. It wasn't Sibyl who had returned to the cave, but Ts'ikil.

The couatl sat coiled on a ledge beside the river at the bottom of the bluff, her head drooping with exhaustion. Her body was badly burned in several places. Scorched feathers stood stiffly out from seared red flesh. Sibyl's black cloud had left oozing brown patches elsewhere along the couatl's length. Her remaining feathers had lost their rainbow luster and her wings were tattered. She held one wing at an awkward angle, as if it were broken.

Arvin opened his mouth to call out to her then hesitated. Maybe he should just sneak away while his invisibility lasted, strike out on his own and try to find the Dmetrio-seed. Unfortunately, even though Arvin had learned his psionics from Hlondeth's best tracker, he didn't have any powers that would allow him to hunt the seed down. He'd concentrated, instead, on learning powers that would help him infiltrate Sibyl's lair.

For what must have been the hundredth time, Arvin wished he hadn't broken the dorje Tanju had given him the winter before. It would have pointed, like a lodestone, directly at the Dmetrio-seed. What Arvin needed was a power that could do the same thing or—he glanced at Pakal's still form—a spell. Pakal had been able to track down the upper half of the Circled Serpent back in Sibyl's lair. Perhaps he could do the same with the seed.

The trouble was, he'd probably continue to insist on destroying the artifact.

Ts'ikil, on the other hand, had at least seemed sympathetic to Karrell's plight. Perhaps she might yet be persuaded.

Arvin negated his invisibility. "Ts'ikil!" he called. "Up here!"

It took several more shouts before the couatl raised her head. Either the cascade of the river below was drowning out Arvin's voice, or she was as far gone as Pakal was.

Arvin! Her voice was faint, weak. *What has happened?*

"Pakal is badly wounded," Arvin shouted. "Dmetrio has taken the Circled Serpent. He has both halves."

Arvin knew he was taking a huge gamble. If Ts'ikil had magic that could locate the Dmetrio-seed, she might go after him and leave Arvin behind, assuming she could still fly.

He felt Ts'ikil's mind slide deep into his awareness. Her mental intrusion was a mere tickle—far gentler than the pummeling Zelia had given him in her rooftop garden as she rifled through his thoughts. Memories flickered past in reverse order: the psychic impressions Arvin had picked up from the cavern, his encounter with the dog-man, Pakal's battle with the shadow asps.

"He looks bad," Arvin told her. He spoke in a normal voice, certain she was still listening in on his thoughts. "He's . . . alive, but his skin's turning black. Can you help him?"

I will try. Can you lower him to me?

"Yes."

That said, he uncoiled his trollgut rope. He repositioned Pakal's belt across his chest, just under the arms, and made sure it was securely buckled. He attached his rope to it, passing a loop under each of the dwarf's legs to turn it into a sling. He carried Pakal to the mouth of the cave, eased him over the edge, and stood holding the end of the trollgut rope. "*Augesto*," he commanded. It lengthened, slowly lowering Pakal to the ledge below.

When the rope went slack, Arvin tossed the other end of it down. He stowed the magical net back inside his pack and slipped the pack on, then activated his bracelet. By the time he climbed down to the ledge, Ts'ikil was bending over Pakal, touching his wounds with a wingtip. She hissed softly as her feathers brushed across the puncture marks. In full daylight, Arvin got a better look at the blackness that surrounded each of the wounds. He'd assumed it to be bruising, but it was something much worse. The darkened areas on Pakal's legs seemed somehow insubstantial—shadows that clung to him, even in the full glare of direct sunlight. As Ts'ikil's wingtip touched them, it sank into nothingness.

"That's not good, is it?" Arvin said. Despite the wound in his shoulder, he bore the dwarf no ill will. Pakal had only been doing what he felt he must—just as Arvin had been.

For several moments, Ts'ikil said nothing. The river surged past them, a pace or two away, sounding like one long, constant sigh. From somewhere in the distant jungle came a faint scream: a monkey's cry. The stone of the ledge felt hot, even through the soles of Arvin's boots. He wondered if they shouldn't be moving Pakal into the shade.

No, Ts'ikil said. *Sunlight will hasten the cure.* She gave Pakal's wounds one last touch, trilled aloud—a melody as beautiful and haunting as that of a songbird—then sank back into a loose coil. *There. I have done all I can.*

"When will he regain consciousness?" Arvin asked.

A day. Perhaps two.

Arvin frowned. "That's too long. We need him to find Dmetrio now." He glanced up at Ts'ikil. "Can you—"

No. Pakal and Karrell were my eyes.

"Aren't there others you can call upon?"

None close by.

Arvin closed his eyes and let out a long sigh. "So that's it, then. The Dmetrio-seed has gotten away."

We will find him.

"How? You said—"

He will go to the door.

"Yes—but there's just one problem," Arvin said. "We don't know where the door is." He paused. "Do we?"

No mortal does.

Her choice of words gave him a surge of hope. "What about the gods?" he asked. "Can they tell us where it is?"

We have petitioned both Ubtao and Thard Harr. They do not know its location.

"What now?" Arvin asked.

We rest and gather strength. And wait.

"Here?" Arvin said. He glanced up at the sky. "What if Sibyl returns?"

She won't, not for some time. She was even more grievously wounded than I.

"She's not dead?" Arvin said. Part of him felt disappointed by the news, but another, larger part of him was glad. He wanted to be the one to kill Sibyl. To exact revenge for what she had done to Naulg, and for what her marilith had done to Karrell. He shrugged off his pack and set it on the ledge by his feet. "What, exactly, are we waiting for?" he asked.

You already know the answer to that question. We await a dream that Sseth will send to the yuan-ti. When it comes, we must act swiftly.

Arvin snapped his fingers. "The dream will provide the location of the door, won't it?" he said. "Then all we have to do is beat the Dmetrio-seed to it and lay an ambush."

Yes.

"A good plan, except for one thing," Arvin said. Feeling a little foolish—surely he was pointing out the obvious—he made a gesture that included Ts'ikil, Pakal, and himself. "None of us is yuan-ti." He hesitated, looking at the couatl's serpent body. "Are we?"

Laughter trilled into his mind. *Not me,* Ts'ikil said. *You.*

Arvin blinked. "You think *I'm* yuan-ti?" he asked. He shook his head. "I'm human."

Yuan-ti blood flows in your veins.

Arvin snorted. "Why do you think that?"

That should be obvious.

"Well it isn't—and I'm not yuan-ti," Arvin said, "unless the potion the Pox forced me to drink left some lingering traces." He stared at Ts'ikil. "You know what I'm talking about, right? You saw that in my memories?"

The couatl nodded.

"That potion was purged from my body a year ago," Arvin continued. "Zelia neutralized it the night she found me in the sewers."

I was not referring to the potion.

Arvin thought a moment. "Ah. You mean the mind seed. It was purged, too, but a little of Zelia's knowledge still remains. Gemstones, for example. I know their value, both in coin and as raw material for constructing dorjes and power stones." He realized he was babbling, but couldn't stop himself. "Is that what you mean? Will my having been seeded a year ago enable me to receive Sseth's dream-message when it comes?"

Despite the couatl's frail condition, there was a twinkle in her eye. *I thought I spoke plainly, but I see that you haven't understood,* she said. *Once again: there is yuan-ti blood in your veins.*

She stared at his injured hand. "This?" Arvin asked, raising it. "Are you trying to say that the viper that bit me—Juz'la's pet—was a yuan-ti?"

The couatl sighed aloud. *Don't you wonder why its venom didn't kill you?*

"I got lucky," Arvin said, touching the crystal at his throat. "Tymora be thanked."

The viper was one of the most deadly in the Black Jungle. You have a strong resistance to snake venom.

"So?" Arvin was starting to get irritated by Ts'ikil's persistence.

Such a strong natural resistance is typically found only in those humans who are part yuan-ti.

"My mother was human!" Arvin said, his temper making his words louder than he'd intended.

And your father?

Arvin balled his fists. His father had been a bard named Salim. Arvin's mother had described him as a gifted singer whose voice could still a tavern full of boisterous drunks to rapt silence. That was where Arvin's mother had met Salim: in a tavern in Hlondeth, one she'd stopped at in the course of her wanderings. He wasn't a psion like her, or even an adventurer, but she fell deeply in love with him. They remained together only for a handful of tendays, but in that time they conceived a child. Then, one night, a vision had come to Arvin's mother in a dream: Salim, drowning, dragging Arvin's mother down with him.

Salim had been planning a voyage to Reth to sing at the gladiatorial games. It was an important commission—one not to be refused if he wanted other business to follow. He had already asked Arvin's mother to accompany him. He refused to believe that her dream was a premonition, but he had not known her long enough to know the extent of her powers. She had already made her dislike of gladiatorial games known, so Salim thought she was simply refusing to accompany him. He boarded a ship bound for Reth and drowned along with everyone else on board, just as she had foretold, when it sank in the stormy waters of the Vilhon Reach. Had Arvin's mother gone with him, she too would have drowned, and Arvin—still in her womb— would never have been born.

That was the extent of what Arvin's mother had told him about his father. She had described Salim as tall and agile, with dark brown hair and eyes, just like Arvin's. She'd never mentioned scales, slit pupils, or any other hint that there might have been yuan-ti in his blood.

Arvin didn't believe that his mother would have lied to him, but what if she herself hadn't known Salim wasn't fully human? What if Arvin really did have a trace of yuan-ti in his ancestry?

Impossible, he told himself. He had been inspected by Gonthril, leader of the rebels of Hlondeth, and pronounced wholly human. Humans with yuan-ti ancestry always had a hint of serpent about them, like the scales that freckled Karrell's breasts. If Arvin's father had been part yuan-ti, surely his mother would have noticed something.

Then again, perhaps she had. Maybe it hadn't mattered to her enough to mention it.

Why does the idea of having a yuan-ti heritage frighten you?

"It doesn't," Arvin snapped, "and get out of my head."

He felt the couatl's awareness slide away.

The intense heat of the jungle had made Arvin sticky with sweat. He stalked over to the lip of the ledge, kneeled, and pulled off what remained of his shirt. He splashed river water on his face and chest. It cooled him but didn't help him to feel any cleaner. He dunked the top of his head into the water, letting it soak his hair, then flipped his hair back. It still didn't help.

He didn't *want* to be part yuan-ti—he'd only recently gotten used to the idea that his children would be part serpent. He'd learned, by falling in love with Karrell, that not all yuan-ti were cruel and cold, but growing up in Hlondeth had taught him to be wary of the race. Yuan-ti were the masters, and humans were slaves and servants. Inferiors. Yet humans, despite being downtrodden, had a fierce pride. They *knew* they were better than yuan-ti. Less arrogant, less vicious, on the whole. Yuan-ti rarely laughed or cried and certainly never caroused or howled with grief. They were incapable of the depths of joy and sorrow that humans felt. They were emotionally detached.

Just as Arvin himself was.

The realization hit him like an ice-cold blast of wind. He sat, utterly motionless, water dripping onto his shoulders from his wet hair. Aside from the feelings Karrell stirred in him, when was the last time he'd been utterly *passionate* about something? He could count the number of true friends he'd had in his life on one hand. If he was brutally honest, they narrowed down to just one: Naulg, who had defended him at the orphanage when they were both just boys. After Arvin had escaped from the Pox, he'd set about trying to rescue Naulg and had eventually succeeded—but just a little too late to save his friend's life. If Arvin had been a little more zealous in his efforts, a little more passionate about his friend's welfare, might Naulg have survived? Was a lack of strong emotion the reason why Arvin had been so reluctant to take up the worship of Hoar, god of vengeance, as the cleric Nicco had urged?

Was Arvin, indeed, as cold-blooded and dispassionate as any full-blooded yuan-ti?

No, he told himself sternly. He wasn't. There was Karrell. He loved her. The need to rescue her burned in him, not just to rescue her, but to save the children he'd fathered. They *mattered* to him.

The fact remained that he *was* part yuan-ti. He couldn't deny it any longer, even to himself. It explained so much: why it felt so natural to morph into a flying snake, why his psionics were so powerful. Yuan-ti had a number of inborn magical abilities that mimicked psionic powers. Their ability to charm humans, for example. That was one of the first powers Arvin had learned. It had just come naturally to him.

Because he had yuan-ti blood.

He squared his shoulders. So what, he told himself. It doesn't change anything. I'm still the person I've always been. I just understand myself a little better now.

He turned, saw Ts'ikil watching him. "Were you listening to my thoughts?"

No.

"Thank you." He stood. "Tell me about the Circled Serpent. If I'm going after the Dmetrio-seed, I'll need to know as much about it as he does."

It is ancient—it was made at the height of the Mhairshaulk Empire. It was one of several keys, the rest of which have been lost in the intervening millennia. The sarrukh, creators of the yuan-ti and other reptilian races, erected a series of gates to other planes of existence. The keys could be used to open any of them.

"How?"

Ts'ikil ignored the question. *You think you can survive in Smaragd.*

"Karrell has for six months, pregnant and alone."

Not alone. Karrell is one of the k'aaxlaat. Ubtao watches over her.

"Even in Smaragd?"

Even there. Ts'ikil's eyes bored into Arvin's. *You, on the other hand, have yet to choose a god.*

Arvin touched the crystal at his throat. "I worship Tymora."

When it suits you.

"That's as much as most mortals can say."

That is true, but the fact remains: you are not a cleric. You will have no protection in Smaragd.

It took Arvin a moment to realize what Ts'ikil had just said. Hope surged through him. "You . . . you're going to let me do it, aren't you? Enter Smaragd." He tilted his head. "What changed your mind?"

I have not changed my mind. The Circled Serpent must be destroyed. A key that can release Dendar—that can bring about the destruction of this world—can not be permitted to remain in existence. She lifted her unbroken wing. Feathers hung from it in tatters. *I am injured; my part in this has diminished.*

She lowered her wing. *Fortunately, so has Sibyl's. She was equally weakened by our battle, and she does not know that Zelia's seed has the key.*

It has come down to a race between yourself and the Dmetrio-seed. If he reaches the door first and opens it, I fully expect that you will follow him inside. You must, if you are to save Karrell's life.

"That much is obvious," Arvin said.

Yes, but the course of action you must pursue is not. You will be tempted to rush to find Karrell first. Don't. Once the seed enters Smaragd, he will hurry to Sseth's side. You must concentrate on stopping him from reaching the god instead. If he succeeds in freeing Sseth, Karrell will be the first to die. She is the cleric of his enemy, and Sseth will know—immediately—where she is within his realm. With a thought, he will destroy her.

Despite the sticky heat, Arvin shivered. "What if I manage to take the Circled Serpent from the seed and open the door with it?"

If you did, you would open a way for any who wished to follow.

"Couldn't I close the door behind me?" Arvin asked.

Not from inside Smaragd. The door can only be opened—or closed—from this plane.

Arvin thought for a moment. "I could leave the Circled Serpent outside with someone else, someone who could close the door behind me and open it again once I've gotten Karrell."

The couatl's laughter trilled softly through his mind. *With me, perhaps? Assuming I let you use the door and closed it after you, how would you let me know when it is time to open it?*

Arvin opened his mouth then closed it again. He already knew his lapis lazuli wasn't capable of penetrating Smaragd. It probably wouldn't allow him to do a sending from within that layer of the Abyss, either. Once inside, he'd be on his own.

"Can the key be carried into Smaragd then out again?"

To Arvin's surprise, the couatl answered. *It can, but if it is lost there, we would lose the opportunity to destroy it, and the gate would remain open.* Ts'ikil paused—long enough for Arvin to silently acknowledge what she meant by "lost." His death. *One of Sseth's faithful would eventually free him, and the key would fall into Sseth's coils. The god of serpents will be sorely tempted to release Dendar. The Night Serpent would readily agree to feed on the faithful of other gods until only Sseth's worshipers remain.*

Without worshipers to sustain them, the gods themselves would fade, Ts'ikil continued. *Only Sseth would remain.* She paused. *Is the life of one woman— however precious that life might be—worth such a risk?*

Arvin squeezed his eyes shut. It was—to him—but who was he to make that decision? He shook his head at the irony. He had hoped to persuade Ts'ikil into supporting a rescue attempt. Instead she was coming close to talking him into abandoning it and without, as far as he could tell, the use of so much as a simple charm spell.

"What if Sseth's faithful can't free him?" Arvin asked. "I'm no cleric, but I do know that only a god is powerful enough to bind another god. That binding is going to be hard to break."

That is true, but one of Sseth's mortal worshipers could accomplish it, if his faith was strong enough.

Arvin brightened at that. "Zelia's only a lay worshiper; she's no cleric," he told Ts'ikil. "If her seed's faith isn't strong enough to do the job, there's little danger in letting him open the door."

What if it is strong enough? Are you really willing to take so large a gamble, when it is souls that you are wagering with?

Arvin hesitated. The soul that mattered most to him was Karrell's.

Her future is assured, continued the couatl. *She is one of Ubtao's faithful, and her soul will be lifted to his domain from the Fugue Plain after she dies. Knowing that, you must ask yourself if rescuing the body that holds that soul is an act of love . . . or selfishness.*

"And our children?" Arvin said. "Would Ubtao accept their souls as well? Or would they be condemned to the torments of the Fugue Plain forever?"

The couatl said nothing for several moments. It was answer enough. She stared at Arvin's crystal.

Their fate is in Tymora's hands, she said at last, *because, in the end, it will all come down to a toss of her coin——to whether the Dmetrio-seed reaches the door before you. If it is open when you arrive, and you can stop him from freeing Sseth, you will get an opportunity to rescue Karrell.* She held up a cautioning wingtip. *Before you start praying to Tymora, you had better weigh the dangers and decide if one woman's life is worth the terrible consequences should you fail.*

Arvin closed his eyes. His heart tipped the balance heavily in one direction, his head another. Logic warred with emotion. He wasn't sure which would triumph——the human passion that surged in him whenever he thought about Karrell and the children he had fathered with her, or the cold, hard logic of the serpent that coiled around his family tree.

Only one thing was clear: he needed to find out where the door was. One way to do that would be to sleep, dream, and hope that one of his nightmares might contain a message from Sseth. He was so worked up by his conversation with Ts'ikil, however, he was pacing. Sleep would be almost impossible. He thought of the dog-man and his ability to render others unconscious and halted abruptly.

"Can you do that?" he asked Ts'ikil. "Put me to sleep with magic?"

The couatl gave him a sad smile. *I could, but your sleep would be deep and dreamless.*

Arvin paused. "I just realized something. If the Dmetrio-seed uses *osssra——*"

Ts'ikil looked grim. *He will enter a dream state more swiftly, and his dreams will be clearer than yours.*

"I don't suppose you're carrying any *osssra,* by any chance?" Arvin asked.

The couatl shook her head. *I came unprepared. Unlike you, I am not a psion.*

That made Arvin pause. Ts'ikil had used the right word——most people called him a "mind mage"——but had made the usual incorrect assumption. Not all psions could see the future. Arvin could catch glimpses, in a limited fashion. From Tanju, he had learned how to choose the better of two possible courses of action——to gain a psionic inkling of the immediate future, events no more than a heartbeat or two distant.

Ts'ikil had reminded him of one thing, however——his meditations. By using them, he could still his mind and force it into a state between waking and sleep. He could listen to his dreams, perhaps even seek out the ones Sseth was sending.

"You know," he said aloud. "That just might work."

Without explaining—the couatl could continue to read his mind, if she wanted to know what he was doing—Arvin lay down on his stomach on the ledge. Its stone was rough, so hot it felt as though it would burn right through the fabric of his trousers, but he paid it no heed. He was used to meditating in worse conditions, and had long since learned to block such trivial discomforts from his mind. He assumed the *bhujang asana*, arching his upper torso and head back like a rearing cobra. In a small corner of his mind, he smiled. No wonder he'd preferred that *asana* to the cross-legged position his mother used for meditation. He, unlike her, had serpent blood flowing in his veins.

And he was about to find out if it was enough to hear what Sseth had to say.

Ψ

Arvin went deep. Deeper than his usual meditations, deeper even than he'd gone while under Tanju's instruction a year before in the abandoned quarry. He viewed his mind as he'd seen it then, as an intricately knotted net of memories and thoughts. But he viewed the strands as if through a magnifying lens. He could see not only the cords that were braided into each rope, but the individual thought fibers that made up each cord. A handful were a pale yellow-tan, mottled with irregular spots of black: hair-thin serpents with unblinking eyes and flickering tongues. Though he was reminded of the tendrils that Zelia's mind seed had insinuated, the sight of those serpents didn't stir up any unpleasant emotions. They were the legacy of his father's yuan-ti blood. Judging by the triangular shape of the head, Salim's ancestors had been pythons in their serpent form.

Bulges pulsed along the bodies of the hair-thin snakes like mice passing through a serpent's gullet: individual thoughts flowing through Arvin's mind. With deep, even breaths, he slowed them, putting his mind ever more at peace. He was distantly aware of his body sinking into a state much like sleep. His breathing and heartbeat slowed, and despite the fierce jungle heat, his body cooled slightly. His arms, however, remained rigid, supporting the *asana*.

Dreamlike images began to crowd into the darkness behind his closed eyelids. Fragments of memory floated by. Karrell's face and her voice, the word in her language for kiss: *tsu*. The warehouse and workshop Arvin had been forced to abandon a year ago, after the militia discovered the plague-riddled body of the cultist who had died there. And memories from farther back. Of the day he'd learned that Naulg had escaped from the orphanage, and the sorrow Arvin had felt at his friend not saying good-bye. Of his mother's face, the day she'd departed on what was to be her last job as a guide, and the tight hug she'd given him after placing around his neck the bead that enclosed the crystal he wore ever since.

He was distantly aware of his body, of a tear trickling down his cheek. It vanished quickly in the intense jungle heat.

He waited, watching the shifting images, drifting. Eventually, they began to blend in the way that dreams will. He was lying in a bed with Karrell, tenderly stroking her cheek, not in the room they'd shared in Ormpetarr but at the orphanage. The bed was small and narrow and hard, its straw-filled mattress scratchy. One of the clerics stood over them, frowning. The gray robe held out his hands, and Arvin saw that they were bound not with the traditional red cord, but with a serpent whose body was a tube of molten lava.

The smell of burned flesh and hair was thick in the room, coming from a lump of *osssra* that burned in a brazier in the corner. The brazier fell over, spilling a wave of lava across the floor. The *osssra* lay in the middle of it—a severed snake head. Its tongue flickered out of its mouth and wrapped around Arvin's wrist. He yanked it free but found himself trapped in the embrace of a six-armed creature—Sibyl, with Karrell's face.

Her stomach bulged like a dead body rotting in the sun. Tiny human hands erupted from it, the fingers seeding themselves like tendrils in his own stomach. He could feel them growing into him, burning their way up his veins toward his heart, which Karrell held in her hand. It pulsed, then lay quivering, then pulsed, then quivered again. She bit into it like an apple, blood-juice running down her chin and throat. Then she laughed with Sibyl's voice, a gurgling hiss like water bubbling through a sewer.

Stink surrounded Arvin, the stench of his own rotting flesh. The plague had found him. It had crept, disguised as his mother, into his bed, and rushed into his nostrils. Deep in his lungs, it festered. Inside his stomach, it grew, forming child-sized tumors that would burst and spread their seeds.

A scream echoed in his ears: his own. Dimly, he could sense Ts'ikil bending over him, touching his shoulder with a wingtip. That steadied him. The nightmare had left his arms trembling, his heart pounding faster than a rattler's shaking tail, his body drenched in sweat. In the momentary reprieve granted by Ts'ikil, he was aware of the ache in his left hand, the crusted blood on his right shoulder.

Then he plunged back into nightmare.

It was as horrible as what had come before: twisted images of Karrell blended with Zelia, Naulg was swallowed whole by Sibyl, a silver snake coiled around Arvin's neck and tightened, slowly and remorselessly. In his dream, he saw his body convulse, his back wrenching backward in agony like a serpent's, until he was staring at his feet.

The image was unmistakable: the Circled Serpent, but was it a message from Sseth or just his own feverish imagination?

A heartbeat later, it was gone, replaced by scenes of infants impaled on fang-shaped stakes, a priest yanking Arvin's head back and forcing him to consume raw sewage while reciting his prayers at the same time, and Karrell—except that when Arvin tried to embrace her, she turned to shadow-stuff.

Nowhere, in any of the imagery, did he see a door.

It was getting increasingly difficult to continue. Had it been a normal dream, he would have woken up screaming long ago. Only the discipline imposed by a year's practice at meditation allowed him to continue for so long. That, and the lingering traces of Zelia's credo.

Control, he told himself savagely. If you want to see Karrell again, you've got to persevere.

The small portion of his mind that remained detached from his nightmares wondered what images Zelia's seed was experiencing. What would his nightmares be like? He doubted there was anyone Zelia cared for, save for herself. Certainly no one she loved. If Zelia herself was sleeping at that moment, she would probably be dreaming about her seeds turning on her.

The thought made Arvin smile. It gave him the strength to carry on.

The images swept relentlessly past. Arvin waded through a river of blood in which screaming human heads bobbed, suddenly found himself a winged snake stripped of his wings and plunging to his death, and saw a boil of pestilence rise on his stomach. He scratched it and a marilith erupted from the wounds his fingers clawed. He realized, suddenly and viscerally, how terrible a place sleep would be if Dendar did not feed on nightmares.

He had no idea how much time was passing. A tiny corner of his mind told him the sun still beat down on his prone body but with less intensity. There was a distant pang of hunger in his stomach and a full sensation that told him he would need to urinate soon. He fought a battle, however, and such things were trivial. The Dmetrio-seed had *osssra* on his side. Arvin had only his own will.

The nightmare images pummeled him, weakened him, wearing down his resolve. His body could endure the strain he was putting it under by holding the *bhujang asana* for so long, but his mind would soon snap. Already he could see the ropes that made up his mental net starting to fray. The sun's heat was making him lightheaded, and he would need to drink soon or he would faint.

A feather brushed his lips, bringing with it a trickle of water— Ts'ikil, lifting water to his mouth. Arvin sucked it greedily down—and saw, in his nightmare, himself suckling at Karrell's breast, only to find his head impaled by cold flat steel as the marilith shoved one of her swords through Karrell's back.

No! In his nightmare, he wrenched his head away. His eyes fluttered open, too-bright sunlight and the riotous colors of Ts'ikil's feathers swam before him, and his arms trembled. He collapsed, slamming his chest down onto hot, rough stone. For a moment, full wakefulness claimed him; he squeezed his eyes shut and straightened his arms, forcing himself back into the *asana*, forcing his mind back into the realm of nightmare.

Then he was aware of something that he hadn't noticed before. His forehead tingled. Either the iron cobra was closing in, or . . .

Or someone else was scrying on him and trying to communicate with him.

Sseth.

With a croaked whisper, Arvin activated the lapis lazuli. He pictured Sseth as the god had been depicted in the Temple of Emerald Scales in Hlondeth—an enormous winged serpent with green and bronze scales looming over his worshipers. Distantly, he felt his mouth form silent words.

"Sseth. I am one of . . ." he hesitated, fearful of telling an outright lie to a god, "one of your people. Tell me how to reach you."

The mental image Arvin had formed suddenly shifted. The statue he had pictured became flesh, and the face of a sleeping serpent filled his mind. Thick vegetation covered it: a tangle of leafy vines, bulging white rootlets, and interwoven tree branches and roots. Arvin's breathing faltered as he realized he was looking at the face of a god.

The eye opened. A slit pupil swiveled to stare at Arvin through the constricting lace of foliage. Arvin gasped as his awareness tumbled into it.

Into Sseth's own nightmares.

Sseth lay in his jungle domain, basking under a brooding purple sky, surrounded by his minions—the souls of his yuan-ti priests. His merest whim should have produced fervent, fawning service, but they had turned their backs on him. Without a word—ignoring even his commands—they slithered away. As they did, the jungle around Sseth came to life. Tree trunks glowed red then turned into tubes of lava. Vines became streamers of molten rock. These flowed over Sseth, burning him. The immense heat curled his scales like dead leaves. Then they crystallized, trapping him in solid stone. Trapped like an insect in amber—him! A god! He tried to open his mouth, but it would not move. The petrified vines had bound it shut.

He stared in mute fury as a dog-headed giant wearing a starched white kilt and golden sandals strode toward him, each of his steps crunching the petrified vegetation underfoot. Around the usurpur's head was the symbol of his power: a golden diadem of a rearing cobra.

The awareness that was Arvin had no idea who the dog-headed giant was, save that he was reminiscent of the dog-man who had followed Arvin all the way from Hlondeth. The awareness that was Sseth, however, understood that the head was not that of a dog, but of a jackal, a scavenger of the desert. It conveyed to Arvin the full extent of what that meant. It was no giant who strode toward him with an evil leer on his lips but a rival god, Set, Lord of Carrion, brother to jackals and serpents, King of Malice and Lord of Evil, slayer of his own kin.

Sseth raged. An angry hiss slipped between his clenched jaws.

Set grabbed his mouth in his massive hands and forced it open. He placed a golden sandal on Sseth's forked tongue, stilling it. Then he stepped inside.

Sseth tried to thrash away, but to no avail; the petrified vegetation held him fast. He felt Set force his way down his gullet. For a heartbeat, all was still. Then came a tearing sensation. To Arvin, it felt as though the skin were being flayed from his body. To Sseth, who had a deeper understanding, it was recognized as skin sloughing free. Never before, however, had the shedding of his skin been so painful.

When it was done, Set stood before him, clad in Sseth's own green-and-bronze skin. A serpent head cloaked his own; through its gaping jaws Set's jackal grin could be seen. Then the rival god vanished.

Sseth tried to follow but could not move. His jaw, however, was still open. He snapped it shut, only to feel a tooth break against one of the petrified vines that bound him. Looking down, he saw that the tooth was embedded in the ground. It stood upright, like a miniature volcano, blood flowing from the broken tip like lava. Then the molten rock crystalized. Sseth stared at it, focusing his entire attention upon the tooth. Upon the crater at its tip. *Thisss . . .*

A sudden clarity came to Arvin's mind. He recognized that shape. The tooth had the exact contours of the volcano he'd viewed from the air while trying to get his bearings after coming through the portal. The broken top of the tooth had the same jagged edges as the crater at the volcano's peak. Sseth's message was clear: the door was inside that crater.

Yes, Sseth hissed. *Yesss.*

"How do I open it?" Arvin asked.

Too late. The sending was over. Blackness descended.

When consciousness returned, Arvin found himself lying face down on the ground. He must have collapsed a second time. Blood trickled from his upper lip where a tooth had torn it. The tooth felt loose in his mouth when he worried it with his tongue.

Ts'ikil bent over him, her expression anxious. *Did you learn where the door is?*

Arvin rose, shaking, to his feet. "You weren't listening to my thoughts?"

Sseth might not have spoken if I had.

The sun was low enough in the west that shadows from the cliff across the river had started to creep across the ledge on which they stood. Arvin turned and looked north. Peeking above the treetops was the distant mountain he had seen in Sseth's dreams. Inside its crater lay the door to Smaragd—the door that led to Karrell.

Ts'ikil turned in that direction. Her awareness slid into Arvin's mind. After a moment, she spoke. *Have you enough magic left to fly?*

Arvin had just been worrying about that. He'd taken the time to replenish his *muladhara* at the beginning of his meditation, but the numerous manifestations the metamorphosis power would require to carry him such a distance would certainly deplete it again. If he was going to do battle with the Dmetrio-seed, he'd need to conserve his power.

Ts'ikil extended her good wing. Only one of her flight feathers remained intact and unbent; she nodded at it. *Take it.*

Arvin started. "You want me to pull your feather out?"

It will allow you to reach the volcano without wasting your power.

Arvin grasped it then hesitated. Was it some sort of trick? Would him having the feather somehow allow Ts'ikil to come along for the ride? To reach the door and prevent him from opening it?

No.

"Then why help me?"

Ts'ikil nodded at Pakal. The dwarf lay on the stone, the patches on his legs only slightly more insubstantial than the shadows that crept toward him. Then she stared at Arvin. *I help you because, even though I know what is in your heart, there is still a chance*—her lips quirked—*albeit only a coin's toss chance, that you will choose the correct path through the labyrinth that lies ahead.*

Arvin nodded. He grasped the feather and pulled. It slid cleanly from Ts'ikil's wing. He felt his feet drift away from the ground. He was flying.

Gripping the feather tightly, he took a deep breath. "I'll make the right choice," he promised Ts'ikil.

Though whether right for himself and Karrell—or for the world—remained to be seen.

CHAPTER 11

ARVIN APPROACHED THE VOLCANIC CRATER WARILY. HE HAD morphed his body into that of a flying snake as soon as he drew close enough to the volcano for a single manifestation to carry him the rest of the distance. The couatl feather was tucked inside his pack.

The lower slopes of the mountain were covered in thick jungle that gave way near its peak to bare black rock where nothing grew. Ancient lava flows had overlapped one another, leaving rounded puddles of frozen stone that looked like layered scales. The peak itself was a crater perhaps fifty paces across with a floor that looked like ropy, wrinkled black skin. Wisps of white vapor hissed from cracks in the rock, tingeing the air with a rotten-egg smell. The walls of the crater appeared thin and fragile. In several places, chunks of stone had broken away and fallen down the mountainside, giving the peak its jagged, broken appearance.

There was no sign of the Dmetrio-seed. Nor was there any indication of exactly where the door might be. Arvin had expected to see something like the portal he and Pakal had used or the circular dais in Sibyl's lair, but the crater appeared wholly natural.

He probed the area for any sign of psionic manifestations. There were none. Nor could he detect any thoughts.

He landed in a spot away from the venting gas, on hot black stone. Folding his wings against his body, he shifted the color of his scales from greenish brown to glossy black. He waited, one finger of his awareness touching his *muladhara*, ready at an instant's notice to manifest a power should the Dmetrio-seed arrive. As shadows crept across the crater's floor, he kept an eye on the sky.

After a time, he felt the tingling in his body that meant his metamorphosis was about to end. Still there was no sign of the Dmetrio-seed. He waited until his body had shifted back into human form before he scrambled to the lip of the crater. It would have been a difficult climb without his magical bracelet, for the rock was indeed as fragile as it appeared. He took a look around but saw nothing that might have been a flying carpet. No matter which direction he peered in, the sky was empty.

Perhaps the seed hadn't received Sseth's message.

Arvin laughed at the irony—that he, the last person who would ever embrace the serpent god, had been the only one to understand Sseth's plea.

He was growing impatient. Gods only knew what was happening to Karrell. She'd put on a brave front when Arvin had used Zelia's power stone to speak with her, but he had seen the toll that mere survival had taken on her. That had been days ago. Anything might have happened in the meantime. Karrell might be . . .

He couldn't bring himself to contemplate it. Not there, not when he was so close. If only the Dmetrio-seed would show up, Arvin could get on with it. The waiting was the hardest part. When would the Dmetrio-seed figure out Sseth's message?

Another possiblity occurred to Arvin. Maybe the seed *had* figured it out. Maybe he'd decided not to betray Zelia but to convey the Circled Serpent to her as ordered. When Arvin had probed the seed's thoughts, a final decision had yet to be made. For all he knew, the Dmetrio-seed had decided to obey Zelia after all. The seed might be making his way back to Hlondeth even then . . .

Arvin rubbed the scar on his forehead. There was one way to find out.

The scents of saffron and ginger mingled with the rotten-egg smell of the volcano as Arvin manifested a metamorphosis. Ectoplasm slimed his skin, adding to the discomfort of assuming a form even more distasteful than that of a flying snake. His body became slender, developing curves and breasts. His face took on a serpentine appearance. Even without a mirror to guide him, he could easily visualize his hair turning red as it lengthened, his tongue developing a bluish tinge as it forked. The scales that blossomed on his hands and face were the exact shade of green he remembered. He fought the urge to scratch his itching skin, venting his discomfort instead in a soft, feminine hiss.

Then he manifested his sending.

The Dmetrio-seed's face took several moments to coalesce in Arvin's mind. Eventually, it came into focus: dark hair that swept back from a high forehead, narrow nose and thin lips. His face was dappled in leaf-shaped shadow; he was somewhere outdoors. Eyelids drooped low over slit-pupiled eyes, and it looked as though the seed had just wakened. He lay on the ground, his body coiled around something that gave off smoke that caused his body to blur then become clear again, probably a brazier filled with burning *osssra*. That surprised Arvin. Perhaps the seed *had* decided to find the door and use it himself.

Arvin wasted no time on preliminaries; Zelia certainly wouldn't. He concentrated on the memory of her voice and shaped his own mental words with the inflections she would use.

The door is a volcanic crater at the head of the River Chun, he sent. *I am there. How quickly can you reach me?*

The Dmetrio-seed looked startled then wary. For a moment, Arvin wondered if something in his tone had given him away. *You want me to . . . ?* he started to ask, then caught himself. A sly smile crept across his face. *I will be there by sunset.*

The sending ended as he bent over and picked up the object he had been lying on—the flying carpet.

Arvin took a deep breath, glanced at the sun, then smiled. "I'll be ready for you," he promised. Then he began his preparations.

❧

The Dmetrio-seed arrived exactly at sunset, when the sky to the west was a deep purplish red and the crater gloomy with shadow. He circled the peak on the flying carpet, staring down into the crater. Arvin, circling higher above in flying snake form, couldn't make out the expression on the seed's face but could imagine it. The seed, expecting a meeting with Zelia, would be puzzled at finding the crater empty. He would be probing for psionic energies or scanning the area for thoughts, perhaps even surveying the seemingly empty crater with a power that would banish illusions.

Arvin waited well out of range, not yet daring to make his move. He'd managed to lure the Dmetrio-seed there, but had the seed brought the Circled Serpent with him?

The flying carpet landed inside the crater. The seed stepped off it, hesitated, then pulled out a box that had been tucked inside his shirt. The seed looked around warily then shouted something, but Arvin was too high above to make out the words. Then the seed opened the box. Arvin saw a gleam of silver inside. He watched as the seed tossed the box aside and began to fit the two halves of the key together. While the seed was busy assembling the Circled Serpent, was the best moment to strike.

Arvin stiffened his wings and dived.

As he hurtled toward the crater, he clawed ectoplasm out of the air around him and shaped it into a flying snake that hurtled through the air next to him. A loud droning noise surrounded him as he gave his construct a single mental command—*seize it!*—and aimed it like an arrow at the Circled Serpent. Then he attacked.

Imagining his arms lashing forward, he sent strands of mental energy whipping through the air toward the Dmetrio-seed. The seed sent his mind slithering away into emptiness that left Arvin's attack with nothing to latch onto, then countered Arvin's attack with one of his own—a psychic crush that crashed through the mental shield Arvin had erected in front of himself and looped tightly around his mind. Arvin was barely able to remain conscious as it constricted, squeezing his thoughts together like the broken bones of a mouse in a serpent's coils. He tumbled through the air, his mind no longer in control of his body. Suddenly, he was human again. He slammed into the crater floor, knocking the air from his lungs. Dazed, he looked up.

The Dmetrio-seed was at the other side of the crater, struggling with Arvin's construct. It had seized the Circled Serpent in its mouth and was tugging on it while the seed clung grimly to it. Arvin forced himself to his knees, waving a hand. *That way*, he commanded. The construct obeyed, dragging the seed with it. At last, it wrenched the Circled Serpent from the seed's hands—but even as it did, a loud hissing filled the air. The seed glared at the construct and it exploded into a mist of ectoplasm. The Circled Serpent clattered to the floor of the crater, practically at the seed's feet.

Instead of picking it up, the seed whirled toward the real threat: Arvin. Surprise flickered across his face as he recognized his attacker. He visibly relaxed, then crooked a finger at Arvin—just as Zelia had done in the rooftop garden. Arvin felt a hollow open at the base of his spine; his *muladhara* opening, preparing to spill its psionic energies to the winds.

He smiled. The seed, just as he'd hoped, had chosen to toy with him instead of killing him outright. Arvin knew better than to use his psionics.

"*Augesto!*" he shouted.

The Dmetio-seed reacted immediately. A sharp hissing filled the air—his secondary display. His psionic attack struck Arvin even as it sounded, and Arvin felt the air rush from his lungs in an explosive breath. His lungs strained as he tried to inhale, but it was as if an invisible rope had cinched tight around his chest. Only by concentrating was he able to draw a thin, gasping breath.

The seed picked up the Circled Serpent, twisted it back into a circle, then bared his fangs in a delighted smile.

"This time, you won't have to play dead, Arvin," he hissed. "You'll be—"

A rumbling noise from the crater wall behind him interrupted his gloating. The seed whirled—just as a teetering slab of stone crashed down on him. Dmetrio vanished underneath the slab, which shattered explosively as it struck the crater floor.

Immediately, Arvin could breathe again. "Nine lives," he breathed, touching the crystal at his neck. Then he ran toward the fallen rock.

The seed lay in the middle of a scattering of broken stone—he either hadn't known any powers that would whisk him away or hadn't had time to manifest them. The falling slab must have struck him square on the head. His high forehead was caved in, and his jaw hung loose, attached only at one side. The arms and legs were likewise broken and bent, fragments of white bone protruding through bloody flesh. Even so, Arvin bent and touched a finger to the seed's twisted throat. As he expected, there was no sign of life.

Jumbled together with the stone were fragments of Arvin's trollgut rope. His trap had worked just as he'd hoped it would. He had tied off the slab of stone with his rope, then loosened it until the rope was all that held it in place. The astral construct had lured the Dmetrio-seed into position, and upon Arvin's command, the rope had lengthened, allowing the stone to fall.

Only one thing had not gone according to plan: the construct was supposed to have carried the Circled Serpent out of the way before the stone fell. Falling to his knees, Arvin scrabbled at the broken rock, clearing it away from the seed's body. The Circled Serpent was supposed to be indestructable, but a part of him worried, even so, that the rock might have dented it, preventing it from being used.

He heaved a sigh of relief when he saw where it had landed: inside a fold of stone that sheltered it from the crush of falling rock. They key was undented. Whole. Closing his eyes, he whispered a prayer to Tymora. He silently promised the goddess of fortune a hundred gold coins—no, a thousand—for her benevolence, then ended it with the plea that she extend the run of good fortune just a little bit longer.

"Just long enough for me to rescue Karrell," he said.

Then he stood. Slowly, he twisted the Circled Serpent back into a circle again. He was careful not to press the head toward the tail; that, he had learned from Pakal, would cause it to consume itself.

When it was a circle again, he walked to the center of the crater, a confident smile on his lips. Last summer, one of Gonthril's rebels had used a magical device to open a secret passage in the Extaminos gardens. The Circled Serpent, Arvin reasoned, had to work in the same manner. Just as Chorl had done with his hollow metal tube that night, Arvin bent and lightly tapped the Circled Serpent against the ground. Instead of emitting a musical tone as the tube had done, the Circled Serpent struck the stone with a dull clank.

He waited, but no door opened.

Arvin tried again.

Nothing happened.

Arvin stood, thinking. He tried holding the Circled Serpent parallel with the crater floor, then turned it a right angle to it, then held it parallel again. He tried walking in a circle around the crater, first in one direction, then the other. He tried drawing a circle on the stone with the Circled Serpent.

Still nothing happened.

The sun had disappeared below the horizon, and stars started to appear in the sky above. Inside the crater, all was in shadow. Arvin was worried but refused to admit defeat. He would solve the puzzle. Perhaps the Circled Serpent worked more like Naneth's teleportation ring. He tried gently tugging it, then laid it on the ground and stood inside it, on tiptoe, with both feet, but wasn't transported anywhere.

He tried to recall everything he had ever gleaned from the guild about opening magical doors. He tossed the Circled Serpent into the air, spinning, but nothing happened. He rolled it around the circumference of the crater—a task made difficult by the pile of broken stone covering the Dmetrio-seed's body—but neither action triggered its magic.

Though the night air was cooling, he could feel anxious sweat beading on his forehead. There *had* to be a way in—but how? Perhaps, like the portal he and Pakal had used, the door to Smaragd would only open at certain times of day, or maybe it could only be opened by a follower of Sseth. Was that why Ts'ikil had seemed so unconcerned about the key winding up in Arvin's hands?

If that was the case, why all the dire warnings about what would happen if Arvin were to enter Smaragd? Those only made sense if there was a way Arvin could use the key.

He pondered. How would one of Sseth's faithful use the key to open the door?

He felt a familiar tickle in his forehead: the lapis lazuli, warning him that someone was scrying on him. Ts'ikil? If so, her timing was impeccable. Arvin had just located, in one of Zelia's memories, a possible solution to his problem.

"If you're watching, Ts'ikil, it's too late," he announced. "I've made my decision."

Bracing his feet, he held the Circled Serpent out at arm's length in his right hand. Then—imitating the motion he'd seen in Zelia's dream-memory of her visit to the temple in Hlondeth—Arvin moved it in an undulating motion.

The sign of Sseth.

A ring of glowing red appeared around the edge of the crater. A wave of heat pressed in upon Arvin from all sides. He saw he was surrounded by a thin line of lava. It formed a perfect circle around the edge of the crater. The line of red expanded. As Arvin watched, it grew to the width of a palm, charring the Dmetrio seed's body with its intense heat. One of the fragments of the rock that had fallen from the lip of the crater above began to melt.

Arvin grinned. He'd done it! He'd opened the door. But—he shot a glance at the lava that bubbled inside the circle that surrounded him—did the entrance to Smaragd indeed lie through the molten interior of a volcano? If so, only an immortal would survive the passage through it.

The floor of the crater tilted suddenly, sending him staggering to the side. He clung to the Circled Serpent, and after an unsteady step or two, found his balance again. It felt as though the floor of the crater had become detached—was it floating on a bed of lava? The crack widened farther still, its edge creeping inward toward the spot where Arvin stood. Already the moat of lava was nearly a pace wide.

The tickling in his forehead continued to intensify until it felt like a hot ember burned within his scar. Something made him look up: a flicker of darkness against the starry sky near the lip of the crater. With a start, he saw a hooded serpent peering down at him. As it humped its body up over the edge of the crater, he heard a scraping sound—the rasp of metal against stone.

The iron cobra.

It slithered into the crater, its battered metal body scraping against the stone. Arvin backed away from it but was forced to halt as the unsteady floor tipped still further. The cobra, too, halted, just on the other side of the circle of lava. It stared at Arvin across the molten rock, its dented face illuminated from below by the red glow. Then it drew back into a coil, preparing to spring across the gap.

Swiftly, Arvin drew energy into his third eye. He hurled a line of sparkling silver at the iron cobra, looping it around the serpent's neck. As the iron cobra began to move, he yanked.

Unbalanced, the cobra toppled into the lava. It thrashed, trying to escape, but began to melt. Soon nothing remained except a bubbling layer of melted metal. For a heartbeat or two, gleaming red eyes glared out of the glowing puddle. Then, with an angry hiss, they vanished.

So did the sensation in Arvin's forehead.

The iron cobra had been following Arvin. Had it given Sibyl his location?

If so, there was little Arvin could do about it now. He teetered on the circular slab of stone. The heat grew steadily more intense. The ever-present damp had long since evaporated from his clothes. His skin felt hot and dry. He could use the couatl feather to fly above the crater, but if he did—if his feet weren't touching it when it at last opened—would he lose his chance to enter Smaragd?

If indeed that door did lead to Smaragd. What if it opened onto another plane—the Elemental Plane of Fire, for example?

Or even just the interior of a volcano, which would just as certainly kill him.

The circle of stone tilted, throwing Arvin to his knees. He started to slide toward the lava, then found a toehold and handhold and scrambled back up the tilting surface, balancing it once more, but not for long. The crack of lava was several paces wide, steadily closing in on the spot where he huddled.

A flapping sound, high overhead, made Arvin look up. He saw a winged serpent silhouetted against the sky. Ts'ikil—or Sibyl? It flew awkwardly, with sudden lurches, perhaps due to a broken wing.

As it wheeled above the crater, Arvin recognized it as Sibyl. The abomination's black wings were tattered and her body was crisscrossed with deep lash marks and burns from her battle with the couatl, but her face was alight with a wicked grin as she suddenly dived toward the spot where Arvin lay.

Arvin tried to wrestle his backpack off, hoping to get at the net it contained. At the very least, he could ensure Sibyl's death before he himself died. It was impossible to hold the Circled Serpent, cling to the rock and reach his pack all at the same time. Something had to go. The Circled Serpent, he decided, hurling it beyond the line of lava, but even as he wrenched his backpack in front of him and tore the flap open, Sibyl struck the edge of the circle of stone. It flipped upside down like a pot lid, spilling Arvin not into lava but into a black nothingness. He fell, still clinging to his pack, and saw Sibyl dive past him. Above them both was a circle of bright, flaming red in an otherwise purple and brooding sky. Below was thick jungle.

A *long* way below. Far enough for the fall to kill him.

Arvin fumbled desperately inside his pack, searching for the couatl feather, as he fell toward the trees below.

Karrell awoke with a scream. For several moments, she struggled to escape from the dream that clung to her like a heavy shroud, blocking all sensation of the waking world. She had been swimming in a bowl of venom, trying desperately to keep her head above water to prevent the deadly poison from slipping past her lips. The pool, at the same time, was an acid that ate into her flesh. It was gnawing a hole through her stomach, which pulsed as her children struggled to free themselves. If they did break free, however, they would die. Their first breath would be a lungful of liquid poison.

Arvin was in her dream as well. He stood at the side of the pool, holding a silver rope in his hands. He twisted it, tying it into a loop, then threw it. Karrell caught it and looped it around her wrist, but it coiled around her tooth instead. Arvin yanked the silver rope he held, forcing her mouth open. The venom rushed in, gagging and drowning her, and . . .

With a whispered prayer to Ubtao, Karrell shoved the dream memories aside. She sat up, expecting to find the marilith hovering over her. Instead the demon's attention was fixed upon the sky. It was difficult to see details through the thick screen of jungle, but something was happening up there, almost directly above them. The dark purple clouds swirled in a spiral around a circle that glowed a dull red.

"What's—" Karrell gasped as a contraction twisted her gut, "happening?" she managed to finish at last.

The demon gave no answer. Fortunately, it hadn't noticed her flinch. It watched, transfixed, as a bulge appeared below the circle of red in the sky. The bulge lengthened like dripping sap, then fell toward the jungle below in a bright red, bubbling streak. An explosive hiss of steam rose from the jungle as it struck.

Whatever was happening, Karrell was thankful for the distraction. After their earlier discussion, she'd pretended to take the demon's advice. She'd closed her eyes, feigning sleep, hoping that the demon would attribute any grimaces she made to nightmares and not to a pain that it didn't feel. Exhausted, Karrell had actually fallen into a restless slumber, but when she was awake she was unable to hide the agony that cramped her stomach every few moments. Her face, she was certain, was as pale as parchment. Sweat trickled onto her lips, leaving the faint taste of acid on them.

714 ❧ LISA SMEDMAN

When the demon turned to her, Karrell glanced up at the sky, redirecting its attention there. "Are we in danger?" she asked, hoping the demon would interpret her look of discomfort as fear.

"Stay here," was the demon's only answer. It gestured, and half a dozen dretches appeared. "Watch her," it instructed them. "See that she doesn't leave this spot. Use your magical fear to herd her back here, but do not harm her."

The dretches nodded their bulbous heads and grunted. One or two of them fixed beady eyes on Karrell and smiled, revealing teeth like broken needles.

The marilith disappeared.

Karrell tried to stand, but a wave of agony forced her back to her knees. She could feel an intense pressure deep in her pelvis; her children, straining to be born.

"Ubtao," she panted. "Not in this place. Not now. Not *here*."

The layers of rotted vegetation beneath her hands and knees quivered as she spoke her god's name, turning to slime. Acid ate into her palms. Staggering upright, she wiped them on a nearby tree. The bark sprouted needles that tore her skin. The ground underfoot continued to liquefy, and Karrell sank into putrid water past her knees before her feet finally settled on something solid.

The dretches giggled—a loathsome, gurgling sound as vile as the bubbles rising through the putrid water in which they stood. The slimy stuff lapped at their bulging bellies, but they didn't seem to mind it. One of them bent over and slurped some into its mouth.

When her contraction ended, Karrell stared, panting, at the dretches. They stood in a circle around her, scratching their bellies, sniffing. They were stupid creatures—her success in avoiding them after her escape had already proved that—but they had powerful magic at their command. She'd seen how they'd driven the souls of the faithful.

She could hear more explosions in the jungle as yet more streaks of red fell from the sky. The circle of red in the clouds was brightening, bathing the clouds around it in an eerie glow. It was, she was certain, a gate—though why it was opening was anyone's guess. If it connected with the Prime Material Plane, however, she might at last be able to summon a creature that could help her.

"Ubtao, hear me," she said. "Send me allies in my time of need."

She trailed a hand in the murky water and pictured the animals she hoped to summon. Small and swift, with silver scales.

She felt her awareness shift. It flew up through the jungle canopy into the sky. Toward the circle in the clouds and through it. Somewhere in the world beyond, it plunged into a river that flowed through the jungle, and . . .

Tiny motes of silver burst from Karrell's fingertips, rapidly expanding into full-sized fish. A school of fish, blunt-faced and silver, with gaping mouths filled with teeth jagged as broken glass soon swarmed toward the dretches and bit before the demons even had time to blink. By the time Karrell lifted her dripping hand from the water, the pool in which they stood had turned from murky green to bright red.

The dretches wailed, gurgled, swatted at the water that boiled around their legs and bellies, but to little effect. One of them went down immediately, yanked sideways by its own entrails. Another thrust a finger into the water, loosing a cloud of noxious vapors into it, but though one or two of the piranha floated to the surface, belly up, the rest continued their savage attack. Another dretch went down screaming, then a third.

Karrell staggered out of the pool, gagging on the fumes from the dretch's spell. A lash of fear struck her as one of the remaining dretches cast a spell at her, but it only hastened her onward. She had to stop a moment later, when another contraction struck, but when she continued, walking unsteadily, there were no sounds of pursuit. The allies she had summoned from her homeland had done their work.

She staggered on and a few moments later came to the spot where the first drip from the sky had landed. It had punched a hole through the trees, smashing them aside and scorching its way down through leaves and vines as it fell. It lay in a crackling red heap, lumpy and soft as bread dough, its edges a crusty black. Steam hissed from the jungle all around it, and even from a distance of several paces, Karrell could feel its intense heat.

Lava? What was lava doing dripping from a gate in the sky?

She glanced up at the circle of red; it was bright enough that it hurt to look at it. She had a better idea of who might have opened it—someone important enough for the marilith to have abandoned Karrell to the dubious guardianship of its dretches.

The circle in the sky suddenly flipped open, revealing a clear patch of starry sky. Two shapes tumbled through: a black, winged serpent with four arms, and a human, arms and legs flailing as he fell.

"Arvin!" Karrell cried, certain it was he.

He crashed into the jungle, not far from the spot where she stood. Karrell winced and felt a pang deep inside. She whispered Ubtao's name, praying that Arvin had survived. If she could reach him, use her healing magic . . .

Another contraction gripped her, forcing her to her knees.

When it was done, she glanced up. The winged serpent flew in an uneven spiral. It lurched sideways every few wingbeats like a drunken man. It was close enough that Karrell could see who it was.

Sibyl. Wounded or unwell, but there. In Smaragd.

Karrell felt a cold fear wash through her. Her head spun and she thought she was going to be sick. Sibyl had achieved her goal. She had found a way into Smaragd. Unless something was done—immediately—she would free Sseth and become his avatar. Karrell's mother's people—the humans of the Chultan Peninsula—would be crushed like mice in a serpent's coils. For unlike the Time of Troubles, Ubtao would not also walk the world in avatar form. There would be no one to battle Sibyl, save the *K'aaxlaat* and any other mortals brave and foolish enough to stand with them. Even these an avatar would sweep aside.

Another contraction gripped her, bringing tears to her eyes. She clung to the tree next to her, but its bark suddenly became spongy and gave way. She tried to climb to her feet but could not. She simply didn't have the strength to rise.

"Ubtao," she whispered. "Help me, not for my sake, or even for . . ." she clutched her stomach as another contraction wrenched at it. Something tore between her legs; she felt warm blood running down them. "For my children," she gasped, "but for all my people. Lend me . . . your power. Send me the weapons . . . I need . . . to stop . . ."

The marilith's voice boomed out over the jungle. "Sibyl!" it cried. "This way! Sseth lies here!"

Another wave of pain forced Karrell's eyes shut. As they closed, one of the trees adjacent to the crackling lump of lava burst into flame. From behind closed eyelids, she could see the flicker of the flames, but by then the pain inside her was too great for her to care. She groaned, panted, then groaned again, waiting for her children to be born.

❦

Arvin, barely conscious, lay in a tangle of vines and broken branches. He had found the couatl feather at the last moment, slowing his fall just enough to avoid being killed—but not enough to avoid being injured. He was dimly aware that one leg was twisted uncomfortably beneath him, that his face and arms were scratched and bleeding, that there was more blood in his mouth and a ringing in his ears, but he couldn't summon up enough energy to care about it.

Something sticky dripped onto his face from a broken branch above his head, something that gummed his nostrils and lips and tasted faintly of acid. The air he breathed had a sickly sweet odor, like rotting fruit. The stench was worse than the sewers of Hlondeth.

He didn't care.

A swarm of tiny flies buzzed around him, landing and walking with sticky feet through the smears of blood and sap that covered his face, then rising again, buzzing around his ears and into his nostrils.

He didn't care.

Somewhere nearby, someone shouted Sibyl's name, a booming, demonic voice that brought back terrible memories.

His eyes flickered open.

He sat up, noticed that the couatl feather was still in his hand. As he stood, a streak of fire raced through the jungle toward him. He gasped, tried to activate the feather's magic, but before he could rise into the air the fire reached him. At the last moment it zigzagged around him, setting a tree a few paces away on fire, then continued on its way. He watched it go, his mouth hanging open in surprise. It was no ordinary fire, but one that scribed a neat line through the jungle, igniting only those trees and bushes in its path—magical flame that burned the vegetation it fed on to ash then continued to burn in empty air.

Arvin touched a hand to the flame. It was like touching an illusion: he felt no heat, no pain.

He shook his head, and blinked. Was he dreaming? Was it another of the nightmares Dendar had failed to consume?

"Sibyl!" the voice cried again—more strident. "*This* way!"

Glancing up, Arvin saw the gate the Circled Serpent had opened—a circle of bubbling lava, framing a patch of clean, starry sky.

It was no dream. He'd done it. He'd entered Smaragd.

A shape swept by overhead. Dark wings against a purple sky.

So had Sibyl.

A second line of fire rushed through the forest, crisscrossing the first. A heartbeat later, Sibyl swept past. She seemed to be following it. Craning his neck, Arvin watched as she flew away with ragged wingbeats, wheeling and twisting in the sky, pursuing what must have been a twisting, convoluted path.

"Sibyl!" the voice cried again from somewhere to his right. "Over here! Under the swords!"

The cry was followed by a whirring, crashing sound. It sounded as though the jungle was being hacked to pieces, as well as set on fire.

There was no time to wonder what was happening, or why. Arvin struggled to his feet and discovered he'd been lying on his backpack. He picked it up. The net was still inside, and he thanked Tymora for that. And for breaking his fall without breaking his bones. "Nine—"

Halfway to his crystal, his hand paused as the realization finally sank home. He was in *Smaragd*.

Mentally reaching for his lapis lazuli instead, he pictured Karrell's face. It came to him immediately. Her eyes were screwed shut, her mouth open and gasping. A grimace of pain etched deep lines into her cheeks and forehead. Her hair hung around her face in a disheveled mess. As he watched, she gagged and was nearly sick.

It didn't matter. Joy surged through him, fierce as the fire that bathed him in its glowing light. Karrell was alive!

Karrrel, he sent. *It's Arvin. I'm in Smaragd. Tell me where you are.*

Karrell's eyes opened briefly. Then she screamed. And panted. Grimaced. Then spoke in a ragged voice. *Ubtao's fire,* she gasped. *Follow . . .*

Of course! The fire. Slinging his pack over one shoulder, Arvin held out the feather. He rose into the air, then flew along the path the fire had burned through the forest. Wary of Sibyl spotting him, he flew within the flame. It blurred his vision and filled his ears with a roaring crackle. More than once, he came to places where the path doubled back across itself. He chose a direction at random the first three times, then realized he was lost in a maze. He paused, hovering in the air, uncertain which way to go. He didn't have much time. If he was to rescue Karrell and stop Sibyl from freeing Sseth, he had to move quickly, to decide quickly.

Saffron and ginger wafted through the flame and a droning noise rose above the crackle of flame as Arvin manifested his power. Which way? he asked himself. Straight ahead, left, or right?

He turned to the right, and an eyeblink-quick flash of a possible future flashed through his mind: him flying on and on through the jungle, until the fire finally died, then a scream, Karrell's.

Straight ahead and he got a flash of the marilith demon, swords whirling above its head, a pair of hands cupped to its lips as it shouted. Behind it was an enormous serpent head under a netlike tangle of vines. The ground beneath Arvin's feet trembled as the serpent's mouth craned open. Its eye fixed on Arvin, somehow seeing him through the slit Arvin's power had sliced through time.

My child, it hissed. *Free me. Join me.*

Arvin hung, transfixed, on the words. The god had spoken directly to him, mind to mind. Sseth's voice entered a place, deep inside Arvin, that he had not known existed, found it empty, and filled it with an overwhelming, almost sexual desire. Arvin was yuan-ti. He was *worthy*, worthy of power beyond his wildest dreams, power that would grant him anything—*anything*—his heart desired.

Karrell? he pleaded. *Karrell can live?*

Yes! the voice hissed. *Yes, yes! She will be yours, for eternity. Yours!*

"You lie," Arvin gritted.

The vision ended. Taking a deep, shuddering breath, he shook it off. Then he turned left and flew on.

He spotted Karrell a moment later. The line of fire ended where she hunkered down on all fours and in rags, trembling against the pain of giving birth. Already Arvin could see the head of one of the children crowning. A few moments more, and he—or she—would be born.

"Karrell!" he shouted, landing and enfolding her in his arms. "I'm here."

She sagged against him, and for a moment they simply held each other.

"Our children?" Arvin asked. "Are they—"

"Soon," Karrell gasped.

Arvin glanced up. The gate was still open but was far overhead, out of reach. He could fly up to it with the couatl feather—might even be able to do so while holding Karrell—but not while she was giving birth.

She clutched his hand. "Arvin," she gasped. "Be . . . you . . ."

"Hush," he told her. "We're together." He forced a smile. "I'll figure out a way to get us both out of here."

Karrell shook her head. "Behind . . ."

Belatedly realizing Karrell had been trying to warn him, Arvin turned . . .

Just in time to see Sibyl reach the end of the line of fire and skid to a landing behind him.

CHAPTER 12

Sibyl landed awkwardly in a loose coil. Arvin could see now why she had been flying so unevenly. There was a trickle of dried blood under each of her ears. Ts'ikil's cry must have burst both of Sibyl's eardrums. As she folded her wings against her back and steadied herself against a tree with two of her four hands, Arvin scrambled for his pack. Ripping it open, he found that tendrils of musk creeper had once again grown into the leather. Cursing, he slashed these with his dagger.

Sibyl's magical fear struck him.

Arvin fought back, even as the fear drove him to his knees. Forcing his will against it was like trying to shoulder his way through an icy wall of water. It slammed against him, trying to shove his mind back into a tiny corner of itself where it screamed, cringed, and wept.

He fought it down. Like a man staggering under a massive weight, he rose to his feet. Hands shaking, he hauled the net from the pack and lifted it to shoulder height, preparing to throw . . .

Sibyl's glare intensified. So did the magical fear. Arvin felt tears pour down his face. The net sagged in his arms then slid from his hands.

Sibyl bared her fangs in triumph. Then she turned her attention to Karrell.

"Well, well," she hissed. "A cleric of Ubtao, in Smaragd? How stupid of you to reveal your position with that spell. I would tell you to prepare to meet your god, but there's only a hungry serpent where you're going." She laughed, then cocked her head, savoring the pain of Karrell's labor. "Go on," she taunted. "Try to run."

Arvin stared at the net that lay at his feet, his entire body quaking. Control, he urged himself. Fight back! Reaching deep inside his *muladhara*, he grasped a thread of energy and yanked it up into his chest. He breathed out, heard a droning noise fill the air, and imagined a protective shield in front of him.

Sibyl's magical fear broke upon it and was deflected to either side.

Arvin scooped up the net and hurled it. The throw was perfect. The net opened in mid-flight and landed on Sibyl's head and shoulders.

"*Absu—*"

Sibyl was swifter. She shifted into a tiny flying snake.

"*—mo!*" Arvin shouted, completing his command.

Too late. Sibyl escaped through the large weave of the net. She hovered above where it lay on the ground. She darted sideways then reappeared in her humanoid form next to Arvin. She towered over him, easily three times his height.

"You may have escaped my temple," she hissed, "but you won't escape Smaragd."

She flicked her tail. A lightning bolt shot from it, striking Arvin square in the chest. He was hurled backward into a vine-draped tree. At a spoken word from Sibyl the vines came to life, whipping themselves around him. He managed to wrench one arm free, tearing his skin as the suckers of the vine were ripped from it, but the vine wrapped around it once more. He tried morphing into flying snake form, but the tendrils tightened instantly, holding him fast. Abandoning that manifestation, he resumed his human form. Sibyl watched with unblinking eyes, smirking at his struggles.

The net lay on the ground a palm's breadth from Karrell, yellow flowers blossoming from its knotwork. Its fibers began to unweave, sending pale green tendrils questing up into the air, searching for a mind to drain.

Karrell continued with her labor, her head down and hair trailing, grunting as another contraction gripped her.

Struggling against the vines was futile, but Arvin's mind was still free. He clawed ectoplasm out of the air and shaped it into a construct with great hooked claws and a mouth that gaped wider than a serpent's and sent it hurtling toward Sibyl in a sparkle of silver that clouded his vision.

Sibyl met it with a shouted word in Draconic. The construct exploded into a cloud of tiny, shimmering flies that circled harmlessly around her head. With a shrug of one wing, she brushed them aside.

Sibyl was even more powerful than Arvin had feared. Had she already become an avatar? No, there hadn't been time, but the thought gave him an idea.

A droning filled the air around him as he tried to force his way into her mind. If he could convince her, even for an instant, that she had heard an unconditional summons from her god, she might leave. A simple splicing of her memories would be all it took. He pushed against her will, looking for the tiniest chink in her mental armor through which his own mind could slip.

Sibyl forced him back. Then she hissed. Her tail began to glow with an unbearably bright light then whipped forward. As the tip of it slapped against Arvin's face the brightness exploded, filling his entire vision. He blinked but could see nothing but white. He was blind.

He could no longer see Karrell, but he could hear her deep, shuddering groans. He could also hear, over Sibyl's hissing laughter, the soft pops of the flowers on his net releasing their compelling dust. Sibyl, he had seen in the instant before he was blinded, was still too far away from the net to be affected by the dust, but Karrell was close. Too close.

"Karrell," he shouted again. "Get away from the—"

His teeth slammed together as what must have been a second lightning bolt struck him. Muscles rigid, he fought against the blackness that threatened to swallow him. He had been foolish, he realized, to attempt to rescue Karrell alone. He should have tried harder to convince Ts'ikil to come with him. He pictured the couatl as he'd left her on the ledge, realized he should have at least told her he was entering Smaragd. Even wounded, the couatl was the one creature who might actually be a match for—

No. There was one other who might be able to beat Sibyl in a head-to-head fight.

The marilith demon. Arvin knew just which card to play to get it on his side: the fate link.

Allowing his body to go limp—playing dead—Arvin pictured the demon in his mind. The face was easy to visualize. It had seared itself into Arvin's memory on that terrible day that Karrell had been drawn into the Abyss. Sulfur-yellow hair framing an angular face with wide lips and a **V**-shaped frown, the hair whipping about in an invisible current. The body, female from the waist up, but with six arms. Below the waist, a writhing serpent's tail covered in green scales that shimmered as though they had been dipped in oil.

As Arvin made contact, he saw the marilith whirl, a hiss on its lips. Its mouth silently framed a word: "You!"

Sibyl is about to kill Karrell, Arvin sent. *Teleport to Karrell. Now!*

The demon didn't bother making a reply; its image simply vanished from Arvin's mind. A heartbeat later, he heard a *whoosh* of displaced air that announced its arrival. He was already busy manifesting a power. His face felt cool where ectoplasm coated it. Blurry images filtered in through the skin of his forehead and cheeks as they became sensitive to light. Two towering shapes, confronting one another.

Suddenly he could see again.

The marilith cuffed Sibyl away from Karrell and screeched something at it in Draconic. Sibyl hissed angrily and snaked her tail toward Karrell. The marilith flung out all six hands, and swords appeared in them.

Arvin smiled. Drawing air deep into his lungs, he charged his breath with psionic energy, then he blew the scents of saffron and ginger, first at the marilith, then at Sibyl, linking their fates.

The shouting was dying down and the marilith was lowering her swords. Time to stir the pot a little. Arvin manifested a second power, insinuating himself inside the demon's mind. It was an ugly mind, volatile and irrational, filled with violent fantasies that centered on what it would do to the worthless dretches—the creatures that were its minions—who had clearly shirked their duties. It bubbled with loathing over the fact that Sibyl—an insignificant *half*-demon— possessed the one necessary quality that would allow her to become Sseth's avatar: a mortal soul. But the anger that had boiled like lava through the marilith just an instant before was already cooling. Sibyl had agreed to deal with Ubtao's worm later, *after* she became Sseth's avatar. Once the chains that bound the human's fate with the marilith's had been severed, the impudent cleric and her squirming, loathsome spawn could be safely crushed. The marilith, Sibyl had just promised, had nothing to fear.

Fear, Arvin thought. He seized the emotion and braided it together with the marilith's frustration and her ideas of how minions should be treated to form a new memory: Sibyl telling the demon that it had better learn to obey her, and that the demon—worthless dretch!—had better learn that its needs were insignificant, that Sibyl was Sseth's chosen one, that she would deal with Ubtao's cleric when it suited her, and if that time had already come, and if that meant the marilith's miserable life would end, well then—

A scream of utter fury ripped through the demon's mind. *Ungrateful spawn! I should never have agreed to—*

A sword slashed down. Connected. Blood sprayed as one of Sibyl's forearms was sliced open from elbow to wrist. Marilith and abomination screamed as one. The demon stared at the identical wound on its own arm. Arvin felt a shadow of the demon's pain and gasped. He clung grimly to its mind. Swift as thought, he added a new memory: Sibyl, grabbing the demon's arm as the sword descended and deliberately twisting it so the blade struck Karrell, instead—causing a wound to spring up magically on the marilith's arm—then Sibyl somehow being wounded in the arm herself by the sword as the demon yanked it away from her again.

It was a crude image, one the demon would have recognized for false in an instant just by glancing down at Karrell, but its blood was up, anger frothing through its mind. Screaming, it launched itself at Sibyl, all six blades flashing.

The demon was lightning-fast, but Sibyl moved even more swiftly. Serpent body writhing, she avoided the slashes. Twin streaks of red shot from Sibyl's eyes. They plunged into the demon's chest, punching hot red holes. Identical wounds appeared on Sibyl's chest. She reeled back, glanced down at them—then at Arvin. Her tail twitched toward him, but before she could blast him with another lightning bolt, the marilith lopped off the tip of Sibyl's tail. Sibyl screamed at it in Draconic, but the demon was in full fury and did not notice that its own tail had been severed as well.

Sibyl, however, had learned something from the exchange. Instead of fighting back, a dark shimmer pulsed from her body: magical fear. It slowed but didn't stop the marilith's attacks. Jungle vines whipped around the demon's body. It sliced them apart and kept coming. In the distance, Arvin could hear wings flapping—another demon, summoned by the marilith to join in the fray?

The vines holding Arvin had loosened somewhat, and he strained against them, trying to get free. Sibyl and the demon were in the way, and he couldn't see Karrell. Had she breathed in the dust and fallen victim to the musk creeper's compulsion?

He caught a glimpse of Karrell crawling toward the net. She reached out, grasped it with both hands, drew it closer to her.

"No!" Arvin shouted.

Karrell staggered to her feet, drawing the net still closer to her. Tendrils reached eagerly for her head.

Arvin tore at the vines. If those tendrils rooted in her scalp. . . .

Sibyl flicked her tail, smearing blood across the marilith as it slapped home, and shouted something in Draconic. The demon was transformed. One moment, it was a massive creature with six arms and a serpent's tail; the next, an ordinary human with six swords lying at her feet—a human who gaped down at the smoking holes in her chest, the blood draining from her lacerated arm, and the abbreviated stump of her left foot . . . then collapsed.

Arvin ripped free of the vines at last and raced for Karrell. "The net!" he screamed at her. "Throw it at Sibyl!"

She did. The net sailed out of her arms—and missed its target. It landed on the now-human demon, enveloping it.

Karrell's face went white. Then another contraction staggered her. Grunting, she sank back into a crouch.

Sibyl whipped around, hissing, her red eyes furious. Her tail lashed forward, catching Arvin around the chest, trapping his arms against his sides. It squeezed . . .

"Karrell," Arvin cried. "I—"

The squeezing forced the air out of his lungs, preventing him from saying more. Then, abruptly, it stopped.

Arvin tore his eyes away from Karrell and looked up at Sibyl. The abomination stared over his head, a vacant look on her face. Like a suddenly loosened cloak, her coils fell away from Arvin. He stepped out of them and saw, behind Sibyl, the marilith demon. Still in the human form Sibyl had transformed it into, it lay, draped by the net, its eyes empty. Strands of yellow musk creeper had rooted in its scalp and wormed their way in through its ears, nose, and mouth. They pulsed as they drained the last vestiges of its mind. Already it had been rendered an empty husk.

Sibyl, linked to it by Arvin's psionics, had suffered the same fate. The abomination's chest still rose and fell, but her mind was a gaping ruin. She was as good as dead.

Arvin ran past both abomination and demon and lifted Karrell in his arms. He felt tears streaming down his cheeks. "The net," he said. "I thought . . ."

"Ubtao," Karrell whispered—though whether it was an explanation or a plea, Arvin couldn't tell. She groaned—deep and long—and her body shuddered.

Arvin glanced up at the sky. The circle of red was still open, and the wingbeats he'd heard a moment before had grown closer.

"We've got to get out of here," he said, knowing even as he spoke that there was no hope of escape.

A shadow fell across them. Arvin reached for the dregs of energy that remained in his almost depleted *muladhara*, then glanced up.

"Ts'ikil!"

The couatl landed gracefully, despite its injured wing. Her condition had improved. New feathers had sprouted in several of the bare patches and her wings were less tattered. Ts'ikil trilled softly as she stared at Karrell, then touched her with a wingtip.

Arvin stared up at the couatl. "How . . . ?"

Your sending.

"But I didn't . . ."

Ts'ikil smiled. *Yes, you did. You called out to me, asking me for aid—then very unflatteringly compared me to a demon.*

"I did?"

Karrell groaned, reminding Arvin of more urgent concerns. "Can you fly Karrell out of here?" he asked. "Quickly, before she—"

I can do better than that, now that the door is open, the couatl said, pointing up at the hole in the sky. She extended her other wingtip to Arvin. *I can take her home. Take her hand, and touch me. We will step between the planes.*

Arvin scrambled across hot, black stone to the spot where he'd thrown the Circled Serpent. The trip to Karrell's village had taken less time than a heartbeat. They'd spent only enough time there to explain what was going on to Karrell's startled clan and see her safely into a hut. Then Ts'ikil and Arvin raced back to the crater again. The gate to Smaragd had already started to close; a thin crust of wrinkled, almost-hard stone covered the opening. It crackled and steamed, releasing hot gases that stung Arvin's eyes.

He blinked, clearing them, and spotted the Circled Serpent lying near the edge of the cooling lava.

"There it is," he told Ts'ikil.

He started to pick it up, then yanked his hand back. The silver didn't look hot, but it had burned his fingers. He blew on them, then manifested a power that lifted the Circled Serpent into the air.

Ts'ikil hovered above, her wings fanning away the worst of the heat. Arvin moved the Circled Serpent toward her, but the couatl shook her head.

You should be the one to destroy it, she said. *You have earned the right.*

Arvin nodded. He enlarged the invisible psionic hand he had created, then squeezed, forcing the tail of the Circled Serpent into its mouth. He felt a sudden tug, and the artifact yanked itself free. A hissing filled the air—louder than the crackling of the cooling lava—as the Circled Serpent spun in mid-air. Arvin backed away, one hand raised to shield his face. Faster and faster the Circled Serpent spun, the head following the tail, until it was a blur of silver in the air. Then it disappeared.

The volcano gave a shuddering rumble. Then all was quiet. Arvin lowered his arm and looked down, and saw that what had been crusted lava a moment ago was cold, solid stone. A breeze blew across the peak of the volcano, cooling the sweat on Arvin's face.

He glanced at Ts'ikil. "That's it?" he asked. He had expected something more.

The couatl smiled, then nodded. *It is done.*

"Then let's go. I want to see my children."

❧

Arvin leaned back against the wall of the hut, his infant son cradled in his arms. The boy was quiet, but earlier he had been competing with his sister in a crying contest. The twins were small—the combined effects of sharing the same womb and the lean nourishment Karrell had found in Smaragd—but they seemed strong enough, and they had powerful lungs.

The boy had brown eyes, like Arvin, a fuzz of brown hair, and a pattern on his smooth skin that might one day become scales. The girl had Karrell's high cheekbones, darker hair, and a slightly forked tongue. Both had human arms and legs, but what was most important was that both had survived.

So had Karrell, though the labor had been hard on her. She lay in a hammock, nursing their daughter. Arvin watched as two women of the Chex'en clan fussed over the new mother, fanning her and offering sips of cool water. They looked like Karrell—close enough in appearance to have been her mother and sister, though Karrell had said they were only the clan midwife and her apprentice, both distant cousins. Each of them had Karrell's long black hair and dusky skin.

It had been some time since Arvin had slept, even though three days had passed since Ts'ikil had spirited them out of Smaragd. The birthing had taken the remainder of that first night, and the days and nights since then had slipped past in a blur. Arvin hovered somewhere between dozing and wakefulness. The heat of the jungle didn't help, nor did the fact that he kept slipping, in his drowsy state, into the minds of his son and daughter. The link with them came so easily it was like breathing. One moment his thoughts were his own—the next, his mind was overflowing with simple sensation: the sweet slide of milk down his throat, the gentle touch of a warm body against his, the blur of his mother's or father's face as they stared down at him with adoration.

It was easy to let his mind drift. The worst was over. Sibyl and the marilith were as good as dead, their minds empty shells. Sseth was securely contained within his domain, bound and brooding. Pakal had recovered from his shadow wounds and gone back to his people, and Ts'ikil had also fully healed.

Yet . . .

The younger woman came to Arvin and said something to him in her own language, then gently lifted his son from his arms. It was time for Karrell to feed him. Arvin reluctantly relinquished his son. He had been enjoying the feel of the infant's soft breathing against his bare chest. He stood and straightened the loincloth one of the Tabaxi men had given him, then crossed the hut to Karrell's hammock. As he brushed his lips against her forehead, she gave him an exhausted smile.

"We did it," she whispered. "We stopped Sibyl. It's over now."

"Yes," he said.

Yet . . .

He needed to think, to shake the lethargy from his mind. He stroked his daughter's head, and his son's, then squeezed Karrell's hand.

"I'll be outside," he told her.

The hut was circular, made of saplings that had been bound together. The roof was a rough dome covered with broad leaves, laid in a pattern like shingles. It was one of perhaps a dozen huts occupying an oval clearing that had been hacked from the jungle. At one end of the clearing stood a pitted chunk of black volcanic stone, studded with "thunder lizard" claws—an altar sacred to both Ubtao and Thard Harr. One of the wild dwarves who also made their home in that part of the jungle was prostrated in front of it, his hands extended toward the stone, fingers curled like claws. The clan's meeting house was at the opposite end of the clearing. In the distance behind it, smoke rose from the trees. That was where the rest of the clan was, clearing new land for crops. Arvin could just hear the faint thudding of their axes. Lulled by the sound, Arvin stood, staring at the jungle.

A woman's shrill cry from inside the hut jerked him out of his half-doze. He raced inside, nearly colliding with the midwife. She shouted something at him in her own language, pointed at her assistant, who knelt on the ground next to Karrell. The assistant lifted one of the twins—their son—and blew air into his open mouth in short, rapid puffs. Arvin's entire body went cold at the sight.

"What's wrong?" he cried.

Karrell didn't answer. Her lips were moving rapidly as she bent over their daughter. She gave Arvin a quick, terrified glance as she whispered a prayer. Arvin clenched his fists. Something had gone wrong. Both twins had stopped breathing, but Karrell's magic would save their children. It *had* to.

Then Karrell exhaled, as sharply and violently as if she had vomited the air from her lungs. She clutched at her chest and struggled to inhale.

"What's *wrong?*" Arvin shouted.

Karrell shook her head. She tried to speak, but couldn't. She made a frantic gesture at their daughter. The girl's lips were starting to turn blue. Arvin scooped the girl up, only to have her wrenched from his hands by the midwife. The elderly woman began blowing air into the infant's lungs.

Karrell swayed, still trying to gasp air into her lungs. Her eyelids fluttered.

Magic. It had to be, but why?

No, not magic. A memory hovered dimly at the back of Arvin's mind. Of himself gloating as he manifested that very same power.

No, not himself.

Zelia.

A droning hum filled the air as Arvin manifested a power. Silver sparkled from his eyes; a thread of it led out the door. He raced after it across the clearing. It led where he'd half expected it to: to the dwarf who stood, a smirk on his face, next to the holy stone.

One of Zelia's seeds.

Arvin hurled a manifestation at the dwarf-seed as he ran. Droning filled the air around him as he tried to batter his way through the seed's defenses, to crush his opponent's mind to dust, but the seed was ready. His mind slithered away from Arvin, leaving him grasping emptiness. Then the seed attacked. A fist of mental energy punched its way through Arvin's defenses then coiled around his mind. Too late, Arvin tried to throw up a shield against it. He could feel strands of energy moving this way and that inside his mind, weaving a net that held him fast. There was a quick, sharp tug—and the net closed, trapping his consciousness inside. Arvin could feel himself standing, was aware of his chest rapidly rising and falling, of his heart pounding in his ears—but the will that normally controlled his actions was tightly confined. He could imagine himself manifesting a power, but his *muladhara* seemed far away. His mind couldn't reach out to it from behind the net that had trapped it. Made stupid by a lack of sleep and the urgency of stopping the attack on Karrell and the children, he'd done just what the seed wanted—rushed blindly into psionic combat.

The dwarf-seed smiled, as if reading his thoughts. For all Arvin knew, it was.

"Arvin," the seed said in a husky voice that was unsettlingly similar to Pakal's, except for its smirking tone. "How obliging of you to run right into my coils."

Arvin tried to talk. All he could manage was a low moan. He felt drool trickle from the edge of his mouth.

The seed smiled. "Where is Dmetrio? Where is the Circled Serpent?" Silver flashed from his eyes as he spoke.

Arvin tried to resist the awareness that slid deep into his mind but couldn't. In another moment, the seed would learn that Dmetrio was dead and the Circled Serpent destroyed. The worst of it was that Arvin knew exactly how the seed would react—with rage at the fact that Zelia's plans had been thwarted—and with gleeful satisfaction at having caused Arvin the greatest anguish possible by killing the children and Karrell.

Then it would kill him.

If Arvin could have closed his eyes, he would have. He didn't want to see the dwarf-seed gloating.

What he did see surprised him. The seed suddenly jerked and his eyes widened. He whirled, and as his back came into Arvin's view, Arvin saw the dart that had lodged in the seed's neck.

"No!" the seed gasped. "Not—"

Then he fell.

As the rigid body struck the ground, Arvin felt the net that held his mind fray then suddenly loosen. He saw Pakal step from the jungle, blowpipe in hand. Astonished, he gaped at the dwarf—but only for a heartbeat.

Karrell, he thought. The *children* . . .

He turned and raced back toward the hut.

As he neared it, he heard a baby's cry. Then another. Then Karrell's voice, thanking Ubtao. He plunged inside and saw Karrell holding both children in her arms, tears streaming down her cheeks. The midwife and her assistant stood nearby, relieved looks on their faces.

Arvin fell to his knees beside Karrell. "By the gods," he said. "I thought I'd lost all three of you."

Karrell closed her eyes and took a shuddering breath. The children in her arms continued to cry, strong, healthy wails. Arvin gently stroked his son's hair then his daughter's. They were *alive*. He touched a hand to the stone that hung at his neck.

"Nine lives," he whispered to himself.

Karrell's eyes opened. They bored into Arvin's "It was her, wasn't it?"

Arvin nodded grimly. "One of her seeds."

"Is it—"

"Dead?" Arvin asked. "Yes, Tymora be praised. By a stroke of her luck, Pakal happened to be—"

Hearing something behind him, Arvin turned. Pakal stood in the doorway, arms folded.

Arvin crossed the hut and squatted in front of the dwarf. "You saved my life," he said, "and Karrell's, and our children's." He let out a long sigh. "I thought you'd gone back to your people. How did you manage to show up in just the right place and at just the right time?"

Pakal grunted. He said something in his own language—a brief prayer—then spoke in the common tongue. His eyes were smiling. "Having me watch the village was your idea. You anticipated that a seed might come."

"My idea?" Arvin echoed.

Pakal nodded. He touched a thick finger to Arvin's temple. "The memory. You erased it."

"Ah," Arvin said. Suddenly understanding his lingering unease.

Karrell passed the twins to the other women and rose to her feet. "You *knew* that a seed would attack us?" she said, rounding on Arvin. "You might have told me."

"He could not, Karrell," Pakal said. "The seed might have probed your thoughts and learned that I was lying in wait for it."

Karrell continued to rage. "You risked our children's lives, just to eliminate one seed?" she shouted. "You might have killed this one, but what now? Will you erase all of our memories of what just happened and send Pakal back into the jungle to wait until the next seed comes? And the next? And the one after that?"

Arvin balled his fists. Karrell was right. More seeds would come. Arvin and Karrell might flee, but there would be no guarantee that wherever they chose to hide wouldn't be home to another of Zelia's seeds, and once Zelia learned the Circled Serpent had been destroyed, she'd stop at nothing to have her revenge. As she'd demonstrated, killing Arvin alone wouldn't be enough.

Pakal interrupted that grim thought. "There *is* a way to end this," he said. He turned to Arvin. "Before you erased your memory, you told me to remind you of this: one year ago, you stripped away Zelia's power to create seeds at will. Since then, she has been able to seed only two people: Naneth and Dmetrio. Both are dead. All of her other seeds—those created before Zelia met you—do not share her animosity toward you. They simply do as Zelia orders. To them, you are just another target for them to kill. Eliminate Zelia, and no more such orders will be given."

"That much is obvious," Arvin said, "but it raises one big question. Did I happen to tell you why I didn't set out for Hlondeth at once?" He glanced at the twins. "Aside from the obvious reason?"

Pakal smiled. "Before confronting Zelia in her tower, you needed to learn more about its defences," Pakal answered. "I have a spell that allows me to question the dead—and the dead cannot lie."

Arvin smiled. "Not a bad plan," he said. "I wish I'd thought of it."

Pakal grinned. "You did."

Arvin glanced at Karrell. The anger had fled from her eyes; determination had replaced it. "I'll come too," she said. "My magic—"

"Is needed to protect the children," Arvin said. "If another seed should find them while I'm gone. . . ."

Karrell's mouth tightened. She held his eyes a moment longer, then nodded. "Do it," she said. "Kill her. End this."

❦

Arvin and Pakal strode across the flagstone plaza toward the pyramid that dominated the center of the city. Ss'inthee'ssaree was as ancient as Ss'yin, but unlike the Jenestaa, the Se'sehen had worked hard to reclaim it from the jungle. The buildings that ringed the plaza had been repaired and restored to their former glory, their stonework cleaned and remortared. The serpents that twined on their carved facades had been repainted in bright colors. The flagstones underfoot were smooth and even, without so much as a tendril of vine growing between their cracks.

They were also stained with dried blood. House Extaminos had not only triumphed over the Se'sehen in Hlondeth but had carried the fight to the Black Jungle. Sibyl had inadvertently shown them the way, when she used the portal on Mount Ugruth to follow Arvin and Pakal. House Extaminos controlled what had once been the Se'sehen stronghold.

Flies rose lazily into the air as Arvin skirted the largest of the dark brown stains that marked the plaza. The corpses of those who had fallen in battle had been carried away, but the smell of death still rose from the sun-hot stones.

A score of Hlondeth's militia stood guard in front of Arvin's destination: the pyramid that housed the Pit of Vipers, a temple identical to the one that had been Sibyl's lair, a temple that contained the one-way portal the Se'sehen had used to reach Hlondeth.

Though they were sweltering in bronze chain mail and flared helmets, the Hlondeth militia was alert. They lowered their crossbows and snapped to attention as Arvin approached. Their officer—a halfblood with a narrow, black-scaled face that echoed those of the twined serpents embossed on his breastplate—touched his sword hilt to his chest, then bowed low.

"Lord Extaminos," he said. "We thought—"

"You are paid to obey, not think, Captain Vreshni," Arvin said, neatly plucking the officer's name from the man's mind. He raised his chin haughtily, as Dmetrio would have done. His forked tongue gave his words an imperious hiss. "Accompany me to the portal. I have urgent business in Hlondeth."

"Yes, Lord Extaminos," the officer said, bowing a second time. He sheathed his sword and gestured at the pyramid. "This way."

Arvin turned to Pakal, who had also disguised himself as a yuan-ti. The dwarf's illusion was perfect; his body appeared twice as tall as it really was and slender as a serpent's. The tattoos on his body had become a pattern of snake scales, his matted braids were gone, and the necklace of claws and teeth around his neck had become a ring of tiny, sparkling jewels set into the scales of his chest, shoulders, and back. The only detail untouched by his illusion was the armband of gold, set with a turquoise stone, on his upper right arm.

"You may go," Arvin told Pakal in a cold voice. Using his lapis lazuli, however, he bade the dwarf a more pleasant farewell. *Thank you. For everything.*

Pakal returned his grim smile. *Thard Harr watch over you,* he sent back. *And . . . good luck.* He bowed then strode away.

Arvin followed the officer, moving his feet with a sliding motion as Dmetrio had done. The metamorphosis had been an easy one; Dmetrio's appearance was still fresh in his mind. The club-toed feet, however, were tricky to walk on.

The pyramid was tall and narrow. It resembled a series of ever-smaller blocks set one upon the other. Each of the four sides was dominated by a stone serpent that seemed to be slithering down the stonework, its head resting upon the ground, and their four tails twined together at the top of the pyramid. The serpent that decorated the front of the pyramid had its mouth open wide, and its fangs looked as though they were solid silver.

Arvin suppressed his shudder as he followed the officer into the mouth. It reminded him a little too closely of Sseth. The mouth was open wide enough that Arvin could walk upright, but an edge of the officer's flared helmet scraped against one of the silver fangs, causing him to duck.

A smooth ramp led down to a chamber filled with soft green light. The walls were carved to resemble scales. A forest of serpent-shaped columns held the weight of the pyramid above at bay. A sweet scent lingered in the air under the heavy musk of snake—*osssra*, Arvin realized a moment later. Though the braziers that dotted the floor were cold and dark, the stone walls were impregnated with the stuff.

More militia—six halfblood officers, two of them armed with wands—stood guard in front of a gilded statue: one of the stations of Sseth. The god was depicted in his twin-tailed form, his tails encircling a black obsidian globe that represented the world. Wings flared out from his shoulders, and under each wing was an arched entry. These led to corridors that curved away to the right and left.

The officers bowed as Arvin approached. One of them touched a hand to his helm. "Shall I inform Lady Dediana of your imminent arrival, Lord Extaminos?"

"No," Arvin ordered. "Tell no one."

Confusion flitted across the officer's face but was quickly hidden by his bow. "As you command, Lord Extaminos."

Arvin waited for Captain Vreshni to indicate which of the corridors led to the portal. The captain did a moment later by turning slightly toward the left entrance. Arvin strode into it as if he'd known all along which route to take. The captain scurried after him.

The corridor spiraled down past slit windows that opened onto a central room. Just like the room in the temple under Hlondeth, it was dominated by a dais of black obsidian. The snakes that had once slithered around it were dead. They'd been reduced to ash; a burned stench lingered in the air. Judging by the scorches on the walls, someone must have let loose a blast of magical fire—one of House Extaminos's wizards, perhaps.

Just as in Sibyl's lair in Hlondeth, the portal room's only other exit was framed by the beastlord's snarling face—it probably led to a similar temple. More militia stood guard in front of the exit, looking alert and watchful. Captain Vreshni indicated a path had been cleared through the ash, allowing passage to the dais.

"If you please, Lord Extaminos."

Arvin started to thank him, then remembered whom he was impersonating. "Go," he said curtly, dismissing him.

The captain bowed his way out of the room.

Arvin took a deep breath then stepped onto the dais. For several heartbeats, nothing happened. Then the portal activated. He felt a dizzying lurch—and found himself standing in the same room as before.

No, not the same. The corridor beyond the beastlord's face was choked with rubble and the lantern light was stronger here. Arvin could hear soft breathing and the creak of a crossbow being drawn. Whoever was guarding this room was invisible.

Refusing to flinch, Arvin drew himself up and glanced imperiously around the seemingly empty chamber. As he did, he manifested the power that would allow him to listen in on their thoughts.

There—one of them was casting a spell. It was divination magic: a spell that would confirm whether the visitor who had arrived so abruptly was, indeed, Hlondeth's missing prince. As the spell quickened, Arvin slid deeper into her mind and neatly snipped out the memory of what her magic had revealed: a human who bore no resemblance whatsoever to Lord Dmetrio. He spliced an image of his metamorphosed form into the hole he'd just created then withdrew.

"Show yourself," he commanded.

A yuan-ti appeared before him. She was a dark-haired woman with yellow scales, wearing the high-collared robe of Sseth's clergy. One hand held a snake-headed staff that rested on the floor. She frowned for a moment, like someone who'd just walked into a room and forgotten what they'd been looking for, then bowed.

"Lord Extaminos," she said. "Welcome back. Your mother will be pleased to hear that you have returned."

"Do not inform her . . . quite yet," Arvin said.

The cleric, straightening, arched an eyebrow.

"There is someone else I must speak with first."

Her thoughts bubbled with curiosity. She held her tongue—but not her magic. Arvin felt energy surge from Karrell's ring, up through his arm and into his mind, shielding it. For just an instant, he slipped the ring from his finger and concentrated on a familiar face—Zelia's—filling his mind with it until the image crowded every other thought out. Then the ring was back on his finger again.

The cleric's lips parted in a smile, baring the tips of her fangs. She hid it behind a bow. "I will escort you, Lord Extaminos. During the attack by the Se'sehen, a number of humans took the opportunity to . . . cause some problems. The streets are still not entirely secure."

She was thinking about Gonthril. The rebel leader and his followers had been stirring up trouble, it seemed. More than that, several sections of the city, including a stretch of its waterfront, had fallen into human hands, but once the militia returned from down south, she was thinking, all that would end. The uprising would be crushed and the slaves who had dared to claim their freedom would be put back in their place.

"You will show me to the surface, then resume your duties here," Arvin commanded.

"As you wish," the cleric demurred.

Her thoughts told him much more. Lady Dediana had grown suspicious of Zelia of late, suspicious of the hold the mind mage seemed to have over the royal son. The queen suspected a plot—and "Dmetrio's" insistence on not telling his mother about his return had confirmed it. He would be watched. Carefully.

Arvin smiled to himself. Years of working for the Guild had taught him how to slip away from even the most persistent watchers, and his psionics would take care of any who was armed with magic. Meanwhile, the cleric would confirm Lady Dediana's fears. If Arvin was unsuccessful in his bid to take Zelia down, House Extaminos would surely finish the job.

For the moment, however, there was someone he needed to make contact with, someone he needed to persuade to help if his plan was to come to fruition.

"Your concern for my well being is . . . appreciated," he told the cleric, "but also unfounded. I can take care of myself."

☜

Arvin stared across the table at Gonthril. The rebel leader hadn't bothered to disguise himself, save for the cloak hood he'd just allowed to fall back against his shoulders. His rebels—for the moment—had control of the waterfront, including one particular tavern.

The Mortal Coil.

Arvin smiled when Gonthril had suggested it as a meeting place. When Arvin had used a sending to contact Gonthril, he'd wondered if the rebel leader would bother to reply. It had been a year since they'd last seen one another. That they were meeting in the place where Arvin's troubles had begun was ironic. The head of the serpent was closing in on the tail.

Though the harbor outside was nearly empty of ships—most had fled when the Se'sehen attack began—the tavern was just as Arvin remembered it. Pipe smoke had stained the coiled-rope ceiling that had given the place its name, and the air still smelled of unwashed sailors and ale. The circular walls were still damp and the benches were as hard as ever. The only "patrons," however, were Gonthril's people, who stood alert and ready, crossbows in hand. Nobody was behind the bar—and nobody was drinking.

Gonthril looked the same but somehow older, aged by a year of hiding and fighting. Arvin, too, had aged. The two men still looked as close as brothers. Gonthril's eyes, however, were blue, and the little finger of his left hand was whole.

"You said you had something to offer me?" he asked. "Something I would find valuable?"

Arvin nodded and leaned forward in his chair. "Information."

"About what?"

"House Extaminos. Its secrets . . . and its weaknesses. Everything your uprising needs to succeed."

Gonthril's eyes glittered. "Tell me more."

"There's a yuan-ti," Arvin began, "a mind mage named Zelia."

"I've never heard the name."

Arvin smiled. "That doesn't surprise me. Zelia makes a point of keeping out of the public eye. She controls a network of spies who have infiltrated not just House Extaminos but every major yuan-ti House in Hlondeth."

"How?"

"By passing themselves off as members of those Houses. The family members are eliminated, and the spies take their place."

Gonthril frowned, and thought a moment. "These spies—are they dopplegangers?"

Arvin's eyesbrows raised. The rebel leader had a quicker mind than he'd expected. "In a manner of speaking, yes."

"The information they have gathered—is it written down?"

"No," Arvin said. "It's all inside Zelia's head, but there's a way to get it out."

"How?" Gonthril asked, skepticism plain in his voice.

"By killing her. Once that's done, I can put you in touch with a cleric who can speak with the dead."

Gonthril's eyes bored into Arvin's. "Why do *you* want this woman dead?"

"For several reasons," Arvin answered. "The simple answer is that if I don't kill her, she'll kill me." He spread his hands. "That's not what really concerns me. Zelia won't stop there. She'll also make sure my wife and children die."

Gonthril's eyebrows rose. "You've been busy, this past year."

Arvin had to smile.

Gonthril's expression turned serious again. "What if the information in Zelia's head turns out to be of no use to the Secession?" Gonthril said, "I'll have wasted my resources. There's an entire city of yuan-ti that need killing and precious few humans bold enough to do the job."

Arvin fought to keep his smile from wavering. Gonthril's hatred of the serpent folk ran deep. If he realized that Arvin was part yuan-ti—and that the wife and children Arvin was trying to protect were as well—the only "help" forthcoming would be a crossbow bolt in the back. He was glad, yet again, that Karrell's ring was still on his finger.

"Zelia is worth killing for other reasons," he said.

"Convince me."

"You've heard that Sibyl is dead?" Arvin asked.

Gonthril nodded. "So House Extaminos says."

"It's true," Arvin assured him. "Now Zelia is trying to pick up where Sibyl left off. Sibyl was only pretending to be Sseth's avatar, but Zelia actually stands a chance at becoming just that."

"How?"

"It's complicated, but the short answer is this: Sseth is bound inside his domain. He needs someone to free him. Whoever does this will be rewarded with anything they ask for. Zelia knows of an artifact called the Circled Serpent—a key that opens a door to Sseth's domain. Using it, she can free him—and become his avatar."

Gonthril whistled under his breath. He sat in silence a moment, then reached inside his shirt and pulled out a chain that was looped through a ring—a wide band of silver, set with deep blue sapphires. He took it off the chain and slid it across the table to Arvin. "Put it on."

Arvin did, reluctantly. He remembered the last time he'd worn it. With the ring on, he'd be unable to tell a lie. If Gonthril asked directly about the Circled Serpent, Arvin would have to tell him it had already been destroyed. Gonthril would assume everything Arvin had just told him was a lie, and Arvin would have to fight his way out of the Mortal Coil.

He resisted the urge to glance at the half-dozen crossbows pointed at him. Instead he took a deep breath. Control, he urged himself. He didn't need to tell the whole truth about the Circled Serpent—he just had to concentrate on answering Gonthril's questions as succinctly as possible.

Gonthril looked him square in the eye. "Do you work for House Extaminos?" he asked.

Relief washed through Arvin as he saw the tack Gonthril's questions would take. He smiled. "No," he answered, his voice firm and level. "As I told you when you asked me that question a year ago, I work for myself."

This time, it was the truth.

"Is the story about wanting to kill Zelia a ruse to trap me?"

"No."

"Is your name really Arvin?"

Arvin frowned. "Of course."

"Are you a doppleganger?"

Arvin laughed. "No. What you see is what you get. I'm—" He was about to say "human" but checked himself just in time. He shrugged. "I'm Arvin."

Gonthril nodded then gestured for Arvin to take off the ring.

Arvin did and passed it back to Gonthril. The rebel leader slipped it back on the chain and hung it around his neck.

"What's the Seccession's part in your plan?" the rebel leader asked. "What do you need us to do?"

"Not the Seccession," Arvin said. "You. I need someone who can pass as me without having to resort to magical disguises. I'll be playing the part of one of Zelia's spies—a spy that has 'captured' Arvin. It will be dangerous and unpleasant, but if Zelia reacts as I expect her to—and believe me, I know her well—it will give me the chance to take her completely by surprise."

"I see," Gonthril said. For several moments, there was silence. Gonthril glanced at one of his rebels. The man gave a slight shrug then nodded.

Arvin waited for the rebel leader's reply.

"I'll need to know more details, of course," Gonthril said, "but so far, you've got my interest."

Arvin heaved a mental sigh of relief. He hesitated then decided to broach the question that had been nagging at him for some time. "Before we get into the details, there's one thing I neglected to ask the last time we met," he said, his voice low enough that Gonthril's people wouldn't hear it.

"Go on," Gonthril said.

Arvin waved a hand between them. "We look enough alike to be brothers," he whispered. "Is there any chance that we might be?"

Gonthril gave a tight smile. "My mother had a very strong spirit. When I was growing up, I often heard her tell my father she wouldn't be bound to any one man. We may—you and I—very well have been fathered by the same man."

"Did your mother ever mention a bard named Salim?"

"No."

"Then your father—"

"The only man who earned the right to be called 'father' was the man who raised me," Gonthril said in a stern voice. His expression was grim. For a moment, Arvin was worried he'd offended Gonthril.

"That man is dead," Gonthril continued, "as is my mother. They died in the so-called 'Plaza of Justice' the year I turned thirteen, executed for a crime they did not commit, but that didn't matter. They were human, and 'insolent to their betters.' Even as they were led to their deaths, they refused to go quietly and shouted insults at the yuan-ti who had condemned them." His eyes grew fierce. "I decided to carry on that tradition of defiance. That same year, I joined the Secession."

Arvin listened quietly, surprised by how much he and Gonthril had in common. Each of them had been forced to make his way in the world alone. Their lives, however, had taken very different paths.

Gonthril shrugged. "You don't need to convince me that we're related," he said. "I'm helping you for the good of Hlondeth—for the benefit of humans everywhere—not because of some blood tie we may or may not share."

Arvin nodded, his face neutral, but his heart was beating quickly. Was the man across the table from him really his brother? Arvin's mother had believed that Arvin was the only child Salim had ever fathered—but what if the bard had been lying to her—or simply hadn't realized that a previous liaison had produced a child?

It would be ironic indeed if the leader of a group dedicated to returning Hlondeth to human hands turned out to be part yuan-ti.

Gonthril had already moved on; he leaned across the table in a conspiratorial hunch. "Now tell me your plan. In detail."

Chapter 13

Arvin walked toward Zelia's tower, herding his captive ahead of him. Gonthril had a blindfold over his eyes and his hands were bound behind his back. His feet were hobbled, so he staggered when Arvin shoved him forward. The bonds looked and felt tight but were special knots that could be loosened in an instant by tugging the right strand. The rebel leader played his part to perfection, never once complaining about Arvin's rough handling.

When they reached the door, Arvin waited. Tension knotted his stomach. The seed Pakal had killed in Karrell's village had told him of the tower's defences—about the strip of copper hidden within the doorframe that would manifest a catapsi on any psionicist who entered and the invisible mage mark designed to take care of non-psionic intruders. The seed had also told him how to get past them. A pressure plate high above had to be pushed with a far hand manifestation as one stepped through the door. It had alerted Arvin to the dangers that lay within. Even so, Arvin had to steel himself as he knocked then waited for the door to open. The bottle he held in his left hand was slippery with sweat.

Control, he told himself. Then he smiled. He was thinking like Zelia—which was just what he wanted.

Arvin's crystal hung around Gonthril's neck and Karrell's ring was on one of the fingers of Gonthril's right hand. A glove on his left hand hid the fact that his little finger was whole. The disguise wouldn't stand up to scrutiny, but if all went well, Zelia wouldn't get a chance to make a close inspection.

As the door swung open, Arvin grabbed Gonthril by the hair and forced him to his knees.

He had been expecting some minion to answer his knock, and was surprised to find Zelia herself staring out at him. Then he realized that it was probably one of her duplicates.

It looked like Zelia, though, down to the last pore. Long red hair glowed in the light of the setting sun, and her green eyes matched the color of the scales that freckled her cheeks and hands. She wore a yellow dress of watered silk that plunged low between her breasts and left her arms bare. The scales that covered her body were a deep sea green. She glanced briefly at Arvin, then at the captive. Her eyes flashed silver as she manifested a power. Then she frowned.

"It's the ring," Arvin told her, "but let him think what he likes— he's powerless. I drained him with a catapsi."

His voice sounded strange in his ears. It matched the form he'd metamorphosed into: Dmetrio. He'd spent extra care in shaping his body, down to the last detail. The hair that framed his high forehead was thinner and darker than his own, and his scales were the exact shade Dmetrio's were. His body was leaner, his groin a smooth surface with his genitals tucked inside a flap of skin. His posture and movements were fully those of a yuan-ti. He swayed, rather than standing square on his two stub feet, and kept his lips parted, tasting the air with his tongue.

A hissing filled the air, though Zelia's lips remained closed. "You're right," she said a moment later. "His aura is empty."

"If it wasn't, the door frame would have drained him," Arvin chuckled.

Abruptly, she looked up at Arvin. He was ready for her. As her eyes flashed silver a second time, he pulled energy into his throat and imagined his hands sweeping through the air in front of his face, washing his thoughts clean. At the same time he concentrated, simultaneously manifesting the power that allowed him to shape sound. The droning of his secondary display became a sharp hissing noise—the sound the Dmetrio-seed would have made, had it been the one manifesting the empty-mind defense.

Zelia *tsk-tsked*, shaking her head.

Arvin shrugged, adding a feminine sway to the gesture. "What did you expect?" he said. "None of us like to reveal all of our playing pieces at once, do we?" He glanced past Zelia into the tower. "Where is she?"

The duplicate didn't bother to pretend she didn't know who he was talking about. "In the study."

She opened the door wider, an invitation for Arvin to step inside. He did, taking care to deactivate the traps in the door as he passed through it. Zelia hung back, waiting for him to prove that he knew where he was going, which he didn't. Her body language, however, spoke volumes to someone trained by the guild. The slight turn of her hips plus her deliberately averted eyes pointed him in the right direction. Shoving Gonthril ahead of him, Arvin crossed the entryway and made for a door on the right. The handle was trapped with a venomed needle, so Arvin pushed the secret button as he turned it, preventing the needle from springing.

The study had a basking pit and walls hung with slitherglows that filled the room with soft, shifting rainbows. The scent of oil lingered in the air. The only piece of furniture was a small cabinet opposite the door. The room was unoccupied; the basking pit was empty. Arvin turned as Zelia closed the door behind her. One hand still knotted in Gonthril's hair, he forced his "captive" back to his knees.

"Where's Zelia?" Arvin asked.

Zelia cocked her head. "Right here," she said, touching her chest with a slender finger.

Arvin didn't believe it for a moment.

Gonthril shifted suddenly, twisting in Arvin's grip. "You bitch!" he shouted, rearing to his feet. "You killed Karrell! I'll—"

Arvin manifested a simple power, shaping the sounds in the room. As a loud hissing filled the air, he shifted one of the fingers of the hand that held Gonthril's head, giving a two-tap code. Gonthril reacted according to plan, writhing and moaning as if his brain were burning. Arvin wrenched Gonthril's head back, exposing his throat, and bared his fangs.

Zelia caught his arm. "Don't be so hasty," she hissed. "Let him suffer a little more. Let's savor this."

Arvin twisted his lips into a sadistic smile. "I know," he said. "Let's fuse him."

"No!" Gonthril cried. "Not that!" He tried to force his way to his feet but Arvin shoved him down.

As Arvin pretended to be busy subduing Gonthril, he heard a chuckle from the seemingly empty air next to the cabinet. A second Zelia appeared in the room, standing next to it. She was dressed identically to the first—aside from their positions in the room, it was impossible to tell them apart. Arvin was almost certain it was the original, or maybe the first Zelia was the original and the second was the duplicate. It would be just the sort of mind game she would enjoy.

This second Zelia stepped swiftly forward and flicked her fingers against Gonthril's face. Silver flashed in her eyes a third time. Gonthril's shouts of protest became muffled howls as his lips fused together. The flesh of his legs joined, and his arms melded with his torso. He crumpled downward into a ball, his body smoothing and folding in upon itself until it resembled a wrinkled lump of clay through which the ropes that had bound him passed. Hair and fingernails were still visible, as were the two holes in what had once been his nose. Gonthril breathed through these rapidly.

Arvin felt a dull horror as he glanced down at the lump that had, a moment before, been a man, but so far, his plan was holding together. Zelia had swallowed the bait he'd tossed her and had repeated her previous error, fusing Gonthril's fingers together, ensuring that Karrell's ring could not be removed. It was up to Arvin to keep her occupied, so she would not slice it free.

The first Zelia gestured toward the far wall. "Roll him over there," she ordered.

Arvin obliged. As he tumbled Gonthril against the wall, he kept one wary eye on the Zelias. At the first hint of suspicion on their part, he would begin his attack.

The second Zelia regarded him with unblinking eyes. "So, 'Dmetrio,' " she said. Why haven't I been able to reach you? Where have you been?"

Arvin turned. "I had a run-in with an old friend of ours," he answered. "Juz'la."

The second Zelia gave him a sharp glance. "What of her?"

"She, too, quit the Hall of Mental Spendor," Arvin said. "She's working for Sibyl now."

Zelia's eyes widened.

"Or perhaps I should say, Juz'la *was* working for Sibyl," Arvin said. He ended with one of Zelia's gloating smiles.

The first Zelia cocked her head. Her tongue flickered from her lips. "You'll have to tell me all about that," she said. "Later."

As if at some unspoken signal, both Zelias swayed toward him. The first one ran a hand down his bare chest, toying with his scales; her tongue flickered out again, touching his chest.

"Interesting perfume," she said. "It tastes like ginger."

Arvin forced himself not to recoil though his skin crawled. He nodded. "I thought you might like it."

The second Zelia lifted the hand that held the bottle. "What's this?" she asked.

"The best wine in House Extaminos' cellars: a truly exotic vintage," Arvin answered. He nodded at the lump that was Gonthril. "I thought it would be appropriate to celebrate before we swat the gnat."

Out of the corner of his eye, Arvin caught a flash of silver from the Zelia who had moved slightly behind him. She was manifesting a power!

Despite knowing that he was already a heartbeat too late, he plunged into his *muladhara* and started to draw energy into—

The cork popped from the bottle, startling him. As it drifted over the shoulder of the Zelia whose eyes had flashed, Arvin realized what power she'd just manifested—a simple far hand to pull the cork. She would have been suspecting treachery from her seed—contact poison on the neck of the bottle, perhaps.

"Drink," she said.

The first Zelia stared up at him, the tips of the fangs showing as she smiled. One hand continued to stroke his chest. Behind her, Gonthril rocked back and forth in a futile effort to free himself, moaning softly.

Arvin lifted the bottle in a toast first to one Zelia, then the other. "To the sweet taste of victory," he said. He drank deeply. The wine was indeed a fine vintage, better than any he'd drunk before, but all he tasted was the *hassaael*'s perfumey flavor, which prickled his nose. That, and a faintly bitter undertone that was his own blood.

He licked his lips with a forked tongue. He glanced between the two Zelias, as if uncertain which to pass the bottle to first. He still couldn't be certain which was the real Zelia and which was merely a duplicate. The one giving the orders might be the original—or she might just be playing a clever game. For all he knew, both women were duplicates.

He hoped not. Two Zelias were enough to deal with.

The one stroking his chest took the bottle. A cabinet opened, and three delicate crystal glasses floated through the air toward her. She poured the wine into them, set the bottle down, and passed one glass to Arvin, the other two to the second Zelia—then took Arvin's face in both hands and kissed him. It took all of Arvin's self control not to flinch away from her and still more effort to return the kiss. Their forked tongues entwined briefly, then she pulled away. She glanced at the first Zelia, nodded, then took one glass and raised it in a toast. The other Zelia returned it but didn't drink the wine herself until the first had swallowed hers.

That decided it. The Zelia standing slightly behind Arvin had to be the original. The one that had met him at the door was taking the chances, tasting his mouth to see if he'd really consumed the wine, then drinking it herself.

The second Zelia clinked her glass against Arvin's then drank. Arvin resisted the urge to smile as he sipped from his own glass. His guess had been right: the Dmetrio-seed hadn't known what *hassaael* was, and neither did Zelia.

Lowering her glass, the second Zelia stared with a smile on her lips for several moments at Arvin—then coiled an arm around his neck and drew him close.

"You said you have both halves?" she breathed, her breath heavy with the scent of the potion.

Arvin smiled. "Yes." He nodded down at Gonthril. "Your plan worked beautifully."

"Where are they?"

"In a safe place." He raised his glass to his lips and started to drink—

The arm around his neck tightened, preventing him from

swallowing. Zelia's green eyes blazed. "You weren't thinking about trying to keep it for yourself," she hissed. "Were you?"

The grip eased enough for Arvin to swallow the wine that was in his mouth. "The thought never even entered my mind," he answered.

"Liar," she spat. She gave him a steely look. "You know what happens to seeds who defy me. You'll deliver them, as promised, and we'll reap our reward." Then she smiled "Before we deal with that, let's have a little fun."

That surprised Arvin. He'd expected her to demand that he hand over the Circled Serpent immediately. That was, in part, why he'd tricked her into drinking the *hassaael*—so that he could persuade her to wait. His deception was going even better than he'd hoped, and that worried him. There was something he was missing—but what?

The second Zelia had dropped to her knees. Feeling her fingers on the laces of his breeches, Arvin stiffened, then forced his body to relax. He looked down and faked a lustful smile as he choked down his revulsion. There was a time he might have found Zelia alluring— but that was long passed.

Time to plant the suggestion and let the potion do its work. He pulled the first Zelia close, pretending to kiss her. "I don't want to share you," he whispered, deliberately making his words just loud enough for the second Zelia to hear. "Get rid of her."

As he spoke, he manifested a fate link between the two. The scent of saffron and ginger rose in the air, and he scratched his chest. He'd never manifested a power in her presence that caused that particular secondary display, and he counted on them to mistake the smell for his "perfume."

If either woman recognized it as a secondary display, they made no comment. They were too busy matching each other, glare for glare.

"What are you waiting for?" Arvin cried at the standing Zelia. "Strike!"

Each of the Zelias hesitated for a heartbeat. Then the air filled with a loud hissing. Under the influence of *hassaael*—and goaded by their own suspicious natures—they attacked each other. Each reeled back as the other's power struck. The kneeling Zelia's eyes rolled back in her head, and the standing Zelia blinked, then shook her head. Eyes flashed silver, hissing lashed through the air and ectoplasm sheened first one then the other woman as powers were hurled back and forth.

Arvin tossed in an attack of his own. He lashed the mind of one Zelia with a whip of psionic energy, then sent tendrils of thought into the mind of the other, constricting and crushing her mind. His concentration held for the first attack, but in the middle of the second, the sound he'd been shaping into a hiss reverted back to a low drone.

One of the Zelias whirled. "Arvin!" she shouted, pointing at the lump that was Gonthril. "He's using his psionics. He's used a suggestion to turn us against each other!"

In the heartbeat of silence that followed, Arvin heard a faint crunch. He knew at once what it was: Gonthril biting down on the thin-walled ceramic vial he'd been holding in his mouth—the potion Arvin had purchased from Drin earlier that evening. Arvin silently cursed.

Not now! Arvin sent. *They're both looking right at you!*

Too late.

The magic dispelling potion inside the vial did its work. Gonthril's arms and legs sprang apart. A quick twist of his hands—just as Arvin had taught him—freed the bonds around his wrists, and a sharp kick freed his ankles. He tore off the blindfold and spat out the remains of the vial, then leaped to his feet.

Arvin lunged for Gonthril, dragging him to the side. "I'll deal with him!" he shouted at one of the Zelias. "*She's* the one who manifested a suggestion on you."

Instead of resuming their attack as he'd hoped, the Zelias turned toward him.

"Do you want to become an avatar or not?" Arvin screamed at the duplicate. "Kill her!"

The Zelias exchanged a knowing look, and Arvin suddenly worried that he'd mistaken the original for the duplicate. Before he could correct the error, both women's eyes flashed silver. Their mouths parted slightly in surprise, one a heartbeat after the other, as they glanced between Arvin and Gontrhil.

"He's split himself," they hissed as one.

Arvin felt the blood drain from his face. They'd just seen through his metamorphosis. Releasing Gonthril and shouting, "Attack them!" he threw up a mental shield. Next to him, Gonthril leaped forward, shouting the word that would turn the rope that had bound him to stone. He whipped this improvised weapon around like a staff, aiming at the closest Zelia's head.

She ducked, but the other Zelia had time to manifest a power. A wall of psionic energy slammed into Arvin, knocking him to the ground. Out of the corner of his eye he saw Gonthril crumple too, his nose and mouth leaking blood like he'd just been smashed in the face with a brick. Despite the roaring in his ears, Arvin heard what sounded like the tinkle of tiny bells—a hallucinatory noise that was another of Zelia's secondary displays. Dazed, he tried to mount a psionic defense—only to feel his *muladhara* open and spill all of its stored energy in a swirling rush.

The Zelias must have seen the distress in his eyes. They smiled.

"You . . . haven't won," Arvin gasped. "I destroyed . . . the Circled Serpent. You'll never become . . ."

The eyes of the Zelia on the left flashed. Arvin felt her awareness enter his mind. Powerless to stop her, he felt her rifle through his thoughts. The memories she was looking for floated to the surface of Arvin's mind—memories of the Circled Serpent being destroyed. She probed further, and earlier memories floated to the surface of Arvin's mind: the dog-headed man confronting him in the cavern, then a skip ahead to Arvin learning that the Dmetrio-seed had killed him and fled with the Circled Serpent.

"So he did betray me," hissed the Zelia whose eyes had flashed. "The fool. He could have ruled Hlondeth."

The other Zelia cocked her head, still staring mockingly at Arvin. "What made you think I *wanted* to become an avatar?" she asked.

Frowning took too much effort. Arvin's entire body felt like one big bruise. Something felt loose inside his chest. Intense agony shot through him with each breath. He couldn't muster the strength to lever himself off the floor; he could barely raise his head. Beside him, Gonthril lay still. Dead or unconscious, Arvin couldn't tell.

"Why . . . wouldn't you?" Arvin asked.

He was surprised that the Zelias hadn't killed him yet. They wanted to gloat over their victory, it seemed. If he could keep them talking, maybe he could still make the *hassaael* work for him.

The Zelia on the left—Arvin had lost track of which one was the original but suspected that she was the one—answered. "Because Set's followers will reward me so well for destroying the key."

"Set's . . . followers?" Arvin repeated dazedly. Then he understood. The dog-man who had followed him up Mount Ugruth—Zelia was working with him. Working *for* him. Arvin had been wrong. She hadn't wanted to become an avatar at all.

"Exactly," she hissed, obviously still listening in on his thoughts. "The Dmetrio-seed was merely supposed to rule Hlondeth, once Dediana was out of the way." She *tsk-tsked*. "A pity that he grew greedy." She sighed melodramatically. "They all do in the end."

The Zelia to the right had been silent for some time; Arvin noticed her frown, as if concentrating on something intensely. Then her eyes slid sideways in a furtive glance that was directed at the first Zelia.

Odd that he couldn't feel both Zelias inside his head. It was almost as if . . .

He spoke quickly, even as the thought formed in his mind. "She's drained you," he gasped. "She's going to kill you. She said 'me,' not 'us.' If you kill her first, she—"

Zelia, too, must have known how to control sound. Arvin heard a hissing and no more words emerged, even though he was still talking.

He smiled. Zelia had just played right into his hand.

Swifter than a cobra, the duplicate twisted and bit the other in the throat. The original Zelia recoiled, one hand pressed to her wound. She removed it, then blinked in surprise at the twin beads of blood on her fingers.

Both women began breathing with tight, shallow gasps; their faces a bright red. Blood trickled from the nose of the original Zelia.

"You fool!" she hissed at the duplicate. "Can't you see what he's done? He fate linked us! You're going to die now, too." She shook her head. "Why did you . . . I would never . . ."

"Yes, you would," the duplicate panted back. A blue forked tongue flicked away the blood that flowed from her own nose. Her lips twisted in a wry grimace. "In fact . . . you just . . . did."

The first turned to Arvin, her eyes wild. "Set . . . curse you," the original panted, "and drag . . . your soul . . . to the . . . Abyss!" Then she collapsed.

A heartbeat later, the duplicate fell on top of her. For a moment, both bodies were still. Then, like dough melting in the rain, they flowed into one another until only one Zelia remained.

Dead.

A brittle laugh erupted from Arvin's lips. He no longer cared about the agony in his chest. Victory sang in his ears. He'd done it! Defeated Zelia! Karrell and his children were safe.

"I've already been to the Abyss," he whispered, "and back again. Now it's your turn."

Still lying on his back, he reached out with one hand. He was able—barely—to reach Gonthril's neck. Under his fingers he felt a faint lifebeat. Gonthril was alive.

Arvin let his fingers linger on the crystal at the rebel leader's throat. "Nine lives," he said.

He chuckled weakly. It had taken him at least that many to claim his revenge, but he was alive and Zelia, dead.

Arvin used the stone in his forehead to manifest a sending. When it was done, he closed his eyes. In a moment or two, once he'd rallied his strength again, he would manifest another sending, calling upon the Secession to rescue him and Gonthril. But for the time being, he would rest. His part was, at last, over.

Out over the Vilhon Reach, thunder grumbled once then stilled.

In a hut deep in the Black Jungles, an infant finished suckling at his mother's breast then fell asleep beside his sister.

Their mother smiled.

Richard Lee Byers

The Haunted Lands

Epic magic • Unholy alliances • Armies of undead
The battle for Thay has begun.

Book I	Book II	Book III
Unclean	**Undead**	**Unholy**

Anthology
Realms of the Dead
Edited by Susan J. Morris
January 2010

"This is Thay as it's never been shown before . . . Dark,
sinister, foreboding and downright disturbing!"
—Alaundo, Candlekeep.com on *Unclean*

MARK SEHESTEDT

Chosen of Nendawen

The consumer, the despoiler, has come to Narfell. His followers
have taken Highwatch and slain all who held it—save one.

Vengeance will be yours, the Master of the Hunt promises.
If you survive.

FORGOTTEN REALMS

THOMAS M. REID

THE EMPYREAN ODYSSEY

What could bring a demon to the gates of heaven?

Book I
The Gossamer Plain

Book II
The Fractured Sky

Book III
The Crystal Mountain
July 2009

What could bring heaven to the depths of hell?

"Reid is proving himself to be one of the best up and coming authors in the FORGOTTEN REALMS universe."
—fantasy-fan.org